HARLAN COBEN
Three Great Novels

Harlan Coben is widely recognized as one of the most exciting talents in American crime writing. He was the first ever author to win all three major US crime awards, and has established a bestselling series of crime novels starring his powerful creation, Myron Bolitar. His latest novel, *Tell No One* has been a massive success both sides of the Atlantic and is currently being made into a Hollywood feature film.

Harlan lives in New Jersey with his wife and four children.

Harlan Coben

Deal Breaker
Drop Shot
Fade Away

Deal Breaker Copyright © 1995 Harlan Coben
Drop Shot Copyright © 1996 Harlan Coben
Fade Away Copyright © 1996 Harlan Coben

All rights reserved

The right of Harlan Coben to be identified as the author
of this work has been asserted by him in accordance
with the Copyright, Designs and Patents Act 1988.

All rights reserved. No part of this publication may be
reproduced, stored in a retrieval system, or transmitted,
in any form or by any means, electronic, mechanical,
photocopying, recording, or otherwise, without the prior
permission of the copyright owner.

First published in Great Britain in 2001 by
Orion Books
An imprint of The Orion Publishing Group,
Orion House, 5 Upper St Martin's Lane,
London WC2H 9EA

An Hachette Livre UK Company

9 10

A CIP catalogue record for this book
is available from the British Library

ISBN 978 0 75284 733 7

Typeset at The Spartan Press Ltd,
Lymington, Hants
Printed and bound in Great Britain by
Clays Ltd, St Ives plc

The Orion Publishing Group's policy is to use papers
that are natural, renewable and recyclable products and
made from wood grown in sustainable forests. The logging
and manufacturing processes are expected to conform
to the environmental regulations of the country of origin.

www.orionbooks.co.uk

Contents

Deal Breaker

This, like everything else, is for Anne

Acknowledgement

The author wishes to thank Sunandan B. Singh, MD, Chief Medical Examiner of Bergen County, New Jersey; Bob Richter; Rich Henshaw; Richard Curtis; Jacob Hoye; Shawn Coyne; and, of course, Dave Bolt.

1

Otto Burke, the Wizard of Schmooze, raised his game another level.

'Come on, Myron,' he urged with neoreligious fervor. 'I'm sure we can come to an understanding here. You give a little. We give a little. The Titans are a team. In some larger sense I would like all of us to be a team. You included. Let's be a real team, Myron. What do you say?'

Myron Bolitar steepled his fingers. He had read somewhere that steepled fingers made you look like a thoughtful person. He felt foolish.

'I'd like nothing more, Otto,' he said, returning the pointless volley for the umpteenth time. 'Really I would. But we've given as much as we can. It's your turn now.'

Otto nodded vigorously, as if he had just heard some philosophical whimsy that put Socrates to shame. He tilted his head, angling the painted-on smile toward his team's general manager. 'Larry, what do you think?'

Taking his cue, Larry Hanson pounded the conference table with a fist hairy enough to be a gerbil. 'Bolitar can go to hell!' he shouted, playing enraged to the hilt. 'You hear me, Bolitar? You understand what I'm telling you? Go to hell.'

'Go to hell,' Myron repeated with a nod. 'Got it.'

'You being a wiseass with me? Huh? Answer me, dammit! You being a wiseass?'

Myron looked at him. 'You have a poppy seed stuck in your teeth.'

'Goddamn wiseass.'

'And you're beautiful when you're angry. Your whole face lights up.'

Larry Hanson's eyes widened. He swung his line of vision toward his boss, then back to Myron. 'You're out of your league here, Bolitar. And you fucking know it.'

Myron said nothing. The truth of the matter was, Larry Hanson was partially right. Myron was out of his league. He had been in sports representation for only two years now. Most of his clients were borderline cases – guys who were lucky to make the cut and grabbed the league's minimum. And football was far from his specialty. He had only three NFL players, only one of whom was a starter. Now Myron sat across from thirty-one-year-old wunderkind Otto Burke, the youngest owner in the NFL, and Larry Hanson, former-football-legend-turned-exec, negotiating a contract that even in his inexperienced hands would be the biggest rookie contract in NFL history.

Yes, he – Myron Bolitar – had landed Christian 'Hot Prop' Steele. Two-time Heisman trophy-winning quarterback. Three straight AP and UPI number-one rankings. All-American four years in a row. If that wasn't enough, the kid was an endorsement wet dream. An A student, good-looking, articulate, polite, and white (hey, it mattered).

Best of all, he was Myron's.

'The offer is on the table, gentlemen,' Myron continued. 'We think it's more than fair.'

Otto Burke shook his head.

'It's a load of crap!' Larry Hanson shouted. 'You're a goddamn idiot, Bolitar. You're going to flush this kid's career down the toilet.'

Myron spread his arms. 'How about a group hug?'

Larry was about to offer up another expletive, but Otto stopped him with a raised hand. In Larry's playing days Dick Butkus and Ray Nitzchke couldn't stop him with body blows. Now this one-hundred-fifty-pound Harvard grad could silence him with but a wave.

Otto Burke leaned forward. He hadn't stopped smiling, hadn't stopped the hand gestures, hadn't stopped the eye contact – like an Anthony Robbins Personal Power infomercial come to life. Disconcerting as all hell. Otto was a small, fragile-looking man with the tiniest fingers Myron had ever seen. His hair was dark and heavy-metal long, flowing to his shoulders. He was baby-faced with a silly goatee that looked as if it'd been sketched on in pencil. He smoked a very long cigarette, or maybe it just appeared long against his tiny fingers.

'Now, Myron,' Otto said, 'let's speak rationally here, okay?'

'Rationally. Let's.'

'Great, Myron, that'll be helpful. The truth is, Christian Steele is an unknown, untested quantity. He hasn't even put on a pro uniform yet. He may be the bust of the century.'

Larry snorted. 'You should know something about that, Bolitar – about players who amount to nothing. Who crap out.'

Myron ignored him. He had heard the insult before. It no longer bothered him. Sticks and stones and all that. 'We are talking about perhaps the greatest quarterback prospect in history,' he replied steadily. 'You made three trades and gave up six players to get his rights. You didn't do all that if you didn't believe he has what it takes.'

'But this proposal' – Otto stopped, looked up as though searching the ceiling tiles for the right word – 'it's not sound.'

'Crap is more like it,' Larry added.

'It's final,' Myron said.

Otto shook his head, the smile unfazed. 'Let's talk this through, okay? Let's look at it from every conceivable angle. You're new at this, Myron – an ex-jock reaching for the executive brass ring. I respect that. You're a young guy trying to give it a go. Heck, I admire that. Really.'

Myron bit down. He could have pointed out that he and Otto were the same age, but he so loved being patronized. Didn't everybody?

'If you make a mistake on this,' Otto continued, 'it could be the sort of thing that destroys your career. Do you know what I mean? Plenty of people already feel that you're not up to this – to handling such a high-profile client. Not me, of course. I think you're a very bright guy. Shrewd. But the way you're acting . . .' He shook his head like a teacher disenchanted with a favorite pupil.

Larry stood, glowering down at Myron. 'Why don't you give the kid some good advice?' he said. 'Tell him to get a real agent.'

Myron had expected this whole good-cop, bad-cop routine. He had, in fact, expected worse; Larry Hanson had not yet attacked the sexual appetites of anyone's mother. Still, Myron preferred the bad cop to the good cop. Larry Hanson was a frontal assault, easily spotted and handled. Otto Burke was the snake-infested high grass with buried land mines.

'Then I guess we have nothing more to discuss,' Myron said.

'I believe a holdout would be unwise, Myron,' Otto said. 'It might soil Christian's squeaky-clean image. Hurt his endorsements. Cost you both a great deal of money. You don't want to lose money, Myron.'

Myron looked at him. 'I don't?'

'No, you don't.'

'Can I jot that down?' He picked up a pencil and began scribbling. 'Don't . . . want . . . to . . . lose . . . money.' He grinned at both men. 'Am I picking up pointers today or what?'

Larry mumbled, 'Goddamn wiseass.'

Otto's smile remained locked on autopilot. 'If I may be so bold,' he continued, 'I would think Christian would want to collect quickly.'

'Oh?'

'There are those who have serious reservations about Christian Steele's future. There are those' – Otto drew deeply on his cigarette – 'who believe he may have had something to do with that girl's disappearance.'

'Ah,' Myron said, 'that's more like it.'

'More like what?'

'You're starting to fling mud. For a second there I thought I wasn't asking for enough.'

Larry Hanson stuck a thumb in Myron's direction. 'Do you believe this fucking sliver of pond film we're sitting with? You raise a legitimate issue about Christian's ex-bimbo, one that goes to the heart of his value as a public relations commodity—'

'Pitiful rumors,' Myron interrupted. 'No one believed them. If anything,

9

they made the public more sympathetic to Christian's tragedy. And don't call Kathy Culver a bimbo.'

Larry raised an eyebrow. 'Well, well, aren't we touchy,' he said, 'for a low-life pissant.'

Myron's expression did not change. He had met Kathy Culver five years ago when she was a sophomore in high school, already a budding beauty. Like her sister Jessica. Eighteen months ago Kathy had mysteriously vanished from the campus of Reston University. To this day no one knew where she was or what had happened to her. The story had all the media's favorite tasty morsels – a gorgeous co-ed, the fiancée of football star Christian Steele, the sister of novelist Jessica Culver, a strong hint of sexual assault for extra seasoning. The press could not help themselves. They attacked like ravenous relatives around a buffet table.

But just recently a second tragedy had befallen the Culver family. Adam Culver, Kathy's father, had been murdered three nights earlier in what police were calling a 'botched robbery.' Myron wanted very much to contact the family, to do more than merely offer simple condolences, but he had decided to stay away, not knowing if he was welcome, fairly certain he wasn't.

'Now if—'

There was a knock on the door. It opened a crack, and Esperanza stuck her head in. 'Call for you, Myron,' she said.

'Take a message.'

'I think you'll want to take it.'

Esperanza stayed in the doorway. Her dark eyes gave away nothing, but he understood.

'I'll be right there,' he said.

She slipped back through the door.

Larry Hanson gave an appreciative whistle. 'She's a babe, Bolitar.'

'Gee, thanks, Larry. That means a lot coming from you.' He rose. 'I'll be right back.'

'We don't have all goddamn day to jerk off here.'

'I'm sure you don't.'

He left the conference room and met up with Esperanza at her desk.

'The Meal Ticket,' she told him. 'He said it was urgent.'

Christian Steele.

From her petite frame most would not guess that Esperanza used to be a professional wrestler. For three years she had been known on the circuit as Little Pocahontas. The fact that Esperanza Diaz was Latino, without a trace of American Indian blood, did not seem to bother the FLOW (Fabulous Ladies of Wrestling) organization. A minor detail, they said. Latino, Indian, what's the difference?

At the height of her pro wrestling career, the same script was played out every week in arenas all over the US of A. Esperanza ('Pocahontas') would enter the ring wearing moccasins, a suede-fringed dress, and a headband that lassoed her long black hair away from her dark face. The suede dress came off before the fight, leaving a somewhat flimsier and less traditional Native American garb in its stead.

Professional wrestling has a pretty simple plot with painfully few variations. Some wrestlers are bad. Some are good. Pocahontas was good, a crowd favorite. She was cute and small and quick and had a tight little body. Everyone loved her. She would always be winning the fight on skill when her opponent would do something illegal – throw sand in her eyes, use a dreaded foreign object that everyone in the free world except the referee could see – to turn the tide. Then the bad wrestler would bring in a couple of extra cronies, ganging up three against one on poor Pocahontas, pounding mercilessly on the brave beauty to the unequivocal shock and chagrin of the announcers, who had seen the same thing happen last week and the week before.

Just when it seemed there was no hope, Big Chief Mama, a mammoth creature, charged out of the locker room and threw the beasts off the defenseless Pocahontas. Then together Big Chief Mama and Little Pocahontas would defeat the forces of evil.

Massively entertaining.

'I'll take it in my office,' Myron said.

As he entered he saw the nameplate on his desk, a gift from his parents.

MYRON BOLITAR
SPORTS AGENT

He shook his head. Myron Bolitar. He still couldn't believe someone would name a kid Myron. When his family first moved to New Jersey, he had told everyone in his new high school that his name was Mike. Nope, no dice. Then he tried to nickname himself Mickey. Unh-unh. Everyone reverted to Myron; the name was like a horror-movie monster that would not die.

To answer the obvious question: No, he never forgave his parents.

He picked up the phone. 'Christian?'

'Mr Bolitar? Is that you?'

'Yes. And please call me . . . Myron.' Acceptance of the inevitable, a sign of a wise man.

'I'm sorry to interrupt you. I know how busy you are.'

'I'm busy negotiating your contract. I have Otto Burke and Larry Hanson in the next room.'

'I appreciate that, Mr Bolitar, but this is very important.' His voice was trembling. 'I have to see you right away.'

He switched hands. 'Something wrong, Christian?' Mr Perceptive.

'I – I'd rather not discuss it over the phone. Would you be able to meet me at my room on campus?'

'Sure, no problem. What time?'

'Now, please. I – I don't know what to make of this. I want you to see it.'

Myron took a deep breath. 'No problem. I'll throw Otto and Larry out. It'll be good for the negotiations. I'll be there in an hour.'

It look a lot longer.

Myron entered the Kinney garage on Forty-sixth Street, not too far from his Park Avenue office. He nodded to Mario, the garage attendant, walked past the pricing sheet, which had a small disclaimer on the bottom that read 'not including 97% tax,' and headed to his car on the lower level. A Ford Taurus. Your basic Babe Magnet.

He was about to unlock the door when he heard a hissing sound. Like a snake. Or more likely, air escaping from a tire. The sound emanated from his back right tire. A quick examination told Myron that it had been slashed.

'Hi, Myron.'

He spun around. Two men grinned at him. One was the size of a small Third World nation. Myron was big – nearly six-four and two hundred twenty pounds – but he guessed that this guy must have been six-six and closing in on three hundred. A heavy-duty weight lifter, his whole body was puffed up as if he were wearing inflatable life vests under his clothes. The second man was of average build. He wore a fedora.

The big man lumbered toward Myron's car. His arms swung stiffly at his sides. He kept tilting his head, cracking the part of the anatomy that on a normal human being might be called a neck.

'Having some car trouble?' he asked with a chuckle.

'Flat tire,' Myron said. 'There's a spare in the trunk. Change it.'

'I don't think so, Bolitar. This was just a little warning.'

'Oh?'

The human edifice grabbed the lapels of Myron's jacket. 'Stay away from Chaz Landreaux. He's already signed.'

'First change my tire.'

The grin increased. It was a stupid, cruel grin. 'Next time I won't be so nice.' He grabbed a little tighter, bunching up the suit and tie. 'Understand?'

'You are aware, of course, that steroids make your balls shrink.'

The man's face reddened. 'Oh, yeah? Maybe I oughta smash your face in, huh? Maybe I oughta pulverize you into oatmeal.'

'Oatmeal?'

'Yeah.'

'Nice image, really.'

'Fuck you.'

Myron sighed. Then his whole body seemed to snap into motion at the same time. He started with a head-butt that landed square on the big man's

12

nose. There was a squelching noise like beetles being stepped on. Blood gushed from the nose.

'Son of a—'

Myron cradled the back of the big man's head for leverage and smashed his elbow into the sweet of the Adam's apple, nearly caving the windpipe all the way in. There was a painful, gurgling choke. Then silence. Myron followed up with a knife-hand strike to the back of the neck below the skull.

The big man slid to the ground like wet sand.

'Okay, that's enough!'

The man with the fedora stepped closer, a gun drawn and pointed at Myron's chest.

'Back away from him. Now!'

Myron squinted at him. 'Is that really a fedora?'

'I said, back off!'

'Okay, okay, I'm backing.'

'You didn't have to do that,' the smaller man said with almost childlike hurt. 'He was just doing his job.'

'A misunderstood youth,' Myron added. 'Now I feel terrible.'

'Just stay away from Chaz Landreaux, okay?'

'Not okay. Tell Roy O'Connor I said it's not okay.'

'Hey, I ain't hired to get no answer. I'm just delivering.'

Without another word the man with the fedora helped his fallen colleague to his feet. The big man stumbled to their car, one hand on his nose, the other massaging his windpipe. His nose was busted, but his throat would hurt even worse, especially when he swallowed.

They got in and quickly drove away. They did not stop to change Myron's tire.

2

Myron dialed Chaz Landreaux's number on his car phone.

Not being what one would call mechanically inclined, it had taken Myron half an hour to change the tire. He rode slowly for the first few miles, fearing his handiwork would encourage the tire to slip off and flee. When he felt more confident, he accelerated and started back on the road to Christian's.

When Chaz answered, Myron quickly explained what happened.

'They was already here,' Chaz told him. Lots of noise in the background. An infant cried. Something fell and broke. Children laughed. Chaz shouted for quiet.

'When?' Myron asked.

'Hour ago. Three men.'

'Did they hurt you?'

'Nah. Just held me down and made threats. Said they was going to break my legs if I didn't honor my contract.'

Breaking legs, Myron thought. How original.

Chaz Landreaux was a senior basketball player at Georgia State and a probable first-round NBA pick. He was a poor kid from the streets of Philadelphia. He had six brothers, two sisters, no father. The ten of them lived in an area that – if daringly improved – might one day be charitably dubbed 'poor ghetto.'

During his freshman year, an underling of a big-time agent named Roy O'Connor had approached Chaz – four years before Chaz was eligible to talk to an agent. The man offered Chaz a five-thousand-dollar 'retainer' up front, with monthly payments of $250, if he signed a contract making O'Connor his agent when he turned pro.

Chaz was confused. He knew that NCAA rules forbade him from signing a contract while he still had eligibility. The contract would be declared null and void. But Roy's man assured him this would be no problem. They would simply postdate the contract to make it appear Chaz had signed on after his final year of eligibility. They'd keep the contract in a safety deposit box until the proper time arrived. No one would be the wiser.

Chaz was not sure. He knew it was illegal, but he also knew what that kind of money would mean to his mom and eight siblings living in a two-room hellhole. Roy O'Connor then entered the picture and pitched the final inducement: If Chaz changed his mind at some future date, he could repay the money and tear up the contract.

Four years later Chaz changed his mind. He promised to pay back every cent. No way, said Roy O'Connor. You have a contract with us. You'll stick with it.

This was not an uncommon setup. Dozens of agents did it. Norby Walters and Lloyd Bloom, two of the country's biggest agents, had been arrested for it. Threats too were not uncommon. But that was where it usually ended: with threats. No agent wanted to risk being exposed. If a kid stood firm, the agent backed off.

But not Roy O'Connor. Roy O'Connor was using muscle. Myron was surprised.

'I want you out of town for a little while,' Myron continued. 'You got someplace to lay low?'

'Yeah, I'll crash with a friend in Washington. But what we going to do?'

'I'll take care of it. Just stay out of sight.'

'Okay, yeah, I hear ya.' Then: 'Oh, Myron, one other thing.'

'What?'

'One of the dudes who held me down said he knew you. A monster, man. I mean, huge. Slick-looking motherfucker.'

'Did he say his name?'

'Aaron. He said to tell you Aaron said hi.'

Myron's shoulders slumped. Aaron. A name from his past. Not a good name either. Roy O'Connor not only had muscle behind him – he had serious muscle.

Three hours after leaving his office, Myron shook off all thoughts about the garage incident and knocked on Christian's door. Despite the fact that he'd graduated two months earlier, Christian still lived in the same campus dorm he had occupied throughout his senior year, working as a counselor at Reston U's football summer camp. The Titans' minicamp, however, started in two days, and Christian would be there. Myron had no intention of having Christian hold out.

Christian opened the door immediately. Before Myron had a chance to explain his tardiness, Christian said, 'Thanks for getting here so fast.'

'Uh, sure. No problem.'

Christian's face was completely devoid of its usual healthy color. Gone were the rosy cheeks that dimpled when Christian smiled. Gone was the wide-open, aw-shucks smile that made the co-eds swoon. Even the famed steady hands were noticeably quaking.

'Come on in,' he said.

'Thanks.'

Christian's room looked more like a 1950s sitcom set than a modern-day campus dorm room. For one thing, the place was neat. The bed was made, the shoes in a row beneath it. There were no socks on the floor, no underwear, no jock straps. On the walls were pennants. Actual pennants. Myron couldn't believe it. No posters, no calendars with Claudia Schiffer or Cindy Crawford or the Barbi twins. Just old-fashioned pennants. Myron felt as if he'd just stepped into Wally Cleaver's dormitory.

Christian didn't say anything at first. They both stood there uncomfortably, like two strangers stuck together at some cocktail party with no drinks in their hands. Christian kept his eyes lowered to the floor like a scolded child. He hadn't commented on the blood on Myron's suit. He probably hadn't noticed it.

Myron decided to try one of his patented silver-tongued ice-breakers. 'What's up?'

Christian began to pace – no easy accomplishment in a room slightly larger than the average armoire. Myron could see that Christian's eyes were red. He'd been crying, his cheeks still showing small traces of the tear tracks.

'Did Mr Burke get mad about canceling the meeting?' Christian asked.

Myron shrugged. 'He had a major conniption, but he'll survive. Means nothing, don't worry about it.'

'Minicamp starts Thursday?'

Myron nodded. 'Are you nervous?'

'A little, maybe.'

'Is that why you wanted to see me?'

Christian shook his head. He hesitated and then said, 'I – I don't understand it, Mr Bolitar.'

Every time he called him mister, Myron looked for his father.

'Don't understand what, Christian? What's all this about?'

He hesitated again. 'It's . . .' He stopped, took a deep breath, started again. 'It's about Kathy.'

Myron thought he'd heard wrong. 'Kathy Culver?'

'You knew her,' Christian said. Myron couldn't tell if it was a statement or a question.

'A long time ago,' Myron replied.

'When you were with Jessica.'

'Yes.'

'Then maybe you'll understand. I miss Kathy. More than anyone can ever know. She was very special.'

Myron nodded, encouraging. Very Phil Donahue.

Christian took a step back, nearly banging his head into a bookshelf. 'Everybody sensationalized what happened to her,' he began. 'They put it in tabloids, had stories about the disappearance on *A Current Affair*. It was like a game to everyone. A TV show. They kept calling us "idyllic," the "idyllic couple."' He made quote marks in the air with his fingers. 'As if *idyllic* meant unreal. Unfeeling. Everyone kept saying I was young, I'd get over it

16

quickly. Kathy was just a pretty blonde, millions more like her for a guy like me. I was expected to get on with my life. She was gone. It was over and done with.'

Christian's boyish quality – something that Myron thought would help make him the future endorsement king – had suddenly taken on a new dimension. Instead of the sky, gee-whiz, modest little Kansas boy, Myron saw reality: a scared child huddled in a corner, a child whose parents were dead, who had no real family, probably no real friends, just hero-worshipers, and those who wanted a piece of him (like Myron himself?).

Myron shook his head. No way. Other agents, yes, but not him. Myron wasn't like that. But still something akin to guilt stayed there, poking a sharp finger into his ribs.

'I never really believed Kathy was dead,' Christian continued. 'That was part of the problem, I guess. The not-knowing gets to you after a while. Part of me – part of me almost hoped they'd find her body already, anything to end it. Is that an awful thing to say, Mr Bolitar?'

'I don't think so, no.'

Christian looked at him solemnly. 'I kept thinking about the panties. You know about that?'

Myron nodded. The lone clue in the mystery was Kathy's ripped panties, found on top of a campus Dumpster. Rumor had it that they were covered with semen and blood. To the world at large, the panties had confirmed what had long been suspected: Kathy Culver was dead. It was a sad though not uncommon story. She had been raped and murdered by a random psychopath. Her body would probably never be found – or maybe some hunters would stumble across the skeletal remains in the woods one day, giving the press a great eleven o'clock commercial teaser, bringing the cameras back into the story with undying hopes of catching a grief-stricken relative on film.

'They made it seem like it was a dirty thing,' Christian continued. ' "Pink," they said. "Silk," they said. They never called them underwear or undergarments or even just plain panties. It was always pink silk panties. Like that was important. One TV station even interviewed a Victoria's Secret model for her comment on them. Pink silk panties. Like that meant she was asking for it. Trashing Kathy like that . . .'

His voice sort of faded away then. Myron said nothing. Christian was working up to something. Myron only hoped it wasn't a breakdown.

'I guess I should get to the point,' Christian finally said.

'Take your time. I'm not going anywhere.'

'I saw something today. I—' Christian stopped and swung his eyes toward Myron's. They looked at him, pleading. 'Kathy may still be alive.'

His words hit Myron like a wet slap. Whatever Myron had been preparing himself for, whatever he imagined Christian was leading up to, hearing Kathy Culver might still be alive was not a part of the equation.

'What?'

Christian reached behind him and opened his desk drawer. The desk too was something out of *Leave It to Beaver*. Completely uncluttered. Two cans, one with Bic pens, the other with sharpened number-two pencils. Gooseneck lamp. Desk blotter with calendar. Dictionary, thesaurus, and *The Elements of Style* all in a row between two globe bookends.

'This came in the mail today.'

He handed Myron a magazine. On the cover was a naked woman. Calling her well-endowed would be tantamount to calling World War II a skirmish. Most men are somewhat mammary obsessed, and Myron was not above having similar sentiments, but this was positively freakish. The woman's face was far from pretty, kind of harsh looking. She was giving the camera a look that was supposed to be come-hither but looked more like constipation. Her tongue was licking her lips, her legs spread, her finger beckoning the reader to come closer.

Very subtle effect, Myron thought.

The magazine was called *Nips*. The lead story, according to the words emblazoned across her right breast: 'How to Get Her to Shave Dat Thang.'

Myron looked up sharply. 'What's this all about?'

'The paper clip.'

'What?'

But Christian seemed too weak to repeat it. He just pointed. On the top of the magazine Myron spotted a glint of silver. A paper clip was being used as a bookmark.

'It came with that on there,' Christian said in way of explanation.

Myron fingered through the pages, catching quick glimpses of flesh, until he arrived at the page marked off by the paper clip. His eyes squinted in confusion. It was an ad page, though it had as many erotic photos as any other. The top of the page read:

Live Fantasy Phone – Pick Your Girl!

There were three rows, four girls in each row, all the way down the page. Myron's eyes scanned down. He could not believe what he was seeing. 'Oriental Girls Are Waiting!' 'Wet and Juicy Lesbos!' 'Spank Me, Please!' 'Bitches in Heat!' 'Tiny Titties!' (for those who didn't like the cover shot, no doubt) 'I Want You to Ride Me!' 'Pick My Cherry!' 'Make Me Beg for More!' 'Wanted: Robocock.' 'Mistress Savannah Demands You Call Now!' 'Horny Housewife!' 'Overweight Men Wanted.' Each with matching photo – provocative poses involving telephones.

There were some that were far more raunchy. Cross-dressers. Women with men's equipment. There were some Myron could not even understand. Like unfathomable science experiments. The telephone numbers were what you'd expect. 1-800-888-SLUT. 1-900-46-TRAMP. 1-800-REAM-MEE. 1-900-BAD-GIRL.

Myron made a face. He wanted to wash his hands.

Then he saw it.

It was in the bottom row, second from the right. It read, 'I'll Do Anything!' The phone number was 1-900-344-LUST. $3.99 per minute. Discreetly billed to your telephone or charge card. Visa/MC accepted.

The woman in the picture was Kathy Culver.

Myron felt a coldness seep into him. He turned back to the cover and checked the date. It was the current issue.

'When did you get this?'

'It came in today's mail,' Christian said, picking up an envelope. 'In this.'

Myron's head began to swim. He tried to fight the dizziness and get some kind of footing, but the picture of Kathy kept tipping him back over. The envelope was plain manila. There was no return address – that would have been too easy. It was not postmarked and had no stamps, merely reading:

CHRISTIAN STEELE
BOX 488

No city, no state. That meant it'd been mailed on campus. The address had been handwritten.

'You get lots of fan mail, right?' Myron asked.

Christian nodded. 'But they go somewhere else. This was in my private box. The number is unlisted.'

Myron handled the envelope carefully, trying not to smudge any potential fingerprints. 'It could be trick photography,' Myron added. 'Someone might have superimposed her head on—'

Christian stopped him with a shake of his head. His eyes were back on the floor. 'It's not just her face, Mr Bolitar,' he said, embarrassed.

'Oh,' Myron said, ever swift on the uptake. 'I see.'

'Do you think we should give this to the police?' Christian asked.

'Perhaps.'

'I want to do the right thing,' Christian said, his hands balling into fists. 'But I won't let them drag Kathy through the mud again. You saw what they did when she was the victim. What will they do when they see this?'

'They'll go animal,' he agreed.

Christian nodded.

'But it's probably just a prank,' Myron continued. 'I'll check it out before we do anything else.'

'How?'

'Let me worry about that.'

'There's one other thing,' Christian said. 'The handwriting on the envelope.'

Myron glanced at it again. 'What about it?'

'I can't say for sure, but it looks a lot like Kathy's.'

19

3

Myron stopped short when he saw her.

He had just stumbled into the bar in something of a daydream, his mind like a movie camera that couldn't stay in focus. He tried to sift through what he had just seen and learned from Christian, tried to compute the facts and form a solid, well-conceived conclusion.

He came up with nothing.

The magazine was jammed into the right pocket of his trench coat. Porn mag and trench coat, Myron thought. Jesus. The same questions echoed ad nauseam in his head: Could Kathy Culver still be alive? And if she was, what had happened to her? What could have led Kathy from the innocence of her dorm room to the back pages of *Nips* magazine?

That was when he spotted the most beautiful woman he had ever seen.

She was sitting on a stool, her long legs crossed, sipping gently at her drink. She wore a white blouse opened at the throat, a short gray skirt, and black stockings. Everything clung just right. For a fleeting moment Myron thought she was just a by-product of his daydream, a dazzling vision to tantalize the senses. But the knot in his stomach made him quickly dismiss that notion. His throat went dry. Deep, dormant emotions crashed down upon him like a surprise wave at the beach.

He managed to swallow and commanded his legs to move forward. She was, quite simply, breathtaking. Everything else in the bar faded into the background, as though they were only stage props set for her.

Myron approached. 'Come here often?' he asked.

She looked at him like he was an old man jogging in a Speedo. 'Original line,' she said. 'Very creative.'

'Maybe not,' he said. 'But what a delivery.' He smiled. Winningly, he thought.

'Glad you think so.' She turned back to her drink. 'Please leave.'

'Playing hard to get?'

'Get lost.'

Myron grinned. 'Stop it already. You're embarrassing yourself.'

'Pardon me.'

'It's obvious to everyone in this bar.'

'Oh?' she remarked. 'Do enlighten.'

'You want me. Bad.'

She almost smiled. 'That obvious, huh?'

'Don't blame yourself. I'm irresistible.'

'Uh-huh. Catch me if I swoon.'

'I'm right here, sweetcakes.'

She sighed deeply. She was as beautiful as ever, as beautiful as the day she had walked out on him. He hadn't seen her in four years, but it still hurt to think about her. It hurt even more to look at her. Their weekend at Win's house on Martha's Vineyard came to him. He could still remember the way the ocean breeze blew her hair, the way she tilted her head when he spoke, the way she looked and felt in his old sweat shirt. Simple fragile bliss. The knot in his stomach tightened.

'Hello, Myron,' she said.

'Hello, Jessica. You're looking well.'

'What are you doing here?' she asked.

'My office is upstairs. I practically live here.'

She smiled. 'Oh, that's right. You represent athletes now, don't you?'

'Yes.'

'Better than working all that undercover stuff?'

Myron did not bother answering. She glanced at him but did not hold the gaze.

'I'm waiting for someone,' Jessica said suddenly.

'A male someone?'

'Myron . . .'

'Sorry. Old reflex.' He looked at her left hand. His heart back-flipped when he saw no rings. 'You never married what's-his-name?' he asked.

'Doug.'

'That's right. Doug. Or was it Dougie?'

'You're making fun of someone's name?'

Myron shrugged. She had a point. 'So what happened to him?'

Her eyes studied a beer ring on the bar. 'It wasn't about him,' she said. 'You know that.'

He opened his mouth and then closed it. Rehashing the bitter past was not going to do any good. 'So what brings you back to the city?'

'I'm going to be teaching a semester at NYU.'

His heart sped up again. 'You moved back to Manhattan?'

'Last month.'

'I'm really sorry about your father's—'

'We got your flowers,' she interrupted.

'I wanted to do more.'

'Better you didn't.' She finished her drink. 'I have to go. It was nice seeing you.'

'I thought you were meeting someone.'

21

'My mistake, then.'

'I still love you, you know.'

She stood, nodded.

'Let's try again,' he said.

'No.'

She walked away.

'Jess?'

'What?'

He considered telling her about her sister's picture in the magazine. 'Can we have lunch sometime?' he asked. 'Just talk, okay?'

'No.'

Jessica turned and left him. Again.

Windsor Horne Lockwood III listened to Myron's story with his fingers steepled. Steepling looked good on Win, a lot better than on Myron. When Myron finished, Win said nothing for a few moments, doing more of that steepled-hands-concentration thing. Finally he rested his hands on the desk.

'My, my, haven't we had a special day?'

Myron rented his space from his old college roommate, Windsor Horne Lockwood III. People often said that Myron looked nothing like his name – an observation Myron took as high praise; Windsor Horne Lockwood III, however, looked exactly like his name. Blond hair, perfect length, parted on the left side. His features were classical patrician, almost too handsome, like something crafted in porcelain.

His attire was always thoroughbred prep – pink shirts, polo shirts, monogrammed shirts, khaki pants, golf (read, ugly) pants, white bucks (Memorial Day to Labor Day) or wing tips (Labor Day to Memorial Day) on his feet. Win even had that creepy accent, the one that did not originate from any particular geographical location as much as from certain prep schools like Andover and Exeter. (Win had gone to Exeter.) He played a mean game of golf. He had a three handicap and was the fifth-generation member of stuffy Merion Golf Club in Philadelphia and third-generation at equally stuffy Pine Valley in southern New Jersey. He had a perennial golf tan, one of those where the color could be found only on the arms (short-sleeve shirts) and a V-shape in the neck (open alligator shirt), though Win's lily-white skin never tanned. It burned.

Win was full-fledged whitebread. He made star quarterback Christian Steele look like a Mediterranean houseboy.

Myron had hated Windsor on sight. Most people did. Win was used to it. People liked to form and keep an immediate impression. In Win's case that impression was old money, elitist, arrogant – in a phrase, a flaming asshole. There was nothing Win could do about it. People who relied solely on first impressions meant little to him.

Win gestured to the magazine on his desk. 'You chose not to tell Jessica about this?'

Myron stood, paced, and then sat back down. 'What was I going to say? "Hi, I love you, come back to me, here's a photo of your supposedly dead sister advertising a sex phone in a porno mag?"'

Win thought a moment. 'I'd refine the wording a bit,' he said.

He flipped through the porno rag, his eyebrow arched as if to say Hmmm. Myron watched. He had decided not to tell Win about Chaz Landreaux or the incident in the garage. Not yet anyway. Win had a funny way of reacting when someone tried to hurt Myron. It wasn't always pretty. Better to save it for later, when Myron would know exactly how he wanted to handle Roy O'Connor. And Aaron.

Win dropped the magazine on his desk. 'Shall we begin?'

'Begin what?'

'Investigating. That is what you planned for us, correct?'

'You want to help?'

Win smiled. 'But of course.' He turned his phone around so that it faced Myron. 'Dial.'

'The number in the magazine?'

'Well, golly, Myron, I thought we'd call the White House,' Win said dryly. 'See if we can get Hillary to talk dirty.'

Myron took hold of the phone. 'You ever call one of these lines?'

'I?' Win feigned shock. 'The Debutantes' Darling? The Society Stud? Surely you jest.'

'Neither have I.'

'Perhaps you'd like to be alone, then,' Win said. 'Loosen your belt, pull down your trousers, that kind of thing.'

'Very funny.'

Myron dialed the 900 number under Kathy's photograph. He had made thousands of investigative calls, both during his years in the FBI and in his private work for team owners and commissioners. But this was the first time he'd felt self-conscious.

An awful bleeping noise blasted his ear, followed by an operator: 'We're sorry. Your call is being blocked.'

Myron looked up. 'The call won't go through.'

Win nodded. 'I forgot. We have a block on all 900 calls. Employees were calling them all the time and ringing up quite a bill – not just the sex phones but astrologers, sports lines, psychics, recipes, even dial-a-prayers.' He reached behind him and pulled out another phone. 'Use this one. It's my private line. No blocks.'

Myron redialed. The phone rang twice before being picked up. A woman's voice on tape husked, 'Hello, there. You've reached the fantasy phone line. If you're under eighteen or do not wish to pay for this call, please hang up now.' Less than a second passed before she continued.

'Welcome to the fantasy phone line, where you can talk to the sexiest, most willing, most beautiful, most desirous women in the world.'

Myron noticed that the taped voice was speaking far more slowly now, as if she were reading to a kindergarten class. Each word was its own sentence.

'*Welcome. To. The. Fantasy . . .*'

'In a moment you will talk directly to one of our wondrous, gorgeous, voluptuous, hot girls who are here to heighten your pleasure to new boundaries of ecstasy. One-on-one private conversation. Discreetly billed to your phone. You will talk live with your personal fantasy girl.' The voice droned on with its own form of iambic pentameter. Finally the tape gave instructions; 'If you have a touch-tone phone, press one if you'd like to talk about the secret confessions of a naughty schoolteacher. Press two if . . .'

Myron looked up at Win. 'How long have I been on?'

'Six minutes.'

'Twenty-four dollars already,' Myron said. 'Does the term "total scam" mean anything to you?'

Win nodded. 'Talk about jerking off.'

Myron pressed a button, anything to get off this revolving tape. The phone rang ten times – Christ, they knew how to stretch the time – before he heard another female voice say, 'Hi, there. How are you today?'

Her voice was exactly what Myron had expected. Low and husky.

'Uh, hi,' Myron fumbled. 'Look, I'd like—'

'What's your name, honey?' she asked.

'Myron.' He slapped his forehead and held back a profanity. Had he really been stupid enough to use his real name?

'Mmmmm, Myron,' she said as if testing it out. 'I like that name. It's so sexy.'

'Yeah, well, thanks—'

'My name is Tawny.'

Tawny. Sure.

'How did you get my number, Myron?'

'I saw it in a magazine.'

'What magazine, Myron?'

The constant use of his name was beginning to unnerve him. '*Nips*.'

'Oooo. I like that magazine. It makes me so, you know.'

A way with words. 'Listen, uh, Tawny, I'd like to ask you about your ad.'

'Myron?'

'Yes.'

'I love your voice. You sound really hot. Do you want to know what I look like?'

'No, not real—'

'I have brown eyes. I have long brown hair, kinda wavy. I'm five-six. And I'm a 36–24–36. C cup. Sometimes a D.'

'You must be very proud but—'

'What do you like to do, Myron?'

'Do?'

'For fun.'

'Look, Tawny, you seem very nice, really, but can I talk to the girl in the ad?'

'I am the girl in the ad,' she said.

'No, I mean, the girl whose picture is in the magazine on top of this phone number.'

'That's me, Myron. I'm that girl.'

'The girl in the photo is a blonde with blue eyes,' Myron said. 'You said you had brown eyes and brown hair.'

Win gave him a thumbs-up, scoring one for the detailed eye of Myron Bolitar, ace investigator.

'Did I say that?' Tawny asked. 'I meant blonde with blue eyes.'

'I need to talk to the girl in the ad. It's very important.'

Her voice went down another octave. 'I'm better, Myron. I'm the best.'

'I don't doubt that, Tawny. You sound very professional. But right now I need to talk to the girl in the ad.'

'She's not here, Myron.'

'When will she be back?'

'I'm not sure, Myron. But just sit back and relax. We're going to have fun—'

'I don't want to be rude, but I'm really not interested. Can I talk to your boss?'

'My boss?'

'Yes.'

Her tone was different now. More matter-of-fact. 'You're kidding, right?'

'No. I'm serious. Please put your boss on.'

'Okay, then,' she said. 'Hold on a second.'

A minute passed. Then two. Win said, 'She's not coming back. She's just going to see how long the chump will stay on the line and pour dollars down her pants.'

'I don't think so,' Myron said. 'She liked my voice, said I sounded hot.'

'Oh, I didn't realize. Probably the first time she's ever said that.'

'My thinking exactly.' A few minutes later Myron put the receiver back in its cradle. 'How long was I on for?'

Win looked at his watch. 'Twenty-three minutes.' He grabbed a calculator. 'Twenty-three minutes times three ninety-nine per minute.' He punched in the numbers. 'That call cost you ninety-one dollars and seventy-seven cents.'

'A rare bargain,' Myron said. 'You want to hear something weird? She never said anything dirty.'

'What?'

'The girl on the phone. She never said anything dirty.'

'And you're disappointed.'

'Don't you find that a bit strange?'

Win shrugged, skimming through the magazine. 'Have you looked through this at all?'

'No.'

'Half the pages are advertisements for sex phones. This is clearly big business.'

'Safe sex,' Myron said. 'The safest.'

There was a knock on the door.

'Enter,' Win called out.

Esperanza opened the door. 'Call for you. Otto Burke.'

'Tell him I'll be right there.'

She nodded and left.

'I have some time on my hands,' Win said. 'I'll try to find out who placed the ad. We'll also need a sample of Kathy Culver's handwriting for comparison.'

'I'll see what I can come up with.'

Win steepled his hands, bouncing the fingertips gently against one another. 'You do realize,' he began, 'that this photograph probably means nothing. Chances are there is a very simple explanation for all this.'

'Maybe,' Myron agreed, rising from his chair. He had been telling himself the same thing for the past two hours. He no longer believed it.

'Myron?'

'What?'

'You don't think it was a coincidence – Jessica being in the bar downstairs, I mean.'

'No,' Myron said. 'I guess I don't.'

Win nodded. 'Be careful,' he said. 'A word to the wise.'

4

Damn him.

Jessica Culver sat in her family's kitchen, in the very seat she had sat in innumerable times as a child.

She should have known better. She should have thought it through, should have come prepared for any occurrence. But what had she done instead? She had gotten nervous. She had hesitated. She had stopped for a drink in the bar below his office.

Stupid, stupid.

But that wasn't all. He had surprised her, and she had panicked.

Why?

She should have told Myron the truth. She should have told him in a plain unemotional voice the real reason she was there. But she hadn't. She had been drinking unaware, and suddenly he had appeared, looking so handsome and yet so hurt and—

Oh shit, Jessie, you are one fucked-up chick . . .

She nodded to herself. Yup. Fucked-up. Self-destructive. And a few other hyphenated words she couldn't come up with right now. Her publisher and agent did not see it that way, of course. They loved her 'foibles' (their term – Jessie preferred 'fuck-ups'), even encouraged them. They were what made Jessica Culver such an exceptional writer. They were what gave Jessica Culver's writing that certain 'edge' (again, their term).

Perhaps that was so. Jessie really couldn't say. But one thing was certain: These foibling fuck-ups had turned her life to shit.

Oh, pity the suffering artist! Thy heart bleeds for such torment!

She dismissed the mocking tone with a shake of her head. She was unusually introspective today, but that was understandable. She had seen Myron, and that had led to a lot of 'what if-ing' – a veritable avalanche of useless 'what if-ing' from every conceivable height and angle.

What if. She pondered it yet again.

In her typically self-centered way, she had seen the 'what if-ing' only in terms of herself, not Myron. Now she wondered about him, about what his life had really been like since the world crumbled down upon him – not all at once – but in small, decaying bits. Four years. She had not seen him in four years. She had shoved Myron into some back closet in her mind and locked the door. She'd thought (hoped?) that would be the end of it, that the door could stand up to a little pressure without opening. But seeing him today, seeing the kind, handsome face high above those broad shoulders, seeing the still why-me stare in his eyes – the door had blown off its hinges like something in a gas explosion.

Jessica had been overwhelmed by her feelings. She wanted to be with him so badly that she knew she had to get out right away.

Makes sense, she thought, *if you're a total fuck-up.*

Jessica glanced out the window. She was waiting for Paul's arrival. Bergen County police Lieutenant Paul Duncan – Uncle Paul to her, since infancy – was two years away from retirement. He had been her father's closest friend, the executor of Adam Culver's will. They had both worked in law enforcement – Paul as a cop, Adam as the county medical examiner – for more than twenty-five years.

Paul was coming to finalize the details for her father's memorial service. No funeral for Adam Culver. He wouldn't hear of it. But Jessica wanted to talk to Paul about another matter. Alone. She did not like what was going on.

'Hi, honey.'

She turned to the voice. 'Hi, Mom.'

Her mother came up through the basement. She was wearing an apron, her fingers fiddling with the large wooden cross around her neck. 'I put his chair in storage,' she explained in a forced matter-of-fact tone. 'Just cluttering space up here.'

For the first time Jessica realized that her father's chair – the one her mother must have been referring to – was gone from the kitchen table. The simple unpadded four-legged chair her father had sat in for as long as Jessica could remember, the one closest to the refrigerator, so close that her father could turn around, open the door, and stretch for the milk on the top shelf without getting up, had been taken away, stored in some cobwebbed corner of the basement.

But not so Kathy's.

Jessie's gaze touched down on the chair to her immediate right. Kathy's chair. It was still here. Her mother had not touched it. Her father, well, he was dead. But Kathy – who knew? Kathy could, in theory, walk through the back door right this very minute, banging it against the wall as she always did, smile brightly, and join them for dinner. The dead were dead. When you lived with a medical examiner, you understood just how useless the dead were. Dead and buried. The soul, well, that was another matter. Jessie's mom was a devout Catholic, attending mass every morning, and during crises like these her religious tenacity paid off – like someone who spent time in a gym finally finding a use for their new muscles. She could believe without question in a divine and joyous afterlife. Such a comfort. Jessica wished she could do the same, but over the years her religious fervor had become a strict couch potato.

Except, of course, Kathy might not be dead. Ergo the chair – Mom's lantern kept lit to guide her youngest back home.

Jessica awoke most mornings bolting upright in her bed, thinking about – no, inventing new possibilities for – her younger sister. Was Kathy lying dead in a pit somewhere? Buried under brush in the woods? A skeleton gnawed on by animals and inhabited by maggots? Was Kathy's corpse stuck in some cement foundation? Was it weighed down in the bottom of some river like the little undersea man in the living-room aquarium? Had she died painlessly? Had she been tortured? Had her body been chopped into small bits, burned, broken down with acid . . .

Or was she still alive?

That eternal spring.

Had Kathy possibly been kidnapped? Was she living in white slavery under the thumb of some Middle East sheikh? Or was she living chained to a radiator on a farm in Wisconsin like something on *Geraldo*? Could she have banged her head, forgotten who she was, and was now living as a street person with amnesia? Or had she simply run away to a different world?

The possibilities were endless. Even those lacking creativity can come up with a million different horrors when their loved one suddenly vanishes – or more painfully, a million different hopes.

Jessica's thoughts were chased away by the tired chugging of a car engine. A familiar Chevy Caprice blanketed with tiny dents pulled up. It looked like a retrieval car at a driving range. She stood and hurried out the front door.

Paul Duncan was a stocky man, compact, with salt-and-pepper hair now turning defiantly toward salt. He walked purposefully, the way cops do. He greeted her on the front stoop with a big smile and kiss on the cheek. 'Hey, beautiful! How are you!'

She hugged him. 'I'm okay, Uncle Paul,' she said.

'You look great.'

'Thanks.'

Paul shaded his eyes from the sun. 'Come on, let's go inside. It's hot as hell out here.'

'In a minute,' she said, putting a hand on his forearm. 'I want to talk to you first.'

'What about?'

'My father's case.'

'I'm not handling that, honey. I don't do homicides anymore, you know that. Besides, it would be a conflict of interest – me being Adam's friend and all.'

'But you have to know what's going on.'

Paul Duncan nodded slowly. 'I do.'

'Mom said the police think he was killed in a robbery attempt.'

'That's right.'

'You don't believe that, do you?'

'Your father was robbed,' he said. 'His wallet was gone. His watch. Even his rings. The guy stripped him clean.'

'To make it look like a robbery.'

Paul smiled then, gently – the way, she remembered, he had at her confirmation and Sweet Sixteen party and high school graduation. 'What are you getting at, Jess?'

'You don't find this whole thing odd?' she asked. 'You don't see a connection between this and Kathy?'

He stumbled a step back, as if her words had given him a gentle push. 'What connection? Your sister vanished from her college campus. Your father was murdered by a robber a year and a half later. Where do you see a connection?'

'Do you really believe that they have nothing to do with each other?' she asked. 'Do you honestly believe that lightning struck twice in the same place?'

He put his hands in his pockets. 'If you mean do I think your family has been the victim of two separate awful tragedies, the answer is yes. It happens all the time, Jess. Life is rarely fair. God doesn't go around divvying out the bad in equal doses. Some families go through life with nary a scratch. Some get too much. Like yours.'

'So it's fate,' she said. 'That's your answer. Fate.'

He threw his hands up. 'Fate, lightning striking twice – these are your phrases. You're the writer here, not me. I just call it a tragedy. I just call it a tragic, somewhat bizarre coincidence. I've seen a lot stranger. So had your dad.'

The front door opened. Mom stood in the doorway. 'What's going on?'

'It's nothing, Carol. We were just talking.'

Carol looked at her daughter. 'Jessica?'

Her eyes stayed on Paul's, probing. 'Just talking, Mom.'

Jessica turned away and stepped back inside. Paul Duncan watched her, letting loose a silent breath. He had suspected she would be a problem – Jessica never accepted easy solutions to anything in life, even when the answer was simple. Yep, he had hoped it wouldn't happen, but he had definitely foreseen this possibility.

He just wasn't sure what he should do about it.

Midnight.

At ten P.M. Christian Steele had crawled under the blanket, read for ten minutes, and then switched off the light. Since then he had lain on his back in the dark, staring at the ceiling, not moving, not fooling himself into even hoping that sleep was imminent.

'Kathy,' he said out loud.

His mind floated about aimlessly, settling like a butterfly for only brief moments before moving on. Darkness surrounded him, but not silence. There was no such thing as silence at football camp. Christian heard kegs being thrown, loud music, laughter, singing, swearing. He could distinctly hear Charles and Eddie, his offensive tackles, in the next room. They were permanently set on loud, like a radio turned up before the knob was ripped out. Christian was not above partying too, having fun by consuming alcohol until he hugged the porcelain god and puked up his offering. But not tonight.

God, not tonight.

'Kathy,' he said again.

Was it possible? After all this time . . .

So many things were happening at once. School was over. The Titans' minicamp began the day after tomorrow. The scrutiny of the press had grown more intense than ever. He liked the attention, liked being on the cover of *Sports Illustrated*, liked the awe in people's faces when they spoke to him. Nice kid, they always said. Real nice. As though they expected him to be rude just because he could throw a pigskin with precision. As though he should somehow feel as though he belonged to a higher species, far above them, because he happened to be a good athlete.

Christian was excited. He was scared. He knew he had to think about the future. Myron had told him of the dangers and of how short-lived fame could be. Myron was, after all, a classic example. He had told Christian about the importance of cashing in now, that his career would at best last ten years. So much was at stake. So much. He was famous now, but there was a big difference between college famous and pro famous. Soon he'd have it all. Competition. Fame. Real money – not just the alumni secret handouts . . .

But so what?

'Kathy . . .'

His phone rang.

Christian shot up, his heart beating like a rabbit's. Fast reflexes. Sometimes they played against you. It was only the phone. Probably Charles or Eddie telling him, hey, it's party time! They'd both gotten drafted too. Charles had gone in the second round to Dallas. Eddie in the fifth to the Rams.

He picked up the phone. 'Hello?'

No response.

'Hello?' he said again.

Nothing. But the phone had not been hung up. Someone was there, silently holding the receiver to their ear.

'Who is this?'

Nothing.

Christian hung up. He began to lie back down when the phone rang again. He picked up the receiver.

'Hello?'

Silence again. Christian tried to listen more closely. Nothing. Or – or was that breathing? Panic seized him. He couldn't say why. It was just a prankster calling on his unlisted phone. It might even be Charles or Eddie playing some kind of joke. Nothing to get upset about.

Except he was upset.

He cleared his throat. 'What do you want?'

Still nothing.

'If you call back again, I'll call the cops.'

He slammed the phone down. His hand shook. He was just about to try to settle back down when he remembered something.

Star. Six. Nine.

The phone company had sent something in the mail today. There had been advertisements on the TV – a pregnant woman trying to get to the ringing phone, trudging across the room toward the phone, but when she arrived the caller had already hung up. Then what? She picked up the phone and the voice-over – Cliff Robertson's or someone like that – said something like 'You just missed the call. Was it important? Was it someone you wanted to talk to? There is only one way to find out. Press the star and then six and nine.' They demonstrated it on the screen now, in case anyone wasn't sure how to use a phone. Then the voice-over continued. 'You'll be connected to your previous caller, even if the number is busy. We'll keep dialing for you, leaving your phone line free to make or receive other calls.'

The pregnant woman listened to a phone ring and then spoke to her relieved husband, who was working on some drafting board at work.

Christian picked up the phone. Then he hit the star, the six, and the nine.

The phone rang.

He rubbed his chin. A moment later a robotic operator came on. 'The number is currently busy. We will ring you back when the line is free. Thank you.'

Christian replaced the receiver. He sat up and waited. The partying was still going on. He could hear three or four distinct partying areas. Someone shouted, 'Yahooo!' A window crashed. People cheered. His larger team-mates were playing keg toss, a sort of discus throw involving beer kegs.

The phone rang.

He snatched the receiver as if it were a loose ball on the turf. The phone was ringing back the number – just like the pregnant lady's on the television. After the fourth ring the phone was picked up.

An answering machine.

A voice said, 'Hi. We're not in right now. Please leave a message at the beep, and we'll be sure to call you back. Thanks.'

The phone slipped from Christian's grip. A chilly hand caressed the back of his neck. A sound – some kind of choking voice – escaped his lips. Christian tried to form words but he couldn't.

The answering machine. The voice.

It was Kathy.

5

Myron staggered into his office, punch-drunk from lack of sleep. He had not even bothered climbing into bed the night before. He tried to read, but the words swam in front of his eyes in meaningless waves. He put on the television. Nick at Nite, the cultural equivalent of aerosol cheese. Back-to-back episodes of *F Troop* for three hours. Larry Storch's portrayal of Agarn was, in a phrase, pure thespian genius. Who knew that hitting someone repeatedly with a big hat could be so funny?

But not even such highbrow entertainment could stop his mind from going back to one thought: Jess was back. And like Win had said, it was no coincidence.

At midnight his mother had come down in her robe.

'Hon, you all right?'

'I'm fine, Mom.'

'You seemed distracted all night.'

'It's nothing. Just have a lot of work.'

She looked at him with her a-mother-is-psychic-and-knows look of disbelief. 'Whatever you say.'

At the age of thirty-one Myron still lived at home. True, he had his own space, his own bedroom and bathroom in the basement. But there was no denying it. Myron still lived with Mommy and Daddy.

Five minutes after his mother had gone back to bed, Christian Steele called Myron on his private line, the one that rang softly in the basement so as not to wake up his parents, both of whom slept so lightly, Myron was sure they'd been some kind of ghetto lookouts in a previous life. He filled Myron in on the weird phone calls.

Myron was familiar with the star-six-nine, known as Return Call. The phone company charged on a 'pay-per-use' basis – around seventy-five cents per use. The problem was, Return Call did not trace the number. It automatically redialed the number of the last incoming call received, not letting you know the number. Star-five-seven – Call Trace – would have done the job, though the number is merely reported to the local phone company, which gives it only to the proper authorities.

Still, Myron would call some of his old sources at the phone company, see what he could find out. He knew that star-six-nine worked only for certain local areas. That meant the call was not long distance. A start. Better than nothing. He would also put Caller ID or a trace on Christian's phone. Taps were no longer like you saw on television, the hero anxiously trying to get the caller to stay on the line until it was completed. They were automatic. Caller ID actually showed you the incoming number before you picked up the phone.

But of course, none of that answered the larger questions:

Was it really Kathy's voice Christian had heard? And if so, what did that mean?

Lots of *preguntas.* Not too many answers.

He approached Esperanza's desk. 'How's it going?'

She pierced him with a glare, shook her head in disgust, and looked back down at her desk.

'Back on decaf?' he asked.

Another glare. Myron shrugged. 'Any messages?'

A head shake. Esperanza muttered something. Myron thought he picked up the Spanish equivalent of 'ass-wipe.'

'You want to tell me why you're so upset?'

'Right,' she said bitingly. 'Like you don't know.'

'I don't.'

The glare was back. Women had a talent for glares. Esperanza had a divine gift.

'Forget it,' he said. 'Just get me Otto Burke on the phone.'

'Now?' Esperanza said, her voice dripping with sarcasm. 'Won't you be busy?'

'Just do it, please, okay? You're starting to piss me off.'

'Oooo. I'm quaking.'

Myron shook his head. He had no time for her moods right now. He crossed the room and opened his office door. He stopped short.

'Hi.'

He cleared his throat and closed the door behind him. 'Hello, Jessica.'

For most athletes, Jessica thought, the spotlight fades slowly. But for a tragic few, it vanishes as though from a sudden power failure, bathing the athlete in dazzling darkness.

Such was the case with Myron.

For most athletes the expectation game helps dim the light gradually. A high school star becomes a college bench warmer. The light dims. A college starter realizes he will not be the team's high scorer. The light dims. The college superstar realizes he will never make it to the pros. The light dims. And then there are those very few, those who are one in a million, those with almost Wolfean 'right stuff,' who become professional athletes.

For those, the light is blinding, forever damaging the vision of the ones

35

who stare directly into it. That was what made the dimming so important. An athlete could get used to losing the light slowly. His career would peak before tapering off just slightly. He would brighten from the inexperienced rookie to the player in his prime, and then the light would begin to fade as he moved past seasoned vet.

For Myron that had not happened.

He had been one of those select few who basked in the most potent wattage imaginable, as if the spotlight shone on him and from inside of him. His basketball talent had first become apparent in the sixth grade. He had gone on to break every scoring and rebounding record in Essex County, New Jersey, a perennial basketball stronghold. Myron was short for a forward, a program six-six (really only six-four), but he was a physical brute, a bull, and a hell of a leaper for a white man. He was highly recruited, chose Duke, and won two NCAA titles in four years.

The Boston Celtics had drafted him in the first round, the eighth pick overall. Myron's spotlight grew impossibly bright.

And then the fuse blew.

A freak injury, they called it. It was a preseason game against the Washington Bullets. Two players weighing a combined six hundred pounds sandwiched the rookie Myron Bolitar. The doctors threw all kind of terms at the man-child who had never been injured before, not even a twisted ankle. Multiple fractures, they said. Shattered kneecap. Casts. Wheelchair. Crutches. Cane.

Years.

Sixteen months later Myron could walk, though the limp lasted another two years. He never came back. His career was over. The only life he had ever known had been stripped from him. The press had done a story or two, but Myron was quickly forgotten.

Complete blackout.

Jessica frowned. Spotlight. Bad metaphor. Too cliché and inaccurate. She shook her head and looked up at him.

'That explains it,' Myron said.

'Explains what?'

'Esperanza's mood.'

'Oh.' She smiled at him. 'I told her we had an appointment. She didn't seem pleased to see me.'

'No kidding.'

'She'd still kill me for a nickel, huh?'

'Or half that much,' he replied. 'Want some coffee?'

'Sure.'

He picked up his phone. 'Can you get me a black coffee? Thanks.' He put the receiver back in its cradle and looked up at her.

'How's Win?' she asked.

'Good.'

36

'His family owns the building?'

'Yes.'

'I understand Win's become quite a financial whiz – despite himself.'

Myron nodded, waited.

'So you're still hanging around with Win,' she continued. 'You still have Esperanza. Not a lot changes.'

'Plenty changes,' he said.

Esperanza appeared at the door, the scowl still on her face. 'Otto Burke was in a meeting.'

'Try Larry Hanson.'

She handed the coffee to Jessica, smiled eerily, and left. Jessica studied the cup. 'Think she spat in it?'

'Probably,' Myron replied.

She put it down. 'I need to cut back anyway.'

Myron moved around his desk and sat down. The wall behind him was covered with theater posters. All musicals. His fingers drummed the desk.

'I'm sorry about yesterday,' she said. 'I wanted to surprise you, catch you off guard. Not the other way around.'

'Still seeking the upper hand?'

'I guess so, yeah. Old habit.'

He shrugged but said nothing.

'I need your help,' she said.

He waited.

She took a breath and plunged. 'The police say my father was killed in a robbery attempt. I don't believe it.'

'What do you believe?' he asked.

'I think his murder has something to do with Kathy.'

Myron was not surprised. He leaned forward, his eyes never staying on hers for very long. 'What makes you say that?'

'The police dismiss it as a coincidence,' she said simply. 'I'm not big on coincidences.'

'What about your dad's friend on the force, what's-his-name?'

'Paul Duncan.'

'Right, him. Have you spoken to him?'

'Yes.'

'And?'

She began tapping her foot, an old, subconscious, annoying habit. She made herself stop. 'Paul says it was a robbery too. He spews out all the facts about the crime scene, the missing wallet, the missing jewelry, that kind of thing. He is perfectly logical and objective, which is not his way.'

'What do you mean?'

'Paul Duncan is a passionate man. A hothead. Here his best friend has been murdered, and he seems almost blasé about it. It's not like him.' She stopped, shifted in her chair. 'Something isn't right here, I don't know how else to explain it.'

Myron rubbed his chin but kept quiet.

'Look, you know I was never very close to my father,' she continued. 'He wasn't an easy man to love. He was far better with his corpses than with breathing entities. He liked the ideal of family, the concept – it was the actual execution he found wearisome. But I still have to find out the truth. For Kathy.'

'How did your father and Kathy get along?' Myron asked.

She thought about it for a moment. 'Better lately. When we were kids, they weren't very close. Kathy was a mama's girl, always hanging around my mom, wanting to be like her, the whole bit. But when she vanished, I'd venture to guess she was closer to my dad than my mom. He was crushed when she disappeared. He became obsessed. No, "obsessed" isn't strong enough. All of us were obsessed, of course. But not like my father. It consumed him entirely. Everything about him changed. He had always been the quiet county medical examiner, the man who made no waves. Now he was using his position to keep the pressure on twenty-four hours a day. He became paranoid, convinced the police weren't doing all they could do to find her. He even started his own investigation.'

'Did he find anything?'

'No. Not that I know of.'

Myron looked away. At the far wall. A movie still of the Marx Brothers. *A Night at the Opera.* Groucho looked back but offered no answers.

'What is it?' she asked.

'Nothing. Go on.'

'There isn't much else. I can only tell you that my father was acting very strangely the past few weeks. He started calling me all the time when previously we'd only talked maybe three times a year, sounding a little teary. It was like he was play-acting the part of perfect Daddy with renewed vigor. I couldn't tell if it was a serious change or just a phase.'

Myron nodded, looking off again. He said nothing. Jessica almost thought he'd completely drifted off when he finally spoke, his voice almost inaudibly soft. 'What do you think happened to Kathy?' he asked.

'I don't know.'

'Do you think she's dead?'

'I—' She stopped. 'I miss her. It's . . . I don't want to think she's dead.'

He nodded again. 'So what do you want me to do?'

'Look into it. Find out what's going on.'

'Assuming something is going on.'

'Right.'

'Why me?'

She thought about it a moment. 'I'm not sure,' she said. 'I thought you'd believe me. I thought you'd help.'

38

'I'll help,' he said. 'But understand one thing: I have an important business interest in settling this whole thing.'

'Christian?'

'I'm his agent,' he continued. 'I'm responsible for his well-being.'

'He still misses my sister,' she said.

'Yes.'

'Is he okay?'

Myron's face remained set. 'He's fine.'

'He's a good kid. I like him.'

Myron nodded.

Jessica rose and stepped toward the window. Myron averted his eyes. He did not like to look at her for too long at one time. She understood. It hurt her too. She looked down at Park Avenue, twelve stories below. A taxi driver with a turban was shaking his fist at an old woman with a cane. The old woman whacked him and ran. The driver fell. The turban did not even shift.

'Hiding your feelings from me has never been your forte,' she said, still staring out the window. 'What don't you want to tell me?'

He did not reply.

'Myron . . .'

Esperanza saved him, bursting through the door without knocking. 'Larry Hanson is out of the office,' she said.

Win came in behind her. 'I got something for us on that magazine . . .' His voice died out when he saw Jessica.

'Hi, Win,' she said.

'Hello, Jessica Culver.' They embraced. 'My goodness, you look utterly fantastic. I read an article on you the other day, calling you the Literary Sex Symbol.'

'You shouldn't read such trash.'

'It was in my dentist's waiting room. Honest.'

An uncomfortable pause followed. Esperanza broke it by pointing at Jessica, making a gagging motion by sticking her finger in her mouth, and then storming out.

'Ever the enchantress,' Jessica muttered.

Myron stood. 'Where are you staying?'

'At my mom's.'

'Same number?'

'Yes.'

'I'll call you later. Right now I've got to go with Win.'

Jessica looked toward Win. He grinned at her. His face, as always, gave away nothing. 'I have a meeting with my editor this afternoon,' she said. 'But I'll be home all night.'

'Fine. I'll call you then.'

An awkward impasse. No one knew exactly how to say good-bye. A wave? A handshake? A kiss?

'We've got to go,' Myron said. He sprinted past her, never getting too close. Win shrugged at her in a what-can-you-do fashion and followed. She watched them disappear around the corner. Batman and Robin heading to the Bat-poles.

She left then. She had seen Myron twice now, and they had not yet touched – not even brushed up against one another.

It was an odd thing to wonder about.

6

'What did you find out?' Myron asked.

Win whipped the wheel to the right. The Jag XJR responded with nary a squeal. They had been driving without speaking for the past ten minutes, Win's CD player the only sound. Win favored show tunes. *Man of La Mancha* was on now. Don Quixote serenaded his beloved Dulcinea.

'*Nips* magazine is published by HDP,' Win answered.

'HDP?'

'Hot Desire Press.' Another Bat-turn. The Jag accelerated past eighty.

'Speed limits,' Myron said. 'Heard of them?'

Win ignored him. 'Their editorial office is located in Fort Lee, New Jersey.'

'Editorial office?'

'Whatever. We have an appointment with Mr Fred Nickler, managing editor.'

'His mother must be proud.'

'Moralizing,' Win mused. 'Nice.'

'What did you tell Mr Nickler?' Myron asked.

'Nothing. I called and asked if we could see him. He said yes. Seemed like a very pleasant fellow.'

'I'm sure he's a prince.' Myron looked out the window. Buildings blurred. They fell back into silence. 'You're probably wondering what Jessica was doing in my office.'

Win gave a half-hearted shrug. It was not his way to pry.

'It's her father's murder. The police say it was a robbery. She thinks otherwise.'

'How does she see it?'

'She thinks there's a connection between his murder and Kathy.'

'So the plot thickens. Are we going to help her?'

'Yes.'

'Goodie. So do we think there is a connection?'

'Yes.'

'Yes,' Win agreed.

They pulled into the driveway of a building that could have been either a nice warehouse or low-rent office space. No elevator, but then again, only three levels. HDP, Inc., was on the second floor. When they entered the outer office, Myron was a bit surprised. He was not sure what he'd expected, but he had thought the dwellings of a sleaze merchant would not be so . . . nondescript. The walls were white with inexpensive but tastefully framed art posters – McKnight, Fanch, Behrens. Mostly scenery shots of beaches and sunset. Nothing with naked breasts. Surprise number one. Surprise number two was the unremarkable receptionist. She was strictly standard issue, not an over-aged, bleach-blond, flabby ex-bunny/ sexpot/porno starlet with breathy giggle and seductive wink.

Myron was almost disappointed.

'May I help you?' the receptionist asked.

Win said, 'We're here to see Mr Nickler.'

'Your names, please?'

'Windsor Lockwood and Myron Bolitar.'

She picked up the phone, buzzed in, and a moment later said, 'Right through that door.'

Nickler greeted them with a firm handshake. He was dressed in a blue suit, red tie, white shirt – conservative as a Republican senatorial candidate. Surprise number three. Myron had expected gold chains or a Joey Buttafuoco earring or at the very least a pinkie ring. But Fred Nickler wore no jewelry, except for a plain wedding band. His hair was gray, his complexion a bit washed out.

Win whispered, 'He looks like your uncle Sid.'

It was true. The publisher of *Nips* magazine looked like Sidney Griffin, popular suburban orthodontist.

'Please have a seat,' Nickler said, moving back behind his desk. He smiled at Myron. 'I was at the Final Fours when you guys beat Kansas. Twenty-seven points including the game winner. Hell of a performance. Incredible.'

'Thank you,' Myron said.

'Never seen anything like it. The way that final shot kissed the back-board.'

'Thank you.'

'Just incredible.' Nickler renewed his smile, shaking his head in awe at the memory. Then he sat back. 'So, what can I do for you gentlemen?'

Myron said, 'We have a couple of questions about an ad in one of your, uh, publications.'

'Which one?'

'*Nips*.' Saying the word felt grungy. Myron tried not to make a face.

'Interesting,' Nickler replied.

'What makes you say that?'

'*Nips* is a relatively new publication, and it's doing poorly – far and away the worst of HDP's monthlies. I'm going to give it another month or two, and then it'll probably fold.'

'How many magazines do you publish?'

'Six.'

'Are they all like *Nips*?'

Nickler chuckled lightly. 'They are all pornographic magazines, yes. And they are all completely legal.'

Myron handed him the magazine Christian had given him. 'When was this printed?'

Fred Nickler barely glanced at it. 'Four days ago.'

'That's all?'

'It's our most recent issue – they've barely hit the stands. I'm surprised you found one.'

Myron opened to the proper page. 'We'd like to know who paid for this advertisement.'

Nickler put on a pair of half-moon glasses. 'Which one?'

'Bottom row. The Lust Line.'

'Oh,' he said. 'A sex phone.'

'Is there a problem?'

'No. But this ad wasn't paid for.'

'What do you mean?'

'It's the nature of the business,' Nickler explained. 'Someone calls me up to place an ad for a dial-a-porn line. I tell him it costs X amount. He says, wow, I'm just starting out, I can't afford it. So if it looks like a good idea, I go in fifty-fifty with him. In other words, I take care of the marketing, if you will, while my partner takes care of the technical side – phones, cables, girls to work the phones, whatever else. Then we split it down the middle. It limits both of our risks.'

'Do you do this a lot?'

He nodded. 'Ninety percent of my advertising comes for fantasy lines. I'd say I have a piece of the action in three-quarters of them.'

'Can you give us the name of your partner on this particular venture?'

Nickler studied the picture in the magazine. 'You're not with the police, are you?'

'No.'

'Private investigators?'

'No.'

He took off his glasses. 'I'm fairly small-time,' he said. 'I have my own little niche. It's the way I like it. No one bothers me, and I don't bother anybody else. I have no interest in a lot of publicity.'

Myron shot a glance at Win. Nickler had a family, probably a nice house in Tenafly, told the neighbors he was in publishing. Pressure could be applied. 'I'll be frank with you,' Myron said. 'If you don't help us out, it may blow up into something major. Newspapers, TV, the works.'

'Is that a threat?'

'Absolutely not.' Myron reached into his wallet and took out a fifty-dollar bill. He placed it on the desk. 'We just want to know who put this ad in.'

Nickler pushed the bill back toward Myron, his expression suddenly irritated. 'What is this, a movie? I don't need a payoff. If the guy has done something wrong, I want no part of him. This business has enough problems as it is. I run a straight operation. No underage girls, nothing illegal in any way, shape, or form.'

Myron looked at Win. 'Told you he was a prince.'

'Think what you want,' Nickler said in a voice that said he'd been down this road many times before. 'This is a business like any other. I'm just an honest guy trying to make an honest buck.'

'Real American of you.'

He shrugged. 'Look, I don't defend everything about this business. But there are plenty worse. IBM, Exxon, Union Carbide – these are the real monsters, the real exploiters. I don't steal. I don't lie. I satisfy a societal need.'

Myron had a quick comeback, but Win stopped him with a shake of his head. He was right. What was the point in antagonizing the guy?

'Could we have the name and address, please?' Myron asked.

Nickler opened a drawer behind him and pulled out a file. 'Is he in some sort of trouble?'

'We just need to talk to him.'

'Can you tell me why?'

Win spoke to Nickler for the first time. 'You don't want to know.'

Fred Nickler hesitated, saw Win's steady gaze, then nodded. 'The company is called ABC. They have a p.o. box in Hoboken, number 785. The guy's name is Jerry. I don't know anything else about him.'

'Thanks,' Myron said, standing. 'One more question if you don't mind: Have you ever seen the girl in the ad?'

'No.'

'You're sure?'

'Positive.'

'If you do or if you think of anything else, will you give me a call?' Myron handed him a card.

Nickler looked as if he wanted to ask a question, his gaze continually drifting back to Kathy's photograph, but he settled for saying 'Sure.'

Once outside, Win asked, 'What do you think?'

'He's lying,' Myron said.

Back in the car Myron asked, 'Can I use the phone?'

Win nodded, his foot not slackening on the pedal. The speedometer was hovering at seventy-five. Myron watched it as if it were a taxi meter on a long ride, keeping his gaze averted from the blur of a street.

Myron dialed the office. Esperanza answered the phone after one ring.

'MB SportReps.'

MB SportReps. The M stood for Myron, the B for Bolitar. Myron had thought of the name himself, though he rarely bragged about it. 'Did Otto Burke or Larry Hanson call?'

'No. But you have lots of messages.'

'Nothing from Burke or Hanson?'

'You deaf?'

'I'll be back in a little while.'

Myron hung up. Otto and Larry should have called by now. They were avoiding him. The question was, why?

'Trouble?' Win asked.

'Maybe.'

'I believe we need a rejuvenation.'

Myron looked up. He recognized the street immediately. 'Not now, Win.'

'Now.'

'I have to get back to the office.'

'It'll keep. You need inner energy. You need focus. You need balance.'

'I hate it when you talk like that.'

Win smiled, pulling into the parking lot. 'Come along now. I'd hate to kick your ass right here in the car.'

The sign read MASTER KWAN'S TAE KWON DO SCHOOL. Kwan was nearing seventy now and rarely conducted classes any longer, choosing instead to hire well-tutored underlings to handle that work. Master Kwan stayed in his high-tech office, surrounded by four television screens so he could monitor the classes. Occasionally he leaned forward and barked something into a microphone, scaring some poor student into attention. Like something out of *The Wizard of Oz*.

If Master Kwan's English improved a bit, it might reach the level of pidgin. Win had brought him over from Korea fourteen years ago, when Win was only seventeen. It seemed to Myron that Master Kwan had spoken better English back then.

Win and Myron changed into their white uniforms called *dobok*. Both men wrapped black belts around their stomachs. Win was a sixth-degree black belt, about as high a ranking as anybody in the United States. He had been studying tae kwon do since the age of seven. Myron had picked it up in college, giving him a dozen years of studying and a third-degree black belt.

They approached Master Kwan's door, paused in the doorway until he acknowledged their presence, then bowed at the waist. 'Good afternoon, Master Kwan,' they said in unison.

Kwan smiled toothlessly. 'You here early.'

'Yes, sir,' Win replied.

'Need help?'

'No, sir.'

Kwan dismissed them by spinning back to his television screens. Myron and Win bowed once more and moved into the private *dojang* for the upper-ranked black belts. They began with meditation, something Myron had never quite gotten the full grasp of. Win loved it. He did it for at least an hour a day. Win folded himself into a lotus position. Myron settled for sitting Indian style. Both men closed their eyes, placed their thumbs on the palm directly below the pinkie, and tilted their palms toward the ceiling. They rested their hands on their knees. Instructions echoed through Myron's mind like a mantra. Back straight. Bottom of tongue curled up against the back of the upper teeth. He breathed in through his nose for six seconds, concentrating on pushing the air down into the pit of his gut, making sure that his chest did not move, that only his abdomen expanded. Then he held the air down deep, counting to himself to prevent his mind from wandering. After seven seconds he slowly released the air through the mouth for a ten count, making sure to empty completely his contracting gut. Then he waited four seconds before breathing in again.

Win did this painlessly. He did not count. His mind went black. Myron always counted, needing it to keep his mind from wandering back to the problems of the day – especially on a day like today. But in spite of himself he began to relax, to feel the tension leave his body with every long exhalation. It almost tingled.

They meditated for ten minutes before Win opened his eyes and said, '*Barro.*' Korean for stop.

They performed deep stretching exercises for the next twenty minutes. Win had the flexibility of a ballet dancer, performing full splits effortlessly. Myron had gained a lot of flexibility since taking up tae kwon do. He believed it had helped him gain six inches on his vertical leap in college. He could almost do a full split, but he couldn't hold it long.

In short Myron was flexible; Win was Gumby.

They went through their forms or *poomse* next, a complicated set of moves not unlike a violent dance step. What many exercise-crazed junkies never realized is that the martial arts are the ultimate aerobic workout. You are in constant motion – jumping, turning, spinning – propelling both arms and both legs nonstop for a half-hour at a time. Low block and front kick, high block and punch, middle block and round-house kick. Inside blocks, outside blocks, knife-hand, fists, palm strikes, knees and elbows. It was an exhausting and exhilarating workout.

Win moved through his routine flawlessly – ever the contradiction and deception. See Win on the street, and people said arrogant WASPy wimp who couldn't bruise a peach with his best punch. See him in a *dojang*, and he struck fear and awe. Tae kwon do is considered a martial art. Art. The word was not used by accident. Win was an artist, the best Myron had ever seen.

Myron remembered the first time he'd seen Win demonstrate his talent. They were freshmen in college. A group of large football players decided to shave Win's blond locks because they didn't like the way he looked. Five of them sneaked into Win's room late at night – four to hold down his arms and legs and one to carry the razor and shaving cream.

Simply put, the football team had a poor season that year. Too many guys on the injured list.

Myron and Win finished up with light free sparring. Then they dropped to the mat and performed one hundred push-ups on their fists – Win counting out loud in Korean. That done, they sat again for meditation, this time lasting fifteen minutes.

'*Barro*,' Win said.

Both men opened their eyes.

'Feeling more focused?' Win asked. 'Feeling the flow of energy? The balance?'

'Yes, Grasshopper. You want me to snatch the pebble from your hand now?'

Win moved from his lotus position into full stance in one graceful, effortless move. 'So,' he said, 'have you reached any decisions?'

'Yes.' Myron struggled to stand in one motion, tipping from side to side as he ascended. 'I'm going to tell Jessica everything.'

7

Yellow stick-on phone messages swarmed Myron's phone like locusts on a carcass. Myron peeled them away and shuffled through them. Nothing from Otto Burke or Larry Hanson or anyone in the Titans organization.

Not good.

He strapped on his headset telephone. He had resisted using one for a long time, figuring they were more suited for air traffic controllers than agents, but he quickly learned that an agent is but a fetus, his office a womb, his telephone an umbilical cord. It was easier with the headset. He could walk around; he could keep his hands free; he could forgo neck cramps from cradling a phone against his shoulder.

His first call was to the advertising director for BurgerCity, a new fast-food chain. They wanted to sign up Christian and were offering pretty good money, but Myron wasn't sure about it. BurgerCity was only regional. A national chain might come up with a better offer. Sometimes the hardest part of the job was saying no. He'd discuss the pros and cons with Christian, let him make the final decision. In the end it was his name. His money.

Myron had already signed Christian to several very lucrative endorsement deals. Wheaties would have Christian's likeness on cereal boxes starting in October. Diet Pepsi was coming up with some promotion involving Christian throwing a two-liter bottle on a perfect spiral to nubile women. Nike was developing a sweat-suit line and cleats known as the Steele Trap.

Christian stood to earn millions from endorsements, far more than he would make playing for the Titans, no matter how reasonable Otto Burke wanted to be. It was strange in a way. Fans grew agitated at the idea of a player trying to get the most out of his playing contract. They called him boorish, selfish, and egomaniacal when he demanded a great deal of money from a wealthy team owner – but they had no problem when he grabbed vaultloads from Pepsi or Nike or Wheaties for promoting products he'd probably never used or even liked. It made no sense. Christian would make more money for spending three days shooting a thirty-second hypocritical spot than he would for spending the season getting blindsided by drooling men with overactive pituitary glands – and that was how the fans wanted it.

No agent minded that setup. Most agents got between three and five percent of their players' total negotiated salary (Myron took four percent), compared with twenty or twenty-five percent for all endorsement money. (Myron took fifteen percent – hey, he was new.) In other words, sign a million-dollar deal with a team, and the agent gets around forty grand. Sign him for a million-dollar commercial, and the agent can nab as much as a quarter mil.

Myron's second call was to Ricky Lane, a running back for the New York Jets and a former college teammate of Christian's. Ricky was one of his most important clients, and Myron was fairly certain it had been Ricky who'd convinced Christian to hire him in the first place.

'I have a kids' camp appearance for you,' Myron began. 'They're paying five grand.'

'Sounds good,' Ricky said. 'How long do I have to be there?'

'Couple hours. Do a little talk, sign a few autographs, that kind of thing.'

'When?'

'A week from Saturday.'

'What about that mall appearance?'

'That's Sunday,' Myron said. 'Livingston Mall. Morley's Sporting Goods.' Ricky would get paid another five thousand dollars for sitting at a table for two hours and signing autographs.

'Cool.'

'You want me to send a limo to pick you up?'

'No, I'll drive. You hear anything about next year's contract yet?'

'We're getting there, Ricky. Another week at the most. Listen, I want you to come in and see Win soon, okay?'

'Yeah, sure.'

'You in shape?'

'The best of my life,' Ricky said. 'I want that starting job.'

'Keep working. And don't forget to make that appointment with Win.'

'Will do. Later, Myron.'

'Yeah, later.'

The calls continued, one blurring into another. He returned calls from the press. They all wanted to know about a pending deal between the Titans and Christian. Myron politely no-commented. Occasionally it was good to use the media as leverage in negotiating, but not with Otto Burke. Matters were proceeding, he told them. An agreement could be expected at any time.

He then called Joe Norris, an old-time Yankee who appeared almost every weekend at a baseball card show. Joe made more in a month now than he had in an entire season in his heyday.

Next up with Linda Regal, a tennis pro who had just cracked the top ten. Linda was worried about aging, offended because a broadcaster had referred to her as a 'familiar veteran.' Linda was almost twenty.

Eric Kramer, a UCLA senior and probable second round NFL draft pick, was in town. Myron managed to arrange a dinner with him. That meant Myron was a finalist – he and a zillion other agents. The competition was incredible. Example: There are twelve hundred NFL-authorized agents who court the two hundred college players who will be drafted in April. Something has to give. It's usually ethics.

Myron called the New York Jets general manager, Sam Logan, to discuss Ricky Lane's contract.

'The kid is in the best shape of his career,' Myron raved. He stood and paced. Myron had a large, fairly gorgeous office on Park Avenue between Forty-sixth and Forty-seventh streets. It impressed people, and appearance was important in a business dominated by sleazeballs. 'I've never seen anything like it. I'm telling you, Sam, the kid is Gayle Sayers all over again. It's amazing, really.'

'He's too small,' Logan said.

'What are you talking about? Is Barry Sanders too small? Is Emmitt Smith too small? Ricky's bigger than both of them. And he's been lifting. I'm telling you, he's going to be a great one.'

'Uh-huh. Look, Myron, he's a nice kid. He works hard. But I can't go any higher than . . .'

The number was still too low. But it was better.

The calls continued without a break. Sometime during the day Esperanza brought him a sandwich, which he inhaled.

At eight o'clock Myron placed his final office call of the day.

Jessica answered. 'Hello?'

'I'll be at your house in an hour,' Myron said. 'We need to talk.'

Myron watched Jessica's face for a reaction. She kept looking at the magazine as if it were just another issue of *Newsweek*, her expression frighteningly passive. Every once in a while she nodded, looked over the rest of the page, and glanced at the front and back covers of the magazine, always returning to the picture of Kathy. She was so nonchalant, Myron almost expected her to whistle.

Only her knuckles gave her away. They were bloodless white, the pages crinkling in her death grip.

'Are you okay?' he asked.

'I'm fine,' she said, her voice calm, almost soothing. 'You said Christian got this in the mail?'

'Yes.'

'And you and Win spoke to the man who publishes this' – she hesitated, her face finally showing some signs of disgust – 'this thing?'

'Yes.'

She nodded. 'Did he give you the address of whoever put this ad in?'

'Just a p.o. box. I'm going to scout it out tomorrow, see who picks up the mail.'

She looked up for the first time. 'I'll go with you.'

He almost protested but stopped himself. He didn't stand a chance. 'Okay.'

'When did Christian give this to you?'

'Yesterday.'

That got her attention. 'You knew about this yesterday?'

He nodded.

'And you didn't tell me?' she snapped. 'I was pouring my heart out to you, feeling like some paranoid schizophrenic, and you knew about this the whole time?'

'I wasn't sure how to tell you.'

'Anything else you haven't told me?'

'Christian got a phone call last night. He thinks it was from Kathy.'

'What?'

He quickly told her about it. When he reached the part about Christian hearing Kathy's voice, her face drained of all color.

'Has your friend at the phone company learned anything?' she asked.

'No. But we know Return Call only works for specific towns within the 201 area codes.'

'How many towns?'

'About three-quarters of them.'

'So you're talking about three-quarters of the northern part of New Jersey, the most densely populated state in the US? That limits it down to what, two, three million people?'

'It's not a big help,' he admitted, 'but it's something.'

Her eyes settled back on the magazine. 'I didn't mean to jump all over you. It's just—'

'Forget it.'

'You're the best person I've ever known,' she said. 'I mean that.'

'And you're the biggest pain in the ass.'

'Tough to argue that one,' she said, but there was a hint of a smile.

'Do you want to tell the police about this?' he asked. 'Or Paul Duncan?'

She thought a moment. 'I'm not sure.'

'The press will eat it up,' he said. 'They'll drag Kathy through the mud.'

'I don't give a rat's ass what the press does.'

'I'm just telling you,' Myron said.

'They can call her a slut a million different ways. I don't care.'

'What about your mom?'

'I don't give a rat's ass what she wants either. I just want Kathy found.'

'So you want to tell them,' Myron said.

'No.'

He looked at her, confused. 'Care to elaborate?'

Her words came slow, measured, the ideas coming to her even as she spoke. 'Kathy has been gone for more than a year now,' she began. 'In all that time the cops and the press have come up with zip. Not one thing. She's just vanished without a trace.'

'So?'

'But now we get this magazine. Someone sent it to Christian, which means someone – maybe Kathy, maybe not – is trying to make contact. Think about it. For the first time in over a year there is a form of communication. I don't want that taken away. I don't want a lot of attention scaring away whoever is out there. Kathy might disappear again. This' – she held up the magazine – 'this thing is disgusting, but it's also encouraging. It's something. Don't get me wrong. I'm shocked by this. But it's a solid thread – a thread as confusing as all hell, but nonetheless a thread of hope. If the cops and the press are called in, whoever did this might get scared and vanish again. Permanently this time. I can't risk that. We have to keep this to ourselves.'

Myron nodded. 'Makes sense.'

'So what's next?' she asked.

'We go to the post office in Hoboken. I'll pick you up early. Say six.'

8

Jessica smelled great.

They were at Uptown Station in Hoboken. She stood very close to him. Her hair had that freshly washed smell he had tried for four years to forget. Inhaling made him feel light-headed.

'So this is playing detective,' she said.

'Exciting, isn't it?'

They had been trying to look inconspicuous – no easy task when a man is six-four and a woman is a total knee-knocker – for the better part of an hour, having arrived at the post office at six-thirty in the morning. No one had touched Box 785 yet.

Boredom set in quickly. Jessica looked over the prices of different mailing containers. Not very interesting. She read the wanted ads, all of them, found them a bit more interesting. Wanted posters in a post office. Like they wanted you to write the guy a letter.

'You sure know how to show a girl a good time,' she said.

'That's why they call me Captain Fun.'

She laughed. The melodic sound twisted his stomach.

'Do you like being an agent, Captain Fun?'

'Very much.'

'I always thought of agents as a bunch of sleazeballs.'

'Thank you.'

'You know what I mean. Leeches. Vipers. Greedy, money-hungry, bloodsucking parasites, swindling naïve jocks, doing lunch at Le Cirque, destroying everything that's good about sports—'

'The problems in the Middle East,' he interrupted. 'That's our fault too. And the budget deficit.'

'Right. But you're not any of those things.'

'Not a leech, viper, or parasite. That's quite a rave.'

'You know what I mean.'

He shrugged. 'There are plenty of sleazy agents. There are also plenty of sleazy doctors, lawyers—' He stopped, the words sounding familiar. Hadn't Fred Nickler used the same argument in justifying his magazines? 'Agents are a necessary evil,' he continued. 'Without them, athletes get taken advantage of.'

'By whom?'

'Owners, management. Agents have done some good for the athletes. They've helped raise their salaries, assure free agency, get them endorsement money.'

'So what's the problem?'

Myron thought a moment. 'Two things,' he said. 'First of all, some agents are crooks. Plain and simple. They see a young, rich kid, and they take advantage. But as the athletes get more sophisticated, as more stories like what happened to Kareem Abdul-Jabar become known, most of the crooks will be weeded out.'

'And second?'

'Agents have to wear too many hats,' he said. 'We're negotiators, accountants, financial planners, hand-holders, travel agents, family counselors, marriage counselors, errand boys, lackeys – whatever it takes to get the business.'

'So how do you do it all?'

'I give two of the biggest hats to Win – accountant and financial planner. I'm the lawyer. He's the MBA. Plus we have Esperanza, who can do almost anything. It works well. We all check and balance one another.'

'Just like the branches of the federal government.'

He nodded. 'Jefferson and Madison would be proud.'

A hand reached out and opened Box 785.

'Show time,' Myron said.

Jessica snapped her head around to look. The man was slim. Everything about him was too long, eerily elongated, as if he had spent time on a medieval rack. Even his face seemed stretched like a cartoon imprint on Silly Putty.

'Recognize him?' Myron asked.

She hesitated. 'Something about him . . . but I don't think so.'

'Come on, let's get out of here.'

They hurried down the steps and got in the car. Myron had parked illegally in front of the building, putting a police emergency sign in his front windshield. A gift from a friend on the force. The emergency sign came in handy – especially during sale days at the mall.

The slim man came out two minutes later. He got into a yellow Oldsmobile. New Jersey plates. Myron shifted into drive and followed. Slim took Route 3 to the Garden State Parkway north.

'We've been driving almost twenty minutes,' Jessica said. 'Why would he go to a mailbox so far from his home?'

'Could be that he's not going to his house. Maybe he's going to work.'

'The dial-a-porn office?'

'Maybe,' Myron said. 'Or it could be that he travels a long way so no one will see him.'

He got off at Exit 160, jumped on Route 208 heading north, and pulled off at Lincoln Avenue, Ridgewood.

Jessica sat up. 'This is my exit,' she said.

'I know.'

'What the hell is going on here?'

The yellow Oldsmobile turned left at the end of the ramp. They were now within three miles of Jessica's house. If he took Lincoln Avenue all the way to Godwin Road, they'd be . . .

Nope.

Mr Slim turned on Kenmore Road, a half-mile before the Ridgewood border. They were still in the heart of suburbia – the suburb in question being Glen Rock, New Jersey. Glen Rock was so named because of a giant rock that sat on Rock Road. The key word here is *rock*.

The yellow Olds pulled into a driveway. 78 Kenmore Road.

'Look casual,' he said. 'Don't stare.'

'What?'

He didn't answer. He drove past the house without pausing, turned at the next street, and stopped the car behind some shrubs. He picked up the car phone and dialed the office. It was picked up midway through the first ring.

'MB SportReps,' Esperanza said.

'Get me all you can on 78 Kenmore Street, Glen Rock, New Jersey. Owner's name, credit check, the works.'

'Got it.' Click.

He dialed another number. 'My friend at the phone company,' he explained to Jessica. Then: 'Lisa? It's Myron. Look, I need a favor. Seventy eight Kenmore Road, Glen Rock, New Jersey. I don't know how many lines the guy has, but I need you to check them all. I want to know every number he calls for the next two hours. Right. Hey, what did you find out about that 900 number? What? Oh, okay, I understand. Thanks.'

He hung up.

'What did she say?'

'The 900 number isn't operated by the phone company. Some small outfit out of South Carolina takes care of it. She can't get anything on it.'

'So what do we do now?' she asked. 'Just watch his house?'

'No. I go inside. You wait here.'

She arched an eyebrow. 'Excuse me?'

'You were the one who didn't want to scare anyone away,' he continued. 'If this guy has something to do with your sister how do you think he'll react to seeing you?'

She folded her arms across her chest and fumed. She knew he was right, but that didn't mean she had to be happy about it. 'Go,' she said.

He got out of the car. It was one of those no-variety neighborhoods, each house cookie-cut from the same mold – split-levels on three-quarters of an acre. Sometimes the house was backward, the kitchen on the right instead of the left. Most had aluminum siding. The street reeked of middle class.

Myron knocked. The thin man opened the door.

'Jerry?'

Slim's face registered confusion. Up close he was better looking, his face more brooding than freakish. Give him a cigarette and a black turtleneck, and he could be reading poetry in a village café. 'May I help you?'

'Jerry, I'm—'

'You must have the wrong house. My name isn't Jerry.'

'You look like Jerry.'

Something dark crossed his face. 'I'm sorry,' he said, closing the door. 'I really don't have time right now.'

'Sure about that, Jer?'

'I already told you—'

'Do you know Kathy Culver?'

It was a sneak attack. And it drew blood. 'Wha— what's this all about?' he snapped.

'I think you know.'

'Who are you?'

'My name is Myron Bolitar.'

'Am I supposed to know you?'

'Well, if you're a big basketball fan . . . actually, no. But I'd like to ask you a few questions.'

'I have nothing to say.'

Ace of spades time. Myron pulled out the magazine. 'Sure about that, Jerry?'

The whites of Slim's eyes grew tenfold, looking like Wedgwood china on the elongated face. 'You have me mixed up with someone else. Good-bye.'

He slammed the door.

Myron shrugged, headed back to the car.

'Well?' Jessica asked.

'We shook him,' Myron said. 'Let's see what falls out.'

The neighborhood newsstand.

Win remembered a time when the phrase conjured up nostalgia and Rockwellian images of real America. No more. Any street, any corner, any hickville town was the same. Candy, newspapers, greeting cards – and porno mags. Kids could pick up a Snickers bar and get an eyeful, all in one. Porno had become a staple of American life. Hardcore porn. The kind of porn that made *Penthouse* look like *Highlights* magazine.

Win approached the man behind the lottery ticket dispenser. 'Pardon me,' Win said.

'Yeah?'

'Would you be able to tell me if you have the most recent issues of *Climaxx, Jiz, Orgasm Today, Licks, Quim,* and *Nips*?'

An elderly woman gasped and gave him an icy stare. Win smiled at her. 'Let me guess,' he said. 'Playmate of the Month, June 1926?'

She made a harumph noise and turned away.

'Check over there,' the man said. 'Between the comic books and Disney videos.'

'Thank you.'

Win found three of them – *Climaxx, Orgasm Today,* and *Quim.* He tried three other newsstands and was able to pick up *Lick,* but there was no sign of *Jiz* or *Nips.* He finally found copies of them at a hardcore shop on Forty-second Street called King David's Smut Palace. They had a big sign out front that said OPEN 24 HOURS. How very convenient. Win considered himself fairly worldly, but the items and photographs in the 'palace' proved that both his life experiences and his imagination had at best been limited.

It was almost noon when he exited the palace. A productive and quasi-educational morning.

With a total of six magazines lodged under his arm, Win caught a taxi to midtown. He skimmed through a few in the backseat.

'So far so good,' he said out loud.

The driver glanced at him in the rearview mirror, shrugged, looked back to the road.

When Win arrived at his office, he spread the magazines across the vast breadth of his desk. He studied them closely, comparing them. Incredible. His suspicion had been sound. It was just as he thought.

Five minutes later, Win put the magazines in his desk drawer. Then he buzzed Esperanza.

'Kindly send Myron to my office as soon as he comes in.'

9

'I have a confession,' Jessica said.

They were coming out of the Kinney garage on Fifty-second Street, the smell of fumes and urine dissipating as they hit the relatively fresh air on the sidewalk. They turned down Fifth Avenue. The line for passports stretched past the statue of Atlas. A black man with long dreadlocks sneezed repeatedly, his hair flapping about like dozens of snakes. A woman behind him tsk-tsked a complaint. Many of the people waiting faced St Patrick's across the street as though pleading for divine intervention, their faces lined with anguish. Japanese tourists took pictures of both the statue and the line.

'I'm listening,' Myron replied.

They kept walking. Jessica did not face him, her gaze fixed on nothing straight ahead. 'We weren't close anymore. In fact, Kathy and I barely spoke.'

Myron was surprised. 'Since when?'

'The last three years or so.'

'What happened?'

She shook her head, but she still did not look at him. 'I don't know exactly. She changed. Or maybe she just grew up and I couldn't handle it. We just drifted apart. When we saw each other, it was as if she couldn't stand to be in the same room with me.'

'I'm sorry to hear that.'

'Yeah, well, it's no big thing. Except Kathy called me the night she disappeared. First time in I don't know how long.'

'What did she want?'

'I don't know. I was on my way out the door. I rushed her off.'

They fell into silence the rest of the way to Myron's office.

When they got off the elevator, Esperanza handed him a sheet of paper and said, 'Win wants to see you right away.' She glared at Jessica the way a linebacker might glare at a limping quarterback on a blindside blitz.

'Otto Burke or Larry Hanson call?' Myron asked.

She swerved her glare toward Myron. 'No. Win wants to see you right away.'

'I heard you the first time. Tell him I'll be up in five minutes.'

They moved into Myron's office. He closed the door and skimmed over the sheet. Jessica sat in front of him. She crossed her legs the way few women could, turning an ordinary event into a moment of sexual intrigue. Myron tried not to stare. He also tried not to remember the luscious feel of those legs in bed. He was unsuccessful in both endeavors.

'What's it say?' she asked.

He snapped to. 'Our slim friend on Kenmore Road in Glen Rock is named Gary Grady.'

Jessica squinted. 'The name sounds familiar.' She shook her head. 'But I can't place it.'

'He's been married seven years, wife Allison. No kids. Has a $110,000 mortgage on that house, pays it on time. Nothing else yet. We should know more in a little while.' He put the paper on his desk. 'I think we have to start attacking this on a few different fronts.'

'How?'

'We have to go back to the night your sister disappeared. Start with that, and move forward. The whole case needs to be reinvestigated. The same with your father's murder. I'm not saying the cops weren't thorough. They probably were. But we now know some things they don't.'

'The magazine,' she said.

'Exactly.'

'How can I help?' she asked.

'Start finding out all you can about what she was up to when she disappeared. Talk to her friends, roommates, sorority sisters, fellow cheerleaders – anyone.'

'Okay.'

'Also get her school records. Let's see if there's anything there. I want to see what courses she was taking, what activities she was involved with, anything.'

Esperanza threw open the door. 'Meal Ticket. Line two.'

Myron checked his watch. Christian should be in the middle of practice by now. He picked up the phone. 'Christian?'

'Mr Bolitar, I don't understand what's going on.'

Myron could barely hear him. It sounded as if he were standing in a wind tunnel. 'Where are you?'

'A pay phone outside Titans Stadium.'

'What's the matter?'

'They won't let me in.'

Jessica stayed in the office to make a few calls. Myron rushed out. Fifty-seventh Street to the West Side Highway was unusually clear. He called Otto Burke and Larry Hanson from the car. Neither one was in. Myron was not astounded.

Then he dialed an unlisted phone number in Washington. Few people had this particular number.

'Hello?' the voice answered politely.

'Hi, P.T.'

'Ah shit, Myron, what the fuck do you want?'

'I need a favor.'

'Perfect. I was telling someone, gee, I wish Bolitar would call so I could do him a favor. Few things bring me such joy.'

P.T. worked for the FBI. FBI chiefs come and go. P.T. was a constant. The press didn't know about him, but every president since Nixon had had his number on their speed dial.

'The Kathy Culver case,' Myron said. 'Who's the best guy to talk to about it?'

'The local cop,' P.T. answered without hesitation. 'He's an elected sheriff or something. Great guy, good friend of mine. I forget his name.'

'Can you get me an appointment?' Myron asked.

'Why not? Serving your needs gives my life a sense of purpose.'

'I owe you.'

'You already owe me. More than you can pay. I'll call you when I have something.'

Myron hung up. The traffic was still clear. Amazing. He crossed the Washington Bridge and arrived at the Meadowlands in record time.

The Meadowlands Sports Authority was built on useless swampland off the New Jersey Turnpike in a place called East Rutherford. From west to east stood the Meadowlands Race Track, Titans Stadium, and the Brendan Byrne Arena, named for the former governor who was about as well liked as a whitehead on prom night. Angry protests equal to the French Revolution had erupted over the name, but to no avail. Mere revolutions are hardly worthy adversaries for a politician's ego.

'Oh, Christ.'

Christian's car – or he assumed it was Christian's – was barely visible under the blanket of reporters. Myron had expected this. He had told Christian to lock himself in his car and not say a word. Driving away would have been useless. The press would have just followed, and Myron was not up for a car chase.

He parked nearby. The reporters turned toward him like lions smelling a wounded lamb.

'What's going on, Myron?'

'Why isn't Christian at practice?'

'You pulling a holdout or what?'

'What's happening with his contract?'

Myron no-commented them, swimming through the sea of micro-phones, cameras, and flesh, squeezing his way into the car without allowing any of the slime to ooze in with him.

'Drive off,' Myron said.

Christian started the car and pulled out. The reporters parted grudgingly. 'I'm sorry, Mr Bolitar.'

'What happened?'

'The guard wouldn't let me in. He said he had orders to keep me out.'

'Son of a bitch,' Myron muttered. Otto Burke and his damn tactics. Little weasel. Myron should have been looking for something like this. But a lockout? That seemed a tad extreme, even by Otto Burke's standards. Despite the posturing, they had been fairly close to signing. Burke had expressed strong interest in getting Christian to minicamp as soon as possible, to get him ready for the season.

So why would he lock Christian out?

Myron didn't like it.

'Do you have a car phone?' he asked.

'No, sir.'

It didn't matter. 'Turn back around,' Myron said. 'Park by Gate C.'

'What are you going to do?'

'Just come with me.'

The guard tried to stop them, but Myron pushed Christian past him. 'Hey, you're not allowed in there!' he called after them. 'Hey, stop!'

'Shoot us,' Myron said without stopping.

They strode onto the field. Players were hitting the tackle dummies hard. Very hard. No one was holding back. These were tryouts. Most of these guys were fighting for a spot on the team. Most had been high school and college superstars, accustomed to unadulterated greatness on the field. Most would get cut. Most would not allow the dream to end there, scrounging other teams' rosters for a possible opening, holding on, slipping endlessly, dying slowly all the while.

A glamour profession.

The coaches blew whistles. The running backs practiced wind sprints. Kickers were knocking down field goals at the far goal post. Punters boomed slow lazy arcs high into the air. Several players turned and spotted Christian. A buzz developed. Myron ignored it. He had spotted his target, sitting in the first row on the fifty-yard line.

Otto Burke sat like Caesar at the Colosseum, that damn smile still plastered to his face, his arms spread over the seats on either side of him. Behind him sat Larry Hanson and a few other executives. Caesar's senate. Occasionally Otto would lean back and award his entourage a comment that brought on aneurysm-like fits of laughter.

'Myron!' Otto called out pleasantly, waving one of those tiny hands. 'Come on over. Have a seat.'

'Wait here,' Myron told Christian. He climbed the steps. The entourage, led by Larry Hanson, stood in unison and marched away.

Myron snapped a salute at them. 'Hut two, three, four. Right face.' No one laughed. Big surprise.

'Sit down, Myron,' Otto said, beaming. 'Let's have a chat.'

'You haven't been returning my calls,' Myron said.

'Did you call?' He shook his head. 'I'll have to get on my secretary about that.'

Myron let out a deep breath and sat. 'Why was Christian locked out?'

'Well, Myron, it's pretty simple, actually. Christian hasn't signed his contract yet. The Titans don't have time to invest in someone who may not be part of our future.' He nodded toward the field. 'Do you see who's here for a tryout? Neil Decker from Cincinnati. Fine quarterback.'

'Yeah, he's great. He can almost throw a spiral.'

Otto chuckled. 'That's funny, Myron. You're a very amusing man.'

'I'm so glad you think so. Mind telling me what's going on?'

Otto Burke nodded. 'That's fair, Myron. So let's talk frankly, shall we?'

'Rationally, frankly, whatever you want.'

'Great. We'd like to renegotiate your client's contract,' he said. 'Downward.'

'I see.'

'We feel your client's value has depreciated.'

'Uh-huh.'

Burke studied him. 'You don't seem surprised, Myron.'

'So what is it this time?' Myron asked.

'What is what this time?'

'Well, let's start with Benny Keleher. You invited him to your house, plied him with booze, then had a cop arrest him on his ride home for drunk driving.'

Otto looked properly shocked. 'I had nothing to do with that.'

'Amazing how he signed the next day. And then there's Eddie Smith. You had compromising photographs of him taken by a private eye and threatened to send them to his wife.'

'Another lie.'

'Fine, a lie. So let's cut to the chase, then. What has caused this sudden devaluation?'

Otto sat back. He withdrew a cigarette from a gold case with a Titans emblem on the cover. 'It's something I saw in a rather lewd magazine,' he said. 'Something that truly disheartened me.' He didn't look disheartened. He looked rather pleased.

'A new low,' Myron said. 'You should be proud.'

'Pardon me?'

'You set it up. The magazine.'

Otto smiled. 'Ah, so you knew about it.'

'How did you get that picture?'

'What picture?'

'The one in the ad.'

'I had nothing to do with it.'

'Sure,' Myron said. 'I guess you're just a charter subscriber to *Nips*.'

'I had nothing to do with that ad, Myron. Honestly.'

'Then how did you get a hold of the magazine?'

'Someone pointed it out to me.'

'Who?'

'I am not at liberty to discuss it.'

'Very convenient.'

'I'm not sure I like your tone, Myron. And let me tell you something else: You're the one who has done wrong in the case. If you knew about the magazine, you had an ethical responsibility to tell me.'

Myron looked up at the sky. 'You used the word *ethical*. Lightning did not strike. There is no God.'

The smile flickered but stayed on. 'Much as we'd like to, Myron, we can't just wish this away. The magazine exists, and it must be dealt with. So let me tell you what I've come up with.'

'I'm all ears.'

'You're going to take our current offer and knock it down by a third. If not, the picture of Ms Culver goes public. Think about it. You have three days to decide.' Otto watched Neil Decker throw a pass. It looked like a duck with a broken wing, crashing well short of the receiver. He frowned, stroked his goatee. 'Make that two days.'

10

Dean of Students Harrison Gordon made sure the door to his office was locked. Double-locked, in fact. He was taking no chances. Not with this.

He sat back down and stared out his office window. Esteemed Reston University in all its glory. The view was a mesh of green grass and brick buildings. No ivy adorned these towers of learning, but it should have. The students were gone for summer break, but the commons still had a sprinkling of people on it – campers from the football and tennis camps, local people who used the campus as a park, the old throwback hippies who pilgrimage to liberal arts institutions like Moslems to Mecca. Lots of red bandannas and ponchos and granola-types. A bearded man tossed a Frisbee. A small boy caught it.

Harrison Gordon saw none of it. He had not spun his chair around to enjoy the view. He had done so to avert his gaze from the . . . thing on his desk. He wanted simply to destroy the damn thing and forget about it. But he couldn't. Something held him back. And something kept drawing him toward it, toward that page near the back.

Destroy it, you fool. If somebody finds it . . .

What?

He did not know. He spun his chair back around, keeping his eyes away from the magazine. The student file marked CULVER, KATHERINE lay to the right. He swallowed. With a shaking hand he sifted through the stacks of transcripts and recommendation letters. It was an impressive file, but Harrison had no time for that now.

The buzz of his intercom – a horrid noise – startled him upright.

'Dean Gordon?'

'Yes,' he said, nearly shouting. His heart was beating like a rabbit's.

'I have someone here to see you. She doesn't have an appointment, but I thought you might want to see her.'

Edith's voice was hushed, a church-whisper.

'Who is it?' he asked.

'It's Jessica Culver. She's Kathy's sister.'

Panic punctured his heart like an icicle.

'Dean Gordon?'

He clamped his hand over his mouth, afraid he might scream.

'Dean Gordon? Are you there?'

There were no true options. He would have to see her and find out what she wanted. To act in any other manner would raise suspicion.

He opened his bottom drawer and scooped the contents of his desk into it. He shut it, took out his key ring, and locked his desk. Better safe than sorry. Last, he unbolted his door.

'Send Ms Culver in,' he said.

Jessica was at least as beautiful as her sister, which was saying something quite extraordinary. He debated on how to greet her and settled for funeral director mode – detached sympathy, warm professionalism.

He shook her hand with gentle firmness. 'Miss Culver, I'm so sorry we have to meet under such circumstances. Our prayers are with your family during this difficult time.'

'Thank you for seeing me without an appointment.'

He waved his hand as if to scoff, It's nothing. 'Please have a seat. Can I get you something to drink? Coffee, soda?'

'No, thank you.'

He moved back to his chair. He sat and folded his hands on the desk. 'Is there something I can do for you?'

'I need my sister's file,' Jessica replied.

Harrison felt his fingers bunch, but he kept his face steady. 'Your sister's school file?'

'Yes.'

'May I inquire as to why?'

'It involves her disappearance.'

'I see,' he said slowly. His voice, he was surprised to hear, remained calm. 'I believe the police were very thorough with the file. They made copies of everything in it—'

'I understand that. I'd like to see the file for myself.'

'I see,' he said again.

Several seconds passed. Jessica shifted in her chair. 'Is there a problem?' she asked.

'No, no. Well, perhaps. I'm afraid it may not be possible to give you the file.'

'What?'

'What I mean to say is, I'm not sure you have any legal right to it. Parents certainly do. But I'm not sure about siblings. I'll need to check this with a university attorney.'

'I'll wait,' Jessica said.

'Uh, fine. Would you mind waiting in the other room, please?'

She stood, turned, stopped. She looked back over her shoulder at him. 'You knew my sister, didn't you, Dean Gordon?'

He managed a smile. 'Yes, I did. Wonderful young lady.'

'Kathy worked for you.'

'Filing, answering the phone, that sort of thing,' he said quickly. 'She was a terrific worker. We all miss her very much.'

'Did she seem okay to you?'

'Okay?'

'Before she disappeared,' Jessica continued, her eyes boring into his. 'Was she acting strangely?'

Beads of sweat popped onto his forehead, but he dared not wipe them away. 'No, not that I could see. She seemed perfectly fine. Why do you ask?'

'Just checking. I'll wait out front.'

'Thank you.'

She closed the door.

Harrison let loose a long breath. What now? He would have to give her the file; to do otherwise would do far more than merely raise suspicion. But he could not, of course, just pull the file out of his bottom drawer and hand it to Jessica. No, he would wait a few minutes, walk down to the filing room to handle her case 'personally,' then return with the file.

Why, he wondered, did Jessica Culver need the file? Was there something he had missed?

No. He was sure of that.

Harrison had spent the last year hoping, praying, that it was over. But he should have known better. Matters like this never truly die. They hide, take root, grow stronger, prepare for a fresh onslaught.

Kathy Culver was not dead and buried. Like some gothic ghost, she had arisen, haunting him, crying out from some great beyond.

For vengeance.

Myron returned to the office.

'Win buzzed down twice,' Esperanza said. 'He wants to see you. Now.'

'On my way.'

'Myron?'

'What?'

Esperanza's lovely dark eyes were solemn. 'Is she back? Jessica, I mean.'

'No. She's just visiting.'

Her face registered doubt. Myron did not press it. He no longer knew what to think himself.

He ran up the stairs two at a time. Win was two floors above him, but he might as well have been in another dimension. As soon as he opened the big steel door, the tireless clamor swarmed in, attacking. The large open space was in perpetual motion. Two, maybe three hundred desks covered the huge floor like throw rugs. Every desk had at least two computer terminals on it. There were no partitions. Hundreds of men sat and stood at every angle, each wearing a white button-down shirt with tie and suspenders, suit jackets draped from the back of their chairs. There were painfully few women. The men were all on the phone, most covering the mouthpiece to scream at someone else. They all looked alike. They all sounded alike. They were all pretty much the same person.

Welcome to Lock-Horne Investments & Securities.

All six floors were exactly the same. In fact, Myron often suspected that Lock-Horne had only one floor and that the elevator was set to stop on the same floor no matter which number you hit from floor fourteen to floor nineteen, giving the illusion of a bigger company.

Office after office made up the compound's perimeter. These were saved for the head honchos, the top dogs, the numero unos, or in securities talk, the Big Producers. The BPs all had windows and sunshine, unlike the peons on the inside, who sickened and paled from the unnatural light.

Win had a corner office with a view of both Forty-seventh Street and Park Avenue – a view that screamed major dinero. His office was decorated in Early American WASP. Dark-paneled walls. Forest green carpet. Wing-back chairs. Paintings of a fox hunt on the wall. Like Win had ever seen a fox.

Win looked up from his massive oak desk when Myron entered. The desk weighed slightly less than a cement mixer. He'd been studying a computer print-out, one of those never-ending reams with green and white stripes. The desk was blanketed with them. They sort of matched the carpet.

'How did your morning rendezvous go with our friend Jerry the Phone-icator?' Win asked.

'Phone-icator?'

Win smiled. 'I spent the whole morning working that one.'

'It was worth it,' Myron said.

He filled Win in on his encounter with Gary 'Jerry' Grady. Win sat back and steepled. Myron then filled him in on his encounter with Otto Burke. Win leaned forward and unsteepled.

'Otto Burke,' Win said, his voice measured, 'is a scoundrel. Perhaps I should pay him a private visit.' He looked up at Myron hopefully.

'No. Not yet. Please.'

'Are you quite positive?'

'Yes. Promise me, Win. No visits.'

He was clearly disappointed. 'Fine,' Win said, grudgingly.

'So what did you want to see me about?'

'Ah.' Win's face lit up again. 'Take a look at this.'

He lifted the reams of computer print-outs and unceremoniously dumped them on the floor. Underneath were a pile of magazines. The top one was called *Climaxx*. The subheadline read, 'Double Xs for Double the Pleasure.' Nifty sales technique. Win fanned them out as if he were doing a card trick.

'Six magazines,' he said.

Myron read the titles. *Climaxx, Licks, Jiz, Quim, Orgasm Today*, and of course, *Nips*. 'Nickler's publications?'

'God, you are good,' Win said.

'Years of training. So what about them?'

'Take a look at the pages I have marked off.'

Myron started with *Climaxx*. The cover featured another freakishly endowed woman, this time licking her own nipple. Handy. Win had used leather bookmarks to mark the page. Leather bookmarks in porno magazines. Like cigarettes in an aerobics class.

The page marked off was already too familiar. Myron felt his stomach churn all over again.

Live Fantasy Phone – Pick Your Girl

There were still three rows, still four in each row. His eyes immediately moved down to the bottom row, second from the right. It still read, 'I'll Do Anything!' The phone number was still 1-900-344-LUST. Still $3.99 per minute. Still discreetly billed to your telephone or charge card, Visa and MasterCard accepted.

But the woman in the picture was not Kathy Culver.

He quickly scanned the rest of the page. Nothing else was different. The same Oriental girl was still waiting. The same buttock still craved a spanking. 'Tiny Titties' had not pubesced.

'This same advertising page is in all six magazines,' Win explained. 'But only *Nips* has Kathy Culver's picture.'

'Interesting.' Myron thought a moment. 'Nickler probably sells package deals to advertisers – buy space in six for the price of three, that kind of thing.'

'Precisely. I would venture to say that all six magazines have the exact same ads.'

'But someone stuck Kathy's picture in *Nips*.' Myron was getting used to saying the name of the magazine. It no longer felt grimy on his lips, which in itself made him feel grimier.

Win said, 'Do you remember Nickler telling us that *Nips* was doing poorly?'

Myron nodded.

'Well, I had a devil of a time locating it. Most of the other rags were fairly easy to find on corner newsstands. But I had to go to a hardcore porno palace on Forty-second Street to come up with *Nips*.'

'Yet,' Myron added, 'Otto Burke was able to get a copy.'

'Precisely. I am sure you've considered the possibility that Mr Burke is behind it.'

'The idea has crossed my mind.'

There was a knock on the door. Esperanza entered.

'Your handwriting expert is on the phone,' she said. 'I put it on Win's line.'

Win picked up the receiver and handed it to Myron.

'Hello.'

'Hey, Myron, it's Swindler. I just went over the two samples you gave me.'

Myron had given Swindler the envelope *Nips* had come in as well as a letter in Kathy's handwriting.

'Well?'

'They match. It's her or a very professional forgery.'

Myron felt his stomach dive. 'You're sure?'

'Positive.'

'Thanks for calling.'

'Yeah, no problem.'

Myron handed the receiver back to Win.

'A match?' Win asked.

'Yep.'

Win tilted back in his chair and smiled. 'Yowzer.'

11

Myron ran into Ricky Lane in the corridor. He hadn't seen him in three months. Ricky looked a lot bigger. The Jets would be pleased.

'What are you doing here?' Myron asked.

'I made an appointment with Win,' Ricky said with a big grin. 'Just like my agent advised.'

'Good to see you listen to your agent.'

'Always. The man is brilliant.'

'And he never argues with a client.'

Ricky laughed. 'Say, I heard Christian got locked out of camp.'

News traveled fast. 'Where did you hear that?'

'The FAN.'

WFAN was New York's all-sports radio station. 'Have you spoken to him lately?'

Ricky made a face. 'Christian?'

'Yeah.'

'Not since my last college football game, what, year and a half ago.'

'I thought you were friends.' Myron had, in fact, assumed that Ricky had recommended his services to Christian.

'We were teammates,' Ricky replied steadily. 'We were never friends.'

'You don't like him?'

Ricky shrugged. 'Not really. None of us did.'

'Who is "us"?'

'Guys on the team.'

'What's wrong with him?'

'Long story, man. Not worth telling.'

'I'd be interested.'

'Put it like this,' Ricky said. 'Christian was a little too perfect for most of us, okay?'

'An egomaniac?'

Ricky paused, considering. 'Not really. I mean, to be straight, I guess a lot of it was jealousy. Christian wasn't just good. Shit, he wasn't even just great. He was incredible. Best I ever seen.'

'So?'

'So he expected the same from everyone else.'

'He got on people's case when they made mistakes?'

Ricky paused again, shook his head. 'No, that ain't it either.'

'You're being a tad obtuse, Ricky.'

Ricky Lane looked up, looked down, looked left, looked right, looked very uneasy. 'I can't explain it,' he said. 'It's going to sound like a lot of griping, but the guys weren't crazy about all the attention he was getting. I mean, we won two national championships, and the only guy they ever talked to was Christian.'

'I heard those interviews. He always gave his teammates all the credit.'

'Yeah, a real gentleman,' Ricky replied with more than a hint of sarcasm. 'All that "it's a team effort" bullshit just made the press love him even more. Guys on the team thought he was a promo-hog, you know? His own best PR firm. They blamed him for being too popular.'

'Did you?'

'I don't know. Maybe. Truth was, I just didn't really like him. We had nothing in common except football. He's a pure Midwest white-boy. I'm a city-slicking black man. It ain't a winning combination.'

'That's all it was?'

He gave a half-shrug. 'I guess so. But man, this is all ancient history. I don't know why I brought it up. It don't matter no more. Christian just didn't fit in, okay. He was a nice guy, I guess. He was always polite. But that don't play so well in a locker room, you know?'

Myron knew. Juvenile, sexist, homophobic bantering – that was the stuff of locker room popularity.

'I gotta go, man. Win will be wondering where I am.'

'Okay. I'll see you around.'

Ricky had almost turned away when Myron thought of something else. 'What can you tell me about Kathy Culver?'

Ricky's face blanched. 'What about her?'

'Did you know her?'

'A little, I guess. I mean, she was a cheerleader and dated the quarterback. But we never hung out or anything.' He looked very unhappy now. 'Why you asking?'

'Was she popular? Or was she hated too?'

Ricky's eyes darted about like birds trying to find a safe place to land. 'Look, Myron, you always been straight with me. I always been straight with you, right?'

'Right.'

'I don't want to say nothing else. She's dead. Might as well let her be.'

'What does that mean?'

'Nothing. I just don't like talking about her, okay. It's kinda creepy. I'll see you later.'

71

Ricky hurried down the corridor as if Reggie White were chasing him. Myron watched him. He debated following him but decided against it. Ricky would say no more today.

12

Esperanza stuck her head in the door. 'Someone – or something – is here to see you.'

Myron held up a silencing hand. The headset had been on since his return to his office. 'Look, I have to go,' he said. 'See if you can get him upgraded to first class. He's a big guy. Thanks.' He took off the headset. 'Who is it?'

She made a face. 'Aaron. He didn't give a last name.'

He didn't have to. 'Send him in.'

Seeing Aaron was like falling into a time warp. He was as big as Myron remembered, as big as the lummox in the garage. He was dressed in a freshly pressed white suit, but he wore no shirt with it, displaying plenty of tan pectoral cleavage. He wasn't wearing socks either. Nifty haircut, the swept-back look à la Pat Riley. A saunter for a walk. Designer sunglasses. Designer cologne that smelled suspiciously like insect repellent. Aaron was the pure definition of 'super-smooth' – just ask him, he'd tell you.

He smiled widely. 'Nice to see you, Myron.'

They shook hands. Myron did not squeeze. He was far too mature. That, and Aaron could probably squeeze harder. 'Have a seat.'

'Wonderful.' Aaron made a production of it, spreading out his arms as if he were wearing a cloak. He removed his sunglasses with an audible snap. 'I like your office. It's really great.'

'Thank you.'

'Great address. Great view.'

The password is *great*. 'You looking to rent space?'

Aaron laughed as if that were the gem of gems. 'No,' he said. 'I don't like being cooped in an office. It's not my style. I like my freedom. I like being out on my own, on the road. I wouldn't do well chained to a desk.'

'Wow, that's fascinating, Aaron. Really.'

He laughed again. 'Ah, Myron, you haven't changed a bit. I'm glad to see it.'

They hadn't seen each other since high school. Myron had gone to Livingston High School in New Jersey. Aaron had gone to his archenemy,

West Orange High. The teams played each other twice a year, and it was rarely a pleasant encounter.

In those days Myron's best friend was a huge ox named Todd Midron. Todd was a big, softhearted, simple kid with a lisp. He played Lenny to Myron's George. He was also the toughest kid Myron had ever met.

Todd never lost a fight. Never. No one ever came close to him. He was just too powerful. During a game in their senior year, Aaron undercut and nearly injured Myron. Todd took exception. He went after Aaron. Aaron destroyed him. Myron tried to help his friend, but Aaron shrugged Myron off like a dandruff flake. He continued to pulverize Todd, steadily, methodically, glaring at Myron the whole time, not even glancing at his limp victim. The beating was ferocious. By the time it ended, Todd's face was an unrecognizable pulpy mess. Todd spent four months in a hospital. His jaw was wired shut for nearly a year.

'Hey,' Aaron said. He pointed to a movie still on the wall. 'That's Woody Allen and what's-her-name.'

'Diane Keaton.'

'Right, Diane Keaton.'

'Is there something I can do for you?' Myron asked.

Aaron turned his whole body toward Myron. The glare from his shaved chest was nearly blinding. 'I think there is, Myron. In fact, I think there's something we can do for each other.'

'Oh?'

'I represent a competitor of yours. A certain dispute has arisen between the two of you. My client wishes to settle it peacefully.'

'Are you an attorney now, Aaron?'

He smiled. 'Not likely.'

'Oh.'

'I am referring to a young man named Chaz Landreaux. He recently signed a contract with your company, MB SportReps.'

'I thought of the name myself.'

'Pardon me.'

'MB SportReps. I came up with the name by myself.'

Aaron renewed his smile. It was a good smile. Lots of teeth. 'There is a problem with the contract.'

'Do tell.'

'You see, Mr Landreaux has also signed a contract with Roy O'Connor at TruPro Enterprises, Incorporated. The contract predates yours. So you see the problem: Your contract is invalid.'

'Why don't we let a court of law decide that?'

He sighed deeply. 'My client feels it is in everyone's best interest to avoid litigation.'

'Gee, what a surprise. So what does your client suggest?'

'Mr O'Connor would be willing to pay you for your time.'

'Very generous of him.'

'Yes.'

'And if I say no?'

'We hope it won't come to that.'

'But if it does?'

Aaron sighed, stood, leaned on Myron's desk. 'I'll be forced to make you disappear.'

'Like in a magic trick?'

'Like in dead.'

Myron put his hand to his chest. 'Gasp. Oh. Gasp.'

Aaron laughed again, this time without humor. 'I know all about your tae kwon do display in the garage. But that guy was a stupid musclehead. I am not. I boxed professionally. I'm a black belt in jujitsu and a grand master in aikido. I've killed people.'

'I bet that looks good on a résumé,' Myron said.

'Let me put this in very simple terms for you, Myron: You fuck with us, I'll kill you.'

'Shiver. Tremble.' Myron was not quite as confident as his sarcasm, but he knew better than to show fear. Guys like Aaron are like dogs. They smell fear, they pounce.

Aaron laughed again. He was laughing a lot today. He was either very amused or had been sniffing gas. He turned his back and walked to the door. 'This is your final warning,' he said. 'Landreaux honors his contract with Mr O'Connor, or both of you end up worm food.'

Worm food. First oatmeal. Now worm food.

'I like you, Myron. I'd really hate to see something bad happen. But you understand.'

'Business is business.'

'Exactly.'

Esperanza appeared at the door.

Aaron gave her a sharklike smile. 'Well, well,' he said. Then he followed up with his best big-guy wink. Esperanza managed to keep her clothes on. Amazing restraint.

'Pick up line two,' she said.

'Listen to this call closely, Myron,' Aaron added with a final grin. 'Appreciate the gravity of the situation. And remember. Worm food.'

'Worm food. I'll keep it in mind.'

Aaron winked at Esperanza again, blew her a kiss, and left.

'Charming,' she said.

'Who's on the phone?'

'Chaz Landreaux.'

Myron picked up the headset. 'Hello.'

'Motherfuckers were at my mom's!' Chaz shouted. 'They told her they were going to cut off my nuts and send them to her in a box! My mother, man! They said this to my mother!'

Myron felt his fingers tighten into fists. 'I'll take care of it,' he said slowly. 'They won't bother her again.'

Enough game playing. It was time to act.

It was time to tell Win about Roy O'Connor.

Win smiled like a kid on a snow day listening to the radio for a school closing. 'Roy O'Connor,' he said.

'I don't want him hurt. Promise me.'

Win's eyes drifted dreamily. He might have nodded a yes, but Myron couldn't say for sure.

13

Baumgart's on Palisades Avenue. Their old stomping grounds.

Peter Chin greeted them at the door, his eyes widening in delight and surprise when he spotted Jessica. 'Miss Culver! How wonderful to see you again.'

'Nice to see you, Peter.'

'You look as lovely as ever. You beautify my restaurant.'

Myron said, 'Hi, Peter.'

'Yeah, whatever.' He dismissed Myron with a hand wave. His full attention was on Jessica; a crocodile gnawing on his foot wouldn't have changed that. 'You look a little too thin, Miss Culver.'

'The food's not as good in Washington.'

'Funny,' Myron said. 'I was thinking she looked a little chunky.'

Jessica eyed him. 'Dead man.'

Baumgart's was an institution in Englewood, New Jersey. For fifty years it was an old Jewish deli and soda fountain, noted for its superb ice cream and desserts. When Peter Chin bought it eight years ago, he kept all of the tradition but added the best nouvelle Chinese cuisine in the state. The combination was a smash. The normal order might consist of Peking duck, sesame noodles, chocolate milk shake, french fries and a death-by-chocolate sundae for dessert. When Myron and Jessica had lived together, they ate at Baumgart's at least once a week.

Myron still came once a week. Usually with Win or Esperanza. Sometimes alone. He never brought a date here.

Peter walked them past the soda fountain and put them in a booth under a huge painting. Modern art. It was a portrait of either Cher or Barbara Bush. Maybe both. Very esoteric.

Myron and Jessica sat across the table from each other, silently. The moment seemed weighed down, overwhelming. Being here together again – they had expected it to generate some light nostalgia. But the effect was more like a body blow.

'I've missed this place,' she said.

'Yes.'

She reached her hand across the table and took his. 'I've missed you.'

Her face was aglow, the way it used to be when she looked at him as though he were the only person in the entire world. Myron felt something squeeze his heart, making it nearly impossible to breathe. The rest of the world broke apart, diffused. There were only the two of them.

'I'm not sure what to say.'

She smiled. 'What? Myron Bolitar at a loss for words?'

'Ripley's, huh?'

Peter came by. Without preamble, he said, 'You'll start with the crispy duck appetizer and squab package with pine nuts. For your main course you'll have softshell crab in special sauce and the Baumgart lobster and shrimp.'

'Can we choose dessert?' Myron asked.

'No. Myron, you'll have the pecan pie à la mode. And for Miss Culver.' He stopped, building suspense like a game-show host.

She smiled expectantly. 'You don't mean . . .'

Peter nodded. 'Banana pudding cake with vanilla wafers. There's only one piece left, but I put it away for you.'

'Bless you, Peter.'

'Each man does what he can. You didn't bring wine?' Baumgart's was BYO.

'We forgot,' Jessica said. She was dazzling Peter with her smile. Not fair. Jessica's looks were like a *Star Trek* laser set on stun. Her smile, kill.

'I'll send someone across the street to get a bottle. Kendall-Jackson Chardonnay?'

'You have a good memory,' she said.

'No. I just remember what is important.' Myron rolled his eyes. Peter bowed slightly and left.

She turned the smile back to Myron. He felt frightened and helpless and deliriously happy.

'I'm sorry,' she said.

He shook his head. He was afraid to open his mouth.

'I never meant—' She was unsure how to continue. 'I made a lot of mistakes in my life,' she said. 'I am dumb. I am self-destructive.'

'No,' Myron said. 'You're perfect.'

Her voice grew dramatic, her hand against her chest. 'Take the blinders from your eyes and see me as I really am.'

He thought a moment. 'Dulcinea to Don Quixote in *Man of La Mancha*. And it's "take the clouds," not blinders.'

'Very impressive.'

'Win was playing it in the car.' This was an old game of theirs. Guess the Quote.

She fiddled with her water glass, making little water circles and then inspecting them for clarity and definition. Eventually she created an aquatic Olympics logo. 'I'm not sure what I'm trying to say to you,' she said at last.

'I'm not sure what I want to happen here.' She looked up. 'One last confession, okay?'

He nodded.

'I came to you because I thought you would help. That was true. But that wasn't the only reason.'

'I know,' he said. 'I try not to think about it too much. It terrifies me.'

'So what do we do now?'

His chance. He hoped there would be others. 'Did you get your sister's file?'

'Yes.'

'Have you gone through it yet?'

'No. I just picked it up.'

'Then why don't we open it now?'

She nodded. The crispy duck and squab package with pine nuts appeared. Jessica took out a manila envelope and slit the seal. 'Why don't you look at it first?'

'Okay,' he said. 'But save me some food.'

'Chance.'

He started sifting through the papers. The top page was Kathy's high school transcript. After her junior year her ranking had been twelfth in a class of three hundred. Not bad. But by the end of senior year her ranking had slipped considerably – to fifty-eighth.

'Her grades dropped senior year of high school,' Myron said.

'Whose didn't drop senior year?' Jess countered. 'She was probably just goofing off.'

'Probably.' But usually that meant A students got Bs or Cs. Kathy had gotten one A, three Ds and an F in her final semester. Her clean record was also muddied with several detentions – all in her senior year. Strange. But probably meaningless.

'Do you want to fill me in on what happened today?' Jessica asked between bites.

She was even beautiful when pigging out. Amazing. He started by telling her about Win's discovery in the six magazines.

'So what does it mean,' she asked, 'her picture being only in that one rag?'

'I'm not sure.'

'But you have an idea?'

He did. But it was too early to say anything. 'Not yet.'

'Did you hear from your friend at the phone company?'

He nodded. 'Gary Grady placed two calls after we left. One was to Fred Nickler's office at Hot Desire Press. The other was someplace in the city. There was no answer when we called it. We got the information kind of late in the day.'

'And the handwriting analyst?'

Best to dive right in. 'The handwriting matches. It's either Kathy's or a very good forger.'

That slowed her chopsticks. 'My God.'

'Yes.'

'Then she's alive?'

'It's still just a possibility. Nothing more. That envelope could have been written before she died. Or like I said, it could be a clever forgery.'

'You're reaching.'

'I'm not so sure,' he said. 'If she's alive, where is she? Why is she doing all this?'

'Maybe she's been kidnapped. Maybe she's being forced to.'

'Forced to address envelopes? Now who's reaching?'

'Do you have a better explanation?' she asked.

'Not yet. But I'm working on it.' He started looking through the file again. 'You ever hear of a guy named Otto Burke?'

'The big record company magnate who owns the Titans?'

'Right. He also knew about the magazine.' Myron quickly summarized his visit to Titans Stadium.

'So you think Otto Burke might be behind it?' she asked.

'Otto has a motive: knocking down Christian's asking price. He certainly has the resources: lots of money. And it would also explain why Christian got a copy in the mail.'

'He was sending Christian a message,' she added.

'Right.'

'But how would Burke forge my sister's handwriting?'

'He could have hired an expert.'

'Where did he get a writing sample?'

'Who knows? It can't be that difficult.'

Her eyes glazed over. 'So this was all a hoax? This was all some plot to gain leverage in a negotiation?'

'It's possible. But I don't think so.'

'Why not?'

'Something just doesn't mesh. Why would Burke go through all that trouble? He could have blackmailed us with just the photo. He didn't have to put it in a magazine. The photo was enough.'

She grasped on to his hope as if it were a life preserver. 'Good point,' she said.

'The question then becomes,' he continued, 'how did Otto get a copy of the magazine?'

'Maybe someone in his organization picked up a copy at a news-stand.'

'Very unlikely. *Nips*' – the word felt grungy again, good – 'has a very low circulation rate. The chances that someone in the Titans organization bought that particular magazine, had time to read it carefully, somehow spotted Kathy's picture in the bottom row on a page of ads in the back – it's fairly remote at best.'

Jessica snapped her fingers. 'Someone mailed it to him too.'

He nodded. 'Why should Christian have been the only one? For all we know, dozens of people were sent that magazine.'

'How do we find out?'

'I'm working on it.'

He managed to salvage a sliver of crispy duck before it was sucked into the black hole. It was delicious. He turned his attention back to Kathy's files. Her bad grades continued during her first semester at Reston. By second semester, her grades had picked up considerably. He asked Jessica about this.

'She settled into college life, I guess,' she said. 'She joined the drama group, became a cheerleader, started dating Christian. She went through culture shock in her first semester. It's not uncommon.'

'No. I guess not.'

'You don't sound convinced.'

He shrugged. Myron Bolitar, Señor Skepticalo.

Kathy's recommendation letters were next. Three of them. Her high school guidance counselor called her 'unusually gifted.' Her tenth-grade history teacher said, 'Her enthusiasm for life is contagious.' Her twelfth-grade English teacher said, 'Kathy Culver is bright, witty, and fun-spirited. She will be a welcome addition to any institution of learning.' Nice comments. He scanned down to the bottom of the page.

'Uh-oh,' he said.

'What is it?'

He handed her the glowing recommendation letter from Kathy's twelfth-grade English teacher at Ridgewood High School. A Mr Grady.

A Mr Gary, aka 'Jerry' Grady.

14

Myron was startled awake by the telephone. He'd been dreaming about Jessica. He tried to remember specifics, but the details disintegrated into small pieces and blew away, leaving behind only a few frustrating snippets. The clock on his nightstand read seven o'clock. Someone was calling him at home at seven o'clock in the morning. Myron had a pretty good idea who it was.

'Hello?'

'Good morning, Myron. I hope I didn't wake you.'

Myron recognized the voice. He smiled and asked, 'Who is this?'

'It's Roy O'Connor.'

'*The* Roy O'Connor?'

'Uh, yes, I guess so. Roy O'Connor, the agent.'

'The superagent,' Myron corrected. 'To what do I owe this honor, Roy?'

'Would it be possible for us to meet this morning?' The voice had a discernible quake to it.

'Sure thing, Roy. My office, okay?'

'Uh, no.'

'Your office, Roy?'

'Uh, no.'

Myron sat up. 'Should I keep guessing places and you can say hotter or colder?'

'You know Reilly's Pub on Fourteenth Street?'

'Yes.'

'I'll be in the booth in the back right-hand corner. One o'clock. We'll have lunch. If that's okay with you.'

'Peachy, Roy. Want me to wear anything special?'

'Uh, no.'

Myron hung up, smiled. A night visit from Win, usually while sleeping soundly in your bedroom, your innermost sanctuary. Worked every time.

He got out of bed. He heard his mother in the kitchen above him, his father in the den watching television. Early morning at the Bolitar house. The basement door opened.

'Are you awake, Myron?' his mother shouted.

Myron. What a goddamn awful name. He hated it with a passion. The way he looked at it, he'd been born with all his fingers and toes, he didn't have a harelip nor a cauliflower ear nor a limp of any kind – so to compensate for his lack of ill fortune, his parents had christened him Myron.

'I'm awake,' he answered.

'Daddy bought some fresh bagels. They're on the table.'

'Thanks.'

He got out of bed and climbed the steps. With one hand he felt the rough beard he'd have to shave; with the other he picked the yellow sleep-buggers out of the corner of his eyes. His father was sprawled on the den couch like a wet sock, wearing an Adidas sweat suit and eating a bagel oozing with whitefish spread. As he did every morning, Myron's father was watching a videocassette of people exercising. Getting in shape through osmosis.

'Good morning, Myron. There're some bagels on the table.'

'Uh, thanks.' It was like one parent never heard the other.

He entered the kitchen. His mom was nearly sixty, but she looked much younger. Say, forty-five. She acted much younger too. Say, sixteen.

'You came in late last night,' she said.

Myron made a grunting noise.

'What time did you finally get home?'

'Really late. It was almost ten.' Myron Bolitar, the late-night scream machine.

'So,' Mom began, struggling to look and sound casual, 'who were you out with?' Mistress of the Subtle.

'Nobody,' he said.

'Nobody? You were out all night with nobody?'

Myron looked left and right. 'When are you going to bring in the hot lights and jumper cables?'

'Fine, Myron. If you don't want to tell me—'

'I don't want to tell you.'

'Fine. Was it a girl?'

'Mom . . .'

'Okay, forget I asked.'

Myron reached for the phone and dialed Win's number. After the eighth ring he began to hang up when a weak, distant voice coughed. 'Hello?'

'Win?'

'Yeah.'

'You okay?'

'Hello?'

'Win?'

'Yeah.'

'What took you so long to answer the phone?'

'Hello?'

'Win?'

'Who is this?'

'Myron.'

'Myron Bolitar?'

'How many Myrons do you know?'

'Myron Bolitar?'

'No, Myron Rockefeller.'

'Something's wrong,' Win said.

'What?'

'Terribly wrong.'

'What are you talking about?'

'Some asshole is calling me at seven in the morning pretending to be my best friend.'

'Sorry, I forgot the time.' Win was not what one would call a morning person. During their years at Duke, Win was never out of bed before noon – even on the days he had a morning class. He was, in fact, the heaviest sleeper Myron had ever known or imagined. Myron's parents, on the other hand, woke up when somebody in the Western hemisphere farted. Before Myron moved into the basement, the same scenario was played out nightly:

Around three in the morning, Myron would get out of bed to go to the bathroom. As he tiptoed past his parents' bedroom, his father would stir ever so slowly, as though someone had dropped a Popsicle on his crotch.

'Who's that?' his father would shout.

'Just me, Dad.'

'Is that you, Myron?'

'Yes, Dad.'

'Are you okay, son?'

'Fine, Dad.'

'What are you doing up? You sick or something?'

'I'm just going to the bathroom, Dad. I've been going to the bathroom by myself since I was fourteen.'

During their sophomore year at Duke, Myron and Win lived in the smallest double on campus with a bunk bed that Win said 'creaks slightly' and Myron said 'sounds like a duck being run over by a back hoe.' One morning, when the bed was quiet and he and Win were asleep, a baseball crashed through their window. The noise was so deafening that their entire dorm jumped out of bed and rushed to see if Myron and Win had survived the wrath of whatever gigantic meteorite had fallen through the roof. Myron rushed to the window to yell obscenities. Dorm members stamped across the underwear-carpeted floor to join in the tirade. The ensuing reverberations were loud enough to disturb a diner waitress on her coffee break.

Win just lay asleep, a blanket of broken glass strewn over his blanket.

The next night, Myron called through the darkness of his bottom bunk. 'Win?'

'Yes.'

'How do you sleep so soundly?' But Win didn't answer because he'd fallen asleep.

On the phone Win asked, 'What do you want?'

'Did all go well last night?'

'Mr O'Connor hasn't called you yet?'

'He has.' End of subject. Myron didn't want details.

'I know,' Win continued, 'that you did not awaken me to question my effectiveness.'

'Kathy Culver got only one A in her senior year at Ridgewood High. Guess who her teacher was.'

'Who?'

'Gary Grady.'

'Hmm. Dial-a-porn and high school English. Interesting vocational mix.'

'I was thinking we could go see Mr Grady this morning.'

'At the school?'

'Sure. The two of us can pretend we're concerned parents.'

'For the same kid?'

'Putting the rainbow curriculum to the test.'

Win laughed. 'This is going to be fun.'

15

'How do we find him?' Win asked.

They arrived at Ridgewood High School at nine-thirty. It was a warm June day, the kind of day where you stared at the window and daydreamed about the end of school. Not much movement around the building – as though the entire school, even the edifice, were coasting toward summer vacation.

Myron remembered how miserable such days were. It gave him an idea.

'Let's pull the fire alarm,' he said.

'I beg your pardon.'

'We'll get everyone outside. It'll be easier to spot him.'

'Idiotically ingenious,' Win said.

'Besides, I always wanted to pull a fire alarm.'

'Walk on the wild side.'

No one noticed them when they entered the school. There were no guards, no locks on the door, no hall monitors of any kind. This was not an urban high school. Myron found a fire alarm not too far from the entrance.

'Kids, don't try this at home,' Myron said. He pulled. Bells went off. Then cheers from the kids. Myron felt good about his deed. He thought about pulling alarms more often but decided some might construe the act as immature.

Win held the door open and pretended to be a fire marshal. 'Single file,' he told the students. 'And remember: Only you can prevent fires.'

Myron spotted Grady. 'Bingo.'

'Where?'

'Turning the corner. On the left. Mr Fashion.'

Gary Grady was wearing a yellow Century 21-like blazer with Keith Partridge orange-striped pants. Win looked visibly pained at the sight. They made their approach.

'Hi, Jerry.'

Grady's head shot around. 'That's not my name.'

'Yeah, you told me. It's your alias, right? When you do business with Fred Nickler. Your real name is Gary Grady.'

Nearby students stopped walking.

'Keep moving!' Gary snapped.

The students restarted their grudging trudge.

'Impatient teachers,' Myron said.

'Sad,' Win agreed.

Gary's thin face seemed to stretch even further. He stepped closer so that no one could overhear.

'Perhaps we can continue this conversation later,' he whispered.

'I don't think so, Gary.'

'I'm in the middle of a class.'

'Tough tittie,' Myron said.

Win arched an eyebrow. 'Tough tittie?'

'Something about being back in high school,' Myron said. 'Besides, I thought it appropriate considering the situation.'

Win considered for a moment. 'Okay, I can accept that.'

Myron turned back to Gary. 'The fire drill will last a little while. Then it will take a little while for the kids to file back in. Then they'll want to goof around in the halls for a while. By then we'll be all done.'

Gary crossed his arms over his chest. 'No.'

'Option two, then.' Myron took out a copy of *Nips*. 'We can play Show and Tell with the principal.'

Grady coughed into his fist. A loud fire whistle sounded. Sirens came closer. 'I don't know what you're talking about,' he said, taking a few more steps away from the kids.

'I followed you.'

'What?'

Myron sighed, gave him exasperation. 'You were in Hoboken yesterday morning. You picked up the mail at an address used for advertising sex lines in porno rags. Then you went home to Glen Rock, saw me, panicked, and called Fred Nickler, the managing editor of said rags.'

'Amateur,' Win added with disgust.

'Now, we can discuss this with you or with the school board. Up to you.'

Gary glanced at his watch. 'You have two minutes.'

'Fine.' Myron gestured to the right. 'Why don't we step into the teachers' lavatory? I assume you have a key.'

'Yes.'

He opened the door. Myron had always wanted to see a teachers' bathroom, see how the other half lives. It was unremarkable in every way.

'Okay, you have me here,' Gary said. 'What do you want?'

'Tell me about this ad.'

Gary swallowed. His enlarged Adam's apple bobbed up and down like a boxer's head avoiding jabs. 'I don't know anything about it.'

Myron and Win exchanged a glance.

'Can I stick his head in a toilet?' Win asked.

Gary straightened his back. 'If you are trying to frighten me, it won't work.'

Win's voice was semipleading. 'One quick dunk?'

'Not yet.' Myron turned his attention back to Gary. 'I have no interest in busting you, Gary. You're a perv, that's your business. I want to know about your connection with Kathy Culver.'

Sweat appeared above Gary's upper lip. 'She was a student of mine.'

'I know. Why is her picture in *Nips*? In your ad?'

'I have no idea. I saw it for the first time yesterday.'

'But that's your ad, right?'

He hesitated, giving silent half-shrugs to no one in particular. 'Okay,' he said. 'I admit it. I advertise in Mr Nickler's publications. No law against that. But I did not put that picture of Kathy in the ad.'

'Who did?'

'I don't know.'

'But you admit operating sex lines?'

'Yes. It's harmless. I do it to make extra money. Nobody gets hurt.'

'Another prince,' Myron said. 'How much extra money?'

'In the business's heyday I was making twenty thousand dollars a month.'

Myron wasn't sure he heard right. 'Twenty thousand dollars a month from phone sex?'

'In the mid-eighties, yes. Before the government got involved and began to crack down on 900 lines. Now I'm lucky to clear eight grand a month.'

'Damn bureaucrats,' Myron said. 'So how does Kathy Culver fit into all this?'

'What do you mean?'

'Gee, Gary, a naked picture of her is in your ad this month. Maybe that's what I mean.'

'I already told you. I had nothing to do with that.'

'Then I guess it's a coincidence, her being a student of yours and all.'

'Yes.'

'I won't hold him under long,' Win promised. 'Please.'

Myron shook his head. 'You wrote her a glowing recommendation letter for college, correct?'

'Kathy was a wonderful student,' Gary replied.

'And what else?'

'If you are suggesting that my relationship with Kathy was something other than student-teacher—'

'That's exactly what I'm suggesting.'

Once again he crossed his arms over his chest. 'I will not dignify that with a response. And I am now terminating this conversation.'

Gary was addressing them in that way teachers do. Sometimes teachers forget that life is not a classroom.

'Dunk him,' Myron said.

'With pleasure.'

Gary probably had two inches on Win. He leaned up on his toes and gave Win his most withering glare.

'I'm not afraid of you,' Gary said.

'Mistake number one.'

Win moved with a speed that videocameras would not catch. He took hold of Gary's hand, twisted it, and pulled down. Hapkido move. Gary dropped to the tile floor. Win pressed his knee against the point of Gary's elbow. Gently. Not too much pain. Just enough to let him know who was in control.

'Damn,' Win said.

'What?'

'All the toilets are clean. I hate when that happens.'

'Anything to add before the dunk?' Myron asked.

Gary's face was white. 'Promise me you won't tell anyone,' he managed.

'You'll tell us the truth?'

'Yes. But you have to swear you won't tell anyone. Not the principal, no one.'

'Okay.' Myron nodded to Win. Win let go. Gary took back his hand and caressed it as though it were an abused puppy.

'Kathy and I had an affair,' he said.

'When?'

'Her senior year. It lasted a few months, that's all. I haven't seen her since, I swear.'

'And that's everything?'

He nodded. 'I don't know anything else. Somebody else put that picture in the ad.'

'If you're lying, Gary—'

'I'm not. Hand to God.'

'Okay,' Myron said. 'You can go.'

Gary rushed out. He had not even paused to check his hair in the mirror.

'Scum,' Myron said. 'The man is pure unadulterated scum. Seduces his students, operates a dial-a-porn line.'

'But a snappy dresser,' Win said. 'So what next?'

'We finish the investigation. Then we go to the school board. We tell them all about Mr Grady's extra-curricular activities.'

'Didn't you just promise him you weren't going to tell?'

Myron shrugged. 'I lied.'

16

In something of a trance, Jessica thanked Myron and hung up the phone. She half-stumbled into the kitchen and sat down. Her mother and her younger brother Edward looked up.

'Honey,' Carol Culver began, 'are you okay?'

'Fine,' she managed.

'Who was on the phone?'

'Myron.'

Silence.

'We were talking about Kathy,' she continued.

'What about her?' Edward asked.

Her brother had always been Edward, not Ed or Eddie or Ted. He was only a year out of college and already he owned a successful computer business, IMCS (Interactive Management Computer Systems), which developed software systems for several prestigious corporations. Edward wore only jeans, even in the office, and obnoxious T-shirts, the kind with chintzy iron-on decals that say stuff like 'Keep on Truckin'.' He didn't own a tie. He had a wide, almost-feminine face with delicate porcelain features. Women would kill for his eyelashes. Only the buzz-cut hair – and the pithy phrase on his T-shirt – hinted at what Edward was proud to be: COMPUTER WEENIES HAVE THE BEST HARDWARE.

Jessica took a deep breath. She could not be concerned with delicacies or feelings anymore. She opened her purse and pulled out a copy of *Nips*. 'This magazine hit the stands a few days ago,' she said.

She tossed it on the table, cover up. A cross between puzzlement and disgust blanketed her mother's face.

Edward remained stoic. 'What the hell is this?' he asked.

Jessica flipped to the page in the back. 'There,' she said simply, pointing to the picture of Kathy in the bottom row.

It took a few moments for them to comprehend what they were seeing, as though the information had been waylaid somewhere between the eye and brain. Then Carol Culver let out a groan. Her hand flew to her mouth, smothering a scream. Edward's eyes narrowed into thin slits.

Jessica did not give her time to recover. 'There's more,' she said.

Her mother looked up at her with hollow, haunted eyes. There was no life behind them anymore, as though a final cold gust had put out a flickering flame.

'A handwriting expert checked the envelope it came in. The writing matches Kathy's.'

Edward inhaled sharply. Carol's legs finally gave out, folding at the knees. She landed hard in her chair and crossed herself. Tears came to her eyes.

'She's alive?' Carol managed.

'I don't know.'

'But there's a chance?' Edward followed up.

Jessica nodded. 'There's always been a chance.'

Stunned silence.

'But I need some information,' Jessica continued. 'I need to know what happened to Kathy. What made her change.'

Edward's eyes narrowed again. 'What do you mean?'

'Kathy had an affair with her high school English teacher. Senior year.'

More silence. Jessica was not so sure it was stunned.

'The teacher, a maggot named Gary Grady, has admitted it.'

'No,' her mother said weakly. She lowered her head, her crucifix dangling like a pendulum. She began to weep. 'Sweet Jesus, not my baby . . .'

Edward stood. 'That's enough, Jess.'

'It's not enough.'

Edward grabbed his jacket. 'I'm out of here.'

'Wait. Where are you going?'

'Good-bye.'

'We need to talk this out.'

'The hell we do.'

'Edward—'

He ran out the back door, slamming it behind him.

Jessica turned back to her mother. Her sobs were gut-wrenching. Jessica watched for a minute or two. Then she turned and left the kitchen.

Roy O'Connor was already in the back booth when Myron arrived. His glass was empty, and he was sucking on an ice cube. He sounded like an aardvark near an anthill.

'Hey, Roy.'

O'Connor nodded to the seat across the table, not bothering to stand. He wore gold rings that disappeared under the folds of flesh in his chubby unstained hands. His fingernails were manicured. He was somewhere between forty-five and fifty-five years old, but it was impossible to tell where. He was balding, wearing the ever-desirable swept-over look, parting his hair just below the armpit.

'Nice place, Roy,' Myron said. 'A table in the back, low lights, soft romantic music. If I didn't know better—'

O'Connor shook his head. 'Look, Bolitar, I know you think you're a regular Buddy Hackett, but give it a rest, okay?'

'I guess flowers are out, then.' Pause. Then: 'Buddy Hackett?'

'We need to talk.'

'I'm all ears.'

A waitress came over. 'Can I get you gentlemen something to drink?'

'Another,' Roy said, pointing to his glass.

'And for you?'

'Do you have Yoo-hoo?' Myron asked.

'I think so.'

'Great. I'll have one.'

She left. Roy shook his head. 'A fucking Yoo-hoo,' he mumbled.

'Did you say something?'

'Your goon visited me last night.'

'Your goons visited me first,' Myron said.

'I had nothing to do with that.'

Myron gave him his best 'come off it' look of pure skepticism. The waitress put down the drinks. Roy scooped up his martini as if it held a life-saving antidote. Myron, by contrast, sipped his Yoo-hoo daintily. Ever the gentleman.

'Look, Myron,' O'Connor continued, 'it's like this. I signed Landreaux. I gave him money up front. I gave him money every month. I kept my part of the bargain.'

'You signed him illegally.'

'I'm not the first guy to do it,' he said.

'Nor the last. What's your point, Roy?'

'Look, you know me. You know how I operate.'

Myron nodded. 'You're a chicken-shitted crook.'

'I might have threatened the kid. Fine. I've done that before. But that's it. I'd never really hurt anybody.'

'Uh-huh.'

'Word would get out to the athletes. I'd be ruined.'

'Damn shame that would be.'

'Bolitar, you're not making this any easier.'

'I'm not trying to.'

O'Connor grabbed the drink again. He finished it and signaled to the waitress for another. 'I've gotten involved with the wrong people,' he said.

'What do you mean?'

'I worked up some big-time gambling debts. Debts I couldn't pay off.'

'So they took a piece of your business.'

Roy nodded. 'They control me now. Your – your friend from last night.' A Geiger counter could have registered the quake in his voice when he mentioned Win. 'I want to do just what he said, but I don't have the power anymore.'

Myron took another sip of his Yoo-hoo, hoping he wasn't getting one of those chocolate mustaches. 'My friend won't be pleased to hear that.'

'You have to tell him it's not me.'

'Then who is it?'

Roy sat back, shaking his head. 'I can't say. But I can tell you they play for keeps. And they don't understand a thing about this business. They think they can just scare everyone into compliance. They want to make an example out of someone.'

'And Landreaux is the example?'

'Landreaux. And you. They want to hurt Landreaux. They want to kill you. They're putting out a contract on your head.'

Another cool sip. Myron said nothing.

'You don't seem very worried,' Roy said.

'I laugh in the face of death,' Myron replied. 'Well, maybe not laugh. More like a snicker. A quiet snicker.'

'Jesus, you're a lunatic.'

'And I wouldn't do it directly in death's face. So it's more like a quiet snicker behind his back.'

'Bolitar, this isn't funny.'

'No,' Myron agreed. 'It's not. I strongly suggest you call them off.'

'Haven't you heard a word I've said? I got no control here.'

'If something happens to me, my friend will be very upset. He'll take it out on you.'

Roy swallowed. 'But I'm powerless. You have to believe that.'

'Then tell me who's calling the shots.'

'I can't.'

Myron shrugged. 'Maybe we can be buried next to one another. One of those romantic tragedy things.'

'They'll kill me if I say anything.'

'What do you think my friend will do to you?'

Roy shuddered. He sucked on the ice again, trying to salvage the last remnants of the martini. 'Where is that damn bimbo with my drink?'

'Who's calling the shots, Roy?'

'You didn't hear it from me, right?'

'Right.'

'You won't tell them?'

'Mum's the word.'

One more ice suck. Then Roy said, 'Ache.'

'Herman Ache?' Myron asked, surprised. 'Herman Ache is behind this?'

Roy shook his head. 'His younger brother. Frank. He's out of control. I don't know what the psycho will do next.'

Frank Ache. It made sense. Herman Ache was one of New York's leading mobsters, responsible for countless misery. But next to his younger brother

Frank, Herman was an Alan Alda clone. Aaron would enjoy working for someone like Frank.

This was not good news. Myron toyed with the idea of dropping the snicker altogether. 'Anything else you can tell me?'

'No. I just don't want anyone hurt.'

'You're some guy, Roy. So selfless.'

O'Connor stood. 'I got nothing more to say.'

'I thought we were going to have lunch.'

'Have it by yourself,' O'Connor said. 'It's on my tab.'

'Won't be the same without your company.'

'Yet somehow you'll muddle through.'

Myron picked up the menu. 'I'll try.'

17

Who else to call?

The answer, Jessica realized, was obvious.

Nancy Serat. Kathy's roommate and closest friend.

Jessica sat at her father's desk. The lights were turned off, the shades were pulled down, but the sunlight was still strong enough to sneak through and cast shadows.

Adam Culver had done everything he could to make his home office radically different from the cement, institutional, macabre feel of the county morgue. The results were mixed. The converted bedroom had bright yellow walls, plenty of windows, silk flowers, white Formica desk. Teddy bears encircled the room. William Shakesbear. Rhett Beartler with Scarlett O'Beara. Bear Ruth. Bearlock Holmes. Humphrey Beargart with Lauren Bearcall. The whole atmosphere was cheerful, albeit a forced cheerful, like a clown you laugh at but find a little scary.

She took her phone book from her purse. Nancy had sent the family a card a few weeks ago. She had won some fellowship and was staying on campus to work in admissions. Jessica looked up her number and dialed.

On the third ring the answering machine picked up. Jessica left a message and hung up. She was about to start going through the drawers when a voice stopped her.

'Jessica.'

She looked up. Her mother stood in the doorway. Her eyes were sunken, her face a skeletal death mask. Her body swayed as though she were about to topple over.

'What are you doing in here?' Carol asked.

'Just looking around,' she said.

Carol nodded, her head bobbing on the string that was her neck. 'Find anything?'

'Not yet.'

Carol sat down. She stared straight ahead, her eyes unfocused. 'She was always such a happy child,' she said slowly. Her fingers fiddled with prayer beads, her gaze still far off. 'Kathy never stopped smiling. She had such a wonderful, happy smile. It lit up any room she entered. You and Edward, well, you were both more brooding. But Kathy – she had a smile for everyone and everything. Do you remember?'

'Yes,' Jessica said. 'I remember.'

'Your father used to joke that she had the personality of a born-again cheerleader,' Carol added, chuckling at the memory. 'Nothing ever brought her down.' She stopped, the chuckle fading away. 'Except, I guess, me.'

'Kathy loved you, Mom.'

She sighed deeply, her chest heaving as though even a sigh took great effort. 'I was a strict mother with you girls. Too strict, I guess. I was old-fashioned.'

Jessica did not reply.

'I just didn't want you or your sister to . . .' She lowered her head.

'To what?'

She shook her head. Her fingers moved across the beads at a more fervid pace. For a long time neither of them spoke. Then Carol said, 'You were right before, Jessica. Kathy changed.'

'When?'

'Her senior year.'

'What happened?'

Tears sprang to Carol's eyes. Her mouth tried to form words, her hands moving in gestures of helplessness. 'The smile,' she replied with something like a shrug. 'One day it was gone.'

'Why?'

Her mother wiped her eyes. Her lower lip quivered. Jessica's heart reached out to her, but for some reason the rest of her couldn't. She sat and watched her suffering, strangely uninvolved, as if she were watching a late-night tearjerker on cable.

'I'm not trying to hurt you,' Jessica said. 'I just want to find Kathy.'

'I know, sweetheart.'

'I think,' Jessica continued, 'that whatever changed Kathy is connected to her disappearance.'

Her mother's shoulders sagged. 'Merciful God.'

'I know it hurts,' Jessica said. 'But if we can find Kathy, if we can find who killed Dad—'

Carol's head shot up. 'Your father was killed in a robbery.'

'I don't think so. I think it's all connected. Kathy's disappearance, Dad's murder, everything.'

'But – how?'

'I don't know yet. Myron is helping me find out.'

The doorbell rang.

'That'll be Uncle Paul,' her mother said, heading for the door.

'Mom?'

Carol stopped but did not turn around.

'What's going on? What are you afraid to tell me?'

The doorbell rang again.

'I better get that,' Carol said. She hurried down the stairs.

'So,' Win began, 'Frank Ache wants to kill you.'

Myron nodded. 'Seems so.'

'A shame.'

'If he'd only get to know me. The real me.'

They sat in the front row at Titans Stadium. Out of the goodness of his heart, Otto had agreed to let Christian practice. That, and the fact that veteran quarterback Neil Decker was beyond horrendous.

The morning session had been a lot of wind sprints and walking through plays. The afternoon session, however, was a bit of a surprise. The players were in full gear, almost unheard of this early on in the year.

'Frank Ache is not a kind fellow,' Win said.

'He likes torturing animals.'

'Excuse me?'

'A friend of mine knew him growing up,' Myron explained. 'Frank Ache's favorite hobby was to chase down cats and dogs and bash in their heads with a baseball bat.'

'I bet that impressed the girls,' Win said.

Myron nodded.

'I assume, then, that you will be in need of my unique services.'

'For a few days, anyway,' Myron replied.

'Goodie. May I also assume that you have a plan?'

'I'm working on it. Feverishly.'

Christian jogged out on the field. He moved in that effortless way great athletes do. He got into the huddle, broke it, and approached the line of scrimmage.

'Full contact!' a coach yelled out.

Myron looked at Win. 'I don't like this.'

'What?'

'Full contact on the first day.'

Christian started calling out numbers. Then he gave a few hut-huts before the ball was snapped to him. He faded back to pass.

'Oh, shit,' Myron said.

Tommy Lawrence, the Titans' All-Pro linebacker, charged forward unblocked. Christian saw him too late. Tommy placed his helmet into Christian's sternum and slammed him to the ground – the kind of tackle that hurts like hell but doesn't do any permanent damage. Two other defenders piled on.

Christian got up, wincing and holding his chest. Nobody helped him.

Myron stood.

Win stopped him with a shake of his head. 'Sit down, Myron.'

Otto Burke came down the stairs, entourage in tow.

97

Myron glared at him. Otto smiled brightly. He made a tsk-tsk noise. 'I traded a lot of popular veterans to get him,' he said. 'It looks like some of the guys aren't too thrilled.'

'Sit down, Myron,' Win repeated.

Myron hesitated, then complied.

Christian limped back to the huddle. He called the next play and again approached the line of scrimmage. He surveyed the defense, yelled out numbers and hut-huts, then took the snap from the center. He stepped back. Tommy Lawrence blitzed again over left guard, completely untouched. Christian froze. Tommy bore down on him. He leaped like a panther, his arms stretched out for a bone-crushing tackle. Christian moved at the very last moment. Not a big move. Just a slight shift, actually. Tommy flew by him and landed on the ground. Christian pumped and threw a bomb.

Complete pass.

Myron turned around, grinning. 'Hey, Otto?'

'What?'

'Kiss my grits.'

Otto's smile did not falter. Myron wondered how he did that, if his mouth was frozen that way, like the threat a little kid hears from his mom when he's making faces. Otto nodded and walked away. His entourage followed in a row, like a family of mallard ducks.

Win looked at Myron. 'Kiss my grits?'

Shrug. 'Paying homage to Flo on *Alice*.'

'You watch too much television.'

'Listen, I've been thinking.'

'Oh?'

'About Gary Grady,' Myron said.

'What about him?'

'He has an affair with a student. She vanishes a year or so later. Time passes and her picture ends up in a porno ad he runs.'

'Your point being?'

'It's crazy.'

'So is everything about this case.'

Myron shook his head. 'Think about it. Grady admits having an affair with Kathy, right? So what would be the last thing he'd want to do?'

'Publicize it.'

'Yet her picture ends up in his ad.'

'Ah.' Win nodded. 'You believe someone is setting him up.'

'Exactly.'

'Who?'

'Fred Nickler would be my bet,' Myron said.

'Hmm. He did hand over Grady's p.o. box without much debate.'

'And he has the power to switch photos in his own magazine.'

'So what do you suggest?' Win asked.

'I'd like you to check out Mr Fred Nickler very thoroughly. Maybe talk to him again. *Talk*,' Myron repeated. 'Not visit.'

On the field Christian was fading back again. For the third straight time Tommy Lawrence blitzed over left guard untouched. In fact, the left guard stood with his hands on his hips and watched.

'Christian's own lineman is setting him up,' Myron said.

Christian side-stepped Tommy Lawrence, cocked his arms, and whipped the ball with unearthly velocity directly into his left guard's groin. There was a short *oomph* sound. The left guard collapsed like a folding chair.

'Ouch,' Win said.

Myron almost clapped. '*The Longest Yard* revisited.'

The left guard was, of course, wearing a cup. But a cup was far from full protection against a speeding missile. He rolled on the ground, back curved fetal-like, eyes wide. Every man in the general vicinity gave a collective, sympathetic 'Ooo.'

Christian walked over to his left guard – a man weighing in excess of 275 pounds – and offered him a hand. The left guard took it. He limped back to the huddle.

'Christian has balls,' Myron said.

Win nodded. 'But can the same be said of the left guard?'

18

As soon as Myron entered the Reston University campus, his car phone rang.

'Listen, putz, I got what you want,' P.T. said. 'My friend's name is Jake Courter. He's the town sheriff.'

'Sheriff Jake,' Myron said. 'You're kidding, right?'

'Hey, don't let the title fool you. Jake used to work homicide in Philly, Boston, and New York. Good man. He said he'd meet with you today at three.'

Myron checked his watch. It was one o'clock now. The station was five minutes away. 'Thanks, P.T.'

'Can I ask you something, Myron?'

'Shoot.'

'Why you looking into this?'

'It's a long story, P.T.'

'This have to do with her sister? That great piece of tail you used to nail?' He cackled.

'You're all class, P.T.'

'Hey, Myron, I want to hear about it sometime. The whole story.'

'It's a promise.'

Myron parked the car and headed into the old athletic center. The corridor was a bit more beaten up than Myron had expected. Three rows of framed photographs of past athletic teams – some from as far back as a hundred years ago – lined the walls. Myron approached a beaded-glass door that looked like something out of an old Sam Spade film. The word FOOTBALL was stenciled in black. He knocked.

The voice was like an old tire on an unpaved road. 'What?'

Myron stuck his head in. 'Busy, Coach?'

Reston University football coach Danny Clarke looked up from his computer. 'Who the hell are you?' he rasped.

'Fine, thanks. But let's dispense with the pleasantries.'

'That supposed to be funny?'

Myron tilted his head. 'You didn't think so?'

'I'll ask one more time. Who the hell are you?'

'Myron Bolitar.'

The coach's scowl did not change. 'Am I supposed to know you?'

It was a hot summer day, the campus was practically empty, and here sat the school's legendary football coach wearing a suit and tie, watching videotapes of high school prospects. A suit and tie and no air conditioning. If the heat bothered Danny Clarke, it didn't show. Everything about him was well groomed and tidy. He was shelling and eating peanuts, but no mess was visible. His jaw muscles bunched as he chewed, making little knobs appear and disappear near his ears. He had a prominent vein in his forehead.

'I'm a sports agent.'

He flicked his eyes away like a ruler dismissing an underling. 'Get out of here. I'm busy.'

'We need to talk.'

'Out of here, asshole. Now.'

'I just—'

'Listen up, shithead.' He pointed a coach finger at Myron. 'I don't talk to bottom-feeders. Ever. I run a clean program with clean players. I don't take payoffs from so-called agents or any of that bullshit. So if you got an envelope stuffed with green, you can go shove it up your ass.'

Myron clapped. 'Beautiful. I laughed, I cried, it became a part of me.'

Danny Clarke looked up sharply. He wasn't used to having his orders questioned, but part of him seemed almost amused by it. 'Get the hell out of here,' he growled, but more gently now. He turned back to the television. On the screen a young quarterback threw a long, tight spiral. Caught. Touchdown.

Myron decided to disarm him with tact. 'The kid looks pretty good,' he said.

'Yeah, well, it's a good thing you're a scum-sucking leech and not a scout. The kid can't play a lick. Now take a hike.'

'I want to talk to you about Christian Steele.'

That got his attention. 'What about him?'

'I'm his agent.'

'Oh,' Danny Clarke said. 'Now I remember. You're the old basketball player. The one who hurt his knee.'

'At your service,' Myron said.

'Is Christian okay?'

Myron tried to look noncommittal. 'I understand he didn't get along with his teammates.'

'So? You his social coordinator?'

'What was the problem?'

'I can't see how it matters now,' he said.

'Then humor me.'

It took the coach some time to relax his glare. 'It was a lot of things,' he said. 'But I guess Horty was the main problem.'

'Horty?' Clever interrogation techniques. Pay attention.

'Junior Horton,' he explained. 'A defensive lineman. Good speed, good size, good talent. The brains of a citrus beverage.'

'So what does this Horty have to do with Christian?'

'They didn't see eye to eye.'

'How come?'

Danny Clarke thought a moment. 'I don't know. Something to do with that girl who disappeared.'

'Kathy Culver?'

'Right. Her.'

'What about her?'

He turned back to the VCR and changed tapes. Then he typed something on his computer. 'I think maybe she dated Horty before Christian. Something like that.'

'So what happened?'

'Horty was a bad apple from the get-go. In his senior year I found out he was pushing drugs to my players: cocaine, dope, Lord knows what else. So I bounced him. Later, I heard he'd been supplying the guys with steroids for three years.'

Later my ass, Myron thought. But for once he kept the thought to himself. 'So what does this have to do with Christian?'

'Rumors started circulating that Christian had gotten Horty thrown off the team. Horty fueled them, you know, telling the guys that Christian was turning them all in for using steroids, stuff like that.'

'Was that true?'

'Nope. Two of my best players showed up game day so stoned, they could barely see. That's when I took action. Christian had nothing to do with it. But you know how it is. They all figured Christian was the star. If he wanted his ass wiped, the coaches asked Charmin or Downy.'

'Did you tell your guys Christian had nothing to do with it?'

He made a face. 'You think that would have helped? They would have thought I was covering for him, protecting him. They would have hated him even more. As long as it didn't affect their play – and it didn't – it was not my concern. I just let it be.'

'You're a real character developer, Coach.'

He gave Myron his best intimidate-the-freshman glare. The forehead vein started pulsing. 'You're out of line, Bolitar.'

'Wouldn't be the first time.'

'I care about my boys.'

'Yeah, I can tell. You let Horty stay as long as he pumped your boys with dangerous albeit play-enhancing drugs. When he graduated to the big leagues – to the stuff that had a negative on-the-field impact – all of a sudden you became a righteous drug czar.'

'I don't have to listen to this bullshit,' Danny Clarke ranted. 'Especially from a no-good, bloodsucking vampire. Get the hell out of my office. Now.'

Myron said, 'You want to catch a movie together sometime? Maybe a Broadway show?'

'Out!'

Myron left. Another day, another friend. Charm was the key.

He had plenty of time to kill before he visited Sheriff Jake, so he decided to take a stroll. The campus was like a ghost town, except no tumbleweeds were skittering along the ground. The students were gone for summer break. The buildings stood lifeless and sad. In the distance a stereo was playing Elvis Costello. Two girls appeared in the distance. Co-ed types wearing crotch-riding shorts and halter tops. They were walking a hairy little dog – a Shih Tzu. It looked like Cousin It after one too many spins in the dryer. Myron smiled and nodded as the girls passed him. Neither one fainted or disrobed. Astonishing. The little dog, however, snarled at him. Cujo.

He was nearly at his car when he spotted the sign:

Campus Post Office

He stopped, looked around the grounds, saw nobody. Hmm. It was worth a try.

The inside of the post office was painted institutional green, the same color as the school bathroom. A long V-shaped corridor was wallpapered with p.o. boxes. He heard the distant sound of a radio. He couldn't make out the song, just a strong, monotonous bass beat.

Myron approached the mail window. A kid sat with his feet up. The music was coming from the kid's ears. He was listening to one of those Walkman clones with the minispeakers that bypass the ears and plug directly into the cerebrum. His black high-tops rested on a desk, his baseball hat tipped down like a sombrero at siesta time. There was a book on his lap. Philip Roth's *Operation Shylock*.

'Good book,' Myron said.

The kid did not look up.

'Good book,' Myron said again, this time yelling.

The kid pulled the speakers out of his ears with a sucking pop. He was pale and red-haired. When he took off his hat, his hair was Afro-wild. Bernie from *Room 222*.

'What?'

'I said, good book.'

'You read it?'

Myron nodded. 'Without moving my lips.'

The kid stood. He was tall and lanky.

'You play basketball?' Myron asked.

'Yeah,' the kid said. 'Just finished my freshman year. Didn't play much.'

'I'm Myron Bolitar.'

The kid looked at him blankly.

'I played ball for Duke.'

Blink, blink.

'No autographs, please.'

'How long ago did you play?' the kid asked.

'Graduated ten years ago.'

'Oh,' the kid replied, as though that explained everything. Myron did some quick math in his head. The kid had been seven or eight when Myron won the national title. He suddenly felt very old.

'We used peach baskets back then.'

'What?'

'Never mind. Can I ask you a few questions?'

The kid shrugged. 'Go ahead.'

'How often are you on duty in the post office?'

'Five days a week in the summer, nine to five.'

'Is it always this quiet?'

'This time of year, yeah. No students, so there's almost no mail.'

'Do you do the mail sorting?'

'Sure.'

'Do you do pick-ups?'

'Pick-ups?'

'Campus mail.'

'Yeah, but there's only that slot by the front door.'

'That's the only campus mailbox?'

'Um-hmm.'

'Been getting a lot of campus mail lately?'

'Next to none. Three, four letters a day.'

'Do you know Christian Steele?'

'Heard of him,' the kid said. 'Who hasn't?'

'He got a big manila envelope in his box a few days ago. There was no postmark, so it had to be mailed from campus.'

'Yeah, I remember. What about it?'

'Did you see who mailed it?' Myron asked.

'No,' the kid said. 'But they were the only pieces of mail I got that whole day.'

Myron cocked his head. 'They?'

'What?'

'You said "they. They were the only pieces." '

'Right. Two big envelopes. Exact same except for the address.'

'Do you remember who the other one was addressed to?'

'Sure,' the kid said. 'Harrison Gordon. He's the dean of students.'

19

Nancy Serat dropped her suitcase on the floor and rewound the answering machine. The tape raced back, shrieking all the way. She had spent the weekend in Cancún, a final vacation before starting her fellowship at Reston University, her alma mater.

The first message was from her mother.

'I don't want to disturb you on vacation, dear. But I thought you'd want to know that Kathy Culver's father died yesterday. He was stabbed by a mugger. Awful. Anyway, I thought you'd want to know. Give us a call when you get back in. Your father and I want to take you out to dinner for your birthday.'

Nancy's legs felt weak. She collapsed into the chair, barely hearing the next two messages – one from her dentist's office reminding her of a teeth cleaning on Friday, the other from a friend planning a party.

Adam Culver was dead. She couldn't believe it. Her mother had said it was a mugger. Nancy wondered. Was it really random? Or did it have something to do with his visit on . . . ?

She calculated the days.

Kathy's father had visited on the day he died.

A voice on the machine jarred her back to the present.

'Hello, Nancy. This is Jessica Culver, Kathy's sister. When you get in, please give me a call. I need to talk to you as soon as possible. I'm staying with my mom. The number here is 555-1477. It's kind of important. Thank you.'

Nancy suddenly felt very cold. She listened to the rest of the messages. Then she sat without moving for several minutes, debating her options. Kathy was dead – or so everyone believed. And now her father, hours after talking to Nancy, was dead too.

What did it mean?

She remained very still, the only sound her own breaths coming in short, hitching gasps. Then she picked up the phone and dialed Jessica's number.

The dean's office was closed, so Myron proceeded straight to his house. It was an old Victorian with cedar shingles on the west end of the campus. He rang the doorbell. A very attractive woman opened the door. She smiled solicitously.

'May I help you?'

She wore a tailored cream suit. She was not young, but she had a grace and beauty and sex appeal that made Myron's mouth a little dry. In front of such a lady Myron wanted to remove his hat, except he wasn't wearing one.

'Good afternoon,' he said. 'I'm looking for Dean Gordon. My name is Myron Bolitar, and—'

'The basketball player?' she interrupted. 'Of course, I should have recognized you right away.'

To grace, beauty, and sex appeal, add knowledge of basketball.

'I remember watching you in the NCAAs,' she continued. 'I cheered you all the way.'

'Thank you—'

'When you got hurt—' She stopped, shook the head attached to the Audrey Hepburn neck. 'I cried. I felt like a part of me was hurt too.'

Grace, beauty, sex appeal, basketball knowledge, and alas, sensitivity. She was also long-legged and curvy. All in all, a nice package.

'That's very kind of you, thank you.'

'It's a pleasure to meet you, Myron.'

Even his first name sounded good coming from those lips. 'And you must be Dean Gordon's wife. The lovely dean-nessa.'

She laughed at the Woody Allen rip-off. 'Yes, I'm Madelaine Gordon. And no, my husband is not home at the moment.'

'Are you expecting him soon?'

She smiled as though the question were a double entendre. Then she gave him a look that flushed his cheeks. 'No,' she said slowly. 'He won't be home for hours.'

Heavy accent on the word *hours*.

'Well then, I won't bother you anymore.'

'It's no bother.'

'I'll come by another time,' he said.

Madelaine (he liked that name) nodded demurely. 'I'll look forward to it.'

'Nice meeting you.' With Myron, every line was a lady-slayer.

'Nice meeting you too,' she singsonged. 'Good-bye, Myron.'

The door closed slowly, teasingly. He stood there for another moment, took a few deep breaths, and hurried back to his car. Whew.

He checked his watch. Time to meet Sheriff Jake.

Jake Courter was alone in the station, which looked like something out of Mayberry RFD. Except Jake was black. There were never any blacks in Mayberry. Or Green Acres. Or any of those places. No Jews, Latinos, Asians, ethnics of any kind. Would have been a nice touch. Maybe have a Greek diner or a guy named Abdul working for Sam Drucker at the grocery store.

Myron estimated Jake to be in his mid-fifties. He was in plainclothes, his jacket off, his tie loosened. A big gut spilled forward like something that belonged to someone else. Manila files were scattered across Jake's desk, along with the remnants of what might be a sandwich and an apple core. Jake gave a tired shrug and wiped his nose with what looked like a dishrag.

'Got a call,' he said by way of introduction. 'I'm supposed to help you out.'

'I'd appreciate it,' Myron said.

Jake leaned back and put his feet on the desk. 'You played ball against my son, Gerard. Michigan State.'

'Sure,' Myron said. 'I remember him. Tough kid. Monster on the boards. Defensive specialist.'

Jake nodded proudly. 'That's him. Couldn't shoot worth a lick, but you always knew he was there.'

'An enforcer,' Myron added.

'Yep. He's a cop now. In New York. Made detective second grade already. Good cop.'

'Like his old man.'

Jake smiled. 'Yeah.'

'Give him my regards,' Myron said. 'Better yet, give him an elbow to the rib cage. I still owe him a few.'

Jake threw back his head and laughed. 'That's Gerard. Finesse was never his forte.' He blew his nose into the dishrag. 'But I'm sure you didn't come all this way to talk basketball.'

'No, I guess not.'

'So why don't you tell me what this is all about, Myron?'

'The Kathy Culver case,' he said. 'I'm looking into it. Very surreptitiously.'

'Surreptitiously,' Jake repeated with a raised eyebrow. 'Awfully big word, Myron.'

'I've been listening to self-improvement tapes in the car.'

'That right?' Jake blew his nose again. Sounded like a ewe's mating call. 'So what's your interest in this – aside from the fact that you represent Christian Steele and you used to have a thing for Kathy's sister.'

Myron said, 'You're thorough.'

He took a bite out of the half-eaten sandwich on his desk, smiled. 'Man does love to be flattered.'

'It's like you said. Christian Steele. He's a client. I'm trying to help him out.'

Jake studied him, waiting again. It was an old trick. Stay silent long enough, and the witness would start talking again, elaborating. Myron did not bite.

After a full minute had passed Jake said, 'So let me get this straight. Christian Steele signs on with you. One day you start chatting. He said, "You know, Myron, the way you been licking my lily-white ass and all, I'd like you to go play Dick Fuckin' Tracy and find my old squeeze who's been missing for the last year and a half and the cops and feds can't find." That how it went, Myron?'

'Christian doesn't curse,' Myron said.

'Okay, fine, you want to skip the dance? Let's skip it. You want me to give, you have to give back.'

'That's fair enough,' Myron said. 'But I can't. Not yet, anyhow.'

'Why not?'

'It could hurt a lot of people,' Myron said. 'And it's probably nothing.'

He made a face. 'What do you mean, hurt?'

'I can't elaborate.'

'Fuck you can't.'

'I'm telling you, Jake. I can't say anything.'

Jake studied him again. 'Let me tell you something, Bolitar. I'm no glory hound. I'm like my son was on the court. Not flashy but a workhorse. I don't look for clippings so I can climb up the ladder. I'm fifty-three years old. My ladder don't go no higher. Now this may seem a bit old-fashioned to you, but I believe in justice. I like to see truth prevail. I've lived with Kathy Culver's disappearance for eighteen months. I know her inside and out. And I have no idea what happened that night.'

'What do you think happened?' Myron asked.

Jake picked up a pencil and tapped it on the desk. 'Best guess based on the evidence?'

Myron nodded.

'She's a runaway.'

Myron was surprised. 'What makes you say that?'

A slow smile spread across Jake's face. 'That's for me to know and you to find out.'

'P.T. said you would help.'

Jake shrugged and took another bite from yet another sandwich scrap. 'What about Kathy's sister? I understand you two were pretty heavy.'

'We're friends now.'

Jake gave a low whistle. 'I've seen her on TV,' he said. 'Hard to be friends with a woman who looks like that.'

'You're a real nineties guy, Jake.'

'Yeah, well, I forgot to renew my subscription to *Cosmo*.'

They stared at each other for a while. Jake settled back in his chair and examined his fingernails. 'What do you want to know?'

'Everything,' Myron said. 'From the beginning.'

Jake folded his arms across his chest. He took a deep breath and let it loose slowly. 'Campus security got a call from Kathy Culver's roommate,

Nancy Serat. Kathy and Nancy lived in the Psi Omega sorority house. Nice house. All pretty white girls with blond hair and white teeth. Kind that all look alike and sound alike. You get the picture.'

Myron nodded. He noticed that Jake was not reading or even consulting a file. This was coming from memory.

'Nancy Serat told the rent-a-cop that Kathy Culver hadn't returned to her room for three days.'

'Why did Nancy wait so long to call?' Myron asked.

'Seems Kathy wasn't spending too many nights in the sorority house anyhow. She slept in your client's room most of the time. You know, the one who doesn't like to curse.' Brief smile. 'Anyhow, your boy and Nancy got to talking one day, both figuring Kathy had been spending all her time with the other. That's when they realized she was missing and called campus security.

'Campus security told us about it, but no one got very excited at first. A co-ed missing for a few days is hardly an earth-shattering event. But then one of the rent-a-cops found the panties on top of a waste bin, and well, you know what happened then. The story spread like a grease stain on Elvis's pillow.'

'I read there was blood on the panties,' Myron said.

'A media exaggeration. There was a bloodstain, dry, probably from a menstrual cycle. We typed it. B negative. Same type as Kathy Culver's. But there was also semen. Enough antibodies for a DNA and blood test.'

'Did you have any suspects?'

'Only one,' Jake said. 'Your boy, Christian Steele.'

'Why him?'

'Usual reasons. He was the boyfriend. She was on her way to see him when she vanished. Nothing very specific or damaging. But the DNA test on the semen cleared him.' He opened a small refrigerator behind him. 'Want a Coke?'

'No, thanks.'

Jake grabbed a can and snapped it open. 'Here's what you probably read in the papers,' he continued. 'Kathy is at a sorority cocktail party. She has a drink or two, nothing serious, leaves at ten P.M. to meet Christian, and disappears. End of story. But now let me fill it in a little.'

Myron leaned forward. Jake took a swig of Coke and wiped his mouth with a forearm the size of an oak trunk.

'According to several of her sorority sisters,' he said, 'Kathy was distracted. Not herself. We also know she got a phone call a few minutes before she left the house. She told Nancy Serat the call was from Christian and she was going to meet him. Christian denies making the call. These were all intracampus calls, so there is no way for us to tell. But the roommate says Kathy sounded strained on the phone, not like she was talking to her true love, Mr Clean-Mouth.

'Kathy hung up the phone and went back downstairs with Nancy. Then she posed for the now-famous last photograph before leaving for good.'

He opened his desk drawer and handed Myron the photograph. Myron had, of course, seen it countless times before. Every media outlet in the country had run the photograph with morbid fascination. A picture of twelve sorority sisters. Kathy stood second from the left. She wore a blue sweater and skirt. Pearls adorned her neck. Very preppy. According to Kathy's sorority sisters, Kathy left the house alone immediately after the picture was taken. She never returned.

'Okay,' Jake said, 'so she leaves the cocktail party. Only one person saw her for sure after that.'

'Who?' Myron asked.

'Team trainer. Guy named Tony Gardola. He saw her, strangely enough, entering the team's locker room around quarter after ten. The locker room was supposed to be empty at that hour. Only reason Tony was there was that he forgot something. He asked her what she was doing there, and she said she was meeting Christian. Tony figured what the hell, kids today. Might be having a kinky locker-room encounter. Tony decided it was in his best interest not to ask too many questions.

'That's our last *firm* report on her whereabouts. We have a possible sighting of her on the western edge of campus at around eleven P.M. Someone saw a blond woman wearing a blue sweater and skirt. It was too dark to make a positive ID. The witness said he wouldn't have even noticed, except she seemed in a rush. Not running but doing one of those quick-walks.'

'Where on the western edge of campus?' Myron asked.

Jake opened a file and took out a map, still studying Myron's face as though it held a clue. He spread the map out and pointed. 'Here,' he said. 'In front of Miliken Hall.'

'What's Miliken Hall?' Myron asked.

'Math building. Locked tight by nine o'clock. But the witness said she was moving west.'

Myron's eyes traced a path to the west. There were four other buildings labeled FACULTY HOUSING. Myron remembered the spot.

It was where Dean Gordon lived.

'What is it?' Jake asked.

'Nothing.'

'Bullshit, Bolitar. You see something.'

'It's nothing.'

Jake's eyebrows furrowed. 'Fine. You want to play it that way? Then get the fuck out. I still got my ace in the hole, and I ain't showing it.'

Myron had planned for this. Jake Courter would have to be given something. That was fine, as long as Myron could turn it to his advantage.

'It seems to me,' Myron said slowly, 'that Kathy was walking in the general direction of the dean's house.'

'So?'

Myron said nothing.

'She worked for him,' Jake said.

Myron nodded.

'What's the connection?'

'Oh, I'm sure it's completely innocent,' Myron said. 'But you might want to ask him about it. You being so thorough and all.'

'Are you saying—'

'I'm not saying anything. I am merely making an observation.'

Again Jake studied him. Myron looked back coolly. A visit from Jake Courter would probably not crack Dean Gordon, but it should soften him a bit. 'Now about that ace in the hole . . . ?'

Jake hesitated. 'Kathy Culver inherited money from her grandmother,' he said.

'Twenty-five grand,' Myron added. 'All three kids got the same. They're sitting in a trust account.'

'Not exactly,' Jake said. He stood, hitched his pants up. 'You want to know why I said the evidence pointed to Kathy being a runaway?'

Myron nodded.

'The day Kathy Culver vanished, she visited the bank,' Jake continued. 'She cleared out her inheritance. Every penny.'

20

Myron started back toward New York. He flipped on the radio. Wham's classic hit 'Careless Whisper' was playing. George Michael was bemoaning the fact that he would never dance again because 'guilty feet have got no rhythm.' Deep, Myron thought. Very deep.

He picked up the car phone and dialed Esperanza.

'What's up?' he asked.

'You coming back to the office?'

'I'm on my way there now.'

'I wouldn't make any stops,' she said.

'Why?'

'You have a surprise client waiting for you.'

'Who?'

'Chaz Landreaux.'

'He's supposed to be hiding in Washington.'

'Well, he's here. And he looks like shit.'

'Tell him to sit tight. I'm on my way.'

'It's like this,' Chaz began. 'I want to cancel our contract.'

He paced the office like an expectant father, and he did indeed look like shit. The cocky grin was nowhere to be seen. The swagger was more like a hunch. He kept licking his lips, darting his eyes, bunching and unbunching his fingers.

'Why don't you start at the beginning?' Myron tried.

'Ain't no beginning,' Chaz snapped. 'I want out. You gonna fight me on it?'

'What happened?'

'Nothing happened. I changed my mind, is all. I want to go with Roy O'Connor at TruPro now. They're big-time. You're a nice guy, Myron, but you don't have their connections.'

'Uh-huh.'

Silence. More pacing.

'Can I have the contract or what?'

'How did they get to you, Chaz?'

'I don't know what the fuck you're talking about. How many times do I have to say it? I don't want you, okay?' Chaz was on the edge and teetering. 'I want TruPro.'

'It's not that easy,' Myron said.

'You gonna fight me on this?' he asked again.

'They won't stop with this, Chaz. You're in over your head. You have to let me help you.'

He stopped. 'Help me? You wanna help me? Then give me back my contract. And don't pretend you give a shit about me. You just want your piece.'

'Do you really believe that?' Myron asked.

He shook his head. 'You don't get it, man. I don't want you. I want to go with TruPro.'

'I get it. And like I said before, it's not that easy. These guys got you by the balls. You think you can make them let go by doing what they say. But you can't. Not for good anyway. Whenever they want something, they'll just reach back into your pants and give another squeeze. They won't stop, Chaz. Not until they've squeezed you for everything they can.'

'Man, you don't know shit. I don't have to explain nothing to you.' He approached the desk, but his eyes looked away. 'I want that goddamn contract. I want it now.'

Myron picked up his phone. 'Esperanza, bring me Chaz's contract. The original.' He hung up. 'It'll just be a moment.'

Chaz said nothing.

'You don't know what you're mixed up in,' Myron continued.

'Fuck off, man. I know exactly what I'm mixed up in.'

'Let me help, Chaz.'

He snorted. 'What can you do?'

'I can stop them.'

'Oh yeah, I can tell. You done a great job so far.'

'What happened?'

But he just shook his head.

Esperanza came in and handed Myron the contract. Myron in turn handed it to Chaz. He grabbed it and hurried to the door.

'Sorry, Myron. But this is business.'

'You can't beat them, Chaz. Not on your own. They'll suck you dry.'

'Don't worry about me. I can take care of myself.'

'I don't think you can.'

'Just stay the fuck out. It ain't your business no more.'

He took off without a backward glance. When he was gone, Win opened the door between the conference room and Myron's office. 'Interesting conversation,' Win said.

Myron nodded, thinking.

'We've lost a client,' Win said. 'Too bad.'

'It's not that simple, Win.'

'That's where you're mistaken,' Win replied steadily. 'It's just that simple. He dumped you for another agency. As he so eloquently put it, "It ain't your business no more."'

'Chaz is being pressured.'

'And you offered to help him. He refused.'

'He's a scared kid.'

'He's an adult who makes his own decisions. One of which was to tell you to fuck off.'

Myron looked up. 'You know what they'll do to him.'

'It's a world of free will, Myron. Landreaux chose to take the money in college. And he chose to go back to them now.'

'Will you follow him?'

'Pardon?'

'Follow Chaz. See where he takes those contracts.'

'You complicate the simple, Myron. Just let it be.'

'I can't. You know I can't.'

Win nodded. 'I guess I do.' He thought a moment. 'I'll do it for the sake of our business,' he said. 'For the added revenue. If we get Landreaux back in our stable, it will be very profitable. You may enjoy playing superhero, but as far as I'm concerned, this is no moral crusade. I am doing this for the money. That is the only reason. The money.'

Myron nodded. 'I wouldn't want it any other way.'

'Fine. As long as we are clear on that point. And I want you to take this.'

Win handed him a Smith & Wesson .38 and a shoulder holster. Myron put it on. Carrying a gun was incredibly uncomfortable, yet the weight felt good, like a reminder of some kind of protective bubble. Sometimes the sensation made you feel heady, invincible even.

That was usually when you got popped.

'Be extra careful,' Win said. 'The word has hit the streets.'

'What word?'

'A price has officially been put on your head,' Win said, as if it were amusing cocktail conversation. 'Thirty thousand dollars to the man who takes you out.'

Myron made a face. 'Thirty thousand? Hell, I used to be a fed. I should be worth sixty, seventy grand minimum.'

'Bad economy. Times are tough.'

'I'm being discounted?'

'Appears so, yes.'

Myron opened the revolver and checked the bullets. Just as he suspected. Win had loaded the gun with dum-dums – bullets with cross-hatched tips to expose the lead. Wasn't enough to be using hollow-point Winchester Silvertip bullets. Win had to doctor them for that extra little crunch. 'These are illegal.'

Win put his hand against his chest. 'My. Oh. My. How. Awful.'

'And unnecessary.'

'If you say so.'

'I say so.'

'They are effective.'

'I don't want them,' Myron said.

'Fine.' He handed Myron uncut bullets. 'Be a wimp.'

21

Jessica listened to the message on the answering machine.

'Hi, Jessica. It's Nancy Serat. I'm so sorry to hear about your father. He was such a nice man. I can't believe it. He was here the morning he died. So weird. He was so nostalgic that day. He told me all about that favorite yellow sweater he gave Kathy. Such a sweet story. I wish I could have been more helpful. I just can't believe – well, I'm rambling, sorry. I do that when I'm nervous. Anyway I'll be out until ten o'clock tonight. You can come by then or give me a call. Bye.'

Jessica rewound the message and played it back. Then a third time. Nancy Serat had seen her father on the morning of his murder.

Another coincidence?

She thought not.

Myron called his mother. 'I won't be home for a few days.'

'What?'

'I'm going to stay with Win.'

'In the city?'

'Yes.'

'New York City?'

'No, Mom. Kuwait City.'

'Don't be such a wise guy with your mother, save it for your friends,' she said. 'So why are you staying in the city?'

Hmm. Should he tell her the truth? *Because, Mom, a mobster has a contract out on my head and I don't want to put you and Dad in danger.* Nah. Might make her worry. 'I'm going to be working late the next few nights.'

'You sure about this?'

'Yes.'

'Be careful, Myron. Don't walk around alone at night.'

Esperanza opened the door. 'Urgent call on line three,' she said, loud enough for Myron's mother to hear.

'Mom, I gotta go. Urgent call.'

'Call us.'

'I will.' He hung up and looked up at Esperanza. 'Thanks.'

'Don't mention it.'

'Is there anyone on the phone?'

She nodded. 'Timmy Simpson again. I tried to handle it, but he says his problem needs your particular expertise.'

Timmy Simpson was a rookie shortstop for the Red Sox. A major-league pain in the ass.

'Hi, Timmy.'

'Hey, Myron, I've been waiting here two goddamn hours for your call.'

'I was out. What's the problem?'

'I'm here in Toronto, okay, at the Hilton. And this hotel's got no hot water.'

Myron waited. Then he said, 'Did I hear you correctly, Timmy? Did you say—'

'Unfuckinbelievable, ain't it?' Timmy shouted. 'I go in the shower, right, wait five minutes, then ten minutes. The water's fucking freezing, Myron. Ice cold. So finally I call down to the front desk, right? Some pissant manager tells me they're having some kind of plumbing problem. Plumbing problem, Myron, like I'm staying in a fuckin' trailer park or something. So I say, when's it going to be fixed? He gives me this whole long spiel how he don't know. Can you believe this shit?'

No, Myron thought. 'Timmy, why exactly are you calling me?'

'Jesus Christ, Myron, I'm a pro, right? And I'm stuck in this hellhole with no hot water. I mean, isn't there something in my contract about that?'

'A hot water clause, perhaps?' Myron tried.

'Or something. I mean, come on. Where do they get off? I need a shower before a game. A *hot* shower. Is that too much to expect? I mean, what am I going to do?'

Stick your head in the toilet and flush, Myron thought, massaging his temples with his fingertips. 'I'll see what I can do, Timmy.'

'Talk to the hotel manager, Myron. Make him understand the importance.'

'As far as I'm concerned,' Myron said, 'those orphans in Eastern Europe are a minor annoyance in comparison to this. But if the hot water doesn't come back on soon, check into another hotel. We'll send the bill to the Red Sox.'

'Good idea. Thanks, Myron.'

Click.

Myron stared at the phone. Unbelievable. He leaned back and wondered how to handle his three big problems: Chaz Landreaux's sudden departure, Kathy Culver's possible re-emergence, and the Toronto Hilton's plumbing. He decided to forgo the last. Only so much one man can do.

Problem 1: Chaz Landreaux was climbing into bed with Frank Ache. There was only one way out of that. Big brother Herman.

Myron picked up the phone and dialed. He still knew the number by heart. It was picked up on the first ring. 'Clancy's Tavern.'

'It's Myron Bolitar. I'd like to see Herman.'

'Hold on.' Five minutes passed before the voice came back on. 'Tomorrow. Two o'clock.'

Click. No need to wait for an answer. Whatever time Herman Ache agreed to see you, you were free.

Problem 2: Kathy Culver. *Nips* magazine had been mailed from a campus box. It had been mailed not only to Christian Steele but also to Dean Harrison Gordon. Why? Myron knew that Kathy had worked for the dean. Was there more to her job than just filing? An affair, perhaps? And what about the dean's lovely wife? Did she wear underwear?

But Myron was digressing.

The catalyst of this whole thing was the ad in *Nips*. Gary Grady claimed he had nothing to do with it. Maybe. Maybe not. But either way the picture had to go through Fred Nickler. Good ol' Freddy was at the center of this.

Myron looked up the number and dialed.

'HDP. May I help you?'

'I'd like to speak to Fred Nickler.'

'Whom shall I say is calling?'

'Myron Bolitar.'

'Please hold.'

A minute passed. Then Fred Nickler came on. 'Hello?'

'Mr Nickler, this is Myron Bolitar.'

'Yes, Myron. What can I do for you?'

'I'd like to come by and ask you a few more questions about the ad.'

'I'm afraid I'm quite busy right now, Myron. Why don't you give me a call tomorrow? Maybe we can set something up.'

Silence.

'Myron? You there?'

'Do you know who took that picture, Mr Nickler?'

'Of course not.'

'You friend Jerry denies any knowledge of it.'

'Myron, please. You're a man of the world. What did you expect him to say?'

'He says he had nothing to do with putting that picture in the ad.'

'Well, that's quite impossible. He was the advertiser. He submitted the photograph.'

'Then you have a copy of the photo?'

Pause. 'It has to be in the file somewhere.'

'Maybe you can pull it out, and I'll come pick it up.'

'Listen, Myron, I hate to be rude, but I'm really busy right now. It will just be the same photograph you already saw.'

'Kathy's picture was only in *Nips*,' Myron said.

'Pardon me?'

'Her picture. It wasn't in any of your other magazines. Only *Nips*.'

Pause. 'So?' But his voice was suddenly tottery.

'So the same ad was in all six magazines. The same exact page with the same exact pictures. Except for one small change in *Nips*. Someone had changed just one photograph in the bottom row. Someone had switched pictures for just that one magazine and not the others. Why?'

Fred Nickler coughed. 'I really don't know, Myron. Tell you what: I'll check on it and let you know. Gotta zillion calls waiting. Gotta run. Bye.'

Another click.

Myron sat back. Fred Nickler was starting to panic.

With a shaking hand Fred Nickler dialed the number. After three rings the phone was picked up.

'County police.'

Fred cleared his throat. 'Paul Duncan, please.'

22

Nine P.M.

Myron called Jessica. He filled her in on his dean discovery.

'Do you really think Kathy was having an affair with the dean?' Jessica asked.

'I don't know. But after seeing his wife, I'd tend to doubt it.'

'Good-looking?'

'Very,' Myron said. 'And she knows her basketball. She even cried when I got hurt.'

Jessica made a noise. 'The perfect woman.'

'Do I detect a note of jealousy?'

'Dream on,' Jessica said. 'The fact that a man is married to a beautiful woman does not preclude him from having affairs with pretty co-eds.'

'True enough. So the question is: How did Dean Gordon get his name on this infamous mailing list?'

'I haven't got a clue,' she said. 'But I too found out something interesting today. My father visited Nancy Serat, Kathy's roommate, the morning he died.'

'Why?'

'I don't know yet. Nancy just left a message on my machine. I'm meeting her in an hour.'

'Good. Call me if you hear anything else.'

'Where are you going to be?' she asked.

'I work nights at Chippendale's,' Myron said. 'Stage name Zorro.'

'Should be Tiny.'

'Ouch.'

An uncomfortable silence engulfed them. Jessica finally broke it. 'Why don't you come by the house tonight?' she asked, struggling to keep her tone level.

Myron's heart pounded. 'It'll be late.'

'That's okay. I'm not sleeping much. Just knock on my bedroom window. Zorro.'

She hung up. For the next five minutes Myron sat perfectly still and thought about Jessica. They had first started dating a month before his career ended. She stayed with him. She nursed him. She loved him. He pushed her away under some macho disguise of protecting her. But she wouldn't leave. Not then, anyway.

Esperanza opened the door without knocking. She looked at him and snapped, 'Stop it.'

'What?'

'You're making that face again.'

'What face?'

She imitated him. 'That repulsive lovesick-puppy face.'

'I wasn't making any face.'

'Right. You disgust me, Myron.'

'Thank you.'

'You know what I think? I think you're more interested in getting back in Jessica's pants than you are in finding her sister.'

'Jesus, what the hell is with you?'

'I was there, remember? When she left.'

'Hey, I'm a big boy. I can take care of myself.'

Esperanza shook her head. 'Déjà vu all over again.'

'What?'

'Take care of yourself. Bullshit. You sound just like Chaz Landreaux. Both of you have your head up your ass.'

Esperanza's dark face reminded him of Spanish nights, golden sand, full moons against starless skies. There had been moments of temptation between them, but one or the other had always realized what it would mean and stopped it. Such temptations no longer came their way anymore. Aside from Win, Esperanza was his closest friend. Her concern, Myron knew, was genuine.

He changed subjects. 'Was there a reason for your unannounced entrance?'

'I found something.'

'What?'

She read from a steno pad. Why she had a steno pad he could not say. She could not take dictation or type a lick. 'I finally tracked down the other number Gary Grady called after your visit. It belongs to a photography studio called – get this – Global Globes Photos. Located off Tenth Avenue, near the tunnel.'

'Sleazy area.'

'The sleaziest,' she said. 'I think the studio specializes in pornography.'

'Nice to have a specialty.' Myron checked his watch. 'Any word from Win?'

'Not yet.'

'Leave the photographer's address on his voice mail. Maybe he'll finish in time to meet me.'

'You going tonight?' she asked.

'Yes.'

Esperanza closed the pad with a snap. 'Mind if I tag along?'

'To the photography studio?'

'Yes.'

'Don't you have class tonight?' Esperanza was getting her law degree from NYU at night.

'No. And I've done all my homework, Daddy. Really I have.'

'Shut up and come on.'

23

Hookerville.

There were all kinds. White, Black, Asian, Latino – a verifiable United Nations of prostitutes. Most were young, very young, stumbling on too-high heels, like children playing dress-up, which in a real sense they were. Most were thin, dried-up, needle tracks covering their arms like dozens of tiny insects, their skin pulled tightly around cheekbones, giving their faces a haunted skull look. Their eyes were hollow and set deep, their hair lifeless and strawlike.

Myron muttered, ' "Don't they know they're making love to what's already dead?" '

Esperanza paused, thinking. 'Don't know that one.'

'Fontine in *Les Misérables*. The musical.'

'I can't afford Broadway musicals. My boss is cheap.'

'But cute.'

He watched a blond girl in sixties hot-pants negotiate with a sleazeball in a Ford station wagon. He knew her story. He had seen girls (boys sometimes) just like her get off the bus at the Port Authority, a Greyhound bus that had originated in West Virginia or western Pennsylvania or that great, barren mono-expanse New Yorkers simply referred to as the Midwest. She had run away from home – maybe to avoid abuse, but more likely because she was bored and 'belonged' in a big city. She had high-stepped off the bus with a wide smile, mesmerized, without a penny. Pimps would eye her and wait with the patience of a vulture. When the time was right, they would sweep down and claim their carcass. They'd introduce her to the Big Apple, get her a place to stay, some food, a hot shower, maybe a room with a Jacuzzi and dazzling lights and a cool CD player and cable TV with a remote. They'd promise to set her up with a photographer, get her a few modeling gigs. Then they'd teach her how to party, *really* party, not that candy-ass shit she'd done in Hicks Falls with some beer and a zit-infested senior pawing at her in the backseat of a pick-up. They'd show her how to have a good time with the prime stuff, the numero-uno white powder.

But things would change. Someone would have to pay for all these good times. The modeling job would fall through, and she couldn't just be a freeloader. Besides, the partying was more a need now than a luxury. Like food or breathing. She could no longer exist without a snort or a pinch from her favorite needle.

It didn't take long to plummet and hit bottom. And once there she didn't have the strength – not even the desire, really – to get up.

She ended up here.

Myron parked. He and Esperanza got out of the car silently. Myron felt his stomach churn. It was night, of course. Places like this existed only at night. They fled with the onslaught of sunlight.

Myron had never been with a whore, but he knew Win had engaged their services on plenty of occasions. Win liked the convenience. His favorite spot was an Asian whorehouse on Eighth Street called Noble House. Back in the mid-eighties, Win and a few friends would have what they called 'Chinese night' in Win's apartment – Hunan Garden would deliver food, Noble House women. The truth was, Win had no feelings for women. He didn't trust them. Whores were what he wanted. It wasn't just the lack of attachment. Win never let women attach. But prostitutes were throwaways. Disposable.

Myron didn't think Win still partook in such events – not in this disease-ridden era – but he didn't know for sure. They never talked about it.

'Pretty spot,' Myron said. 'Scenic.'

Esperanza nodded.

They passed a nightclub of some sort. The music was loud enough to crack the sidewalk. A teen – Myron couldn't say if it was male or female – with green spiked hair bumped into him. Looked like the Statue of Liberty. There were lots of motorcycles, ear and nipple rings, tattoos, chain jewelry. A constant whore chorus of 'Hey, baby' pelted him from every conceivable angle, their faces blurring into one mass of human debris. The place was like a carnival freak show.

The sign above the door read CLUB F.U. The logo was a raised middle finger. Subtle. A chalkboard read the following:

HEAVY 'MEDICAL' NIGHT!
LIVE BANDS!
Featuring the only local appearances by:
PAP SMEAR
AND RECTAL THERMOMETER

Myron could see through the open door. People weren't dancing. They were jumping up and down, heads lolling lifelessly as if their necks were rubber bands, their arms tucked against their sides. Myron focused in on one kid, maybe fifteen years old, lost in the violet bliss, sweat matting his long hair to his face. He wondered if the group onstage was Pap Smear or Rectal Thermometer. Didn't matter. Sounded like someone had jammed a rutting pig into a Cuisinart.

The whole scene was like Dickens meets *Blade Runner*.

'The studio is next door,' Esperanza said.

The building was either a disastrous brownstone or a small warehouse. Whores hung out the windows like shreds of leftover Christmas decorations.

'This is it?' Myron asked.

'Third floor,' Esperanza answered. She did not seem intimidated by the surroundings in the least, but she had come from streets not much better than this. Her face remained a placid pool. Esperanza never showed weakness. Her temper flared often, but for all their times together, Myron had never seen her cry. She could not say the same of him.

Myron approached the stoop. An overweight whore stuffed into a bodysuit that doubled as sausage casing licked her lips and stepped in front of him.

'Hey, yo, want a blow job? Fifty bucks.'

Myron tried not to close his eyes. 'No,' he said softly, lowering his head. He wanted to offer words of wisdom, words that could transform her, change her circumstances. But he just said, 'I'm sorry,' and hurried past. The fat girl shrugged and moved on.

It was a walk-up. No surprise there. The stairwells were littered with people, most unconscious or maybe dead. Myron and Esperanza carefully climbed over them. A cacophony of music – everything from Neil Diamond to what might have been Pap Smear bellowed through the corridor. There were other sounds too. Broken bottles, shouts, curses, crashing, a baby crying. An orchestra from hell.

When they reached the third floor, they saw a glassed-in office. No one was inside, but the pictures on the wall – not to mention the bullwhip and handcuffs – left little doubt that they had arrived at the right place. Myron tried the knob. It turned.

'You stay out here,' he said.

'Okay.'

He moved in. 'Hello?'

No one answered him, but the music was coming from the other room. Sounded like calypso music. He called out again and stepped into the studio.

Myron was struck by how professional the setup was. It was clean, brightly lit, with one of those big white umbrella things you always see in photo studios. There were half a dozen cameras set up on tripods, and overhead was a variety of different-colored lights.

Of course, the setting was not the first thing that struck him. Other things caught his eye first. The naked woman sitting on a motorbike, for example. To be accurate, she wasn't fully naked – she had on a pair of black boots. Nothing else. Not a look every woman could pull off, but it seemed to work for her. She had not seen him yet, studying the magazine in her hand. *The*

National Sun. Headline: Boy 16 Becomes Grandmother. Hmm. He stepped closer. She was big-breasted, very Russ Meyer, but Myron could see scars under the large swellings. Implants, the fashion accessory of the eighties.

She looked up, startled.

Myron smiled warmly. 'Hi.'

She screamed. Piercingly. 'Get the fuck out of here!' she shrieked, covering her chest. Modesty. So rare nowadays. It was nice to see.

Myron said, 'My name—'

Another piercing scream. Myron heard a noise behind him and spun. A skinny kid wearing no shirt stood smiling. He popped open a switchblade, a maniacal grin plastered across his face. His Bruce Lee-like build shimmered in the light. He crouched low and beckoned Myron forward. Very *West Side Story*. If only the kid would snap his fingers.

Another door opened, and red light leaked out. A woman stepped into view. She had what looked like curly red hair, but Myron couldn't be sure if that was her color or if it just appeared red because of the light from the darkroom.

'You're trespassing,' she said to Myron. 'Hector has the right to kill you where you stand.'

'I don't know where you got your law degree,' Myron said, 'but if Hector isn't careful, I'm going to take away his toy and shove it where the sun don't shine.'

Hector giggled. He began to toss the knife back and forth between his hands.

'Wow,' Myron said.

The topless model fled to the dressing room, which was cleverly marked UNDRESSING ROOM. The woman from the darkroom stepped fully into the studio and closed the darkroom door. Her hair was indeed red, more like burnt auburn actually. Her skin was what some might call peaches and cream. She was maybe thirty and looked, strange as it might sound, perky. The Katie Couric of the porno world.

'Are you the owner?' Myron asked.

'Hector is very good with a blade,' she replied coolly. 'He could slice out a man's heart and show it to him before he died.'

'That must liven a party.'

Hector stepped closer. Myron did not move.

'I could demonstrate my skills in the martial arts,' Myron began. He quickly withdrew his gun and aimed it at Hector's chest. 'But I just showered.'

Hector's eyes widened in surprise.

'Let this be a lesson to you, Blade Boy,' Myron continued. 'Half the people in this building probably carry guns. You go around waving that toy, and someone without my tender heart will ace you.'

The redhead did not seem taken aback by the gun. 'Get out of here,' she said to Myron. 'Now.'

'Are you the owner?' Myron tried again.

'You got a warrant?'

'I'm not a cop.'

'Then get your ass out of here.' She undulated a lot when she talked. Her hips and legs in constant motion. She signaled to Hector, who closed up the switchblade. 'You can go, Hector.'

'Not so fast, Hector,' Myron said. 'Get in the darkroom. I don't want you getting any ideas about coming back with a gun.'

Hector looked toward the redhead. She nodded, and he went.

'Close the door,' Myron said.

He closed it. Myron walked over and pulled the dead bolt.

The redhead put her hands on her hips. 'Happy now?'

'Nearly ecstatic.'

'Now get out.'

'Listen,' Myron said with his melt-'em, warm smile, 'I don't want any trouble. I'm just here to buy some photographs. My name is Bernie Worley. I work for a new porno magazine.'

She made a face. 'Do I really look that stupid? Bernie Worley, here to buy some photographs. Give me a fuckin' break.'

There was a sudden noise. People. Lots of them. A commotion, even by this place's standard. In the corridor. Right where he had left Esperanza. Alone.

Myron turned and ran, feeling his heart leap to his throat. If something had happened to her—

He threw open the door. Dozens of people surrounded Esperanza, most kneeling. She stood in the middle, smiling and – he couldn't believe it – signing autographs.

'It's Pocahontas!' someone shouted.

'Make mine out "With love to Manuel." '

'You're still my favorite!'

'I remember when you beat Queen Carimba. What a fight!'

'That Highway Hannah. Such a dirty fighter. When she threw salt in your eyes, I could have killed her.'

Esperanza caught Myron's eye, shrugged, went back to signing old matchbooks and scraps of paper. The redhead followed him out the door. When she saw Esperanza, her entire being lit up. 'Poco?'

Esperanza looked back up. 'Lucy?'

They hugged. They stepped back into the studio, Myron following.

'Where you been, girl?' Lucy asked.

'Here, there.'

The two women kissed. On the lips. A little too long. Esperanza turned around. 'Myron?'

'Huh?'

'Your eyes are bulging.'

'They are?'

'I don't tell you everything.'

'Apparently not,' he said. 'But at least I know why my startling good looks didn't faze your friend.'

Both women found that laughable. 'Lucy, this is Myron Bolitar.'

Lucy looked him up and down. 'He your boyfriend?'

'No. Just a good friend. And my boss.'

'He looks like a guy I know, worked a kinky show at a club down the street. He had this act where he peed on different women.'

'It wasn't me,' Myron assured her. 'I have enough trouble peeing in a public urinal.'

Lucky turned her attention to Esperanza. 'You look good, Poco.'

'Thanks.'

'Out of the wrestling game, huh?'

'Completely.'

'But you're still working out?'

'As often as I can.'

'Nautilus?'

'Um-hmm.'

'It shows,' Lucy said with a wicked smile. 'You really look hot.'

Myron cleared his throat. 'Hey, how about those Knicks?'

The women ignored him. 'You still taking pictures of the wrestlers?' Esperanza asked.

'Not much anymore. I'm mostly into this shit.'

Esperanza looked back at Myron. 'Lucy – that isn't her real name, we just call her that because of her hair – she used to do the promo photos of all the wrestlers.'

'So I gathered,' Myron said. 'Do you think she can help us out?'

'What do you want to know?' Lucy asked.

Myron handed her the copy of *Nips*. He pointed to Kathy's picture. 'I want to know about this,' he said.

Lucy studied the photograph for a second. 'He a cop?' she asked Esperanza.

'A sports agent.'

'Oh.' She did not ask for further elaboration. 'Because this could get us in trouble.'

'How so?' Myron asked.

'The photograph. The girl is topless.'

'So?'

'So it's illegal. Topless girls aren't allowed in 900 ads. We're going to get screwed if the government sees this.'

'We?' Myron repeated. Again the clever interrogation techniques.

'I'm one of the owners of these dial-a-porn companies. A lot of the lines work out of this building.'

'I'm not sure I understand,' Myron said. 'What do you mean, topless girls are illegal? Almost every girl in that magazine is naked.'

'Not in the ads for 900 lines,' Lucy corrected. 'Couple years back a law was passed. Nine hundred lines had to go clean. Look here.' She turned a page and pointed at another ad. 'The girl might look suggestive, but she can't be naked. And look at the name of the lines. Stuff like "Secret Confessions" or "Talk to Girls." Now look at the ones for the 800 lines. Hard core. "Cum Between My Tits," stuff like that.'

Myron remembered his conversation with Tawny on the 900 line. He had been struck by the fact that she said nothing dirty. 'So you can only have phone sex on the other lines?'

'Right. You see, you need real permission for those. That's how the government sees it. Any asshole can call a 900 line. The charges are automatic. They start almost immediately after your call is answered. But not with an 800 line or one of the other numbers. You have to use either your credit card or a callback. That's the way you get billed.'

'So all that talk about 900 lines being dirty—'

'Is bullshit,' Lucy finished. 'They're cons. We can't say one dirty thing on those lines. We use them as lures mostly, because they're so easy to use. A guy just has to dial. No credit card. No callbacks. Most of the time we talk about skinny-dipping or massages – suggestive but not sexual. Get him excited, you know what I mean?'

'I think so, yes.'

'These guys call horny anyway. I mean, most are so hard up, they'll stick it in a knothole to get relief. What we try to do is get him to say the first dirty word, which usually isn't too difficult. Once he does, we say, "Oh, baby, I can't talk dirty on this line, but you should call me back at X number with a credit card." The guys calls it and gets charged all over again.'

'Aren't they afraid of how it'll look on their credit card bill?' Myron asked.

Lucy shook her head. She was still undulating. It was a combination of irritating and erotic. 'The company names are usually pretty discreet,' she explained. 'We bill under names like Norwood Incorporate or Telemark – not Hot Lesbos or Sucking Starlet. You want to see it?'

'See what?'

'The operation upstairs. Where we answer some of the calls. Lots of people work out of their homes, but I got a crew of six or seven working the lines now.'

Myron shrugged. 'Yeah, sure.'

Lucy took them up one level. Some sort of sickening stench engulfed the stairwell. When they reached the landing, Lucy opened a door. They stepped through and quickly closed it behind them.

'This is Fantasies Forever Lines,' Lucy said. 'Not to mention Dick-a-Lick, Hootersline, Telefun, and a dozen others.'

Myron could not believe what he was seeing. His mouth dropped open. He had expected ugly women or fat women or old women. But he had not expected this.

They were men. All but one of the workers were male.

'Gay lines?' Myron asked.

Lucy shook her head, smiling. 'Very few gay calls come in. Maybe one in a hundred.'

'But . . . these are men.'

Myron Bolitar, the essence of keen observation.

He heard a man in a gruff, truck-driver voice say, 'Yeah, big man, slide it all the way in. That's it. Oh, yeah, that feels good.'

Lucy smiled at the man. The man rolled his eyes and continued, 'Don't stop, Stallion. Ride me.'

Esperanza, Myron was glad to see, looked equally confused. 'What's going on, Lucy?' she asked.

'It's the times,' Lucy said. 'In this economy men are a cheaper source of labor. Most of the girls are on the streets. These are brothers, cousins, street kids.'

'But their voices—'

'They use a voice changer. Sharper Image sells them, but I get them cheaper in the Village. You can make little girls sound like Barry White, or vice versa. These guys can become a husky woman, a teenage virgin, a little girl – whatever the line calls for.'

Myron was stunned. 'Do the customers know this?'

'Of course not.' She turned to Esperanza. 'Dumb. But he is kinda cute.'

Myron Bolitar, Lesbian Fantasy Man.

The room looked like any telemarketing office. The phones were high-tech. Dozens of lines lit up, each marked for what role was to be played. Horny Housewife. Dominatrix. Cross-dressers. Busty Babes. Even Foot Fetish. Each employee also had another phone for Visa and MasterCard verification.

'The lines with a C next to them got to be kept clean,' Lucy explained. 'We also have another hundred or so people working phones from their homes. Most of those are women.'

'Horny housewives?'

'Some of them. Most are just plain housewives. Anyway, that's why I found the ad strange. A 900 line shouldn't have a topless girl.'

They left the room and walked back down to the studio. Myron almost tripped over a wino who chose the moment Myron was stepping over him to stand up.

'Is ABC one of the companies upstairs?' Myron asked.

'Yeah.'

'And we know Gary Grady called you yesterday. Can you tell us why?'

'Who?'

'Gary Grady.'

Lucy shook her head. 'Don't know him.'

'How about Jerry?'

'Oh yeah, him.' She gave a small laugh. 'I figured that wasn't his real name. He was always real secretive.'

'So what did he want?'

She nodded as though something had just occurred to her. 'I get it now.'

'Get what?'

'He was asking me about a photograph I'd taken a couple years back.'

'This one?' Myron asked, pointing to Kathy's picture again.

'Yeah. One of his girls.'

Myron and Esperanza exchanged a glance. 'You mean there were others?'

'Few. Half dozen, maybe more.'

Myron felt the rage consume again. 'Underage girls?'

'How the fuck am I supposed to know?'

'You didn't ask?' Myron asked.

'Do I look like a cop? Look, man, if you're here to hassle me—'

'He's not,' Esperanza said. 'You can trust him.'

'The fuck I can, Poco. He comes busting in here with a fucking gun, scares the piss out of my model.'

'We need your help,' Esperanza said. '*I* need your help.'

'I don't want to hurt you, Lucy,' Myron said. 'I'm just interested in the girl in the picture.'

Lucy hesitated. 'All right,' she said at last. 'But back off.'

Myron gave a quick nod of agreement. 'Jerry brought this girl to you?'

'Yeah, when I had my other studio a couple blocks away. Like I said, he brought in a few girls over the years. He wanted their photos for all kinds of stuff. Porno mags, smut film stills, that kind of thing. Most were a cut or two above the average hosebag who comes through the door. But he usually keeps the photos under wraps until they're a little older. Legal age, I guess.'

The rage again. Myron's hands tightened into fists. 'So Jerry asked you about this picture yesterday?'

'Yeah.'

'What did he want to know?'

'If I sold any copies recently.'

'Have you?'

Pause. 'Yeah. Couple months ago.'

'Who bought them?'

'You think I keep records?'

'A he or a she?'

'A he.'

'Do you remember what he looks like?'

She took out a cigarette, lit it, took a deep puff. 'I'm not real good with faces.'

'Anything, Lucy,' Esperanza added. 'Young, old, anything you can remember.'

Another puff. Then: 'Old. Not ancient, but not a young guy. Might have been my father's age. And he knew what he was doing.' She looked at Myron. 'Not like you. Bernie Worley. Jesus.'

Myron pressed on. 'What do you mean, he knew what he was doing?'

'The man paid me top dollar under one condition: I hand over every photo and negative in front of him right now. Smart. He wanted to make sure I didn't have time to make any extra copies or an extra set of negatives.'

'How much did he pay you?'

'Sixty-five hundred altogether. In cash. Five grand for the photos and negatives. Plus another grand for Jerry's phone number. Said he wanted to get in touch with the girl personally. Then he gave me another five hundred if I didn't say anything to Jerry.'

In the background there was yet another blood-curdling scream. It went ignored. 'Would you know the man if you saw him again?' Myron asked.

'I don't know,' she said. 'I can't picture him now, but if we met up face to face . . . who knows?' There was a pounding noise from the darkroom. 'Mind if I let Hector out now?'

'We were just leaving,' Myron said. He handed her a card. 'If you remember anything else—'

'Yeah, I'll call.' She looked over to Esperanza. 'Don't be a stranger, Poco.'

Esperanza nodded but said nothing. They were quiet the entire way down. When they stepped into the hot air, surrounded by the night street, she said, 'Didn't mean to shock you in there.'

'Not my business,' he said. 'I was a little surprised, that's all.'

'Lucy is a lesbian. I experimented with it a little. Long time ago.'

'You don't have to explain,' he said. But he was glad she told him. Myron had no secrets from Esperanza. He didn't like thinking she had some from him.

They were about to head back to the car when Myron felt the muzzle of a gun against his ribs.

A voice said, 'Stay cool, Myron.'

It was the man with the fedora hat from the garage. He reached into Myron's jacket and took out the .38. A second man, this one with a Gene Shalit-like mustache, grabbed Esperanza and pressed his gun against her temple.

'If Myron moves,' Fedora said to the other man, 'blow the bitch's brains all over the sidewalk.'

The man nodded, half-smiling.

'Come on,' Fedora said, nudging Myron forward with the gun. 'Let's take a little walk.'

24

Jessica parked in front of the house Nancy Serat was renting for the semester. It was more a cottage really, located at the end of a dark street about a mile from the campus of Reston University. Even at night Jessica could see the house's salmon-pink hue, which seemed to clash with the planet earth. The landscape looked like the trees had vomited – the front yard of *The Munsters*. A faded 118 ACRE STREET was stenciled on the weatherbeaten sign. A blue Honda Accord with a Reston University bumper sticker sat in the driveway.

Jessica headed down the broken remnants of what must have once been a cement path. She rang the bell and immediately heard a scurrying sound. Several seconds passed. No one approached the door. She tried again. No scurrying sound this time. No sound at all.

'Nancy?' she called out. 'It's Jessica Culver.'

She hit the bell a few more times, though in a house this small there was not much chance she hadn't been heard. Unless Nancy was in the shower. A possibility. The lights, she could see through the window shades, were on. The car was in the driveway. Jessica had heard movement.

Nancy had to be home.

Jessica reached out for the knob. Under normal conditions some filter in her mind would probably have stopped her from simply trying to open the door of a virtual stranger (she had only met Nancy once). But these conditions were hardly normal. She took hold of the knob and turned.

Locked.

Now what?

She stood at the door five more minutes ringing the bell. Still nothing. Jessica circled the house, using a distant streetlight and the house's glow-in-the-dark properties to guide her. She stumbled over a tricycle that looked like something recovered from an archaeological dig. Her feet got tangled in the high grass, the prickly ends tickling her calves. As she circled, Jessica peeked through the small openings in the window shades. She could make out rooms and spotted an occasional piece of furniture or wall hanging, but no people.

In the backyard she saw the shades were not pulled down in the kitchen.

The lights were off too. It was pitch black here, the pink not getting the illumination of the streetlight to cast its glow. She peered through the kitchen window, cupping her hands around her face to cut off the reflection. A sliver of light from the front room slashed across the room. On the table sat a purse. And a set of keys.

Someone was home.

A sound behind her made her jump. Jessica spun, but it was too dark to make out what it was. Her heart beat wildly in her chest. Crickets singsonged unceasingly. She pounded on the door with both fists.

'Nancy! Nancy!'

She heard the panic in her voice and scolded herself for it. *Get a grip. You're spooking yourself.*

She stopped, took a few deep breaths, felt herself relax. She took another look through the window, pressing her face right up against the glass. She was watching the sliver of light when it happened.

Someone walked by.

Jessica jumped back. She hadn't seen the person, hadn't seen anything, except the sliver of light disappear for the briefest of seconds. She looked again. Nothing. But someone had gone past and blocked off the light. She put her hand on the kitchen doorknob.

This time the door was not locked. The knob turned easily.

Don't just go in, dodo! Call the cops!

And say what? I knocked on a door and no one answered? That I then started peeking through windows and saw someone moving around?

That doesn't sound so bad.

Sounds bad enough to me. Besides, I'd have to find a phone. By the time I do that, whatever is going on may be over. I may have lost my one opportunity . . .

Opportunity for what?

She pushed the voice away. Then she opened the door. She waited for the door to squeak madly, but it slid open with remarkable silence. She stepped into the kitchen and left the door open. Better for the quick getaway.

'Nancy?'

'Kathy?'

She clasped her hand over her mouth. She hadn't meant that. Kathy wasn't here. Jessica wished like hell she were, but that would be too easy. Kathy wasn't here. And if she were, she certainly would not be afraid to open the door for her sister. Her baby sister. The sister with the bright smile. The sister whom she loved . . .

The sister you let slip away. The sister you impatiently rushed off the line the night she vanished.

For several minutes Jessica just stayed in the kitchen. There were no sounds, except those maddening crickets. No running water. No shower. No scurrying. No footsteps. She opened the purse and extracted the wallet.

Driver's license and assorted credit cards – all in the name of Nancy Serat. She flipped to the back and stopped suddenly at a wallet-size photograph.

The picture. The sorority sisters picture. The last picture of Kathy.

She dropped the wallet as though it were something scaly and alive. Enough, Jessica said to herself. She moved toward the light. One foot slid out, the other followed. In a matter of seconds Jessica was at the door. It was open a crack, allowing the light to cast its sliver now unimpeded. She pushed through, crouching like a cop with a gun, preparing for the worst.

And the worst was what she got.

Jessica stumbled back. 'Jesus Christ—'

Nancy lay flat on her back, her hands at her sides. Her eyes stuck out like two golf balls, staring at Jessica. Her face was a deep purplish-blue, like a giant bruise. Her mouth was wide and twisted in pure agony. The tongue lolled out like a dead fish. Nancy Serat's entire expression was still frozen in a look that begged and screamed with its every cell for oxygen. A thin line of still-wet saliva clung to her chin.

A cord of some kind – no, a wire – was wrapped around Nancy's neck, barely visible. Most of it had sliced clean through the skin and was embedded deep in the flesh. A circling lash of blood marked the spot where the wire had entered.

Jessica stared, lost. The world vanished for several moments, leaving behind only the horror. She forgot about the scurrying when she first rang the bell. She forgot the shadow that had cut off the sliver of light.

Jessica did not hear the approaching footsteps. Still staring at Nancy's face, unable to tear her eyes away, she felt a sudden, sharp pain in her head. She saw white flashes. Her body folded at the waist and pitched forward. A tingling numbness followed.

Then nothing.

25

Fedora Hat knew what he was doing.

'Stay a few steps behind me,' he barked at his new partner.

In the garage Fedora and Musclehead (who, Myron was happy to see, seemed to be out of commission) had underestimated Myron, Fedora would not make the same mistake twice. Not only had he always kept eyes and gun on Myron but he was making sure that his new partner (the Mustache) kept both himself and Esperanza a safe distance away.

Smart.

Myron had been tempted to make a move, but even his best move was useless in this circumstance. If he managed to get the gun way from Fedora, there was no way he'd be able to turn it on the Mustache before he'd shoot either him or Esperanza.

He would have to wait and watch. He knew what Fedora and Mustache intended to do. They hadn't been hired to buy him ice cream or teach line dancing or even beat him up. Not this time.

'Let her go,' Myron said. 'She has nothing to do with this.'

'Keep moving,' Fedora replied.

'You don't need her.'

'Move.'

Mustache spoke for the first time. 'I might want a little company later,' he sneered. Then he stopped and pressed the gun against Esperanza's right cheek while he licked – actually licked – her left cheek with a wet cowlike tongue. Esperanza stiffened. Mustache looked at Myron. 'You got a problem with that, pal?'

Myron knew words would be either superfluous or harmful at this stage. He kept his mouth shut.

They turned a corner. The stench of garbage was overwhelming. It was piled at least six feet high on both sides of the narrow alley. Fedora quickly scanned the area. It appeared to be abandoned.

'Go,' he said, giving Myron another poke with the gun. 'End of the alley.'

Myron felt as if he were walking a plank. He tried to take it as slowly as possible.

'What are we going to do with the piece of ass?' Mustache asked.

Fedora's eyes never left Myron. 'She's seen us,' he said. 'She's a witness.'

'But we weren't hired to ace her,' Mustache whined.

'So?'

'So let's not just waste a piece like this' – he smiled – 'especially when we can fuck it first.'

Mustache laughed at his suggestion. Fedora did not. He stepped back, aiming the gun at Myron's back. Myron turned to face him. They were separated by about six feet. Myron was against the back wall. There was no avenue of escape. The nearest window was at least twelve feet off the ground. No room to move at all.

Fedora raised the gun so that it stared Myron right in the face. Myron did not blink. He looked into Fedora's eyes.

And then they were gone. Fedora's eyes were gone. Along with half his head.

The bullet had ripped off the skull at the midway point, splitting Fedora's head open like a coconut. He slid to the ground, the fedora floating down after him.

A dum-dum bullet.

Mustache cried out and dropped the gun. He held his hands up. 'I surrender!'

Myron ran forward. 'Don't! He's surren—'

But the gun exploded again. Mustache's face disappeared in a spray of red mist. Myron stopped, closed his eyes. Mustache joined Fedora on the filthy cement. Esperanza came over and wrapped her arms around Myron. They both turned toward the alley's entrance.

Win stepped into view, studying his handiwork as though it were a statue he wasn't sure he liked. He was dressed in a gray suit, his red tie still in a perfect Windsor knot. His blond hair was neat, conservative, parted as always on the left. The .44 was in his right hand. His cheeks were rosy, and there was just a hint of a smile on his face.

'Good evening,' Win said.

'How long have you been here?' Myron asked. He hadn't spotted Win when they exited the photography studio. But he had known he was there. With Win you just knew. One of life's constants.

'I arrived as you entered the dwelling of ill repute,' Win answered. He smiled. 'But I wanted my appearance to have that flair of drama.'

Myron let go of Esperanza.

'We better get moving,' Win said. 'Before the authorities arrive.'

They walked away from the corpses in silence. Esperanza was shaking. Myron did not feel so hot either. Only Win seemed completely unaffected by what had transpired. As they approached the car, the same fat young prostitute clad in sausage casing approached Win.

'Hey, yo, want a blow job? Fifty bucks.'

Win looked at her. 'I would rather have my semen sucked out with a catheter.'

'Okay,' the girl said. 'Forty bucks.'

Win laughed and walked away.

26

'All units. One-eighteen Acre Street. All units. One-eighteen Acre Street.'

Paul Duncan heard the call on his police scanner. He was only a few blocks from the scene, but this was not his district. Far from it. He could certainly not answer the call. That would only draw attention and questions. Questions like what was he doing here.

Pieces were starting to come together. Fred Nickler, the publisher of those sleazy rags, had called him earlier in the day. What he had told Paul explained a lot. Not everything. Not by a long shot. But he now understood Jessica's behavior the other night. She had learned about Kathy's picture. Myron Bolitar must have told her.

But how had Myron gotten a copy of it?

Not important. Not really. What was important was that Myron Bolitar was involved. He could not be underestimated. Jessica was a big enough pain in the ass on her own. But now she had Myron on her side and probably that Win Lockwood, Myron's psychotic Tonto. Paul knew something about their past work for the feds. Not a lot. Myron and Win had answered only to top government officials. Their work was almost always classified. But Paul knew their reputations. That was enough.

A police car sped past Paul, sirens screaming. They were probably on their way to 118 Acre Street. Paul turned up his scanner. He wanted to hear every word that was said.

He debated calling Carol, but what could he tell her? She hadn't been specific on the phone, just telling him about the phone message from Nancy to Jessica. So what did Jessica know? How had she found out?

And what would Carol ultimately be pressured into saying?

Two ambulances flew by him. They too had their sirens on full blast. Paul swallowed. He wanted to pull over, but he wanted more to drive as far away as possible.

Once again Paul Duncan thought of his friend Adam Culver. Dead. Murdered. With everything that had happened, there had been no time for Paul to mourn.

Yes, mourn.

That might sound strange – Paul Duncan mourning Adam Culver.

Especially if anyone knew how Adam had spent the last precious hours of his life.

Win and Myron dropped Esperanza off at the apartment she shared with her sister and cousin in the east part of Greenwich Village. Myron escorted her to the door.

'You okay?'

She nodded. Her face was deathly pale. She had not spoken a word since the shooting. 'Win—' She stopped, shook her head. It took her a full minute to pull herself together. 'He saved us. I guess that's what counts.'

'Yes.'

'I'll see you in the morning.'

Myron returned to the car. He called Jessica. She wasn't home yet, but Myron did manage to wake her mother. They drove to a twenty-four-hour diner on Sixth Avenue – one of those Greek diners with a menu the approximate length of a Tolstoy novel. Win was a vegetarian. He ordered a salad and french fries. Myron ordered a Diet Coke. He couldn't eat.

After they were settled in, Myron asked, 'What happened with Chaz?'

Win was picking at a basket of stale bread. His face registered displeasure, but he settled on a small packet of Saltines. 'Mr Landreaux hurried straight from our esteemed offices to a building at 466 Fifth Avenue,' he began. 'He took the elevator to the eighth floor, which is rented by Roy O'Connor and TruPro Enterprises. When Landreaux entered the elevator, he had your contract tightly clutched in his paw. When he exited, the contract was no longer visible. He had no pockets that could hold such a document. Conclusion: Mr Landreaux gave the contract to someone at TruPro Enterprises.'

'Your powers of deduction,' Myron said. 'In a word: uncanny.'

Win smiled. 'I assume you are feeling better.'

Myron shrugged.

'We are not the same, you and I,' Win added. 'You call it execution, what I did to that vermin. I call it extermination.'

'You didn't have to kill him.'

'I *wanted* to kill him,' Win said with flat inflection. 'And I doubt any of us will mourn his death for very long.'

True enough, but the argument did not ease Myron's mind. He wanted to drop the subject. 'Where did Chaz go after he left TruPro?'

Win took a dainty bite out of the corner of the Saltine. 'Before I get into that, I should point out that Mr Landreaux was escorted from the building by a large man who fit the description of your friend Aaron. Large. Confident. Athletic. Suit with no shirt. Sunglasses, though the sun had already set.'

'Sounds like Aaron.'

'They split up on the street. Aaron got into a stretch limousine. Chaz Landreaux walked to the Omni Hotel.'

'Which Omni?' Myron asked. Manhattan had several.

'The one near Carnegie Hall. Landreaux met up with his mother in the lobby. Their reunion was rather moving. Mother and son embraced. Both were crying.'

'Hmm,' Myron said.

The waitress arrived with the food and drinks. She put them down, scratched her butt with a pencil, and returned to the kitchen.

'So where did they go after that?'

'Upstairs. They ordered room service.'

Myron thought a moment. 'What is Chaz's mother doing up from Philadelphia?'

'I would assume,' Win said, pulling a napkin out of the dispenser and spreading it on his lap, 'based on their mutual anguish, that Frank Ache reached Chaz Landreaux through a family member.'

'A kidnapping?'

Win shrugged. 'A possibility. Frank just sent two men to try to kill you. I highly doubt he is going to become squeamish over a ghetto abduction.'

Silence.

'We're wading in some deep doo-doo,' Myron said.

'Indeed. Too deep.'

Chaz had a big family. If Frank really wanted to hit him where he lived, he'd take one of his siblings. 'We'll settle it tomorrow,' Myron said. 'I scheduled a meeting with Herman Ache. Two o'clock. Usual place.'

'Should I attend?'

'Most definitely.'

Win ate his salad. 'You do know that this won't be easy.'

Myron nodded.

'Herman Ache does not like to intervene in his brother's business.'

'I know.'

Win put down his fork. 'If I may be so bold as to offer a suggestion.'

'I'm listening.'

'Frank Ache sent two professionals after you. Their untimely deaths will not dissuade him from trying again.'

'Uh-huh. So what's your suggestion?'

'Cut your losses now. Make an exchange. You let them keep Landreaux. They call off the contract on your head.'

'I can't do that.'

'You can. You choose not to.'

'Semantics.'

'You don't have to help him.'

'I *want* to help him,' Myron answered.

Win sighed. 'A man must try to illuminate even those who prefer to sit in the darkness. Do you have a plan yet?'

'I'm still working on it.'

'Feverishly?'

Myron nodded.

'In the meantime,' Win said, 'what did you learn from the photographer?'

Myron filled him in on the meeting with Lucy.

'So who bought the nude pictures?' Win asked.

'A name springs to mind,' Myron said.

'Who?'

'Adam Culver.'

'Kathy's father?'

Myron nodded. 'Think about it. The buyer was in his fifties. He wanted all copies and all negatives on the spot. He left nothing to chance.'

'The father protecting the daughter?'

'It makes sense,' Myron said.

'But Kathy was missing for over a year. How did Adam Culver suddenly learn about the photographs?'

'Maybe he knew about them all along.'

'Then why did he wait so long to buy them?'

Myron shrugged. 'We'll know more tomorrow. I'm going to send Esperanza over to the studio with a picture of Adam, see if Lucy recognizes him.'

Win took another bite of his salad. 'It's a rather strange development.'

'Yes.'

'But' – Win stopped to finish chewing – 'here is something else you may not have considered: If Adam Culver purchased all the pictures and negatives in order to protect his daughter, how did her photograph end up in the magazine?'

Myron had considered that. He just didn't have an answer.

The waitress put down the check. Myron picked up the tab for both of them. The total was $8.50. Mr Magnanimous. They drove uptown. Win lived in the San Remo building overlooking Central Park West. Very fancy address. They were on Seventy-second Street when the car phone rang.

Myron looked at his multicolored Swatch. A gift from Esperanza.

Past midnight.

'Rather late for a call to your car,' Win noted.

Myron picked up the phone. 'Hello?'

The voice came fast. 'Bolitar, it's Jake Courter. Get your ass down to St Barnabas Hospital in Livingston right away.'

'What happened?'

'Just get down here. Now.'

27

'We got the call around eleven-thirty,' Jake said, ushering Myron through the lobby of St Barnabas. Jake's face was set, his eyes red and puffy. They hurried past the circular visitors' desk and waited for an elevator.

'Is Jessica okay?' Myron asked.

'She is going to be fine,' he said. Then he added, 'Wish I could say the same about Nancy Serat.'

'What happened?'

'She was garroted with a wire.' The elevator arrived. Jake pressed the button for the fifth floor. 'When no one answered the door, Jessica let herself in through the back. The killer must have still been there. He knocked her over the head and ran. When she came to, she called us. I'd say she's pretty lucky the perp didn't waste her.'

The elevator opened with a *ding*. 'What room is she in?' Myron asked.

'Five fifteen.'

Myron sprinted down the corridor. He turned the corner. Jessica was in the bed, her face ashen. A doctor stood next to her, preparing a needle. Jake came up behind Myron but stayed in the doorway.

Her voice was wobbly. 'Myron?'

'I'm here,' he said, taking her hand. She looked small and frail and alone. 'I won't leave.'

The doctor pricked her with the needle. 'You need your rest,' he said.

'I'm fine,' Jessica insisted weakly. 'I want to get out of here.'

'We think it's best if you stay overnight for observation.'

'But—'

'Listen to him, Jess,' Myron interrupted. 'There's nothing we can do tonight.'

The drug began to take effect. Her eyes fluttered back. 'Nancy . . .'

'It's okay,' Myron soothed.

'Her face was blue . . .'

'Shhh.'

Jessica slipped into unconsciousness. Myron looked up at the doctor. 'Is she going to be okay?'

'She'll be fine. I think the shock of what she saw was worse than the blow to her head.'

Jake put his hand on Myron's shoulder. 'Come on, I'll buy you a cup of coffee.'

'I want to stay.'

'You can come back later. Right now we need to talk.'

Myron gazed down at Jessica. She was deep in sleep.

'She'll be out for a while,' the doctor assured him.

They walked down the corridor silently and took the elevator back to the lobby. The place had that hospital smell – the unique combo of something antiseptic and the hospital food. Win had parked the car and was now sitting in the waiting area. He stood when he saw them.

'That your friend Win?' Jake asked, motioning with his chin. 'The one P.T. told me about?'

'Yes.'

'Tell him to stay here. I want to talk to you alone.'

Myron signaled to Win. Win nodded, sat back down, picked up a newspaper, crossed his legs. Jake looked him over for a minute. 'He as crazy as P.T. says?'

'Pretty much.'

'Come on.'

They grabbed coffee and found a table in the corner. 'The crime scene unit is going over Nancy's house now. They'll beep me if they find anything.'

'So what do you know so far?' Myron asked.

'Not much. Nancy spent the last few days in Cancún – a graduation present from her parents.'

'Have they been told?'

He shook his head. 'I'm going over there right after we talk.'

Silence. Jake broke it. 'So how did Jessica get involved in this?'

'She wanted me to look into her father's murder. She didn't buy the fact that he was killed in a botched robbery.'

Jake nodded. 'She thought her old man's murder had something to do with her sister.'

'Yes.'

'I figured as much. I got the file in the car.'

Myron sat up. 'Adam Culver's homicide file?'

'Hey, I ain't an idiot, Bolitar. You start investigating after eighteen months. Why? Had to be the father's murder. You saw a connection. But I gotta be honest. I don't see it. No connections in that file at all. A few inconsistencies maybe. But no connection.'

'What sort of inconsistencies?' Myron asked.

'Adam Culver was supposed to be in Denver when he was killed. At a medical examiners' conference at the Hyatt Regency. But he never showed, missed his morning flight.'

'Does the file say why?'

'Adam didn't feel well. A reasonable explanation.'

'Who told them that?'

'His wife.'

Pause. 'What else?'

'Nothing else. The crime scene – a quiet street – was unremarkable. He was stabbed through the heart.'

'What was he doing out?'

'The wife said he went out to buy some groceries.'

Myron chewed that one over for a moment. 'Odd thing to do,' he said, 'when you're not feeling well.'

'Yeah, that's easy for us to say, sitting here like this. But the cops were concentrating on finding a mugger. No one really gave a shit about a missed flight or what it might mean.'

'Any witnesses to the murder?'

'None. The file is pretty bare-bone.' Jake leaned forward and tried to stare Myron down. Myron did not look away. 'Now,' Jake said slowly, 'you start talking to me. And don't give me no "I don't want no one hurt" crap. Too late for that now. Why are you really involved in all this?'

'I told you. Jessica.'

Jake leaned farther forward until their faces were only inches apart. 'Stop jerking me around,' he hissed. 'I ain't blind. I can see Jessica Culver is great tail. But don't start giving me this bullshit that you just decided to drop everything and help on a whim. You ain't that hard up.'

'There was also Christian to consider,' Myron said.

'What about him?'

'He's my top client. He was still upset about his fiancée's disappearance.'

Jake made a snorting noise. 'Yeah, I bet.'

'What's that supposed to mean?'

'It means,' Jake said, 'that I'm not convinced Christian is completely innocent in all this.'

'But you said the DNA test on the semen—'

'I'm not saying he raped her.'

'Then what are you saying?'

'That he might be involved,' Jake replied. 'Your client had no solid alibi for the time of the disappearance. He claims he was in bed at eleven o'clock, but no one can confirm it.'

'He has a single room,' Myron said. 'Who's going to confirm he was in bed when he lived alone?'

'It's suspicious,' Jake replied.

'How? Kathy Culver was seen entering the team locker room after ten, right?'

Jake nodded.

'And you know Christian was meeting with the offensive coordinator until ten-thirty,' Myron continued. 'That's confirmed.'

'But that's where his alibi ends.'

'He went to bed after that. Kathy was seen wandering around on the other side of the campus at eleven o'clock. I don't see the connection.'

'Maybe there is none,' Jake said simply. 'But he's the boyfriend. The boyfriend is always a prime suspect. And there was something else.'

'What?'

'His teammates.'

'What about them?'

'They were cooperative, I guess, but some of them seemed awfully vague. Nothing I could pin down, but some of them looked more nervous than they should. Like they were covering something up. Like maybe, just maybe, they were protecting their star quarterback before the big game.'

Except, Myron thought, nobody on the team liked Christian. His teammates would not have gone out of their way to protect him. Just the opposite, in fact.

So, why were they nervous?

Jake settled back and smiled, marking a change in tactics. 'Now, Myron, I've been awfully sweet, haven't I? I've told you all I know, and you're still holding back on me. That ain't nice. Something else – something you haven't shared with me yet – put a real hairy bug in your ass. Now I visited our friend Dean Gordon a few hours ago, just like you suggested. The man was cordial, friendly, not at all a pompous ass. Which ain't like him. In fact, I think he was scared shitless. Now why's that?'

'Did he tell you anything?'

'Oh, he was real helpful. Kathy was a wonderful girl, an honor student, a hard worker, blah, blah, blah. Oh, yeah. He also told me your ex upstairs paid him a visit. Seems Jessica wanted her sister's file. Imagine that.'

'We were trying to gather as much info as possible.'

'Information on what?'

Myron eyed his coffee. It looked like sewer sludge. 'On the morning Adam Culver was murdered, he visited Nancy Serat.'

Jake's eyes widened bit. 'How do you know that?'

'Nancy left a message on Jessica's phone to meet her at ten o'clock tonight. She also said that she'd seen Adam Culver on the morning of the murder.'

'Jesus Christ.' Jake crossed his arms, resting them on his belly. 'So Adam Culver visits Nancy Serat in the morning. He finds something out. Something big. Something so big he cancels his trip.'

'Something so big,' Myron added, 'it gets him killed.'

Jake nodded, thinking. 'Then the killer has to get rid of the source.'

'Nancy Serat.'

'Right.' Jake stopped. 'But I questioned that girl for hours. I asked her everything . . .' His voice faded off, and a shadow crossed his face. Myron knew what he was wondering. Any cop worth a damn would be asking the same questions. *Did I fuck up? Did I miss something? Is a young girl dead because of me?*

'If Nancy knew something that important,' Myron said, 'the killer wouldn't have waited eighteen months to silence her. I think it's a little more complicated than our scenario. I think Adam Culver had already put most of it together. Nancy had the final piece, a piece that by itself meant nothing to anyone – except Adam Culver.'

'You trying to make me feel better?'

'No. It's how I see it. If I thought you fucked up, I'd say so.'

'You didn't see her body,' Jake said quietly. 'Strangulation ain't pretty. The damn wire nearly sliced her head off. Not a nice way to go, Myron.' He stopped, shook his head. 'After seeing that, I know what Jessica is asking herself, because I keep asking myself the same thing.'

'What's that?'

'Did Kathy meet a similar fate?'

Silence. They drank some coffee. Myron's was already cold, but he didn't complain. Cold, sludgelike coffee seemed to fit the occasion.

'P.T. told me all about you,' Jake said after a massive slurp. 'Said you were smart, that I could trust you. He don't say that about too many folks. Said you and that Win fella were as good as they come. A little too maverick, but right now I could use that. I'm a cop. I have to follow rules. You don't. More power to you. But this is my territory, and I ain't gonna sit around like some fucking movie extra.' He put his hands on the table. They were big and callused and had no rings. 'So now I want you to tell me everything, Myron. Right now. Just you and me. It won't get out, you have my word. Don't hold anything back. You understand?'

Myron nodded.

'So start talking, boy. I'm all ears.'

Myron took out the magazine and handed it to Jake. 'It all started with this.'

28

The morning papers had no mention of Nancy Serat's murder, but the radio was beginning to pick up early reports of a murdered woman. Just a question of time. Myron took Route 280 east to the New Jersey Turnpike north. Scenic road. Like driving through west Beirut on a good day. Problem was, people unfairly judged New Jersey by this road. It was like judging a woman's beauty by the size of her feet.

Billy Joel was on the radio, singing, 'I love you just the way you are.' Big talk, Myron mused, when you've been married to Christie Brinkley.

Exit 16W led him directly into the Meadowlands parking lot. Murder and intrigue were all well and good, but agenting paid the bills. He had a meeting with Otto Burke. Otto was expecting a response to his demand vis-à-vis Christian's contract. Myron had prepared one for him.

He had spent the night in Jessica's hospital room, trying to get comfortable in a chair that doubled as a medieval torture device. But he had not minded. He liked watching her sleep. It brought back memories. He'd always hoped they'd one day sleep together again, though last night was not precisely what he had had in mind.

Jess had woken up two hours ago. Belligerent. Testy. Demanding. In a word: herself. Before her brother Edward took her home, Myron had told her all he knew – especially about his visit to Lucy's photo studio. She had given him a photograph of her father to show Lucy. Myron was surprised to see Jessica carried one in her wallet. But he was far more surprised to catch a fleeting glimpse of a picture from four summers ago – a picture she tried to skip past without his seeing. But he had seen it, and he remembered the precise moment it had been taken. Their last weekend in Martha's Vineyard. Just the two of them. Tan, happy, relaxed. A barbecue at Win's summer house: The pinnacle before the inevitable slide.

Myron had not had a chance to change clothes. He looked as if he'd spent the evening in the bottom of a laundry hamper.

Otto was waiting for him in the owner's box on Titans Stadium mezzanine level. Larry Hanson was with him. Otto greeted Myron with a bony handshake and a wide smile. Mr Sunshine. Larry offered a quick wave. He did not meet Myron's eye. It was no wonder. Larry Hanson was a tough guy, a loud brute even, but he tried to play fair. He didn't like to cheat, and he did not like what Otto was doing now. He looked, in fact, as if he wanted to blend into the wall.

'Please, Myron,' Otto said, spreading his arms like Carol Merrill on *Let's Make a Deal*, 'sit wherever you like.'

'Always the perfect host, Otto.'

'I do try, Myron. Thank you for noticing.'

'Sarcasm, Otto. It's called sarcasm.'

Otto kept the smile aglow. His goatee was exactly the same as always, never heavier or lighter. Must trim it every day, Myron thought. They sat in two seats facing the field. Fifty-yard line. Fans would kill for these seats. Down below, players were scattered across the field. Myron spotted Christian walking toward the sideline. His helmet was off, his head held high. Christian didn't know about Nancy Serat's murder – her name had not yet been released – but the press would be all over him soon enough. Myron could protect him only so much, though he did entertain hopes that the news of Christian's signing would deflect some attention away from the murder.

'So,' Otto said with clap of his hands, 'are you ready to sign?'

Down on the field Christian was being introduced to a bunch of long-haired men. Myron recognized the men from video on MTV. They were Otto Records' latest find. A group called StillLife. Good sound, but did they have the raw talent, of, say Pap Smear?

'Sure,' Myron said. 'We would like nothing more.'

'Great. I have a pen.'

'How handy. I have a contract.' He handed it to Otto. Otto read it quickly. His mouth was smiling, but his eyes frowned. He passed it to Larry Hanson.

'I'm confused, Myron. This looks like your last offer.'

'Very perceptive, Otto.'

'I thought we had an agreement,' he said.

'We do. There it is.'

'I think you're forgetting' – he paused, searching for the right word – 'Christian's sudden devaluation.'

'You make him sound like a foreign currency.'

Otto laughed. He looked over to Larry as if to say, laugh too. Larry could only muster a smile. 'Okay, Myron, I'll accept that. We are all, to some extent, commodities. Your client, however, is now trading at a lower rate against the U.S. dollar.'

'Thanks for keeping within the metaphor, Otto, but I don't see it that way.' Myron looked at Larry Hanson. 'How's his play been, Larry?'

'Well, it's very early,' Larry said, clearing his throat. 'You really can't tell too much after such a short time period.'

'But if you had to grade him so far?'

Another throat clear. 'Let's just say,' he replied, 'that Christian's play has not been a disappointment.'

'There you go,' Myron said, matching Otto's smile. 'His value has, if anything, increased with his recent on-the-field display. You have now had a tasty morsel of his potential. I don't see how you could expect us to drop our asking price.'

Otto rose, nodding his head. He clasped his hands behind his back and walked to the bar. 'Care for a drink, Myron?'

'Do you have any Yoo-hoo?'

'No, I don't.'

'Nothing, then.'

Otto poured himself a 7-Up. He did not ask Larry Hanson if he wanted anything. 'I will admit,' Otto said, 'that Christian's play so far has been impressive, though I must caution you, Myron – and you too, Larry – that there is a big difference between practice and games. Between how an athlete performs in a scrimmage and how he performs in a pressure situation.'

Myron and Larry exchanged a glance. The glance said, Pretentious asshole.

'But let me also add,' Otto continued, 'that our product is dependent on more than just performance. If, for example, our team were to win the Super Bowl but were also involved in a major drug or sex scandal, the overall value of the product may decline.'

'Can you demonstrate that with a graph?' Myron asked. 'I'm not sure I understand.'

'It means,' Otto said, 'that the photograph in that sleazy publication makes Christian worth less money to us.'

'But it's not a picture of him.'

'It's a picture of his fiancée.'

'Ex-fiancée.'

'His fiancée who vanished under mysterious circumstances.'

'Christian and I are willing to take the chance,' Myron said. 'It was in a small publication. It hasn't gotten out so far. We don't think it will.'

Otto sipped his 7-Up. He seemed to enjoy it, even adding an 'aaah' like he was taping a commercial. 'But the press might find out.'

'I don't think so,' Myron said. 'I've discussed it with Christian. We both feel the same.'

'Then you are both fools.'

The facade had dropped open a crack.

'Now, Otto, that wasn't very nice.'

The facade slid back up, smooth as an electric car window. 'Let me remind you of our previous discussion on this very subject, Myron. See if you can follow this. You were to take our agreement and knock it down by a third. If not, the picture of the au naturel Ms Culver goes public, thereby ruining your player's endorsement career.'

'But he didn't do anything, Otto. It's only a picture of Kathy Culver.'

'It doesn't matter. Advertisers do not like the smallest whiff of controversy. Remember this, Myron: In business, appearance is far more important than reality.'

'Appearance versus reality,' Myron said. 'That I have to write down.'

Otto took out a contract of his own. 'Sign it,' he said. 'Now.'

Myron just smiled at him.

'Sign it, Myron. Or I'll ruin you.'

'I don't think so, Otto.'

Myron began to unbutton his shirt.

'What do you think you're doing?'

'Don't get excited, Otto. I'm stopping after the third button. Just enough to show you this.' He pointed to the small microphone on his chest.

'What the hell—?'

'It's a wire, Otto. It leads to a tape recorder stuck in my belt. You can make the picture public, that's up to you. It may damage Christian, it may not. I, in turn, will make this tape public. I will also sue your sorry ass for any damages Christian may have suffered because of your actions, and I will also see to it that you are arrested for extortion and blackmail.' Myron smiled. 'I always wanted to own a record company. Chicks dig that, don't they, Otto?'

Otto looked at him coolly. 'Larry?'

'Yes, Mr Burke.'

'Take the tape away from him. Forcibly, if necessary.'

Myron looked at Hanson. 'You're a big guy, Larry,' Myron said. 'And I know you were one of the toughest fullbacks ever to play this game. But if you get out of that chair, I'll put you in a body cast.'

Larry Hanson merely nodded. Not afraid, but not moving either.

'There are two of us,' Otto urged. 'I can call in security guards to help.'

'I don't think so, Mr Burke.' Larry was almost smiling. 'And I don't think a few security guards are going to scare him very much. Are they, Myron?'

'Not likely.'

'I think we should sign his contract, Mr Burke. I think it's best for all.'

'I've even drawn up a press release,' Myron said. 'Says how happy Christian is to be playing for such an outstanding and reputable organization as the Titans.'

Otto thought a moment. 'If I sign,' he said, 'you'll hand over the tape?'

'Not likely.'

'Why not?'

'You keep the magazine and I keep the tape. Think of it as our own little balance of terror. A throwback to the cold war.'

'But you have my word—'

'Please, Otto, it hurts when I laugh.'

Otto thought a moment. He was shaken but calm. A guy his age doesn't reach this level without learning to take a few knocks.

'Myron?'

'Yes.'

'I can't tell you how thrilled the Titans are to have Christian Steele, the quarterback of the future, with us.'

'Just sign right here, Otto.'

'My pleasure, Myron.'

'No, Otto. Mine.'

Otto signed. Myron and Otto shook hands. The deal was done.

'Shall we meet the press jointly, Myron?'

'Sounds wondrous, Otto.'

'There's a shower downstairs. I'll make sure you're provided with shaving equipment, if you like.'

'Very kind of you.'

Otto's smile was back. The man was never down long. He picked up the phone. 'Christian Steele has been signed,' Otto said. Then, looking back and winking at Myron, he added, 'At the highest salary ever given to a rookie.'

Myron winked back and gave him the thumbs up. Lifelong chums. He checked his watch. There would be just enough time to shower and do the press conference before he would have to head back into the city for his meeting with Herman Ache.

He had no idea how he was going to handle the evil Ache brothers. But he was still working on it. Feverishly.

29

Jessica arrived at the house in Ridgewood at ten o'clock. The doctor had wanted to run some more tests in the morning. Jessica refused. They finally reached a compromise whereby Jessica promised to visit him in his office sometime during the week. Edward had driven her home in silence.

When they arrived, Jessica noted that her mother's car was not in the driveway. Good. Not in much of a mood to handle a hysterical mother on top of everything else, Jessica had insisted that no one tell her mother about last night's incident. Mom had enough on her mind. No reason to get her unnecessarily upset.

Jessica headed straight for the study. Her father had been up to something, that much was clear. There were too many weird happenings for it to have been any other way. He had visited Nancy Serat on the morning of his death. He had skipped out on a medical examiners' convention in Denver because he hadn't felt well – something he would never do. He had possibly even purchased nude photographs of Kathy.

You didn't have to be Sherlock Holmes to realize something was amiss.

She flicked on the track lights, illuminating the room a bit too harshly for her taste. She used the dimmer. Downstairs, Edward was in the kitchen opening the refrigerator.

She began to rifle through her father's drawers. She had no idea what she was looking for. Perhaps a small box with the words BIG CLUE scrawled across the top. That would be nice. She tried not to think about Nancy Serat, about her blue face frozen in terror, but the thought stayed anchored front and center. She thought of more pleasant things, like waking to see Myron folded up in that hospital chair like a contortionist from Le Cirque du Soleil. The image made her smile.

In the file drawer she found a folder marked CMA. Her father's Merrill Lynch Cash Management Account. She pulled it out. The CMA statement is a financial instrument of great beauty. Everything in one statement – your stocks, bonds, other holdings, checks, Visa card transactions. Jessica had one of her own.

She checked the charges and checks cleared on the most recent statement.

Nothing unusual. Problem was, the statement ended three weeks ago. She needed something more recent.

She flipped to the last page. On the bottom in small print it read 'You have an alphabetic character in your Merrill Lynch account number. Please use nine-eight-two-three-three-four as your account access number for CMA-DATA.'

CMA-DATA. The 800 line. She had used it before with her own account, whenever she found a discrepancy. She dialed the number and immediately heard a taped voice say, 'Welcome to the Merrill Lynch Financial Service Center. Enter your Merrill Lynch account number or your account access number.'

Jessica entered the number.

'Enter your selection. You may interrupt the dialogue at any time. For your current balance and purchasing power, enter one. For check clearing information, enter two. For most recent funds received, enter three. For most recent Visa transactions, enter six.'

She decided to start with the charges and then look at the checks. She pressed six.

The voice said, 'Visa draft for $28.50 is on delay debit as of May twenty-eighth. Visa draft for $14.75 is on delay debit as of May twenty-eighth.'

The machine was not telling her where the charges were coming from. The same would be true for the checks. Knowing just the amounts would do her no good.

'Visa draft for $3,478.44 is on delay debit as of May twenty-seventh.'

She froze. Three thousand dollars? For what? She hung up, hit the redial button, and put in the account access number.

'Enter your selection.'

This time she pressed zero for a customer service representative.

'Good morning,' a pleasant-voiced woman singsonged. 'May I help you?'

'Yes, there's a Visa charge on my account for over three thousand dollars. I'd like to know where the charge came from.'

'Your account number, please?'

'Nine-eight-two-three-three-four.'

There was some keyboard clacking in the background. 'And you are?' the rep asked.

Jessica checked the statement. A joint account, thank God. 'Carol Culver,' she said.

'Hold one moment, Mrs Culver.'

More clacking. 'Yes, I have it here. $3,478.44. Eye-Spy Shop in Manhattan.'

Eye-Spy? What the hell was that all about?

'Thank you,' Jessica said.

'Anything else today, Mrs Culver?'

'Yes. My husband and I have all our records on a personal computer, and I'm afraid the computer has had a disk failure. Can I ask you to give me the most recent checks that have been written against the account?'

'Certainly.'

More clacking. 'Check one-nineteen for $295 to Volvo Finance written on May twenty-fifth.'

Car payment.

'Check one-eighteen for $649 to Getaway Realty, also written on May twenty-fifth.'

Hold the phone. 'Did you say Getaway Realty?'

'Yes, that's correct.'

'Does it say where they're located?'

'I'm afraid I don't have that information.'

They went through the rest of the month's checks. Nothing unusual. Jessica thanked the woman and hung up.

$649 to Getaway Realty? $3,478.44 to Eye-Spy? More and more amiss.

Edward knocked on the door. 'Hi,' he said.

'Hi.'

He stepped into their father's study, head lowered.

'I'm sorry about the other day,' Edward said. He blinked several times, his to-die-for eyelashes waving up and down. 'About running out like that.'

'It's okay.'

'You hit a raw nerve,' he said. 'Asking all those questions and everything.'

'They need to be asked,' she replied. 'I think everything is connected. What happened to Kathy. What happened to Dad. What made Kathy change.'

Edward flinched at the word *change*. Then he shook his head. His T shirt of the day featured Beavis and Butt-head. 'You're wrong,' he said. 'It doesn't have anything to do with what happened to her.'

'Maybe,' she said. 'Only way to find out is if you tell me.'

'I don't feel comfortable about it. It's painful.'

'I'm your sister. You can trust me.'

'We were never very close,' he said bluntly. 'Not like you and Kathy.'

'Or you and Kathy,' Jessica said. 'But I still love you.'

She waited.

'I don't know where to begin exactly,' he said. 'It started her senior year of high school. You had just moved to Washington. I was at Columbia. I was living off campus with my friend Matt. Remember him?'

'Of course. Kathy dated him for two years.'

'Almost three,' Edward corrected. 'Matt and Kathy were like something out of another century. They were together three years, and he never got, well, below the neck. I mean, never. And it wasn't just from a lack of trying. Matt was as strait-laced as any guy I knew, but that didn't mean he didn't push it now and again. But Kathy held him off.'

Jessica nodded, remembering. Kathy had still been confiding in her at that stage.

'Mom loved Matt,' Edward continued. 'She thought he was the greatest. She used to invite him over for tea like something out of *The Glass Menagerie*. A gentleman caller sitting on the porch with the youngest daughter. Dad liked him too. Everything seemed to be going well. They planned on getting engaged in another year, married after he graduated, the whole Chevy-and-apple-pie love story. Then one day Kathy called him on the phone and just dumped him. No explanation.

'Matt was shocked. He tried to talk to her, but Kathy wouldn't see him. I tried to talk to her too, but she just blew me off. Then I started hearing rumors.'

Jessica shifted in her chair. 'What kind of rumors?' she asked.

'The kind,' Edward said slowly, 'a brother doesn't like to hear about his sister.'

'Oh.'

'Worse than oh. Guys were trashing her nonstop. Someone had finally found the key to Miss Prude's chastity belt, they said, and now they couldn't get it back closed. I even got into a fight. Got the shit beaten out of me protecting Kathy's honor.' He spat out the word *honor* as though it had an offensive taste.

'She changed at home too. She never went to mass anymore. I thought Mom would have a stroke – you know how she gets about stuff like that.'

Jessica nodded. She knew only too well.

'But she never said a word. Kathy started staying out late. She went to college parties. Some nights she wouldn't even come home.'

'Didn't Mom stop her?' Jessica asked.

'She couldn't, Jess. It was unbelievable. Kathy had spent her entire life in fear of the woman. Now it was like Kathy had found Kryptonite. Mom couldn't touch her.'

'What about Dad?'

'He was never as strict as Mom, you know that. He wanted to be everyone's buddy, not the bad guy. But strangely enough, Kathy grew closer to Dad during all this. He was thrilled by the sudden attention. I think he was afraid if he laid down the law, he'd push her away from him.'

Sounded like her father. 'What did you do?' she asked.

'I confronted her.'

'What did she say?'

'Nothing really. She wouldn't deny it or admit it. She would just stand there and smile eerily. She said I didn't understand, that I was "naïve." Naïve. Can you believe Kathy could call someone else naïve?'

Jessica thought a minute. 'But none of that explains what started it, what made her change in the first place.'

Edward opened his mouth, stopped. He spread his hands, then dropped them back to his sides as though they were too heavy to hold up. His voice was barely audible. 'Something with Mom,' he said.

'What with Mom?'

'I don't know. I think maybe Mom does. Kathy became withdrawn from you and me. But she still loved us. It was Mom got the brunt of it.'

Jessica leaned back in her father's chair, considering his last comment. 'I knew Kathy had changed the last couple of years, but I had no idea . . .' Her voice sort of faded away.

'But it ended, Jess. You have to remember that.'

'What ended?' she asked.

'This stage Kathy went through. That's why I don't think it's related to her disappearance. By the time she disappeared, it was all in the past.'

'What do you mean, in the past?'

'She changed back. Oh, I don't mean she started going to mass every Sunday or became buddies with Mom. But whatever had twisted her out of shape had finally let go. She was regaining her old self. I think Christian had a lot to do with that. I think he helped bring her back from the edge. The slutty behavior certainly stopped. So did the drugs, the drinking, the partying. Other things too. The smile even came back a little.'

Jessica remembered Kathy's school transcript. The terrible grades in her senior year and the beginning of college. Then the sudden turnabout back toward excellence that had started her second semester freshman year – when she met Christian. It added up with what Edward was saying.

So was the past irrelevant? Was this period of her life, as Edward had insisted, all behind her? Perhaps. But Jessica doubted it. If it were truly dead and buried, why was her picture now appearing in a pornographic magazine? And that of course led to the central question in all this:

What had made Kathy change in the first place?

Jessica still did not know. But she now had a pretty good idea who might.

30

There were several things Myron enjoyed more than visiting Herman Ache. Having his eyeball removed with a grapefruit spoon, for example.

'I heard your press conference on the radio,' Win said. The top was down on Win's racing-green Jaguar XJR. Myron was not big on having the top down. It was just a question of time before a bug got stuck in his teeth. 'I trust that Christian was pleased with the deal.'

'Very.'

'The press still hasn't picked up on Nancy Serat.'

'Jake hasn't released her name yet. Once they do—'

'Party time.'

'Exactly.'

'Does Christian know?' Win asked.

'Not yet. He was so damn happy. I just wanted to let him enjoy it a little longer.'

'You should warn him.'

'I will. Jake promised to let me know the second it got out.'

'You seem to like this Jake fellow,' Win noted.

'He's a good man. We can trust him.'

Win wiggled his fingers, regripped the wheel, accelerated. 'I don't trust officers of the law,' Win said. 'It's safer that way.'

The car was going very fast. The West Side Highway was not built for such speed – a four-lane highway with traffic lights every twenty yards. Plus the 'ongoing' construction didn't help. The construction had been going on for as long as anyone could remember. History books stated that Peter Minuit, the Dutchman who purchased Manhattan from the Indians in 1626, often complained about the delays around Fifty-seventh Street.

But none of that deterred Win's hefty accelerator foot. The Javits Center was a blur. So was the Hudson River, for that matter.

Myron said, 'Could you slow down a tad?'

'No need to worry. The car has a driver-side air bag.'

'Wonderful.'

They were getting closer to Ache's office. Myron's stomach knotted – not helped by the smog blasting into his face because the top was down. His nerves were as taut as a freshly strung tennis racket. Win, on the other hand, looked relaxed. Then again, Frank Ache didn't have a contract out on his head.

Win's car phone rang. He picked it up. 'Hello?' He handed the phone to Myron. 'It's P.T.'

Myron took the receiver. 'What's up?'

'Hey, Myron, how you feeling today?'

'Can't complain.'

'Glad to hear it. Say, you'll never guess what happened last night.'

'What?'

'Two of New York's finest hit men were found dead in an alley. Sad, ain't it?'

'Tragic,' Myron agreed.

'They worked for Frank Ache.'

'That a fact?'

'Forty-four Magnum with dum-dum bullets were used. Blew their heads clean off.'

'Such a loss.'

'Yeah, I'm losing sleep over it too. Anyway, word out on the street is, this ain't over. Corpses don't exactly waylay the wants of a guy like Frank Ache. The contract is still out on whatever ugly slob pissed Frank off.'

Myron said, 'Ugly?'

'Well, it's been nice talking to you, Myron. Take care.'

'You too, P.T.'

Myron hung up.

'The contract is still in place?' Win asked.

'Yep.'

'They won't hit you in Herman's office,' Win said. 'He would never allow it.'

Myron knew that was true. There was a certain code, even among men who have probably ordered the deaths of hundreds of people. Some idiots believed that these codes were based on some sort of ethics. Not even close. The codes were two things to mobsters: 1. a device to make them appear almost human, and 2. a way of protecting themselves and their position. Ethics are to a mobster what honesty is to a politician.

A construction site slowed them near Twelfth Street, but they still made it with time to spare. The air smelled of pizza – probably because they parked in front of a pizzeria called The First Original Ray's Pizza of New York, Really, We're Not Kidding, Honest, We're It. A tall woman in a blue business suit and fancy sunglasses strolled purposefully down the sidewalk. Myron smiled at her, and she returned it. He would have preferred a faint or even a small swoon, but you can't have everything.

At two in the afternoon Clancy's Tavern was already in full swing. Myron stopped right outside the door, fixed his hair, turned left, smiled, turned right, smiled, looked up, smiled.

Win looked a question at him.

'The feds take pictures of everyone who comes in here,' Myron said. 'I just wanted to look my best.'

'Now you tell me. I look like hell.'

Clancy's patrons were all men. Not exactly a swinging pick-up joint. A jukebox played Bob Seger. The decor was Early American Beer. Lots of those neon signs, the ones that spell out company names. Budweiser, Bud Light, Miller, Miller Lite, Schlitz. A clock courtesy of Michelob. A mirror from Coors. Coasters from Pabst. The mugs had Rolling Rock logos emblazoned across them.

Myron knew that there were probably a million FBI bugging devices in here. Herman Ache didn't care. Anybody who said something truly damaging in the tavern itself was beyond stupid and deserved to get nailed. The real talk went on in the back rooms. Ache made sure they were swept for bugs every day.

Win drew a few curious glances when they entered. Prep was not exactly the 'in' style of Clancy's clientele. But no one stared too long. This was a bar where no one stared at anyone too long.

'Is that your friend Aaron?' Win asked.

Aaron was at the back of the bar wearing his customary white suit. This time he wore a shirt, albeit one of those pectoral-displaying sleeveless muscle Ts. It was as if Aaron's wardrobe had entered some molecular transformer with issues of *GQ* and *Pumping Iron*. Aaron waved them to come forward with a hand the size of a manhole cover.

'Hello, Myron,' Aaron said. 'A genuine pleasure to see you again.'

Myron Bolitar, Mr Popularity. 'Aaron, I'd like you to meet Win Lockwood.'

Aaron angled the smile at Win. 'Pleasure, Win.' They shook hands with death stares, each sizing the other man up. Neither flinched.

'They're waiting in the back,' Aaron said. 'Come on.'

Aaron led them to a locked door with a one-way mirror. The door opened immediately. They entered. Two hoods stood stonefaced. In front of them was a long corridor. There was – and this was new – a metal detector, like at the airport.

Aaron shrugged, as if to say, A sign of the times. 'Hand over your weapons, if you'd be so kind. Then step through.'

Myron took out his thirty-eight, Win a brand-new forty-four. Last night's forty-four had no doubt been destroyed. They stepped through. The metal detector did not ding, but the two hoods still searched with one of those gizmos that looked suspiciously like vibrators. Then they searched again, this time by hand.

'Very thorough,' Win said.

'Almost enjoyable,' Myron added. 'I thought he was going to ask me to turn my head and cough.'

'Hey, funny man,' one of the hoods groused, 'this way.'

The two hoods took over, escorting them down the corridor. Aaron stayed back and watched. Myron did not like that. The walls were white, the carpet office-orange. Lithographs of the French Riviera lined the walls. The front of Clancy's Tavern looked like a dive; the back like a dentist's office.

Two other men appeared at the other end of the corridor. They were both carrying guns.

Myron leaned forward toward Win's ear. 'Uh-oh.'

Win nodded.

The two men pointed their guns at Myron and Win. One barked, 'Hey, you, Goldilocks. Get over here.'

Win looked at Myron. 'Goldilocks?'

'I think he means you.'

'Oh. The blond hair. I get it now.'

'Yeah, Goldie, get your butt down here.'

'Later,' Win said. He moved down the corridor. The two hoods from the metal detector took out their guns. Four men, four guns. Lots of firepower. Not taking any chances after last night.

'Hands on your head. Let's go.'

Win and Myron, separated by approximately ten feet, did as they were told. One of the hoods from the metal detector approached Myron. Without warning, he punched the butt of his gun against Myron's kidney.

Myron dropped to his knees. Nausea swam through him. The man followed up with a kick to the ribs. Then another. Myron slid to the ground. The other man joined in. He stomped on Myron's upper legs like they were small brushfires. One stomp landed on the already-sore kidney. Myron thought he was going to vomit.

In something of a haze Myron spotted Win. He had not moved, his face displaying something akin to non-interest. He had sized up the situation and made a quick determination: There was nothing he could do to help. Worrying and fretting were worthless. Win was spending his time calmly studying the men. He didn't like to forget a face.

The kicks came in a nonstop flurry. Myron curled into a fetal position and tried to ride it out. The kicks hurt like hell, but they were too rushed to do serious damage. One landed near his eye. He'd have a shiner for sure.

Then a voice shouted, 'What the hell— Stop this moment!'

The kicks halted immediately.

'Get away from him!'

The men backed off. 'Sorry, Mr Ache.'

Myron rolled onto his back. With some effort he managed to sit up. Herman Ache stood by an open door. 'Are you okay, Myron?'

Myron winced. 'Never better, Herman.'

'I can't tell you how sorry I am,' Herman Ache said. Then glaring at his men. 'But some people will be even sorrier.'

The men cowered away from the older man. Myron almost rolled his eyes. This was all an act. Herman Ache's men did not beat up men in Herman's corridor without permission. This had been a setup. Now Myron supposedly owed Herman, even before the negotiating started. Not to mention the fact that pain is a great fear-inducer, the perfect prenegotiation cocktail.

Aaron came down the hall. He helped Myron to his feet and sort of half-shrugged as if to say Cheap move, but what can you do?

'Come,' Herman beckoned. 'Let's talk in my office.'

Myron moved tentatively into the office. He had not been here in several years, but not much had changed. Golf was still the theme. LeRoy Neiman painting of some golf course on the main wall. Lots of those stupid cartoon/artworks of old-fashioned golfers. Aerial photographs of golf courses. In one corner of the office was a movie screen showing a shot of a fairway. In front of the screen was a golf tee. The player hits the ball against the screen. A computer then calculates where it would have landed and changes the image on the screen to match that. Then the player takes his second shot. Fun city.

'Nice office,' Win said.

Figures.

'Thank you, son.' Herman Ache smiled. Capped teeth. He was in his early sixties, tan, fit, wearing white pants and a yellow golf shirt with a Nicklaus golden bear where an alligator normally went – as if he were on his way to a gin tournament in Miami Beach. Herman Ache had gray hair. Not his own. A toupee or one of those Hair Club systems, a good one, one most people would probably not spot. He had liver spots on his hands. His face was wrinkle free, probably from collagen shots or a face-lift. The neck gave him away. The flesh was baggy and Reaganesque. Looked like a big scrotum.

'Please, gentlemen, have a seat.'

They did so. The door was closed behind them. Aaron, two new hoods, and Herman Ache. Nausea's grip on Myron's stomach began to slacken.

Herman picked up a golf club and sat on the edge of his desk. 'I understand,' he said, 'that you and Frank are having a misunderstanding, Myron.'

'That's what I wanted to talk to you about.'

Herman nodded. 'Frank?'

The door opened. Frank entered. You could tell that they were brothers, both having almost identical facial features, but that was where the similarities ended. Frank had at least twenty pounds on his older brother. He was pear-shaped with small Paul Schaefer shoulders and a rubber tire that would be the envy of the Michelin Man. Frank was completely bald,

162

forgoing the hair weave. His teeth were black with spaces between them. His face was permanently set on angry scowl.

Both brothers had grown up on the streets. Both had started out as small-time hoods and worked their way up. Both had seen their own children gunned down over the years. Both had gunned down plenty of other people's children. Herman liked to pretend that he dwelled on a loftier plane than his coarse younger brother – a plane of fine books, the arts, golf. But the escape was not that easy. Two sides of the same coin. Frank gratingly reminded Herman of his origins and perhaps true nature. But Frank was comfortable and accepted in his world. Herman was not.

Frank was dressed in a powder blue sweat suit with neon yellow trim. The jacket was unzipped and – taking a fashion tip from Yves St Aaron – he wore no shirt. His chest hairs were matted with either some type of oil or sweat. Quite a turn-on. The form-fitting pants were a few sizes too small, outlining a bulge in his crotch. Myron started feeling nauseous again.

Frank did not speak. He sat at his brother's desk and waited.

'Now, Myron,' Herman continued, 'I understand this is all about some black boy who plays basketball.'

'Chaz Landreaux,' Myron said. 'And I'm not sure he'd be crazy about being called "boy." '

'Pardon an old man who is not up on all the politically correct terms. I meant no disrespect.'

Win sat quietly, studying his surroundings.

'Let me tell you how I see it,' Herman continued. 'And I'm trying to be objective here. Your Mr Landreaux made a deal. He took the money. For four years he helped his family with that money. Then when it was time to pay up, he reneged.'

'That's objective? Chaz Landreaux is just a kid—'

'Spare me the lecture,' Herman interrupted gently. 'We're not social workers here. You know that. We are businessmen. We made an investment in this young man. We risked several thousand dollars on him. The investment was finally about to pay dividends when you interfered.'

'I didn't interfere. He came to me. He's a scared kid. O'Connor got his hooks in him when he was eighteen. There are rules against approaching kids that young for a reason. Now the kid's trying to get out before he slides in too deep.'

Herman looked skeptical. 'Oh, come on now, Myron. Kids grow up fast nowadays. He knew exactly what he was doing. So it was against the rules – big deal. The kid knew the rules. He wanted the money anyway.'

'He'll pay it back.'

Frank Ache spoke for the first time. 'Fuck he will.'

Myron waved. 'Hi, Frank. Boss threads.'

'And fuck you too, bug shit. Deal's a deal.'

Myron turned to Win. 'Bug shit?'

163

Win shrugged.

'The deal,' Myron continued, 'was that Chaz could back out at any time and pay back the money. Roy O'Connor told him that.'

'I don't give a fuck what O'Connor said.'

Herman said, 'Please, Frank, we don't need to get hostile.'

'Ah, fuck him, Herman. This asshole wants to fuck me over. He wants to steal food off my fucking table. Not just this Landreaux nigger. That's just the start. We got dozens of prospects signed like this. We lose one, we lose them all. I say we let the other agents know we ain't to be messed with. I say we waste Bolitar right now.'

Myron said, 'I don't like that idea.'

'Who the fuck asked you?'

'Just giving my opinion.'

'Please, Frank, this isn't helping. You promised to let me handle this.'

'Handle what? Kill the son of a bitch. End of story.'

'Wait in the other room. I'll take care of it, I promise.'

Frank glared at Myron. Myron did not bother glaring back. He knew this was part of the act. He knew that they were trying to intimidate him in much the same way Otto Burke and Larry Hanson had. But for some odd reason, the air of death gave the Mutt and Jeff routine a whole new dynamic.

Win, however, remained pensive.

'Come on, Aaron,' Frank growled. 'Let's get the fuck out of here.' He stood. 'But the contract is still on.'

'Fine,' Herman said. 'If you want to kill him, I won't get in the way.'

'He's as good as dead.'

Frank and Aaron left. Frank slammed the door. Overacting, Myron thought, but an effective cameo appearance.

Myron said, 'He's fun.'

Herman moved to the corner of the room. He took a slow practice swing with the club. 'I wouldn't mess with him, Myron. Frank is really angry. Me, I've always liked you. From the early days. But I'm not sure I can help you on this one.'

The 'early days' had begun Myron's sophomore year at Duke. It was not something he liked to remember. His father had been gambling. And losing. On the day before a game against Georgia State, Myron returned to his dorm to find his father and two of Herman Ache's hoods. The two hoods told Myron that if Georgia State did not cover the twelve-point spread, his father would lose a finger. His father was crying, the first time Myron had ever seen his father cry. Myron made three turnovers in the last forty seconds to make sure Duke won by only ten.

Father and son never talked about it.

'Why is this kid, this Chaz Landreaux, so important to you, Myron?'

'I think he's worth saving.'

'Saving from what?'

'He's just a kid, Herman. Frank is putting the screws to him. I want it to stop.'

Herman smiled, changed clubs, took a few more swings. Then he picked up his putter. 'Still a crusader, eh, Myron?'

'Hardly. I'm just trying to help the kid.'

'And yourself.'

'Fine. And myself.'

Myron realized that Herman Ache was wearing golf cleats. Jesus. To most people golf is an idiotic excuse for a sport. For others it's a life-consuming obsession. There is no in between.

'I don't think,' Herman said, reading the break in his carpet, 'I can stop Frank. He's very determined.'

'You run the show,' Myron said. 'Everyone knows that.'

'But Frank is my brother. I don't step on his toes unless it's absolutely necessary. I don't think that's the case here.'

'What did Frank do to him?'

'Pardon?'

'How did he scare the kid?'

'Oh,' Herman said. Another club changed. This time he exchanged the putter for a wood. 'He kidnapped his sister. Twin sister, I think.'

Myron felt his stomach dive anew. They'd been right. Not much satisfaction in that. 'Is she okay?'

'Oh, I wouldn't worry,' Herman said, as if that were a truly foolish question. 'They won't hurt her. Long as Landreaux continues to cooperate.'

'When are they going to let her go?'

'Two more days. Something about making sure the contract is official and Landreaux doesn't have second thoughts.'

'What do you want, Herman? What's it going to cost to get Frank off?'

He put on a golf glove and took a very deliberate swing, watching his hands. 'I'm an old man, Myron. A *rich* old man. What could you possibly give me?'

Win sat forward, moving for the first time. 'Your club is too far open on your swing, Mr Ache. Try turning your wrists a little more. Shift your grip to the right a little.'

The sudden change in subject caught everyone by surprise. Herman looked at Win. 'I'm sorry. I never caught the name.'

'Windsor Horne Lockwood III.'

'Ah, so you are the immortal Win. Not exactly what I expected.' He tested the new grip. 'Feels odd.'

'Give it a few weeks,' Win said. 'Do you play often?'

'As often as I can. It's more than just a game to me. It's . . .'

'Sacred,' Win finished for him.

His eyes livened. 'Exactly. You play, Mr Lockwood?'

165

'Yes.'

'Nothing like it, is there?'

'Nothing,' Win agreed. 'Where do you play?'

'Not easy for my kind to find good courses. I joined a club in Westchester. St Anthony's. You know it?'

'No.'

'It's not much of a course. Eighteen holes, of course. Very rocky. You have to be half mountain goat.'

Golf stories. Myron loved them. Didn't everyone?

'I don't understand something,' Myron said, playing along. 'With all your, uh, influence, why don't you play anywhere you want?'

Herman and Win looked at him as though he were a naked infidel praying in the Vatican. 'Excuse him,' Win said. 'Myron does not understand golf. He thinks a nine iron is a vitamin supplement.'

Herman laughed. The hoods joined suit. Myron didn't get it.

'I understand fine,' Myron said. 'Golf is a bunch of silly-dressed men using massive tracts of real estate to play with a ball and stick.'

Myron laughed. No one joined suit. Golfers are not known for their sense of humor.

Herman put the club back in the bag. 'A man does not force or buy or bully his way onto a golf course,' he explained. 'I have too much respect for the game, for the traditions, to do anything so crass. It would be like putting a gun against a priest's head to get the front pew.'

'Sacrilege,' Win said.

'Exactly. No *real* golfer would do it.'

'He has to be invited,' Win added.

'Right. And you don't merely play a great course. You pay homage to it. I'd love to be invited to one of the world's great courses. It would be my dream. But it is not meant to be.'

'How about being invited to two of them?' Win asked.

'Two—' Herman stopped. His eyes widened for a millisecond, then quickly dimmed as though afraid he was being teased. 'What do you mean?'

Win pointed to a picture on the left wall. 'Merion Golf Club,' he said. Then he pointed to a picture on the far wall. 'And Pine Valley.'

'What about them?'

'I assume you've heard of them?'

'Heard of them?' Herman repeated. 'They're the top two courses on the East Coast, two of the best in the world. Name a hole. Go ahead, any hole, either course.'

'Sixth hole at Merion.'

Herman's face glowed like a little kid's on Christmas morning. 'One of the most underrated holes anywhere. It sets up with a semiblind tee-shot to a fairway that favors a soft fade. Start your tee-shot at middle bunker, then cut back to the center, keeping clear of the boundary, which comes in on the right. Long-to-middle iron to the modestly elevated green, careful of the bunkers on the left and right.'

Win smiled. 'Very impressive.'

Snore.

'Don't tell me, Mr Lockwood, that you've played Merion and Pine Valley.' Something well past awe resonated in Herman's voice.

'I'm a member of both.'

Herman inhaled sharply. Myron half-expected him to cross himself. 'A member,' he began incredulously, 'of both?'

'I'm a three handicap at Merion,' Win continued. 'A five handicap at Pine Valley. And I'd like you to be my guest at both for a weekend. We'll try to get in seventy-two holes a day, thirty-six at each course. We'll start at five A.M. Unless that's too early.'

Herman shook his head. Myron thought his eyes looked teary. 'Not too early,' he managed.

'Next weekend okay for you?' Win asked.

Herman picked up the phone. 'Let the girl go,' he said. 'And the contract is off. Anyone touches Myron Bolitar, they're dead.'

31

Win and Myron went back to the office. Myron felt sore from the beating, but nothing was broken. He would persevere. He was that kind of guy. Terribly brave.

Esperanza said, 'You look like shit.'

'You're so hung up on appearances.'

He tossed her the photograph of Adam Culver. 'See if your friend Lucy recognizes him.'

She snapped a salute. '*Jawohl, Kommandant.*' Of all the old shows, Esperanza's favorite was *Hogan's Heroes*. Myron was not a big fan, though he always wished he could have been there when some young TV hotshot said, 'Hey, I got an idea for a sitcom! Set it in a POW camp in Nazi Germany. Laughs galore.'

'How many calls?' he asked.

'About a million. Mostly the press wanting your comments on Christian's signing.' She smiled. 'Nice job on that one.'

'Thank you.'

'That Otto Burke,' she said, a pencil near her mouth. 'Is he single?'

Myron looked at her, horrified. 'Why would you want to know?'

'He's kinda cute.'

The nausea was back. 'You're hitting me up for a raise, aren't you? Please say yes.'

Esperanza smiled coyly but said nothing. He started for his office.

'Hold it,' she said. 'A strange message just came in for you a few minutes ago.'

'From?'

'A woman named Madelaine. Wouldn't give her last name. Sounded sultry.'

The dean-nessa. Hmm.

'She leave a number?'

Esperanza nodded, handed it to him. 'Remember: The condom is your friend.'

'Thanks, Mom.'

'Speaking of which, your mother called twice, your father once. I think they're worried about you.'

He entered his office. His little private sanctuary. He liked it in here. Myron held most of his negotiations and important meetings in the traditionally decorated conference room, freeing him up to make his office whatever he wanted it to be. He had, of course, his view of the Manhattan skyline to his left. On the wall behind his desk he had framed posters from Broadway musicals: *Fiddler on the Roof, The Pajama Game, How to Succeed in Business Without Really Trying, Man of La Mancha, Les Misérables, La Cage aux Folles, A Chorus Line, West Side Story, Phantom.*

Another wall had movie stills: Humphrey Bogart and Ingrid Bergman in *Casablanca*, Woody Allen and Diane Keaton in *Annie Hall*. Katharine Hepburn and Spencer Tracy in *Adam's Rib*. Groucho, Chico, and Harpo in *A Night at the Opera*. Adam West and Burt Ward in *Batman*, the TV show, the real Batman, the one where Burgess Meredith played the Penguin and Cesar Romero played the Joker. The Golden Age of Television.

The final wall had photographs of Myron's clients. In a few days Christian Steele cloaked in Titans blue would join the group.

He dialed Madelaine Gordon's number. The answering machine picked up. Her silky voice. Hearing it again made his throat dry. He hung up, not leaving a message. He checked the time on the far wall. The clock was shaped like a giant watch with a Boston Celtics insignia in the center.

Three-thirty.

Still time to get to the campus. Madelaine was not important, but Myron very much wanted to see the dean. And he wanted to show up unexpectedly.

At Esperanza's desk he said, 'I'm going out for a while. You can reach me in the car.'

'Are you limping?' she asked.

'A little. Ache's men roughed me up.'

'Oh. See you later.'

'Hurts like hell, but I can take it.'

'Uh-huh.'

'Don't make a scene.'

'Inside,' she said, 'I'm dying.'

'Please see if you can reach Chaz Landreaux. Tell him we need to talk.'

'Okay.'

He left. He picked up his car in the garage. Win was into cars. He loved his racing-green Jag. Myron drove a blue Ford Taurus. He was not what one might call a car man. A car got him from point A to point B, that was all. It was not a status symbol. It was not a second home. It was not his baby.

The drive didn't take long. Myron took the Lincoln Tunnel. He passed the famed York Motel. Long sign:

$11.99 PER HOUR
$95 PER WEEK
MIRRORED ROOMS
NOW FEATURING SHEETS!

He paid the toll on the Parkway. The woman in the booth was very friendly. She almost looked at him when she tossed him the change.

He called his mother on the car phone and reassured her he was okay. She told him to call his father, he was the worried one. Myron called his father and reassured him he was okay. He told him to call his mother, she was the worried one. Great communication. The secret to a happy marriage.

He thought about Kathy Culver. He thought about Adam Culver. He thought about Nancy Serat. He tried to draw little lines, connecting them. The lines were tenuous at best. He was sure Fred Nickler, Sir Sleaze Rag, was one line. That picture hadn't sneaked into *Nips* by itself. Fred seemed to run a tight operation. He had to know more than he was saying. Win was digging into his background, seeing what he could unearth.

Half an hour later, Myron arrived at the campus. Extra-deserted today. No one on the commons. Very few cars. He parked near the dean's house and knocked on the door. Madelaine (he still liked the name) answered. She smiled when she saw him, clearly pleased, tilting her head a little. 'Well, hello, Myron.'

'Hi.' The Return of Mr Smooth.

Madelaine Gordon was dressed for tennis. Short white skirt. Great legs. White shirt. He noticed that the shirt was see-through. Keen observation, the signs of a master investigator. Madelaine noticed him noticing. She did not seem particularly offended.

'I'm sorry to intrude,' Myron said.

'No intrusion,' she said. 'I was just about to take a shower.'

Hmm. 'Your husband's not in, is he?'

She crossed her hands under breasts. 'Not for hours yet,' she said. 'You got my message?'

He nodded.

'Would you care to come inside?'

Myron said, 'Mrs Robinson, you're trying to seduce me, aren't you?'

'Pardon me?'

'*The Graduate.*'

'Oh.' Madelaine wet her lips. She had a very sexy mouth. People overlook the mouth. They talk about the nose, the chin, the eyes, the cheekbones. Myron was a mouth man. 'I guess I should be offended,' she continued. 'I mean, I'm not that much older than you, Myron.'

'Good point. Quote withdrawn.'

'So,' she said. 'I'll ask again. Would you like to come inside?'

Myron said, 'Sure.' Bowling her over with quick wit. What chance did she have against such sparkling repartee?

She disappeared back into the house, creating an air vacuum that sucked Myron – against his will, of course – in after her. The inside was nice, the kind of house that obviously saw plenty of company. Big open room on the left. Tiffany lamps. Persian rugs. Busts of French guys with long, curly hair. Grandfather clock. Painted portraits of stern-faced men.

'Care to sit down?' she said.

'Thank you.'

Sultry. That had been the word Esperanza used. It fit. Not just Madelaine's voice but her mannerisms, her walk, her eyes, her persona.

'How about a drink?' she asked.

He noticed she already had one made for herself. 'Sure, whatever you're having.'

'A vodka tonic.'

'Sounds good.' Myron hated the taste of vodka.

She mixed the drink. He sipped it, trying not to make a face. He wasn't sure if he was successful. She sat down next to him. 'I've never been this forward before,' she said.

'That a fact?'

'But I'm very attracted to you. It's one of the reasons I loved watching you play. You're really very handsome. I'm sure you're sick of hearing that.'

'Well, I don't know if *sick* is the right word.'

Madelaine crossed her legs. It wasn't Jessica's leg cross, but it was still worth watching. 'When you came to the door yesterday, I didn't want to miss out on the opportunity. I decided to throw caution to the wind and just go for it.'

Myron could not stop grinning. 'I see.'

She stood and reached out her hand to him. 'Now how about that shower?'

'Uh, can we talk first?'

Puzzlement shadowed her face. 'Is there something wrong?'

Myron feigned embarrassment. 'Aren't you married?'

'And that bothers you?'

Not really. 'Yes. I guess it does.'

'Admirable,' she said.

'Thank you.'

'Stupid too.'

'Thank you.'

She laughed. 'Actually, it's sweet. But Dean Gordon and I have what we call a semi-open marriage.'

Hmm. 'Could you elaborate a little?'

'Elaborate?'

'Just to make me feel more comfortable about all this.'

She sat back down. The white skirt might as well not have been there. Her

171

legs could best be described as scrumptious. 'I've never had to elaborate before,' she said.

'I realize that. But I'm interested.'

Arched eyebrow. 'In?'

'Can we start with your definition of *semi-open*?'

She sighed. 'My husband and I have been close friends since childhood. Our parents summered together in Hyannis Port. We were both from the "right families." ' She made little quote marks in the air when she said 'right families.' 'We thought that would be enough. But it wasn't.'

'So why not divorce?'

She looked a question. 'Why am I telling you this?'

'My honest blue eyes,' he said. 'They're hypnotic.'

'Maybe they are.'

Now Myron gave her aw-shucks modesty. Mr Adaptable Face.

'My husband is politically connected. He was an ambassador. He's next in line to be university president. If we get divorced—'

'That ends,' Myron finished.

'Yes. Even these days, the hint of scandal can destroy a career and a lifestyle. But more than that, Harrison and I are still dear friends. Best friends, really. It's just that we need limited outside stimulation.'

'Limited?'

'Once every two months,' she said.

Yikes. 'How did you come up with that number?' he asked. 'Some kind of new algorithm, perhaps?'

She smiled. 'Lots of discussions. Negotiations, really. Once a month seemed like too much. Once a semester too little.'

Myron nodded at her. *Toto, we're not in Kansas anymore.*

'And we always use a condom,' she added. 'That's part of the arrangement.'

'I see.'

'Do you have one?' she asked. 'A condom.'

'On?'

She smiled. 'I have some upstairs.'

'Can I ask one more thing?'

'If you must.'

'How do you and your husband know that the other had kept to their, er, limit?'

'Easy,' she said. 'We tell each other. Everything. Helps spice things up a little.'

Madelaine was seriously strange, which only made her more attractive to Myron.

'Your husband. Does he ever fool around with co-eds?'

She leaned forward and put her hand on his thigh. Upper thigh. Upper, upper thigh. 'That kind of thing turn you on?'

'Yeah.' He tried a rakish smile. But rakish was not him. He could see in her eyes that she wasn't buying it.

Madelaine took back her hand. 'What are you up too, Myron?' she asked.

'Up to?'

'I feel like I'm being used,' she said. 'But not the way I had in mind.'

Man. 'Just getting in the mood.'

'I don't think so, Myron.' She studied him for moment. 'Be honest for a second. Are we going to go to bed?'

'No,' he said. 'We're not.'

'I've never been turned down before.'

'And I've never turned down a proposition like this before,' Myron said. 'Come to think of it, I've never had a proposition like this before.'

'Is it because I'm married?'

'No.'

'Are you involved with someone else?' she asked.

'Worse. I'm on the cusp of something that means a great deal to me. I don't know which way I'm going to fall. I'm confused.'

'That's sweet.'

Again he gave her aw-shucks.

'If it doesn't work out . . . ?' she said.

'I'll be back.'

She kissed him then. Hard. It was a damn good kiss. He felt it in his toes.

'Just the overture,' she said.

He'd be dead before the second scene. 'I really do have to talk to your husband. Do you know when he'll be home?'

'Not for a while. But he's at the office across campus. By himself. You'll have to knock loudly for him to hear you.'

He rose. 'Thanks.'

'Myron?'

'Yes?'

'We never use names when we discuss our affairs. I don't know if Harrison fools around with co-eds. I would doubt it highly.'

'How about Kathy Culver?'

She visibly jumped. Her face stiffened. 'I think you better leave now.'

'The honest blue eyes,' Myron said. 'Watch the honest blue eyes.'

'Not this time. And when I watched you play, it wasn't your eyes I looked at.'

'Oh?'

'Your ass,' she said. 'It looked nice in those little shorts.'

Myron felt cheap. Or ecstatic. Probably ecstatic. 'Were they having an affair?' he asked.

She said nothing.

'I'll shake my ass if I have to.'

'They weren't having an affair,' she said firmly. 'That much I know.'

'So why did you get all bent out of shape?'

'You were asking if my husband had an illicit affair with a co-ed who was probably murdered. I was taken aback.'

'Did you know Kathy Culver?'

'No.'

'Did your husband ever talk about her?'

'Not really. I just know she worked in his office.' She looked at the grandfather clock, stood, and led him to the door. 'Talk to my husband, Myron. He's a good man. He'll tell you everything you need to know.'

'Like?'

She shook her head. 'Thanks for visiting.'

Madelaine was in shutdown mode. Probably hurt by his interrogation technique. Using his brawny body to get his way. Myron had never done that before. He liked it. Better than pistol-whipping a suspect, anyway.

He turned and left. Madelaine was probably watching his ass. He put a little wiggle in his step and hurried across campus.

32

Jessica found Getaway Realty in the Bergen County Yellow Pages. Their office was a converted cottage next to a McDonald's off Route 17 on the New Jersey side of the New York–New Jersey border. The drive was only twenty minutes, but it felt as if she'd arrived in the rural past. She actually saw a feed store.

Only one person was in the office.

'Well, hello there,' the man said with a too-wide smile. He was mid-fifties, bald, with a long, scraggly gray beard, like a college professor's. He wore a flannel shirt, black tie, Levi's jeans, and red Chuck Taylor Converse sneakers.

'I'm Tom Corbett, president of Getaway Realty.' He handed her a card. 'What can I do for you today?'

'I'm Dr Adam Culver's daughter,' she said. 'He wrote a check to your office on May twenty-fifth for $649.'

'Yeah, so?'

'He passed away recently. I'd like to know what it was for.'

Corbett took a step back. 'I'm awfully sorry to hear that,' he said. 'Nice man, your father.'

'Thank you. Can you tell me why he came to you?'

He thought a moment, shrugged. 'Don't see why not. He rented a cabin.'

'Near here?'

'Five, six miles. In the woods.'

'For how long?'

'A month. Starting May twenty-fifth. Still has it for a few more weeks, if you'd like to use it.'

'What kind of cabin?' she asked.

'What kind? Well, it's pretty small. One bedroom, one bathroom with shower stall, living room, kitchenette.'

This made no sense. 'Do you think you could give me the directions and a spare key?'

He thought that one over too, chewing on the inside of his mouth. 'It's a bit remote,' he said. 'Kinda hard to find, darling.'

Aside from *babe* and *honey-bun*, there were few things Jessica enjoyed

175

being called more than *darling*. But now was not the time to explain her sentiments. She bit her lip and held back.

'The cottage's away from it all,' Tom continued. 'Way away, if you know what I mean. A little hunting, a little fishing, but mostly just peace and quiet.' He picked up a key chain as heavy as a barbell. 'I'll drive you.'

'Thank you.'

He drove a Toyota LandCruiser and chatted the whole way, as though she were a client. 'Here's our local grocery store.'

It was an enormous A&P Superstore.

She was surprised when he turned onto an unpaved road. They were heading straight into the woods.

'Nice, ain't it? Real pretty.'

'Uh-huh.'

Green foliage surrounded them. Jessica was not much of the outdoor sort. To her, the great outdoors meant bugs and humidity and dirt and no running water and no bathroom. Man had evolved for millions of years to escape the woods. Why rush back? But more important, her father had felt the same. He hated the woods.

Why would he rent a cabin out here?

Tom pointed to a gully up ahead. 'Two years ago, guy got killed by a hunter over there. Accident. The hunter thought he was a deer, shot him in the head.'

'Uh-huh.'

'Couple of dead bodies been found in the woods. Three in the past two years, I think. Found one girl just a couple months back. Runaway, they guessed. Hard to tell 'cause she was all decayed and stuff.'

'You're a hell of a salesman, Tom.'

He laughed. 'Yeah, well, I can tell when someone ain't a buyer.'

Jessica, of course, knew all about the bodies. The police hadn't caught the killer, but the general consensus was that the psychopath had gotten hold of one more young girl, one that had not yet been found:

Kathy Culver.

Could Kathy's fate have been that simple and that horrible? Had she been another victim of a random psychopath, just as everyone thought?

No, Jessica told herself. Too many holes.

'When I was a kid growing up around here,' Tom said, 'these woods were filled with legends. Guy with a hook hand lived in here, the old-timers said, used to kidnap bad little boys and gut them with his hook.'

'Charming.'

'Sometimes I wonder if he moved on to young ladies.'

Jessica said nothing.

'Used to call him Dr Hook,' he continued.

'What?'

'Dr Hook. That's what we all called him.'

'Isn't that a singer?' she asked.

'A what?'

'Never mind.'

They drove another mile away from civilization. 'That's the house,' Tom said. 'Up there behind the trees.'

It was a small wooden cabin with a big front porch.

'Rustic, ain't it?'

Decrepit would have been a better adjective. Jessica checked the porch, but there were no toothless hillbillies playing dueling banjos.

'Did my father say why he wanted to rent this cabin?'

'Just said he needed someplace to get away from it all in these woods.'

It still made no sense. Dad was going to be gone at a medical examiners' conference for a week out of the month, anyway. And Adam Culver was not the get-away-from-it-all type. He dealt with the dead. On vacations he wanted to be in Vegas or Atlantic City or someplace with lots of people and action. Now he was renting the Waltons' cabin.

Tom used the key to unlock the door. He pushed it open and said, 'After you.'

Jessica stepped into the living room. And stopped short.

Tom came in behind her. His voice was a whisper. 'What the hell is this?' he asked.

33

Dean Gordon's office was in Compton Hall. The building was only three stories high but wide. Greek columns out front screamed House of Learning. Brick exterior. White double doors. Directly inside was a bulletin board filled with old notices. Meetings of the usual campus groups: the African American Change Committee, the Gay-Lesbian Alliance, the Liberators of Palestine, the Coalition to Stop the Domination of Womyn (never spell *woman*, for the sexism the name implies), the South African Freedom Fighters – all taking the summer off. College fun days.

There was no one inside the huge lobby. The motif was marble. Marble floors, banisters, columns. The walls were covered with huge portraits of men in graduation robes, most of whom would flip if they could read the bulletin board. All the lights were on. Myron's footsteps clacked and reverberated in the still room. He wanted to shout 'Echo,' but was far too adult.

The dean of students' office suite was at the end of the left corridor. The door was locked. Myron knocked hard. 'Dean Gordon?'

Shuffling behind the dark-paneled doors. Several seconds later, the door opened. Dean Gordon was wearing tortoiseshell glasses. He had wispy hair, conservatively cut, a handsome face with clear brown eyes. His features were gentle, as though the facial bones had been rounded off to soften his appearance. He looked kind, trustworthy. Myron hated that.

'I'm sorry,' the dean said. 'The office is closed until tomorrow morning.'

'We need to talk.'

Confusion crossed his face. 'Do I know you?'

'I don't think so.'

'You're not a student here.'

'Hardly.'

'May I ask who you are?'

Myron looked at him steadily. 'You know who I am. And you know what I want to talk about.'

'I don't have the slightest idea to what you are referring, but I am really quite busy—'

'Read any good magazines lately?'

178

Dean Gordon's whole body twitched. 'What did you say?'

'I guess I could come back when the office was crowded. Maybe bring some reading material for the school's trustees, though I understand they only read the articles.'

No response.

Myron smiled – knowingly. At least, he hoped that was how it looked. Myron had no idea what part the dean played in this little mystery. He had to step tentatively here.

The dean coughed into his fist. Not a real cough or throat-clear. Just something to stall, give him a chance to think. Finally he said, 'Please come in.'

He disappeared back into his office. No sucking vacuum this time, but Myron still followed. They passed a few chairs in the waiting room, a secretary's desk. The typewriter was hidden by a khaki-colored dust cover. Camouflaged in the event of war.

Dean Gordon's office was cookie-cut university executive. Lots of wood. Diplomas. Old sketches of the Reston University chapel. Lucite blocks with clippings or awards on the desk. Bookshelves with all nonfiction titles. The books hadn't been touched. They were props, creating the mood of tradition, professionalism, competence. The prerequisite picture of the family. Madelaine and a girl who looked about twelve or thirteen years old. Myron picked up the photograph.

'Nice family,' he said. Nice wife.

'Thank you. Please have a seat.'

Myron sat. 'Say, where did Kathy work?'

The dean stopped in midseat. 'Pardon me?'

'Where was her desk?'

'Whose?'

'Kathy Culver's.'

Dean Gordon lowered himself the rest of the way, slowly, as into a hot tub of water. 'She shared a desk with another student in the room next door.'

Myron said, 'Convenient.'

Dean Gordon's eyebrows frowned. 'I'm sorry. I missed your name.'

'Deluise. Dom Deluise.'

The dean allowed himself a small brittle smile. He looked tight enough to pop a wine cork with his butt. No doubt being sent the magazine had put the screws in. No doubt Jake's visit yesterday had tightened them a little. 'What, Mr Deluise, can I do for you?'

'I think you know.' Again the knowing smile. Combined with the honest blue eyes. If Dean Gordon were female, he'd be naked by now.

'I'm afraid I don't have the slightest idea,' the dean said.

Myron continued the knowing smile. He felt like an idiot or a morning network weatherman, if there was a difference. This was an old trick he was trying. Pretend you know more than you do. Get him talking. Play it by ear. Impromptu.

The dean folded his hands and put them on his desk. Trying to look as if he were in control. 'This whole conversation is very strange. Perhaps you could explain why you're here.'

'I thought we should chat.'

'About?'

'Your English department, for starters. Do you still make students read *Beowulf*?'

'Please, whatever your name is, I don't have time for games.'

'Neither do I.' Myron took out his copy of *Nips* and tossed it on the desk. The magazine was starting to look creased and worn from all the handling, as if it belonged to a hormonal adolescent.

The dean barely glanced at it. 'What is this?'

'Now who's playing games?'

Dean Gordon leaned back, his fingers fiddling with his chin. 'Who are you?' he asked. 'Really.'

'It's not important. I am merely a messenger.'

'Messenger for who?'

'For *whom*,' Myron corrected. 'Prepositional phrase. And you a college dean.'

'I don't need any smart talk, young man.'

Myron looked at him. 'Get real.'

The dean sucked in air as if he were about to plunge underwater. 'What do you want?'

'Isn't the pleasure of your company enough?'

'This is not a joking matter.'

'No, it's not.'

'So kindly stop playing games. What do you want with me?'

Myron tried the knowing smile again. Dean Gordon looked puzzled for a brief moment but then returned the smile. It too was knowing.

'Or should I say,' the dean added, 'how much?'

He seemed more in control now. He had dealt with the blow and was carrying on. A problem had arisen. But there was a solution. There always was in his world.

Money.

He took out a checkbook from his top drawer. 'Well?'

'Not that simple,' Myron said.

'What do you mean?'

'Don't you think someone should pay?'

He shrugged. 'Let's talk figures.'

'Don't you think this is worth something more than just money?'

He looked bewildered, as though Myron had just denied the existence of gravity. 'I don't understand what you mean.'

'What about justice?' Myron asked. 'Kathy is owed. Big-time.'

'I agree. And I am willing to pay. But what good is revenge going to do her now? You are the messenger, are you not?'

'I am.'

'Then go back and tell Kathy to take the money.'

Myron's heart collapsed. This man, a man who was clearly involved in what had happened that night, believed Myron was a messenger for a living, breathing Kathy Culver. Tread gently, fair Myron. Ever gently.

But how to play this . . .

'Kathy is not happy with you,' he tried.

'I meant her no harm.'

Myron put his hand on his chest and lifted his head dramatically. 'Be thy intents wicked or charitable, thou com'st in such a questionable shape.'

'What's that supposed to mean?'

Myron shrugged. 'I like to work Shakespeare into conversations. Makes me sound smart, don't you think?'

The dean made a face. 'Can we return to the matter at hand?'

'Sure.'

'You say Kathy does not want money.'

'Yup.'

'What then does she want?'

Good question. 'She wants the truth to come out.' Noncommittal, vague, open-ended.

'What truth?'

'Stop playing dumb,' Myron snapped, feigning annoyance. 'You weren't about to write a check to her favorite charity, were you?'

'But I didn't do anything,' he half-whined. 'Kathy took off that night. I haven't seen her since. How was I supposed to know what to think or do?'

Myron gave him a skeptical look. He did that because he had no idea what else to do. He was now playing Jake's game, the keep-silent-and-hope-he-ties-his-own-noose game. This worked especially well with political types. They're born with a defective chromosome that will not allow for prolonged silence.

'She has to understand,' he continued. 'I did my best. She disappeared. What was I supposed to do? Go to the police? Was that what she wanted? I didn't know anymore. I was thinking of her. She might have changed her mind. I didn't know. I was trying to consider her interests.'

The skeptical look came easier after that last sentence. Myron only wished he knew what the hell the dean was talking about. They sat there staring at one another. Then something happened to Dean Gordon's face. Myron wasn't sure exactly what it was, but his whole demeanor seemed to slump. His eyes grew twisted, pained. He shook his head.

'Enough,' he said in a quiet voice.

'What's enough?'

He closed the checkbook. 'I won't pay,' he said. 'Tell Kathy I'll do whatever she wants. I'll stand by her no matter what the cost. This has gone on long enough. I can't live like this. I am not an evil man. She's a sick girl. She needs help. I want to help.'

Myron had not expected this. 'Do you mean that?'

'Yes. Very much.'

'You want to help your former lover?'

His head shot up. 'What did you say?'

Myron had been skating blindly on thin ice. His last comment, it seemed, had been something of a blowtorch.

'Did you say "lover"?'

Uh-oh.

'Kathy didn't send you,' he continued. 'She has nothing to do with you, does she?'

Myron said nothing.

'Who are you? What is your real name?'

'Myron Bolitar.'

'Who?'

'Myron Bolitar.'

'Are you a police officer?'

'No.'

'Then what exactly are you?'

'A sports agent.'

'A what?'

'I represent athletes.'

'You— So what do you have to do with this?'

'I'm a friend,' Myron said. 'I'm trying to find Kathy.'

'Is she alive?'

'I don't know. But you seem to think so.'

Dean Gordon opened his bottom drawer, took out a cigarette, lit it.

'Bad for you,' Myron said.

'I quit smoking five years ago. Or so everyone thinks.'

'Another little secret?'

He smiled without humor. 'So you were the one who sent me the magazine.'

Myron shook his head. 'Nope.'

'Then who?'

'I don't know. I'm trying to figure that out. But I know about it. And now I also know you're hiding something about Kathy's disappearance.'

He inhaled deeply and let loose a long stream of smoke. 'I could deny it. I could deny everything we said here today.'

'You could,' Myron countered. 'But of course I have the magazine. I have no reason to lie. And I also have a friend in Sheriff Jake Courter. But you're right. In the end it would be my word against yours.'

Dean Gordon took off his glasses and rubbed his eyes. 'No,' he said slowly, 'it won't come down to that. I meant what I said before. I want to help her. I *need* to help her.'

Myron was not sure what to think. The man looked in genuine pain, but Myron had seen performances that would put Olivier to shame. Was his guilt real? Was his sudden catharsis the result of having a conscience, or was it self-preservation? Myron didn't know. He didn't much care either, as long as he got to the truth.

'When was the last time you saw Kathy?' Myron asked.

'The night she vanished,' he said.

'She came to your house?'

He nodded. 'It was late. I guess around eleven, eleven-thirty. I was in my study. My wife was upstairs in bed. The doorbell rang. Not once. Repeatedly, urgently. Interspersed with heavy door-pounding. It was Kathy.'

His voice was on autopilot, as if he were reading a fairy tale to a child. 'She was crying. Or rather she was sobbing uncontrollably. So much so that she couldn't speak. I brought her into my study. I poured her some brandy and wrapped an afghan around her shoulders. She looked' – he stopped, considered – 'very small. Helpless. I sat down across from her and took her hand. She jerked it back. That was when the tears stopped. Not slowly, but all at once, as though a switch had been thrown. She became very still. Her face was completely blank, no emotion whatsoever. Then she started talking.'

He reached into the drawer for another cigarette. He put it in his mouth. The match lit on the fourth try.

'She started from the beginning,' he continued. 'Her voice was remarkably steady. It never cracked or wavered – uncanny, when you consider the fact that she was hysterical just moments earlier. But her words belied her placid tone. She told me stories—' He stopped again, shook his head. 'They were surprising, to say the least. I had known Kathy for almost a year. I considered her a thoughtful, sweet, proper young woman. I am not making moral judgments here. But she had always been what I considered old-fashioned. And here she was telling me stories that would make a sailor blush.

'She started by telling me that she used to be everything I always thought she was. The girl next door. Everyone's favorite. But then she changed. She became, in her own words, "a free-wheeling slut." She started with some boys in her high school class. But she quickly moved onto bigger things. Adults, teachers, friends of her parents. Biracial, homosexual, two-on-ones, even orgies. She took pictures of her encounters. For posterity, she said with a sneer.'

'Did she mention any names?' Myron asked. 'Of the teachers or adults or anyone?'

'No. No names.'

They fell into silence. Dean Gordon looked exhausted.

'What happened next?' Myron prompted.

He lifted his head slowly, as though it took great effort. 'Her story began to change direction,' he said. 'For the better. She said she realized that what she was doing was wrong and stupid. She began, she said, to work through her problems. That was when she met Christian and fell in love. She wanted to put it all behind her, but it wasn't easy. The past wouldn't just go away. She tried and tried, and then . . .' His voice trailed off.

'And then?' Myron prompted.

'Then Kathy just looked at me – I'll never forget this – and she said, "I was raped tonight." Just like that. Out of nowhere. I was stunned, of course. There were six of them, she said. Or seven, she wasn't sure. A gang-rape in the locker room. I asked her when. She told me it had started less than an hour ago. She had gone to the locker room to meet someone. A blackmailer, she said. A former, uh, suitor, who had threatened to reveal her past. She was going to pay for his silence.'

The big cash withdrawal from her trust account, Myron thought.

'But when she got to the locker room, the blackmailer wasn't alone. Several of his teammates were with him, including another past suitor. They didn't hit her, she said. They didn't beat her. And she didn't fight. There were too many of them, and they were too strong.' He closed his eyes, his voice a whisper. 'They took turns with her.'

Silence.

'As I said before, Kathy told me all this in the most dispassionate tone I had ever heard her use. Her eyes were clear, determined. She told me there was only one way to bury her past. Once and for all. She would have to confront it head-on. She'd have to push it out into the bright sunshine where it would wither and die like a medieval vampire. She said she knew what she had to do.'

More silence.

'What?' Myron asked.

'Prosecute the boys who raped her. Face up to her past and then put it behind her. Otherwise it would follow her around for the rest of her life.'

'What did you say?'

Dean Gordon winced at the question. He stamped out the cigarette. He glanced down at the bottom drawer but didn't reach for another. 'I told her to calm down.' He laughed at the memory. 'Calm down. By now, the girl was so unemotional, so detached, that she could have been reading a telephone directory. And I told her to calm down. Jesus.'

'What else?'

'I told her that I thought she was still in shock. I meant that too. I told her that she should consider everything, weigh all her options, not rush into a decision that would undoubtedly affect the rest of her life. I told her to think about what it would mean to have her past dragged out – to her family, to her friends, to her fiancé, to herself.'

'In other words,' Myron said, 'you tried to talk her out of pressing charges.'

'Perhaps. But I never said what I was really thinking. A self-described free-wheeling slut who had gotten involved in pornography and wild sex was going to claim she was raped by a group of college boys, two of whom she admitted having past liaisons with. I wanted her to think about all that before she did something rash.'

'Don't be so easy on yourself,' Myron said. 'You didn't give a damn about her. She came to you for help, and you thought about everything but her. You thought about your precious institution. You thought about the scandal. You thought about the football team on the eve of a national championship. You thought about your own career, how it would come out that she worked for you, how she felt comfortable visiting your house late at night. You'd be tied in. People would investigate you closer, maybe unearth your unusual marital arrangement.'

That prodded him upright. 'What about my marital arrangement?'

'Does the phrase "once every two months" mean anything to you?'

His mouth dropped open. 'How . . . ?' He stopped, almost smiled. 'You are a very well-informed young man.'

'All-knowing,' Myron corrected. 'Godlike.'

'I won't comment on my marriage, but I would be less than honest if I did not admit that those selfish considerations crossed my mind. But I was also concerned for Kathy. A mistake like this—'

'A rape, Dean. Not a mistake. Kathy was raped. She didn't make a "mistake." She wasn't the victim of an indiscretion. A bunch of football players pinned her down in a locker room and took turns with her against her will.'

'You're simplifying the situation.'

'You're the one who simplified the situation. You just put Kathy last.'

'That's not true.'

Myron shook his head. No time for this now. 'So what happened after you bestowed your stellar counsel upon Kathy?'

He tried to shrug but couldn't pull it off. 'She looked at me funny, as though I had betrayed her when all I was trying to do was help. Or maybe she saw in my words the same thing you did. I don't know. She stood up then and said that she would be back tomorrow morning to press charges. Then she left. I never heard from her again until that magazine came in the mail. And the phone call a few nights ago.'

'What phone call?'

'A few nights ago, very late, I got a phone call. A female voice – maybe Kathy's, maybe not – said, "Enjoy the magazine. Come and get me. I survived." '

' "Come and get me, I survived"?'

'Something like that, yes.'

'What did she mean?'

'I haven't the slightest idea.'

'What did you think when you first heard about Kathy's disappearance?'

'That she ran away. Decided it was all too much. I thought she'd come back when she was ready. The police thought that too, until they found her undergarments. Then they suspected violence. But I knew the undergarments were probably from the rape, not the disappearance. So in my mind I still considered her a runaway.'

'Didn't the possibility that the rapists wanted to silence her cross your mind?'

'It crossed my mind, yes. But these boys weren't capable of—'

'Rapists,' Myron corrected. ' "Boys" who gang-raped a young girl who never did them any harm. You didn't think they had the capability to commit murder?'

'If they wanted her dead, they would never have let her go,' the dean countered steadily. 'That's what I thought.'

'So you kept your mouth shut.'

He nodded. 'That was a mistake. I know that now. I was hoping she had just run away for a few days to straighten herself out. When a week passed, I realized it was too late to say anything.'

'You chose to live with the lie.'

'Yes.'

'She was just a student, after all. She came to you for help during the hardest time of her life. And you turned her away.'

'Don't you think I know that?' he shouted. 'Don't you think this has been tearing me apart for the past year and a half?'

'Yeah, you're a real humanitarian.'

'What the hell do you want from me, Bolitar?'

Myron stood. 'Resign. Immediately.'

'And if I refuse?'

'Then I'll drag you down, and it'll be uglier than you ever imagined. First thing tomorrow morning. Turn in your letter of resignation.'

He looked up, his fingers supporting his chin. Time passed. His face began to soften as though from a masseur's touch. His eyes closed, and his shoulders slumped. Then he nodded slowly. 'All right,' he said. 'Thank you.'

'This isn't penitence. You don't get off that easy.'

'I understand.'

'One last thing. Did Kathy mention any names at all?'

'Names?'

'Of the rapists?'

He hesitated. 'No.'

'But you have a guess?'

186

'It's not based on anything concrete.'

'Go on.'

'A few days after she disappeared, I noticed a certain student was tossing around a lot of money. A troublemaker. He bought a new BMW convertible that came to my attention because he drove it across the commons. Ripped up a lot of grass.'

'Who?'

'An ex-football player. He was kicked off the team for selling drugs. His name was Junior Horton. They call him—'

'Horty.'

Myron left without another word, hurrying to get out of the building. It was a beautiful day. Warm but not humid, the sun weakening in the late afternoon but not quite ready to set. The air smelled of freshly cut grass and blooming cherry blossom trees. Myron wanted to spread out a blanket. He wanted to lie down and think about Kathy Culver.

No time.

The phone in his Ford Taurus was ringing when he unlocked the door. It was Esperanza.

'Dead end with Lucy,' she said. 'Adam Culver wasn't the guy who bought the pictures.'

Another theory blown to hell. He was about to start his car when he heard Jake Courter's voice.

'Thought I might find you here.'

Myron looked out the open window. 'What's up, Jake?'

'We're about to release Nancy Serat's name to the press.'

Myron nodded. 'Thanks for letting me know.'

'That's not why I'm here.'

Myron did not like his tone.

'We also have a suspect,' Jake continued. 'We've brought him in for questioning.'

'Who?'

'Your client,' Jake said. 'Christian Steele.'

34

'What about Christian?' Myron asked.

'Nancy Serat had just rented that house a week ago,' Jake replied, 'a day or two before she left for Cancún. She hadn't even unpacked yet.'

'So?'

'So how come Christian Steele's fingerprints – clean, fresh prints – are all over the place? On the front doorknob. On a drinking glass. On the fireplace mantel.'

Myron tried not to look stunned. 'Come on, Jake. You can't make an arrest on something like that. The press will eat him alive.'

'Like I give a flying shit.'

'You have nothing.'

'We can place him at the scene.'

'So what? You can place Jessica at the scene. Gonna arrest her too?'

Jake unbuttoned his jacket, allowing his belly to expand. He was wearing a brown suit, circa 1972. In a word: lapels. No slave to fashion, that Jake. 'Okay, smart-boy,' he said, 'you want to tell me what your client was doing at Nancy Serat's house?'

'We'll ask him. He'll talk to you. Christian's a good kid, Jake. Don't ruin him on speculation.'

'Yeah. I'd hate to ruin your commissions.'

'Low blow, Jake.'

'You're not objective, Bolitar. The kid's your most valuable client, your ticket to the bigs. You don't want him to be guilty.'

Myron looked at him but said nothing.

'Leave your car here,' Jake said. 'I'll drive you to the station.'

It was only a mile away. When they pulled into the lot, Jake said, 'The new DA is here. Young hotshot named Roland.'

Uh-oh. 'Cary Roland?' Myron asked. 'Curly hair?'

'You know him?'

'Yeah.'

'He's a publicity hound,' Jake said. 'Get's a hard-on watching himself on TV. He practically creamed when he heard Christian's name.'

Myron could imagine. Old buddies, he and Cary Roland. This was not a good development. 'Has he released Christian's name?'

'Not yet,' Jake said. 'Cary decided to put it off until eleven. Gets a live feed from all the networks that way.'

'And plenty of time to tighten the perm.'

'That too.'

Christian was sitting in a small room, no bigger than eight by eight. He sat in a chair behind a desk. No hot lights. No one else was in the room.

'Where's Roland?' Myron asked.

'Behind the mirror.'

One-way glass, even in a rinky-dink station like this. Myron stepped into the room, looked in the mirror, adjusted his tie, and refrained from giving Roland the finger. Mr Mature strikes again.

'Mr Bolitar?'

Myron turned. Christian waved to him as if he'd spotted a familiar face in the stands.

'You okay?' Myron asked.

'I'm fine,' Christian said. 'I just don't understand what I'm doing here.'

A uniformed officer came in with a tape recorder. Myron turned to Jake. 'Is he under arrest?'

Jake grinned. 'I almost forgot, Bolitar. You're a lawyer too. Nice to be dealing with a professional.'

'Is he under arrest?' Myron repeated.

'Not yet. We'd just like to ask him a few questions.'

The uniformed officer took care of the preliminaries. Then Jake started. 'My name is Sheriff Jake Courter, Mr Steele. Do you remember me?'

'Yes, sir. You're handling my fiancée's disappearance.'

'That's correct. Now, Mr Steele, do you know a woman named Nancy Serat?'

'She was Kathy's roommate at Reston.'

'Are you aware that Nancy Serat was murdered last night?'

Christian's eyes widened. He turned to Myron. Myron nodded. 'My God . . . no.'

'Were you friends with Nancy Serat?'

His voice was hollow. 'Yes, sir.'

'Mr Steele, can you tell us where you were last night?'

Myron interrupted. 'What time last night?'

'From the time he left practice till he went to sleep.'

Myron hesitated. This was a trap. He could try to defuse it, or he could let Christian handle it on his own. Under most circumstances Myron would have stepped in and sounded a subtle warning of what the wrong answer might mean. But this time he sat back and watched.

'If you want to know if I was with Nancy Serat last night,' Christian said slowly, 'the answer is yes.'

Myron breathed again. He looked back at the one-way mirror and stuck out his tongue. The demise of Mr Mature.

'What time was that?' Jake asked.

'Around nine o'clock.'

'Where did you see her?'

'At her house.'

'The one at 118 Acre Street?'

'Yes, sir.'

'What was the purpose of your visit?'

'Nancy returned from a trip that morning. She called and said she needed to talk to me.'

'Did she tell you why?'

'She said it had something to do with Kathy. She wouldn't tell me anything else over the phone.'

'What happened when you arrived at the house at 118 Acre Street?'

'Nancy practically shoved me out the door. She said I had to leave right away.'

'Did she say why?'

'No, sir. I asked Nancy what was going on, but she was insistent. She promised to call me in a day or two and tell me everything, but for now I had to go.'

'What did you do?'

'I argued with her for a minute or two. She started getting upset and saying stuff that made no sense. I finally just gave up and left.'

'What sort of "stuff" was she saying?'

'Something about sisters reuniting.'

Myron sat up.

Jake asked, 'What about sisters reuniting?'

'I don't remember exactly. Something like "Time for sisters to reunite." She really wasn't making much sense, sir.'

Jake looked at Myron. Myron looked back.

'Do you remember anything else she said?'

'No, sir.'

'Did you go straight home after that?'

'Yes, sir.'

'What time did you arrive home?'

'Ten-fifteen, I guess. Maybe a little later.'

'Is there anybody who can confirm the time?'

'I don't think so. I just moved into a condominium in Englewood. Maybe a neighbor saw me, I don't know.'

'Would you mind waiting here for a minute?'

Jake signaled for Myron to follow him. Myron nodded, leaned over to Christian. 'Don't say another word until I get back.'

Christian nodded.

They stepped into the other room. The other side of the mirror, so to speak. County District Attorney Cary Roland had gone to Harvard Law School with Myron. A bright guy. Law review. Clerk for a Supreme Court justice. Cary Roland had first shown signs of political ambition while exiting his mother's womb.

He looked the same. Gray suit with vest (yes, he'd worn suits to class). Hook nose. Small, dark eyes. Loose curly hair, like a seventies Peter Frampton's, only shorter.

Roland shook his head. Then he made a noise of disgusted belief. 'Creative client, Bolitar.'

'Not as creative,' Myron said, 'as your barber.'

Jake held back a laugh.

'I say we book him,' Roland continued. 'We'll announce it at the press conference.'

'Now I see it,' Myron said.

'See what?'

'The hard-on. When you said "press."'

Snickers.

Roland fumed. 'Still a comedian, eh, Bolitar? Well, your client is about to go down.'

'I don't think so, Cary.'

'I don't care what you think.'

Myron sighed. 'Christian gave you a reasonable explanation for being at Nancy Serat's house. You got nothing else, ergo you got nothing. Besides, imagine the headlines if Christian's innocent. Young DA Makes Major Blunder. Tarnishes Name of Local Hero for Own Gain. Hurts Titans' Chances for Super Bowl. Becomes Most Hated Man in State.'

Roland swallowed. He hadn't considered that. Blinded by the lights. The TV lights. 'Sheriff Courter, what do you think?'

Backpedal time.

'We have no choice,' Jake said. 'We have to let him go.'

'Do you believe his story?'

Jake shrugged. 'Who the hell knows? But we don't have enough to keep him.'

'Okay,' Roland said with a weighty nod. Important man. 'He's free to go. But he better not leave town.'

Myron looked at Jake. 'Not leave town?' He laughed. Hard. 'Did he just say not to leave town?'

Jake was trying to hold it in. But his lip was quivering pretty good.

Roland's face turned red. 'Infantile,' he spat out. 'Sheriff, I want daily updates on this case.'

'Yes, sir.'

Roland gave everyone his most frightening glare. No one fell to their knees. He stormed out.

'Must be nonstop laughs,' Myron said, 'working with him.'

'Gobs of fun.'

'Can Christian and I go now?'

Jake shook his head. 'Not until I hear all about your visit with Dean Gordon.'

35

Myron filled Jake in. Then he drove Christian home. On the way he filled Christian in too. On everything. Christian wanted to know. Myron wanted to spare him, but he knew he didn't have the right to keep things from him.

Christian did not interrupt with questions. In fact, he said nothing. On the field he was famous for his composure under any situation. Right now, Christian had on his best game face.

When Myron finished, neither spoke for several minutes. Then Myron said, 'Are you okay?'

Christian nodded. His face was pale. 'Thank you for being up-front with me,' he said.

'Kathy loved you,' Myron said. 'Very much. Don't forget that.'

He nodded again. 'We have to find her.'

'I'm trying.'

Christian shifted in the car seat so he could face Myron. 'When I was being wooed by all these big agencies, the whole process felt – I don't know – so impersonal. It was all about money. Still is, I know that. I'm not being naïve here, but you were different. I instinctively knew I could trust you. I guess what I'm trying to say is, you've become more than just an agent to me. I'm glad I chose you.'

'Me too,' Myron said. 'This might not be the best time to ask, but how did you hear about me in the first place?'

'Someone gave you a glowing recommendation.'

'Who?'

Christian smiled. 'You don't know?'

'A client?'

'No.'

Myron shook his head. 'I have no idea.'

Christian settled back in his seat. 'Jessica,' he said. 'She told me your life history. About your playing days, your injury, what you went through, how you worked for the FBI, how you went back to school. She said you were the best person she knew.'

'Jessica doesn't get out much.'

They fell back into silence. The New Jersey Turnpike had a center-lane closure, slowing them down to a crawl. Should have taken the western spur. Myron was about to change lanes when Christian said something that almost made him slam on the brakes.

'My mother once posed in the nude.'

Myron thought he'd heard wrong. 'What?'

'When I was a little kid. I don't know if they were ever printed in a magazine or anything. I doubt it. She wasn't very attractive by then. She was twenty-five but looked sixty. She worked as a prostitute in New York. On the streets. I don't know who my father was. She figured he was one of the guys at a bachelor party, but she had no idea which one.'

Myron sneaked a glance at him. Christian stared straight ahead. The game face was still on.

'I thought your mother and father raised you in Kansas,' Myron said carefully.

Christian shook his head. 'Those were my grandparents. My mom died when I was seven. They legally adopted me. We had the same last name, so I just pretended they were my real parents.'

Myron said, 'I didn't know. I'm sorry.'

'Don't be. They were wonderful parents. I guess they made a lot of mistakes with my mom, the way she ended up and all. But they were kind and loving to me. I miss them a lot.'

The silence was heavier now. They drove past the Meadowlands. Myron paid the toll at the end of the turnpike and followed the signs to the George Washington Bridge. Christian had bought a place two miles before the bridge, six miles from Titans Stadium. A set of three hundred prefab condos loftily labeled Cross Creek Pointe, one of those New Jersey housing developments that looked like something out of *Poltergeist*.

As they cruised to a stop, the car phone rang. Myron picked it up.

'Hello?'

'Where are you?'

It was Jessica.

'In Englewood.'

'Take Route four west to seventeen north,' she said quickly. 'I'll meet you in the Pathmark parking lot in Ramsey.'

'What's going on?'

'Just meet me there. Now.'

36

The moment Myron saw Jessica standing in the dusky glow of the Pathmark fluorescent parking lights, looking achingly beautiful in a pair of hip-hugging blue jeans and a red blouse open at the throat, he knew there was trouble. Big trouble.

'Very bad?' he asked her.

She opened the car door and slid in next to him. 'Worse.'

He couldn't help it. He couldn't stop thinking of how beautiful she was. She looked a little pale, her eyes a bit too sunken. She did not have crow's-feet quite yet, but new lines had etched their way into her face. Had they been there yesterday or the day she visited his office? He wasn't sure. But he thought she had never looked so devastating. The imperfections, if you wanted to call them that, just made her more real and hence more desirable. Myron had thought Dean-nessa Madelaine was attractive, but she was nary a penlight next to Jessica's blinding beacon.

'Want to tell me about it?'

She shook her head. 'I'd rather just show you.' She started giving directions. When they reached a road appropriately called Red Dirt Path, she said, 'My father rented a cabin out here.'

'In these woods?'

'Yes.'

'When?'

'Two weeks ago. He had it for the month. According to the realtor, he wanted some peace and quiet. A place to get away from it all.'

'Doesn't sound much like your father,' Myron said.

'Not like him at all,' she agreed.

A few minutes later, they arrived at the cabin. Myron had a hard time believing that Adam Culver, a man he had gotten to know fairly well during his time with Jessica, would want to vacation out here. The man liked to gamble. He liked the ponies, the roulette wheel, the blackjack table. He liked action. His idea of a quiet time was a Tony Bennett concert at the Sands.

Jessica got out of the car. Myron followed. Her posture was arrow-perfect. So was the walk, something Myron had always loved to watch in the past. But there was an unmistakable teeter in her step, as though her legs were not sure they could sustain the lovely torso over the long haul.

Their footsteps creaked on the steps of the wooden porch. Myron spotted plenty of dry rot. Jessica unlocked the front door and pushed it open.

'Take a look,' she said.

He did. He said nothing. He could feel her eyes on him.

'I checked his charge card,' she said. 'He spent over three thousand dollars at a place in the city called Eye-Spy.'

Myron knew the store. This was definitely their handiwork. Three videocameras were sprawled across the couch. Panasonic. All with mounting material, so they could be hung up somewhere. There were also three small television monitors. Also Panasonic. The kind you might see at a high-rise's security station. Two VCRs. Toshiba. Lots of cables and wires and stuff like that.

But that stuff wasn't the most bothersome thing he saw. Alone, those electronic goods could have meant one of several things. But two other items – items that drew Myron's eye and held it like a baby near a shiny coin – changed everything. They were the added catalyst. They completed a mixture that was far too noxious to be ignored.

Propped against the wall was a rifle. And on the floor next to it, a set of handcuffs.

Jessica said, 'What the hell was he doing?'

He knew what she was thinking. The dead girls found near here. The television images of their battered, decayed bodies hovered above them like the most haunting of ghosts.

'When did he buy this stuff?' Myron asked.

'Two weeks ago.' Her eyes were clear, controlled. 'Listen, I've had time to think about this. Even if our worst fears are true, it doesn't explain anything. What about the picture in the magazine? Or Kathy's handwriting on that envelope? Or the phone calls? Or for that matter his murder?'

Myron looked at her. He knew she was seeking an explanation – any explanation but the one that stared them straight in the face. 'Are you okay?' he asked.

She crossed her arms under her breasts, a hand on each elbow, as if she were hugging herself. 'I feel,' she said, 'unanchored.'

'Can you take more?'

Her hands dropped to her sides. 'Why? What is it?'

He hesitated.

She exploded. 'Goddamn it, don't coddle me!'

'Jess—'

'You know I hate that protect-the-little-lady bullshit of yours! Tell me what the hell is going on!'

'Kathy was gang-raped by some of Christian's teammates on the night she disappeared.'

Jessica looked as if she'd just been slapped with an open hand. Myron reached out. 'I'm sorry,' he said.

'Just tell me what happened. Everything.'

He did. Her clear, controlled eyes went blank, lifeless. She remained uncharacteristically silent.

'Bastards,' she managed. 'The goddamn bastards.'

He nodded.

'One of them killed her,' she said. 'Or all of them. To shut her up.'

'It's possible.'

She paused, thinking. Then the eyes came back to life. 'Suppose,' she began slowly, 'that my father learned about the rape.'

Myron nodded.

'What would he do?' she continued. 'How would you react – if it was your daughter?'

'I'd be enraged,' Myron replied.

'Would you be able to control yourself?'

'Kathy is not my daughter,' he said. 'And I'm still not sure I can control myself.'

Jessica nodded. 'So maybe, just maybe, that explains this whole setup. The electronics, the cuffs, the rifle. Maybe he was using this hideaway, deep in the woods, so he could grab a rapist and exact a little private justice.'

'Kathy was gang-raped. There were six of them. This place looks built for one.'

'But,' she continued with the hint of an eerie smile, 'suppose my father was in the exact same position we are in now.'

'I don't follow.'

'Suppose he knew the name of only one rapist. Maybe this Horton guy. What might he do then? What might *you* do then?'

'I might,' Myron said, 'kidnap him and make him tell.'

'Exactly.'

'But it's a hell of a reach. Why would I videotape it? Why would I need cameras and monitors?'

'Tape the confession, make sure no one comes down the road, I don't know. You have a better scenario?'

He did not. 'Have you gone through the rest of the house yet?'

'I didn't have a chance. The realtor brought me here. He practically burst a blood vessel when he saw this stuff.'

'What did you tell him?'

'That I knew all this was here. That my father was a private investigator working undercover.'

Myron made a face.

'Hey, it was the best I could come up with.'

'And he bought that?'

'I think so.'

Myron shook his head. 'I thought you were a writer.'

'I'm not good with spur-of-the-moment. I'm a lot better with the written than the oral.'

'Based on past experience,' he said, 'I'd have to disagree.'

'Nice time,' she said, 'for a come-on.'

He shrugged. 'Just trying to keep things loose.'

She almost smiled.

'Let's look around,' he said.

There wasn't much to search. The living room had no drawers or closets. Everything was in plain view – the electronic equipment, the handcuffs, the rifle. The kitchenette held no surprises. Same with the bathroom. That left the bedroom.

It was small. The size of a guest bedroom at a beach house. The double bed took up almost the entire room. There were reading lights on either side of the bed, attached to the wall because there was no room for night tables. No dressers either. The bed was made with flannel sheets. They checked the closet.

Bingo.

Black pants, black T-shirt, black sweat shirt. And worst of all, a black ski mask.

'Ski mask in June?' Myron said.

'He might have needed it to kidnap Horton,' she tried. But her tone would not make the leap.

Myron dropped to the floor and looked underneath the bed. He saw a plastic bag. He stretched out his hand, grabbed it, and dragged it along the dust-blanketed floor toward him. The bag was red. The initials BCME were emblazoned across the front.

'Bergen County Medical Examiner,' Jessica explained.

It looked like one of those old Lord and Taylor's bags, the kind that snapped closed on the top. Myron pulled it back. The bag opened with a pop. He pulled out a pair of gray no-frills sweat pants with a drawstring. Then he reached back in and withdrew a yellow pullover with the letter T in red. Both were covered with caked-on dirt.

'Recognize these?' he asked.

'Just the yellow sweater,' she said. 'It's my dad's old varsity sweater from Tarlow High School.'

'Funny thing to hide under a bed up here.'

Jessica's eyes lit up. 'Nancy's message! Jesus Christ, she said my dad told her all about Kathy's yellow sweater.'

'Whoa, slow down a second. What did Nancy say exactly?'

'She said – and I quote verbatim – "He told me all about that favorite yellow sweater he gave Kathy. Such a sweet story." Those were her exact words. My father never wore it. Kathy did. Like a nightshirt or kick-around-the-house shirt.'

'Did your dad give it to her?'

'Yes.'

'So how did he get it back?'

'I don't know. I imagine it was in her personal belongings at school.'

'Which doesn't explain why he asked Nancy Serat about it. Or why it's hidden under his bed.'

They stood in silence.

'We're missing something here,' she said.

'Maybe your father saw something in these clothes we can't see yet.'

'What do you mean?'

'I don't know,' Myron admitted. 'But these clothes were clearly significant to him. Maybe he found them somewhere unusual. Or maybe the police found them.'

'But Kathy was wearing blue the night she left. That's been established.'

Myron remembered the testimony of the sorority sisters and the photograph. But then again . . .

'One way to check on that.'

'How?'

He ran out to the car. Darkness had finally laid claim on the long summer day. He turned on the phone, hoping they weren't too far out of a calling area. Three of those little bars lit up. Enough for the phone to work. He tried Dean Gordon's office. It rang twenty times. No answer. He tried the dean's house. It was picked up on the third ring.

Dean Gordon said, 'Hello?'

'What was Kathy wearing when she came to your house?' No need for identification or pleasantries.

'Wearing? A sweater and skirt of some kind.'

'What color?'

'Blue. I think the sweater was ripped a bit.'

Myron hung up.

Jessica said, 'Back to square one.'

Maybe, Myron thought. But the flash of an image seared across his mind. He couldn't grasp it, couldn't even make out what it was exactly. But it had been there, and it would come back.

'Let's go,' she said softly, taking his hand. The car light provided enough illumination to see the look in her eyes. They were beautiful eyes, so light colored they were almost yellow. 'I want to get away from here.'

He closed the car door, feeling suddenly choked up. The car light went out, basking them in darkness. He couldn't see her face anymore. 'Where do you want to go?'

From the darkness he heard her voice. 'Someplace,' she said, 'where we can be alone.'

37

They found a high-rise Hilton in Mahwah.

Myron checked them in to the best available suite. Jessica stood next to him. The hotel concierge swung his line of vision from Myron to Jessica, eyeing her lustily and Myron jealously. A formal affair was in full swing in the lobby. Men in tuxes, women in long gowns. But every man stared agog at Jessica, who was dressed in jeans and a button-down red blouse.

Myron was used to it. When they were first together, he had taken an almost perverse pleasure in seeing men stare, the familiar you-look-but-I-touch-ha-ha school of macho sneering. But then he started seeing things in the looks that weren't there, and the even more familiar male insecurity burrowed through his rationality.

Jessica was practiced at this. She knew how to ignore the looks without looking cold, bothered, or interested.

Their room was on the sixth floor. They had barely closed the door when they kissed. Jessica's tongue circled and gently darted, making his whole body spasm helplessly. He began to unbutton her blouse. His mouth went dry. He actually gasped when he saw her again. Breathlessness made him heady. He cupped a warm breast, feeling the delicious weight in his hand. She moaned into his mouth.

They moved to the bed.

Their lovemaking had always been intense, all-consuming, but this was somehow more animalistic, needier, and yet more tender.

Later, much later, Jessica sat up, kissed him gently on the cheek. 'That,' she said, 'was awesome.'

Myron shrugged. 'Not bad.'

'Not bad?'

'For me. For you it was awesome.'

She swung her legs out of bed and slipped into a hotel robe. 'I did enjoy myself,' she said.

'Sounded like it.'

'I was a tad noisy, huh?'

'The Who in concert is a tad noisy. You were loud.'

She stood above the bed, smiling. The robe was tied loosely, showing

200

plenty of cleavage and legs that were so long, they were almost intimidating. 'I didn't hear you complain.'

'How could you,' Myron said, 'over all your screaming?'

'What time is it?'

'Midnight.' He reached for the phone. 'Hungry?'

She gave him a look he felt in his toes. Well, not exactly his toes. 'Famished,' she said.

'For food, Jess. Food.'

'Oh.'

'Ever learn about the male's "time for recovery" in health class?'

'Must have been absent that day.'

'The three Rs. Replenishment, restoration, recuperation.' He looked at the menu. 'Damn.'

'What?'

'No oysters.'

'Myron?'

'Yes.'

'There's a hot tub in the bathroom.'

'Jess . . .'

She looked at him with who-me innocence. 'We can soak until the food comes. Recuperate. One of the three Rs.'

'Just soak?'

'Just soak.'

She had said soak. He was sure of it. Soak. Not soap. But that was how it started. She soaped him back to life. Myron tried to fight it, almost afraid of how good it felt. But he couldn't. Jess toyed with him, pushed him to the edge, let him teeter, then pulled him back. Myron was helpless. Words like *heaven, ecstasy, paradise, ambrosia* floated through his mind.

Total surrender.

With a whispered 'Now,' she let him go. His nerve endings surged and sung. The white-hot explosion was so powerful, his ears popped. The bright light hurt his eyes.

'Awesome,' he managed.

She lay back, smiling. 'Not bad.'

There was a knock on the door. Probably room service. Neither one of them moved.

'Why don't you get it,' she said.

'My legs,' he said. 'They can't move. I may never walk again.'

Another knock.

'I'm not dressed,' she said.

'And what am I, ready for a press conference?'

'Bet you'd get good coverage.'

Myron moaned at the joke.

Another knock.

'Come on, Myron. Just throw a towel around your shapely ass and get moving.'

The second woman to mention his ass in the same day. Yowzer. He grabbed the bath towel and headed for the door. Another knock.

'One second.'

He opened the door. It wasn't their food.

'Maid service,' Win said. 'May I turn down your bed?'

'Didn't you see the Do Not Disturb sign?'

Win glanced at the doorknob. 'Sorry. No speaka da English.'

'How the hell did you find us?'

'I traced down your charge card,' he said, as though it were the most natural thing in the world. 'You checked in here at eight twenty-two P.M.' Win leaned his head in the doorway. 'Hello, Jessica.'

From the bathroom. 'Hi, Win.' Myron heard her stepping out of the Jacuzzi. The image of water cascading down her naked body came to him like a deep punch.

'Come on in,' he grumbled.

'Thank you.' Win handed him a manila folder. 'Thought you might want to take a look at this.'

Jessica came in from the bathroom. The robe was tied tighter. She was drying her hair with a towel. 'What's up?' she asked.

'The police rap sheet of one Fred Nickler, aka Nick Fredericks,' Win said.

'Imaginative alias,' Myron said.

'For an imaginative fellow.'

Jessica sat on the bed. 'He's the porno publisher, right?'

Myron nodded. The rap sheet was not very long. He started with the most recent dates. Traffic violations, two DWIs, one arrest for mail fraud.

'Nineteen seventy-eight,' Win said.

Myron skipped down. June 30, 1978. Fred Nickler had been arrested for endangering the welfare of a child. Charges dropped.

'So?'

'Mr Nickler was involved in kiddie porn,' Win explained. 'He was only a small-time photographer back then. But he was nabbed with his hand, so to speak, in the cookie jar. More precisely, taking photographs of an eight-year-old boy.'

Jessica said, 'Jesus.'

Myron remembered their meeting. 'Just an honest guy trying to make an honest buck.'

'Indeed.'

Jessica asked, 'Why were the charges dropped?'

'Ah,' Win said, pointing a finger in the air, 'that's where things get interesting. In many ways it's not an uncommon story. Fred Nickler was only the photographer. A little fish. The authorities wanted the bigger fish. The little fish ratted out the big fish in exchange for leniency.'

'And they dropped the charges completely?' Myron said. 'Not even a misdemeanor?'

'Not even. It seems that Mr Nickler also agreed to help out the police from time to time.'

'So what's the significance?'

'This entire arrangement was negotiated between Nickler and the officer in charge of the investigation,' Win said. He shot a quick glance at Jessica.

'The officer in charge of the investigation was your friend Paul Duncan.'

38

'That's our man,' Win said. 'Mr Junior Horton.'

Horty looked like an ex-football player. Big and wide, all veins and bulges. His arms looked like corded wood. He was dressed for a rap video. His button-down St Louis Cardinals baseball shirt was untucked. His baggy shorts reached down past his knees. No socks. Black Reebok high-tops. A Chicago White Sox baseball cap. Dark sunglasses and lots of jewelry.

It was nine in the morning. One Hundred Thirty-second Street in Manhattan. The street was quiet. Horty was making a drug deal. He had been in and out of jail plenty of times, his one long stint of freedom during his time at Reston U. Drugs, mostly. Armed robbery, once. Two sexual assault charges. Twenty-four years old and a complete punk. Like most inmates he had spent his prison time lifting weights. Pumping iron. Our penal institutions develop violent men's physical strength, so when they get out, they'll be able to intimidate and maim with far greater skill. Nice system.

Jessica was not with them. She was packing her father's office – that is, the morgue – and checking for any additional bombshells. Myron had managed to talk her out of confronting Paul Duncan until they knew a little more. She listened grudgingly, but that was how Jessica usually listened anyway.

Horty finished the transaction with a kid who looked no older than twelve, slapped him five, headed west. He wasn't wearing a Walkman, but he walked as though he were. Very jittery. His eyes were red. Every few steps he would snort the air and wipe his nose with the back of his hand.

'Boys and girls, can you say "Cokehead"?'

'Probably has the flu,' Win said.

'The Colombian strain.'

They ducked out of sight as he approached. When Horty reached the lip of the alley, Myron stepped in front of him.

'Junior Horton?'

Horty gave him a scornful street glare. 'Who the fuck wants to know?'

'Snappy comeback,' Myron said.

'Get the fuck out of my way or I kick your ass.' He spotted Win. 'Both your ass.'

'Asses,' Win corrected. 'One ass. Two asses. Plural.'

'What the fuck—'

'We want to talk to you,' Myron said.

'Hey, fuck you, man.'

Myron turned to Win. 'He's a real badass.'

'Indeed,' Win said. 'I may wet myself.'

Horty stepped toward Win. He had at least six inches and sixty pounds on him. Horty probably thought he was being clever, going after and intimidating the little guy. Myron tried not to smile when Horty spat, 'Gonna fuck you up big-time.'

'If you curse again,' Win said in the tone of pre-school teacher, 'I will be forced to silence you.'

'You?' Horty laughed heartily. He flexed for a moment and then lowered his nose until it almost touched Win's. Win did not move. 'Little piece of upper-crust whitebread gonna shut me up? Fuck—'

Win barely moved. His arm shot up, delivered a palm strike to the solar plexus, and was back at his side in what seemed like a tenth of a second. Horty stumbled back, gasping, unable to get any oxygen into his lungs.

'I asked you not to curse,' Win said.

It took Horty nearly half a minute to recover. When he did, the lips started flapping again. 'Fucking cheapshot motherfucker,' he said rising. 'I gonna tear you a brand-new asshole.'

He charged Win, his arms outstretched as though tackling a fullback. Win sidestepped him and delivered a quick roundhouse kick, again hitting the solar plexus. Horty folded and went down. His face was a mixture of fury, pain, surprise, and of course, embarrassment. He looked around to make sure nobody was watching. He was, after all, getting his butt whipped by Mr Wonderbread.

'There are two hundred and six bones in the body,' Win said evenly. 'Next time I break one.'

But Horty wasn't listening. His eyes bulged. Rage twisted his face – not to mention his limited ability to reason. Horty stood, stumbling, pretending he was more hurt than he was. The element of surprise. When Horty was close enough, he made his move.

He must have been really coked up, Myron mused. Or really stupid. Probably both.

Win leaned away and snapped a sidekick toward Horty's lower leg. There was a cracking sound, like stepping on a dry twig. Horty screamed and went down. Win raised his leg for an ax kick, but Myron stopped him with a shake of his head.

'Two hundred five,' Win said, lowering his foot gently, 'and counting.'

'You broke my f—' He stopped, holding his leg and rolling back and forth. 'You broke my leg!'

'Your right tibia,' Win corrected.

'Who the – who are you?'

Myron said, 'We're going to ask you a few questions. You're going to answer them.'

'My leg, man. I need a doctor.'

'When we're finished.'

'Look, I just work for Terrell. He gave me this territory. You gotta a problem with that, you speak to him, okay?'

'We don't want to talk to you about that.'

'Please, man, I'm begging you. My leg.'

'You used to attend Reston University.'

A surprised look replaced the pained one. 'Yeah, so? You want my résumé?'

'You knew Kathy Culver.'

Panic now. 'You guys cops?'

'No.'

Silence.

'You knew Kathy Culver.'

'Kathy who?'

Win said, 'Number two-oh-five. The left femur. The femur is the largest bone in the body—'

'Okay, I knew her. So what?'

'How did you meet?' Myron asked.

'At a party. Her first week of school.'

'Did you ever date?'

'Date?' Horty laughed at that one. 'No. She wasn't the kind you date.'

'What kind was she?'

'The kind who sucked off my Johnson first night. Willie's too.'

'Who is Willie?'

'My roomie.'

'He play football?'

'Yeah.' Then he added, 'But only special teams,' as if that made him a lower species of being.

'Go on.'

'Man, why you want to hear this?'

'Go on.'

Horty shrugged. The leg was swelling badly, but the coke was numbing the pain enough to keep him going. 'You see, we had this party. At Moore House. Where all the brothers lived. Kathy, she was like the only white chick there. So she comes in dressed like a prime-time ho. I mean, she was all that, you know? We start rapping and shit, you know. Did a little nose-candy like a Hoover vac. She liked the stuff. Then we start slow-dancing.' The grin returned with the memory. 'Grinding, you know. She put her hand on the Black Blade right there on the dance floor. Starts rubbing it and shit. So I take her upstairs, and she sucks me off. But that ain't all. She takes a camera – a fucking camera! – out of her bag and asks me to take pictures. No shit! Close-ups, she wants, of her and the Black Blade.'

Myron's stomach began to churn again. Win looked on with his usual noninterest.

Horty continued. 'Next night, she come back. Takes on me and Willie at the same time. We take more pictures, have a good old time. 'Cept this time I had my camera too.'

'So you took some pictures of your own.'

'Shit, yeah.'

'Did you and Kathy have any more, uh, encounters?'

'Nope. She moved on to other dudes, though. Prime-looking babe for such a ho. All blond and built and shit.'

'You talk to her after that?'

He shrugged. 'Little. Not much. But once she started up with Christian, man, it was a whole other story.'

'What do you mean?'

'She be all nose up in the air, like her shit don't stink no more. Two of them all lovey-dovey and shit, like they was going steady on a TV show. All of a sudden the slut thinks she's some fucking pure-ass cherry. I mean, the ho been riding the Blade like a fucking bronco, and now she don't even say how-do. That ain't right. That just ain't right.'

Mr Etiquette.

'So you decided to blackmail her,' Myron said.

'No way. Unh-unh.'

'We know about it, Horty. We know she paid you for the pictures.'

Horty made a snorting sound. 'Aw, shit, that ain't blackmail. That's a business transaction. I just called her one day and told her I might have to knock her down a few pegs. And then I said a picture was worth a thousand words. She kinda agreed with all that and said she'd be willing to pay for such wonderful pictures. I told her they was real valuable to me. Had a lot of sentimental value and shit. But we finally reached an agreement. A mutually beneficial agreement,' he stressed, 'not blackmail.' He took hold of his leg and winced. 'End of story, man.'

'You left something out.'

'What?'

'The gang-rape in the locker room.'

He did not seem surprised. He half-smiled and said, 'Rape? Man, you ain't listening. This woman had Horty's Three Hs: Hot, Horny, Ho. Shit, she'd jump naked into a rock pile if she thought they'd be a snake in it. She loved it. We all had a good time.'

Win looked at Myron. The look said Keep your cool.

'How many of you?' Myron asked.

'Six.'

'Why,' he said in a low voice, 'didn't you just take the money, Horty? Why did you have to rape her?'

'I just told you, man—'

'She didn't come to that locker room for consensual sex with six people. You raped her.'

'Can't be, man,' he said with a shake of his head. 'She a ho through and through. And once a ho, always a ho. That's just the way it is. Fucking cunt acting all high and prissy and shit. Quarterback's girl. Miss fucking all-American cheerleader. Who the fuck did she think she was? So yeah, I showed her. I reminded her where she come from, what she really is. Not some fucking prom queen. A slut. A dick-loving ho.'

Win now stepped in front of Myron. Preventive measures.

''Sides,' Horty continued, 'I owed her boyfriend. Big-time.'

'Christian Steele?'

'Yeah. He did me wrong. I did him wrong. Passed around his little ho. Just a little payback, my man. To the prick who got me thrown off the team.'

'No,' Myron said. 'It wasn't Christian.'

'What you talking about?'

'I spoke with Coach Clarke. Two guys showed up for a game high. That's why you were thrown off. Christian had nothing to do with it.'

'Oh,' Horty said with a shrug. 'Ain't that something.'

'Your remorse,' Myron said, 'is very touching.'

'I gotta get to a doctor, man. My leg is killing me.'

'Weren't you worried about getting caught?'

'What?'

'Weren't you afraid she'd report the rape?'

Horty made a face as if Myron had suddenly started speaking Japanese. 'You crazy, man? Who she gonna tell? She just gave me major cash to keep it all quiet. She say anything, it all gets out. The whole ugly truth. Everyone would know – Christian, her mammy, her pappy, her teachers. Everyone would know what she just paid all that money to hide. And what if she was dumb enough to tell? There were pictures and witnesses of her doing Willie and me at the party. Who gonna believe she was raped after seeing that?'

Dean Gordon had made the same argument, Myron remembered. Great minds thinking alike.

'Hey, look, man, my leg's killing me.'

'Did you ever see Kathy again?' Myron managed.

'Nope.'

'Were you the one who threw away the panties?'

'Nope. One of the other guys had them. Thought he'd keep them as a souvenir. When he heard she was missing, he got scared, threw them away.'

'Who?'

'I ain't giving names.'

'Yes,' Win said. 'You are.' He rested his foot against the broken tibia. That was enough.

'Okay, okay. Like I said, they was six of us. Three brothers, two white dudes, one chink.'

Equal opportunity rapists.

'One was the place kicker. Guy named Tommy Wu. Then there was Ed Woods, Bobby Taylor, Willie and me.'

'That's five.'

Horty hesitated. 'Give me a break, man. The other dude was the one who threw away the panties. But he's a friend, man. Still give me money when I'm down, you know. I can't just give him up. He's big-time.'

'What do you mean, big-time?'

'Plays pro ball and shit. I can't give you his name.'

Win put the slightest pressure on the leg. Horty bucked.

'Ricky Lane.'

Myron froze. 'The running back for the Jets?' Dumb question. How many Ricky Lanes who now play pro football went to Reston University?

'Yeah. Now look, man, that's all I know.'

Win said to Myron, 'Do you have any other questions for him?'

Myron shook his head.

'Then leave,' Win said.

Myron did not move.

'I said,' Win continued, 'leave.'

'No.'

'You heard what he said. You'll never convict him. He pushes drugs to kids, rapes innocent women, blackmails, steals, whatever, and laughs about it.'

Horty sat up. 'What the fuck is this?'

'Leave,' Win repeated.

Myron hesitated.

'Yo, man, I told you everything I know.' There was a tremble in Horty's voice.

Myron did not move.

Horty shouted, 'Don't leave me alone with this crazy motherfucker!'

'Leave,' Win said.

Myron shook his head. 'No. I'll stay.'

Win studied Myron. Then he nodded and approached Horty, who was trying to claw away but not getting far.

'Don't kill him,' Myron said.

Win nodded. He went to work with the careful precision of a surgeon. His face never changed expression. If he heard Horty's cries, he never showed it.

After a short time Myron told him to stop. Reluctantly Win stepped away.

They left.

39

Ricky Lane lived in a New Jersey condo development similar to Christian's. Win waited in the car. As Myron approached the door, he felt rather than heard the bass from Ricky's stereo. It took three rings of the bell and several knocks before Ricky appeared.

'Hey, Myron.'

He was wearing a silk shirt that was either very fashionable or a pajama top. Hard to tell. The shirt was unbuttoned, revealing a well-defined physique. His pants were held up by a drawstring. He was also wearing slippers. Maybe they were pajamas. Or lounging clothes. Or he was trying out for a walk-on role on *I Dream of Jeannie*.

'We need to talk,' Myron said.

'Come on in.'

The music was deafening and awful. Made Pap Smear sound like Brahms. The motif was sleek modern. Lots of Fiberglas. Lots of black and white. Lots of rounded edges. The stereo took up a whole wall. The lights on the equalizer looked like something on *Star Trek*.

Ricky flipped the stereo off. The silence was abrupt. Myron felt his chest stop vibrating.

'So what's up?' Ricky asked.

Myron tossed him a glass jar. Ricky caught it, looked a question.

'Pee in it,' Myron said.

'What?'

'I want you to urinate into this jar.'

Ricky looked at the jar. Then at Myron. 'I don't get it.'

'Your new size,' Myron said. 'You're taking steroids.'

'No way, man. Not me.'

'Then give me a urine sample. Right now. I'll have it tested at a lab.'

Ricky stared at the jar. He said nothing.

'Go ahead, Ricky. I don't have all day.'

'You're my agent, Myron. You ain't my mother.'

'True enough. Are you taking steroids?'

'It's none of your business.'

'I'll take that as a yes.'

'Take it any way you'd like.'

'Did Horty sell them to you? Or have you gotten a new supplier since college?'

Silence.

Ricky said, 'You're fired, Myron.'

'I'm devastated. Now tell me about raping Kathy Culver.'

More silence. Ricky was struggling to look casual, but his body language was all wrong.

'I know all about it,' Myron continued. 'Your buddy Horty told all. Nice guy, by the way. A real sweetheart.'

Ricky stumbled back. He put the jar down on a shiny cube that Myron guessed was a table. He turned away. His voice was barely audible. 'I never touched her.'

'Bullshit. You and five other guys jumped her in the locker room. You took turns raping her.'

'No. That's not how it happened.'

Myron waited. Ricky buttoned his shirt, his back still facing Myron. He took a CD out of the stereo and tucked it back into its case.

'I was there,' Ricky began, his voice low. 'In the locker room. I was stoned. We all were. Stoned out of our minds. Horty had just gotten in a new supply, and . . .' He sort of shrugged away the rest of the sentence.

'It started as a dare, you know. We knew we'd never go through with it. We figured we'd walk right to the edge but never jump. We kept waiting for someone to call it off.' He stopped again.

Myron said, 'But no one called it off.'

He nodded slowly. 'It stopped. But too late. It stopped when it was my turn, and I said no.'

'After all the others had gone?'

'Yes. I stood there and watched them. I even cheered.'

Silence.

'You kept her panties?'

'Yes.'

'When you heard the police were investigating, you tossed them in that garbage bin.'

He faced Myron. 'No,' he said with something close to a hint of a smile. 'I wouldn't have been stupid enough to leave them on top of a Dumpster. I'd have burned them.'

Myron considered that for a moment. It was, he thought, an excellent point. 'Then who threw them away?'

Ricky shrugged. 'Kathy, I guess. I gave them to her.'

'When?'

'Later.'

'What time later?'

'Around midnight, I think. After it happened . . . after she left the locker room, it was like someone had given us the antidote. Or like someone turned on the lights, and we finally saw what we'd done. We all went silent and just drifted away. Except Horty. He was laughing like a goddamn hyena, getting more and more stoned. The rest of us went back to our rooms. None of us said one word. I got into bed, for a little while anyway. Then I got dressed and went back out. I didn't have a plan. Not really. I just wanted to find her. Say something to her. I just wanted to . . . shit, I don't know.'

His fingers were playing with his hair, twisting it like a little kid. He looked smaller now. 'I finally found her.'

'Where?'

'Crossing the campus.'

'Where specifically?'

'The middle, I guess. On the commons.'

'What direction was she walking in?'

He thought a moment. 'South.'

'Like maybe she was coming from the faculty housing?'

'Yes.'

After she left Dean Gordon's, he thought.

'Go on.'

'I approached her. Called out her name. I thought she'd just run away, you know. It was dark and all. But she didn't. She just turned and stared at me. She wasn't scared. She wasn't shaking. She just stood there and stared me down. I said I was sorry. She didn't say anything. I gave her the panties. I told her she could use them as evidence. I even told her I'd testify. I didn't plan on saying that. It just came out. Kathy took the panties and walked away. She never said anything.'

'Was that the last time you saw her?'

'Yes.'

'What was she wearing?'

'Wearing?'

'When you last saw her?'

He looked up, trying to recall. 'Something blue, I think.'

'Not yellow?'

'No. Definitely not yellow.'

'She hadn't changed clothes since the rape?'

'I don't think so. No, they were the same clothes.'

Myron headed for the door. 'You're going to need more than a new agent, Ricky. You're also going to need a good lawyer.'

40

Jake was sitting next to Esperanza in the waiting area. He stood when Myron and Win entered.

'Got a minute?'

Myron nodded. 'My office.'

Jake said, 'Alone.'

Without a word Win spun and left.

'Nothing personal,' Jake said. 'But the guy gives me the creeps.'

'Come on in.' He stopped at Esperanza's desk.

'Did you reach Chaz?'

'Not yet.'

He handed her an envelope. 'There's a photograph inside. Bring it to Lucy. See if she recognizes him.'

Esperanza nodded.

Myron followed Jake into his office. The air conditioning was on full blast. It felt good.

'So what brings you to the Big Apple, Jake?'

'I was over at John Jay,' he said, 'checking something out.'

'The crime lab?'

'Yup.'

'Find something?' Myron asked.

Jake did not reply. He examined the pictures on the client wall, leaning forward and squinting. 'Heard of some of these guys,' he said. 'But no superstars up here.'

'No, no superstars.'

'Nothing like Christian Steele.'

Myron sat down. He threw his legs up on the desk. 'You still think he killed Nancy Serat?'

Jake did something with his shoulders. Might have been a shrug. 'Let's just say Christian is no longer our main suspect.'

'Who is?'

Jake moved away from the client wall. He sat down and crossed his legs. 'I've been poking into Adam Culver's homicide. Found out something interesting. Seems the cops concentrated solely on the murder scene and

214

surrounding neighborhood. No reason for them to check anything else. They were convinced he was a victim of random street violence. I took a different avenue. I canvassed Culver's neighborhood in Ridgewood. Nice town. Real white. No brothers at all. You been there, I assume?'

Myron nodded.

'Anyway, I talked to a guy who lives two houses down from the Culvers. He says he was walking his dog on the night in question. He wasn't sure of the time, but he guessed it was eight o'clock or so. Seems he heard a big fight going on at the Culvers' house. Major blowup. He said he'd never heard anything like that before. It was so bad he almost called the cops, but he didn't want to pry. They'd been neighbors for twenty years and all. So he just let it slide.'

'Did he know what the fight was about?'

Jake shook his head. 'Nope. Just loud voices. Adam's and Carol's.'

Myron sat quietly, still leaning back in his chair. Adam and Carol Culver had fought hours before Adam's murder. Myron tried to put it together with what he already knew. For the first time things were beginning to fit.

'What else do you got?' Myron asked.

'On Adam Culver's murder? Nothing.'

Silence.

'There were,' Jake continued, 'a few hairs found at Nancy Serat's murder scene. On the body itself. More specifically, clutched in Nancy's hand.'

Myron sat up. 'Like maybe she tore them off the killer?'

'Maybe,' Jake said. 'But we checked the hairs at our own facilities and got a confirmation this morning at John Jay. There's no question. The hairs belong to Kathy Culver.'

Myron felt his flesh turn to cold stone. He couldn't speak.

'We had some of her hairs on file,' Jake continued. 'From before. In case we ever found a body or wanted to check a location. Got them from her hairbrush at school. Both labs have done every comparison test conceivable. Neither one has any doubt. They're Kathy's hairs.'

Myron shook his head. He felt dizzy. Inside his head the Robot from *Lost in Space* was shouting 'That does not compute!' over and over again.

'You have any thoughts on this, Myron?'

'Just the same ones you're having.'

Jake nodded. 'What Christian said.'

' "Time for sisters to reunite," ' Myron quoted.

'Yup. Kinda takes on a whole new meaning now, don't it.'

'But it still doesn't explain anything,' Myron said. 'Let's assume Kathy Culver is alive. Let's assume that Nancy Serat knows this. Why would Kathy kill her?'

Jake shrugged. 'Sounds to me like Kathy may have gone off the deep end. I mean, first she's got this whole weird past. Then she falls in love with a guy. Then she's blackmailed. Then she's gang-raped. Then the dean turns his back on her. She cracks. Has a breakdown. Runs away. Maybe she tells Nancy Serat, maybe she doesn't. But somehow Nancy finds out. Nancy arranges a reunion – probably a surprise reunion – between sisters. Kathy gets there early. She's not happy about Nancy's surprise.'

'So she kills her?'

'Could be,' Jake said. 'Kathy's loony-tunes. She doesn't want to be found. Shit, she probably killed her old man for the same reason. She's nuts. Maybe she wants revenge for some reason. On her father, on her best friend – even on Christian and Dean Gordon and whoever else she sent that nutty magazine to.'

Didn't feel right to Myron. 'Then what about the big fight between Adam and Carol Culver? How does that fit in?'

'Hell if I know,' Jake said. 'I'm making this shit up as I go along. Maybe the fight was just a coincidence. Maybe ol' Adam was on edge because he was about to meet with his daughter. Maybe the mother knows more than she's saying.'

Myron thought about it. It was confusing, but the last part made sense. Maybe Carol Culver did know more than she was saying. More than maybe. Myron even had some idea now of what she was hiding.

It was time to pay Carol Culver a visit.

41

Myron pulled up in front of the familiar Victorian house on Heights Road in Ridgewood. He hesitated. He should have told Jessica about this, but there are things a woman might be more willing to tell a casual acquaintance than a daughter. This might be one of them.

Carol Culver answered the door. She was wearing an apron and those industrial rubber gloves. She smiled when she saw him, but the smile did not reach her eyes. 'Hello, Myron.'

'Hello, Mrs Culver.'

'Jessica isn't home right now.'

'I know. I wanted to talk to you, if you have a minute.'

The smile stayed. But a shadow crossed over the face. 'Come on in,' she said. 'Can I get you something to drink? Maybe a little tea?'

'That would be nice.'

He stepped inside. He and Jessica had not visited here often during their time together. A major holiday or two, that was it. Myron never liked the house. Something about it was stifling, as though the air were too heavy for normal breathing.

He sat down on a couch that was hard as a park bench. The decor was solemn. Lots of religious memorabilia. Lots of madonnas and crosses and gold-leaf paintings. Lots of halos and serene faces looking skyward.

Two minutes later Carol reappeared, minus the gloves and apron, plus some tea and shortbread cookies. She was an attractive woman. She didn't really look like her daughters, but Myron had seen pieces of her in both of them. Jessica's straight posture. Kathy's shy laugh.

'So how have been you?' she asked.

'Fine, thank you.'

'It's been a long time since we've seen you, Myron.'

'Yes.'

'Are you and Jessica . . . ?' She feigned embarrassment. She did that a lot. 'I'm sorry. That's none of my business.'

She poured the tea. Myron sipped it and nibbled on a cookie. Carol Culver did likewise.

'Tomorrow's the memorial service,' she said. 'Adam donated his corpse to a medical school, you know. The spirit was all that mattered to him. The body was worthless tissue. I guess that's part of being a pathologist.'

Myron nodded, took another sip.

'Well, I just can't believe this weather,' she rambled, a distracted smile frozen to her face. 'It's so hot out. If we don't have rain soon, the whole front lawn will be brown. And we just paid to have it reseeded last season—'

'The police will be here soon,' Myron interrupted. 'I thought we should talk first.'

She put her hand to her chest. 'The police?'

'They'll want to talk to you.'

'Me? What about?'

'They know about the fight,' he said. 'A neighbor was walking a dog. He heard you and Dr Culver.'

She stiffened. Myron waited, but she said nothing.

'Dr Culver wasn't feeling sick that night, was he?'

The color ebbed from her face. She put down her cup of tea and dabbed the corners of her mouth with a cloth napkin.

'He never intended to go to that medical conference in Denver, isn't that right, Mrs Culver?'

She lowered her head.

'Mrs Culver?'

No movement.

'I know this isn't easy,' Myron said gently. 'But I'm trying to find Kathy.'

Her eyes remained on the floor. 'Do you really think you can, Myron?'

'It's possible. I don't want to give you false hope, but I think it's possible.'

'Then you think she might be alive?'

'There's a chance, yes.'

She finally raised her head. The eyes were wet. 'You do what you have to do to find her, Myron.' Her voice was surprisingly steady and strong. 'She's my daughter. My baby. She has to come first. No matter what.'

Myron waited for Carol Culver to continue, but she fell back into silence. After nearly a full minute, Myron said, 'Dr Culver just pretended he was going to that medical conference.'

She took a deep breath and nodded.

'You thought he'd left that morning.'

Another androidlike nod.

'Then he surprised you here.'

'Yes.'

Myron's soft voice seemed to boom in the room. An antique clock ticked maddeningly. 'Mrs Culver, what did he see when he arrived?'

Tears began to flow. She lowered her head again.

'Did he see you,' Myron continued, 'with another man?'

Nothing.

'Was the man Paul Duncan?'

She lifted her head. Her eyes met his. 'Yes,' she said. 'I was with Paul.'

Myron waited again.

'Adam set a trap,' she continued, 'and we got caught.' The words were once again steady and strong. 'He had become suspicious. I don't know how. So he did just what you said – pretended to go to a conference in Denver. He even had me arrange his flights, so I would be sure he was gone.'

'What happened when your husband saw you?'

Shaking fingers rubbed her cheeks. She stood, turned away. 'Exactly what you'd expect to happen when a man finds his wife and best friend in bed. Adam went crazy. He'd been drinking pretty heavily, which didn't help matters. He shouted at me, called me horrible names. I deserved that. I deserved a lot worse. He threatened Paul. We tried to calm him down, but of course that was impossible.'

She picked up the tea again. Each word was making her a little stronger, making it a little easier to breathe. 'Adam stormed out. I was scared. Paul went after him. But Adam drove off. Paul left after that.'

'How long have you and Paul Duncan . . . ?' His voice just sort of mumbled away.

'Six years.'

'Did anybody else know?'

Her composure gave way. Not slowly. But as if a small bomb had blown it off her face. She crumbled, weeping freely. A realization came to Myron. He felt his blood freeze.

'Kathy,' he whispered. 'Kathy knew.'

The sobbing grew more intense.

'She found out,' he continued, 'during her senior year.'

Carol tried to stop her tears, but that took time. Myron remembered how Kathy had worshiped her mother, the perfect woman, the woman who balanced old-fashioned values with a sense of the modern. Carol Culver had been a homemaker and a shop owner. She had raised three beautiful children. She had instilled in her children more than just a sense of what is now popularly called 'family values.' For her values had been a rigid doctrine that she insisted her children follow. Jessica had rebelled. So had Edward. Only Kathy had been successfully locked in, like a lion kept in too small a cage.

And she had finally broken free.

'Kathy . . .' Carol Culver stopped, shut her eyes tightly. 'She walked in on us.'

'And that was when she changed,' Myron finished.

Carol Culver nodded, her eyes still squeezed closed. 'I did that to her. Everything that happened was because of me. God forgive me.' Then she shook her head. 'No. I don't deserve forgiveness. I don't want it. I just want my baby back.'

'What did Kathy do when she saw you two?'

'Nothing. At first. She just turned and ran away. But the next day she broke up with her boyfriend Matt. And from there – she made sure I paid for what I'd done. For all the years I'd been a hypocrite. For all the years I lied to her. She wanted to hurt me in the worst way possible.'

'She began to sleep around,' Myron said.

'Yes. And she made sure I knew all about it.'

'By telling you?'

Carol Culver shook her head. 'Kathy wouldn't talk to me anymore.'

'So how did you find out?'

She hesitated. Her face was drawn, her skin pulled tight against her cheekbones. 'Photographs,' she said simply.

Something else clicked into place. Horty and the camera. 'She gave you photos of herself with men.'

'Yes.'

'White men, black men, sometimes more than one.'

Her eyes closed again, but she managed to say, 'And not just men. It started slowly. A couple of nude pictures of her. Like the one in that magazine.'

'You saw that same picture before?'

'Yes. It even had the name of a photographer stamped on the back.'

'Global Globes Photos?'

'No. It was something like Forbidden Fruit.'

'Do you still have the picture?'

She shook her head.

'You threw them away?'

She shook her head again. 'I wanted to destroy them. I wanted to burn them and pretend I'd never seen them. But I couldn't. Kathy was punishing me. Keeping them was a form of penitence. I never told anyone about them, but I couldn't just throw them away. You see that, Myron, don't you?'

He nodded.

'So I hid them in the attic. In an old storage box. I thought they'd be safe there.'

Myron saw where this was going. 'Your husband found them.'

'Yes.'

'When?'

'A few months ago. He never told me about it. But of course I knew by the way he was acting. I checked the attic. The pictures were gone. Adam assumed that Kathy had hidden them up there. He had no idea she'd sent them to me. Or maybe he did. Maybe that's how he became suspicious of Paul and me. I don't know.'

'Do you know what your husband did with those pictures, Mrs Culver?'

'No. They were so awful. So painful to look at. I think Adam destroyed them.'

Myron doubted it. They both sat in silence for several minutes. Finally Myron said, 'Jessica is going to want to know.'

Carol Culver nodded. 'You tell her, Myron.'

She showed him to the door. He stopped at his car and turned back around. He studied the gray Victorian house. Twenty-six years ago a young family had moved in. They'd put up swings in the backyard and a basketball hoop in the driveway. They'd owned a station wagon, carpooled to Little League and choir practice, attended PTA meetings, hosted birthday parties. Myron could almost see it all happening, like a life insurance commercial playing in his head.

He slid into his car and drove away.

42

Myron was thinking about threads again.

Threads like Gary Grady. Dean Gordon. Nancy Serat. Carol Culver. Christian Steele, Fred Nickler. Paul Duncan. Ricky Lane. Horty and the thugs. But there was one thread he had overlooked.

Otto Burke.

Suppose Jake was right. Suppose the magazines had been sent out to wreak vengeance or maybe to satisfy some misguided or irrational anger. Either way, it meant that everyone who had received a copy of *Nips* was in some way connected to Kathy Culver.

Except Otto Burke.

How did he fit in? Otto hadn't even known Kathy Culver.

Or had he?

Myron got off Route 4 at the Garden State Plaza Mall and took Route 17 south to Route 3. New Jersey, land of routes. He pulled into the Meadowlands and parked near the Titans' executive offices. He found the general manager's office and asked for Larry Hanson.

He was let in almost immediately. He quickly explained the reason for his visit.

Larry Hanson watched him without expression. His huge hands were folded on his desk. His neck strained the top button. Larry was about fifty, but he hadn't gone to flab. He looked, Myron thought not for the first time, like Sergeant Rock in the old comic strips. Should have been chewing on a big cigar.

The office was adorned with trophies. Larry had been named league MVP twice. He'd been All-Pro twelve times. He had been elected into the Football Hall of Fame on the first ballot. There were plenty of his old football photos, from high school through college and into the pros. Black-and-whites and colors. Same crew cut. Same gritty smile. Different poses, including plenty of knee-up, straight-arm favorites from yesteryear.

When Myron finished, Larry studied his big hands for a minute, as if they were something he'd never noticed before.

'Why ask me?' he said. 'Why don't you ask Otto Burke about the magazine?'

'Because he won't tell me.'

'And what makes you think I will?'

'Because you're not a complete asshole.'

Larry's mouth twitched toward a smile, but he caught himself. 'Coming from you,' he said, 'that really means a lot.'

Myron said nothing.

'This is important, huh?'

Myron nodded.

Larry sat back. 'Burke didn't get the magazine in the mail. He heard about it from a private detective.'

Myron shifted in his chair. 'Otto was having Christian investigated?'

Larry's tone was flat. 'A man of Otto Burke's unquestionable integrity would never stoop to such a level.'

'Under the desk,' Myron said, 'you're crossing your fingers.'

Again the twitch/smile. 'This doesn't leave this room, Bolitar. You understand?'

'Cross my heart.' Myron motioned such with his hand.

'Burke has a whole security division,' Larry explained. 'They poke into everyone on the payroll. Including yours truly. They also have a source network all over the place. The credo is pretty simple: If you got dirt on a Titan, Burke will pay top dollar for it. So one of these sources came across the magazine.'

'How?'

'I don't know. Maybe he's a steady reader.'

'Do you know his name?'

'Brian Sanford. A true sleazeball. He works out of Atlantic City. The casino route. Spies on gamblers, that kind of thing. A Titan puts a quarter in a slot machine, he reports it, especially since that whole Michael Jordon thing started. Burke likes to be kept informed. Gives him the edge in negotiating.'

Myron stood. 'Thanks. I appreciate it.'

'Hey, Bolitar. This don't make us buddies or nothing. We talk again, I still hate your guts. You got it?'

Myron said, 'We're having a warm moment now, aren't we, Larry?'

Hanson leaned his elbows on the desk, pointing a finger at Myron. 'I still think you're a little pissant piece of dog shit. And next time I see you, I'll prove it.'

Myron spread his arms. 'Come on, Larry. How about that hug now?'

'Wiseass.'

'Does that mean no?'

'Do me a favor, Bolitar.'

'Name it, bright eyes.'

'Get the fuck out of my office.'

43

Myron called Brian Sanford. Answering machine. Myron said he had a real big case, one that paid ten grand, and he'd stop by his office tonight at seven o'clock. Brian Sanford would be there. For ten grand, a guy like Sanford would let his mother take a bullet in the gut.

Myron dialed his office.

Esperanza said, 'MB SportReps.'

'Did you show Lucy the photo?'

'Yep.'

'And?'

'You found your buyer.'

Myron said, 'Lucy was sure?'

'Positive.'

'Thanks.'

He hung up. An hour to kill. Myron headed over to the county medical examiner's office – Dr Adam Culver's old office. Just a hunch, but worth checking out.

The building was a one-level brick building. Institutional, almost like a small elementary school. The furniture was metal chairs with thin padding, again like a schoolteacher's. The waiting room magazines were pre-Watergate. The tiled floor was worn and yellowed with age, like the 'before' shot on a Mr Clean commercial. There was nothing even remotely decorative.

'Is Dr Li in?' he asked the receptionist.

'I'll buzz her.'

Sally Li was dressed in hospital scrubs, but there was no blood or anything on them. She was Chinese, approaching forty, but she could have passed for much younger. She wore bifocals. A pack of cigarettes was stashed in her front pocket. Cigarettes with a surgeon's gown. Like bowling shoes with a tuxedo.

They had met a couple of times in the past. Sally Li came to many Culver family functions. She had been Adam's right-hand woman for the past decade. Myron greeted her with a kiss on the cheek.

'Jessica told me you were looking into Adam's death,' she said without preamble.

He nodded. 'Can we talk for a minute?'

'Sure.' She led him to her office. Again, institutional. No personal stuff. Lots of pathology textbooks. A metal desk. Metal chair. A small tape recorder she probably used during autopsies. Her degrees on the wall. She wasn't married, had no children, so there was no picture on the desk. Big ashtray, though. Overflowing.

She struck a match, lit up, and said, 'How's tricks?'

'An MD smoking,' Myron said. 'Tsk, tsk.'

'My patients never complain.'

'Good point.'

She took a deep drag. 'So what do you want to know?'

'Did you and Adam ever have an affair?'

'Yes.' No hesitation. She looked him right in the eye. 'About four years ago. Lasted a week.'

'Did Adam have a lot of affairs?'

'Got me. A few, I guess. Why do you ask?'

'I'm just trying to put a few things together.'

'Vis-à-vis his murder?'

'Right.'

She took off her glasses. 'What does Adam's love life have to do with it?'

'Probably nothing,' Myron admitted. 'How had Adam been acting the last couple months?'

'A bit wacko,' she said. Again no hesitation.

'In what way?'

She gave that one some thought. 'Businesswise, he wasn't letting me help him on a lot of big cases. He was keeping them all to himself.'

'And that was unusual?'

'That was unheard of. We always worked the big cases together.'

'These cases,' Myron said. 'Were they the girls found in the woods upstate?'

She looked at him. 'You want to tell me how you knew that?'

'Just a guess.'

'Hell of a guess, Myron.'

'You said big cases. I read the papers. Those are the big cases they keep talking about.'

Sally didn't believe him, but she didn't push it either.

Myron said, 'So what else was there?'

She took another deep drag. 'He was very distracted. You'd talk to him, he'd nod, but he wouldn't listen.'

'Anything else?'

Sally crushed out the cigarette, though it still had plenty to go. She lit another. 'A new way to quit smoking,' she said. 'I smoke the same amount of cigarettes, but I take less puffs each day. Gradual slowdown until I quit entirely. At this rate it should take no more than twelve years.'

'Good luck.'

'Thanks.'

'So what else was there?'

Another puff. 'Adam was ordering a lot of weird tests on the last girl they found in the woods.'

'What do you mean, weird tests?'

'Superfluous tests. In my opinion, anyway.'

Myron said, 'You never got a positive ID on her, right?'

'Right.'

'So maybe he was running the tests to see if he could get a handle on her whereabouts.'

'Maybe. But he sent them out one at a time. He'd wait for one test to come back before he'd ask for the next one. Anthropological measurements, shape and size of cranium, pelvic bones, ossification of the bones, fusing of sutures on the skull – all one at a time.'

'So what do you make of that?'

She shrugged again. 'I don't make anything out of that. It's just an example of what I meant by acting strangely. Distracted. The case was a weird one to start off. The girl's skull had been crushed by the perp, but that wasn't what killed her. In other words, she had been buried alive in those woods. She died trying to claw her way out.'

Silence.

'This girl,' Myron said, 'what was she wearing?'

Sally stiffened a little. Then she leaned forward. 'Okay, Myron, what's going on?'

'Nothing. Why?'

'You know why.'

Myron stopped. 'The girl's clothes are missing.'

'Yes.'

He felt his heart crash into the pit of his stomach, like a skydiver with a ripped parachute. 'Oh, shit.'

'What is it?'

'Sally, I need you to run a test for me.'

44

The address of Brian Sanford, private investigator, was a go-go bar conveniently located one block from Merv Griffin's Resorts. Atlantic City was like that. The big hotels were like beautiful flowers untouched and unbothered by the unseemly weeds of poverty and sleaze that surrounded them. The big flowers had not beautified the neighborhood as promised by the casino owners. The contrast, if anything, had made the weeds more glaringly hideous.

The go-go bar was called Eager Beaver, and it was exactly what one would expect. Blinking sign with missing letters on the outside. Lots of lowlights around the bar, lots of bright spotlights on the stage. Bored women danced in shifts, most of them unattractive. Lots of flab. Lots of implants. Lots of herpes.

Myron make the key mistake of entering what might loosely be designated a bathroom. The urinals were stuffed with ice cubes – an adequate substitute, Myron supposed, for an actual flushing mechanism. No doors were on the stalls, which did not deter the defecators at all. One man smiled and waved to Myron from a squat.

Myron decided he could wait.

He called over a bartender. 'Could you tell me how to get to Brian Sanford's office?'

'Michelob, Bud, Bud Light, Coors.'

'I just want to know—'

'Michelob, Bud, Bud Light, Coors.'

Myron took out five dollars. The bartender pocketed it.

'Door in the back. Take the stairs up a level.'

He didn't wait for Myron to thank him. Capitalism.

A dancer on break approached him. She smiled. Each tooth was angled in a different direction, as if her mouth were the masterwork of a mad orthodontist.

'Hi,' she said.

'Hi.'

'You're really cute.'

'I don't have any money.'

She spun and walked away. Ah, romance.

The stairs did not creak. They cracked. Myron kept waiting for them to collapse. On the landing there was only one door. It was open. Myron knocked on the wall and peeked in.

Myron called out, 'Hello.'

A man he assumed was Brian Sanford came to the door. All smiles. Dressed in a beige suit that had last been pressed during the Bay of Pigs. 'You the guy who left the message?'

'Yes.'

The office was a minicasino. No desk but a roulette table. A one-armed bandit in the corner. Decks of cards everywhere. Souvenir dice, the kind that have a hole drilled in them, littered the floor. So did racing forms. Keno cards too.

The man put out his hand. 'Brian Sanford. But everyone calls me Blackjack. You know who gave me that nickname?'

Myron shook his head.

'Frankie. That's what I call Frank Sinatra. Frankie. Not Frank. Frankie, I call him.' He paused, waited.

Myron said, 'Good nickname.'

'See, Frankie and me were playing at the Sands one night, right, and I was on one of my streaks, you know. And Frankie turns to me and says, "Yo, check out Blackjack. He can't lose." Just like that. Frankie says, "Hey, Blackjack." Out of nowhere. The name stuck. Now everyone calls me Blackjack. All 'cause of Frankie.'

'Great story,' Myron said.

'Yeah, well, you know how it is. So what can I do for you, Mr . . . ?'

'Olson. Merlin Olson.'

Blackjack smiled knowingly. 'Okay, I can play it that way. Have a seat, Mr Olson.'

Myron sat.

'But before we start, Mr Olson, I have to tell you one thing right up front.'

He was holding dice in his hand, moving them around in his hands the way some people do with those Chinese balls that are supposed to help circulation.

'What's that?'

'I'm a very busy man. Lots of big stuff going on right now. You know how I started in this business?'

Myron shook his head.

'I used to be chief of security for Caesars Palace in Vegas. Head chief. You know how it is. I was in Vegas, right? But Donny – that's what I call Donald Trump, Donny – Donny asked me to head up security for his first hotel on the strip. Then he started nagging me to set up the Taj Mahal's security. I told him, I said, "Donny, I got too much on my plate, you know?" '

Myron looked up. A small crop plane flew overhead, leaving mucho cow manure in its wake.

'So my problem is this, you see. I got a meeting tomorrow morning with Stevie – Steve Wynn. First thing, seven A.M. sharp. Great guy, Stevie. Morning guy. Up at five every day. You know he's practically blind? Got cataracts or something. He keeps it hidden. Only tells his closest friend. So anyway Stevie wants me to do something for him. Normally I'd tell him no, but it's a personal favor and Stevie's a good friend. Not like Donny. I'm not crazy about Donny. Thinks he's some hot stud now that he's got Marla.'

'Mr Blackjack—'

'Please,' he said throwing up his hands, 'just call me Blackjack.'

'I'd like to ask you a few questions, uh, Blackjack. I need your particular expertise on an important matter.'

He nodded. Very understanding. He didn't hitch up his pants importantly, but he should have. 'What's this all about?'

'You performed some work for a friend of mine recently,' Myron said. 'Mr Otto Burke.'

A big smile now. 'Sure. Otto. Swell kid. Smart as a whip. He calls me whenever he comes down.'

Probably calls him Ottie, Myron thought.

'You gave him a magazine a few days ago. An issue of *Nips*.'

Blackjack looked wary now. He rolled the dice on the table. A three. 'What about it?'

'We need to know how you located it.'

'Who is "we"?'

'I work with Mr Burke.' Even saying it made Myron feel nauseous.

'So why didn't Ken call? He's the usual contact.'

Myron leaned forward. Conspiratorial. 'This is bigger than Ken, Blackjack. We don't feel anyone can be trusted with this but you.'

He nodded. Again very understanding.

'Frankly, Blackjack – and this has to remain hush-hush.'

'Of course.'

'You're our first choice to replace Ken. But we know how busy you are.'

His eyes gleamed a bit. 'I appreciate that, Mr Olson, but for someone like Otto Burke, I could try to open—'

'Let's talk about this case first, okay? How did you come across the magazine?'

The wary look again. 'Don't take this the wrong way,' he said, 'but how do I know you work with Otto? How do I know you're not some schmo off the street?'

Myron smiled. 'I knew it.'

'What?'

'I told Otto you were the right guy for the job. You're not sloppy. You're careful. We like that. We need that.'

Blackjack shrugged. He picked up the dice, gave another roll. Snake eyes. 'I'm a professional,' he said.

'Clearly,' Myron agreed. 'So why don't you call Otto yourself on the private line? He'll confirm everything. I'm sure you know the number.'

That slowed him down a bit. He swallowed, trying to disguise it, looked around like a cornered rabbit. Myron could see the wheels churning. 'Uh, no reason to bother Otto with this,' Blackjack said. 'You know how he hates that. I can tell you're an honest Joe. Besides, how would you know about the magazine if Otto hadn't told you?'

Myron shook his head. 'You're an amazing man, Blackjack.'

He waved a hand of modesty.

'How did you find the magazine?' Myron asked.

'Shouldn't we talk about my fee? On the phone you said something about ten grand.'

'Otto said you were a trustworthy guy. He said to bill him through Ken. Whatever you think is fair.'

Another nod. He picked up the dice. Rolled again. Another three. Practice, practice. 'I didn't find the magazine,' Blackjack said. 'It found me.'

'What do you mean?'

'I was hired to do a job. Part of it was to send out copies of that mag to some people.'

'Was Christian Steele one of those people?'

'Yup. That's how I got suspicious. I mean, the envelopes were given to me already addressed and sealed. I didn't recognize any of the names except Christian's. Otto had already put out word he wanted anything, *anything*, on Steele. So I opened it up and took a peek. That's when I saw the picture.'

'Who hired you to mail out the magazines?'

Blackjack placed one chip on red, one chip on odd. He spun the roulette wheel. 'You wanna put down a couple of chips?'

'No. Who hired you?'

'Well, that's the weird part. I don't know. I got this big package in the mail with very specific instructions. Plus cash. But no name.'

'Any return address?'

'Nope. Just a postmark.'

'From where?'

'Right here in Atlantic City. I got it about ten, twelve days ago.'

The roulette wheel stopped. Twenty-two. Black.

Blackjack said, 'Damn.'

'Do you still have the instructions?'

'Yeah, sure.' He opened a drawer and handed him a piece of paper. 'Here.'

The letter had been typed:

Dear Mr Sanford,

For the sum of $5,000 (plus expenses) I would like you to perform the following services:

1. Enclosed find seven envelopes. Two of them should be mailed from the campus mail box at Reston University on Friday. The other three should be mailed from a post office box in their respective towns.

2. Please mail out the following New Jersey Bell literature to each person on the list at the same time.

3. Please arrange a phone number in the 201 area code, one that will work on Return Call. This number should be immediately disconnected should anyone call it back or answer it. I would like you to hook up an answering machine with the enclosed tape to that phone. I would then like you to make calls to each of the numbers listed below from that number. On the first two nights – Saturday and Sunday – you will simply call repeatedly, hold the line when they answer, and say nothing until they hang up. On Monday, you will call and say the following: 'Enjoy the magazine. Come and get me. I survived.' Please make your voice sound female and vague. (As you know, there are phones that can disguise voices and make them sound female.)

4. Enclosed is a money order for $3,000. Upon completion of this exercise I will contact you personally on or around the ninth of the month and pay off the remaining $2,000 plus expenses.

My name must remain anonymous. Thank you for understanding.

Myron looked up. 'I assume the New Jersey Bell literature explained Return Call.'

Nod.

'Who were the seven people?'

Blackjack shrugged. The dice were rolled yet again. Another snake eyes. The guy had the touch. 'I don't remember. Christian was one. Some dean was another. I mailed another from a town called Glen Rock.'

'To a Gary Grady.'

'Yeah, that's the name. I also mailed three from New York.'

'One of those to Junior Horton?'

'Uh, yeah, I think so. Junior. That rings a bell.'

'And the last one?'

'Some other place in New Jersey. Near Glen Rock.'

Myron stopped. 'Ridgewood?'

'Yeah. Something-wood anyway. A woman's name. I remember because all the rest were men.'

Myron said, 'Carol Culver?'

He thought a moment. 'Yeah. That's it. A name with two Cs.'

Myron's shoulders slumped.

'Hey, buddy, you all right?'

'Fine,' he said softly. 'What about the phone calls?'

'The numbers were on another page. I threw them away when I finished. I called Steele and hung up a few times. By the time I called him back to give him the message calls, the line was disconnected. Guess he'd moved.'

Myron nodded. Christian had moved from the campus to the condo.

'The guy in New York – Junior – he was never home so I never reached him either. The others all got hang-ups and then the message calls.'

'How many of them used Return Call?'

'Just two. Christian and the guy from Glen Rock. It wouldn't have worked for the guys in New York anyhow. Return Call only works for that area code.'

'Have you heard from your client yet?'

'Nope. And yesterday was the ninth. I tell you, he better not stiff Blackjack Sanford.' Another mental pants-hitch. 'If he knows what's good for him.'

'Uh-huh. Anything else you can tell me?'

'About this case? Nope. Hey, you wanna go over to Merv's? They know me over there. I can get us on a good table. Play a little blackjack maybe. Watch the legend in action.'

Tempting, Myron thought. Like having electrolysis performed on his testicles. 'Maybe some other time.'

'Yeah, okay. Say, how much you think I should bill Otto for? Like you said, I want to be fair.'

'Oh, I'd bill him for the full amount.'

'The whole ten Gs?'

'Yes. You've been very helpful, Blackjack. Thank you.'

'Yeah, take care. Come by anytime.'

'Oh, one more thing.'

'What's that?'

Myron said, 'Mind if I use your bathroom?'

45

It was ten-thirty when Myron arrived at Paul Duncan's house. Lights were still on. Myron had not called to make an appointment. He wanted the element of surprise.

The house was a simple Cape Cod. Needed a new coat of paint maybe. The front yard had lots of budding flower beds. Myron remembered that Paul liked gardening in his down time. Lot of cops did.

Paul Duncan answered the door holding a newspaper. A pair of reading glasses were low on his nose. His gray hair was neatly combed. He wore navy-blue Hagar slacks and a twist-a-flex Speidel watch. The casual man from Sears. A television played in the background. An audience applauded wildly. Paul was alone, except for a sleeping golden retriever curled in front of the television as if it were a fire on a snowy night.

'We need to talk, Paul.'

'Can't this wait until the morning?' His voice was strained. 'After Adam's memorial service?'

Myron shook his head and stepped into the den. The television audience applauded again. Myron glanced at the screen. Ed McMahon's *Star Search*. The spokesmodels weren't on, so Myron turned away.

Paul closed the door. 'What's this all about, Myron?'

A coffee table had *National Geographic* and *TV Guide*. Also two books – the latest Robert Ludlum and the King James Bible. Everything was very neat. A portrait of the golden retriever in its younger days hung on the wall. Lots of little porcelain figurines adorned the room. A couple of Rockwell plates too. Hardly a swinging bachelor pad or den of lust.

'I know about your affair with Carol Culver,' Myron said.

Paul Duncan played stiff-lip. 'I don't know what you're talking about.'

'Then let me try to clarify myself. The affair's been going on for six years. Kathy caught you and Mommy a couple of years back. Adam also caught you two on the night he was murdered. Any of this ring a bell?'

His face went ashen. 'How . . . ?'

'Carol told me.' Myron sat. He picked up the Bible and flipped through it. 'Guess you skipped the part about not coveting your neighbor's wife, huh, Paul?'

'It's not what you think.'

'What's not what I think?'

'I love Carol. She loves me.'

'That sounds swell, Paul.'

'Adam treated her awfully. He gambled. He whored. He was cold to his family.'

'So why didn't Carol divorce him?'

'She couldn't. We're both devout Catholics. The Church wouldn't allow it.'

'The Church prefers marital infidelity?'

'That's not funny.'

'No, it's not.'

'Who are you to judge us? You think any of this was easy?'

Myron shrugged. 'You didn't stop. Not even after Kathy saw you.'

'I love Carol.'

'So you say.'

'Adam Culver was my closest friend. He meant a great deal to me. But when it came to his family, he was a bastard. He provided for them materially, but that's it. Ask Jessica, Myron. She'll tell you. I've always been there. From the time she was a little girl. Who took her to the hospital when she fell off her bike? Me. Who built her swingset? Me. Who drove her down to Duke her freshman year? Me.'

'Did you also dress up as the Easter Bunny?' Myron asked.

He shook his head. 'You don't understand.'

'Correction: I don't give a shit. There's a difference. Now let's go back to the day Kathy caught you two. Tell me what happened.'

His face became irritated. 'You know what happened. She walked in on us.'

'Were you naked?'

'What?'

'Were you and Mrs Culver in the throes of passion?'

'I won't dignify that with an answer.'

Time to rattle his cage a bit. 'What position? Missionary, doggie, what? Were either of you wearing handcuffs or a pig's mask?'

He moved so he was standing directly over Myron. Everyone thought this was tremendously intimidating, towering over a seated foe. Fact was, Myron could deliver a palm strike to the groin before an ordinary man could even cock his fist.

'Watch it, son,' Paul said.

'How did Kathy react to seeing you two lovebirds?'

'There was no reaction. She ran away.'

'Did either of you follow her?'

'No. Frankly, we were both too shocked.'

'I bet. Did you ever discuss the matter with Kathy?'

Paul stepped away, circled, sat in the chair next to Myron. 'She only mentioned it to me once.'

'When?'

'A few months later.'

'What happened?'

He looked away, his eyes darting about, searching for a safe place to land. 'This isn't easy to say.'

Myron nodded, feigned sympathy. 'Go on.'

'Kathy made a pass at me.'

'Did you catch it?'

'What?'

'As in "catch her pass." '

He flashed the irritated face again. 'Of course not.'

'You turned her down?'

'I pretended I didn't know what she was talking about.'

'Did she persist?'

'Yes. But I kept ignoring her.'

'Bet you were real excited, though. Mother and daughter. Both good-lookers. Your fantasies must have been in overdrive.'

Irritation turned to rage. He finally took off his reading glasses. Very dramatically. 'Last warning, pal.'

'Uh-huh. So now tell me about Fred Nickler.'

Piss him off. Quick subject change. Keep him off balance.

'Who?'

'For a cop,' Myron said, 'you're a lousy liar. Nineteen seventy-eight. You let Nickler plea-bargain a kiddie porn charge. I know all about your connection with him, Paul. What I don't know is how he fits into all this.'

'He helped me out from time to time. With cases.'

'Including the disappearance of Kathy Culver?'

'In a manner of speaking, yes.'

'How?'

'I guess there's no reason not to tell you.' He coughed into a shaking fist. The golden retriever opened an eye but didn't move. 'Adam found photographs of Kathy in his attic. He brought them to me in the strictest confidence. On the back of one was the name of a photography studio called Forbidden Fruit. I couldn't find them anywhere. So Adam and I visited Nickler. Nickler told us that Forbidden Fruit was now called Global Globes. He gave me the address.'

'Then you went and bought all the pictures and negatives of Kathy?' A throwaway question. Lucy had already identified Paul Duncan from a photograph.

'Yes. We wanted to protect Kathy's name. But we also wanted the name of the animal that'd brought Kathy to the studio.'

'Gary Grady.'

'You know about that?'

'I am,' Myron said, 'well informed.'

'Well, I checked Grady out completely. He was shady, no question about it. A high school teacher with all those sex lines. He advertised in at least fifty pornographic magazines. I tailed him for a couple of weeks, did a lot of it on my own time. I also had his phone tapped for a while. But in the end we came up with nothing.'

'How did Adam react to that?'

'Not well. Adam was always coming to me with some new angle on Kathy's case, mostly out of pure desperation. I don't blame him. She was his youngest daughter. The one child he had a decent relationship with. Adam was willing to do anything to find her. He even wanted to kidnap Grady and torture him until he talked. I told him I'd do anything to help, but that we had to keep within the limits of the law. He didn't like hearing that.'

'Tell me about the night Adam died.'

Paul took a deep breath. 'He set us up beautifully.'

'I know all about that. What happened after he caught you and Carol in bed?'

Paul Duncan rubbed his eyes with his palms. 'He went berserk. He started calling Carol names. Awful names. We tried to talk to him, but what could we say? After a while he told her he wanted a divorce and ran out.'

'What did you do then?'

'I went home.'

'Did you stop on the way?'

'No.'

'Anybody who can confirm you were home?'

'I live alone.'

'Anybody who can confirm you were home?' Myron repeated.

'No, dammit. That's why Carol and I didn't tell anyone. We know how it would look.'

'Not good,' Myron agreed.

'I didn't kill him. I wronged him. I was a terrible friend. But I didn't kill him.'

Myron gave a small shoulder shrug. 'You seem like a pretty good candidate, Paul. You lied about the night of his murder. You were having a long-term affair with his wife, a wife who could marry you only if her husband died. He confronted you two in his bed on the night of the murder. His missing daughter was the only person who knew about your secret liaison. Her photograph appears in a magazine published by your source. No, Paul, I'd say it looks pretty goddamn shitty.'

'I had nothing to do with any of that.'

'What did you do with Kathy's pictures?'

'I gave them to Adam, of course.'

'Did you keep any for yourself? Maybe as a little souvenir?'

'Of course not!'

'And you never saw any of the pictures again?'

'Never.'

'Yet somehow Kathy's picture ended up in a porno mag.'

Paul nodded slowly.

'A porno mag published by your buddy Fred Nickler.'

Another nod.

'So now comes the big question, Paul: How did Kathy's picture end up in Nickler's magazine?'

Using both arms for leverage Paul Duncan stood. He moved to the television and flicked it off. The junior dancers faded away. The dog did not move. Paul studied the blank screen for a while and then said, 'It's going to sound crazy.'

'I'm listening.'

'Adam arranged it. He put Kathy's picture in that magazine.'

Myron waited. His spine began to tingle.

'I don't understand it, either,' Paul continued. 'Nickler called me yesterday. He was all upset, said you were nosing around and realizing something was up. I had no idea what he was talking about. Then he explained it to me. Adam had told Nickler to put that picture in his magazine. You see, Adam had met Nickler when we were trying to find the photographer's studio. So Adam went back to him, pretended he was still working on a case with me. He told Nickler to put Kathy's picture in Gary Grady's ad. He also told him not to say anything if anybody asked about it – except to give out Gary's alias and address.'

'Enough clues,' Myron said, 'so someone would find Grady.'

'It seems so, yes.'

'Did Nickler tell you why he placed the picture only in *Nips*?'

'No. I can call and ask him, if you'd like.'

Myron shook his head. 'Not necessary.'

'That's all I know. I can't for the life of me figure out what Adam was doing. Maybe he wanted to set up Grady. Or maybe he just snapped. But the truth is, I have no idea why Adam would put his own daughter's picture in that magazine.'

Myron rose. He had a very good idea why.

46

Win gazed into the mirror. Despite the fact that the hour was closing in on midnight, his evening was just beginning. He patted his hair, smiled at his reflection, and said, 'God, I am handsome.'

Myron grunted.

'Are you going to call Jessica?' Win asked.

'I want to go over it again.'

'Now?'

'Now.'

'And make my nubile lass wait?'

'She'll survive.'

'You don't understand. This girl is very special to me.'

'What's her last name?'

Win thought a moment, shrugged. 'Okay, what do you wish to review?'

'I've told you everything I know,' Myron said. 'I want to know how you see it.'

Win turned away from the antique mirror. His Central Park West apartment had been a gift from his grandfather. It was huge, worth millions, and decorated like Versailles. Myron was afraid to touch anything. He was sitting in an antique chair with wooden arms digging into his ribs.

'Do you mind if I break the case down into three separate entities?' Win said.

'Whatever you want.'

'Fine. Then let us begin. Entity one: Kathy Culver's disappearance. During her senior year of high school, Kathy's personality changed for reasons her mother has now revealed to you. Kathy then sought to hurt said mother with promiscuity. Ergo the lewd photographs, which Kathy mailed to Carol. But Kathy Culver did not see the danger in her actions. She took for granted that she could just end it whenever she so desired. But that was not the case. When she wanted to stop – when she met Christian, it seems – she could not just backslide out.'

Myron nodded.

'Enter Mr Junior Horton. He decided to cash in on the new, unsullied Kathy Culver through blackmail. Kathy agreed to pay him in exchange for silence and photographs. On the night in question Mr Horton called Kathy at her sorority house. She agreed to meet him in the locker room. Once there, she was gang-raped by Junior Horton and several cohorts.'

Win stopped and moved toward a decanter. 'Care for a little cognac?'

'No, thanks.'

He poured some into a snifter. 'The rape bent her past the breaking point,' he continued. 'She snapped. She suddenly craved redemption and justice above all else. So she headed immediately to Dean Gordon's office to report the attack. Dean Gordon had been her employer, and she probably considered him a friend. She told him what had happened to her in the locker room. His reaction was either superfluous or detrimental to her resolve. Take your pick.'

'Probably detrimental,' Myron added.

'Yes, probably detrimental. Either way, Kathy left Dean Gordon's house disheartened. She walked around the campus in a sort of catatonic daze, I imagine. Ricky Lane approached her. He apologized and gave her the panties – that is, evidence of the crime against her. After that – who knows? We slam into a big brick wall. The only thing we know for sure is that the panties were found on top of a waste bin several days later. Are there any questions so far?'

Myron shook his head.

'Then let's move on to Entity two: Adam Culver's involvement. Sometime after Kathy disappears, her father finds the lewd photographs of his little princess in the attic. We know that they were hidden there by Carol Culver. But Adam, I am sure, did not realize that. He would have naturally assumed that Kathy had hidden them there. He would also have naturally assumed that the pictures were connected to his daughter's disappearance.'

'Logical,' Myron agreed.

'Yes, quite.' Win twirled his cognac, studying the color. 'Adam Culver then enlists the aid of Paul Duncan in his investigation. They track down the photographs' place of origin with the help of Fred Nickler. They also find out about Gary Grady. They continue their investigation, but nothing new develops. Paul wants to give up. Adam is desperate – so desperate that he tries to draw out the assailant in a most unorthodox manner.'

Win paused, considering. 'Here,' he said, 'is where it gets very interesting. We know Adam Culver had the photographs. We know he arranged to have them put in a pornographic magazine. I find it significant that the picture was placed only in *Nips* magazine.'

Myron leaned forward. They were on the same wavelength. 'The magazine with the smallest – almost nonexistent – circulation.'

'That fact disturbed you from the beginning,' Win said.

Myron nodded. 'Someone didn't want that magazine seen by a lot of people.'

'Like her father.'

'Right.'

'And,' Win continued, 'we know that Adam Culver liked to frequent the casinos of Atlantic City. He might have met your friend Blackjack during one of his visits or at least heard his name. He could have hired someone else to forge his daughter's handwriting. He probably had a tape with her voice from an old answering machine. Ergo, Adam Culver set the whole thing up. He sent out the magazine to everyone who might have been involved in Kathy's disappearance. Her fiancé, for one. People in the picture, like Junior Horton.'

'Why did he send one to his wife?' Myron asked.

'I don't know.'

'And Dean Gordon?'

'Perhaps the dean was in one of those attic photographs. Or perhaps Adam found out about Kathy's visit to the dean's house that night. Most likely Adam was merely considering every possibility. But it's not really that relevant to the case. What is relevant, however, is the question of why Adam did not once again enlist the help of Paul Duncan.'

'Because,' Myron said, 'Adam found out that Paul was sleeping with his wife.'

Win nodded. 'Paul was no longer a friend or trustworthy. Adam was now on his own. He sent the package to Sir Blackjack, making sure it would never be traced back to him. Then Adam set up his second little sting operation, the one on his wife and Paul. He walked in on them, ran out, and was killed.'

'So who murdered him?' Myron said.

Win put down the snifter on a harpsichord from the seventeenth century. He steepled his fingers, bouncing them gently off one another. 'There are two strong possibilities,' he said. 'First, Paul Duncan. We cannot just dismiss him. He had motive and opportunity. Second, Adam wanted to stir up the killer, that much is clear. But perhaps the magazine stirred up more trouble than he'd anticipated.'

'Except for one thing,' Myron interjected. 'The magazines hadn't been sent out yet. Adam was dead two days before Blackjack mailed them.'

'So perhaps someone discovered what Adam was up to before they were mailed?'

'Otto Burke?'

Win shrugged.

'But Otto has no connection to Kathy Culver,' Myron said.

'None that we are aware of. Which leads us to Entity three: the unknowns. A major unknown, as I see it, is Nancy Serat. We can assume that she gave Adam Culver valuable information. But we do not know who killed her. Or what she meant when she told Christian it was time for sisters to reunite. And we especially do not know why Kathy Culver's hair was found on her dead body.'

Win rechecked his hair. Perfect. He smiled, winked, did everything but kiss his own reflection. 'We also have no explanation for Adam Culver's cabin in the woods. He could have become desperate enough to grab suspects and do his own interrogations. Or he could have been seeking retribution for all in the wicked photographs. On someone like Gary Grady. Or Junior Horton. But for some reason my mind cannot fully accept either of these rationales.'

Myron nodded. It didn't feel right to him either.

'And so now we've reached the final unknown. The most significant unknown of all: Miss Kathy Culver herself. Is she alive? Is she behind all this? Is she involved in any way at all?'

Win picked the snifter off the harpsichord. He took a sip of cognac, let it roll around his tongue, swallowed. 'The end.'

They both sat in silence. Myron churned the facts through his head yet again. None of them changed. Win studied his face.

'This was all a mental exercise,' Win said. 'A test drive, as it were.'

Myron said nothing.

'You know what happened. You knew before I said a word.'

Myron handed Win the telephone. 'Cancel your date. We have a lot of work to do.'

47

The memorial service.

Myron slipped in late and ducked behind a pillar. He was in desperate need of a shower, a shave, a nap. And he looked it.

He spotted Jessica in the front pew. She sat on one side of her mother, Edward on the other. All three were crying.

The priest delivered the standard death spiel like an actor who knew his lines too well. Nothing new or original was said. There was no coffin, no well-dressed corpse in peaceful repose. The priest seemed bothered by this, by the absence of his customary prop. He kept motioning down on cue, only to draw back when he realized that there was nothing in front of him.

Myron stayed out of sight. The church was crowded. Paul Duncan sat in the second row, directly behind Carol. Every once in a while Paul would put his hand on her shoulder, but he'd never leave it there for long. Appearances. Christian was next to him, head lowered in prayer. Otto Burke and Larry Hanson were a few rows back. Good PR move. The press would undoubtedly be made aware of Otto Burke's heartfelt concern for his players' personal plights. Again, appearances.

Win was near the back. To his right sat Sally Li. Her face looked drawn, as if she could use a cigarette. Myron had spoken to her late last night. She had done the test. It had come out as he'd suspected.

Dean Gordon and his wife Madelaine were off to the left. Dean Gordon looked grim. Madelaine Gordon looked good in black. Myron recognized a few other faces in the crowd, but he couldn't put a name or place to any of them. It didn't matter.

The priest made a few last comments about the hereafter, God's will, and reuniting with the beloved in Heaven. Jessica's sob racked her whole body. No one put an arm around her. No one comforted her. She looked small and frail. Myron felt a lump rise in his throat.

Here we go.

When the ceremony ended, Myron did not hesitate. He walked purposively down the aisle. Jessica ran toward him without hesitation. They hugged, both closing their eyes. The mourners turned away and began to head for the exit. Win kept close to Otto Burke, Larry Hanson, and Dean Gordon.

Jessica finally released her grip. 'Where were you?' she asked.

Myron swallowed. He nodded to Paul Duncan, shook hands with Edward and Christian, lightly kissed Carol on the cheek.

'I don't know how to say this,' Myron said.

'What's the matter?'

He looked her straight in the eye. 'I found Kathy. She's alive.'

The group went silent.

Jessica opened her mouth, closed it.

'I'm meeting her tonight,' Myron said.

Jessica finally found her voice. 'I don't understand.'

'It's a long story. But she's alive. I'll bring her home to you tonight.'

Jessica looked at Carol. Carol looked back. Everyone looked at everyone else.

'I'll go with you,' Jessica said.

'You can't.'

'Like hell I can't.'

'I promised her,' Myron said. 'Just me. Alone. She's scared.'

'Of what?'

'Of the person who tried to kill her.'

'Who?'

Myron shook his head. 'She wouldn't tell me. Not on the phone.' He took hold of Jessica's hand. It was cold and stiff. Like marble. 'I'll bring her right to the house. I promise. We'll all talk then. But we can't risk scaring her off.'

Jessica shook her head. She looked lost. 'Where are you meeting her?'

'It's in the woods.'

'What woods?' Jessica pulled back a little. 'You're not making any sense.'

'I can't tell you, Jess. I promised her. Kathy said it's the spot where she was left for dead. She wants to show me where it happened.'

More silence.

Paul Duncan said, 'Dear God.'

Carol practically fainted into his arms.

'Where has she been?' Jessica asked.

'I only know bits and pieces from my investigation. She spent most of the time recovering from her injuries. She also spent some time in the Caribbean. An island called Curaçao. I picked up her trail from an entry that night in St Mary Hospital's registry. On the night she vanished, a patient was found unconscious in the middle of a road. She gave her name as Katherine Pierce.'

Carol gasped. 'Pierce? That's my maiden name.'

Myron nodded. 'I don't know all the details yet. She was hit over the head. The blow cracked her skull. The assailant thought she was dead. But

243

she wasn't. He buried her in the woods. She woke up and managed to dig herself out. It's a miracle she survived.'

Jessica's eyes filled with tears. 'She's alive?'

'Yes.'

'You're sure?'

'Yes.'

Jessica hugged her mother then. Edward joined in. Christian and Paul watched dumbfounded. Myron turned toward the door. Win was standing there. His nod was almost imperceptible.

48

Myron parked his car on the dirt road. He was alone. The car's clock read 8:30 P.M. He grabbed his flashlight and headed toward the meeting spot.

The brush was thick. Several branches whipped across his face. He listened for other sounds. Crickets hummed away. Nothing else. The flashlight sliced through the heavy darkness, carving a path for him to follow. Myron heard his feet crunch on twigs and leaves. His mouth felt bone-dry. It always felt that way at moments like this.

He was getting close now, no more than twenty or thirty yards away.

'Kathy?' he called out.

No answer.

'It's Myron, Kathy. I'm alone.'

No reply. But then Myron heard a shuffling from in front of him. Something came into view. A head. A head of long blond hair.

'It's okay,' Myron said gently. 'I'm here alone.'

She stepped toward him tentatively. Her right hand shaded her eyes from the flashlight's harsh glare. Myron pointed the beam away. 'It's all right,' he said.

She continued to move toward him, a dim silhouette. Her steps were slow, plodding, like a B-movie monster come to life.

'It's okay,' Myron said again. 'No one is going to hurt you.'

'I wish that were true.'

The voice had not come from her. It had come from behind him. Myron closed his eyes. His shoulders slumped. 'Hello, Christian.'

'Don't move, Mr Bolitar. Put your hands up.'

'Why bother?'

'What?'

'You're going to kill us. Just like you tried to kill Kathy. Just like you killed her father and Nancy.'

'I never meant to hurt anybody,' he said.

'But you did.'

Christian cocked the gun. 'Hands up. Now.'

Myron raised his hands slowly. 'Kathy opened up to you that night. She told you everything – every sordid detail of her past. She wanted to clean the slate.'

'She lied to me!' Christian shouted. 'All the time we were together – it was all a lie.'

'So you tried to kill her.'

'Kathy wanted me to still love her, Mr Bolitar. But don't you see? I never loved her. I loved a lie. She wanted me to stand beside that lie while she told her story to the world. She wanted me to sell out my teammates, toss away a chance at a national championship and Heisman trophy – all for the sake of a lying whore.'

'A lying whore,' Myron said, 'like your mother.'

He nodded. 'Mr Bolitar, tell her. Tell her what that game meant. In terms of money, fame, pride. You understand, Mr Bolitar. It helped get me that contract.'

'So you hit her over the head.'

'I didn't mean to. It just happened. I thought she was dead. I couldn't find a pulse.'

'So you drove her out here and buried the body. You hoped she'd never be found, but if she were, it'd be blamed on a serial killer.'

Christian stepped closer. He raised the gun. 'Enough talk,' he said. 'I'm not going to let you stall around until someone shows up.'

'No need. Someone's been here all the time.'

Win came out from behind a tree, no more than a yard away from Christian. He pressed the .44 against Christian's ear and said, 'Drop it, or your brain becomes squirrel lunch.'

Christian dropped the gun.

'It's over,' Myron shouted.

From a farther distance two uniformed police arrived. They handcuffed Christian.

Jake Courter stumbled behind them, high-stepping through the long grass. 'Too old for this shit,' he mumbled. When he reached the clearing he said, 'Nice setup, Bolitar.'

'Lots of details. The secret to a good scam.'

'Gonna tell me what's going on now?'

'Sure. Jess?'

Jessica took off the blond wig and stepped forward.

Christian's mouth dropped open. 'What the—'

'You killed Kathy,' Myron said, 'but not from the blow to the head. She suffocated trying to claw her way out of the dirt.'

Jake looked confused. 'Where's the body?'

'In the morgue. Where it's been since the police found it two months ago. Sally Li confirmed the identity last night.'

'So why hadn't it been identified before?'

'Because the county medical examiner was Kathy's father. He knew who it was right away, but he pretended otherwise.'

'Why?'

'Think about it a second, Jake. From Adam Culver's perspective. Your case had gone nowhere in eighteen months. Adam knew that. He also knew the body provided no new clues. So he figured that the only way to catch Kathy's killer was to draw him out. How? By making the killer think Kathy might still be alive. After all, she'd been alive when he dumped her in the woods. So Adam kept the corpse's identity a secret from everyone – the police, his friends, even his own family. He also figured that the nude photographs were tied into all this. So he used them.'

'You mean he put that ad in the magazine?'

Myron nodded. 'Adam Culver arranged everything. Even the mysterious phone calls saying "Come and get me. I survived." He did everything he could to make it look like Kathy was alive.'

Jake nodded. 'So what you guys were just doing—'

'Was finishing up Adam Culver's plan. Our performance at the church this morning sowed the final seeds of doubt.'

'You were forcing Christian to make a play for you.'

'Exactly.'

'Incredible. So everyone was in on this?'

'Jessica was,' Myron said. 'So were her mother and brother. It would have been too cruel to lie to them. But Paul Duncan didn't know. Neither did anybody else, and Win made sure that all the suspects – Otto, the dean, even Gary Grady – knew about Kathy's "survival."'

'Then you weren't sure it was Christian?'

'No, I was sure.'

'You were trying to play it fair.'

Myron nodded. 'That's why I didn't tell you anything. I wanted you to see what happened without any preconceived notions.'

'Fair enough,' Jake said. 'Go on.'

'Adam Culver understood that only the killer would know this spot. If he made the killer think Kathy could still be alive, he or she would have to come back here – just to make sure Kathy was dead. That was why Adam rented that cabin nearby. That was why he had all that electronic equipment. To tape him. To have proof.'

'Catching the killer returning to the scene of the crime,' Jake said.

'Right.'

'But I don't get something. Adam was killed before the magazine was mailed out. How did Christian find out about it?'

'He didn't. Remember, Adam was a pathologist. He wasn't an investigator. He overlooked a very important clue. At first anyway.'

'What clue?'

'Kathy's clothes.'

'What about them?'

'When Kathy's body was found, she was wearing a yellow sweater and a pair of gray sweat pants. Yet the sorority sisters said she was wearing blue when she left the house. The rapists said she was wearing blue. Dean Gordon said she was wearing blue. Ricky Lane said she was wearing blue. The sorority sisters were also positive that Kathy never returned to the house. So the question was: Where did the yellow sweater and gray sweat pants come from?'

Jake shrugged.

'It took Adam a while to realize the significance of the clothes. But when he did, he went to the most obvious source. Kathy's roommate.'

'Nancy Serat.'

'Right. But he didn't want to let on that Kathy's body had been found. So he asked Nancy where he could find her favorite yellow sweater, pretending to be a typical dad on some kind of nostalgic tour. But think about it. If Kathy didn't go back to her sorority house, where did she change clothes?'

Jake saw it now. 'At Christian's,' he said with a snap of the fingers. 'Kathy slept there all the time. She must have kept clothes there.'

'Right.'

'And Nancy and Christian were friends,' Jake said, picking up the thread. 'She'd see nothing wrong with telling Christian all about Adam's visit. Probably thought the whole thing was kinda cute.'

Myron turned toward Christian. 'You got scared when you heard Adam had been asking about the yellow sweater. You knew he was getting close. So you followed him that night. You heard him fight with his wife. You saw him storm out of the house, and you figured this was the ideal opportunity to kill him. Another perfect misdirection.'

Christian said nothing.

Jake said, 'What do you mean, "another perfect misdirection"?'

'When your investigation of Kathy's disappearance began,' Myron said, 'who did you focus in on?'

'Christian,' Jake said. 'Like I said, we always check out the boyfriend.'

'So what did Christian do? With campus security combing the campus for clues, he planted the panties on the top of a garbage bin.'

'The panties,' Jake added, 'with someone else's semen.'

'Proof he didn't do it.'

'Well, I'll be damned.'

'He also misdirected us with Nancy Serat. He strangled Nancy. Then he planted one of Kathy's hairs at the scene.'

'But where did he get the hair?'

'Kathy slept in his room all the time, right? She would have kept other stuff there besides her clothes. Stuff like a hairbrush.'

'Son of a bitch.'

'It was almost perfect. Blame someone who was dead. And if Kathy wasn't dead – if she had indeed survived – he'd make her look like a lunatic. Who'd believe the ravings of a girl who'd killed her old roommate? But Christian didn't count on Jessica showing up at Nancy's. He panicked. He hit her over the head and ran. Problem was, he'd left his fingerprints behind. But Christian was quick. He even used that to his advantage. When you dragged him in the next morning, he immediately admitted to being at Nancy's house. And then he came up with that wonderful story about sisters reuniting.'

'Another perfect misdirection,' Jake said.

'Except he forgot about the glass.'

'What glass?'

'His fingerprints were found in several spots in the house, including a drinking glass. Yet Christian told us Nancy barely let him in the door, that she practically pushed him away mumbling about the reuniting sisters. Under those circumstances, isn't it odd she'd offer him a drink?'

Myron looked at Christian. He lowered his eyes.

'I – I didn't mean to hurt any of them, Mr Bolitar,' he said.

'You were manipulative and calculating,' Myron said. 'You covered all the bases, even when you hired me. I was small-time. I could be controlled. You knew about my background, that I was an experienced investigator. You knew if any trouble arose, I'd keep things quiet. That I'd keep you informed. That I'd try to protect you. You played me for a sucker.'

Everyone remained silent until Jake said, 'All right. Get him out of here.'

The uniformed officers led Christian away.

Myron looked back at Jessica. She still hadn't said a word. Tears slid down her cheeks. None of this morning's tears had been for her father. Maybe some of these were.

Win shook his head. ' "Squirrel lunch." I can't believe I said "squirrel lunch." '

Jessica stopped crying. She even smiled a little. Myron put his arm around her and pulled her in close. Together they made their way back to the car.

49

Three days later Myron drove Jessica to the airport.

'Just drop me off at the terminal,' she said.

'I'll wait with you at the gate.'

'You should head back.'

'I have time.'

'The traffic will be murder.'

'I don't care.'

'Myron?'

'What?'

'Just drop me off. Please. You know I hate scenes.'

'I won't make a scene.'

'You always make a scene.'

Silence.

'What's going to happen to Gary Grady?' she asked.

'I've sent all the information to the school board and the local press. I don't know if he'll spend any time in jail, but he's finished.'

'What about Dean Gordon?'

'He's resigned this morning. He's going to enter the private sector.'

'And the rapists?'

'Cary Roland is the DA. This case means big headlines. He'll do his best. Ricky Lane is going to turn state evidence.'

'You dumped Ricky as a client?'

Myron nodded.

'And you lost Christian.'

Another nod.

'All in all,' she said, 'this case hasn't had a real positive economic effect on you.'

'I'm more worried about the personal effect.'

'Meaning?'

'Meaning you're back in my life.'

'Isn't that a good thing?'

'It is. Except you're leaving.'

'Just for a month or two. It's a book tour.'

He pulled up to the front of the terminal.

'I'll be back,' she said.

He nodded.

Jessica kissed him. He held on. She finally pushed him back. He released her grudgingly.

'I love you,' he said.

'I love you too.' She stepped out of the car. 'And I'll be back.'

He watched her walk toward the entrance. He watched her pass through the sliding glass doors, watched her walk to the ticket gate, watched her disappear down an escalator. When she was out of sight, he still watched until a security guard knocked on his window.

'Unloading zone, bub. Move it!'

Myron looked back one more time. Then he drove back to the office.

Drop Shot

For Anne and Charlotte,
from the luckiest man in the whole world

Acknowledgement

The author wishes to thank the following: my friends and college roommates James Bradbeer Jr and Lawrence Vitale; David Pepe of Pro Agents Inc.; Peter Roisman of Advantage International; my editor and friend Jacob Hoye; Natalie Ayars, MD; E. W. Count; the AOL Writers Club; and, of course, Dave Bolt.

1

'Cesar Romero,' Myron said.

Win looked at him. 'You're not serious.'

'I'm starting off with an easy one.'

On Stadium Court the players were changing sides. Myron's client, Duane Richwood, was shellacking the number-fifteen seed Ivan Something-okov, leading 5–0 in the third set after winning the first two sets 6–0, 6–2. An impressive US Open debut for the unseeded twenty-one-year-old upstart from the streets (literally) of New York.

'Cesar Romero,' Myron repeated. 'Unless you don't know.'

Win sighed. 'The Joker.'

'Frank Gorshin.'

'The Riddler.'

Ninety-second commercial break. Myron and Win were keeping themselves busy with a scintillating game of Name the *Batman* Criminal. The TV *Batman*. The *Batman* starring Adam West and Burt Ward and all those Pow, Bam, Slam balloons. The *real* Batman.

'Who played the second one?' Myron asked.

'The second Riddler?'

Myron nodded.

From across the court Duane Richwood flashed them a cocky smile. He sported garish aviator sunglasses with loud fluorescent green frames. The latest style from Ray•Ban. Duane was never without them. He had become not only identified by the shades but defined by them. Ray•Ban was rather pleased.

Myron and Win sat in one of the two players' boxes reserved for celebrities and players' entourages. For most matches every seat in the box was filled. When Agassi played the night before, the box had overflowed with his family, friends, suck-ups, young lasses, environmentally correct movie stars, hair weaves – like an Aerosmith backstage party. But Duane had only three people in the box: agent Myron, financial consultant Win, and Duane's coach, Henry Hobman. Wanda, the love of Duane's life, got too nervous and preferred to stay home.

'John Astin,' Win answered.

Myron nodded. 'How about Shelley Winters.'

'Ma Parker.'

'Milton Berle.'

'Louie the Lilac.'

'Liberace.'

'Chandell the Great.'

'And?'

Win looked puzzled. 'And what?'

'What other criminal did Liberace play?'

'What are you talking about? Liberace only appeared in that one episode.'

Myron leaned back and smiled. 'Are you sure?'

In his seat next to the umpire's chair Duane happily chugged down a bottle of Evian. He held the bottle so that the sponsor's name could be clearly seen by the television cameras. Smart kid. Knew how to please the sponsor. Myron had recently signed Duane to a simple deal with the natural water giant: during the US Open Duane drank Evian in marked bottles. In return Evian paid him ten grand. That was water rights. Myron was negotiating Duane's soda rights with Pepsi and his electrolyte rights with Gatorade.

Ah, tennis.

'Liberace only appeared in that one episode,' Win announced.

'Is that your final answer?'

'Yes. Liberace only appeared in that one episode.'

Henry Hobman continued to study the court, scrutinizing with intense concentration, his line of vision swinging back and forth. Too bad no one was playing.

'Henry, you want to take a guess?'

Henry ignored them. Nothing new there.

'Liberace only appeared in that one episode,' Win repeated, his nose in the air.

Myron made a soft buzzing sound. 'Sorry, that answer is incorrect. What do we have for our player, Don? Well, Myron, Windsor gets the home version of our game plus a year's supply of Turtle Wax. And thank you for playing our game!'

Win was unmoved. 'Liberace only appeared in that one episode.'

'That your new mantra?'

'Until you prove otherwise.'

Win – full name: Windsor Horne Lockwood III – steepled his manicured fingers. He did that a lot, steepling. Steepling fit him. Win looked like his name. The poster boy for the quintessential WASP. Everything about his appearance reeked arrogance, elitism, *Town and Country* Parties Page, debutantes dressed in monogrammed sweaters and pearls with names like Babs, dry martinis at the clubhouse, stuffy old money – his fine blond hair, his pretty-boy patrician face, his lily-white complexion, his snotty Exeter accent. Except in Win's case some sort of chromosomal abnormality had slipped through the generations of careful breeding. In some ways Win was exactly what he appeared to be. But in many more ways – sometimes very frightening ways – Win was not.

'I'm waiting,' Win said.

'You remember Liberace playing Chandell the Great?' Myron asked.

'Of course.'

'But you forgot that Liberace also played Chandell's evil twin brother, Harry. In the same episode.'

Win made a face. 'You cannot be serious.'

'What?'

'That doesn't count. Evil twin brothers.'

'Where in the rule book does it say that?'

Win set his jutting jaw in that certain way.

The humidity was thick enough to wear as undergarments, especially in Flushing Meadows's windless stadium court. The stadium, named strangely enough for Louis Armstrong, was basically a giant billboard that also happened to have a tennis court in the middle. IBM had a sign above the speedometer that clocked the velocity of each player's serve. Citizen kept both the real time and how long the match had been going on. Visa had its name printed behind the service line. Reebok, Infiniti, Fuji Film, Clairol had their names plastered wherever there was a free spot. So did Heineken.

Heineken, the official beer of the US Open.

The crowd was a complete mix. Down low – in the good seats – people had money. But anything went in the dress department. Some wore full suits and ties (like Win), some wore more casual Banana Republic-type clothes (like Myron), some wore jeans, some wore shorts. But Myron's personal favorite were the fans who came in full tennis gear – shirt, shorts, socks, tennis shoes, warm-up jacket, sweatbands, and tennis racket. Tennis racket. Like they might get called on to play. Like Sampras or Steffi or someone might suddenly point into the stands and say, 'Hey, you with the racket. I need a doubles partner.'

Win's turn. 'Roddy McDowall,' he began.

'The Bookworm.'

'Vincent Price.'

'Egghead.'

'Joan Collins.'

Myron hesitated. 'Joan Collins? As in *Dynasty*?'

'I refuse to offer hints.'

Myron ran episodes through his mind. On the court the umpire announced, 'Time.' The ninety-second commercial break was over. The players rose. Myron couldn't swear to it, but he thought he saw Henry blink.

'Give up?' Win asked.

'Shhh. They're about to play.'

'And you call yourself a *Batman* fan.'

The players took the court. They too were billboards, only smaller. Duane wore Nike sneakers and clothes. He used a Head tennis racket. Logos for McDonald's and Sony adorned his sleeves. His opponent wore Reebok. His logos features Sharp electronics and Bic. Bic. The pen and razor company. Like someone was going to watch a tennis match, see the logo, and buy a pen.

Myron leaned toward Win. 'Okay, I give,' he whispered. 'What criminal did Joan Collins play?'

Win shrugged. 'I don't remember.'

'What?'

'I know she was in an episode. But I don't remember her character's name.'

'You can't do that.'

Win smiled with perfect white teeth. 'Where in the rule book does it say that?'

'You have to know the answer.'

'Why?' Win countered. 'Does Pat Sajak have to know every puzzle on *Wheel of Fortune*? Does Alex Trebeck have to know every question on *Jeopardy!*'

Pause. 'Nice analogy, Win. Really.'

'Thank you.'

Then another voice said, 'The Siren.'

Myron and Win looked around. It seemed to have come from Henry.

'Did you say something?'

Henry's mouth did not appear to be moving. 'The Siren,' he repeated, his eyes still pasted to the court. 'Joan Collins played the Siren. On *Batman.*'

Myron and Win exchanged a glance.

'Nobody likes a know-it-all, Henry.'

Henry's mouth might have moved. Might have been a smile.

On the court Duane opened the game with an ace that nearly bore a hole through a ball boy. The IBM speedometer clocked it at 128 mph. Myron shook his head in disbelief. So did Ivan what's-his-name. Duane was lining up for the second point when Myron's cellular phone rang.

Myron quickly picked it up. He was not the only person in the stands who was talking on a cellular phone. He was, however, the only one in a front row. Myron was about to disconnect the power when he realized it might be Jessica. Jessica. Just the thought quickened his pulse a little.

'Hello.'

'It's not Jessica.' It was Esperanza, his associate.

'I didn't think it was.'

'Right,' she said. 'You always sound like a whimpering puppy when you answer the phone.'

Myron gripped the receiver. The match continued without interruption, but sour faces spun to seek out the origin of the offending ring. 'What do you want?' he whispered. 'I'm in the stadium.'

'I know. But you look like a pretentious asshole. Talking on a cellular phone at the match.'

Now that she mentioned it . . .

The sour faces were glaring daggers now. In their eyes Myron had committed an unpardonable sin. Like molesting a child. Or using the salad fork on the entree. 'What do you want?'

'They're showing you on TV right now. Jesus, it's true.'

'What?'

'The TV does make you look heavier.'

'What do you want?'

'Nothing much. I thought you might want to know I got you a meeting with Eddie Crane.'

'You're kidding.' Eddie Crane, one of the hottest tennis juniors in the country. He was seeing only the big-four agencies. ICM, TruPro, Advantage International, ProServ.

'No joke. Meet him and his parents by court sixteen after Duane's match.'

'I love you, you know.'

'Then pay me more,' she said.

Duane hit a cross-court forehand winner. Thirty-love.

'Anything else?' Myron asked.

'Nothing important. Valerie Simpson. She's called three times.'

'What did she want?'

'She wouldn't say. But the Ice Queen sounded ruffled.'

'Don't call her that.'

'Yeah, whatever.'

Myron hung up. Win looked at him. 'Problem?'

Valerie Simpson. A weird, albeit sad case. The former tennis wunderkind had visited Myron's office two days ago looking for someone – anyone – to represent her. 'Don't think so.'

Duane was up forty-love. Triple match point. Bud Collins, tennis columnist extraordinaire, was already waiting in the gangway for the postmatch interview. Bud's pants, always a Technicolor fashion risk, were particularly hideous today.

Duane took two balls from the ball boy and approached the line. Duane was a rare commodity in tennis. A black man. Not from India or Africa or even France. Duane was from New York City. Unlike just about every other player on the tour, Duane had not spent his life preparing for this moment. He hadn't been pushed by ambitious, carpooling parents. He hadn't worked with the world's top coaches in Florida or California since he was old enough to hold a racket. Duane was on the opposite end of the spectrum: a street kid who had run away at age fifteen and somehow survived on his own. He had learned tennis from the public courts, hanging around all day and challenging anyone who could hold a racket.

He was on the verge of winning his first Grand Slam match when the gunshot sounded.

The sound had been muffled, coming from outside the stadium. Most people did not panic, assuming the sound had come from a firecracker or car backfire. But Myron and Win had heard the sound too often. They were up and moving before the screams. Inside the stadium the crowd began to mumble. More screams ensued. Loud, hysterical screams. The court umpire in his infinite wisdom impatiently shouted 'Quiet, please!' into his microphone.

Myron and Win sprinted up the metallic stairway. They leaped over the white chain, put out by the ushers so that no one could enter or leave the court until the players switched sides, and ran outside. A small crowd was beginning to gather in what was generously dubbed the 'Food Court.' With a lot of work and patience the Food Court hoped to one day reach the gastronomic levels of, say, its mall brethren.

They pushed through the crowd. Some people were indeed hysterical but others hadn't moved at all. This was, after all, New York. The lines for refreshments were long. No one wanted to lose their place.

The girl was lying facedown in front of a stand serving Moët champagne at $7.50 a glass. Myron recognized her immediately, even before he bent down and turned her over. But when he saw her face, when he saw the icy blue eyes stare back at him in a final, unbreakable death gaze, his heart plummeted. He looked back at Win. Win, as usual, had no expression on his face.

'So much,' Win said, 'for her comeback.'

2

'Maybe you should just let it go,' Win said.

He whipped his Jaguar XJR onto the FDR Drive and headed south. The radio was tuned to WMXV, 105.1 FM. They played something called 'Soft Rock.' Michael Bolton was on. He was doing a remake of an old Four Tops classic. Painful. Like Bea Arthur doing a remake of a Marilyn Monroe film.

Maybe Soft Rock meant Really Bad Rock.

'Mind if I put on a cassette?' Myron said.

'Please.'

Win swerved into a lane change. Win's driving could most kindly be described as creative. Myron tried not to look. He pushed in a cassette from the original production of *How to Succeed in Business Without Really Trying*. Like Myron, Win had a huge collection of old Broadway musicals. Robert Morse sang about a girl named Rosemary. But Myron's mind remained fixed on a girl named Valerie Simpson.

Valerie was dead. One bullet to the chest. Someone had shot her in the Food Court of the United States Tennis Association National Tennis Center during the opening round of America's sole Grand Slam event. Yet no one had seen a thing. Or at least no one was talking.

'You're making that face,' Win said.

'What face?'

'The I-want-to-help-the-world face,' Win said. 'She wasn't a client.'

'She was going to be.'

'A large distinction. Her fate does not concern you.'

'She called me three times today,' Myron said. 'When she couldn't reach me, she showed up at the tennis center. And then she was gunned down.'

'A sad tale,' Win said. 'But one that does not concern you.'

The speedometer hovered about eighty. 'Uh, Win?'

'Yes.'

'The left side of the road. It's for oncoming traffic.'

Win spun the wheel, cut across two lanes, and swerved onto a ramp. Minutes later the Jag veered into the Kinney lot on Fifty-second Street. They gave the keys to Mario, the parking attendant. Manhattan was hot. City hot. The sidewalk scorched your feet right through your shoes. Exhaust fumes got stuck in the humidity, hanging in the air like fruit on a tree. Breathing was a chore. Sweating was not. The secret was to keep the sweat to a minimum while walking, hoping that the air conditioning would dry off your clothes without giving you pneumonia.

Myron and Win walked south down Park Avenue toward the high-rise of Lock-Horne Investments & Securities. Win's family owned the building. The elevator stopped on the twelfth floor. Myron stepped out. Win stayed inside. His office at Lock-Horne was two floors up.

Before the elevator closed Win said, 'I knew her.'

'Who?'

'Valerie Simpson. I sent her to you.'

'Why didn't you say anything?'

'No reason to.'

'Were you close?'

'Depends on your definition. She's old money Philadelphia. Like my family. We were members of the same clubs, the same charities, that sort of thing. Our families occasionally summered together when we were kids. But I hadn't heard from her in years.'

'She just called you out of the blue?' Myron asked.

'You could say that.'

'What would you say?'

'Is this an interrogation?'

'No. Do you have any thoughts on who killed her?'

Win stood perfectly still. 'We'll chat later,' he said. 'I have some business matters I must attend to first.'

The elevator door slid closed. Myron waited for a moment, as though expecting the elevator to open again. Then he crossed the corridor and opened a door that read MB SportsReps Inc.

Esperanza looked up from her desk. 'Jesus, you look like hell.'

'You heard about Valerie?'

She nodded. If she felt guilty about calling her the Ice Queen moments before the murder, she didn't show it. 'You have blood on your jacket.'

'I know.'

'Ned Tunwell from Nike is in the conference room.'

'I guess I'll see him,' Myron said. 'No use moping around.'

Esperanza looked at him. No expression.

'Don't get so upset,' he continued. 'I'm okay.'

'I'm putting on a brave front,' she said.

Ms Compassion.

When Myron opened the conference room door, Ned Tunwell charged like a happy puppy. He smiled brightly, shook hands, slapped Myron on the back. Myron half expected him to jump in his lap and lick his face.

Ned Tunwell looked to be in his early thirties, around Myron's age. His entire persona was always upbeat, like a Hare Krishna on speed – or worse,

266

a *Family Feud* contestant. He wore a blue blazer, white shirt, khaki pants, loud tie, and of course, Nike tennis shoes. The new Duane Richwood line. His hair was yellow-blond and he had one of those milk-stain mustaches.

Ned finally calmed down enough to hold up a videotape. 'Wait till you see this!' he raved. 'Myron, you are going to love it. It's fantastic.'

'Let's take a look.'

'I'm telling you, Myron, it's fantastic. Just fantastic. Incredible. It came out better than I ever thought. Blows away the stuff we did with Courier and Agassi. You're gonna love it. It's fantastic. Fantastic, I tell you.'

The key word here: *fantastic.*

Tunwell flipped the television on and put the tape in the VCR. Myron sat down and tried to push away the image of Valerie Simpson's corpse. He needed to concentrate. This – Duane's first national television commercial – was crucial. Truth was, an athlete's image was made more by these commercials than anything else – including how well he played or how he was portrayed by the media. Athletes became defined by the commercials. Everyone knew Michael Jordan as Air Jordan. Most fans couldn't tell you Larry Johnson played for the Charlotte Hornets, but they knew all about his Grandmama character. The right campaign made you. The wrong one could destroy you.

'When is it going to air?' Myron asked.

'During the quarter finals. We're gonna blitz the networks in a very big way.'

The tape finished rewinding. Duane was on the verge of becoming one of the most highly paid tennis players in the world. Not from winning matches, though that would help. But from endorsements. In most sports, the big-name athletes made more money from sponsors than from their teams. In the case of tennis, a lot more. A hell of a lot more. The top ten players made maybe fifteen percent of the money from winning matches. The bulk was from endorsements, exhibition matches, and guarantees – money paid big names to show up at a given tournament no matter how they fared.

Tennis needed new blood, and Duane Richwood was the most exhilarating transfusion to come along in years. Courier and Sampras were about as exciting as dry dog food. The Swedish players were always a snooze-a-thon. Agassi's act was growing wearisome. McEnroe and Connors were history.

So enter Duane Richwood. Colorful, funny, slightly controversial, but not yet hated. He was black and he was from the streets, but he was perceived as 'safe' street, 'safe' black, the kind of guy even racists could get behind to show they are not really racists.

'Just check this baby out, Myron. This spot, I'm telling you, it's . . . it's just . . .' Tunwell looked up, as though searching for the word.

'Fantastic?' Myron tried.

Ned snapped his fingers and pointed. 'Just wait till you see. I get hard watching it. Shit, I get hard just *thinking* about it. Swear to Christ, it's that good.'

He pressed the PLAY button.

Two days ago Valerie Simpson had sat in this very room, coming in on the heels of his meeting with Duane Richwood. The contrast was striking. Both were in their twenties, but while one career was just blossoming, the other had already dried up and blown away. Twenty-four years old and Valerie had long been labeled a 'has been' or 'never-was.' Her behavior had been cold and arrogant (ergo Esperanza's Ice Queen comment), or perhaps she'd just been distant and distracted. Hard to know for sure. And yes, Valerie had been young, but she had not exactly been – to quote a cliché – full of life. Eerie to say it now, but her eyes seemed to have more life in death – more animated while frozen and staring – than when she'd sat across from him in this very room.

Why, Myron wondered, would someone want to kill Valerie Simpson? Why had she tried so desperately to reach him? Why had she gone to the tennis center? To check out the competition? Or to find Myron?

'Watch this, Myron,' Tunwell repeated yet again. 'It's so fantastic, I came. Really, swear to God. Right in my pants.'

'Sorry I missed that,' Myron said.

Ned whooped with pleasure.

The commercial finally began. Duane appeared, wearing his sunglasses, dashing back and forth on a tennis court. Lots of quick cuts, especially to his sneakers. Lots of bright colors. Pounding beat, mixed in with the sound of tennis balls being blasted across the net. Very MTV-like. Could have been a rock video. Then Duane's voice came on.

'Come to my court . . .'

A few more hard ground strokes, a few more quick cuts. Then everything suddenly stopped. Duane vanished. The color faded to black and white. Silence. Scene change. A stern-looking judge glared down from his bench. Duane's voice returned:

'. . . and stay away from his court.'

The rock music started up again. The color returned. The screen cut back to Duane hitting the ball, smiling through his sweat, his sunglasses reflecting the light. A Nike symbol appeared with the words COME TO DUANE'S COURT below them.

Fade to black.

Ned Tunwell groaned – actually groaned – in satisfaction.

'You want a cigarette?' Myron asked.

Tunwell's smile doubled in wattage. 'What did I tell you, Myron? Huh? Fantastic or what?'

Myron nodded. It was good. Very good. Hip, well-made, responsible message but not too preachy. 'I like it,' he said.

'I told you. Didn't I tell you? I'm hard again. Swear to God, that's how much I like it. I might just come again. Right here, right now. As we speak.'

'Good to know.'

Tunwell broke into a seizurelike fit of laughter. He slapped Myron's shoulder.

'Ned?'

Tunwell's laughter faded away like the end of a song. He wiped his eyes. 'You kill me, Myron. I can't stop laughing. You really kill me.'

'Yeah, I'm a scream. Did you hear about Valerie Simpson's murder?'

'Sure. It was on the radio. I used to work with her, you know.' He was still smiling, his eyes wide and bright.

'She was with Nike?' Myron asked.

'Yep. And let me tell you, she cost us a bundle. I mean, Valerie seemed like a sure thing. She was only sixteen years old when we signed her and she'd already reached the finals of the French Open. Plus she was good-looking, all-American, the works. And she was already developed, if you know what I mean. She wasn't a cute little kid who might turn into a beast when she got a little older. Like Capriatti. Valerie was a babe.'

'So what happened?'

Ned Tunwell shrugged. 'She had a breakdown. Shit, it was in all the papers.'

'What caused it?'

'Hell if I know. Lot of rumors.'

'Like?'

He opened his mouth, then closed it. 'I forget.'

'You forget?'

'Look, Myron, most people thought it was just too much, you know? All that pressure. Valerie couldn't hack it. Most of these kids can't. They get it all, you know, reach such big heights and then poof, it's gone. You can't imagine what it's like to lose everything like . . . uh . . .' Ned stammered to a stop. Then he lowered his head. 'Ah, shit.'

Myron remained silent.

'I can't believe I said that, Myron. To you of all people.'

'Forget it.'

'No. I mean, look, I can pretend I didn't just put my foot in my mouth like that, but . . .'

Myron waved him off. 'A knee injury isn't a mental breakdown, Ned.'

'Yeah, I know but still . . .' He stopped again. 'When the Celts drafted you, were you a Nike guy?'

'No. Converse.'

'They dump you? I mean, right away?'

'I have no complaints.'

Esperanza opened the door without knocking. Nothing new there. She

269

never knocked. Ned Tunwell's smile quickly returned. Hard to keep the man down. He stared at Esperanza. Appreciatively. Most men did.

'Can I see you for a second, Myron?'

Ned waved. 'Hi, Esperanza.'

She turned and looked right through him. One of her many talents.

Myron excused himself and followed her out. Esperanza's desk was bare except for two photographs. One was of her dog, an adorable shaggy pooch named Chloe, winning a dog show. Esperanza was into dog shows – a sport not exactly dominated by inner-city Latinos, though she seemed to do pretty well. The desk's other picture showed Esperanza wrestling another woman. Professionally wrestling, that is. The lovely and lithe Esperanza had once wrestled professionally under the name Little Pocahontas, the Indian Princess. For three years Little Pocahontas had been a crowd favorite of the Fabulous Ladies of Wrestling organization, popularly known as FLOW (someone had once suggested calling it the Beautiful Ladies of Wrestling, but the acronym was a problem for the networks). Esperanza's Little Pocahontas was a scantily clad (basically a suede bikini) sexpot whom fans cheered and leered at as she bravely took on enormous evil, cheating nemeses every week. A morality play, some called it. A classic reenactment of Good vs Evil. But to Myron the weekly action was more like those women-in-prison films. Esperanza played the beautiful, naïve prisoner stuck in cell block C. Her opponent was Olga, the sadistic prison matron.

'It's Duane,' Esperanza said.

Myron took the call at her desk. 'Hey, Duane. What's up?'

His voice came fast. 'Get over here, man. Like now.'

'What's the matter?'

'The cops are in my face. They're asking me all kinds of shit.'

'About what?'

'That girl who got shot today. They think I got something to do with it.'

3

'Let me speak to the police officer,' Myron told Duane.

Another voice came on the line. 'This is homicide detective Roland Dimonte,' the voice barked with pure cop impatience. 'Who the hell is this?'

'I'm Myron Bolitar. Mr Richwood's attorney.'

'Attorney, huh? I thought you were his agent.'

'I'm both,' Myron said.

'That a fact?'

'Yes.'

'You got a law degree?'

'It's hanging on my wall. But I can bring it if you'd like.'

Dimonte made a noise. Might have been a snicker. 'Ex-jock. Ex-fed. And now you tell me you're a goddamn lawyer?'

'I'm what you might call a Renaissance man,' Myron said.

'Yeah? Tell me, Bolitar, what law school would let in someone like you?'

'Harvard,' Myron said.

'Whoa, aren't we a big shot.'

'You asked.'

'Well, you got half an hour to get here. Then I drag your boy to the precinct. Got me?'

'I've really enjoyed this little chat, Rolly.'

'You got twenty-nine minutes. And don't call me Rolly.'

'I don't want my client questioned until I'm present. Understood?'

Roland Dimonte didn't answer.

'Understood?' Myron repeated.

Pause. Then: 'Must be a bad connection, Bolitar.' Dimonte hung up.

Pleasant guy.

Myron handed the phone back to Esperanza. 'Mind getting rid of Ned for me?'

'Done.'

Myron took the elevator to the ground floor and sprinted toward the Kinney lot. Someone shouted, 'Go, O.J.!' at him. In New York everyone's a comedian. Mario tossed Myron the keys without glancing up from his newspaper.

Myron's car was parked on the ground floor. Unlike Win, Myron was not what one would label a 'car guy.' A car was a mode of transportation, nothing more. Myron drove a Ford Taurus. A blue Ford Taurus. When he cruised down the street, chicks did not exactly swarm.

He'd driven about twenty blocks when he spotted a powder-blue Cadillac with a canary-yellow roof. Something about it bothered Myron. The color maybe. Powder blue with a yellow roof? In Manhattan? A retirement community in Boca Raton, okay, driven by some guy named Sid who always had his left blinker on. Myron could see that. But not in Manhattan. And more to the point, Myron remembered sprinting past the exact same car on his way to the garage.

Was he being followed?

A possibility, though not a great one. This was mid-town Manhattan and Myron was heading straight down Seventh Avenue. About a million other cars were doing the same. Could be nothing. Probably was. Myron made a quick mental note and proceeded.

Duane had recently rented a place on the corner of Twelfth Street and Sixth Avenue. The John Adams Building, on the fringe of Greenwich Village. Myron illegally parked in front of a Chinese restaurant on Sixth, got passed through by the doorman, and took the elevator to Apartment 7G.

A man who had to be Detective Roland Dimonte answered the door. He was dressed in jeans, paisley green shirt, black leather vest. He also had on the ugliest pair of snakeskin boots – snow-white with flecks of purple – Myron had ever seen. His hair was greasy. Several strands were matted to his forehead like to flypaper. A toothpick – an actual toothpick – was jutting out of his mouth. His eyes were set deep in a pudgy face, like someone had stuck two brown pebbles in at the last minute.

Myron smiled. 'Hi, Rolly.'

'Let's get one thing straight, Bolitar. I know all about you. I know all about your glory days with the feds. I know all about how you like to play cop now. But I don't give a shit about none of that. Nor do I give a shit that your client is a public figure. I gotta job to do. You hear what I'm saying?'

Myron put his hand to his ear. 'Must be a bad connection.'

Roland Dimonte crossed his arms and gave Myron his most withering glare. The snakeskin boots had a high platform of some sort, pushing his height over six foot, but Myron still had a good three or four inches on him. A minute passed. Roland still glared. Then another minute. Roland gnawed on the toothpick. The glare persisted without a blink.

'On the inside,' Myron said, 'I'm quaking in fear.'

'Go fuck yourself, Bolitar.'

'Chewing the toothpick is a nice touch. A little cliché perhaps, but it works for you.'

'Just keep it up, smart-ass.'

'Mind if I come in,' Myron said, ' before I wet my pants?'

Dimonte moved out of the way. Slowly. The death glare was still locked on autopilot.

Myron found Duane sitting on the couch. He was wearing his Ray•Bans, but that was not surprising. He stroked his closely cropped beard with his left hand. Wanda, Duane's girlfriend, stood by the kitchen. She was tall, five-ten or so. Her figure was what was commonly referred to as tight or hard rather than muscular, and she was a stunner. Her eyes kept darting about like birds moving from branch to branch.

It was not a huge apartment. The decor was standard New York rental. Duane and Wanda had moved in only a few weeks ago. Month-to-month lease. No reason to fix the place up. With the money Duane was about to start making they could live anywhere they wanted to soon.

'Did you say anything to them?' Myron asked.

Duane shook his head. 'Not yet.'

'Want to tell me what's going on?'

Duane shook his head again. 'I don't know.'

There was another cop in the room. A younger guy. Much younger. He looked to be about twelve. Probably just made detective. He had his pad out, his pen at the ready.

Myron turned to Roland Dimonte. Dimonte had his hands on his hips, emanating self-importance from every pore. 'What's this all about?' Myron asked.

'We just want to ask your client a few questions.'

'About what?'

'The murder of Valerie Simpson.'

Myron looked over at Duane. 'I don't know nothing,' Duane said.

Dimonte sat down, making a big production out of it. King Lear. 'Then you won't mind answering a few questions?'

Duane said, 'No.' But he didn't sound very confident about it.

'Where were you when the shooting occurred?'

Duane glanced at Myron. Myron nodded. 'I was on Stadium Court.'

'What were you doing?'

'Playing tennis.'

'Who was your opponent?'

Myron nodded. 'You're good, Rolly.'

'Shut the fuck up, Bolitar.'

Duane said, 'Ivan Restovich.'

'Did the match continue after the shooting?'

'Yeah. It was match point anyway.'

'Did you hear the gunshot?'

'Yeah.'

'What did you do?'

'Do?'

'When you heard the shot?'

Duane shrugged. 'Nothing. I just stood there until the umpire told us to keep playing.'

'You never left the court?'

'No.'

The young cop kept scribbling, never looking up.

'Then what did you do?' Dimonte asked.

'When?'

'After the match.'

'I had an interview.'

'Who interviewed you?'

'Bud Collins and Tim Mayotte.'

The young cop looked up for a moment, confused.

'Mayotte,' Myron said. 'M-A-Y-O-T-T-E.'

He nodded and resumed his scribbling.

'What did you talk about?' Roland asked him.

'Huh?'

'During the interview. What did they ask you about?'

Dimonte shot a challenging glare at Myron. Myron responded with his warmest nod and a pilotlike thumbs up.

'I'm not going to tell you again, Bolitar. Cut the shit.'

'Just admiring your technique.'

'You'll admire it from a jail cell in a minute.'

'Gasp!'

Another death glare from Roland Dimonte before he turned back to Duane. 'Do you know Valerie Simpson?'

'Personally?'

'Yes.'

Duane shook his head. 'No.'

'But you've met?'

'No.'

'You don't know her at all?'

'That's right.'

'You've never had any contact with her?'

'Never.'

Roland Dimonte crossed his legs, resting his boot on his knee. His fingers caressed – actually caressed – the white-and-purple snakeskin. Like it was a pet dog. 'How about you, miss?'

Wanda seemed startled. 'Pardon me?'

'Have you ever met Valerie Simpson?'

'No.' Her voice was barely audible.

Dimonte turned back to Duane. 'Had you ever heard of Valerie Simpson before today?'

Myron rolled his eyes. But for once he kept his mouth shut. He didn't want to push it too far. Dimonte was not as dumb as he appeared. No one was. He was trying to lull Duane before the big whammy. Myron's job was to disrupt his rhythm with a few choice interruptions. But not too many.

Myron Bolitar, darling of the tightrope.

Duane said with a shrug, 'Yeah, I heard of her.'

'In what capacity?'

'She used to be on the circuit. Couple years back, I think.'

'The tennis circuit?'

'No, the nightclub circuit,' Myron interjected. 'She used to open for Anthony Newley in Vegas.'

So much for Mr Restraint.

The glare was back. 'Bolitar, you're really starting to piss me off.'

'Are you going to get to the point already?'

'I take my time with interrogations. I don't like to rush.'

'Should do the same,' Myron said, 'when purchasing footwear.'

Dimonte's face reddened. Still glaring at Myron, he said, 'Mr Richwood, how long have you been on the circuit?'

'Six months.'

'And in those six months you never saw Valerie Simpson?'

'That's right.'

'Fine. Now let me see if I got this right: You were playing a match when the gun went off. You finished the match. You shook hands with your opponent. I assume you shook hands with your opponent?'

Duane nodded.

'Then you did an interview.'

'Right.'

'Did you shower before or after the interview?'

Myron held up his hands. 'Okay, that's enough.'

'You got a problem, Bolitar?'

'Yeah. Your questions are beyond idiotic. I'm now advising my client to stop answering them.'

'Why? Your client got something to hide?'

'Yeah, Rolly, you're too clever for us. Duane killed her. Several million people were watching him on national television during the shooting. Several thousand more were watching him in person. But that wasn't him playing. It was really his identical twin, lost since birth. You're just too smart for us, Rolly. We confess.'

'I haven't ruled that out,' Dimonte countered.

'Haven't ruled what out?'

'That "we" stuff. Maybe you had something to do with it. You and that psycho-yuppie friend of yours.'

He meant Win. Lots of cops knew Win. None liked him. The feeling was mutual.

'We were in the stadium at the time of the shooting,' Myron said. 'A dozen witnesses will back that up. And if you really knew anything about Win, you'd know he'd never use a weapon that close up.'

That made Dimonte hesitate. He nodded. Agreeing, for once.

'Are you through with Mr Richwood?' Myron asked.

Dimonte suddenly smiled. It was a happy, expectant smile, like a school kid sitting by the radio on a snow day. Myron didn't like the smile.

'If you'll just humor me for another moment,' he said with syrupy phoniness. He rose and moved toward his partner, the Pad. The Pad kept scribbling.

'Your client claims he didn't know Valerie Simpson.'

'So?'

The Pad finally looked up. His eyes were as vacant as a court stenographer's. Dimonte nodded at him. The Pad handed him a small leather book encased in plastic.

'This is Valerie's calendar book,' Dimonte said. 'The last entry was made yesterday.' His smile widened. His head was held high. His chest puffed out like a rooster about to get laid.

'Okay, poker face,' Myron said. 'What's it say?'

He handed Myron a photocopy. Yesterday's entry was fairly simple. Sprawled across the entire page it read:

D.R. 555-8705 Call!

555-8705. Duane's phone number. D.R. Duane Richwood.

Dimonte appeared gleeful.

'I'd like to talk to my client,' Myron said. 'Alone.'

'No.'

'Excuse me?'

'You're not going to duck away now that I have you on the ropes.'

'I'm his attorney—'

'I don't give a rat's ass if you're the Chief Justice of the Supreme Court. You take him away, I take him downtown in cuffs.'

'You don't have anything,' Myron said. 'His phone number is in her book. Means nothing.'

Dimonte nodded. 'But how would it look? To the press, for example. Or the fans. Duane Richwood, tennis's newest hero, being dragged into the station with handcuffs on. Bet that would be hard to explain to the sponsors.'

'Are you threatening us?'

Dimonte put his hand to his chest. 'Heavens no. Would I do something like that, Krinsky?'

The Pad did not look up. 'Nope.'

'There. You see?'

'I'll sue your ass for wrongful arrest,' Myron said.

'And you might even win, Bolitar. Years from now, when the courts actually hear the case. Lot of good that's going to do you.'

Dimonte looked a lot less stupid now.

Duane quickly stood and crossed the room. He snapped off the Ray•Bans, then, thinking better of it, put them back on. 'Look, man, I don't know why my number is in her book. I don't know her. I never spoke to her on the phone.'

'Your phone is unlisted. Is that correct, Mr Richwood?'

'Yeah.'

'And you just moved in. Your phone's only been hooked up, what, two weeks?'

Wanda said, 'Three.' She was hugging herself now, as though she were cold.

'Three,' Roland Dimonte repeated. 'So how did Valerie get your number, Duane? How come some woman you don't know has your brand-new, unlisted number in her date book?'

'I don't know.'

Roland skipped skeptical and moved directly to absolute disbelief. For the next hour he continued to hammer Duane, but Duane stuck to his story. He never met her, he said. He didn't know her. He never spoke to her. He had no idea how she could have gotten his phone number. Myron watched in silence. The sunglasses made it harder to read Duane, but his body language was all wrong. So was Wanda's.

With an angry sigh Roland Dimonte finally stood up. 'Krinsky?'

The Pad looked up.

'Let's get the hell out of here.'

The Pad closed the pad, joined his partner.

'I'll be back,' Dimonte barked. Then pointing at no one in particular he added, 'You hear me, Bolitar?'

'You'll be back,' Myron said.

'Count on it, asshole.'

'Aren't you going to warn us not to leave town? I love it when you cops do that.'

Dimonte made a gun with his hand. He pointed it at Myron and lowered the thumb/hammer. Then he and the Pad disappeared out the door.

For several minutes no one said anything. Myron was about to break the silence when Duane started laughing. 'You sure showed him, Myron. Tore him a whole new asshole—'

'Duane, we need—'

'I'm tired, Myron.' He feigned a yawn. 'I really need to get some sleep.'

'We need to talk about this.'

'About what?'

Myron looked at him.

Duane said, 'Pretty weird coincidence, huh?'

Myron turned toward Wanda. She looked away, still hugging herself. 'Duane, if you're in some kind of trouble—'

'Hey, tell me about the commercial,' Duane interrupted. 'How did it come out?'

'Good.'

Duane smiled. 'How did I look?'

'Too handsome. I'll be fighting off the movie offers.'

Duane laughed too hard. Much too hard. Wanda did not laugh. Neither did Myron. Then Duane feigned another yawn, stretched and stood. 'I really need to get some rest,' he said. 'Big match coming up. Hate to let all this bullshit distract me.'

He showed Myron to the door. Wanda still had not moved from her spot by the kitchen door. She finally met Myron's eye.

'Good-bye, Myron,' Wanda said.

The door closed. Myron took the elevator back down and walked to his car. A ticket was nestled between the windshield and the wiper. He grabbed it and started the car.

Three blocks away Myron spotted the same powder-blue Cadillac with the canary-yellow top.

4

Yuppieville.

The fourteenth floor of Lock-Horne Investments & Securities reminded Myron of a medieval fortress. There was the vast space in the middle, and a thick, formidable wall – the big producers' offices – safeguarding the perimeter. The open area housed hundreds of mostly men, young men, combat soldiers easily sacrificed and replaced, a seemingly endless sea of them, bobbing and blending into the corporate-gray carpet, the identical desks, the identical rolling chairs, the computer terminals, the telephones, the fax machines. Like soldiers they wore uniforms – white button-down shirts, suspenders, bright ties strangling carotid arteries, suit jackets draped across the backs of the identical rolling chairs. There were loud noises, screams, rings, even something that sounded like death cries. Everyone was in motion. Everyone was scattering, panicked, under constant attack.

Yes, for here was one of the final strongholds of true yuppieism, a place where man was free to practice the religion of eighties greed, greed at all costs, without pretense of doing otherwise. No hypocrisy here. Investment houses were not about helping the world. They were not about providing a service to mankind or doing what was best for all. This haven had a simple, clear-cut, basic goal. Making money. Period.

Win had a spacious corner office overlooking Park and Fifty-second Street. A prime-time view for the company's number one producer. Myron knocked on the door.

'Enter,' Win called out.

He was sitting in a full lotus on the floor, his expression serene, his thumbs and forefingers forming circles in each hand. Meditation. Win did it every day without fail. Usually more than once.

But as with most things with Win, his moments of inner solitude were a tad unconventional. For one, he liked to keep his eyes open when meditating, while most practitioners kept them closed. For another, he didn't imagine idyllic scenes of waterfalls or does in the forest; rather, Win opted for watching home videotapes – videos of himself and an interesting potpourri of lady friends in assorted throes of passion.

Myron made a face. 'You mind turning that off?'

'Lisa Goldstein,' Win said, motioning toward a mound of writhing flesh on the screen.

'Charmed, I'm sure.'

'I don't think you ever met her.'

'Hard to tell,' Myron said. 'I mean, I'm not even sure where her face is.'

'Lovely lass. Jewish, you know.'

'Lisa Goldstein? You're kidding.'

Win smiled. He uncrossed his legs and stood in one fluid motion. He switched off the television, hit the EJECT button, put the tape back in a box marked L.G. He filed the box under the Gs in an oak cabinet. There were a lot of tapes already there.

'You realize,' Myron said, 'that you're quite deranged.'

Win locked the cabinet with a key. Dr Discretion. 'Every man needs a hobby.'

'You're a scratch golfer. You're a champion martial artist. Those are hobbies. This is deranged. Hobbies; deranged. See the difference?'

'Moralizing,' Win said. 'How nice.'

Myron did not respond. They had been down this road many times since they were freshmen at Duke. It never led anywhere.

Win's office was pure, elitist WASP. Paintings of a fox hunt adorned paneled walls. Burgundy leather chairs ideally complemented the deep forest-green carpeting. An antique wooden globe stood next to an oak desk that could double as a squash court. The effect – not a subtle one, at that – could be summed up in two words: Serious. Cash.

Myron sat in one of the leather chairs. 'You got a minute?'

'Of course.' Win opened a cabinet in the bar behind his desk, revealing a small refrigerator. He took out a cold Yoo-hoo and tossed it to Myron. Myron shook the can as per the instructions (*Shake! It's Great!*) while Win mixed himself a very dry martini.

Myron started off by telling Win about the police visit to Duane Richwood. Win remained impassive, allowing himself a small smile when he heard how Dimonte had called him a psycho-yuppie. Then Myron told him about the powder-blue Cadillac. Win sat back and steepled. He listened without interrupting. When Myron finished, Win rose from his seat and picked up a putter.

'So our friend Mr Richwood is holding something back.'

'We can't be sure.'

Win raised a skeptical eyebrow. 'Do you have any thoughts as to how Duane Richwood and Valerie Simpson are connected?'

'Nope. I was hoping you might.'

'*Moi?*'

'You knew her,' Myron said.

'She was an acquaintance.'

'But you have a thought.'

'About a connection between Duane and Valerie? No.'

'Then what?'

Win strolled to a corner. A dozen golf balls were all in a line. He began to putt. 'Are you really intent on pursuing this? Valerie's murder, I mean?'

'Yep.'

'It might be none of your business.'

'Might be,' Myron agreed.

'Or you might unearth something unpleasant. Something you would rather not find.'

'A distinct possibility.'

Win nodded, checked the carpet's lie. 'Wouldn't be the first time.'

'No. Not the first time. Are you in?'

'There is nothing in this for us,' Win said.

'Maybe not,' Myron agreed.

'No financial gain.'

'None at all.'

'In fact there is never any profit in your holy crusades.'

Myron waited.

Win lined up another putt. 'Stop making that face,' he said. 'I'm in.'

'Good. Now tell me what you know about this.'

'Nothing really. It's just a thought.'

'I'm listening.'

'You know, of course, about Valerie's breakdown,' Win said.

'Yes.'

'It was six years ago. She was only eighteen. The official word was that she collapsed under the pressure.'

'The official word?'

'It may be the truth. The pressure on her was indeed awesome. Her rise had been nothing short of meteoric – but nowhere near as meteoric as the tennis world's expectations of her. Her subsequent fall – at least, up until the time of the breakdown – was slow and painful. Not at all like yours. Your fall, if you don't mind me using that word, was far swifter. Guillotine-like. One minute you were the Celtics' number one draft pick. The next minute you were finished. The end. But unlike Valerie, you had a freak injury and were thereby blameless. You were pitied. You cut a sympathetic figure. Valerie's demise, on the other hand, seemed to be of her own doing. She was a failure, ridiculed, but still no more than a child. To the world at large, the fickle finger of fate had ended the career of Myron Bolitar. But in the case of Valerie Simpson, she alone was culpable. In the eyes of the public she did not possess enough mental fortitude. Her fall, thus, was slow, torturous, brutal.'

'So what does this have to do with the murder?'

'Perhaps nothing. But I always found the circumstances surrounding Valerie's mental collapse a bit disturbing.'

'Why?'

'Her game had slipped, that much was true. Her coach – that famous gentleman who plays with all the celebrities . . .'

'Pavel Menansi.'

'Whatever. He still believed Valerie could come back and win again. He said it all the time.'

'Thereby putting more pressure on her.'

Win hesitated. 'Perhaps,' he said slowly. 'But there is another factor. Do you remember the murder of Alexander Cross?'

'The senator's son?'

'The senator from Pennsylvania,' Win added.

'He was killed by robbers at his country club. Five, six years ago.'

'Six. And it was a tennis club.'

'You knew him?'

'Of course,' Win said. 'The Hornes have known every important Pennsylvania politician since William Penn. I grew up with Alexander Cross. We went to Exeter together.'

'So what does he have to do with Valerie Simpson?'

'Alexander and Valerie were, shall we say, an item.'

'A serious item?'

'Quite. They were about to announce their engagement when Alexander was killed. That night, as a matter of fact.'

Myron did some quick mathematics in his head. Six years ago. Valerie would have been eighteen. 'Let me guess. Valerie's breakdown took place right after his murder.'

'Precisely.'

'But I don't get something. The Cross murder was on the news every day for weeks. How come I never heard Valerie's name mentioned?'

'That,' Win said, nailing another putt, 'is why I find the circumstances disturbing.'

Silence.

'We need to talk to Valerie's family,' Myron said. 'Maybe the senator's as well.'

'Yes.'

'You live in that world. You're one of them. They'd be more apt to talk to you.'

Win shook his head. 'They'll never talk to me. Being "one of them," as you put it, is a severe handicap. Their guard will be up with someone like me. But with you they won't be so concerned about facades. They'll perceive you as someone who doesn't matter, as someone inferior, as someone beneath them. A nobody.'

'Gee, that's flattering.'

Win smiled. 'The way of the world, my friend. Many things change, but these people still consider themselves the true, original Americans. You and your kind are just hired help, shipped in from Russia or Eastern Europe or from whatever gulag or ghetto your people originated.'

'I hope they don't hurt my feelings,' Myron said.

'I'll arrange a meeting for you with Valerie's mother for tomorrow morning.'

'You think she'll see me?'

'If I request it, yes.'

'Groovy.'

'Indeed.' Win put down his putter. 'In the meantime what do you suggest we do?'

Myron checked his watch. 'One of Pavel Menansi's protégées is playing on Stadium Court in about an hour. I figured I'd pay him a visit.'

'And *pour moi*?'

'Valerie spent the past week at the Plaza Hotel,' Myron said. 'I'd like you to look around, see if anybody remembers anything. Check her phone calls.'

'See if she did indeed call Duane Richwood?'

'Yes.'

'And if she did?'

'Then we have to look into that too,' Myron said.

5

The USTA National Tennis Center is neatly snuggled into the bosom of Queens' top attractions: Shea Stadium (home of the New York Mets), Flushing Meadows Park (home of the 1964–65 World's Fair) and La Guardia Airport (home of, uh, delays).

Players used to complain about the La Guardia planes flying overhead, for the very simple reason that it made Stadium Court sound like a launch pad during an Apollo liftoff. Then-mayor David Dinkins, never one to let a terrible injustice go unheeded, immediately sprang into action. Using all his political might, the former mayor of New York City – who in a fascinating and almost eerie coincidence was also an enormous tennis fan – had La Guardia's offending runway halt operations for the duration of the Open. Tennis millionaires were grateful. In a show of mutual respect and admiration Mayor David Dinkins returned their gratitude by showing up at the matches every day for the two weeks of play, except – in yet another eerie coincidence – during election years.

Only two courts were used for the night sessions: Stadium Court and the adjacent Grandstand Court. The day sessions, Myron thought, were much more fun. Fifteen or sixteen matches might be going on at the same time. You could cruise around, catch a great five-set match on some obscure court, discover an up-and-coming player, see singles, doubles, and mixed doubles matches all in the glorious sunshine. But at night you basically sat in one seat and watched a match under lights. During the Open's first couple of days this match usually featured a top-seed mercilessly decapitating a qualifier.

Myron parked in the Shea Stadium lot and crossed the walking bridge over the No. 7 train. Someone had set up a booth with a radar gun where spectators could measure the speed of their own serve. Business was brisk. Ticket scalpers were also busy. So were the guys selling knockoff US Open T-shirts. The knockoff T-shirts sold for five dollars, as opposed to the ones inside the gates that went for twenty-five dollars. Not a bad deal on the surface. Of course, after one wash the knockoff T-shirt could only be worn by a Barbie doll. But still.

Pavel Menansi was in one of the players' boxes, the same one Myron and

Win had sat in earlier in the day. It was 6:45 P.M. The final day match was over. The first night match, featuring Pavel's latest protégée, fourteen-year-old Janet Koffman, would not begin until 7:15 P.M. People were milling around during the day-to-night cusp. Myron spotted the usher from the day session.

'How ya doing, Mr Bolitar?' the usher said.

'Fine, Bill. Just wanted to say a quick hello to a friend.'

'Sure, no prob, go right ahead.'

Myron headed down the steps. Without warning a man wearing a blue blazer and aviator sunglasses stepped in front of him. He was a big guy – six-four, two-twenty – just about Myron's size. His neatly combed hair sat above a pleasant though unyielding face. He expanded his chest into a paddleball wall, blocking Myron's path.

His voice said, 'Can I help you, sir?' But his tone said, *Take a hike, bub.*

Myron looked at him. 'Anyone ever tell you you look like Jack Lord?'

No reaction.

'You know,' Myron said. 'Jack Lord? *Hawaii Five-O*?'

'I'll have to ask you to leave, sir.'

'It's not an insult. Many people find Jack Lord very attractive.'

'Sir, this is the last time I'm going to ask nicely.'

Myron studied his face. 'You even have that Jack Lord surly grin. Remember it?' Myron imitated the grin for him, in case he'd never seen the show.

The face twitched. 'Okay, buddy, you're out of here.'

'I just want to speak to Mr Menansi for a moment.'

'I'm afraid that won't be possible at this time.'

'Oh, okay.' He spoke a little louder. 'Just tell Mr Menansi that Duane Richwood's agent wanted to discuss something very important with him. But if he's not interested I'll go elsewhere.'

Pavel Menansi's head jerked around as though pulled by a string. His smile flicked on like a cigarette lighter. He rose, his eyes half open, his whole persona oozing that foreign charm that some women find irresistible and others find nauseating beyond words. Pavel was Romanian, one of tennis's original Bad Boys, the former doubles partner of Ilie 'Nasty' Nastase. He was nearing fifty, his face tanned to the point of leathery. When he smiled, the leather cracked almost audibly.

'Pardon me,' he said. His voice was smooth – part Romanian, part American, part Ricardo Montalban discussing Corinthian leather. 'You are Myron Bolitar, are you not?'

'I am.'

He dismissed Jack Lord with a nod. Big Jack was not happy about it, but he moved out of the way. His body swung to the side like a metal gate, allowing only Myron to enter. Pavel Menansi held out a hand. For a moment Myron thought he wanted him to kiss it, but it ended in a brief handshake.

'Please,' Pavel said. 'Sit here. Next to me.'

Whoever was in the seat quickly made himself scarce. Myron sat. Pavel did likewise. 'I apologize for my guard's zeal, but you must understand. People, they want autographs. Parents, they want to discuss their child's play. But here' – he spread his hands – 'this is not the time or place.'

'I understand,' Myron said.

'I've heard quite a bit about you, Mr Bolitar.'

'Please call me Myron.'

Pavel had the smile of a lifelong smoker, *sans* proper dental hygiene. 'Only if you call me Pavel.'

'Deal.'

'Fine then. You discovered Duane Richwood, did you not?'

'Somebody pointed him out to me.'

'But you saw the potential first,' Pavel insisted. 'He never played in the juniors, never went to college. That's why all the big agencies missed him, am I right?'

'I guess so.'

'So now you have a top tennis contender. You are now competing with the big boys, yes?'

Myron knew that Pavel Menansi worked with TruPro, one of the country's largest sports agencies. Working with TruPro didn't automatically make you a sleazeball, but it brought you awfully close. Pavel was worth millions to them – not because of what he made as much as the young talent he brought in. Pavel got a Svengali-like hold on prodigies at the age of eight or ten, giving TruPro a hell of an advantage in getting them signed. TruPro had never been a reputable agency – almost a contradiction in terms anyway – but over the last year it had become mob-controlled, run by the appropriately named Ache brothers of New York City. The Ache brothers were into all the top mob favorites: drugs, numbers, prostitution, extortion, gambling. Sweethearts, those Aches.

'Your Duane Richwood,' Pavel continued. 'He played a fine match today. Fine match indeed. His potential is quite limitless. You agree?'

'He works very hard,' Myron said.

'I'm sure he does. Tell me, Myron, who is Duane's present coach?' He said *present*, but it came out more like *former*.

'Henry Hobman.'

'Ah.' Pavel nodded with vigor, as though this response explained something very complex. He, of course, already knew who coached Duane. Pavel probably knew who coached every player on the circuit. 'Henry Hobman is a fine man. A competent coach.' He said *competent*, but it came out more like *crappy*.

'But I believe I can help him, Myron.'

'I'm not here to talk about Duane,' Myron said.

A shadow crossed his face. 'Oh?'

'I want to discuss another client. Or should I say a once-potential client.'

'And who would that be?'

'Valerie Simpson.'

Myron looked for a reaction. He got one. Pavel lowered his head into his hands. 'Oh, my God.'

The box rumbled with overwrought concern. Comforting hands found their way to Pavel's shoulders, uttering his name in low voices. But Pavel pushed them away. Very brave.

'Valerie came to me a few days ago,' Myron continued. 'She wanted to make a comeback.'

Pavel took a deep breath. He made a show of putting himself together a piece at a time. When he was able to continue, he said, 'The poor child. I can't believe it. I just can't . . .' He stopped. Overwhelmed again. Then: 'I was her coach, you know. During her glory years.'

Myron nodded.

'To be shot down like that. Like a dog.' He shook his head dramatically.

'When was the last time you saw Valerie?'

'Several years ago,' he said.

'Have you seen her since the breakdown?'

'No. Not since she went into the hospital.'

'Spoken to her? On the phone maybe?'

Pavel shook his head again. Then he lowered it. 'I blame myself for what happened to her. I should have looked out for her better.'

'What do you mean?'

'When you coach one so young, you have responsibilities that go beyond her life on the court. She was a child – a child growing up in the spotlight. The media, they are savages, no? They don't understand what they do to sell papers. I tried to cushion some of their blows. I tried to protect her, to not let it eat her up inside. In the end, I failed.'

He sounded genuine, but Myron knew that meant nothing. People were amazing liars. The more sincere they sounded – the more they held your gaze and looked truthful – the more sociopathic they were. 'Do you have any idea who would have wanted her dead?'

He looked puzzled by the question. 'Why are you asking these questions, Myron?'

'I'm looking into something.'

'Into what? If I may ask.'

'It's kind of personal.'

He studied Myron for a few seconds. The stench of tobacco was heavy on his breath. Myron was forced to inhale through his mouth. 'I will tell you the same thing I told the police,' Pavel said. 'In my opinion Valerie's breakdown was not just from the usual tennis pressures.'

Myron nodded, encouraging him to continue.

Pavel turned his palms toward the sky, as though seeking divine intervention. 'Perhaps I am wrong. Perhaps I want to believe that to – how do you say? – soothe my own guilt. I don't know anymore. But I've had a lot of young people in my camp and never have I experienced anything like what happened to Valerie. No, Myron, her problems were caused by more than the pressures of big-time tennis.'

'What then?'

'I'm not a medical doctor, you understand. I cannot say for sure. But you must remember that Valerie was being menaced.'

Myron waited for him to elaborate. When he didn't, Myron said, 'Menaced?' Probing interrogatories – one of Myron's strong suits.

'Stalked,' he said with a finger snap. 'That's the word they use nowadays. Valerie was being stalked.'

'By whom?'

'A very sick man, Myron. A terrible man. After all these years I still remember his name. Roger Quincy. Crazy animal. He wrote her love letters. He called all the time. He hung around her house, by her hotel, at every match she played.'

'When was this?'

'When she was on the tour, of course. It began – I don't know – six months before she was hospitalized.'

'Did you try to stop him?'

'Of course. We went to the police. They could do nothing. We tried to get a court order, but this Quincy never actually threatened her. He would say "I love you, I want to be with you," things like that. We did our best. We changed hotels, signed in under different aliases. But you have to remember, Valerie was just a child. She became paranoid. The pressure on her was already tremendous. But now she had to look over her shoulder all the time. This Roger Quincy, he was a crazy beast. That's what he was. He was the one who should have been gunned down.'

Myron nodded, waiting a beat. 'How did Alexander Cross react to Roger Quincy?'

The question stunned Pavel like a surprise left hook. Lennox Lewis vs Frank Bruno. He hesitated, trying to regain his footing. The players came out of the tunnel. Applause began to build. The distraction worked like a standing eight count, giving Pavel time to recover.

'Why would you ask that?' he asked.

'Weren't Alexander Cross and Valerie Simpson involved?'

'I guess you could say that.'

'Seriously?'

'She was away a lot. Traveling. But they seemed fond of each other.'

'And I assume their relationship was going on at the same time Quincy was stalking Valerie?'

'I believe the time periods overlapped, yes.'

'So it's a natural question,' Myron said. 'How did Valerie's boyfriend react?'

'Natural, perhaps,' he said. 'But you must admit it is also a bizarre question. Alexander Cross has been dead for several years now. How is his reaction relevant to what happened to Valerie today?'

'For one, they were both murdered.'

'You're not suggesting a connection?'

'I'm not suggesting anything,' Myron said. 'But I don't understand why you don't want to answer my question.'

'It's not a matter of wanting or not wanting,' Pavel replied. 'It's a matter of doing what is right. You are delving into places where you do not belong. Personal places. Places that cannot possibly have any relevance in today's world. I feel like I am betraying confidences. You see?'

'No.'

Pavel looked back at Jack Lord. Jack's mouth twitched. He stood again. The chest self-inflated.

'The match is about to begin,' Pavel said. 'I hate to be rude, but I really must ask you to leave now.'

'Hit a raw nerve, did I?'

'Yes. I cared for Valerie very deeply.'

'That wasn't what I meant.'

'Please leave. I must concentrate on this match.'

Myron did not move. Jack Lord put a big mitt on Myron's shoulder. 'You heard the man,' he said. 'Move out.'

'Let go of my shoulder,' Myron said.

Jack shook his head. 'No more games, pal. It's time for you to get lost.'

'If you don't move your hand,' Myron explained calmly, 'I'll hurt you. Maybe severely.'

From behind his sunglasses Big Jack finally smiled. His grip on Myron's shoulder tightened. Myron quickly reached up with his right hand and grabbed the man's thumb. He locked the joint and pulled it back the wrong way. Jack dropped to one knee.

Myron lowered his mouth toward Jack's ear. 'I don't want to make a scene, so I'm going to let you go,' he whispered. 'If you do anything but smile I will hurt you. Definitely severely. Nod if you understand.'

He nodded, his face pale.

Myron let the thumb go. 'Later, Pavel.'

Pavel said nothing.

Myron walked past Jack. As ordered, Jack was smiling.

'Book 'em, Dann-o,' Myron said.

6

A stalker.

Could it be that simple? Could some deranged fan have put a bullet into Valerie Simpson because a voice told him to? Doesn't explain Duane Richwood's connection. But maybe there was no connection. Or maybe the connection had nothing to do with the murder and, more important, was none of Myron's business.

Myron turned onto Hobart Gap Road. He was only a mile from his home in Livingston, New Jersey. The powder-blue Caddy with the canary-yellow roof finally turned off, jumping on the JFK Parkway. Whoever it was must have figured Myron was going home for the night, and hence there was no reason to keep the tail. But if the Caddy was around tomorrow, Myron would have to take care of it – unmask the true identity of Mr Miami Gin Tournament.

Right now he needed to concentrate on this whole stalker possibility.

If Valerie had been killed by Roger Quincy, then why had ol' Pavel gotten so antsy when Myron mentioned Alexander Cross? Or was it just like Pavel said – he didn't want to betray confidences? When you thought about it, wasn't it a hell of a lot more probable that Pavel just felt it was in his best interest to keep quiet? Senator Cross was an awfully powerful man. Spreading stories about his murdered son wasn't necessarily the wisest course of action. So there could be nothing there. Then again it could be something big. Or something small.

Thoughts like these are what made Myron a brilliant detective.

He parked in the driveway. His mom's car was in the garage. His dad's was nowhere in sight. He opened the door with his key.

'Myron?'

Myron. God, what a name. You'd think he'd be used to it by now, but occasionally the horror hit him anew. He had been dubbed Myron. A last-second decision, his parents claimed. Something Mom came up with at the hospital. But to name a kid Myron Bolitar? Was that fair? Was that ethical?

As a youngster Myron tried giving himself nicknames: Mike, Mickey, even Sweet J, for his famous jumpshot. Okay, maybe it was a good thing that Sweet J didn't stick. But still.

Warning to parents naming children: Let's be careful out there.

His mother called out, 'Myron? Is that you?'

'Yeah, Mom.'

'I'm in the den.' She was wearing an exercise outfit, watching some kind of workout tape. She stood on one leg, crane stance á la *The Karate Kid*. On the television a familiar voice crooned. 'Now flow-step to the left . . .'

David Carradine's T'ai Chi Workout. Wonderful.

'Hi, Mom.'

'You're late,' she said.

'I didn't realize I had a curfew.'

'You said you'd be home by seven. It's past nine.'

'Your point being?'

'I was worried. I saw on the news about that girl getting shot at the Open. How did I know you weren't killed?'

Myron held back a sigh. 'Did the news say I was killed? Did the news say anything about unidentified bodies? Or did they say only one girl named Valerie Simpson was shot?'

'They could have been lying.'

'Excuse me?'

'Happens all the time. The police lie to the reporters until they notify the next of kin.'

'Weren't you home all day?'

'What, the police have my phone number?'

'But they could . . .' He stopped. What was the point? 'Next time a murder takes place within a three-mile radius of my being I'll be sure to call home.'

'Good.' She snapped off the tape. Then she placed a pillow in a corner and stood on her head.

'Mom?'

'What?'

'What are you doing?'

'What's it look like? I'm standing on my head. It's good exercise. Makes the blood flow. Makes me look my best. You know who used to stand on his head every day?'

Myron shook his head.

'David Ben-Gurion.'

'And everyone knows what a looker he was,' Myron said.

'Smart-mouth.'

Mom was a major paradox. On the one hand she'd been a practicing attorney for the past twenty years. She was the first generation born in the United States, her parents coming over from Minsk or somewhere like that, living lives that as near as Myron could tell paralleled *Fiddler on the Roof*. She became a sixties radical, an original bra burner, and experimented with various mind-altering drugs (hence naming a child Myron).

She did not cook. Ever. She had no idea where the vacuum cleaner was stored. She did not know what an iron looked like, never mind whether or not she owned one. In the courtroom her crosses were legendary. She breakfasted on star witnesses. She was bright, frighteningly shrewd, and very modern.

On the other hand, all of this went out the window when it came to her son. She completely decompensated. She became her mother. And her mother before her. Only worse. Murphy Brown became Grandma Tzietl.

'Your father is picking up some Chinese food. I ordered enough for you.'

'I'm not hungry, thanks.'

'Spareribs, Myron. Sesame chicken.' Meaningful pause. 'Shrimp with lobster sauce.'

'I'm really not hungry.'

'Shrimp with lobster sauce,' she repeated.

'Mom . . .'

'From Fong's Dragon House.'

'No thanks.'

'What? You love Fong's shrimp in lobster sauce. You're crazy about it.'

'Maybe a little then.' Easier.

She was still standing on her head. She began to whistle. Very casuallike. 'So,' she said in that strain-to-sound-aloof voice, 'how's Jessica?'

'Butt out, Mom.'

'Who's butting? I just asked a simple question.'

'And I gave you a simple answer. Butt out.'

'Fine. But don't go crying to me if something goes wrong.'

Like that happens.

'Why has she been away so long anyway? What's she doing over there?'

'Thanks for butting out.'

'I'm concerned,' Mom said. 'I just hope she's not up to something.'

'Butt out.'

'Is that all you can say? Butt out? What are you, a parrot? Where is she anyway?'

Myron opened his mouth, wrestled it closed, and stormed into the basement. His dwelling. He was almost thirty-two years old and still lived at home. He hadn't been here much the past few months. Most nights he'd spent at Jessica's place in the city. They had even talked about moving in together but decided to take it slow. Very slow. Easier said than done. The heart don't know from slow. At least Myron's didn't. As usual Mom had drilled into exposed nerve endings. Jessica was in Europe right now, but Myron had no idea where. He hadn't heard from her in two weeks. He missed her. And he was wondering too.

The doorbell rang.

'Your father,' Mom called down. 'Probably forgot his key again. I swear that man is getting senile.'

A few seconds later he heard the basement door open. His mother's feet appeared. Then the rest of her. She beckoned him forward.

'What?'

'There's a young lady here to see you,' she said. Then in a whisper, 'She's black.'

'Gasp!' Myron put his hand to his heart. 'Hope the neighbors don't call the police.'

'That's not what I meant, smart-mouth, and you know it. We have black families in the neighborhood now. The Wilsons. Lovely people. They live on Coventry Drive. In the old Dechtman home.'

'I know, Mom.'

'I was just describing her for you. Like I might say she has blond hair. Or a nice smile. Or a harelip.'

'Uh-huh.'

'Or limp. Or she's tall. Or short. Or fat. Or—'

'I think I get the drift, Mom. Did you ask her name?'

She shook her head. 'I didn't want to pry.'

Right.

Myron headed up the stairs. It was Wanda, Duane's girlfriend. For some reason Myron was not surprised. She smiled nervously, waved quickly.

'I'm sorry to disturb you at home,' she said.

'No problem. Please come in.'

They headed down the basement. Myron had subdivided it into two rooms. One, a small sitting room he basically never used. Hence it was presentable and clean. The inside room, his living quarters, resembled a frat house after a major kegger.

Wanda's eyes darted around again, like they had when Dimonte had been at the apartment. 'You live down here?'

'Only since I was sixteen.'

'I think that's sweet. Living with your parents.'

From upstairs: 'If only you knew.'

'Close the door, Mom.'

Slam.

'Please,' Myron said. 'Sit down.'

Wanda looked unsure but finally settled into a chair. She was wringing her hands nonstop. 'I feel a little foolish,' she said.

Myron gave her an understanding, encouraging smile – the Phil Donahue smile. *Caller, are you there?*

'Duane likes you,' she said. 'A lot.'

'The feeling is mutual.'

'The other agents, they call Duane all the time. All the big ones. They keep saying how you're too small-time to represent Duane. They keep saying they can help him make a lot more money.'

'They might be right,' Myron said.

She shook her head. 'Duane doesn't think so. I don't think so either.'

'That's nice of you to say.'

'You know why Duane won't meet with those other agents?'

'Because he doesn't want to see me weep?'

She smiled at that one. The Master of Levity strikes again. Señor Self-Deprecation. 'No,' she said. 'Duane trusts you.'

'I'm glad.'

'You're not just in it for the money.'

'That's nice of you to say, Wanda, but Duane is making me a lot of money. There's no denying that.'

'I know,' she said. 'I don't want to sound naïve here, but you put him first. Before the money. You look out for Duane Richwood the human being. You care about him.'

Myron said nothing.

'Duane doesn't have many people,' she continued. 'He doesn't have any family. He lived on the streets since he was fifteen, scraping by. He wasn't an angel that whole time. He did some things he'd rather forget. But he never hurt anybody, never did anything serious. His whole life he never had anyone he could rely on. He had to take care of himself.'

Silence.

'Does Duane know you're here?' Myron asked.

'No.'

'Where is he?'

'I don't know. He just took off. He does that sometimes.'

More silence.

'So anyway, like I said, Duane doesn't have anybody else. He trusts you. He trusts Win, too, but only because he's your best friend.'

'Wanda, what you're saying is very nice, but I'm hardly driven by altruism. I'm well paid for what I do.'

'But you care.'

'Henry Hobman cares.'

'Maybe. But his wagon is hitched to Duane's star. Duane is his ticket back to the bigs.'

'Many would say the same for me,' Myron countered. 'Except that part about "back," since I've never been to the bigs. Duane's my only big tennis player. In fact Duane is the only player I've got in the US Open.'

She considered this for a moment, nodding. 'Maybe that's all true,' she said. 'But when push came to shove – when trouble hit today – Duane came to you. And when push came to shove for me tonight, I came to you too. That's the bottom line.'

The basement door opened.

'Would you kids like something to drink?'

'Got any Kool-Aid, Mom?'

Wanda laughed.

'Listen, smart-mouth, maybe your company is hungry.'

'No, thank you, Mrs Bolitar,' Wanda shouted up.

'You sure, hon? Coffee maybe? A Coke?'

'Nothing, really, thank you.'

'How about some Danish? I just bought some fresh at the Swiss House. Myron's favorite.'

'Mom . . .'

'Okay, okay, I can take a hint.'

Right. The Mistress of the Subtle Signal. The basement door closed.

'She's sweet,' Wanda said.

'Yeah, adorable.' Myron leaned forward. 'Why don't you tell me why you're here?'

She started wringing her hands again. 'I'm worried about Duane.'

'If it's about Dimonte's visit, don't let him get to you. Being a horse's ass is part of his job.'

'It's not that,' she said. 'Duane wouldn't hurt anybody. I know that. But something isn't right with him. He's tense all the time. He paces around the apartment. He flies off the handle at the littlest things.'

'He's under a lot of pressure right now. It could just be nerves.'

She shook her head. 'Duane thrives on pressure. He loves competing, you know that. But the last day or two it's different. Something is really bothering him.'

'Any idea what?'

'No.'

Myron leaned forward. 'Let me ask you the obvious question: Did Duane get a call from Valerie Simpson?'

She thought for a moment. 'I don't know.'

'Does he know her?'

'I don't know that either. But I know Duane. We've been together for three years, since we were both eighteen. He was still on the streets when we met. My father freaked out when he heard. He's a chiropractor. He makes a good living, worked hard to keep the bad element away from us. And here I was, dating a street kid, a runaway.'

She chuckled at the memory. Myron sat and waited.

'No one thought it would last,' she continued. 'I left college and got a job so he could pursue tennis. Now he's putting me through NYU. We love each other. We loved each other before all this tennis stuff started and we'll love each other long after he puts down the racket for good. But for the first time he's shutting me out.'

'And you think Valerie Simpson is somehow connected?'

She hesitated. 'I guess I do.'

'How?'

'I have no idea.'

'What do you want me to do?'

She stood, paced in the small room. 'I heard those policemen talking. They said you used to be a big deal with the government. You and Win. Something secretive with the FBI – after you recovered from the knee injury. Is that true?'

'Yes.'

'I thought maybe you could, I don't know, look into it?'

'You want me to investigate Duane?'

'He's hiding something, Myron. It has to come out.'

'You might not like what I find,' he said, echoing Win's earlier words.

'I'm more afraid of going on like this.' Wanda looked up at him. 'Will you help him?'

He nodded. 'I'll do what I can.'

7

The phone rang.

Myron reached out blindly, swimming back to consciousness. He grabbed the receiver and croaked, 'Hello?'

'Is this the Rent-a-Stud hotline?'

Her voice hit him like a jolt. 'Jess?'

'Oh shit,' Jessica said. 'You were sleeping, right?'

'Sleeping?' Myron squinted at his digital. 'At four-thirteen in the morning? Captain Midnight? Surely you jest.'

'Sorry. I forgot about the time difference.'

He sat up. 'Where are you?'

'Greece,' she said. 'I miss you.'

'You're just horny.'

'Well, there's that.'

'Captain Midnight is willing to help,' he said.

'My fearless hero. I suppose you're not even a little horny.'

'Captain Midnight lives chastely.'

'Part of his image?'

'Exactly,' he said.

'It's no fun,' she said. 'Being away from you.'

His heart soared. 'So come home.'

'I am.'

'When?'

'Soon.' Jessica Culver, Miss Specific USA. 'Tell me what's been going on,' she said.

'You hear about the shooting at the Open?'

'Sure. The hotel has CNN.'

Myron told her about Valerie Simpson. When he finished, her first comment was, 'You didn't have to bend that clod's thumb back.'

'But it was all very macho,' Myron said.

'A real turn-on, I'm sure.'

'Guess you had to be there,' he said.

'Guess so. So are you going to find the killer?'

'I'm going to try.'

'For Valerie's sake? Or for Wanda and Duane?'

'For all of them, I guess. But mostly Valerie. You should have seen her, Jess. She tried so hard to be sullen and unpleasant. A girl that young shouldn't have to try that hard.'

'Do you have a plan?'

'Of course. First, I'm going to visit Valerie's mother tomorrow morning. In Philadelphia.'

'And then?'

'Well, the plan isn't really that well developed. But I'm working on it.'

'Please be careful.'

'Captain Midnight is always careful.'

'It's not just Captain Midnight I'm worried about. It's his alter ego.'

'And who might that be?'

'My Love Muffin.'

Myron grinned into the receiver. 'Hey, Jess, did you know Joan Collins was on *Batman*?'

'Of course,' Jessica said. 'She played the Siren.'

'Oh yeah? Well, who did Liberace play?'

8

Myron spent the rest of the night dreaming about Jessica, though as usual he could only remember meaningless scraps in the morning. Jessica was in his life again, but it was still new to him. Too new. He needed to hold back, to tread gently. He was afraid of being crushed under her heel again, of having his heart slammed in the door of love.

Door of love. Christ. He sounded like a bad country song.

He motored south on the famed New Jersey Turnpike. The powder-blue Cadillac with the canary-yellow top was four cars behind him. More than anything else, this stretch of roadway had made New Jersey the butt of so many jokes. He passed Newark Airport. Kind of ugly, but what airport isn't? Then he drove by the turnpike's pièce de résistance, its cause célèbre if you will – an enormous industrial power plant between exits 12 and 13 that closely resembled the futuristic nightmare world in the beginning of the *Terminator* movies. Thick smoke sprang from every orifice. Even in the bright sunshine the place looked dark, metallic, menacing, foreboding.

On the radio a rock group called the Motels were repeatedly singing the ingenious line *Take the L out of lover, and it's over.* Deep. Literal, but still deep. The Motels. Whatever happened to them?

Myron picked up the cellular phone and dialed. A familiar voice answered.

'Sheriff Courter speaking.'

'Hey, Jake, it's Myron.'

'I'm sorry. You must have the wrong number. Bye.'

'Good one,' Myron said. 'Guess those night-school comedy courses are finally starting to pay off.'

'What do you want, Myron?'

'Can't a friend just call and say hello?'

'So this is just a social call?' Jake said.

'Yes.'

'I feel so blessed.'

'Wait. It gets better. I'm going to be in your neck of the woods in a couple of hours.'

'Be still my heart.'

'I thought maybe we could meet for lunch. I'm buying.'

'Uh-huh. You bringing Win?'

'No.'

'Then okay. Guy gives me the creeps.'

'You don't even know him.'

'Cool by me. Now what do you want, Myron? This may be a surprise to you, but I work for a living.'

'You still have friends on the Philadelphia force?'

'Sure.'

'Can you get someone to fax you a homicide file?'

'Recent homicide?'

'Er, not exactly.'

'How old?'

'Six years,' Myron said.

'You're kidding, right?'

'It gets worse. The victim was Alexander Cross.'

'The senator's kid?'

'Right.'

'What the hell do you want that for?'

'I'll tell you about it when I get there.'

'Someone is going to want to know why.'

'Make something up.'

Jake chewed on something that sounded like tree bark. 'Yeah, all right. What time will you be here?'

'Probably around one. I'll call you.'

'You're going to owe me, Myron. Owe me big.'

'Didn't I mention I was buying lunch?'

Jake hung up.

Myron headed off at exit 6. The toll was almost four dollars. He was tempted to pay the Caddy's toll, but four dollars was a bit steep for the gesture. Myron handed the clerk the money. 'I only wanted to drive on the road,' Myron said. 'Not buy it.'

Not even a sympathetic smile. Complaining about toll prices. One of those signs you're becoming your father. Next thing you know Myron'd be screaming at someone for turning up the thermostat.

Altogether the trip to Philadelphia's wealthiest suburb took two hours. Gladwynne was old money. Plymouth Rock old money. Bloodlines were as important as credit lines. The house Valerie Simpson had grown up in was Gatsby-esque with signs of fray. The lawn was not quite manicured. The shrubbery was slightly overgrown. The paint was chipped in certain places. The ivy crawling along the walls seemed a tad too thick.

Still, the estate was huge. Myron parked so far away he almost waited for shuttle service. As he approached the front door Detectives Dimonte and

Krinsky came out. In a major shock, Dimonte did not appear happy to see him. He put his hands on his hips. Important, impatient.

'What the fuck are you doing here?' he barked.

'Do you know what happened to the Motels?' Myron asked.

'The what?'

Myron shook his head. 'How quickly they forget.'

'Goddamn it, Bolitar, I asked you a question. What do you want here?'

'You left your underpants at my house last night,' Myron said. 'Jockey shorts. Size thirty-eight. Little bunny design.'

Dimonte's face grew red. Most cops were homophobes. Best way to needle them was to play on it. 'You better not be playing fucking Hardy Boys with my case, asshole. You and your pal Psycho-yuppie.'

Krinsky laughed at that one. Psycho-yuppie. When ol' Rolly got hold of a good one he didn't let it go.

'Doesn't matter,' Dimonte continued. 'The case is just about wrapped up.'

'And I'll be able to say I knew you when.'

'You'll be happy to know your client is no longer my main suspect.'

Myron nodded. 'Roger Quincy the stalker is.'

That didn't please Dimonte. 'How the fuck do you know about that?'

'I am all-seeing, all-knowing.'

'Doesn't mean your boy is fully in the clear. He's still lying about something. You know it. I know it. Krinsky here knows it.'

Krinsky sort of nodded. Mr Sidekick.

'But now we just figure your boy was porking her. You know, on the side.'

'You have any evidence?'

'Don't need none. Don't give a shit. I want her killer, not her porker.'

'Poetically put, Rolly.'

'Ah screw it, I don't have time for your wit.'

As they passed, Myron gave a little wave. 'Nice talking to you, Krinsky.'

Krinsky nodded.

Myron rang the doorbell. It rang dramatically. Sounded like an orchestra. Tchaikovsky maybe. Maybe not. A man of about thirty came to the door. He was dressed in a pink oxford shirt open at the neck. Ralph Lauren. Big dimple on chin. Hair so black it was almost blue, like Superman's.

He looked at Myron like he was a vagrant urinating on the steps. 'Yes?'

'I'm here to see Mrs Van Slyke.' Valerie's mother had remarried.

'Now is not a good time,' he said.

'I have an appointment.'

'Perhaps you didn't hear me,' he said in that haughty, Win-like accent. 'Now is not a good time.'

'Please tell Mrs Van Slyke that Myron Bolitar is here,' Myron persisted. 'She is expecting me. Windsor Lockwood spoke with her last night.'

'Mrs Van Slyke isn't seeing anybody today. Her daughter was murdered yesterday.'

'I'm aware of that.'

'Then you'll understand—'

'Kenneth?'

A woman's voice.

'It's okay, Helen,' the man said. 'I'm handling the situation.'

'Who is it, Kenneth?'

'No one.'

Myron said, 'Myron Bolitar.'

Kenneth shot Myron a look. Myron held back the temptation to stick out his tongue. It wasn't easy.

She appeared in the foyer. All in black. Her eyes were red with equally red rims. She was an attractive woman, though Myron ventured to guess she was probably a lot more attractive twenty-four hours ago. Late forties. Blond hair, softly colored. Nicely coiffed. Not too bleachy.

'Please come in, Mr Bolitar.'

Kenneth said, 'I don't think that's such a good idea, Helen.'

'It's okay, Kenneth.'

'You need your rest.'

She took Myron's arm. 'Please forgive my husband, Mr Bolitar. He is just trying to protect me.'

Husband? Did she say husband?

'Please follow me.'

She led him into a room slightly larger than the Acropolis. Over the fireplace hung a gigantic portrait of a man with long sideburns and a walrus mustache. Kinda scary. The room was lit by a half dozen of those fixtures that look like candles. The furniture, while old-world tasteful, seemed a tad too worn. There wasn't a silver tea set, but there should have been. Myron sat in an antique chair about as comfortable as an iron lung. Kenneth kept his eye on Myron. Making sure he didn't pocket an ashtray or something.

Helen sat on the couch across from him. Kenneth stood behind her, hands on her shoulders. Would have made a nice photograph. Very regal. A little girl, no more than three or four, toddled into the room. 'This is Cassie,' Helen Van Slyke said. 'Valerie's sister.'

Myron smiled widely and leaned toward the little girl. 'Hello, Cassie.'

The little girl responded by bawling like she'd just been stabbed.

Helen Van Slyke comforted her daughter, and after a few more wails Cassie stopped. She peeked out behind balled-up fists every once in a while to study Myron. Maybe she too feared for the safety of the ashtrays.

'Windsor tells me you're a sports agent,' Helen Van Slyke said.

'Yes.'

'Were you going to represent my daughter?'

'We were discussing the possibility.'

Kenneth said, 'I don't see why this conversation can't wait, Helen.'

She ignored him. 'So why did you want to see me, Mr Bolitar?'

'I'd just like to ask you a few questions.'

'What kind of questions?' Kenneth asked. Sneering suspicion.

Helen silenced him with her hand. 'Please go ahead, Mr Bolitar.'

'I understand Valerie was hospitalized about six years ago.'

'What does that have to do with anything?' Kenneth again.

'Kenneth, please leave us alone.'

'But Helen—'

'Please. Take Cassie for a walk.'

'Are you sure?'

'Yes.'

He protested, but he was no match for her. She closed her eyes, signaling the argument's end. Grudgingly Kenneth took his daughter's hand. When they were out of earshot, she said, 'He is a bit overprotective.'

'It's understandable,' Myron said. 'Under the circumstances.'

'Why do you want to know about Valerie's hospitalization?'

'I'm trying to put some loose ends together.'

She studied his face for a moment. 'You're trying to find my daughter's killer, aren't you?'

'Yes.'

'May I ask why?'

'There are several reasons.'

'I'll accept one.'

'Valerie tried to reach me before the murder,' Myron said. 'She called my office three times.'

'That hardly makes you responsible.'

Myron said nothing.

Helen Van Slyke took a deep breath. 'And you think her murder has something to do with her breakdown?'

'I don't know.'

'The police feel quite certain the killer is a man who stalked Valerie.'

'What do you think?'

She stayed perfectly still. 'I don't know. Roger Quincy seemed harmless enough. But I guess they all seem harmless until something like this happens. He used to write her love letters all the time. They were sort of sweet, in a kooky kind of way.'

'Do you still have them?'

'I just gave them to the police.'

'Do you remember what they said?'

'They vacillated between almost normal courting words and outright obsession. Sometimes he would simply ask her on a date. Other times he would write about eternal love and how they were destined to be together forever.'

'How did Valerie react?'

'Sometimes it scared her. Sometimes it amused her. But mostly she ignored it. We all did. No one took it too seriously.'

'What about Pavel? Was he concerned?'

'Not overly.'

'Did he hire a bodyguard for Valerie?'

'No. He was dead set against the idea. He thought a bodyguard might spook her.'

Myron paused. Valerie hadn't needed a bodyguard against a stalker, yet Pavel needs one against pestering parents and autograph hounds. It made one wonder. 'I'd like to talk about Valerie's breakdown, if that's all right.'

Helen Van Slyke stiffened slightly. 'I think it's best to leave that alone, Mr Bolitar.'

'Why?'

'It was painful. You have no idea how painful. My daughter had a mental collapse, Mr Bolitar. She was only eighteen years old. Beautiful. Talented. A professional athlete. Successful by any rational measure. And she had a breakdown. It was stressful on all of us. We tried our best to help her get well, to keep it from getting in the papers and becoming public. We tried our best to keep it under wraps.'

She stopped then and closed her eyes.

'Mrs Van Slyke.'

'I'm fine,' she said.

Silence.

'You were saying how you tried to keep it under wraps,' Myron prompted.

The eyes reopened. She smiled and sort of smoothed her skirt. 'Yes, well, I didn't want this episode ruining her life. You know how people talk. For the rest of her life people would point and whisper. I didn't want that. And yes, I was embarrassed too. I was younger, Mr Bolitar. I was afraid of how her breakdown would reflect on the Brentman family name.'

'Brentman?'

'My maiden name. This estate is known as Brentman Hall. My first husband was named Simpson. A mistake. A social climber. Kenneth is my second husband. I know tongues wag about our age differences, but the Van Slykes are an old family. His great-great-grandfather and my great-grand-father were partners.'

Good reason to get married. 'How long have you and Kenneth been married?'

'Six years last April.'

'I see. So you got married around the same time Valerie was hospitalized.'

Her eyes narrowed and her words came slower now. 'What exactly are you implying, Mr Bolitar?'

'Nothing,' Myron said. 'I wasn't implying anything. Really.' Well, maybe a little. 'Tell me about Alexander Cross.'

She stiffened again, almost like a spasm. 'What about him?' She sounded annoyed now.

'He and Valerie were serious?'

'Mr Bolitar' – impatience creeping in – 'Windsor Lockwood is an old family friend. He is the reason I agreed to see you. You earlier portrayed yourself as a man concerned with finding my daughter's killer.'

'I am.'

'Then please tell me what Alexander Cross or Valerie's breakdown or my own marriage has to do with your task?'

'I am making an assumption, Mrs Van Slyke. I am assuming that this was not a random killing, that the person who shot your daughter was not a stranger. That means I have to know about her life. All of it. I don't ask these questions to amuse myself. I need to know who would have feared Valerie or hated her or had a lot to gain by her death. That means digging into all the unpleasantries of her life.'

She held his gaze a beat too long and then looked away. 'Just what do you know about my daughter, Mr Bolitar?'

'The basics,' Myron said. 'Valerie became tennis's next wunderkind at the French Open when she was only sixteen. Expectations ran wild, but her play quickly leveled off. Then it grew worse. She was stalked by an obsessive fan named Roger Quincy. She had a relationship with the son of a prominent politician, who was later murdered. Then she had a mental collapse. Now I need to fill in – and illuminate – more pieces of this puzzle.'

'It's very difficult to talk about all this.'

'I understand that,' Myron said gently. He opted now for the Alan Alda smile over the Phil Donahue. More teeth, moister eyes.

'There's nothing more I can tell you, Mr Bolitar. I don't know why anyone would want to kill her.'

'Perhaps you can tell me about the last few months,' Myron said. 'How was Valerie feeling? Did anything unusual happen?'

Helen fiddled with her strand of pearls, twisting them around her fingers until they made a red mark around her neck. 'She finally started getting better,' she said, her voice more of a choke now. 'I think tennis helped. For years she wouldn't touch a racket. Then she started playing. A little at first. Just for fun.'

The facade collapsed then. Helen Van Slyke lost it. The tears came hard. Myron took her hand. Her grip was both strong and shaky.

'I'm sorry,' Myron said.

She shook her head, forcing the words out. 'Valerie started playing every day. It made her stronger. Physically, emotionally. She finally seemed to be putting it all behind her. And then . . .' She stopped again, her eyes suddenly flat. 'That bastard.'

She might have been talking about the unknown killer. But somehow the anger seemed more specific.

'Who?' Myron tried.

'Helen?'

Kenneth was back. He quickly crossed the room and took his wife in his arms. Myron thought he saw her back away at his touch, but he couldn't be sure.

Kenneth looked over her shoulder at Myron. 'See what you've done,' he hissed. 'Get out.'

'Mrs Van Slyke?'

She nodded. 'Please leave, Mr Bolitar. It's for the best.'

'Are you sure?'

Kenneth bellowed again. 'Get out! Now! Before I throw you out!'

Myron looked at him. Not the time or the place. 'I'm sorry for the intrusion, Mrs Van Slyke. My most sincere condolences.'

Myron showed himself out.

9

When Myron entered the small police station Jake's chin was coated with something red and sticky. Might have been from a jelly doughnut. Might have been from a small farm animal. Hard to tell with Jake.

Jake Courter had been elected sheriff of Reston, New Jersey two years before. In view of the fact that Jake was black in an almost entirely white community, most people considered the election result an upset. But not Jake. Reston was a college town. College towns were filled with liberal intellectuals who wanted to lift a black man up. Jake figured his skin color had been enough of a disadvantage over the years, might as well turn the tide. White guilt, he told Myron. The best vote-getter this side of Willie Horton ads.

Jake was in his early fifties. He'd been a cop in a half dozen major cities over the years – New York, Philadelphia, Boston, to name a few. Tired of chasing city scum, he'd moved out to the happy suburbs to chase suburban scum. Myron and Jake met a year ago, investigating the disappearance of Kathy Culver, Jessica's sister, a student at Reston University.

'Hey, Myron.'

'Jake.'

Jake looked, as always, rumpled. Everything about him. His hair. His clothes. Even his desk looked rumpled, like a cotton shirt kept in the bottom of a laundry hamper. The desk also had an assortment of goodies. A Pizza Hut box. A Wendy's bag. A Carvel ice-cream cup. A half-eaten sandwich from Blimpie. And, of course, a tin of Slim-Fast diet powder. Jake was closing in on two hundred and seventy-five pounds. His pants never fit right. They were too small for his stomach, too large for his waist. He was constantly adjusting them, searching for that one elusive point where they'd actually stay in place. The search required a team of top scientists and a really powerful microscope.

'Let's go grab a couple burgers,' Jake said, wiping his face with a moist towelette. 'I'm starving.'

Myron picked up the Slim-Fast can and smiled sweetly. ' "A delicious shake for breakfast. Another for lunch. And then a sensible dinner." '

'Bullshit. I gave it a try. The shit doesn't work.'

307

'How long were you on it?'

'Almost a day. Zip, nothing. Not a pound gone.'

'You should sue.'

'Plus the stuff tastes like used gunpowder.'

'You get the file on Alexander Cross?'

'Yeah, right here. Let's go.'

Myron followed Jake down the street. They stopped at a place very generously dubbed the Royal Court Diner. A pit. If it were totally renovated, it might reach the sanitary status of an interstate public toilet.

Jake smiled. 'Nice, huh?'

'My arteries are hardening from the smell,' Myron said.

'For chrissake, man, don't inhale.'

The table had one of those diner jukeboxes. The records hadn't been changed in a long time. The current number one single, according to the little advertisement, was Elton John's 'Crocodile Rock'.

The waitress was standard diner issue. She was grumpy, mid-fifties, her hair a purplish tint not found anywhere in the state of nature.

'Hey, Millie,' Jake said.

She tossed them menus, not speaking, barely breaking stride.

'That's Millie,' Jake said.

'She seems great,' Myron said. 'Can I see the file?'

'Let's order first.'

Myron picked up the menu. Vinyl. And sticky. Very sticky. Like someone had poured maple syrup on it. There were also bits of coagulated scrambled eggs in the crease. Myron was losing his appetite in a hurry.

Three seconds later Millie returned, sighed. 'What'll it be?'

'Give me a cheeseburger deluxe,' Jake said. 'Double order of fries instead of the coleslaw. And a Diet Coke.'

Millie looked toward Myron. Impatiently.

Myron smiled at her. 'Do you have a vegetarian menu?'

'A what?'

'Stop being an asshole,' Jake said.

'A grilled cheese will be fine,' Myron said.

'Fries with that?'

'No.'

'To drink?'

'A Diet Coke. Like my low-cal buddy.'

Millie eyed Myron, looked him up and down. 'You're kinda cute.'

Myron gave her the modest smile. The one that said, *Aw, shucks.*

'You also look familiar.'

'I have that kind of face,' Myron said. 'Cute yet familiar.'

'You date one of my daughters once? Gloria maybe. She works the night shift.'

'I don't think so.'

She looked him over again. 'You married?'

'I'm involved with someone.'

'Not what I asked you,' she said. 'You married?'

'No.'

'All right then.' She turned and left.

'What was all that about?'

Jake shrugged. 'Hope she's not getting Gloria.'

'Why?'

'She kinda looks like a white version of me,' Jake said. 'Only with a heavier beard.'

'Sounds enticing.'

'You still with Jessica Culver?'

'Guess so.'

Jake shook his head. 'Man, she's something else. I've never seen nothing that looked that good in real life.'

Myron tried not to grin. 'Hard to argue.'

'She also got you wrapped around her finger.'

'Hard to argue.'

'Lots of worse places for a man to be wrapped around.'

'Hard to argue.'

Millie came back with the two Diet Cokes. This time she almost managed to smile at Myron. 'Good-looking man like you shouldn't be single,' she said.

'I'm wanted in several states,' Myron said.

Millie did not seem discouraged. She shrugged, left. Myron turned back to Jake.

'All right,' Myron said. 'Where's the file?'

Jake flipped it open. He handed Myron a picture of a handsome, healthy man. Tan, fit, wearing tennis shorts. Myron had seen the picture in the paper after the murder.

'Meet Alexander Cross,' Jake began. 'Age twenty-four at the time of the murder. Wharton graduate. Son of United States senator Bradley Cross of Pennsylvania. On the night of July twenty-four, six years ago, he was attending a party at a tennis club called Old Oaks in Wayne, Pennsylvania. The esteemed senator was there. It's a pretty ritzy place – fancy food, indoor and outdoor courts, hard court, clay, lit, unlit, the works. Even grass courts.'

'Okay.'

'What happened next is a bit fuzzy, but here's what we have. Alexander Cross and three buddies were taking a walk around the grounds.'

'At night? During a party?'

'Not unheard of.'

'Not common either.'

Jake shrugged. 'Anyway, they heard a noise coming from the western end of the club. They went to check it out. They ran into two suspicious-looking youths.'

'Suspicious-looking?'

'The youths were – what are they calling us today? – African American.'

'Ah,' Myron said. 'Is it safe to assume that Old Oaks did not have a lot of African American members?'

'Like none. It's exclusive.'

'So you and I could never be members.'

'Real shame,' Jake said. 'I bet we'd have loved that party.'

'So what happened next?'

'According to the witnesses, the white youths approached the black youths. One of the black youths – later identified as one Errol Swade – reacted by whipping out a switchblade.'

Myron made a face. 'A switchblade?'

'Yeah, I know. Such a cliché. No imagination. Anyway, an incident ensued. Alexander Cross was stabbed. The two youths ran. A few hours later the police caught up with them in north Philadelphia, not far from where the youths lived. During the apprehension, one of the punks pulled out a gun. A Curtis Yeller. Sixteen years old. A police officer shot him. Yeller's mother was at the scene, from what I understand. She was cradling the kid in her arms when he died.'

'She saw him being shot?'

Jake shrugged. 'Doesn't say.'

'So what happened to Errol Swade?'

'He escaped. A nationwide manhunt began. His mug shot was in all the papers, sent to all the stations. Lot of cops on it, of course – the victim being the son of a U.S. senator and all. But here's where things get interesting.'

Myron sipped the Diet Coke. Flat.

'They never found Errol Swade,' Jake said.

Myron felt his heart sink. 'Never?'

Jake shook his head.

'Are you telling me Swade escaped?'

'Appears so.'

'How old was he?'

'Nineteen at the time of the incident.'

Myron mulled that over a moment. 'That would make him twenty-five now.'

'Whoa. A math major.'

Myron did not smile. Millie brought the food. She made another comment, but Myron did not hear it. Twenty-five years old. Myron couldn't help but wonder. It was a dumb thought. Unforgivable. And maybe even racist. But there it was. Twenty-five years old. Duane claimed to be twenty-one, but who knew for sure?

But no. It can't be.

Myron took another sip of the flat soda. 'What do you know about Errol Swade?' he asked.

'A pedigree punk. He had already been in jail three times. First offense was stealing a car. He was twelve. Assorted felonies followed. Muggings, assaults, car thefts, armed robberies, drugs. Also a member of an ultra-violent street gang. Guess what the gang was called.'

Myron shrugged. 'Josie and the Pussycats?'

'Close. The Stains. Short for Bloodstains. They always wear a shirt dipped in a victim's blood. Kinda like a Boy Scout badge.'

'Charming.'

'Errol Swade and Curtis Yeller were also cousins. Swade had been living with the Yellers since his release a month earlier. Let's see what else. Swade was a dropout. Big surprise. A coke addict. Another shocker. And a major league moron.'

'So how has he eluded the police for so long?'

Jake picked up his burger and took a bite. A big bite. Half the burger vanished. 'He couldn't have,' he said.

'Excuse me?'

'No way he could have stayed out of trouble this long. Impossible.'

'Hold up. Did I miss something here?'

'Officially the police are still looking,' Jake said. 'But unofficially they're sure he's dead. The kid was a dumb punk. He couldn't find his ass with both hands, never mind hide from a nationwide dragnet.'

'So what happened?'

'Rumor has it the senator got a favor from the mob. They knocked him off.'

'Senator Cross put out a hit on him?'

'What, that surprises you? The guy's a politician. That's like a step below child molester.'

'Weren't you *elected* sheriff?'

Jake nodded. 'There you go.'

Myron risked a bite of his sandwich. Tasted a bit like a sink sponge. 'Do you have a physical description of Errol Swade?' he asked, almost hoping the answer was no.

'I got better. I got Swade's mugshot.' Jake dusted his hands off, rubbed them on his shirt for good measure. Then he reached into the folder and withdrew a photograph. He handed it to Myron. Myron tried not to appear too eager.

It wasn't Duane.

Not even close. Not even with plastic surgery. For one, Errol Swade was much lighter skinned. Swade's head was shaped like a block, completely different from Duane's. His eyes were spaced too far apart. Everything was different. His height was listed as six-four, three inches taller than Duane. Can't fake being shorter.

311

Myron almost sighed with relief. 'Does the name Valerie Simpson pop up in that file?' he asked.

Jake's eyes caught a little fire. 'Who?'

'You heard me.'

'Golly, Myron, that wouldn't be the same Valerie Simpson who was murdered yesterday?'

'By coincidence it is. Is her name in there?'

He handed Myron half the file. 'Hell if I know. Help me look.'

They went through it. Valerie's name was only on one sheet. A party guest list. Her name along with a hundred others. Myron jotted down the names and addresses of the witnesses to the murder – three friends of Alexander Cross's. Nothing else of much interest in the file.

'So,' Jake said, 'what does the lovely and dead Valerie Simpson have to do with this?'

'I don't know.'

'Jesus Christ.' Jake shook his head. 'You still yanking my chain?'

'I'm not yanking anything.'

'What have you got so far?'

'Less than nothing.'

'That's what you said about Kathy Culver.'

'But this isn't your case, Jake.'

'Maybe I can help.'

'I really don't have anything. Valerie Simpson visited my office a few days ago. She wanted to make a comeback, but somebody killed her instead. I want to know who, that's all.'

'You're full of shit.'

Myron shrugged.

'The TV said something about a stalker doing the job,' Jake said.

'Might be him. Probably is.'

Silence.

'You're holding back again,' Jake said. 'Just like with Kathy Culver.'

'It's confidential.'

'You're not going to tell me?'

'Nope. It's confidential.'

'Protecting someone again?'

'Confidential,' Myron said. 'As in not to be divulged. Communicated in the strictest of confidence. A secret.'

'Fine, be that way,' Jake said. 'So how's your sandwich?'

Myron nodded. 'Maybe the ambience isn't so good, but at least the food stinks.'

Jake laughed. 'Hey, you got tickets to the Open?'

'Yeah.'

'How about getting me two?'

'For when?'

'The last Saturday.'

The men's semis and women's finals. 'Tough day,' Myron said.

'But not for a big-time agent like yourself.'

'Then we'll be even?'

'Yeah.'

'I'll leave them at the on-call window.'

'Make sure they're good seats.'

'Who you taking?'

'My son Gerard.'

Myron had played ball against Gerard in college. Gerard was a bull. No finesse about his game. 'He still working homicide in New York?'

'Yep.'

'Can he do me a little favor?'

'Shit. Like what?'

'The cop on Valerie's murder is a devout asshole.'

'And you want to know what they have.'

'Yeah.'

'All right. I'll ask Gerard to give you a call.'

10

'Messages?'

Esperanza nodded. 'About a million of them.'

Myron fingered through the pile. 'Any word on Eddie Crane?'

'You're having dinner with him and his folks.'

He looked up. 'When?'

'Tonight. Seven-thirty. At La Reserve. I already made a reservation. Make sure you use Win's name.'

Win's name carried weight at many of New York's finest restaurants. 'You realize, of course, that you're a genius.'

She nodded. 'Yeah.'

'I want you to come too.'

'Can't. School.' Esperanza went to law school at night.

'Is Eddie still being coached by Pavel Menansi?' Myron asked.

'Yeah, why?'

'He and I had a discussion last night at the Open.'

'What about?'

'He used to coach Valerie.'

'And you two "discussed" that?'

Myron nodded.

'May I assume you wowed him with your usual charm?'

'Something like that.'

'So we don't have a chance with Eddie,' she said.

'Not necessarily. If Eddie was really close to Pavel, then TruPro would have him signed by now. Maybe there's some friction there.'

'Almost forgot.' Esperanza picked up a small stack of papers. 'This just came in by fax. They want it signed right away.'

A contract for a baseball prospect named Sandy Repo. A pitcher. The Houston Astros had taken him in the first round. Myron scanned it over. The contract had been orally finalized yesterday morning, but Myron spotted the new paragraph right away. Sandwiched it in on the second-to-last page.

'Cute,' he said.

'Who?'

'The Astros. Get me Bob Wasson on the line.' The Astros' general manager.

Esperanza picked up the phone. 'You're supposed to meet with Burger City tomorrow afternoon.'

'Same time as Duane's match?'

She nodded.

'You mind handling it?' he asked.

'They're not going to like dealing with a receptionist,' she said.

'You're an associate,' Myron corrected. 'A valued associate.'

'Still not the main man. Still not Myron Bolitar.'

'Ah, but who is?'

She rolled her eyes, picked up the phone, began dialing. She purposely did not look at him. 'You really think I'm ready?'

The tone was hard to read. Myron couldn't tell if it signaled sarcasm or insecurity. Probably both.

'They're going to want Duane for their new promo,' he said. 'But Duane wants to wait for a national deal. Try to push someone else on them.'

'Okay.'

Myron went into his office. Home. Tara. He had a nice view of the Manhattan skyline. Not a corner office view like Win's, but not shabby either. On one wall he had movie stills. Everything from Bogie and Bacall to Woody and Diane. Another wall featured Broadway posters. Musicals mostly. Everything from Rodgers and Hammerstein to Andrew Lloyd Webber. The final wall was his client wall. Action photos of each player. He studied the picture of Duane, his body arched in a serving motion.

'What's going on, Duane?' Myron said out loud. 'What are you hiding?'

The photo did not answer. Photos rarely did.

His phone buzzed. Esperanza came on the speaker. 'I have Bob Wasson on the line.'

'Okay.'

'I can put him on hold. Until you're finished talking to your wall.'

'No, I think I'll take it now.' Wiseass. He hit the speakerphone. 'Bob?'

'Goddamn it, Bolitar, take me off the speaker. You're not that goddamn important.'

Myron picked up the receiver. 'That better?'

'Yeah, great. What do you want?'

'I got the contract today.'

'Well, yippee for you. Now, here's what you do next. Step one: Sign it where the X is. You know how to do that, don't you? I had your name typed under the X in case you're unsure of the spelling. And use a pen, Myron. Blue or black ink, please. No crayons. Step two: Put the contract in the enclosed self-addressed envelope. Moisten the flap. With me so far?'

Good ol' Bob. Funny as a case of head lice. 'There's a problem,' Myron said.

'A what?'

'A problem.'

'Look, Bolitar, if you're trying to squeeze me for more dough, you can fuck yourself from behind.'

'Point thirty-seven. Paragraph C.'

'What about it?'

Myron read it out loud. ' "The player agrees that he will not engage in sports endangering his health or safety including, but not limited to, professional boxing or wrestling, motorcycling, moped riding, auto racing, sky-diving, hang gliding, hunting, et cetera, et cetera." '

'Yeah, so? It's a prohibited activities clause. We got it from the NBA.'

'The NBA's contract says nothing about hunting.'

'What?'

'Please, Bob, let's try to pretend I don't have a learning disability. You threw in the word *hunting*. Sneaked it in, if you will.'

'So what's the big deal? Your boy hunts. He hurt himself in a hunting accident two years ago and missed half his junior year. We want to make sure that doesn't happen again.'

'Then you have to compensate him for it,' Myron said.

'What? Don't bust my balls, Bolitar. You want us to pay the kid if he gets hurt, right?'

'Right.'

'So we don't want him hunting. Suppose he shoots himself. Or suppose some other asshole mistakes him for a deer and shoots him. You know what that's going to cost us?'

'Your concern,' Myron said, 'is touching.'

'Oh excuse me. A thousand pardons. I guess I should care more and pay less.'

'Good point. Strike my last statement.'

'So stricken. Can I go now?'

'My client enjoys hunting. It means a great deal to him.'

'And his left arm means a lot to us.'

'So I suggest a fair compromise.'

'What?'

'A bonus. If Sandy doesn't hunt, you agree to pay him twenty thousand dollars at the end of the year.'

Laughter. 'You're out of your mind.'

'Then take that clause out. It's not standard and we don't want it.'

Pause. 'Five grand. Not a penny more.'

'Fifteen.'

'Up yours, Myron. Eight.'

'Fifteen,' Myron said.

'I think you're forgetting how this is played,' Bob said. 'I say a number a little higher. You say a number a little lower. Then we meet somewhere in the middle.'

'Fifteen, Bob. Take it or leave it.'

Win opened the door and came in. He sat down silently, crossed his right ankle over his left thigh, and studied his manicured nails.

'Ten,' Bob said.

'Fifteen.'

The negotiation continued. Win stood, checked his reflection in the mirror behind the door. He was still fixing his hair five minutes later when Myron hung up. Not a blond lock was out of place, but that never seemed to deter Win.

'What was the final number?' Win asked.

'Thirteen five.'

Win nodded. He smiled at his reflection. 'You know what I was just thinking?'

'What?'

'It must suck to be ugly.'

'Uh-huh. Think you can tear yourself away for a second?'

Win sighed. 'It won't be easy.'

'Try to be brave.'

'I guess I can always look again later.'

'Right. It'll give you something to look forward to.'

With one last hair pat, Win turned away and sat down. 'So what's up?'

'The powder-blue Caddy is still following me.'

Win looked pleased. 'And you want me to find out who they are?'

'Something like that,' Myron said.

'Excellent.'

'But I don't want you to move in on them without me there.'

'You don't trust my judgment?'

'Just don't, okay?'

Win shrugged. 'So how was your visit to the Van Slykes' estate?'

'I met Kenneth. The two of us really hit it off.'

'I can imagine.'

'You know him?' Myron asked.

'Oh yes.'

'Is he as big an asshole as I think?'

Win spread his hands wide. 'Of biblical proportions.'

'You know anything else about him?'

'Nothing significant.'

'Can you check him out?'

'But of course. What else did you find out?'

Myron told him about his visits to both the Van Slykes and Jake.

'Curiouser and curiouser,' Win said when he finished.

'Yes.'

'So what's the next step?' Win asked.

'I want to attack this from several directions.'

'Those being?'

'Valerie's psychiatrist, for one.'

'Who will throw all kinds of terms like "doctor-patient confidentiality" at you,' Win said with a dismissive wave. 'A waste of time. Who else?'

'Curtis Yeller's mother witnessed her son's shooting. She's also Errol Swade's aunt. Maybe she has some thoughts on all this.'

'For example?'

'Maybe she knows what happened to Errol.'

'And you – what? – expect her to tell you?'

'You never know.'

Win made a face. 'So basically your plan is to flail about helplessly.'

'Pretty much. I will also need to talk to Senator Cross. Do you think you can arrange it?'

'I can try,' Win said. 'But you're not going to learn anything from him either.'

'Boy, you're a bundle of optimism today.'

'Just telling it like it is.'

'Did you learn anything at the Plaza?'

'As a matter of fact, I did.' Win leaned back and steepled his fingers. 'Valerie made only four calls in the past three days. All were to your office.'

'One to make an appointment to see me,' Myron said. 'The other three on the day she died.'

Win gave a quick whistle. 'Very impressive. First you figure out Kenneth is an asshole and now this.'

'Yeah, sometimes I even scare myself. Is there anything else?'

'A doorman at the Plaza remembered Valerie rather well,' Win continued. 'After I tipped him twenty dollars, he recalled that Valerie took a lot of quick walks. He found it curious, since guests normally leave for hours at a time, rather than scant minutes.'

Myron felt a surge. 'She was using a pay phone.'

Win nodded. 'I called Lisa at NYNEX. By the way, you now owe her two tickets to the Open.'

Great. 'What did she find out?'

'On the day before Valerie's murder, two calls were placed from a nearby pay phone at Fifth and Fifty-ninth to the residence of one Mr Duane Richwood.'

Myron felt a sinking feeling. 'Shit.'

'Indeed.'

'So not only did Valerie call Duane,' Myron said, 'but she went out of her way to make sure no one would know.'

'So it appears.'

Silence.

Win said, 'You'll have to talk to him.'

'I know.'

'Let it wait until after the tournament,' Win added. 'Between the Open and the big Nike campaign, there's no reason to distract him now. It will keep.'

Myron shook his head. 'I'll talk to Duane tomorrow. After his match.'

11

François, the maître d' at La Reserve, flitted about their table like a vulture awaiting death – or worse, a New York maître d' awaiting a very large tip. Since discovering that Myron was a close friend of Windsor Horne Lockwood III's, François had befriended Myron in the same way a dog befriends a man with raw meat in his pocket.

He recommended the thinly sliced salmon appetizer and the chef's special scrod as an entree. Myron took him up on both suggestions. So did the so-far silent Mrs Crane. Mr Crane ordered the onion soup and liver. Myron was not going to be kissing him anytime soon. Eddie ordered the escargot and lobster tails. The kid was learning fast.

François said, 'May I recommend a wine, Mr Bolitar?'

'You may.'

Eighty-five bucks down the drain.

Mr Crane took a sip. Nodded his approval. He had not smiled yet, had barely exchanged a pleasantry. Luckily for Myron, Eddie was a nice kid. Smart. Polite. A pleasure to talk to. But whenever Mr Crane cleared his throat – as he did now – Eddie fell silent.

'I remember your basketball days at Duke, Mr Bolitar,' Crane began.

'Please call me Myron.'

'Fine.' Instead of reciprocating the informality, Crane knitted his eyebrows. The eyebrows were his most prominent feature – unusually thick and angry and constantly undulating above his eyes. They looked like small ferrets furrowing into his forehead. 'You were captain of the team at Duke?' he began.

'For three years,' Myron said.

'And you won two NCAA championships?'

'My team did, yes.'

'I saw you play on several occasions. You were quite good.'

'Thank you.'

He leaned forward. The eyebrows grew somehow bushier. 'If I recall,' Crane continued, 'the Celtics drafted you in the first round.'

Myron nodded.

'How long did you play for them? Not long, as I recall.'

'I hurt my knee during a preseason game my rookie year.'

'You never played again?' It was Eddie. His eyes were young and wide.

'Never,' Myron said steadily. Better lesson than any lecture he could give. Like the funeral of a high school classmate who died because he was DUI.

'Then what did you do with yourself?' Mr Crane asked. 'After the injury?'

The interview. Part of the process. It was harder when you were an ex-jock. People naturally assumed you were dumb.

'I went through rehab for a long while,' Myron said. 'I thought I could beat the odds, defy the doctors, come back. When I was able to face reality, I went to law school.'

'Where?'

'At Harvard.'

'Very impressive.'

Myron tried to look humble. He almost batted his eyes.

'Did you make Law Review?'

'No.'

'Do you have an MBA?'

'No.'

'What did you do upon graduation?'

'I became an agent.'

Mr Crane frowned. 'How long did it take you to graduate?'

'Five years.'

'Why so long?'

'I was working at the same time.'

'Doing what?'

'I worked for the government.' Nice and vague. He hoped Crane didn't push it.

'I see.' Crane frowned again. Every part of him frowned. His mouth, his forehead, even his ears frowned. 'Why did you enter the field of sports representation?'

'Because I thought I'd like it. And I thought I'd be good at it.'

'Your agency is small.'

'True.'

'You don't have the connections of some larger agencies.'

'True.'

'You certainly don't wield the power of ICM or TruPro or Advantage.'

'True.'

'You don't have too many successful tennis players.'

'True.'

Crane gave a disapproving scowl. 'Then tell me, Mr Bolitar, why should we choose you?'

'I'm a lot of fun at parties.'

Mr Crane did not break a smile. Eddie did. He caught himself, smothered the smile behind his hand.

'Is that supposed to be funny?' Crane said.

'Let me ask you a question, Mr Crane. You live in Florida, right?'

'St Petersburg.'

'How did you get up to New York?'

'We flew.'

'No. I mean, who paid for the tickets?'

The Cranes shared a wary glance.

'TruPro bought your tickets, right?'

Mr Crane nodded tentatively.

'They had a limo meet you at the airport?' Myron continued.

Another nod.

'Your jacket, ma'am. It's new?'

'Yes.' First time Mrs Crane had spoken.

'Did one of the big agencies buy it for you?'

'Yes.'

'The big agencies, they have wives or female associates who take you around town, show you the sights, do a little shopping, that sort of thing?'

'Yes.'

'What's your point?' Crane interrupted.

'That kind of thing is not my bag,' Myron said.

'What kind of thing?'

'Ass-kissing. I'm not very good at ass-kissing a client. And I'm terrible at ass-kissing the parents. Eddie?'

'Yes?'

'Did the big agencies promise to have someone at every match?'

He nodded.

'I won't do that,' Myron said. 'If you need me I'm available twenty-four hours a day, seven days a week. But I'm not physically there twenty-four hours a day, seven days a week. If you want your hand held at every match because Agassi's or Chang's is, go with one of the big agencies. They're better at it than I am. If you need someone to run errands or do your laundry, I'm not the guy either.'

The Cranes shared another family glance. 'Well,' Mr Crane said. 'I heard you speak your mind, Mr Bolitar. It appears you are living up to your reputation.'

'You asked for a contrast between me and the others.'

'So I did.'

Myron focused his attention on Eddie. 'My agency is small and simple. I will do all your negotiations – tournament guarantees, appearances, exhibitions, endorsements, whatever. But I won't sign anything you don't want to. Nothing is final until you look it over, understand it, and approve it yourself. Okay so far?'

Eddie nodded.

'As your father pointed out I am not an MBA. But I work with one. His name is Win Lockwood. He's considered one of the best financial consultants in the country. Win's theory is similar to mine: he wants you to understand and approve every investment he makes. I will insist that you meet with him at least five times a year, preferably more, so that you can set up solid, long-term financial and tax plans. I want you to know what your money is doing at all times. Too many athletes get taken advantage of – bad investments, trusting the wrong people, that sort of thing. That won't happen here because *you* – not just me, not just Win, not just your parents, but *you* – won't let it.'

François came by with the appetizers. He smiled brightly while the underlings served. Then he pointed and ordered them about in impatient French, like they couldn't possibly know how to put a plate down in front of a human being without his fretting.

'Is that everything?' François asked.

'I think so.'

François sort of lowered his head. 'If there is any way I can make your dining experience more pleasurable, Mr Bolitar, please do not hesitate to ask.'

Myron looked down at his salmon. 'How about some ketchup?'

François's face lost color. 'Pardon?'

'It's a joke, François.'

'And a funny one at that, Mr Bolitar.'

François slithered away. Myron the Card strikes again.

'How about the young lady who set up this dinner?' Mr Crane asked. 'Miss Diaz. What's her function at your agency?'

'Esperanza is my associate. My right hand.'

'What's her work background?'

'She currently goes to law school nights. That's why she couldn't join us tonight. She was also a professional wrestler.'

That piqued Eddie's interest. 'Really? Which one?'

'Little Pocahontas.'

'The Indian Princess? She and Big Chief Mama used to be the tag team champs.'

'Right.'

'Man, she is hot!'

'Yup.'

Mrs Crane nibbled at her salmon. Mr Crane ignored his onion soup for the moment. 'So tell me,' Mr Crane said, 'what strategy would you employ for Eddie's career?'

'Depends,' Myron said. 'There's no set formula. You have two conflicting factors pulling at your son. On the one hand Eddie is only seventeen. He's a kid. Tennis shouldn't consume him to the point where he hates it. He should still have fun, try to do the things seventeen-year-olds do. On the other hand it's naïve to think that tennis will still be just a game to him. Or that he'll be a "normal" kid. This is about money. Big money. If Eddie does it right, if he makes some sacrifices now and works with Win, he can be financially set for life. It's a delicate balance – how many tournaments and exhibitions to play in, how many appearances, how many endorsements.'

Crane's eyebrows nodded. They seemed to agree.

Myron turned his attention to Eddie. 'You want to score a lot of money early, because you never know what can happen. I'm proof of that. But I don't want you sucked dry. Sometimes the hardest thing in the world is to say no to staggering amounts of money. But in the end it's your decision, not mine. It's your money. If you want to play in every tournament and every exhibition match, it's not my place to stop you. But you can't do it, Eddie. No one can. You're a good kid. You have your head on straight. You were raised right. But if you try to bend too far, you'll break. I've seen it happen too often.

'I want you to make a lot of money. But not every cent out there. I don't want to turn you into a money machine. I want you to have some fun. I want you to enjoy all of this. I want you to realize how lucky you are.'

The Cranes listened in rapt silence.

'That's my theory, Eddie, for what it's worth. You may make more money with the big agencies. I can't deny that. But in the long run, with a long and healthy career, with careful planning, I think you'll be wealthier and better off with MB SportsReps.'

Myron looked at Mr Crane. 'Anything else you care to know?'

Crane sipped his wine, studied its color, put the glass down. He did the eyebrow mambo again. 'You came highly recommended to us, Mr Bolitar. Or should I say to Eddie.'

'Oh?' Myron said. 'By whom?'

Eddie looked away. Mrs Crane put her hand on his arm. Mr Crane provided the answer. 'Valerie Simpson.'

Myron was surprised. 'Valerie recommended me?'

'She thought you'd be good for Eddie.'

'She said that?'

'Yes.'

Myron turned to Eddie. He wasn't crying, but he looked on the verge. 'What else did she say, Eddie?'

Shrug. 'She thought you were honest. That you'd treat me right.'

'How did you know Valerie?'

'They met at Pavel's camp in Florida,' Crane answered. 'She was sixteen when Eddie arrived. He was only nine. I think she looked after him a little.'

'They were quite close,' Mrs Crane added. 'Such a tragedy.'

'Did she say anything else, Eddie?'

Another shrug. Eddie finally looked up. Myron met his gaze, held it steady.

'It's important,' Myron said.

'She told me not to work with TruPro,' he said.

'Why?'

'She didn't say.'

'My theory,' Crane added, 'is that she blamed them for her downfall.'

'What do you think, Eddie?' Myron asked.

Yet another shrug. 'Could be. I don't know.'

'But you don't think so.'

Nothing.

Mrs Crane said, 'I think that's enough for now. Valerie's murder has been very hard on Eddie.'

The conversation slowly drifted back to business. But Eddie was silent now. Every once in a while he would open his mouth, then close it again. When they rose to leave, Eddie leaned toward Myron and whispered, 'Why do you want to know so much about Valerie?'

Myron opted for the truth. 'I'm trying to find out who killed her.'

That widened his eyes. He looked behind him. His parents were busy saying good-bye to François. François kissed Mrs Crane's hand.

'I think you might be able to help,' Myron said.

'Me?' Eddie said. 'I don't know anything.'

'She was your friend. You were close to her.'

'Eddie?'

Mr Crane's voice.

'I have to go, Mr Bolitar. Thank you for everything.'

'Yes, thank you,' Crane added. 'We have a few more agencies to see, but we'll be in touch.'

After they left, François came by with the bill. 'Your tie is very becoming, Mr Bolitar.'

The man knew how to kiss ass. 'You should have been an agent, François.'

'Thank you, sir.'

Myron gave him a Visa card and waited. He turned his cellular phone back on. A message from Win. Myron called him back.

'Where are you?' Myron asked.

'On Twenty-sixth Street, near Eighth,' Win said. 'There were two gentlemen – and I use that term in its absolute loosest sense – in the Cadillac. They followed you to La Reserve, sat outside for a while, and left about half an hour ago. They've just entered a drinking establishment of rather questionable repute.'

'Questionable repute?'

'It's called the Beaver Hunt. Enough said?'

'Stay on them. I'm on my way down.'

12

Win was waiting across the street from the Beaver Hunt. The block was quiet, the only sound was the faint beat of music coming from inside the bar. A large neon sign said TOPLESS!

'Two of them,' Win said. 'The driver was a white man, approximately six-three. Overweight but powerfully built. I think you'll like his fashion sense.'

'Meaning?'

'You'll see. He is with a black man. Six foot. Big scar on his right cheek. I guess you might describe him as thin and wiry.'

Myron looked down the street. 'Where did they park?'

'A lot on Eighth Avenue.'

'Why not on the street? Plenty of spots.'

'I believe our man is quite attached to his charming chariot.' Win smiled. 'If anything happened to it, I bet he'd be very upset.'

'How difficult will it be to break in?'

Win looked insulted. 'I'll pretend you didn't ask that.'

'Fine, you check the car. I'll go inside.'

Win snapped a salute. 'Roger, Wilco.'

They split up. Win headed for the lot, Myron for the bar. Myron would have preferred it the other way around, especially since the two men obviously knew what Myron looked like, but they needed to play their strengths. Win was far better at breaking into cars or handling anything mechanical. Myron was better at, well, this.

He entered the bar with his head lowered, just in case. No need. No one paid him any attention. There was no cover charge here. Myron looked around. Two words came to mind: major dive. The decor's theme was Early American Beer. The walls were ornamented with neon beer signs. The bar and table were crusted with beer rings. Behind the bar were pyramids of beer bottles from all over the land.

Of course, there were topless dancers. They lazily pranced atop small stages that looked like old stage props from *Wonderama*. Most of the dancers were not attractive. Far from it. The exercise craze had not yet hit the Beaver Hunt. Flesh jiggled. The place looked more like a cellulite test center than a male-fantasy cantina.

Myron moved to a corner table and sat by himself. There were a few suits, but for the most part the clientele was blue-collar. The well-to-do usually got their topless kicks at Goldfingers or Score, where the women were far more aesthetically pleasing, though their body parts were about as real as their inflatable brethren's.

Two men were laughing it up by center stage. One black, one white. They fit Win's description. When the dancers rotated stages, the one in front of them stepped off. Her downtime. The boys began to negotiate with her. In places like Goldfingers and Score, you paid about twenty or twenty-five dollars for a table dance. It was basically just what it sounded like. The girl took off her top and danced at your table for maybe five minutes. No touchy, no feely. At the Beaver Hunt, the order of the day was a recent craze known as the Lap Dance, which took place in discreet corners of the bar. The Lap Dance, known to young adolescents as the Dry Hump, consisted of a dancer gyrating on a man's crotch until he, well, orgasmed. Moral repugnancy aside, Myron had several questions about the technical aspects of such an act. Like after the act, how does a guy go around the rest of the night? Does he bring a change of underwear with him?

So many questions. So little time.

The two men and the dancer headed toward Myron's corner. Myron could now see clearly what Win had been talking about. The white guy did indeed have big arms, but he also had a protruding gut and flabby chest. Some of these flaws could be hidden with proper fashion sense, but the white guy was wearing a tight fishnet shirt. Fishnet. As in a lot of holes. As in practically no shirt at all. His chest hairs – and there were lots of them – were jutting through the holes. The hairs seemed unusually long, coiling around – and indeed getting enmeshed in – the many gold chains that were draped about his neck. As he walked by, Myron got a full view of his back, thank you very much, which was even hairier and somewhat oilier than the front.

Myron felt a little ill.

'Fifteen dollars for the first ten minutes,' the girl said. 'I can't do better than that.'

'Don't jerk us around, whore,' Fishnet said. 'There's two of us here. Two for one.'

'Yeah,' the black guy chimed in. 'Two for one.'

'I can't do that,' the girl said. If she seemed insulted by the name calling, it didn't show. Her voice was tired and matter-of-fact, like a diner waitress on the night shift.

Fishnet was not pleased by this. 'Listen, bitch, don't get me angry.'

'I'll get the manager,' she said.

'The fuck you will. You ain't leaving here till I get my rocks off, slut.'

'Yeah,' the black guy added. 'Me too. Slut.'

'Look, I charge more for talking dirty,' the girl said.

Fishnet looked at her in disbelief. 'What did you say?'

'There's a surcharge for talking dirty.'

'A surcharge?' Fishnet shouted. He was enraged now. 'This might come as a surprise to a stupid whore, but we live in the US of A Land of the free, home of the brave. I can say whatever I want, slut – or haven't you ever heard of freedom of speech?'

A constitutional scholar, Myron thought. Nice to see a man defending the First Amendment.

'Look,' the dancer said, 'the price is twelve dollars for five minutes, twenty dollars for ten minutes. Plus tip. That's it.'

'How about this,' Fishnet said. 'You dance on both of us at the same time.'

'Huh?'

'Like you're dancing on me but stroking him. How's that sound, pig?'

'Yeah,' the black guy said. 'Pig.'

'Look, fellas, there's no two-for-one deals,' the dancer said. 'Just let me get another girl. We'll take good care of you.'

Myron stepped into view. 'Will I do?'

No one moved.

'Gee,' Myron said, 'they're both so attractive. I just can't choose.'

Fishnet looked at the black guy. The black guy looked at Fishnet.

Myron turned to the girl. 'Do you have a preference?'

She shook her head no.

'Then I'll take him.' Myron pointed to Fishnet. 'He likes me. I can tell by the erect nipples.'

The black guy said, 'Hey, what's he doing here?'

Fishnet shot him a look.

'I mean, who is this guy?'

Myron nodded. 'Nice recovery. Very smooth.'

'What do you want, mister?' Fishnet asked.

'Actually, I was lying.'

'What?'

'About how I knew you liked me. It wasn't just the erect nipples, though they were a noticeable – albeit nauseating – tip-off.'

'What the fuck are you talking about?'

'Your following me around the past two days, that's what gave it away. Next time try the secret admirer route. Send flowers without signing for them. A nice Hallmark card. That kind of thing.'

'Come on, Jim,' Fishnet said to the black guy, 'this guy's nuts. Let's get out of here.'

The girl said, 'No lap dance?'

'No. We gotta go.'

'Someone's got to pay for this,' the girl said. 'Otherwise the manager's going to fry my ass.'

'Get lost, whore. Or I'll whack you.'

'Whoa, big man,' Myron said.

'Look, mister, I don't got no beef with you. Just get out of my way.'

'No lap dance for me either?'

'You're crazy.'

'I can offer you a special discount,' Myron said.

Fishnet's hands tightened into fists. He'd been ordered to follow Myron, not to be found out or get involved in physical altercation. 'Come on, Jim.'

'Why have you been following me?' Myron asked.

'I don't know what you're talking about.'

'Is it my hypnotic blue eyes? The strong features? The shapely derriere? By the way what do you think of these pants? They're not too tight, are they?'

'Fruitcake.' They moved past him.

'Tell you what,' Myron said. 'You tell me who you're working for and I promise not to tell your boss.'

They kept walking.

'Promise,' Myron said.

They headed out the door. Another day, another friend. Myron had that knack.

Myron followed them out to the street. Fishnet and Jim hurried west.

Win appeared from the shadows across the street. 'This way,' he said.

They cut through an alley and arrived at the lot before Fishnet and Jim. It was an outdoor lot. The parking attendant was in a little booth watching a *Roseanne* rerun on a minuscule black-and-white TV. Win pointed out the Cadillac. They ducked behind an Oldsmobile parked two cars away and waited.

Fishnet and Jim approached the booth. They were still looking down the street. Jim was panicking. 'How did he find us, Lee? Huh?'

'I don't know.'

'What we gonna do?'

'Nothing. We'll change cars. Try again.'

'You got another car, Lee?'

'No,' Fishnet said. 'We'll rent one.'

They paid, got a receipt and their keys. Fishnet had insisted on parking the car himself.

'This,' Win said, 'should be fun.'

When they arrived at the Cadillac, Fishnet put his key in the lock. He stopped, looked down, and began screaming.

'Shit! Goddamn fuck!'

Myron and Win stepped out of the shadows.

'Language, language,' Myron said.

Fishnet stared down at his car in disbelief. Win had drilled a hole under the lock to break in. He didn't use that particular method when neatness counted, but this was an occasion when he thought it necessary. On top of that, Win's hand had 'accidentally' slipped, scratching both driver's-side doors.

'You!' Fishnet shouted. He pointed at Myron, his face red and apoplectic. 'You!'

Win turned to Myron. 'Quite the vocabulary.'

'Yeah, but it's the threads that really make me swoon.'

'You!' Fishnet said. 'You did this to my car?'

'Not him,' Win said. 'Me. And may I say you keep the inside lovely. I felt terrible about spilling that maple syrup all over the velour seats.'

Fishnet's eyes popped. He looked inside, placed his hand on the inside, and screamed. The scream was deafening. It was so loud, the parking lot attendant almost stirred.

Myron looked at Win. 'Maple syrup?'

'Log Cabin.'

'I've always been an Aunt Jemima man myself,' Myron said.

'To each his own.'

'You find anything inside the car?'

'Not very much,' Win said. 'In the glove compartment were several parking stubs.' He handed them to Myron. Myron took a quick glance.

'So,' Myron called out, 'who are you guys working for?'

Fishnet started walking over. 'My car!' he shouted, his face red. 'You . . . my car! My car!'

Win sighed. 'Can we get past this, please? *Très* dull.'

'You motherfucker! You . . .' Fishnet's hands were fists again. He stepped closer, smiling now at Win. It was an ugly smile in every way. 'I'm going to break your fucking face, pretty boy.'

Win looked at Myron. 'Pretty boy?'

Myron shrugged.

Jim stood next to Fishnet. Neither one was armed with a gun, Myron could tell. They might have a blade hidden somewhere, but he wasn't worried.

Fishnet moved to within a yard of Win. Nothing unusual there. The bad guys always honed in on Win. He was smaller than Myron by nearly six inches and thirty-five pounds. Best of all, Win looked like a wimpy rich boy who raised his finger only to call for the butler – everything the discerning bully could want in a punching bag.

Fishnet took one more step and cocked his fist. Whoever had hired these guys had not briefed them well.

The punch whizzed toward Win's nose. He sidestepped it. Sometimes Myron thought Win moved like a cat. But that wasn't accurate. It was more ghostlike. One nanosecond he was there, the next he was two feet to the left. Fishnet tried again. Win blocked it this time. He grabbed Fishnet's fist with one hand and connected with a knife-hand strike to Fishnet's neck. Fishnet backed off, woozy. Jim stepped forward.

'Don't even think about it,' Myron said.

Jim ran.

Myron Bolitar. The Intimidator.

Fishnet regained his footing. He charged Win, head lowered, attempting a tackle. Big mistake. Win hated it when an opponent tried to use superior size against him. Win had introduced Myron to tae kwon do during their freshman year at Duke, but he'd been studying it himself since he was five years old. He'd even spent three years in the Far East studying under some of the world's greatest masters.

'Aaaarrrrghhh!' Fishnet shouted.

Again Win stepped to the side, like the smoothest matador against the clumsiest bull. Win connected on a roundhouse kick to the solar plexus and followed up with a palm strike to the nose. There was a sharp crack and blood flowed. Fishnet screamed and went down. He did not get up again.

Win bent down. 'Who are you working for?'

Fishnet looked at the blood in his hand. 'You broke my nose!' His voice was nasally.

'Wrong answer,' Win said. 'Let me repeat the question. Who are you working for?'

'I ain't saying nothing!'

Win reached down, gripped the broken nose with two fingers. Fishnet's eyes bulged.

'Don't,' Myron said.

Win looked up at him. 'If you can't take it, leave.' He turned his attention back to Fishnet. 'Last chance. Then I start twisting. Who hired you?'

Fishnet said nothing. Win gave the nose a quick squeeze. The small bones grated against one another, making a sound like rain on a skylight. Fishnet bucked in agony. Win stifled his scream with his free hand.

'Enough,' Myron said.

'He hasn't said anything yet.'

'We're the good guys, remember?'

Win made a face. 'You sound like an ACLU lawyer.'

'He doesn't have to say anything.'

'What?'

'He's a two-bit scum. He'd sell out his mother for a nickel.'

'Meaning?'

'Meaning he's more terrified of opening his mouth than the pain.'

Win smiled. 'I can change him.'

Myron held up one of the parking lot stubs. 'This lot is at Fifty-fourth and Madison. It's under TruPro's building. Our pal here is working for the Ache brothers. They're the only ones who could put that kind of scare into a guy.' Fishnet's face was pure white.

'Or Aaron,' Win said.

Aaron.

'What about him?' Myron asked.

'The Aches could be using Aaron. He could put that kind of scare into a guy.'

Aaron.

'He isn't working for Frank Ache anymore,' Myron said. 'At least, that's what I heard.'

Win looked down at Fishnet. 'The name Aaron mean anything to you?'

'No,' he shouted. Quickly. Too quickly.

Myron lowered his head toward Fishnet. 'Start talking or I'll tell Frank Ache you told us all about it.'

'I didn't say anything about no Frank Ache!'

'Triple negative,' Win said. 'Very impressive.'

There were two Ache brothers. Herman and Frank. Herman, the elder, was the boss, a sociopath responsible for countless murders and misery. But next to his whacked-out brother Frank, Herman Ache was Mary Poppins. Unfortunately, Frank ran TruPro.

'I didn't say nothing,' Fishnet repeated. He was petting his nose like it was an abused dog. 'Not a goddamn word.'

'But how's Frank to know?' Myron asked. 'You see, I'll tell Frank you sang like the tastiest of stool pigeons. And you know what? He'll believe me. How else would I know Frank hired you?'

Fishnet's face went from pale-white to a sort of seaweed-green.

'But if you cooperate,' Myron said, 'we'll all pretend this never happened. That I never spotted your tail. You'll be safe. Frank will never have to know about your little screwup.'

Fishnet didn't have to think too long. 'What do you want?'

'One of Ache's men hired you?'

'Yeah.'

'Aaron?'

'No. Just some guy.'

'What were you hired to do?'

'Follow you. Report wherever you went.'

'For what reason?'

'I don't know.'

'When did you get hired?'

'Yesterday afternoon.'

'What time?'

'I don't remember. Two, three o'clock. I was told you were at the tennis match and to get over there right away.'

That would have been almost immediately after Valerie's murder.

'That's all I know. I swear to God. That's it.'

'Bull,' Win said. But Myron waved him off. Fishnet knew nothing more of any real significance.

'Let him go,' Myron said.

13

Myron woke up early. He grabbed some cold cereal from the pantry. Something called Nutri-Grain. Yummy name. He read on the back of the box about the importance of fiber. Snore.

Myron longed for his childhood cereals: Cap'n Crunch, Froot Loops. Quisp. Quisp cereal. Who could forget Quisp, the cute alien who competed on TV commercials with some coal-miner loser named Quake? Quisp vs Quake. Extraterrestrial vs Mr Blue-collar. Interesting concept. What happened to those two rivals? Has even lovable Quisp gone the way of the Motels?

Myron sighed. He was far too young for such bouts of nostalgia.

Esperanza had managed to track down an address for Curtis Yeller's mother. Deanna Yeller lived alone in a recently purchased house in Cherry Hill, New Jersey, a suburb outside Philadelphia. Myron made his way to his car. If he started out now, there would be time to drive to Cherry Hill, meet with Deanna Yeller, and get back to New York in time for Duane's match.

But would Deanna Yeller be home? Best to make sure.

Myron picked up the car phone and dialed. A woman's voice – probably Deanna Yeller – answered. 'Hello?'

'Is Orson there?' Myron asked.

Warning: Clever deductive technique coming up. Those desiring professional pointers should pay strict attention.

'Who?' the woman asked.

'Orson.'

'You have the wrong number.'

'I'm sorry.' Myron hung up.

Deduction: Deanna Yeller was home.

He pulled up to a modest but modern home on a classic New Jersey suburban street. Every house was more or less the same. Different colors maybe. The kitchen might be on the right instead of the left. But genetically they were clones. Nice. A sprinkling of kids on the street. A sprinkling of multicolored bicycles. Couple of squirrels. A far cry from west Philadelphia. It made him wonder.

Myron walked up the little brick walk and knocked on the door. A very attractive black woman answered, a pleasant smile at the ready. Her hair was tied back in a severe bun, emphasizing the high cheekbones. Age lines around the eyes and mouth, but nothing drastic. She was well dressed, kind of conservative. Anne Klein II. Her jewelry was noticeable but not too flashy. The overall impression: classy.

Her smile seemed to fade when she saw him. 'Can I help you?'

'Mrs Yeller?'

She nodded slowly, as though not sure.

'My name is Myron Bolitar. I'd like to ask you a few questions.'

The smile fled completely. 'What about?' Her diction was different now. Less suburban civil. More street suspicious.

'Your son.'

'I ain't got a son.'

'Curtis,' Myron said.

Her eyes narrowed. 'You a cop?'

'No.'

'I ain't got the time. I'm on my way out.'

'It won't take long.'

She put her hands on her hips. 'What's in it for me?'

'Pardon me?'

'Curtis is dead.'

'I realize that.'

'So what good is talking about it gonna do? He still gonna be dead, right?'

'Please, Mrs Yeller, if I could just come in for a moment.'

She thought about it a second or two, glanced around, then shrugged in tired surrender. She checked her watch. Piaget, Myron noticed. Could be a fake, but he doubted it.

The decor was basic. Lot of white. Lot of pinewood. Torchère lamps. Very Ikea. There were no photographs on the shelves or coffee table. Nothing personal at all. Deanna Yeller didn't sit. She didn't invite Myron to either.

Myron offered up his warmest, most trustworthy smile. One part Harry Smith, two parts John Tesh.

She crossed her arms. 'What the hell you grinning at?'

Yep, another minute and she'd be curled up in his lap.

'I want to ask you about the night Curtis died,' Myron said.

'Why? What's this got to do with you?'

'I'm investigating.'

'Investigating what?'

'What really happened the night your son died.'

'You a private eye?'

'No. Not really.'

Silence.

'You got two minutes,' she said. 'That's it.'

'According to the police your son drew a gun on a police officer.'

'So they say.'

'Did he?'

She shrugged. 'Guess so.'

'Did Curtis own a gun?'

Another shrug. 'Guess he did.'

'Did you see it that night?'

'I don't know.'

'Did you ever see it before that night?'

'Maybe. I don't know.'

Boy, was this helpful. 'Why would your son and Errol break into the Old Oaks Club?'

She made a face. 'You serious?'

'Yes.'

'Why you think? To rob the place.'

'Did Curtis do that a lot?'

'Do what?'

'Rob places.'

Another shrug. 'Places, people, whatever.' Her tone was matter-of-fact. No shame, no embarrassment, no surprise, no revulsion.

'Curtis didn't have a record,' Myron said.

Yet another shrug. Her shoulders would tire soon. 'Guess I raised a smart boy,' she said. 'Until that night, anyhow.' She made a show of looking at her watch again. 'I gotta go now.'

'Mrs Yeller, have you heard from your nephew Errol Swade?'

'No.'

'Do you know where he went after your son was shot?'

'No.'

'What do you think happened to Errol?'

'He's dead.' Again matter-of-fact. 'I don't know what you want here, but this thing is finished. Finished a long time ago. No one cares anymore.'

'How about you, Mrs Yeller? Do you care?'

'It's done. Closed.'

'You were there when the police shot your son?'

'No. I got there right after.' Her voice sort of faded away.

'And you saw your son on the ground?'

She nodded.

Myron handed her his business card. 'If you remember anything else . . .'

She didn't take it. 'I won't.'

'But if you do . . .'

'Curtis is dead. Nothing you can do can change that. Best to just forget it.'

'It's that easy?'

'Been six years. Not like anybody misses Curtis.'

335

'How about you, Mrs Yeller? Do you miss him?'

She opened her mouth, closed it, opened it again. 'Not like Curtis was a good kid or nothing. He was trouble.'

'Doesn't mean he should have been killed,' Myron said.

She looked up at him, held his gaze. 'Don't matter. Dead is dead. Can't change that.'

Myron said nothing.

'Can you change that, Mr Bolitar?' she asked, challenging.

'No.'

Deanna Yeller nodded, turned away, picked up her purse. 'I have to go now,' she said. 'Best if you leave now too.'

14

Henry Hobman was the only one in the players' box.

'Hi, Henry,' Myron said.

No one was playing yet, but Henry was still in his coach repose. Without turning away from the court, Henry muttered, 'Heard you had a meeting with Pavel Menansi last night.'

'So?'

'You unhappy with Duane's coaching?'

'No.'

Henry almost nodded. End of conversation.

Duane and his opponent, a French Open finalist named Jacques Potiline, came onto the court. Duane looked himself. No signs of strain. He gave Myron and Henry a big smile, nodded. The weather was perfect for tennis. The sun was out, but a cool breeze gently purled through Stadium Court, staving off the humidity.

Myron glanced around courtside. There was a rather buxom blonde in the next box. She was packed into a white tank top. The word for today, boys and girls, is cleavage. Plenty of men ogled. Not Myron, of course. He was far too worldly. The blonde suddenly turned and caught Myron's eye. She smiled coyly, gave him a little wave. Myron waved back. He wasn't going to do anything about it, but yowzer!

Win materialized in the chair next to Myron. 'She's smiling at me, you know.'

'Dream on.'

'Women find me irresistible,' Win said. 'They see me, they want me. It's a curse I live with every day of my life.'

'Please,' Myron said. 'I just ate.'

'Envy. It's so unattractive.'

'So go for it, stud.'

Win looked over at her. 'Not my type.'

'Gorgeous blondes aren't your type?'

'Her chest is too big. I have a new theory on that.'

'What theory?'

'The bigger the breasts, the lousier the lay.'

'Pardon me?'

'Think about it,' Win said. 'Well-endowed women – I am referring here to ones with mega-fronts – have a habit of laying back and relying on their, er, assets. The effort isn't always what it should be. What do you think?'

Myron shook his head. 'I have several reactions,' he replied, 'but I think I'll stick with my initial one.'

'Which is?'

'You're a pig.'

Win smiled, sat back. 'So how was your visit with Ms Yeller?'

'She's hiding something too.'

'Well, well. The plot doth thicken.'

Myron nodded.

'In my experience,' Win said, 'there is only one thing that can silence the mother of a dead boy.'

'And that is?'

'Cash. A great deal of it.'

Mr Warmth. But in truth the same thought had crossed Myron's mind. 'Deanna Yeller lives in Cherry Hill now. In a house.'

Win leapt on that one. 'A single widow from the dumps of west Philadelphia moving to the 'burbs? Pray tell, how does she afford it?'

'Do you really think she's being bought?'

'Is there another explanation? According to what we know, the woman has no solid means of support. She spent her life in an impoverished area. Now all of a sudden she's Miss Better Homes and Gardens.'

'Could be something else.'

'For example?'

'A guy.'

Win made a scoffing noise. 'A forty-two-year-old ghetto woman does not find that kind of sugar daddy. It just doesn't happen.'

Myron said nothing.

'Now,' Win continued, 'add into that equation Kenneth and Helen Van Slyke, the grieving parents of another dead child.'

'What about them?'

'I've done a bit of checking. They too have no visible signs of support. Kenneth's family was already destitute when they married. As for Helen, whatever money she had Kenneth lost in his business ventures.'

'You mean they're broke?'

'Completely,' Win replied. 'So pray tell, dear friend, how are they managing to carry on at Brentman Hall?'

Myron shook his head. 'There has to be another explanation.'

'Why?'

'One mother being bought off by her child's killer I *might* be able to buy. But two?'

Win said, 'You have a rather rosy view of human nature.'

'And you have a rather dim one.'

'Which is why I'm usually correct in these matters,' Win said.

Myron frowned. 'What about TruPro's connection with this?'

'What about it?'

'Fishnet was hired to follow me immediately after the murder. Why?'

'The Ache brothers know you quite well by now. Perhaps they feared you'd investigate.'

'So? What's their interest?'

Win thought a second. 'Didn't TruPro used to represent Valerie?'

'But that was six years ago,' Myron said. 'Before the Ache brothers had even taken over the agency.'

'Hmm. Perhaps you are barking up the wrong tree.'

'What do you mean?' Myron asked.

'Perhaps there is no connection. TruPro is interested in signing Eddie Crane, correct?'

Myron nodded.

'And Eddie's mentor – this Pavel fellow – is closely associated with TruPro. Perhaps they feel you are moving in on their turf.'

'Which the Ache brothers would not like,' Myron added.

'Precisely.'

A possibility. Myron tried it on and walked around a bit, but it just didn't feel right.

'Oh, one other thing,' said Win.

'What?'

'Aaron is in town.'

Myron felt a quick chill. 'What for?'

'I don't know.'

'Probably just a coincidence,' Myron said.

'Probably.'

Silence.

Win sat back and steepled his fingers. The match began. Duane's play was nothing short of spectacular. He cruised through the first set 6–2. He stumbled a bit in the second, but came on to win it 7–5. Jacques Potiline had had enough. Duane whipped him in the final set 6–1.

Another impressive victory.

As the players left the court, Henry Hobman stood. His face remained locked on grim. He chewed at the inside of his mouth. 'Better,' he said tightly. 'But not great.'

'Stop gushing, Henry. It's embarrassing.'

Ned Tunwell sprinted down the steps toward Myron. His arms were flapping like a kid making windmills in the snow. Several other Nike execs followed him. There were tears in Ned's eyes.

'I knew it!' Ned shouted in glee. He shook Myron's hand, hugged him, turned to Win, pumped his hand too. Win pulled his hand back and wiped it on his pants. 'I just knew it!'

Myron simply nodded.

'Soon! So soon!' Ned cried. 'The promo of the year begins! Everyone is going to know the name Duane Richwood! He was fantastic, utterly fantastic! I can't believe it. I swear, I don't think I've ever been this excited before!'

'You're not going to come again, are you, Ned?'

'Oh, Myron!' He nudged Win playfully with his elbow. 'Is he a kidder or what?'

'A gifted comedian,' Win agreed.

Ned slapped Win's shoulder. Win visibly winced but did not break the offending hand. Amazing restraint for Win.

'Look, guys,' Ned said, 'I'd love to stand here and chat all day. But I gotta run.'

Win managed to hide his disappointment.

'Ciao for now. Myron, we'll talk, okay?'

Myron nodded.

'Bye, guys.' Ned skipped – actually skipped – back up the stairs.

Win watched him depart with something approaching horror. 'What,' he asked, 'was that?'

'A bad dream. I'll meet you back at the office.'

'Where are you going?' Win asked.

'To talk to Duane. I have to ask him about Valerie's call.'

'Let it go until after the tournament.'

Myron shook his head. 'Can't.'

15

Myron waited for the press conference to end. It took some time. Duane was holding court, firmly in his element. The media had a new darling. Duane Richwood. Cocky but not obnoxious. Confident yet gracious. Handsome. American.

When the hordes of press finally ran out of questions, Myron accompanied Duane back to the dressing room. He sat on a chair next to Duane's locker. Duane took off his sunglasses and put them on the top shelf.

'Some match, huh?' Duane said.

Myron nodded.

'Hey, this win oughta make Nike happy.'

'Orgasmic,' Myron agreed.

'They are going to air the ad during my next match, right?'

'Yep.'

Duane shook his head. 'Quarterfinal, at the US Open,' he said in awe. 'I can't believe it, Myron. We're on our way.'

'Duane?'

'Yeah?'

'I know Valerie called you,' Myron said.

Duane stopped. 'What?'

'She called your apartment twice. From a pay phone near her hotel.'

'I don't know what you're talking about.'

Duane quickly reached for the sunglasses, fumbled them, put them on.

'I want to help you, Duane.'

'Nothing to help with me.'

'Duane . . .'

'Just leave me the fuck alone.'

'I can't do that.'

'Look, Myron, I don't need distractions right now. Just drop it.'

'She's dead, Duane. That just won't go away.'

Duane took off his shirt and began toweling off his chest. 'Some stalker killed her,' he said. 'I saw it on the news. Got nothing to do with me.'

'Why did she call you, Duane?'

His hands were clenching and unclenching. 'You work for me, right?'

'Right.'

'Then drop it or you're fired.'

Myron looked at him. 'No,' he said.

Duane sank into a chair, his head in his hands. 'Shit, I'm sorry, Myron. I didn't mean that. It's just the pressure. What with this tournament and that Dimonte cop accusing me and all. Look, just forget I said anything, okay? Just forget this whole conversation happened.'

'No.'

'What?'

'Why did she call you, Duane?'

'Man, don't you listen?'

'Not well.'

'Just stay out of it.'

'No.'

'It's got nothing to do with the murder.'

'Then you admit she called you?'

Duane stood, turned his back toward Myron, leaned against his locker.

'Duane?'

His words were soft. 'Yeah, she called me. So what?'

'Why?'

'Let's just say we were acquainted. Intimately, if you get my drift.'

'You and Valerie . . . ?' Myron made futile hand gestures.

Duane nodded slowly. 'It was no big thing. Just a few times.'

'When did this start?'

'Couple of months ago.'

'Where did you meet?'

He looked at Myron, confused. 'At a tournament.'

'Which one?'

'I don't remember. New Haven, I think. But it was over quick.'

'So why did you lie to the police?'

'Why do you think?' he countered. 'Wanda was standing right there. I love her, man. I made a mistake. I didn't want to hurt her. Is that so wrong?'

'So why wouldn't you tell me?'

'What?'

'When I asked you just now. Why didn't you tell me the truth?'

'Same reason.'

'But Wanda isn't here.'

'I was ashamed, okay?'

'Ashamed?'

'I'm not proud of what I did.'

Myron watched him. With those sunglasses Duane's face looked sleek and robotic. But something wasn't right here. It was a nice sentiment, but twenty-one-year-old professional athletes, no matter how faithful to their partners, were not this ashamed of letting their agents know about an indiscretion. The excuse might be commendable, but it rang hollow. 'If it was over, why was Valerie calling you?'

'I don't know. She wanted to see me again. One last fling, I guess.'

'Did you agree to see her?'

'No. I told her we were finished.'

'What else did you say?'

'Nothing.'

'What else did she say?'

'Nothing.'

'Are you sure? Do you remember anything at all?'

'No. Nothing.'

'Did she seem distressed?'

'Not that I could tell.'

The door opened. Players began to file in, many offering Duane icy congratulations. Rising stars were not big in the locker room. If someone new was joining the ultra-exclusive tennis club known as the 'Top Ten,' another member had to be thrown out. The way it was. No boardroom was this cutthroat. Everyone was a rival here. Everyone was competing for the same dollars and fame. Everyone was an enemy.

Duane suddenly looked very much alone.

'You hungry?' Myron asked.

'Starved,' Duane said.

'You want anything in particular?'

'Pizza,' Duane said. 'Extra cheese and pepperoni.'

'Get dressed. I'll meet you out front.'

16

'Myron Bolitar?'

The car phone. He'd just dropped Duane off at his apartment.

'Yes.'

'This is Gerard Courter with the NYPD. Jake's son.'

'Oh, right. How's it going, Gerard?'

'Can't complain. I doubt you remember but we played against each other once.'

'Michigan State,' Myron said. 'I remember. And I have the bruises to prove it.'

Gerard laughed. Sounded just like his old man. 'Glad I was memorable.'

'That's a polite word for what you were.'

Another Jake-like guffaw. 'My dad said you needed info on the Simpson homicide.'

'I'd appreciate it.'

'You probably heard there's a major suspect. Guy named Roger Quincy.'

'The stalker.'

'Yeah.'

'Is there anything specific tying him to the murder?' Myron asked. 'Besides the stalking?'

'He's on the run, for one thing. When they got to Quincy's apartment he was packed and gone. No one knows where he is.'

'He might have just been scared,' Myron said.

'Good reason to be.'

'Why do you say that?'

'Roger Quincy was at the tennis center on the day of the murder.'

'You have witnesses?'

'Several.'

That slowed Myron down. 'What else?'

'She was shot with a thirty-eight. Very close range. We found the weapon in a garbage can ten yards away from the shooting. Smith & Wesson. It was in a Feron's bag. The bag had a bullet hole in it.'

Feron's. Another tournament sponsor. They were licensed to sell 'official tournament merchandise.' Feron's had at least half a dozen stands selling to a zillion people. No way to trace it back. 'So the killer walked up to her,' Myron said, 'shot her through the bag, kept walking, dumped the gun in the garbage, and headed out.'

'That's how we see it,' Gerard said.

'A cool customer.'

'Very.'

'Any prints on the gun?' Myron asked.

'Nope.'

'Any witnesses to the shooting?'

'Several hundred. Unfortunately all anyone remembers is the sound of the gun, and Valerie toppling over.'

Myron shook his head. 'The killer took a hell of a chance. Shooting her in public like that.'

'Yeah. A major case of brass balls.'

'You got anything else?'

'Just a question,' Gerard said.

'Shoot.'

'Where are our seats for next Saturday?'

17

Esperanza had neatly stacked two piles of six-year-old press clippings on Myron's desk. The pile on the right – the taller pile – was made up of articles on the murder of Alexander Cross. The smaller stack was on the hospitalization of Valerie Simpson.

Myron ignored the third stack – the one with his messages – and started sifting through the pile on Valerie. The story was already familiar to him. Valerie's family had claimed she was 'taking time off,' but a well-placed source leaked the truth to the press: the teen tennis star was actually a patient at the famed Dilworth Mental Health Facility. The family denied it for a few days – until a photograph of Valerie taking a walk on the Dilworth grounds appeared in the papers. A belated statement from the family claimed that Valerie was 'resting from exhaustion caused by external pressures,' whatever that meant.

The media coverage was only mildly intense. Valerie was already a has-been in the tennis world, ergo the press was interested but not ravenous. Still, rumors surfaced, especially in some of the fringe periodicals. One said that Valerie's breakdown had been the result of a sexual assault. Another said she'd been attacked by a stalker. Still another claimed Valerie had murdered someone in cold blood, though the article didn't bother the reader with mundane details – like the victim's name, how he or she was killed, why the police hadn't arrested Valerie, the little things.

But the most interesting rumor, the one that really snared Myron's attention, appeared in two separate papers. According to several 'unnamed sources,' Valerie Simpson had gone into hiding to cover up a pregnancy.

Might be something, might be nothing. Pregnancy rumors always surface when a young woman goes into hiding. Still . . .

He moved on to articles on Alexander Cross's murder. Esperanza had limited her search to Philadelphia area periodicals, but the material was still immense. The stories basically followed the police version. Alexander Cross had been at a party at his snooty tennis club. He stumbled across two burglars, Errol Swade and Curtis Yeller. He took chase, confronted them on the main grass court, and was stabbed by Errol Swade. The blade punctured Alexander's heart. Death was instantaneous.

Senator Cross and his family had not commented on the case. According to the senator's spokesman, the family was 'in seclusion' and was 'relying on law enforcement agencies and the justice system,' whatever that meant.

The press focused on the manhunt for Errol Swade. The police were confident to the point of cocky that Swade would be captured within a matter of hours. But hours turned to days. Editorials harshly criticized the police for not being able to nab one nineteen-year-old drug addict, but the Cross family remained silent. The story provoked the standard public outrage – why, editorials demanded to know, had a lowlife like Errol Swade been let out on parole in the first place?

But the anger fizzled, as it always does in such cases. Other stories began to take precedence. The coverage trickled from front page to back page to oblivion.

Myron checked through the pile again. The police shooting of Curtis Yeller had been neatly glossed over. There was no mention of an internal affairs investigation into the incident. None of the usual reactionaries protested the police 'brutality,' which was strange. Usually some whacko managed to get himself on television, no matter what the facts, especially in the case of a black teen being gunned down by a white cop. But not this time. Or at least it wasn't covered by the press.

Wait. Hold the phone.

An article on Curtis Yeller. Myron had missed it the first time because it'd been printed the day immediately following the murder. Very early for this kind of piece. Probably sneaked in before Senator Cross put his foot down – but that might just be conspiracy paranoia on Myron's part. Hard to tell.

It was a small article on the bottom corner of page 12 in the metro section. Myron read it twice. Then a third time. The article was not on the shooting in west Philly or even the police's role in said shooting. The article was on Curtis Yeller himself.

It started out like any puff piece: Curtis Yeller was described as an 'honor roll student.' Not a big deal really. A psychotic child molester with the IQ of a citrus beverage was suddenly dubbed an honor student when killed prematurely. Very *Bonfire of the Vanities*. But this story went a bit further. Mrs Lucinda Elright, Curtis Yeller's history teacher, described Curtis as her 'best pupil' and a boy who 'had never even gotten a detention.' Mr Bernard Johnson, his English teacher, said Curtis was 'unusually bright and inquisitive,' 'one in a million,' and 'like a son to me.'

The usual death hyperbole?

Perhaps. But school records backed the teachers up. Curtis had never been on report. He also had the best attendance record in his grade. On top of that, his transcript reported a 3.9 average, his sole B coming in some sort of health class. Both teachers firmly believed that Curtis Yeller was incapable of violence. Mrs Elright blamed Curtis's cousin Errol Swade, but no specifics were given.

Myron sat back. He stared at a movie still from *Casablanca* on the far wall. Sam was serenading Bogie and Bergman as the Nazis moved in. Here's looking at you, kid. We'll always have Paris. You're getting on that plane. Myron wondered if young Curtis Yeller had ever seen the movie, if he had had the opportunity to behold the celluloid image of Ingrid Bergman with tears in her eyes at a foggy airport.

He picked up the basketball from behind his desk and began spinning it on his finger. He slapped it at just the right angle to increase the speed rotation without dislodging the ball from its axis. He stared at his handiwork as though it were a Gypsy's crystal ball. He saw an alternate universe, one with a younger version of himself hitting a three-pointer at the buzzer on the Boston Garden's parquet floor. He tried not to let himself dwell on this image too long, but there it stayed, front and center, refusing to leave.

Esperanza came in. She sat down and waited in silence.

The ball stopped spinning. Myron put it down and handed her the article. 'Take a look at this.'

She read it. 'A couple of teachers said something nice about a dead kid. So what? Probably misquoted anyway.'

'But this is more than just a couple of casual comments. Curtis Yeller had no police record, no school record, a nearly perfect attendance record, and a 3.9 GPA. For most kids that's a hell of a statement. But this was a kid from one of the worst parts of Philadelphia.'

Esperanza shrugged. 'I don't see the relevance. What difference does it make if Yeller was Einstein or an idiot?'

'None. Except it's just one more thing that doesn't add up. Why did Curtis's mother say he was a no-good thief?'

'Maybe she knew more than his teachers.'

Myron shook his head. He thought about Deanna Yeller. The proud, beautiful woman who answered the door. The suddenly hostile, defensive woman at the mention of her dead son. 'She was lying.'

'Why?'

'I don't know. Win thinks she's being bought off.'

'Sounds like a good possibility,' Esperanza said.

'What, a mother taking bribes to protect her son's murderer?'

Esperanza shrugged again. 'Sure, why not?'

'You really think a mother . . . ?' Myron stopped. Esperanza's face was totally impassive – another one who believed the worst. 'Just look at this whole scenario for a second,' he tried. 'Curtis Yeller and Errol Swade break into this ritzy tennis club at night. Why? To rob the place? Of what? It was night. It wasn't like they were going to find wallets in the locker room. So what were they going to steal? Some tennis sneakers? A couple of rackets? That's a hell of a long way to go for some tennis equipment.'

'Stereo equipment, maybe,' Esperanza said. 'The clubhouse could have a big-screen TV.'

'Fine. Assume you're right. Problem is, the boys didn't take a car. They took public transportation and walked. How were they going to carry the loot? By hand?'

'Maybe they planned on stealing one.'

'From the club's valet lot?'

She shrugged. 'Could be,' she said. Then: 'Mind if I change subjects for a second?'

'Go ahead.'

'How did it go with Eddie Crane last night?'

'He's a big fan of Little Pocahontas. He said she was "hot." '

'Hot?'

'Yup.'

She shrugged. 'Kid's got taste.'

'Nice too. I liked him. He's smart, got his head on straight. Helluva good kid.'

'You going to adopt him?'

'Uh, no.'

'How about represent him?'

'They said they'll be in touch.'

'What do you think?'

'Hard to say. The kid liked me. The parents are worried about me being small-time.' Pause. 'How did it go with Burger City?'

She handed him some papers. 'Prelim contract for Phil Sorenson.'

'TV commercial?'

'Yeah, but he has to dress up as a burger condiment.'

'Which one?'

'Ketchup, I think. We're still talking.'

'Fine. Just don't let it be mayonnaise or pickle.' He studied the contract. 'Nice work. Good figures.'

Esperanza looked at him.

'Very good, in fact.' He smiled at her. Widely.

'Is this the part where I get all excited by your praise?' she asked.

'Forget I said anything.'

She pointed to the stack of articles. 'I managed to track down Valerie's shrink from her days at Dilworth. Her name is Julie Abramson. She has a private office on Seventy-third Street. She won't see you, of course. Refuses to discuss her patient.'

'A woman doctor,' Myron mused. He put his hands behind his head. 'Maybe I can entice her with my rapier wit and brawny body.'

'Probably,' Esperanza said, 'but on the off chance she's not comatose, I went with an alternative plan.'

'And that is?'

'I called her office back, changed my voice, and pretended you were a patient. I made an appointment for you to see her tomorrow morning. Nine o'clock.'

'What's my psychosis?'

'Chronic priapism,' she said. 'But that's just my opinion.'

'Funny.'

'Actually, you've been much better since what's-her-name left town.'

What's-her-name was Jessica, which Esperanza knew very well. Esperanza did not care much for the love of Myron's life. A casual observer might offer up jealousy as the culprit, but that'd be way off base. True, Esperanza was extraordinarily beautiful. Sure, there'd been moments of temptation between them, but one or the other had always been prudent enough to douse the flames before any real damage was done. There was also the fact that Esperanza liked a bit of diversity when it came to beaus – diversity that went well beyond tall or short, fat or thin, white or black. Right now, for example, Esperanza was dating a photographer. The photographer's name was Lucy. Lucy. As in a female, for those having trouble catching the drift.

No, the reason for her strong dislike was far simpler: Esperanza had been there when Jessica left the first time. She had seen it all firsthand. And Esperanza held grudges.

Myron returned to his original question. 'So what did you tell them was wrong with me?'

'I was vague,' she said. 'You hear voices. You suffer from paranoid schizophrenia, delusions, hallucinations, something like that.'

'How did you get an appointment so fast?'

'You're a very famous movie star.'

'My name?'

'I didn't dare give one,' Esperanza said. 'You're that big.'

18

Dr Julie Abramson's office was on the corner of Seventy-third Street and Central Park West. Ritzy address. One block north, overlooking the park, was the San Remo building. Dustin Hoffman and Diane Keaton lived there. Madonna had tried to move in, but the board decided she was not San Remo material. Win lived a block south, in the Dakota, where John Lennon had lived and literally died. Whenever you entered the Dakota's courtyard you crossed over the spot where Lennon had been gunned down. Myron had walked it a hundred times since the shooting, but he still felt the need to be silent when he did.

There was an ornate, wrought-iron gate on Dr Abramson's door. Protective or decorative? Myron couldn't decide, but he saw some irony in a psychiatric office being guarded by a 'wrought' iron gate.

Okay, not much irony but a little.

Myron pressed a doorbell. He heard the buzzer and let himself in. He was wearing his best pair of sunglasses for the occasion, even though it was cloudy outside. Mr Movie Star.

The receptionist, a neatly attired man wearing fashionable spectacles, folded his hands and said, 'Good morning,' in a supposedly soothing voice that grated like a tortured cat's screech.

'I'm here to see Dr Abramson. I have a nine o'clock appointment.'

'I see.' He perked up now, studying Myron's face, trying to guess who the big movie star was. Myron adjusted his sunglasses but kept them on. The receptionist wanted to ask for a name, but discretion got the better of him. Afraid of insulting the big-time celebrity.

'Could you fill out this form while you're waiting?'

Myron tried to look annoyed by the inconvenience.

'It's just a formality,' the receptionist said. 'I'm sure you understand how these things are.'

Myron sighed. 'Very well then.'

After it was filled out the receptionist asked for it back.

'I'd rather give it directly to Dr Abramson,' Myron said.

'Sir, I assure you—'

'Perhaps I didn't make myself clear.' Mr Difficult. Just like a real movie star. 'I will give it to Dr Abramson personally.'

The receptionist sulked in silence. Several minutes later the intercom buzzed. The receptionist picked up the phone, listened for a second, hung up. 'Right this way please.'

Dr Abramson was tiny – four-ten, tops, and seventy pounds soaking wet. Everything about her looked shrunken, scrunched up. Except for her eyes. They peered out of the diminutive face like two big, radiant, warm beacons that missed nothing.

She placed her child-size hand in his. Her handshake was surprisingly firm. 'Please have a seat,' she said.

Myron did. Dr Abramson sat across from him. Her feet barely reached the ground. 'May I have your sheet?' she asked.

'Of course.' Myron handed it to her. She glanced down for a brief second. 'You're Bruce Willis?'

Myron gave her a cocky side smirk. Very *Die Hard*. 'Didn't recognize me with the sunglasses, huh?'

'You look nothing like Bruce Willis.'

'I would have put Harrison Ford, but he's too old.'

'Still would have been a better choice.' Then studying him a bit more she added, 'Liam Neeson would have been better still.' Dr Abramson did not seem particularly upset by Myron's stunt. Then again, she was a trained psychiatrist and thus used to dealing with abnormal minds. 'Why don't you tell me your real name.'

'Myron Bolitar.'

The little face broke open in a smile nearly as radiant as the eyes. 'I thought I recognized you. You're the basketball star.'

'I wouldn't say "star" exactly.' Blush, blush.

'Please, Mr Bolitar, don't be so modest. First team all-American three years in a row. Two NCAA championships. One College Player of the Year. Eighth pick overall in the draft.'

'You're a fan?'

'And so observant.' She leaned back. Like a small child in a big rocking chair. 'As I recall, you made the cover of *Sports Illustrated* twice. Unusual for a college player. You were also a good student, an academic all-American, popular with the press, and considered quite handsome. Am I correct?'

'Yes,' Myron said. 'Except maybe for that "considered" part.'

She laughed. It was a nice laugh. Her whole body seemed to join in. 'Now why don't you tell me what this is all about, Mr Bolitar.'

'Please call me Myron.'

'Fine. And you can call me Dr Abramson. Now what seems to be the problem?'

'No, I'm fine.'

'I see.' She looked skeptical, but Myron sensed that the good doctor was having a little fun at his expense. 'So you have a "friend" with a problem. Tell me all about it.'

'My friend,' he said, 'is Valerie Simpson.'

That got her attention. 'What?'

'I want to talk to you about Valerie Simpson.'

The open face slammed shut. 'You're not a reporter, are you?'

'No.'

'I thought I read you were a sports agent.'

'I am. Valerie Simpson was about to become a client.'

'I see.'

'When was the last time you saw Valerie?' Myron asked.

Dr Abramson shook her head. 'I can neither confirm nor deny that Valerie Simpson was ever a patient of mine.'

'You don't have to confirm or deny it. I know she was.'

'I repeat: I can neither confirm nor deny that Valerie Simpson was ever a patient of mine.' She studied him for a moment. 'Perhaps you can tell me what your interest is in this.'

'Like I said before, I was going to represent her.'

'That doesn't explain your visiting me incognito.'

'I'm investigating her murder.'

'Investigating?'

Myron nodded.

'Who hired you?'

'No one.'

'Then why are you investigating?'

'I have my reasons.'

She nodded. 'What are those reasons, Myron? I'd like to hear about them.'

Psychiatrists. 'You want me to also tell you about the time I walked in on Mommy and Daddy?'

'If you want.'

'I don't want. What I want is to know what caused Valerie's breakdown.'

Her response was rote. 'I can neither confirm nor deny that Valerie Simpson was ever a patient of mine.'

'Doctor-patient privilege?'

'That's right.'

'But Valerie is dead.'

'That doesn't alter my obligation in the slightest.'

'She's been murdered. Gunned down in cold blood.'

'I understand that. Dramatics will not alter my obligation either.'

'But you may know something helpful.'

'Helpful in what way?'

'In finding the killer.'

She folded the tiny hands in her lap. Like a little girl in church. 'And that's what you're attempting to do? Find this woman's killer?'

'Yes.'

'What about the police? I understand from news reports that they have a suspect.'

'I don't trust authority types,' Myron said.

'Oh?'

'It's one of the reasons I want to help.'

Dr Abramson fixed him with the big eyes. 'I don't think so, Myron.'

'No?'

'You look more like the rescue-complex sort to me. The kind of man who likes to play hero all the time, who sees himself as a knight in shining armor. What do you think?'

'I think we should save my analysis for later.'

She shrugged her little shoulders. 'Just giving my opinion. No extra charge.'

'Fine.' *Extra* charge? 'I'm not so sure the police have the right man.'

'Why not?'

'I was hoping you could help me with that. Valerie must have talked about Roger Quincy's stalking her. Did she think he was dangerous?'

'For the final time, I will neither confirm nor deny—'

'I'm not asking you to. I'm asking about Roger Quincy. You don't have a relationship with him, do you?'

'I also don't know him.'

'Then how about one of those quick opinions. Like you did with me.'

She shook her head. 'I'm sorry.'

'There's no way I can convince you to talk to me?'

'About a possible patient? No.'

'Suppose I got parental consent.'

'You won't.'

Myron waited, watched. She was better at this than him. Her face gave away nothing, but the words couldn't be taken back. 'How do you know that?' he asked.

She remained silent. Her eyes dropped to the floor. Myron wondered if the faux pas had been on purpose.

'They called you already, didn't they?' Myron said.

'I'm not at liberty to discuss any communications between myself and—'

'The family called. They hushed you up.'

'I will neither confirm—'

'The body is barely cold and they're already covering their tracks,' Myron went on. 'You don't see anything wrong with that?'

Dr Abramson cleared her throat. 'I do not know what you're talking about, but I will say this: it is not unreasonable in situations such as the one you've described to me for parents to want to protect their daughter's memory.'

'Protect her memory' – Myron rose, put on his best lawyer-in-summation glower – 'or her murderer?' Mr High Drama.

'Now you're being silly,' she said. 'You surely don't suspect the young woman's family.'

Myron sat back down. He gave his best anything's-possible head tilt. 'Helen Van Slyke's daughter is killed. Within hours the grieving mother calls you to make sure you keep your mouth shut. You don't find that a tad odd?'

'I will neither confirm nor deny that I have ever heard the name Helen Van Slyke.'

'I see,' Myron said. 'So you think this should all be shoved aside. Bottled up. Let the image rule over the reality. Somehow I don't think that sits well with you, Doc.'

She said nothing.

'Your patient is dead,' Myron continued. 'Don't you think your obligation should be to her, not her mother?'

Dr Abramson's hands tightened into small balls for a moment, then relaxed. She took a deep breath, held it, let it out slowly. 'Let us pretend – and just pretend – that I was the psychiatrist for this young woman. Wouldn't I have an obligation not to betray what she told me in the strictest of confidences? If the patient chose not to reveal any of this while alive, wouldn't I have an obligation to uphold that right for her in death?'

Myron stared at her. Dr Abramson stared back. Unyielding. 'Nice speech,' he said. 'But maybe Valerie wanted to reveal something. And maybe someone killed her to deny her that right.'

The bright eyes blinked several times. 'I think you should leave now,' she said.

She pressed a button on her intercom. The receptionist appeared at the door. He crossed his arms and tried to look intimidating. The attempt was hardly a rousing success.

Myron rose. He knew he had planted a seed. He would have to give it time to germinate. 'Will you at least think about it?' he added.

'Good-bye, Myron.'

The receptionist stepped aside, allowing Myron room to pass.

19

Of the three witnesses to the murder of Alexander Cross – all college chums of the deceased – only one lived in the New York area. Gregory Caufield, Jr was now a young associate at daddy's law firm of Stillen, Caufield, and Weston, a high-powered, high-profile firm with offices in several states and foreign countries.

Myron dialed, asked for Gregory Caufield, Jr, and was put on hold. A woman came on the line several seconds later and said, 'I'll put you straight through to Mr Caufield.'

A click. One ring. Then an enthusiastic voice said, 'Well, hi!'

Well, hi?

'Is this Gregory Caufield?'

'Sure is. What can I do for you today?'

'My name is Myron Bolitar.'

'Uh-huh.'

'And I'd like to make an appointment to see you.'

'Sure. When?'

'As soon as possible.'

'How about half an hour from now? Will that be okay?'

'That'll be fine, thank you.'

'Super, Myron. Looking forward to it.'

Click. *Super?*

Fifteen minutes later Myron was on his way. He walked up Park Avenue past the mosque steps where Myron and Win liked to lunch on summer days. Prime woman-watching perch. New York has the most beautiful women in the world, bar none. They wear business attire and sneakers and sunglasses. They walk with cool purpose, with no time to waste. Amazingly, none of the beautiful women checked Myron out. Probably just being discreet. Probably ogling him like crazy from behind those sunglasses.

Myron cut west to Madison Avenue. He passed a couple of electronics stores with the same GOING OUT OF BUSINESS signs they'd had up for at least a year. The sign was always the same – white sign, black letters. A blind man held out a cup. Didn't even give out pencils anymore. His seeing-eye dog looked dead. Two cops were laughing on the corner. They were eating croissants. Not doughnuts. Another cliché blown to hell.

There was a security guard by the elevator in the lobby.

'Yes?'

'Myron Bolitar to see Gregory Caufield.'

'Oh yes, Mr Bolitar. Twenty-second floor.' Didn't call up. Didn't check his list. Hmm.

When the elevator opened, a pleasant-faced woman was standing there. 'Good afternoon, Mr Bolitar. If you'd please follow me.'

Down a long corridor with an office-pink carpet, white walls, McKnight framed posters. No typewriters clicked, but Myron heard the whir of a laser printer. Someone was dialing a number on a speakerphone. A fax machine screeched its call to another fax machine. When they turned the corner, a second, equally pleasant-faced, woman approached. Plastic smiles all around.

'Hello, Mr Bolitar,' the second woman said. 'Nice to see you today.'

'Nice to see you too.' Every line a lady-slayer.

The first woman handed him over to the second. Tag-team style. 'Mr Caufield is waiting for you in conference room C,' the second woman said, her voice low, as if conference room C were a clandestine chamber in the bowels of the Pentagon.

She led him to a door very much like any other except it had a big bronze C on it. In a matter of seconds, Myron managed to deduce that the room was conference room C. The Adventures of Sherlock Bolitar. A man opened the door from the inside. He was young with a thick head of Stephanopoulos-like hair. He pumped Myron's hand enthusiastically. 'Hi, Myron.'

'Hi, Gregory.' Like they actually knew each other.

'Please come in. There's someone here I'd like you to meet.'

Myron stepped fully into the room. Big walnut table with dark leather chairs, the expensive kind, the kind with those little gold buttons on them. Oil portraits of stern-faced men on the walls. The room was empty, except for one man down the other end of the table. Though they had never met, Myron recognized the man immediately. He should have been surprised, but he wasn't.

Senator Bradley Cross.

Gregory did not bother with introductions. In fact he didn't bother staying. He slipped out the door, closing it behind him. The senator stood. His were a far cry from the classic patrician good looks one usually associates with political families. They say people look like their pets; in that case Senator Bradley Cross owned a basset hound. His features were long and malleable. His finely tailored suit did nothing to disguise his exaggerated pear build; on a woman, his hips would be called child-bearing. His hair was wispy gray strands that seemed to be suffering from static cling. He wore thick glasses and an off-center smile. Still, it was an endearing smile – indeed, an endearing, trustworthy face. The kind of face you'd vote for.

Senator Cross slowly put out his hand. 'I'm sorry for the dramatics,' he said, 'but I thought we should meet.'

They shook hands.

'Please have a seat. Make yourself comfortable. Can I get you something?'

'No, thank you,' Myron said.

They sat facing each other. Myron waited. The senator seemed unsure how to begin. He coughed into his fists several times. Each cough made his jowls flap a bit.

'Do you know why I wanted to see you?' he asked.

'No,' Myron said.

'I understand you've been asking a lot of questions about my son. More specifically, about his murder.'

'Where did you hear that?'

'Around. Here and there. I am not without my sources.' He tilted his head the way a basset hound does when he hears a strange sound. 'I'd like to know why.'

'Valerie Simpson was going to be a client of mine,' Myron said.

'So I've been told.'

'I'm looking into her murder.'

'And you believe there might be a connection between Valerie's murder and Alexander's?'

Myron shrugged.

'My son was killed by a random street thug six years ago near Philadelphia. Valerie was killed almost gangland style at the US Open in New York. What possible connection could there be?'

'Maybe none.'

Cross leaned back, fiddled his thumbs. 'I want to be up-front with you, Myron. I've looked into your background a bit. I know about your past work. Not the details, of course, but your reputation. I'm not trying to apply any influence here. It's not my style. I've never been comfortable at playing the tough guy.' He smiled again. His eyes were wet now and there was a discernible quake in his voice. 'I'm talking to you now not as a United States senator but as a grieving father. A grieving father who just wants to let his son rest in peace. I'm asking you to please stop what you're doing.'

The pain in the man's voice was raw. Myron had not expected this. 'I'm not sure I can, Senator.'

The senator rubbed his entire face vigorously, using both hands. 'You see two young people . . .' he began tiredly. 'You see two young people with the whole world in front of them. Practically engaged to one another. And what happens to them? They're murdered in two separate incidents six years apart. The cruel coincidence is too much to fathom. You wonder about that, don't you, Myron?'

Myron nodded.

'So you begin to scrutinize their deaths. You look for something that might explain such a bizarre double tragedy. And in your search you find inconsistencies. You see pieces that just don't add up.'

'Yes.'

'And those inconsistencies lead you to believe that there is a connection between Alexander's murder and Valerie's.'

'Maybe.'

Cross glanced up at the ceiling and rested his index finger on his lip. 'Will you take my word that those inconsistencies have nothing to do with Valerie Simpson?'

'No,' Myron said. 'I can't.'

Senator Cross nodded, more to himself than Myron. 'I didn't suspect you would,' he said. 'You don't have children, do you, Myron?'

'No.'

'It doesn't matter. Even people who have children don't understand. They can't. What happened . . . it's not just the pain. The death is all-consuming. It never lets you go, never gives you a chance to catch your breath. My wife still has to be medicated almost daily. It's like someone scooped out everything inside of her and left behind only a pitiful shell. You can't imagine what it's like to see her like that.'

'I don't mean to hurt anyone, Senator.'

'But you won't stop either. And no matter how careful you are, someone is bound to get wind of your investigation, just as I did.'

'I'll try to be discreet.'

'You know that's impossible.'

'I can't back away now. I'm sorry.'

The senator gave himself the face massage again. He sighed deeply and said, 'You leave me no choice. I'll have to tell you what happened. Maybe then you'll let it go.'

Myron waited.

'You are an attorney, are you not?'

'Yes,' Myron said.

'You're a member of the New York bar?'

'Yes.'

Bradley Cross reached into his suit pocket. Sallow skin hung off his face in uneven clumps. He took out a checkbook. 'I'd like to hire you as my attorney,' he said. 'Will a five-thousand-dollar retainer be enough?'

'I don't understand.'

'As my attorney, what I'm about to tell you falls under the jurisdiction of attorney-client privilege. You will not be allowed, even in a court of law, to repeat what I am about to tell you.'

'You don't need to hire me for that.'

'I'd prefer it.'

'Fine. Make it a hundred dollars.'

Bradley Cross wrote out the check and handed it to Myron.

'My son was on drugs,' he said without preamble. 'Cocaine mostly. Heroin too, but he'd only just started on it. I knew he was on something, but frankly I didn't think it was serious. I saw him high. I saw the red eyes. But I thought it was just marijuana. Hell, I've tried marijuana. Inhaled even.'

Weak smile. Myron returned it, equally weak.

'Alexander and his friends weren't taking a casual stroll around the club grounds that night,' he said. 'They were going to get high. Alexander was found with a syringe in his pocket. There was cocaine found in the bushes not far from where the murder took place. And, of course, there were traces of both heroin and cocaine in Alexander's body. Not just in his fluids but in his tissue. I'm told that shows he'd been using for a while.'

'I thought there was no autopsy,' Myron said.

'It was kept secret. Nothing was reported or filed. It didn't matter anyway. A knife wound ended Alexander's life, not drugs. The fact that my son was taking illegal substances was irrelevant.'

Maybe, Myron thought, keeping his expression blank.

Cross stared off for a while. After some time had passed he asked, 'Where was I?'

'They left the party to get high.'

'Right, thank you.' He cleared his throat, sat up a little straighter. 'The rest of the story is fairly straightforward. The boys stumbled upon Errol Swade and Curtis Yeller on one of the grass courts. The papers talked about how brave Alexander was, how he tried to thwart the evil-doers without concern for his own safety. My spin doctors at their best. But the truth is, he was flying so high he acted irrationally. He swooped in like some kind of superhero. The Yeller boy – the one the police shot – dropped everything and ran. But Errol Swade was a cooler customer. He took out a switchblade and punctured my boy's heart like a balloon. Casually, they say. Non-chalant.'

Senator Cross stopped. Myron waited for him to continue. When it was clear he had reached the end of his saga, Myron asked, 'Why were they at the club?'

'Who?'

'Swade and Yeller.'

Senator Cross looked puzzled. 'They were thieves.'

'How do you know that?'

'What else would they have been doing there?'

Myron shrugged. 'Selling drugs to your son. Dealing. It sounds a lot more plausible than a late-night robbery of a tennis club.'

Cross shook his head. 'They were carrying items. Tennis rackets. Tennis balls.'

'According to whom?'

'According to Gregory and the others. The items were also found at the scene.'

'Tennis rackets and balls?'

'There may have been other things, I don't remember.'

'That's what they were after?' Myron said. 'Some tennis gear?'

'The police believe that my son interrupted them before the robbery was complete.'

'But your son stumbled across them *outside*. If they'd already stolen some gear, then they'd already been inside.'

'So what are you suggesting?' the senator asked sharply. 'That my son was murdered in a drug deal gone bad?'

'I'm just trying to see what sounds most plausible.'

'Would a drug deal murder make a connection with Valerie more likely?'

'No.'

'So what's your point?'

'No point. Just trying out different theories. What happened next? Directly after the murder?'

He looked off again, this time in the general direction of one of the portraits, but Myron didn't think he was actually seeing it. 'Gregory and the other boys came running back into the party,' he said in a hollow voice. 'I followed them outside. Blood was bubbling out of Alexander's mouth. By the time I reached him he was dead.'

Silence.

'You can pretty much figure out the rest. Everything switched over to autopilot. I really didn't do much. Aides did. Gregory's father – he's a senior partner here – helped too. I just stood and nodded numbly. I won't lie to you. I won't tell you I didn't know what was going on. I did. Old habits die hard, Myron. There is no creature more selfish than a politician. We so easily justify our selfishness as the "common good." So the cover-up was done.'

'And if the truth came out now?'

He smiled. 'I'd be destroyed. But I'm not really afraid of that anymore. Or maybe that's a lie too, who knows anymore?' He threw up his hands, lowered them. 'But my wife never learned the truth. I don't know what it would do to her, I really don't. Alexander was a good kid, Mr Bolitar. I don't want his memory ripped to shreds. In the end drugs do not make Errol Swade and Curtis Yeller any less culpable or my son any more guilty. He didn't ask to be stabbed.'

Myron waited a beat. Then the left-field question: 'What about Deanna Yeller?'

Puzzled. 'Who?'

'Curtis Yeller's mother.'

'What about her?'

'You have no relationship with her?'

More puzzled. 'Of course not. Why would you ask something like that?'

'You never paid to keep her silent?'

'About what?'

'About the circumstances of her son's death.'

'No. Why should I?'

'You know there was never an autopsy done on Curtis Yeller either. Strange, don't you think?'

'If you're insinuating that the police did not act strictly within regulations, I can't answer that because I don't know. I don't care either. Yes, I've wondered about the police shooting myself. Perhaps there was a second cover-up that night. If there was, I was not involved in it. And more important, I don't see what possible connection it could have with Valerie Simpson. In fact, I don't see any connection in any of this with Valerie.'

'She was at the party that night?'

'Valerie? Of course.'

'Do you know where she was at the time Alexander was murdered?'

'No.'

'Do you remember how she reacted to his death?'

'She was devastated. Her fiancé had just been killed in cold blood. She was distraught and angry.'

'Did you approve of their relationship?'

'Yes, very much so. I thought Valerie was a bit troubled. A bit too sad. But I liked her. She and Alexander were good together.'

'Valerie's name was never mentioned in connection with your son's murder. Why?'

The jowls were quivering big-time. 'You know why,' he said. 'Valerie Simpson was still something of a celebrity from her tennis days. We felt that there was already enough scrutiny without adding her name to the mix. It wasn't a question of liking or not liking Valerie. We just wanted to minimize the story as much as possible. Keep it off the front pages.'

'You got lucky then.'

'What do you mean?'

'Yeller was killed. Swade vanished.'

Cross blinked several times. 'I'm not sure I understand.'

'If they were alive there would have been a trial. More media attention. Maybe too much media attention for even your spin doctors to handle.'

He smiled. 'I see you've heard the rumors.'

'Rumors?'

'That I had Errol Swade killed. That the mob did me a favor or some such nonsense.'

'You have to admit, Senator, their fates made for a convenient little public relations package. No one to dispute your spin on things.'

'I don't cry over the fate of Curtis Yeller, and if Errol Swade was murdered I doubt I'd shed too many tears about that either. But I don't know any mobsters. That may sound silly, but I wouldn't know the first thing about enlisting the mob's help. I did hire a detective agency to look for Swade.'

'Did they find anything?'

'No. They believe that Swade is dead. So do the police. He was a punk, Myron. He wasn't on a path that led to a long life even before this incident.'

Myron followed up with a few more questions, but there was nothing more to learn. A few minutes later the two men stood.

'Would you mind if I spoke to Gregory Caufield before I leave?' Myron asked.

'I'd prefer it if you didn't.'

'If there's nothing to hide—'

'I don't want him knowing I told you this. Attorney-client privilege, remember? He won't speak honestly to you anyway.'

'He will if you tell him to.'

Cross shook his head. 'Gregory's father controls him. He won't talk.'

Myron shrugged. The senator was probably right. The only leverage he could apply on Gregory would be what Cross just told him. Cross had neatly arranged it so Myron couldn't do that. He'd have to think of a way to end-run that. Caufield was an eyewitness. He'd be worth a few questions.

The two men shook hands, both making serious eye contact. Was Senator Cross a sweet old codger, a grieving father trying to protect his son's memory? Or had he calculated that this would be the most effective strategy for dealing with Myron? Was he cagey or sympathetic or both?

Cross gave him the endearing off-center smile again. 'I hope I've satisfied your curiosity,' he said.

He hadn't. Not even close. But Myron didn't bother telling him that.

20

Myron left the building and strolled down Madison Avenue. Traffic was at a standstill. Big surprise in Manhattan. Five lanes were merging into one on Fifty-fourth Street. The other four lanes were blocked by one of those purely New York construction sites with steam pouring up out of the streets. Very Dante. What was with all that steam anyway?

He was about to cut across Fifty-third Street when he felt a sharp stab in his ribs.

'Give me an excuse, asshole.'

Myron recognized the voice before seeing the taped nose and the black eyes. Fishnet. He was pressing a gun against Myron's rib cage, using his body to hide the gun from any curious onlookers.

'You're wearing the same shirt,' Myron said. 'Jesus Christ, you didn't even change.'

Fishnet gave him a little gun jab. 'You're going to wish you were never born, asshole. Get in the car.'

The car – the powder-blue Caddy with thick scratches on the side – pulled alongside of them. Jim, Fishnet's partner, was driving, but Myron barely noticed him. His eyes immediately locked on the familiar figure in the backseat. The figure smiled and waved.

'Hey, Myron,' he called out. 'How's it going?'

Aaron.

'Bring him here, Lee,' Aaron said.

Fishnet Lee gave Myron a nudge with the gun. 'Let's go, asshole.'

Myron got in the backseat with Aaron. Fishnet Lee joined Jim in the front. The front seats were both covered with plastic where Win had dumped the maple syrup.

Aaron was dressed in his customary garb. Pure-snow-white suit, white shoes. No socks. No shirt. Aaron never wore a shirt, preferring to display his tan pectorals. They gleamed from some sort of oil or grease. He always looked fresh out of the wax salon, his body smooth as a baby's bottom. Aaron was a big man, six-six, two-forty. The weight lifter's build was not merely for show. Aaron moved with a speed and grace that defied the bulk. His black hair was slicked back and tied into a long ponytail.

He gave Myron a game-show-host grin and held it.

Myron said, 'Nice smile, Aaron. Lots of teeth.'

'Proper dental hygiene. It's a passion of mine.'

'You should share your passion with Lee,' Myron said.

Fishnet's head spun. 'What the fuck did you say, asshole?'

'Turn around, Lee,' Aaron said to Fishnet. Fishnet glared a few more daggers. Myron yawned. Jim drove. Aaron sat back. He said nothing, smiling brightly. Every part of him glistened in the sunlight. After two blocks of this Myron pointed at Aaron's cleavage. 'Your electrolysis missed a chest hair.'

To Aaron's credit he didn't look. 'We need to chat, Myron.'

'What about?'

'Valerie Simpson. For once I think we're on the same side.'

'Oh?'

'You want to capture Valerie Simpson's killer. So do we.'

'You do?'

'Yes. Mr Ache is determined to bring her killer to justice.'

'That Frank. Always the good Samaritan.'

Aaron chuckled. 'Still the funny man, eh, Myron? Well, I admit it sounds a bit bizarre, but we'd like to help you.'

'How?'

'We both know that Roger Quincy killed Valerie Simpson. Mr Ache is willing to use his considerable influence to help locate him.'

'And in return?'

Aaron feigned shock. He put a manicured hand the size of a manhole cover to his chest. 'Myron, you wound me. Really. We try to extend the hand of friendship and you slap it away with an insult.'

'Uh-huh.'

'This is one of those rare win-win situations,' Aaron said. 'We're willing to help you get your killer.'

'And you get?'

'Not a thing.' He settled back into his seat. 'If the killer is found, the police will move on to other matters. We will move on to other matters. And you, Myron, should also move on to other matters.'

'Ah.'

'Now, there's no reason to have a problem here,' Aaron added. When the sun hit his chest at a certain angle, the reflection dazzled the eyes. 'This isn't like some of our past encounters. We both want the same thing. We both want to put this tragic episode behind us. For you, that means finding the killer and bringing him to justice. For us, that means ending the investigation as soon as possible.'

'But suppose I'm not convinced Roger Quincy did it,' Myron said.

Aaron raised an eyebrow. 'Come on now, Myron. You've seen the evidence.'

'It's circumstantial.'

'Since when has that bothered you? Oh by the way, a new witness has come forward. We just got wind of it.'

'What kind of witness?' Myron asked.

'A witness who saw Roger Quincy talking to your beloved Valerie within ten minutes of the murder.'

Myron said nothing.

'You doubt my word?'

'Who's the witness, Aaron?'

'Some housewife. She was at the matches with her kids. And to answer your next question we have nothing to do with her.'

'So why the big fear?'

'What fear?'

'What's Ache so concerned about? Why hire Starsky and Hutch up there to follow me?'

Fishnet turned around. 'What the fuck did you call me, asshole?'

'Turn around, Lee,' Aaron said.

'Ah, come off it, Aaron, let me fuck him up a little. You see what the motherfucker did to my car? And look at my fucking nose.' Car first, then nose. Priorities. 'He and his faggot buddy jumped me. Two on one. When I wasn't looking. Let me teach him a little respect.'

'You couldn't, Lee. You and Jim together couldn't.'

'Fuck I couldn't. If I didn't have this busted nose—'

'Shut up, Lee,' Aaron said.

Immediate silence.

Aaron rolled his eyes at Myron and spread his hands. 'Rank amateurs,' he said. 'Frank is always trying to cut corners. Save a buck here. Save a buck there. In the end it always costs more.'

'I thought you stopped working for the Ache brothers,' Myron said.

'I work freelance now.'

'So Frank just brought you in?'

'As of this morning.'

'Must be something big,' Myron said. 'You don't come cheap.'

Aaron gave him the teeth again, adjusted the jacket of his suit. 'You want the best, you have to pay.'

'So why's Frank so bent out of shape about this?'

'I have no idea. But make no mistake about it: Frank wants your investigation to end. Now. No excuses. Look, Myron, we both know you've been something of a pain in the ass to Frank. He doesn't like you. To be honest he'd like to ace you. That's no bullshit. I'm talking man to man here. Friend to friend. We're friends, right? Buddies?'

'Best of chums,' Myron added. Shovel, shovel.

'But Frank is showing incredible restraint with you. Generosity even. He knows, for example, that you took Eddie Crane out to dinner. That alone would be reason for Frank to want you roughed up a bit. But he doesn't. In fact he's decided that if Eddie Crane chooses your agency, he won't get in the way.'

'Big of him.'

'But it *is* big of him,' Aaron insisted. 'He owns the kid's coach, for crying out loud. By all rights he belongs to TruPro. But Frank is willing to let him go, and he's willing to help you bring in Roger Quincy. Two very big favors. Gifts really. In exchange, you do nothing.'

Myron turned his palms up. 'How can I pass up a deal like that?'

'Do I sense a whiff of sarcasm?'

Myron shrugged.

'Frank's trying to be fair, Myron.'

'Yeah, the man's a prince.'

'Don't push him on this. It's not worth it.'

'Can I leave now?'

'I'd like your answer first.'

'I'll have to think about it,' Myron said. 'But I'd be much more willing to let go if I knew what Frank was trying to hide.'

Aaron shook his head. 'Still the same old Myron, huh? You never change. I'm surprised no one has wasted you yet.'

'I'm not easy to kill,' Myron said.

'Maybe not.'

'And I'm also a snazzy dancer. No one likes to kill a snazzy dancer. There's so few of us left.'

Aaron put his hand on Myron's knee and leaned toward him. 'Can we stop the lunatic routine for a moment?'

Myron's eyes flicked down to the knee, then back to Aaron. 'Uh, your hand?'

'You know about the carrot and the stick, Myron?'

'The what?'

'The carrot and the stick.' The hand was still on Myron's knee.

'Oh. Sure. The carrot and the stick.' *What?*

'So far I have shown you only the carrot. I would feel amiss if I did not also show a bit of stick.'

In the front seat Fishnet and Jim shared a chuckle.

Aaron's fingers gave the knee a little squeeze. Like a hawk's talons. 'Now you know me. I'm not a stick man. I'm the gentle sort. I'm kind. I'm nice. I'm . . .' He looked up as though searching for the word.

'A carrot,' Myron finished.

'Right. A carrot.'

Myron had seen Aaron kill a man. Snap his neck as though it were a twig. He'd also seen the results of Aaron's work in venues ranging from boxing rings to morgues. Some carrot.

'But nonetheless I need to add a bit of stick. Just for the record, you understand. It's expected. I know it's not necessary in your case. The stick, I mean.'

'I'm listening,' Myron said.

'Yeah,' Fishnet added, 'tell him, Aaron.' Fishnet and Jim restarted the chuckle. Louder.

'Shut up,' Aaron said softly.

Again immediate silence. Like they'd both been shot in the head.

Aaron swung his line of vision to Myron. His eyes were suddenly dark and hard. 'There will be no further warnings. We will simply strike. I know you don't scare easily. I explained that to Frank. He doesn't care. He suggested striking places that another man might consider taboo.'

'Like?'

'I understand Duane Richwood is playing well. I'd hate to see his career cut short.' He gave the knee a harder squeeze. 'Or take your beautiful Jessica, for example. Now I know she's out of the country right now. In Athens, in case you don't know. The Grand Bretagne Hotel. Room 207. Frank has friends in Greece.'

Myron felt a cold chill. 'Don't even think about it, Aaron.'

'Not my decision.' He finally let go of the knee. 'It's Frank. He's adamant about this. He wants you to let go now. You know what they say about grabbing a tiger by the tail.'

'If he touches her—'

Aaron waved him off. 'Please, Myron, no threats. There's no reason for threats here. You can't win. You know that. The price of victory is too high. You and Win are only two men. Two good men. Two of the best. Worthy adversaries. But Frank has me, for one. And he has others. Many others. As many men as he needs. Men with no scruples. Men who would break into Jessica's room, take turns with her, and then blow her away. Men who would jump Esperanza on her way home from work. Men who would even do unspeakable things to your mother.'

Myron stared at Aaron. Aaron did not blink. 'You can't win, Myron. No matter how tough you are, you can't stand up to that kind of thing. We both know it.'

Silence. The Caddy pulled up to the front of Myron's building.

'Can I have your answer now?' Aaron asked.

Myron tried not to shake as he got out of the car. Without glancing behind him he walked inside.

21

Win worked the heavy bag. He was snapping side kicks that bent the eighty-pound bag almost in half. He threw kicks at every level. The opponent's knee. The abdomen. The neck. The face. He struck with his heel, his toes angled down. Myron went through several katas, or forms, concentrating on the precision of his strikes, imaging a person in front of him rather than the air. Sometimes the person was Aaron.

They were at Master Kwon's new downtown location. The *dojang* was divided into two sections. One looked like a dance studio. Hardwood floor and lots of mirrors. The other section had matted floors, dumbbells, a speed bag, a heavy bag, a jump rope. On the shelf were rubber knives and guns to practice take-away techniques. The American flag and Korean flag were hung near the doorway. Each student bowed to them as they entered and left. School rules were listed on a poster. Myron knew them by heart. His favorite was rule number ten. Always finish what you start.

Hmm. Good advice? Hard to say right now.

There were fourteen school rules in all. Every once in a while Master Kwon added a new one. Number fourteen had been put up two months ago: Do not overeat. 'Students too fat,' Master Kwon had explained. 'Too much put in mouth.' In the twenty years since Win had helped Kwon relocate to the United States, Kwon's English had continually degenerated. Myron suspected it was part of his image as a wise old man from the Far East. Playing Mr Miyagi from the *Karate Kid* movies.

Win stopped. 'Here,' he said, gesturing to the bag. 'You need this more than I do.'

Myron began to hit the bag. Hard. He started with some punches. Tae kwon do's fighting stance is simple and practical, not all that different from a boxer's. Anyone who tried that crane-stance bullshit on the streets usually ended up on their ass. Myron followed up with some elbow and knee strikes. Elbows and knees were useful, particularly for fighting in close. Martial arts movies showed lots of spinning kicks to the head, jumping kicks to the chest, stuff like that. But street fighting was far simpler. You aimed for the groin, the knee, the neck, the nose, the eyes. Occasionally the solar plexus. The rest was wasteful. You get in a real life-or-death situation, you twist the guy's balls. You stick your fingers in his eyes. You throw an elbow to his throat.

Win walked over to a full-length mirror. 'Let's review what we've learned so far,' he said in the mock voice of a kindergarten teacher. He began to play air-golf, practicing his swing in the mirror. He did that a lot. 'One, the esteemed senator from Pennsylvania wants you off this case. Two, a major mobster from New York wants you off this case. Three, your client, the womanizing Duane Richwood, wants you off this case. Have I left anybody out?'

'Deanna Yeller,' Myron said. 'And Helen Van Slyke. Kenneth too, don't forget Kenneth. Pavel Menansi.' Myron thought a moment. 'I think that's it.'

'The police officer,' Win added. 'Detective Dimonte.'

'Oh yeah, right. I forgot about Rolly.'

Win checked the grip on his imaginary club. 'Thus,' he continued, 'your cause is mustering its customary support – i.e., none.'

Myron shrugged, threw a combination. ' "Can't please everyone, so you've got to please yourself." '

Win made a face. 'Quoting Ricky Nelson?'

'It's been a long day.'

'I would say.'

Myron back-kicked. A good countermove to almost any attack. 'So why is everyone so afraid of Valerie Simpson? A Unites States senator sets up a clandestine meeting with me. Frank Ache brings in Aaron. Duane threatens to fire me. Why?'

Win took another air-golf swing in the mirror. He looked up after the shot, squinting, as though following the trajectory of the imaginary ball. He seemed displeased. Golfers.

The door to the *dojang* opened. Wanda peered inside, gave a shy wave.

'Hi,' Myron said.

'Hi.'

Myron smiled. He was happy to see her – someone who did indeed want him to continue his investigation. She wore a patterned, almost little-girlish summer dress. The dress was sleeveless, revealing her nicely toned arms. She wasn't wearing one of those big summer hats, but she should have been. Her makeup had been applied with a light hand. Gold hoop earrings hung from her lobes. She looked young and healthy and quite beautiful.

A sign beside the door read NO SHOES ALLOWED. Wanda obeyed, slipped her flats off before stepping inside the *dojang*. 'Esperanza told me you'd be here,' she said. 'I'm really sorry about disturbing you outside the office again.'

'Don't worry about it,' he said. 'You know Win.'

'Yes,' she said, turning to him. She managed a smile. 'Nice to see you.'

Win gave her an almost indiscernible head tilt. Stoic. Playing Tonto.

Wringing her hands together Wanda asked, 'Can we talk for a moment?'

Win did not need prompting. He moved to the door, bowed deeply at the waist, left. They were alone.

She walked toward him deliberately, glancing around like she was on a house tour but not really interested in buying. 'Do you come here a lot?' she asked.

'Here or one of Master Kwon's other *dojangs*.'

'I thought they were called *dojos*,' she said.

'*Dojo* is Japanese. *Dojang* is Korean.'

She nodded as though this information had some significance in her life. She glanced around a bit more. 'Have you studied this for a long time?'

'Yes.'

'And Win?'

'Even longer.'

'He doesn't look the fighting type,' she said. 'Except maybe in the eyes.'

Myron had heard that before. He waited.

'I just wanted to know if you'd learned anything,' she said. Her eyes flicked left, right, up, down.

'Not much,' he said. Not exactly the truth, but Myron wasn't about to mention Duane's liaisons with Valerie.

She nodded again. Her hands were in constant motion, searching for something to occupy them. 'Duane is acting even stranger,' she said.

'How?'

'Just more of the same, I guess. He's on edge all the time. He keeps getting these calls he takes in another room. When I answer the phone the caller hangs up. And he disappeared again last night. Said he needed some air, but he was gone for two hours.'

'Do you have any thoughts?' he asked.

She shook her head.

Myron aimed for his gentlest voice. 'Could there be someone else?'

Her eyes stopped flicking and flared in his direction. 'I'm not some hooker he picked up off the street.'

'I know that.'

'We love each other.'

'I know that too. But I also know a lot of guys in love who still do dumb things.' Women too. Jessica, for one. Four years ago with a guy named Doug. It still hurt. Guy named Doug. Go figure.

Wanda shook her head again firmly. Convincing herself or Myron? 'It's not like that with us. I know I sound like a gullible idiot, but it's the way it is. I can't explain it.'

'No need to. I was just seeing what you thought.'

'Duane's not having an affair.'

'Okay.'

Her eyes were wet. She took a couple of deep breaths. 'He's not sleeping at night. He paces. I ask him what's wrong, but he won't tell me. I tried eavesdropping on a call, but the only thing I picked up was your name.'

'My name?'

She nodded. 'He said it twice, but that's all I heard.'

Myron thought a moment. 'Suppose I put a tap on your phone.'

'Do it.'

'You don't have a problem with that?'

'No.' The wet eyes broke into tears. She let out two quick sobs, made herself stop. 'It's getting worse, Myron. We have to find out what's going on.'

'I'll do my best.'

She gave him a brief hug. Myron wanted to stroke her hair and say something comforting. He didn't do either. She strode out slowly, head high. Myron watched. As soon as she was out of sight Win returned.

'Well?' Win asked.

'I like her,' Myron said.

Win nodded. 'Very shapely derriere.'

'That's not what I meant. She's a good woman. And she's scared.'

'Of course she's scared. Her meal ticket is about to go bye-bye.'

The Return of Mr Warmth. 'It's not like that, Win. She loves him.'

Win strummed a few notes on an air-violin. Couldn't talk to him about stuff like that. He just didn't get it. 'What did she want?'

Myron filled him in on the conversation. Win spread his legs, dropping into a full split and then sliding back up. He repeated the move several times, faster and faster. Ladies and gentlemen, the Godfather of Soul, Mr James Brown.

When Myron finished, Win said, 'Sounds like Duane is trying to hide more than a quick fling.'

'My thoughts exactly.'

'You want me to watch him?'

'We can take shifts.'

Win shook his head. 'He knows you.'

'He knows you too.'

'Yes,' Win said, 'but I am invisible. I am the wind.'

'Sure you don't mean passing wind?'

Win made a face. 'That was a good one. I'm sure I'll laugh for days.'

Truth was, Win could be nestled in your BVDs for a week and you'd never know. 'Can you start tonight?' Myron asked.

Win nodded. 'I'm already there.'

22

Myron shot baskets on the blacktop off the driveway. The long summer day was finally slipping into darkness, but the basket was illuminated with spotlights. He and his father had installed them when Myron was in the sixth grade. A variety of barbecue smells competed in the still air. Chicken from the Dempseys' house. Burgers from the Weinsteins'. Shish kebab at the Rushkins'.

Myron shot, rebounded, shot again. He got a little rhythm going, the ball back-spinning gently through the basket. Nothing but net. Sweat matted his gray T-shirt to his chest. Myron always did his best thinking out here, but right now his mind was a blank. There was nothing but the ball, the hoop, and the sweet arc after the release. It felt pure.

'Hey, Myron.'

It was Timmy from next door. Timmy was ten.

'Bug off, kid. You're bothering me.'

Timmy laughed and grabbed a rebound. It was an inside joke. Timmy's mother was convinced that her son was bothering Myron and that Myron should send Timmy home whenever he came over. Didn't stop Timmy. He and his friends always came over when Myron was shooting. Once in a while, when they needed an extra body, the kids would knock on the door and ask his mom if Myron could come out and play.

He and Timmy shot around for a while. They talked about stuff that was important to little boys. A few other kids came by. The Daleys' boy. The Cohens' girl. Others. Bikes were parked at the end of the driveway. They started playing a game. Myron was designated steady passer. No one kept score accurately. Everyone laughed a lot. A few fathers came by and joined in. Arnie Stollman. Fred Dempsey. It'd been a while since they'd done this. A bit too Rockwellian for some, but it felt very right to Myron.

It was nearly ten when mothers started to call out for their children. From their front stoops the mothers smiled brightly and waved at Myron. Myron waved back. The kids 'aw, Mom' 'd, but they listened.

Summer and school break. Still a touch of innocence. Kids were supposed to be different now. They had to deal with guns and drugs and crime and AIDS. But a summer night in middle-class suburbia was the great generational equalizer, a place far away from people like Aaron and the Ache brothers. A place far away from young women being murdered.

Valerie would have had fun tonight.

Mom opened the back door. 'Telephone,' she said shortly.

'Who is it?'

Her voice was like a closed fist. 'Jessica.' She made a face when she said it, like the name tasted bad on her lips.

Myron tried not to sprint. He walk/ran up the back steps and into the kitchen. The kitchen had been completely redone last year. Why, Myron couldn't say. No one in the house cooked, unless you count microwaving Celeste frozen pizzas.

'I'll take it in the basement,' he said.

A grunt from Mom. No wisecrack. Like Esperanza, Mom too held grudges. Especially when it came to her little boy.

He closed the door, grabbed the receiver, heard his mother hang up the extension. 'Jess?'

'Is this Stallions "R" Us?'

As usual her voice made him soar. 'Why, yes it is. What can we do for you, ma'am?'

'I'm looking for a true stallion.'

'You called the right place. Any preference?'

'Well hung,' she replied. 'But you'll do.'

'Nice talk.'

There was a lot of noise in the background. 'What took you so long to pick up?' she asked.

'I was outside. Playing with Timmy and the kids.'

'Did I interrupt?'

'Nope. Game just ended.'

'Your mom sounded a tad frosty on the phone.'

'She gets that way,' Myron said.

'She used to like me.'

'She still does.'

'And Esperanza?'

'Esperanza never liked you.'

'Oh yeah,' she said.

'You still at the Grand Bretagne Hotel?' Myron asked. 'Room 207?'

Pause. 'Were you spying on me?'

'No.'

'Then how do you know—'

'Long story. I'll tell you about it when you get home. Where are you?'

'Kennedy Airport. We just landed.'

His heart did a quick twirl. 'You're home?'

'I will be as soon as I find my luggage.' She hesitated. 'Will you come right over?'

'I'm on my way.'

'Wear something I can easily rip off your bod,' she said. 'I'll be waiting in the tub with all kinds of exotic oils from overseas.'

'Hussy.'

There was another hesitation. Then Jessica said, 'I love you, you know. I get funny sometimes, but I do love you.'

'Never mind that. Tell me more about the oils.'

She laughed. 'Hurry now.'

He put the receiver back in its cradle. He quickly stripped down and showered. A cold shower for the time being. He was whistling 'Tonight' from *West Side Story*. He dried himself off and checked out his closet. Something in the easy-to-rip-off family. Found it. Snap buttons. He sprinkled on a little cologne. Myron rarely wore cologne, but Jess liked it. He heard the doorbell ring as he was bounding up the stairs.

'I'll get it,' he called out.

Two uniformed police officers were at the door.

'Are you Myron Bolitar?' the taller one asked.

'Yes.'

'Detective Roland Dimonte sent us. We would appreciate it if you would come with us.'

'Where?'

'Queens Homicide.'

'What for?'

'Roger Quincy has been captured. He's a suspect in the murder of Valerie Simpson.'

'So?'

The shorter cop spoke for the first time. 'Mr Bolitar, do you know Roger Quincy?'

'No.'

'You've never met him?'

'Not to my knowledge.' Not to my knowledge. Lawyer talk for *no*.

The officers exchanged a glance.

'You better come with us,' the taller cop said.

'Why?'

'Because Mr Quincy refuses to make a statement until he talks with you.'

23

Myron called Jessica's place and left a message that he'd be late.

When they arrived at the precinct, Dimonte greeted Myron at the door. He was chewing a wad of gum or maybe it was spitting tobacco. And he was smiling a whole lot. He wore a different pair of boots this time. Still snakeskin, still hideous. But these were bright yellow with blue fringes.

'Glad you could make it,' Dimonte said.

Myron pointed to the boots. 'Mug a cheerleader, Rolly?'

Dimonte laughed. This wasn't good. 'Come on, smart-guy,' he said with something approaching good nature. He led Myron down a corridor, threading between lots of bored-looking cops. Almost every one of them had a cup of coffee in their hands, leaning against a wall or refreshment machine, pleading some pathetic case to a nodding head.

'No press,' Myron noted.

'They haven't been told of Quincy's capture yet,' Dimonte said. 'But it'll leak soon enough.'

'You going to leak it?'

He shrugged happily. 'The public has a right to know.'

'Sure.'

'What about you, Bolitar? You want to come clean?'

'Come clean on what?'

He shrugged again. Mr Carefree. 'Suit yourself.'

'I don't know him, Rolly.'

'Guess he got your name out of the yellow pages, huh?'

Myron stayed silent. No point in arguing now.

Dimonte opened a door into a small interrogation room. Two cops were already in there. Their neckties were loosened low enough to double as a belt. They'd been working Roger Quincy over pretty good, but Quincy did not seem too agitated. In most movies or TV shows a prisoner in a holding cell wears stripes or grays. But in reality they wear loud, fluorescent orange. Better to see them should they opt to flee.

Roger Quincy's eyes lit up when he saw Myron. He was younger than Myron had expected – early thirties, though he probably could have passed for mid-twenties. He was thin, his face pretty in a feminine way. His fingers were graceful and elongated. He looked like a ballet dancer.

From his chair Roger Quincy waved and said, 'Thanks for coming, Myron.'

Myron looked at Dimonte. Dimonte smiled back. 'Don't know him, huh?' He nodded to the other cops. 'Come on, guys. Let's leave the two buddies alone.'

A few quiet snickers later, the cops were gone. Myron sat in the chair across the table from Roger Quincy.

'Do I know you?' Myron asked.

'No, I don't think so.' Quincy extended his hand. 'I'm Roger Quincy.'

Quincy's hand felt like a small bird. Myron gave it a quick shake. 'How do you know my name?'

'Oh, I'm a big sports fan,' he said. 'I know I don't look the type, but I've been one for years. I don't follow basketball that closely anymore. Tennis is my favorite. Do you play at all?'

'Just a little.'

'I'm not very good, but I try.' His eyes lit up again. 'Tennis is such a magnificent sport when you think about it. A competitive acrobatic dance really. A small ball hurls at you with unearthly velocity and you have to move, set your feet, hit the ball back using a racket. Everything has to be calculated in a matter of moments: the speed of the oncoming ball, the spot it will land, the spin on it, the angle of the bounce, the distance between your hand and the center of the racket head, the stroke you will use, the placement of your return. It's amazing when you think about it.'

Two words: Looney Tunes.

'Uh, Roger, you didn't answer my question,' Myron said. 'How do you know me?'

'I'm sorry.' He flashed a shy smile. 'I get overexcited sometimes. Some people think it's a flaw. Me, I'd rather be like that than some couch potato. Did I mention that I'm also a basketball fan?'

'Yes.'

'That's how I know your name. I saw you play at Duke.' He smiled like that explained everything.

'Okay,' Myron said, struggling to keep a patient tone. 'So why did you tell the police you wanted to talk to me?'

'Because I did. Want to talk to you, that is.'

'Why?'

'They think I killed Valerie, Myron.'

'Did you?'

His mouth made a surprised little O. 'Of course not. What kind of man do you think I am?'

Myron shrugged. 'The kind who stalks young girls. The kind who harassed Valerie Simpson, who followed her around, called her repeatedly, wrote her long letters, frightened her.'

He waved Myron off with those long fingers. 'You're exaggerating,' he said. 'I courted Valerie Simpson. I loved her. I cared about her well-being. I was merely a persistent suitor.'

'She wanted you to leave her alone.'

He laughed. 'So she turned me down. Big deal. Am I the first man ever rejected by a beautiful woman? I just don't give up as easily as most. I sent her flowers. I wrote her love letters. I asked her out again. I tried different tactics. Do you ever read romance novels?'

'Not really.'

'The hero and heroine are always rejecting each other. Through wars or pirate attacks or high society parties, the couple fight and claw and seem to hate each other. But deep down they are in love. They're repressing their true feelings, see? That's how it was with Valerie and me. There was an undeniable tension there. A high-voltage surge between us.'

'Uh-huh,' Myron said. 'Roger, why did you want to see me?'

'I thought you could talk to the police for me.'

'And tell them what?'

'That I didn't kill Valerie. That she was in imminent danger from someone else.'

'Who?'

'I thought you knew.'

'What makes you think that?'

'Valerie told me. Right before she was murdered.'

'She told you what exactly?'

'That she was in danger.'

'In danger of what?'

'I thought you'd know.'

Myron raised his hand. 'Slow down a second, okay? Let's start at the beginning. You were at the US Open.'

'Yes.'

'Why?'

'I go every year. I'm a big fan. I love to watch the matches. They're so mesmerizing—'

'I think we covered that already, Roger. So you went as a fan. Your going had nothing to do with Valerie Simpson? You didn't follow her there?'

'Of course not. I had no idea she'd even be there.'

'Okay, so what happened?'

'I was sitting in the stadium watching Duane Richwood demolish Ivan Restovich. Incredible performance. I mean, Duane slaughtered him.' He smiled. 'But why am I telling you this? You're his agent, right?'

'Yes.'

'Can you get me his autograph?'

'Sure.'

'Not tonight, of course. Tomorrow maybe?'

'Maybe.' Earth to Roger. 'But let's stick with Valerie right now. You were watching Duane's match.'

'Exactly.' His voice grew serious. 'I wish I'd known you were Duane Richwood's agent then, Myron. Maybe everything would have been okay then. Maybe Valerie would still be alive and I'd be the hero who saved her and she'd have to stop denying her true feelings and let me into her life and let me protect her forevermore.'

Myron remembered a quote from *Man of La Mancha:* 'I can see the coo-coo singing in the coo-coo berry tree.'

'What happened, Roger?'

'The match was basically over so I checked my program. Arantxa Sanchez-Vicario was about to start her match on court sixteen, so I figured I'd go over there and get a good seat. Arantxa's a wonderful player. Such a hustler. Her brothers Emilio and Javier are pros also. Nice players, but they don't have her heart.'

'So you left the stadium,' Myron tried.

'I left the stadium. I had a few minutes, so I went over to the booth near the front entrance. The one with all the TV monitors giving the scores of the other matches. I saw that Steffi had already won and that Michael Chang had been dragged into a fifth set. I was checking out some doubles matches on the board. Men's doubles, I think. Ken Flach was one of the people. No, it was . . . I can't remember.'

'Stay with me, Roger.'

'Anyway, that's when I saw Valerie.'

'Where?'

'By the front gate. She was trying to get in, but the guard wouldn't let her. She didn't have a ticket. She was very upset, that was clear. You know, the Open is always sold out. Every year. But I still couldn't believe what I was seeing. The guard wouldn't let her in. Valerie Simpson. He didn't even recognize her. So naturally I went to her aid.'

Naturally. 'What did you do?'

'I got my hand stamped by another guard and walked outside the gate. Then I came up behind her and tapped her on the shoulder. When she turned around I couldn't believe what I saw.'

'What?'

'I know Valerie Simpson,' he said, his words slower now. 'Even you will have to concede that. I've seen every match she ever played in. I saw her at work. I saw her at play. I've seen her on the streets, on the court, at her house, practicing with that slimy coach of hers. I've seen her happy and sad, up and down, in triumph and defeat. I saw her progress from an enthusiastic teenager to a fierce competitor to a despondent, lifeless beauty. My heart has ached for her so many times, I've lost count. But I'd never seen her like this.'

'Like what?'

'So scared. She was absolutely terrified.'

Little wonder, Myron thought. Daffy Duck here sneaks up behind her and taps her on her shoulder. 'Did she recognize you?'

'Of course.'

'What did she do then?'

'She asked for my help.'

Myron arched a skeptical eyebrow. He'd learned the technique from Win.

'It's true,' Roger insisted. 'She said she was in danger. She said she needed to get in and see you.'

'She mentioned me by name?'

'Yes. I'm telling you, she was desperate. She pleaded with the guard, but he wouldn't listen. So I came up with an idea.'

'What was that?'

'Scalp a ticket,' he answered. He was clearly pleased with himself. 'There were dozens of scalpers hanging around the subway entrance. I found one. A black man. Nice enough fellow. He wanted a hundred and fifty dollars. I told him that was way too much. They always start high. The scalpers, I mean. You have to negotiate with them. They expect it. But Valerie would have none of that. She just accepted his price. That's Valerie. No head for money. If we'd gotten married, I would have had to handle the finances. She's too impulsive.'

'Focus with me, Roger. What happened after you bought the ticket?'

His face went soft and dreamy. 'She thanked me,' he said, like he'd seen a burning bush. 'It was the first time she ever opened up to me. I knew then that my patience had won out. After all this time I'd finally cracked the face. Funny, isn't it? For years I tried so hard to make her love me. And then when I least expect it, boom! – love crashed into my life.'

I, me, I, me, I, me. Even Valerie's murder he could only see in terms of himself. 'What did she do then?' Myron asked.

'I escorted her through the gates. She asked me if I knew what you looked like. I said, you mean Myron Bolitar the basketball player? She said yes. I said yes, I knew. She said she needed to find you.' He leaned forward. Earnest. 'You see what I mean? If I had known you were Duane's agent I would have known exactly where you were. I would have led her right to you. Then everything would have been all right. I'd have gotten a bigger thank-you and that priceless Valerie Simpson smile all for me. I'd have saved her life. I would have been her hero.' He shook his head for what might have been. 'It would have been perfect.'

'But instead?' Myron tried.

'We split up. She asked me to cover the outside courts while she searched the Food Court and the stadium area. We were going to meet back by the Perrier booth every fifteen minutes. I took off and began my search. I was anxious. Finding you would have proved my undying love—'

'Yeah, I got that part.' This guy must have been gobs of fun for ol' Rolly to interrogate. 'What happened next?'

'I heard a gunshot,' Quincy continued. 'Then I heard screams. I ran back toward the Food Court. By the time I got there a crowd had formed. You were running toward the body. She was on the ground. So still. You bent down and cradled her body. My dreams. My life. My happiness. Dead. I knew what the police would think. They tormented me for courting her. Called me names. Heck, they threatened to put me in jail for asking her out – what were they going to think now? They never understood the bond between us. The attraction.'

'So you ran,' Myron said.

'Yes. I went to my place and packed a bag. Then I took out the maximum amount on my MAC card. I saw on TV once how the police tracked a guy down by where he used his credit cards, so I wanted to make sure I had enough cash. Smart, huh?'

'Ingenious,' Myron agreed. But he felt his heart sink. Valerie Simpson had had no one. She'd been alone. When danger struck she turned to Myron, a man she barely knew. And someone had murdered her. A painful pang consumed him.

'I stayed in crummy motels and used fake names,' Quincy rambled. 'But someone must have recognized me. Well, you know the rest. When they caught me, I asked for you. I thought you'd be able to explain to them what really happened.' Quincy leaned forward, whispered conspiratorially. 'That Detective Dimonte can be rather hostile.'

'Uh-huh.'

'The only time he smiled was when I mentioned your name.'

'Oh?'

'I told him you and I were friends. I hope you don't mind.'

'Not at all,' Myron said.

24

Myron faced Dimonte and sidekick Krinsky in the adjoining interrogation room. It was identical to the other one in every way. Dimonte was still gleeful.

'Would you care for an attorney?' he asked sweetly.

Myron looked at him. 'Your face ·is positively beaming, Rolly. New moisturizer?'

The smile stayed. 'I'll take that as a no.'

'Am I under arrest?'

'Of course not. Have a seat. Care for a drink?'

'Sure.'

'What would you like?' Quite the host, that Rolly. 'Coke? Coffee? Orange juice?'

'Got any Yoo-hoo?'

Dimonte looked at Krinsky. Krinsky shrugged and went to check. Dimonte folded his hands and put them on the table. 'Myron, why did Roger Quincy ask for you?'

'He wanted to speak to me.'

Dimonte smiled. Mr Patience. 'Yes, but why you?'

'I'm afraid I can't answer that.'

'Can't,' Dimonte said. 'Or won't?'

'Can't.'

'Why can't you?'

'I think it falls under attorney-client privilege. I have to check.'

'Check with who?'

'With whom,' Myron said.

'What?'

'Check with whom. Not who, whom. Prepositional phrase.'

Dimonte nodded. 'So it's going to be like that, is it?'

'Like what?'

His voice was a little rougher now. 'You're a suspect, Bolitar. No, check that. You're *the* suspect.'

'What about Roger?'

'He's the trigger man. I'm sure of that. But he's too much of a nut job to have done it on his own. Way we figure it, you set the whole thing up. Had him do the dirty work.'

'Uh-huh. And my motive?'

'Valerie Simpson was having an affair with Duane Richwood. That's why his phone number was in her book. A white girl with a black guy. How would the sponsors have reacted to that?'

'It's the nineties, Rolly. There's even a mixed marriage on the Supreme Court.'

Dimonte put a boot up on a chair and leaned on the raised knee. 'Times may change, Bolitar, but sponsors still don't like black boys boffing white chicks.' He tickled his chin with two fingers. 'Let me run this by you, see how it sounds: Duane is a bit of a coonhound. He sniffs out white meat. He nails Valerie Simpson, but she doesn't fancy the idea of being a one-nighter. We know she's a bit of a fruitcake, spent time in an asylum. Probably a bunny burner to boot.'

'Bunny burner?'

'You seen *Fatal Attraction*?'

Myron nodded. 'Oh. Bunny burner. Right.'

'So like I said, Valerie Simpson is crazy. Her elevator don't stop at every floor. But now she's also pissed off. So she calls up Duane just like it says in her little diary and threatens to go to the press. Duane is scared. Like he was yesterday when I came by. So who does he call? You. That's when you hatch your little scheme.'

Myron nodded. 'That'll hold up in court.'

'What? Greed isn't a good motive?'

'I might as well confess right here.'

'Fine, smart-guy. You play it that way.'

Krinsky returned. He shook his head. No Yoo-hoo.

'You want to tell me why Quincy called you first?' Dimonte continued.

'Nope.'

'Why the hell not?'

'Because you've hurt my feelings.'

'Don't fuck with me, Bolitar. I'll throw your ass into a holding cell with twenty psychos and tell them you're a child molester.' He smiled. 'He'll like that, won't he, Krinsky?'

'Yeah,' Krinsky said, mirroring Dimonte's smile.

Myron nodded. 'Right. Okay, now I say, what do you mean? Then you say, a tasty morsel like you will be popular in the slammer. Then I say, please don't. Then you say, don't bend over to pick up the soap. Then you both give me a cop snicker.'

'What the fuck you talking about?'

'Don't waste my time, Rolly.'

'You think I won't throw your ass in jail?'

Myron stood. 'I know you won't. If you thought you could I'd be handcuffed by now.'

'Where the fuck do you think you're going?'

'Arrest me or get out of my way. I got places to go, people to see.'

'I know you're dirty, Bolitar. That whacko didn't ask for you by accident. He thought you could save him. That's why you've been playing cop with us. Pretending to investigate on your own. You just wanted to stay close, find out what we knew.'

'You got it all figured out, Rolly.'

'We'll grill him and grill him and grill him until he gives you up.'

'No, you won't. As his attorney I am forbidding any interrogation of my client.'

'You can't represent him. Ever heard of conflict of interest?'

'Until I find him someone else I'm still his attorney of record.'

Myron opened the door and stepped into the corridor. He was surprised to see Esperanza. So were the cops. Every one of them up and down the corridor stared at her hungrily. Probably just being careful, Myron mused, afraid maybe Esperanza had a concealed weapon in her tight jeans. Yeah, that was probably it.

'Win called,' she said. 'He's looking for you.'

'What's up?'

'He followed Duane. There's something he thinks you should see.'

25

Esperanza and Myron shared a yellow cab to the Chelsea Hotel on Twenty-third Street between Seventh and Eighth. The cab smelled like a Turkish whorehouse, which was an improvement over most.

'Win will be seated in a red chair near the house phones,' she told him when they stopped. 'It's to the right of the concierge's desk. He'll be reading a newspaper. If he's not reading a newspaper, the coast isn't clear. Ignore him and walk out. He'll meet you at the Billiards Club.'

'Win said that?'

'Yes.'

'Even that part about the coast not being clear?'

'Yes.'

Myron shook his head. 'You want to come?'

'Can't. I still have studying to do.'

'Thanks for finding me.'

She nodded.

Win was seated where advertised. He was reading the *Wall Street Journal* so the coast was clear. Oooo. Win looked exactly like himself, except a black wig covered the blond locks. Dr Disguise. Myron sat next to him and whispered, 'The white rabbit turns yellow when the black dog urinates on him.'

Win continued to read. 'You said to contact you if Duane did anything unusual.'

'Yep.'

'He arrived here about two hours ago. He took the elevator to the third floor and knocked on the door to room 322. A woman answered. They embraced. He entered. The door closed.'

'That's not good,' Myron said.

Win turned the page. Bored.

'Do you know who the woman is?' Myron asked.

He shook his head. 'Black. Five-seven, five-eight. Slim. I took the liberty of booking room 323. The peephole has a view of Duane's door.'

Myron thought of Jessica waiting for him. In a warm tub. With those exotic oils.

385

Damn.

'I'll stay if you want,' Win said.

'No. I'll handle this.'

'Fine.' Win stood. 'I'll see you at the match tomorrow, if our boy isn't too tired to play.'

Myron took the stairs to the third floor. He peered out into the corridor. No one. With key in hand he hurried down to room 323 and went inside. Win, as usual, was right. From the peephole he had a good, albeit convex, view of the door to room 322. Now he had to wait.

But wait for what?

What the hell was he doing here? Jessica was waiting for him in a bathtub filled with exotic oils – the thought made his body both sing and ache – and here he was, playing Peeping Tom over . . .

Over what?

What was he after anyway? Duane had explained his connection to Valerie Simpson. They'd briefly been lovers. What was so weird about that? They were both attractive, both in their early twenties, both tennis players. So what was the big deal? The racial thing? Nothing unusual about that anymore. Hadn't he just pointed that out to Dimonte?

So what was Myron doing with his eye pressed against a peephole? Duane was a client, for chrissake, an important client. What right did Myron have to invade his privacy like this? And for what reason – because his girlfriend didn't like the fact that Duane was having affairs? So what? That wasn't Myron's concern. Myron wasn't Duane's social worker, parole officer, priest, shrink – he was his agent. His job was to get the maximum return for his client, not make morality judgments.

On the other hand, what the hell was Duane doing here? Maybe he liked to play the field, fine and dandy, no problem. But tonight of all nights? It's crazy. Tomorrow was the biggest day of Duane's career. Nationally televised match. His first US Open quarterfinal. His first match against a seeded player. The launching of the Nike spots. Kind of a strange night for a romantic tryst in a hotel room.

Duane Richwood, the Wilt Chamberlain of professional tennis.

Myron didn't like it.

Duane had always been a bit of a mystery. In reality Myron knew nothing about his past. He'd been a runaway, or so Duane said, but who knew for sure? Why had he run in the first place? Where was his family now? Myron had created a spin on the facts – portraying Duane as the poor street kid struggling to escape the shackles of poverty. But was that the truth? Duane seemed like a good kid – intelligent, well-spoken, well-mannered – but could that all be an act? The young man Myron had known would not be spending such an important night screwing in a strange hotel room – which, of course, circled Myron back to the question:

So what?

Myron was his agent. Period. The kid had talent to burn and a terrific court sense. He was good-looking and could make a lot of money in endorsements. In the end, that was all that mattered to an agent. Not a player's love life. The kid was a dream on the court. Who cared what he was like off it? Myron was getting too close to this. He had no perspective anymore. He had a business to run, and spying on one of his biggest clients, invading that client's privacy, was not good business sense.

He should leave. He should go to Jessica and talk to her about it, see what she thought.

Ten more minutes.

He needed only two. He switched eyes just as the door to room 322 opened. Duane appeared, or at least the back of him. Myron saw a woman's arms go around his neck, pulling him down. They embraced. He couldn't see the woman's face, just the arms. Myron thought about Wanda's intuition. She had been so sure of herself, so blind to this possibility. Myron understood. He'd been there. Love has a way of putting on the blinders.

'Putting on the blinders,' Myron muttered to himself. 'Unbelievable.'

After the hug broke, Duane straightened up. The woman's arms dropped out of sight. Duane looked ready to leave. Myron pushed his eye closer to the peephole. Duane spun and looked directly at Myron's door. Myron almost jumped back. For a second it was like Duane was looking right at Myron, like he knew Myron was there.

Once again Myron wondered how he had ended up here. If his job included checking on the promiscuity of every athlete he represented, he would spend his life peering through peepholes. Duane was a kid. Twenty-one years old. He wasn't even married or officially engaged. Nothing Myron was seeing was connected in any way with Valerie Simpson's murder.

Until Duane finally stepped away.

Duane had given the woman one more brief hug. There had been muffled voices, but Myron couldn't make out any specific words. Duane looked left, then right, then moved away. The woman was already starting to close the door, but she glanced out one last time. And that was when Myron saw her.

The woman was Deanna Yeller.

26

The morning.

Myron had not confronted Duane. He'd stumbled to Jessica's in something of a daze. He'd opened the door with his key and said, 'I'm sorry. I had to—'

Jessica shushed him with a kiss. Then a bigger kiss. Hungrier kiss. Myron tried to fight off her advances, though some might call his struggle less than valiant.

He rolled over in the bed. Jessica was gently padding across the room. Naked. She slipped into a silk robe. He watched, as he always did, with utter fascination. 'You're so hot,' he said, 'you make my teeth sweat.'

She smiled. There is something that happens to men when Jessica looks at them. Shallow breathing. Fluttering stomach. A cruel longing. But her smile raised all those symptoms to the tenth power.

'Good morning,' she said. She bent down and kissed him gently. 'How are you feeling?'

'My ears are still popping from last night.'

'Nice to know I still have the touch,' she said.

The understatement of the millennium. 'Tell me about your trip.'

'Tell me about your murder first.'

He did. Jess was a great listener. She never interrupted, except to ask the right question. She looked at him steadily without a lot of that phony head nodding or out-of-context smiling. Her eyes focused in on him as if he were the only person in the world. He felt light-headed and happy and scared.

'This Valerie got to you,' Jessica said when he finished.

'She had no one. Her life was in danger and she had no one.'

'She had you.'

'I only met her once. She wasn't even signed yet.'

'Doesn't matter. She knew what you were. If I were in trouble, you'd be the person I'd run to.' She tilted her head. 'How did you know my room number and hotel?'

'Aaron. He was trying to be intimidating. He succeeded.'

'Aaron threatened to hurt me?'

'You, me, my mom, Esperanza.'

388

She hesitated, thinking. 'Esperanza would be my choice. I mean, if it has to be one of us.'

'I'll tell him.' He took her hand. 'I'm glad you're home.'

'No third degree?'

Myron shook his head.

'But I owe you an explanation.'

'I don't want one,' he said. 'I just want to be with you. I love you. I've always loved you. We are soul mates.'

'Soul mates?'

He nodded.

'When did you decide this?' she asked.

'A long time ago.'

'So why not tell me before now?'

He shrugged. 'I didn't want to scare you off.'

'And now?'

'Now it's more important to tell you how I feel.'

The room was still. 'What am I supposed to say to that?' she asked.

'Nothing.'

'I do love you, Myron. You know that.'

'I know.'

Silence. A long silence.

Jessica crossed the room. Naked. She was not self-conscious about her body. Then again, she had no reason to be. 'It seems to me,' she began, 'there are a lot of weird connections with this murder. But there is one overriding constant.'

Change of subjects. That was okay. Enough had been said for one day. 'What?' Myron asked.

'Tennis,' she said. 'Alexander Cross is killed at a tennis club. Valerie Simpson is murdered at the national tennis center. Valerie and Duane have an affair – both are professional tennis players. Those two kids who supposedly killed Alexander Cross – what's their names?'

'Errol Swade and Curtis Yeller.'

'Swade and Yeller,' she repeated. 'They were both up to no good at a tennis club. The Ache brothers and Aaron are connected to an agency who deals with tennis players. That leaves us with Deanna Yeller.'

'What about her?'

'Her sleeping with Duane. It can't just be a coincidence.'

'So?'

'So how would she have met Duane?'

'I don't know,' Myron said.

'Does she play tennis?'

'What if she does?'

'Keeps things constant.' She stopped. 'I don't know. I'm ranting. It's just that everything circles back to tennis – except for Deanna Yeller.'

Myron thought about it a moment. Nothing clicked, but something did rumble somewhere in the back of his brain.

'Just a thought,' she said.

He sat up. 'Before you said "supposedly" killed Alexander Cross. What did you mean?'

'What real evidence do you have that Swade and Yeller murdered the Cross kid?' she asked. 'They might have just been convenient scapegoats. Think about it a second. Yeller was conveniently killed by the police. Swade has conveniently fallen off the face of the earth. Who better to take the fall?'

'Then who do you think killed Alexander Cross?' he asked.

She shrugged. 'Probably Swade and Yeller. But who knows for sure?'

More rumbling in the brain. But still nothing surfaced. Myron checked his watch. Seven-thirty.

'You in a rush?' she asked.

'A little.'

'I thought Duane Richwood doesn't play until one,' she said.

'I'm trying to land a kid named Eddie Crane. He's playing in the juniors at ten.'

'Can I come along?' she asked.

'Sure.'

'What are your chances of landing him?' she asked.

'I think they're pretty good. His father might be a problem.'

'The father doesn't like you?'

'I think he'd prefer a bigger agency,' Myron said.

'Should I smile sweetly at him?' she asked.

Myron thought a moment. 'Flash a little cleavage. I'm not sure this guy's into subtle.'

'Anything to get a client,' she said.

'Maybe you should practice a little first,' he said.

'Practice what?'

'Flashing cleavage. I'm told it's something of an art.'

'I see. And on whom should I practice?'

Myron spread his hands. 'I'm willing to volunteer my services.'

'The sacrifices you make for clients,' she said. 'It's heroic, really.'

'So what do you say?'

Jessica gave him a look. *The* look, actually. Myron felt it in his toes, to name one place. She leaned toward him. 'No.'

'No?'

She put her lips to his ear. 'Let's try out my new oils first.'

One word: Yowzer.

27

Jessica hadn't need to flash cleavage.

Both Cranes were immediately entranced. Mrs Crane chatted with Jess about her books. Mr Crane couldn't stop smiling and sucking in his gut. At the start of the second set Mr Crane tried to chew down the commission a half-point. A very good sign. Myron made a mental note to bring Jess to more business gatherings.

There were other agents there. Lots of them. Most wore business suits and had their hair slicked back. They ranged in age, but most looked pretty young. Several tried to approach, but Mr Crane shooed them away.

'Vultures,' Jessica whispered to Myron as one forced his card on Mr Crane.

'Just trying to hustle business,' Myron said.

'You're defending them?'

'I do the same thing, Jess. If they're not aggressive they don't have a chance. You think the Cranes are going to come to them?'

'But still. You don't hang around like these guys.'

'What exactly am I doing now?'

Jessica thought a second. 'Yeah, but you're cute.'

Hard to argue. Eddie crushed his opponent 6–0, 6–0, but the match was not as close as the score indicated. Eddie lacked finesse. He relied on power. But what power. His racket ripped through the still air like the reaper's scythe. The ball shot off the strings as though from a bazooka. The finesse would come. But for now the awesome power was more than enough.

After the players shook hands Eddie's parents went onto the court.

'Do me a favor,' Myron said to Jess.

'What?'

'Get rid of the parents for a couple of minutes. I want to talk to Eddie alone.'

She did it with a lunch invitation. Jessica escorted Mr and Mrs Crane to the Racquets restaurant overlooking the Grandstand. Myron accompanied Eddie to the locker room. The kid had barely broken a sweat. Myron had exerted himself more just watching. Eddie walked with big, unhurried steps, a towel draped around his neck, completely relaxed.

'I told TruPro I wasn't interested,' Eddie said.

Myron nodded. That explained Aaron's generous offer to let Myron represent Eddie. 'How did they respond?'

'They were pretty pissed,' Eddie said.

'I bet.'

'I think I want to go with your agency,' he said.

'How do your parents feel?'

'Doesn't matter really. They both know it's my decision.'

They walked a few more steps.

'Eddie, I need to ask you about Valerie.'

He half-smiled. 'Are you really trying to find her killer?'

'Yes.'

'Why?'

'I don't know. It's just something I have to do.'

Eddie nodded. The answer was good enough for him. 'Shoot.'

'You first met Valerie at Pavel's camp in Florida?'

'Right.'

'How did you two become friends?'

'You ever been to Pavel's academy?' Eddie asked.

'No.'

'You might not get it.' Eddie Crane stopped, brushed the hair from his eyes, continued. 'It probably sounds weird – a sixteen-year-old girl and a nine-year-old boy being close friends. That's pretty normal in tennis. You don't make friends with kids your own age. They're the enemy. Val and I were both lonely, I guess. And because of our differences we weren't threats to each other. I guess that's how it started.'

'Did she ever mention Alexander Cross?'

'Yeah, a couple of times. They dated or something.'

'Did you get the impression they were serious?'

He shrugged. The guard checked their passes and let them enter. 'Not really. Tennis was her life. Boyfriends were peripheral.'

'Tell me more about Pavel's academy. What was it like for Valerie?'

'What was it like?' Eddie grinned sadly, shook his head. 'It was like one big game of King of the Mountain. Every kid is trying to knock off every other kid.'

'And Valerie was king of the woman's side?'

Eddie nodded. 'The undisputed king.'

'Did Pavel and Valerie get along?'

'Yeah. At first anyway. He motivated Val like no one else could. She would practice for hours with his assistants, and just when you thought she couldn't take one more step Pavel would come out and boom! It was like an energy boost. Val was a great player, but Pavel knew how to get her competitive juices really flowing. When he was there, she blew away everyone else. Diving, stretching, running down each lob. She was incredible.'

'So when did things start going wrong?'

Eddie shrugged. 'When she started losing.' He said it like it was the most natural thing in the world.

'What happened?'

'I don't know.' He stopped again, thinking. 'She stopped caring, I guess. It happens to a lot of the players. They burn out. Too much pressure too fast.'

'What did Pavel do?'

'He tried all his old tricks. You see, Pavel fostered the whole dog-eat-dog atmosphere. It weeded out the weak, he told me. But Valerie wasn't responding anymore. She still beat most of the girls. But when she played against the game's greats – Steffi, Monica, Gabriela, Martina – she didn't have the heart to beat them anymore.'

Eddie sat in a chair in front of his locker. Very few people were around. The floor, carpeted in an office-brown, was littered with little pieces of wrap and bandaging. Myron sat down next to him. 'You told me you saw Valerie a few days before she died.'

'Yeah,' Eddie said. 'In the lobby of the Plaza.' He took off his shirt. The kid was bony. The kind of bony where it appears the chest concaves into the heart. 'I hadn't seen her in a long time.'

'What did she say to you?'

'She was going to make a comeback. She seemed pretty excited about the idea, kinda like the old Val. Then she gave me your number and told me to stay away from Pavel and TruPro.'

'Did she say why you should stay away?'

'No.'

'Did she say anything else?'

He paused, his mind flashing back. 'Not really. She was kinda in a hurry. She said she had to go out and settle something.'

'Settle what?'

'I don't know. She didn't say.'

'What day was this?' Myron asked.

'Thursday, I think.'

'Do you remember the time?'

'Must have been around six.'

Valerie had called Duane's apartment. Thursday at six-fifteen. Settle something. Settle what? Settle her relationship with Duane? Or expose it? And what if she did threaten that? Would Duane kill her to stop her? Myron didn't think so, especially in light of the fact that Duane was serving a tennis ball in front of several thousand people when she was shot.

Eddie slipped out of his sneakers and socks.

'I got two tickets to the Yankees for Wednesday night,' Myron said. 'You want to go?'

Eddie smiled. 'I thought you didn't do that.'

'Do what?'

'That ass-kissing stuff.'

'I do. Every agent does. I'm not above it. But in this case I actually thought it might be fun.'

Eddie stood. 'Should I be skeptical of your motives?' he asked.

'Only if you're smart.'

Duane liked to be alone before a match. Win had taught him meditation techniques, *sans* the dirty videotapes, and you could usually find him curled up in a corner, sitting in the lotus position with his eyes closed. He didn't like to be disturbed, which was good. Myron wasn't sure he wanted to see him right now anyway. His main responsibility, he knew, was still to help his client perform his best – especially on this, the most important day of Duane's career. Raising the issue of Duane's late-night rendezvous with Deanna Yeller would be a distraction. A major distraction.

It would have to wait.

The crowd was huge. Everyone had been waiting for this match between the upstart American Duane Richwood and the cool Czech Michel Brishny, a former number one player now ranked fifth. Myron and Jessica took their seats in the front row. Jess looked incredible in a simple yellow sundress. Spectators gaped. Nothing new there. Without a doubt, the TV cameras would be getting plenty of shots of the box today. Between Jess's beauty and her fame in the literary world they wouldn't be able to resist.

Myron debated having her hold up one of his business cards. Nah. Too tacky.

A bevy of favorites was already in their seats. Ned Tunwell and other Nike VIPs crowded a corner box. Ned waved like a windmill on LSD. Myron gave a small wave back. Two boxes behind them sat chubby Roy O'Connor, the rotund president of TruPro. Sitting with him was Aaron. Aaron had his face tilted to the sun, soaking up the rays. He was garbed in his usual attire – white suit, no shirt. Across the way Myron also spotted Senator Cross in a box jammed with gray-haired lawyer types – the exception being Gregory Caufield. Myron still wanted to talk to Gregory. Perhaps an opportunity would present itself after the match. The buxom blonde from the other day was back in the same seat. The shapely lass gave Myron another small wave. He didn't wave back.

Myron turned to Jessica. She smiled at him.

'You're beautiful,' he said.

'More beautiful than the blonde with the big boobs?' she asked.

'Who?' Myron said.

'The Silicone She-Beast giving you the eye.'

'I don't know what you mean.' Then: 'How do you know they're silicone?'

The players took the court for warm-ups. Two minutes later Pavel

Menansi made his grand entrance. There was a smattering of applause. Pavel displayed his gratitude with a circular hand gesture. Very popelike. He wore tennis whites, with a green sweater tied around his neck. The smile was on full blast. Pavel made his way toward the TruPro box. Aaron rose, let him in, then sat back down. Pavel and Roy O'Connor shook hands.

It hit Myron like a shot to the solar plexus. 'Oh no,' he said.

'What?' Jessica asked.

Myron stood. 'I've got to go.'

'Now?'

'I'll be back. Make my excuses.'

28

The match was on the car radio. WFAN, 66 AM. From the sound of it Duane was not playing well. He had just dropped the first set 6–3 when Myron pulled into a lot off Central Park West in Manhattan.

Dr Julie Abramson lived in a town house half a block down from her office. Myron rang the bell. There was a buzzing noise and then her voice came over the intercom.

'Who is it?'

'Myron Bolitar. It's urgent.'

There were a few seconds of silence. Then: 'Second floor.' The buzzer sounded again. Myron pushed the door open. Julie Abramson was waiting for him on the stairwell.

'Did you call and hang up on me?' she asked.

'Yes.'

'Why?'

'To see if you were home.'

He arrived at her door. They stood and faced each other. With their height difference – she well under five feet, he six-four – the sight was almost comical.

She looked up. Way up. 'I still can't deny or confirm that Valerie Simpson was ever a patient of mine,' she said.

'That's okay. I want to ask you about a hypothetical situation.'

'A hypothetical situation?'

He nodded.

'And that couldn't wait until Monday?'

'No.'

Dr Abramson sighed. 'Come on in.'

She had the television turned on to the match. 'I should have known,' she said. 'The TV keeps flashing to Jessica Culver in the players' box, but never you.'

'With her there they wouldn't show me anyway.'

'The sportscaster says you two are an item. Is that true?'

Myron shrugged. Noncommittal. 'What's the score now?' he asked.

'Your client lost the first set 6–3,' she said. 'He's down 2–0 in this set.' She switched off the television with the remote and signaled to a chair. They both sat. 'So tell me about your hypothetical situation, Myron.'

'I want to start off with a young girl. Fifteen years old. Pretty. From a well-to-do family, parents divorced, the father absent. She dates a boy from a prominent family. She's also a tennis protégée.'

'This isn't sounding too hypothetical,' Dr Abramson said.

'Just bear with me a second. The young girl is such a great tennis player that her mother ships her off to an academy run by a world-famous tennis coach. When this young girl arrives at the academy she finds the competition cutthroat. Tennis is the most individual of sports. There is no team spirit here. There is no camaraderie. Everybody is vying for the approval of the world-famous coach. Tennis is not conducive to making friends.' Echoing Eddie's words. 'It isolates. Would you say that's true, Doctor?'

'On the level you're talking about, yes.'

'So when this young girl is uprooted from the life she has known and tossed into this rather hostile environment, she is not made to feel welcome. Far from it. The other girls see this new tennis protégée as a threat and when they realize what a magnificent player she is, the threat becomes reality. The other girls shun her all the more. She grows even more isolated.'

'Okay.'

'Now, this world-famous coach, he's a bit Darwinian. Survival of the fittest and all that. He sort of plays a dual role here. On the one hand this isolation will force the girl to search for an escape, a place where she can thrive.'

'The tennis court?' Abramson said.

'Exactly. The young girl begins to practice even harder than before. But at the same time the world-famous coach is nice to her. While everyone else is cruel, the world-famous coach praises her. He spends time with her. He gets the most out of her.'

'Which in turn,' Dr Abramson interjected, 'isolates her from the other girls all the more.'

'Right. The young girl becomes dependent on the coach. She thinks he cares and like any eager student she wants – needs – his approval. She begins to play even harder. She also knows that pleasing the world-famous coach will also please her mother. She tries even harder. The cycle continues.'

Dr Abramson had to see where Myron was going with this, but her face remained blank. 'Go on,' she said.

'The tennis academy is not the real world. It's a secluded domain ruled by the world-famous coach. But he acts like he cares for the young girl. He treats her like she's something special. The young girl plays even harder, pushing herself more than she could ever imagine – not for herself, but to please him. Maybe he offers her a pat on the back after practice. Maybe he rubs her sore shoulders. Maybe they have dinner one night to discuss her tennis. Who knows how it started?'

'How what started?' Abramson asked.

Myron chose to ignore the question. For now. 'The young girl and world-famous coach start touring together,' he continued. 'She starts playing competitive tennis against women who again treat her as a feared rival. But now the young girl and the world-famous coach are alone. On the road. Staying in hotels.'

'More isolation,' Abramson offered.

'She plays well. She's beautiful, she's young, she's American. The press begins to swarm. The sudden attention frightens her. But the world-famous coach is there to protect her.'

'She becomes more dependent on him.'

Myron nodded. 'Now let's remember that the world-famous coach is a former world-famous player himself. He is accustomed to the narcissistic lifestyle that goes along with being a professional athlete. He is used to doing as he pleases. And that's exactly what he does with this girl.'

Silence.

'Could this happen, Doc? In theory?'

Dr Abramson cleared her throat. 'In theory, yes. Whenever a man wields power and authority over a woman the potential for abuse is high. But in your scenario the potential for abuse is maximized. The man is older, the woman no more than a child. A teacher or a boss might control their victim for a few hours a day, but in your scenario the coach is both omnipotent and omnipresent.'

They looked at each other.

'The girl in my scenario,' Myron said softly. 'Her play would deteriorate if he abused her?'

'Without question.'

'What else would happen to her?'

'Every case is different,' Abramson replied as though giving a dissertation. 'But the results would invariably be catastrophic. A scenario like yours would probably start out for the young girl as nothing more than a crush. This sophisticated, older man is nice to her when nobody else is. He understands and cares about her. She probably doesn't have to invite his advances – they just sort of happen. The young girl may encourage them at first, but probably not. She may even resist, but at the same time she feels responsible. She blames herself.'

Myron felt something in the pit of his stomach open wide. 'Which causes more problems.'

'Yes. You talked about how the world-famous coach isolates her,' Abramson continued. 'But in your scenario he does more than that. He dehumanizes her. Her adolescence is turned upside down by her tennis greatness. Her life is not about school and friends and family. It's about money and winning. She's become a commodity. She knows that if she displeases him, the commodity becomes worthless. And her being a commodity makes it easier on him too.'

'How?' Myron asked.

'A commodity is far easier to abuse than a human being.'

Silence.

'So what happens when it's all over?' Myron asked. 'When the world-famous coach uses up the commodity, what happens to her?'

'The young girl would reach out for something – anything – that she thinks might save her.'

'The old boyfriend maybe?'

'Perhaps.'

'She might even want to get engaged right away.'

'That's possible, yes. She may see the old boyfriend as a return to her innocence. In her mind the boyfriend may be raised to savior status.'

'And suppose this boyfriend was murdered?'

'You've pulled out the final block,' Abramson replied softly. 'The young girl was already in need of serious therapy. Now a complete mental breakdown is a very real possibility. Maybe even a likelihood.'

Myron felt his heart crumble.

Dr Abramson looked away for a moment. 'But there are other aspects to your scenario that need to be explored,' she said, trying to sound offhanded.

'Like?'

'Like what actually occurred during the abuse. If, as you say, the world-famous coach was a narcissistic man, he would only concern himself with his pleasure. He wouldn't worry about her. He probably wouldn't, for example, wear protection. And since this girl is rather young and probably not sexually active, she wouldn't be using oral contraceptives.'

Dread flooded Myron's chest. He remembered the rumors. 'He got her pregnant.'

'In the realm of your scenario,' Abramson said, 'that is certainly a possibility.'

'What would happen . . . ?' Myron stopped. The answer was obvious. 'The world-famous coach would make her get an abortion.'

'I imagine so, yes.'

Silence.

Myron felt something well up in his eyes. 'What she went through . . .' He shook his head. 'Everyone thought Valerie was so weak. But in reality—'

'Not Valerie,' Abramson corrected. 'A young girl. A theoretical young girl in a theoretical situation.'

Myron looked up. 'Still trying to protect your ass, Doc?'

'You can't say anything, Myron. It's all hypothetical. I will neither confirm nor deny that Valerie Simpson was ever a patient of mine.'

He shook his head, stood, and headed for the door. When he reached it, he turned back toward her. 'One more hypothetical question,' he said. 'The world-famous coach. If he's willing to abuse one child, how likely is it he'll do it again?'

Dr Abramson did not face him. 'Very likely,' she said.

29

By the time Myron got back to Stadium Court, Duane had dropped the first two sets 6–3, 6–1, and it was 2–2 in the third set. Myron sat between Jessica and Win. Pavel Menansi, he immediately noticed, was no longer in his seat. Aaron was still there. Senator Cross and Gregory Caufield were in their box too. Ned Tunwell still sat with his Nike colleagues. Ned was no longer waving. He was, in fact, crying. The entire Nike box looked like a deflated balloon. Henry Hobman was still as a Rodin.

Myron turned to Jessica. She looked concerned but said nothing. She took his hand and gave it a little squeeze. He squeezed back and gave her a small smile. He noticed that she was now wearing a bright pink Ray•Ban cap.

'What's with the cap?' he asked.

'A guy offered me a thousand dollars to wear it.'

Myron was familiar with the old advertising trick. Companies – in this case, Ray•Ban – paid anyone seated in the players' boxes to wear the caps during matches, figuring, of course, that there was an excellent chance the person and hence the hat would show up on television. Relatively cheap and effective exposure.

Myron looked at Win. 'What about you?'

'I don't do caps,' Win replied. 'They muss my hair.'

'That,' Jessica added, 'and the guy only offered him five hundred dollars.'

Win shrugged. 'Sexual discrimination. It's an ugly thing.'

More like smart business. Five hundred dollars was the normal rate. But somebody at Ray•Ban realized Jess was both attractive and a celebrity – ergo, extra exposure.

Duane dropped another game. Down 3–2 after losing the first two sets. Not good. The players collapsed in their chairs on either side of the umpire for the changeover. Duane toweled down his racket. He changed shirts. Some female fans whistled. Duane did not smile. He glanced over at their box. Unlike just about any other sport in the world, tennis players are not allowed to talk to their coaches during the match. But Henry did move. He took his hand off his chin and made a fist. Duane nodded.

'Time,' the chair ump said.

That was when Pavel made his return.

He entered through the portal on the right near the grandstand carrying an Evian in his hand. Myro's eyes locked on to him. He felt his pulse quicken. Pavel Menansi was still wearing the sweater tied around his neck. He took his seat behind Aaron. Pavel Menansi. He smiled. He laughed. He sipped a cold Evian. He breathed in and out. He lived. People patted his back. Someone asked for an autograph. A young girl. Pavel said something to her. The young girl giggled behind her hand.

'Burgess Meredith,' Win said. He was looking at the court, not Myron.

'What?'

'Burgess Meredith.'

More Name the *Batman* Commercial. 'Not now,' Myron said.

'Now. Burgess Meredith.'

'Why?'

'Because you're staring. Aaron will pick it up.' Win adjusted his sunglasses. 'Burgess Meredith.'

He was right. 'The Penguin.'

'Victor Buono.'

'King Tut.'

'Bruce Lee.'

Jessica leaned over. 'Trick question,' she said.

'No hints,' Win said.

'He played Kato,' Myron said. 'Green Hornet's sidekick. He guest-starred on one episode. I don't know if you could call him a criminal.'

'Correct.' Silence. Then Win said: 'That bad?'

'Worse.'

'The police released Valerie's body,' Win said. 'The funeral is tomorrow.'

Myron nodded. On the court Duane served up an ace. Only his second of the match. Myron said, 'It may get ugly now.'

'How so?'

'I know why the Ache brothers want us out.'

'Ah,' Win said. 'May I assume the Aches will not want you to disseminate this information to the general public?'

'Correct assumption.'

'And may I further assume this information is worth the cost of Aaron and an all-star cast?'

'Another correct assumption.'

Win sat back. He was very still. He was also smiling. Myron turned to Jessica. Her hand still held his.

'If you get killed,' she whispered, 'I'll kill you. Soul mate.'

Silence.

On the court Duane hit two more aces and then an overhead to tie the third set at three games apiece. Duane looked over at the box. The reflection of the sun off his sunglasses was blinding, giving him a sleek, robotic look. But something in his face had changed. Duane made the fist again.

Henry spoke for the first time. 'He's baaack.'

30

Henry Hobman was good as his word. Duane rallied. He took the third set 6–4. Ned Tunwell stopped crying. The fourth set went to a tiebreaker, which Duane won 9–7, saving three match points. Ned started the windmill wave again. Duane won the fifth set 6–2. Ned had to change his underwear.

Final score of the marathon match: 3–6, 1–6, 6–4, 7–6, (9–7), 6–2. Before the combatants had even left the court the word *classic* was being bantered about.

By the time all the congratulations and news conferences ended it was getting late. Jess borrowed Myron's car to visit her mother. Win dropped him off at the office. Esperanza was still there.

'Big win,' she said.

'Yup.'

'Duane played like shit in the first two sets.'

'He had a long night,' Myron said. 'What have we got?'

Esperanza handed him a stack of papers. 'Prenuptial agreement for Jerry Prince. Final copy.'

Ah, the beloved prenup. A necessary evil. Myron hated to recommend them. Marriage should be about love and romance. A prenup, frankly speaking, was about as romantic as licking a litter box. Still, Myron had an obligation to guard the financial well-being of his clients. Too many of these marriages ended in quickie divorces. Gold-digging, it used to be called. Some mistook his concern for sexism. It wasn't. Well-to-do female athletes should do the same.

'What else?' he asked.

'Emmett Roberts wants you to call. He needs your opinion on a car he's buying.'

Myron drove a Ford Taurus, hardly qualifying him as *Motor Trend*'s Man of the Year.

Emmett was a fringe basketball player who bounced between bench-sitting in the NBA and starring in the Continental Basketball Association – a sort of basketball minor league where players do nothing but try to impress NBA scouts. Very few do. There were exceptions. John Starks and Anthony Mason of the Knicks, to name two. But for the most part the CBA gymnasiums were yet another haven of shattered dreams, a bottom rung on the ladder before slipping off altogether.

Myron fingered through his Rolodex. Esperanza was good about keeping it up-to-date and in alphabetical order for him. Raston. Ratner. Rextell. Rippard. Roberts. There. Emmett Roberts.

Myron stopped.

'Where's Duane's card?' he asked.

'What?'

Myron quickly skimmed through the rest of the Rs. 'Duane Richwood isn't in my Rolodex. Could you have misfiled it?'

She dismissed that possibility with a glare. 'Look around. It's probably on your desk someplace.'

Not on the desk. Myron tried the Ds. No Duane.

'I'll make you up a new one,' she said, heading for the door. 'Try not to lose it this time.'

'Thanks a bunch,' he said. Still, the missing card gnawed at him. Another coincidence involving Duane? He dialed Emmett Roberts's phone. Emmett answered.

'Hey, Myron. How's it going?'

'Good, Emmett. What's this about buying a car?'

'I saw this Porsche today. Red. Fully loaded. Seventy Gs. I was thinking about using the playoff bonus money to buy it.'

'If that's what you want,' Myron said.

'Man, you sound like my mother. I wanted your opinion.'

'Buy something cheaper,' Myron said. 'A lot cheaper.'

'But the car is so hot, Myron. If you could just see it . . .'

'Then buy it, Emmett. You're an adult. You don't need my blessing.' Myron hesitated. 'Did I ever tell you about Norm Booker?'

'Who?'

How soon they forget.

'I was maybe fifteen or sixteen years old,' Myron said, 'and I was working at this summer camp in Massachusetts. It was a Celtics camp. They used to have their rookie tryouts there. I was basically a towel boy. I met a lot of the draft picks back then. Cedric Maxwell. Larry Bird. But my first year the Celtics had a first-round pick named Norm Booker. I think he was out of Iowa State.'

'Yeah, so?'

'Norm was a great player. Six-seven, smooth moves, nice touch. Strong as an ox. And nice guy too. He talked to me. Lot of the guys ignored the towel boys, but Norm wasn't like that. I remember he used to shoot foul shots with his back to the basket. He'd toss the ball over his shoulder. He had such a great touch that he could made better than fifty percent that way.'

'So what happened to him?'

'He sat the bench as a rookie. The Celtics cut him the next year. He scrounged around a bit and then he landed with the Portland Trailblazers. He mostly rode the bench, played garbage time, that sort of thing. When the Trailblazers made the playoffs Norm got the usual bonus. He was so excited about it he went out and bought a Rolls-Royce. Dropped every dime he had on the car. But he wasn't worried. There was always next year. And the year after that. Only thing was, Portland cut him. He tried out with a couple of other clubs, but nobody wanted him. Last I heard Norm had to sell the car to feed his family.'

Silence.

After some time passed Emmett said, 'I also saw this Honda Accord. They had a pretty good lease deal.'

'Go for it, Emmett.'

They hung up a few minutes later. Myron hadn't thought about Norm Booker in a long time. He wondered what became of him.

Esperanza came back in. She put a new card for Duane Richwood in his Rolodex. 'Happy?'

'Yes.' He handed her two sheets of paper. 'This is a party list for the night Alexander Cross was killed.'

'What am I looking for?'

'Heck if I know. A familiar name. Something that leaps out at you.'

She nodded. 'You know about the funeral tomorrow?'

Myron nodded.

'You going?' she asked.

'Yes.'

'I tracked down one of the schoolteachers from the article on Curtis Yeller.'

'Which one?'

'Mrs Lucinda Elright. She's retired now, lives in Philadelphia. She'll see you tomorrow afternoon. You can go right after the funeral.'

Myron leaned back. 'I'm not sure that's necessary anymore.'

'You want me to cancel?'

Myron thought a moment. In light of what he'd learned about Pavel Menansi, the connection between Valerie's murder and what happened to Curtis Yeller seemed more tenuous than ever. The murder of Alexander Cross had not caused Valerie's downfall. It wasn't even the final push. Pavel Menansi had pushed Valerie off the cliff years before. He had watched her slowly plummet, tumbling over jagged rocks on her painful way down. Alexander Cross's death had marked the end of the descent. The ground, if you will. The final crash. Nothing more. Clearly there was no connection between Valerie's death and the events of six years ago. There was also no connection between Duane and Valerie other than what Duane had said – they slept together. No big deal.

Except . . .

406

Except for last night's rendezvous between Duane and Curtis Yeller's mother.

If not for that – if Myron hadn't seen them together at the hotel – he would be able to dismiss them both entirely. But Duane and Deanna Yeller having an affair – it was too much of a coincidence. There had to be a connection.

'Don't cancel,' Myron said.

31

Valerie's funeral was strictly cookie-cutter.

The reverend, a porky man with a red nose, hadn't known her with any depth. He listed achievements as though reading from a résumé. He mixed in a few oldies but goodies: loving daughter; so full of life; taken so young; God has a plan. An organ sounded self-righteous indignation. Tacky flowers, like something you'd find draped around a winning horse, adorned the chapel. Stern stain-glass figures peered from above.

The crowd did not linger long. They stopped by Helen and Kenneth Van Slyke, not so much to offer comfort but to be sure they'd been seen and recognized, which was the real reason they'd come in the first place. Helen Van Slyke shook hands with her head high. She did not blink. She did not smile. She did not cry. Her jaw was set. Myron waited in the receiving line with Win. As they got closer they could hear Helen repeat the same phrases – 'Good of you to come, thank you for coming, good of you to come, thank you for coming' – in a singsong voice reminiscent of a flight attendant upon disembarkation.

When it was Myron's turn Helen gripped his hand hard. 'Do you know who hurt Valerie?'

'Yes.' She had said hurt, Myron noted. Not kill.

Helen Van Slyke looked at Win for confirmation. Win nodded.

'Come back to the house,' she said. 'There's going to be a reception.' She turned to the next mourner and hit PLAY on her internal tape recorder. 'Good of you to come, thank you for coming, good of you to come . . .'

Myron and Win did as she asked. The mood at Brentman Hall was neither Irish wake-like nor devastating grief. There were no tears. No laughter. Either would have been more welcome than this room completely void of any emotion. 'Mourners' milled around like they were at an office cocktail party.

'No one cares,' Myron said. 'She's gone and no one cares.'

Win shrugged. 'No one ever does.' The eternal optimist.

The first person to approach them was Kenneth. He was dressed in proper black with well-shined shoes. He greeted Win with a back slap and a firm handshake. He ignored Myron.

'How are you holding up?' Win asked. Like he cared.

'Oh I'm doing okay,' he said with a heavy sigh. Mr Brave. 'But I'm worried about Helen. We've had to medicate her.'

'I'm sorry to hear that,' Myron said.

Kenneth turned to him, as though seeing him for the first time. He made a face like he was sucking on a lemon. 'Do you mean that?' he asked.

Myron and Win shared a glance. 'Yes, I do, Kenneth,' Myron said.

'Then do me the courtesy of staying away from my wife. She was very upset after your visit the other day.'

'I meant no harm.'

'Well, you caused plenty of it, I can tell you. I think it's high time, Mr Bolitar, you showed some respect. Leave my wife alone. We are grieving here. She's lost her daughter and I've lost my stepdaughter.'

Win rolled his eyes.

Myron said, 'You have my word, Kenneth.'

Kenneth nodded a manly nod and moved away.

'His stepdaughter,' Win said in disgust. 'Bah.'

From across the room Myron caught Helen Van Slyke's eye. She made a gesture toward a door on her right and slipped through it. Like they were meeting for a secret liaison.

'Keep Kenneth away,' Myron said.

Win feigned surprise. 'But you gave Kenneth your word.'

'Bah,' Myron said. Whatever that meant.

He ducked through the doorway and followed Helen. She too wore all black, a suit of some sort with the skirt cut just low enough to be sexy yet proper. Good legs, he noticed, and felt like a pig for thinking such a thing at such a time. She led him to a small room down the end of an ornate corridor and closed the door behind them. The room looked like a miniature version of the living room. The chandelier was smaller. The couch was smaller. The fireplace was smaller. The portrait over the mantel was smaller.

'This is the drawing room,' Helen Van Slyke explained.

'Oh,' Myron said. He'd always wanted to know what a drawing room was. Now that he was in one he still had no idea.

'Would you care for some tea?'

'No thanks.'

'Do you mind if I have some?'

'Not at all,' he said.

She sat demurely and poured herself a cup from the silver set on the table. Myron noticed that there were two tea sets on the table. He wondered if that was a clue as to the definition of drawing room.

'Kenneth tells me you're on medication,' he said.

'Kenneth is full of shit.'

Big surprise.

'Are you still investigating Valerie's murder?' she asked. There was almost a mocking quality in her voice. Her words also seemed just a tad slurred, and Myron wondered if perhaps she was indeed being medicated or if she'd added a little home brew to her tea.

'Yes,' he said.

'Do you still feel some chivalrous responsibility toward her?'

'I never did.'

'Then why do you do it?'

Myron shrugged. 'Someone should care.'

She looked up, searching his face for a shred of sarcasm. 'I see,' she said. 'So tell me: what have you learned from your investigation?'

'Pavel Menansi abused your daughter.'

Myron watched for a reaction. Helen Van Slyke smiled semi-teasingly and put a sugar cube in her tea. Not exactly the reaction he had in mind. 'You can't be serious,' she said.

'I am.'

'What do you mean, abused?'

'Sexual abuse.'

'As in rape?'

'You may call it that, yes.'

She made a scoffing noise. 'Come now, Mr Bolitar. Isn't that a tad extreme?'

'No.'

'It is not as though Pavel forced himself on her, is it? They had an affair. It's hardly unheard of.'

'You knew about it?'

'Of course. And frankly, I was quite displeased. Pavel showed poor judgment. But my daughter was sixteen years old at the time – maybe seventeen, I'm not really sure. Anyway, she was certainly of legal age. Calling it rape or sexual abuse, well, I think that's being a tad overdramatic, don't you?'

Maybe both medication and booze. Maybe even mixing them. 'Valerie was a young girl,' he said. 'Pavel Menansi was her coach, a man of nearly fifty.'

'Would it have made it any better if he was forty? Or thirty?'

'No,' Myron said.

'So why bring up their age difference?' She put down the tea. The smile was again toying with her lips. 'Let me ask you a question, Mr Bolitar. If Valerie was a sixteen-year-old boy and he had an affair with a beautiful female coach who was, let's say, thirty – would you call that sexual abuse? Would you call that rape?'

Myron hesitated for a second. It was a second too long.

'I thought so,' she said triumphantly. 'You're a sexist, Mr Bolitar. Valerie had an affair with an older man. It happens all the time.' Again the playful smile. 'To me even.'

'Did you have a breakdown after it was over?'

She raised an eyebrow. 'So that's your definition of abuse?' she asked. 'A breakdown?'

'You entrusted your daughter to this man,' Myron said. 'He was supposed to help her. But he used her instead. He tore her down. He destroyed and discarded her.'

'Tore? Destroyed? Discarded? My, my, Mr Bolitar, we are out for shock effect, aren't we?'

'You don't see anything wrong with what he did?'

She put down her tea and took a cigarette. She lit it, inhaled deeply with her eyes closed, and let it all out. 'If it makes you happy to blame me for what happened, fine, blame me. I was a lousy mother. The worst. Is that better?'

Myron watched her calmly smoking her cigarette and sipping her tea. Too calmly. Did she really buy this crap she was peddling? Or was it an act? Was she just deluding herself or . . .

'Pavel bought you off,' Myron said.

'No.'

'TruPro and Pavel are paying—'

'That's not it at all,' she interrupted.

'We know about the money, Mrs Van Slyke.'

'You don't understand. Pavel blames himself for what happened. He took it upon himself to remedy the situation in the only way he could.'

'By paying you off.'

'By providing us with some of the funds Valerie may have earned had her career continued. He didn't have to do that. The affair wasn't necessarily the cause—'

'It's called hush money.'

'Never,' she said in a near-hiss. 'Valerie was my daughter.'

'And you sold her for cash.'

She shook her head. 'I did what I thought was best for my daughter.'

'He abused her. You took his money. You let him get away with it.'

'There was nothing I could do,' she said. 'We didn't want to make it public. Valerie wanted to put it behind her. She wanted to keep it confidential. We all did.'

'Why?' Myron said. 'It was just an affair with an older man. Happens all the time. To you even.'

She bit down on her lip for a moment. When she spoke again her voice was softer. 'There was nothing I could do,' she repeated. 'It was in everyone's best interest to keep it quiet.'

'Bullshit,' Myron said. He realized he was pushing too hard, but something inside of him wouldn't let him back off. 'You sold your daughter.'

She was silent for a few moments, concentrating only on her cigarette, watching the ash grow longer and longer. In the distance they could hear the low rumble from the funeral crowd. Glasses clinking. A polite titter.

'They threatened Valerie,' she said.

'Who?'

'I don't know. Men who work with Pavel. They made it very clear that if she opened her mouth she was dead.' She looked up, pleading. 'Don't you see? What option did we have? No good could come from talking. They'd kill her. I was afraid for Valerie. Kenneth – well, I think Kenneth was more interested in the money. Hindsight may be twenty-twenty, but at the time I believed it was the best thing.'

'You were protecting your daughter,' Myron said.

'Yes.'

'But she's dead now.'

Helen was puzzled. 'I don't understand.'

'You don't have to worry about her being hurt anymore. She's dead. You're free to do as you please.'

She opened her mouth, closed it, tried again. 'I have another daughter,' she managed. 'I have a husband.'

'So then what was all that talk before about protecting Valerie?'

'It . . . I was trying . . .' Her voice churned to a silence.

'You took the hush money,' Myron said. He tried to remind himself that the woman who sat before him had buried her daughter today, but not even that fact could slow him down. If anything, it seemed to fuel him. 'Don't blame your husband. He's a spineless worm. You were Valerie's mother. You took money to protect a man who abused your daughter. And now you'll keep taking money to protect a man who might have killed her.'

'You have no proof Pavel had anything to do with her murder.'

'The murder, no. His other crimes against Valerie – that's a different story.'

She closed her eyes. 'It's too late.'

'It's not too late. He's still doing it, you know. Guys like Pavel don't stop. They just find new victims.'

'There's nothing I can do.'

'I have a friend,' Myron said. 'Her name is Jessica Culver. She's a writer.'

'I know who she is.'

He handed her Jess's card. 'Tell her the story. She'll write it up. Put it in a major publication. *Sports Illustrated* maybe. It'll be out before Pavel's people even know about it. They're bad men, but they're not wasteful or stupid. Once it's published there'll be no reason to go after your family anymore. It'll end him.'

'I'm sorry.' She lowered her head. 'I can't do it.'

She was crumbling. Her whole body was slumped and shaking. Myron watched her, tried to muster up some pity, couldn't do it. 'You left her alone with him,' he continued. 'You didn't look after her. And when you had the chance to help her, you told her to bury it. You took money.'

Her body racked. Probably from a sob. Attacking a mother at her own daughter's funeral, Myron thought. What could he do for an encore? Drown newborn kittens in the neighbor's pool?

'Perhaps,' he went on, 'Valerie wanted to tell the truth. Maybe she needed that to put it all behind her. And maybe that's why she was murdered.'

Silence. Then without warning Helen Van Slyke raised her head. She stood and left without saying another word. Myron followed. When he reentered the living room he could hear her voice.

'Good of you to come. Thank you for coming.'

32

Lucinda Elright was big and warm with thick, jiggly arms and an easy laugh. The kind of woman that as a child you feared would hug you too hard and as an adult you wish like hell she would.

'Come on in,' she said, shooing several small children away from the door.

'Thank you,' Myron said.

'You want something to eat?'

'No thanks.'

'How about some cookies?' There were at least ten kids in the apartment. All black, none over the age of seven or eight. Some were using a paint set. Some were building a castle out of sugar cubes. One, a boy about six years old, was sticking his tongue out at Myron. 'Not homemade, you understand. I can't cook worth spit.'

'Actually, cookies sound good.'

She smiled. 'I do day care now that I'm retired. Hope you don't mind.'

'Not at all.'

Mrs Elright went into the kitchen. The little boy waited until she was out of the room. Then he stuck his tongue out again. Myron stuck his tongue out back. Mr Mature. The kid giggled.

'Now sit, Myron. Right over there.' She knocked various paraphernalia off the sofa. The plate was full of the classics. Oreos. Chips Ahoys. Fig Newtons.

'Eat,' she said.

Myron reached for a cookie. The little boy stood behind Mrs Elright so he couldn't be seen. He stuck his tongue out again. Without so much as a backward glance Mrs Elright said, 'Gerald, you stick your tongue out one more time, I'll cut it off with my pruning shears.'

Gerald rolled his tongue back. 'What's pruning shears?'

'Never you mind. Just go over there and play now, you hear? And don't you be causing no trouble.'

'Yes, ma'am.'

When he was out of earshot Mrs Elright said, 'I like them better at this age. They break my heart when they get a little older.'

Myron nodded, pulled apart an Oreo. He didn't lick out the cream. Very adult.

'Your friend Esperanza,' Mrs Elright began, grabbing a Fig Newton. 'She said you wanted to talk about Curtis Yeller.'

'Yes, ma'am.' He handed her the article. 'Were you correctly quoted in this article?'

She lifted her half-moon reading glasses from her hefty bosom and scanned the page. 'Yes, I said that.'

'Did you mean it?'

'This wasn't just talk, if that's what you're getting at. I taught high school for twenty-seven years. I've seen lots of kids go to jail. I've seen lots of kids die in the streets. Never said a word to the newspapers about any of them. See this scar?' She pointed to an immense, fleshy bicep.

Myron nodded.

'Knife wound. From a student. I got shot at once too. I've confiscated more weapons than any damn metal detector.' She put her arm down. 'That's what I mean when I say I like them younger. Before they get like that.'

'But Curtis was different?'

'Curtis was more than just a good boy,' she said. 'He was one of the best students I ever had. He was always polite and friendly and never caused a lick of trouble. But he wasn't a sissy either, you understand. He was still popular with the other boys. Good at all kinds of sports. I'm telling you, the boy was one in a million.'

'What about his mother?' Myron asked. 'What was she like?'

'Deanna?' Lucinda sat a little straighter. 'Fine woman. Like so many of them young mothers today. Single. Proud. Did whatever she had to to get by. But Deanna was smart. She set rules. Curtis had a curfew. Kids today don't even know what curfew means anymore. Couple nights ago, a ten-year-old boy got shot at three in the morning. Now you tell me, Myron – what's a ten-year-old boy doing out on the streets at three in the morning?'

'I wish I knew.'

She waved a hand at the air. 'Anyway you don't want to hear no old woman rambling on.'

'I got time.'

'You're a sweet man, but you're here for a reason. A good reason, I think.'

She looked at Myron. He nodded but said nothing.

'Now,' she continued, slapping her thighs with her palms, 'what were we talking about?'

'Deanna Yeller.'

'That's right. Deanna. You know, I think about her a lot too. She was such a caring mother. She came to every open house. She loved parent-teacher conferences. She basked in all that praise we heaped on her boy.'

'Did you talk to her after his death?'

415

'Nope.' She shook her head hard and let out a sigh. 'Never heard from Deanna again, poor woman. No funeral. No nothing. I called her a couple of times, but nobody ever answered. Like she fell off the face of the earth. But I understood. She'd always had it rough. From the start. She used to be a street girl, you know.'

'I didn't know. When?'

'Oh, a long time ago. She doesn't even know who Curtis's father really was. But she quit. Got herself cleaned up. Worked like a dog, any job she could get. All for her boy. And then, just like that . . .' She shook her head. 'Gone.'

'Did you know Errol Swade?' Myron asked.

'Just enough to know he was trouble. In and out of prison his whole life. He was Deanna's sister's boy. The sister was a junkie. Ended up dying of an overdose. Deanna had to take Errol in. He was family. She was a responsible woman.'

'How did Errol get along with Curtis?'

'Actually, they got along pretty good – considering how different they were.'

'Well, maybe they weren't so different,' Myron said.

'What do you mean?'

'Errol got him to break into that tennis club.'

Lucinda Elright watched him a moment before she picked up a cookie and began to nibble. A small smile toyed with her lips. 'Come on, Myron, you know better than that,' she said. 'You're a smart boy. So was Curtis. What would he want to steal way out there? It don't make sense, robbing a place like that at night. Think about it.'

Myron had already. He was glad to see someone else had the same trouble with the official scenario. 'So what do you think happened?'

'I've thought a lot about it, but I don't really know. Nothing makes much sense to me about that whole night. But I do think Curtis and Errol were set up. Even if Curtis decided to steal – and even if he was dumb enough to break in to this club – I can't believe he'd shoot at a police officer. A boy can change, but that's like the tiger changing his stripes. It's just too incredible.' She sat up, adjusting herself on the couch. 'I think some fool thing happened at the rich white club and they needed a couple of black boys to take the fall. Now, I'm not that way. I'm not one of those who think the white man is always plotting against the black man. It's just not in my nature. But in this case I don't know what else could have happened.'

'Thank you, Mrs Elright.'

'Lucinda. And Myron, do me a favor.'

'What?'

'When you find out what really happened to Curtis, let me know.'

33

Myron and Jessica drove out to New Jersey for dinner at Baumgart's. They ate there at least twice a week. Baumgart's was a strange combination. For half a century it had been a popular soda fountain and deli, the kind of place neighbors went for lunch and Archie took Veronica for an after-school smooch. Eight years ago a Chinese immigrant named Peter Li bought the place and turned it into the best Chinese around – but without getting rid of the old soda fountain. You could still twirl on a stool at the counter, surrounded by chrome and blenders and ice-cream scoops in hot water. You could order a milkshake with your dim sum and have french fries with your General Tso's chicken. When they first lived together, Myron and Jess had come at least once a week. Now that they were back together, the tradition had resumed.

'It's the Alexander Cross murder,' Myron said. 'I can't stop thinking about it.'

Before Jess could answer, Peter Li arrived. Myron and Jess never ordered. Peter chose for them. 'Coral shrimp for the beautiful lady,' he said, putting down her plate, 'and Baumgart's Szechuan chicken and eggplant for the man not fit to grovel at her feet.'

'Good one,' Myron said. 'Very funny.'

Peter bowed. 'In my country they consider me a man of great humor.'

'Must be a lot of laughs in your country.' Myron looked down at his plate. 'I hate eggplant, Peter.'

'You'll eat it and beg for more,' he said. He smiled at Jess. 'Enjoy.' He left.

'Okay,' Jess said, 'so what about Alexander Cross?'

'It's not Alexander, per se. It's actually Curtis Yeller. Everyone says he was a great kid. His mom was very involved, loved him like mad, the whole nine yards. Now she acts like nothing happened.'

' "There's a grief that can't be spoken," ' Jessica replied. ' "There's a pain goes on and on." '

Myron thought a second. '*Les Mis*?' The ongoing game of Guess the Quote.

'Correct, but what character said it?'

'Valjean?'

'No, sorry. Marius.'

Myron nodded. 'Either way,' he said, 'it's a lousy quote.'

'I know. I was listening to the tape in the car,' she said. 'But it might not be that far off the mark.'

'A grief that can't be spoken?'

'Yes.'

He took a sip of water. 'So it makes sense to you, the mother acting like nothing happened.'

Jessica shrugged. 'It's been six years. What do you want her to do – break down and cry every time you come around?'

'No,' Myron said, 'but I'd think she'd want to know who killed her son.'

Before touching her shrimp, Jessica reached across the table and forked a piece of Myron's chicken. Not the eggplant. The chicken. 'Maybe she already knows,' Jess said.

'What, you think she's being bought off too?'

Jess shrugged. 'Maybe. But that's not what's really bugging you.'

'Oh?'

Jess chewed daintily. Even the way she chewed food was a thing to behold. 'Seeing Duane in that hotel room with Curtis Yeller's mother,' she replied. 'That's what's got to you.'

'You must admit it's a hell of a coincidence,' he said.

'Do you have a theory?' she asked.

Myron thought a moment. 'No.'

Jessica forked another piece of chicken. 'You could ask Duane,' she said.

'Sure. I could just say, "Gee, Duane, I was following you around and noticed you're shacking up with an older woman. Care to tell me about it?"'

'Yeah, that could be a problem,' she agreed. 'Of course, you could approach it from the other direction.'

'Deanna Yeller?'

Jessica nodded.

Myron took a taste of his chicken. Before Jess finished the whole thing. 'Worth a try,' he said. 'You want to come along?'

'I'll scare her off,' Jess said. 'Just drop me off at my place.'

They finished eating. Myron even ate the eggplant. It was pretty good. Peter brought them a rich chocolate dessert – the kind of dessert you could gain weight just looking at. Jess dove in. Myron held back. They drove back over the George Washington Bridge to the Henry Hudson and down the west side. He dropped her off at her loft on Spring Street in SoHo. She leaned back into the car.

'You'll come by after?' she said.

'Sure. Put on that little French maid's uniform and wait.'

'I don't have a French maid's uniform.'

'Oh.'

'Maybe we can pick one up in the morning,' she said. 'In the meantime I'll find something suitable.'

'Groovy,' Myron said.

Jess got out of the car then. She made her way up the stairs to the third floor. Her loft took up half the floor. She turned the key and entered. When she flicked on the lights she was startled to see Aaron lounging on her couch.

Before she could move, another man – a man with a fishnet shirt – came up behind her and put a gun to her temple. A third man – a black man – locked the door and turned the dead bolt. He too had a gun.

Aaron smiled at her. 'Hello, Jessica.'

34

Myron's car phone rang.

'Hello.'

'*Bubbe*, it's your aunt Clara. Thanks for the referral.'

Clara wasn't really his aunt. Aunt Clara and Uncle Sidney were just longtime friends of his parents. Clara had gone to law school with Myron's mom. Myron had set her up to represent Roger Quincy.

'How's it going?' Myron asked.

'My client wanted me to give you an important message,' Clara said. 'He stressed that I, his attorney, should treat this as my number one priority.'

'What?'

'Mr Quincy said you promised him an autograph of Duane Richwood. Well, he'd like it to be an autographed *picture* of Duane Richwood, not just an autograph. *Color* picture, if that's not too much trouble. And he'd like it inscribed to him, thank you very much. By the way, did he tell you he was a tennis fan?'

'I think he might have mentioned it. Fun guy, huh?'

'A constant party. Laughs galore. My sides are aching from all the laughing. It's like representing Jackie Mason.'

'So what do you think?' Myron asked.

'In legal terms? The man is a major fruitcake. But is he guilty of murder – and more important, can the DA prove it? – that's a different kettle of gefilte.'

'What do they have?'

'Circumstantial nothings. He was at the Open. Big deal, so were a zillion other people. He has a weird past. So what, he never made any overt threats that I'm aware of. No one saw him shoot her. No tests link him to the gun or that Feron's bag with the bullet hole. Like I said, circumstantial nothings.'

'For what's it worth,' Myron said, 'I believe him.'

'Uh-huh.' Clara wouldn't say if she believed him or not. It didn't matter. 'I'll speak to you later, doll-face. Take care of yourself.'

'You too.'

He hung up and dialed Jake.

A gruff voice said, 'Sheriff Courter's office.'

'It's me, Jake.'

'What the fuck do you want now?'

'My, what a charming salutation,' Myron said. 'I must use it sometime.'

'Jesus, you're a pain in the ass.'

'You know,' Myron said, 'I can't for the life of me understand why you're not invited to more parties.'

Jake blew his nose. Loudly. Geese in the tri-state area scattered. 'Before I'm left mortally wounded by your caustic wit,' he said, 'tell me what you want.'

'You still have your copy of the Cross file?' Myron asked.

'Yeah.'

'I'd like to meet the coroner on the case and the cop who shot Yeller,' Myron said. 'Think you can set it up?'

'I thought there was no autopsy.'

'Nothing formal, but the senator said someone did some work on him.'

'Yeah, all right,' Jake said. 'But I know the cop who did the shooting. Jimmy Blaine. A good man, but he ain't gonna talk to you.'

'I'm not interested in bringing him down.'

'That's a big comfort,' Jake said.

'I just want some information.'

'Jimmy won't see you, I'm sure of it. Why do you need all this anyway?'

'I see a connection between Valerie's murder and Alexander Cross's.'

'What connection?'

Myron explained. When he finished, Jake said, 'I still don't see it, but I'll call you if I get something.'

He hung up.

Myron lucked out and found a spot within two blocks of the hotel. He walked in like he belonged and took the elevator to the third floor. He stopped in front of room 322 and knocked.

'Who is it?' Deanna Yeller's voice was cheerful, singsong.

'Bellhop,' Myron said. 'Flowers for you.'

She flung open the door with a wide smile. Just like the first time they'd met. When she saw no flowers – and more to the point, when she saw Myron – the smile fled. Again, just like the first time.

'Enjoying your stay?' Myron said.

She didn't bother hiding her exasperation. 'What do you want?'

'I can't believe you came to town and didn't call me. A less mature man would be insulted.'

'I got nothing to say to you.' She began to close the door.

'Guess who I just spoke to?'

'I don't care.'

'Lucinda Elright.'

The door stopped. With Deanna looking slightly dazed, Myron slid through the opening.

Deanna recovered. 'Who?'

'Lucinda Elright. One of your son's teachers.'

'I don't remember none of his teachers.'

'Oh but she remembers you. She said you were a wonderful mother to Curtis.'

'So?'

'She also said that Curtis was a wonderful student, one of the best she ever had. She said he had a bright future. She said he never got into trouble.'

Deanna Yeller put her hands on her hips. 'There a point to all this?'

'Your son had no police record. He had a perfect school record, not so much as a detention. He was one of the top students in his class, if not *the* top student. You were clearly involved in his activities. You were an excellent mother, raising an excellent young man.'

She looked away. She might have been looking out the window, except the blinds were drawn. The TV was humming softly. A commercial for men's pick-up trucks featuring a soap opera star. Soap opera star, pick-up trucks – what advertising genius came up with that combo?

'This is none of your business,' she whispered.

'Did you love your son, Ms Yeller?'

'What?'

'Did you love your son?'

'Get out. Now.'

'If you cared about him at all, help me find out what happened to him.'

She glared at him. 'Don't give me that,' she countered. 'You don't care about my boy. You're trying to find out who killed that white girl.'

'Maybe. But Valerie Simpson's death and your son's are connected. That's why I need your help.'

She shook her head. 'You don't listen too good, do you? I told you before: Curtis is dead. Can't change that.'

'Your son wasn't the type to rob. He wasn't the type to carry a gun or threaten the police with one. That's just not the boy you raised.'

'Don't matter,' she said. 'He's dead. Can't bring him back.'

'What was he doing at the tennis club that night?'

'I don't know.'

'Where did you suddenly get all your money?'

Pow. Deanna Yeller looked up, startled. The old change-topic attention-getter. Works every time. 'What?'

'Your house in Cherry Hill,' Myron said. 'It was a cash deal four months ago. And your bank account at First Jersey. All cash deposits within the past half-year. Where did the money come from, Deanna?'

Her face grew angry. Then suddenly she relaxed and smiled eerily. 'Maybe I stole it,' she said, 'just like my son. You gonna report me?'

'Or maybe it's a payoff.'

'A payoff? For what?'

'You tell me.'

'No,' she said. 'I don't have to tell you nothing. Get out.'

'Why are you here in New York?'

'To see the sights. Now leave.'

'One of those sights Duane Richwood?'

Double pow. She stopped. 'What?'

'Duane Richwood. The man who was in your room the other night.'

She stared at him. 'You were following us?'

'No. Just him.'

Deanna Yeller looked horror-stricken. 'What kind of man are you?' she said slowly. 'You get off on that kind of thing, watching other people and all? Checking their bank accounts? Following them around like a Peeping Tom?' She opened the door. 'Don't you have no shame at all?'

The argument was a little too close for comfort. 'I'm trying to find a killer,' Myron argued, but his tone rang lamely in his own ears. 'Maybe the person who killed your son.'

'And it don't matter who you hurt to do it, right?'

'That's not true.'

'If you really want to do some good, then just drop this whole thing.'

'What do you mean by that?'

She shook her head. 'Curtis is dead. So is Valerie Simpson. Errol . . .' She stopped. 'It's enough.'

'What's enough? What about Errol?'

But she kept shaking her head. 'Just let it go, Myron. For everyone's sake. Just let it go.'

35

Jessica felt the cold barrel of the gun against her temple.

'What do you want?' she asked.

Aaron signaled. The man behind her covered her mouth with his free hand. He pressed her hard against him. Jessica could feel hot spittle on her neck. It was hard to breathe. She twisted her head back and forth. Her chest hitched as she scrambled for more air. Panic seized her.

Aaron rose off the couch. The black man moved a step closer, his gun still pointed at her.

'No reason for preliminaries,' Aaron said calmly. He took off his white jacket. He wore no shirt underneath, revealing instead the hairless, body-builder physique. He flexed a little. His pectoral muscles made ripples, like a stadium crowd doing the wave. 'If you can still speak when we're through, make sure you tell Myron it was me.' He cracked his knuckles. 'I'd hate for my work to go unaccredited.'

'Should I break her jaw?' the man with the fishnet asked. 'So she can't yell or nothing.'

Aaron thought a moment. 'No,' he said. 'I kind of enjoy a good yell now and again.'

All three men laughed.

'I go second,' the black man said.

'Like hell,' the man with the fishnet countered.

'You always go before me,' the black man whined.

'All right, we'll flip for it.'

'You got a coin? I never carry change.'

'Shut up,' Aaron said.

Silence.

Jessica struggled feverishly, but the man in the fishnet was too strong. She bit down and managed to skim one of his fingers. He yelped and called her a bitch. Then he bent her head back in a way it was never supposed to go. Pain shot down her spine. Her eyes widened.

Aaron was about to unbutton his pants when it happened.

A gunshot. Or more than one gunshot. It sounded to Jessica like only one, but it had to be more. The hand pressed hard against her mouth slackened and slid off. The gun against her temple dropped to the floor. She turned just enough to see the man behind her no longer had a face or even much of a head. He was dead well before his legs realized it and let him cave onto the floor.

At seemingly the same time, the back half of the black man's head flew across the room. He too fell to the floor in a bloody heap.

Aaron's speed was uncanny. Seemingly before the first bullet even hit its target he had rolled into a crouch and whipped out a gun. Everything – the shots, the men going down, Aaron rolling to safety – had taken less than two seconds. Aaron came up aiming his gun at Win, who aimed his right back. Jessica stood frozen. Win must have come in through the terrace window, though how he could have gotten there and how long he'd been there Jessica could not say.

Win smiled casually and gave a half-nod. 'My, my, Aaron, you're looking rather buff.'

'I try to stay in shape,' Aaron said. 'Nice of you to notice.'

The two men continued to aim their guns at each other. Neither blinked. Neither stopped smiling. Jessica had not moved. Her body quaked as though from fever. She felt something sticky on her face and realized it was probably brain matter from the man at her feet.

'I have an idea,' Aaron said.

'An idea?'

'For how to end this deadlock. One I think you'll like, Win.'

'Do tell,' Win said.

'We both put our guns down at the same time.'

'So far it doesn't sound very appealing,' Win said.

'I'm not finished.'

'How rude of me. Please continue.'

'We've both killed men with our bare hands,' Aaron said. 'We both know we like it. A lot. We both know there are very few worthy adversaries in this world. We both know we are rarely if ever seriously challenged.'

'So?'

'So I'm suggesting the ultimate test.' Aaron's grin grew brighter. 'You and me. Man to man, hand-to-hand combat. What do you say?'

Win chewed on his upper lip. 'Intriguing,' he said.

Jessica tried to say something, but her tongue would not obey. She just stood there, stone-faced; the thing that used to wear fishnet shirts bled without a twitch.

'One condition,' Win said.

'What's that?'

'No matter who wins, Jessica goes free.'

Aaron shrugged. 'Doesn't matter. Frank will get her some other time.'

'Maybe. But not tonight.'

'Fine then,' Aaron said. 'But she can't leave until it's over.'

Win nodded at her. 'Wait by the door, Jessica. When the fight ends, run.'

'But you have to wait until it's over,' Aaron added.

Jessica found her voice. 'How will I know when it's over?'

'One of us will be dead,' Win said.

She nodded numbly. She couldn't stop shaking. Both men were still pointing the guns at one another.

'You know the drill?' Aaron asked.

'Of course.'

Still holding the guns, both men placed their hand on the floor. At the same time, they twisted their weapons so that the barrel was no longer pointing at the other man. They both released their weapons at the same time. They both stood at the same time. They both kicked the weapons into a corner at the same time.

Aaron grinned. 'It's done,' he said.

Win nodded.

They approached each other slowly. Aaron's grin spread into something fully maniacal. He got into some weird fighting position – dragon or grasshopper or something – and beckoned with his left hand. His body was sleek, all muscle. He towered over Win. 'You forgot the basic premise of the martial arts,' Aaron said.

'What's that?' Win asked.

'A good big man will always beat a good little man.'

'And you forgot the basic premise of Windsor Horne Lockwood III.'

'Oh?'

'He always carries two guns.'

Almost nonchalantly, Win reached into his leg holster, took out his gun, and fired. Aaron ducked, but the bullet still hit him in the head. The second bullet also hit Aaron's head. So too, Jessica guessed, did the third.

The big man fell to the ground. Win walked over and studied the still figure, tilting his head from side to side like a dog hearing a strange sound.

Jessica watched him in silence.

'Are you okay?' he asked.

'Yes.'

Win continued to look down. He shook his head and made a tsk-tsk noise.

'What is it?' she asked.

Win turned to her, an almost shy smile toying with his lips. He gave a half-shrug. 'I guess I'm not much for fair fights.'

He looked back down at the body and started to laugh.

36

Jessica didn't want to talk about it. She wanted to make love. Myron understood. Death and violence do that to a person. The fine line. There was definitely something to that 'reaffirming life' stuff after facing down the Grim Reaper.

When they were spent, Jessica laid her head on his chest, her hair a wonderful fan. For a long time she didn't say anything. Myron stroked her back. Finally she spoke. 'He enjoys it, doesn't he?'

Myron knew she meant Win. 'Yes.'

'Do you?' she asked.

'Not like Win.'

She lifted her head and looked at him. 'That sounded a tad evasive.'

'Part of me hates it more than you can imagine.'

'And another part of you?' she prompted.

'It's the ultimate test. There's an undeniable rush to that. But it's not like what happens with Win. He craves it. He needs it.'

'And you don't?'

'I like to think I loathe it.'

'But do you?'

'I don't know,' Myron said.

'It was scary,' she said. 'Win was scary.'

'He also saved your life.'

'Yes.'

'It's what Win does. He's good at it – the best I've ever seen. Everything with him is black and white. He has no moral ambiguities. If you cross the line, there is no reprieve, no mercy, no chance to talk your way out of it. You're dead. Period. Those men came to harm you. Win wasn't interested in rehabilitating them. They made their choice. The moment they entered your apartment they were doomed.'

'It sounds like the theory of massive retaliation,' she said. 'You kill one of ours, we kill ten of yours.'

'Colder,' Myron said. 'Win's not interested in teaching a lesson. He sees it as extermination. They're no more than pestering fleas to him.'

'And you agree with that?'

'Not always. But I understand it. Win's moral code is not mine. We've both known that for a long time. But he's my best friend and I'd trust him with my life.'

'Or mine,' she said.

'Right.'

'So what is your moral code?' she asked.

'It's flexible. Let's leave it at that.'

Jessica nodded. She laid her head back down on his chest. The warmth of her felt good against his heartbeat. 'Their heads,' she said. 'They just exploded like melons.'

'Win doctors the bullets to maximize impact.'

'Where did he take the bodies?' she asked.

'I don't know.'

'Will they be found?'

'Only if he wants them to be.'

A few minutes later Jessica's eyes closed and her breathing grew deep. Myron watched her drift into a sound sleep. She cuddled closer to him, looking small and frail. He knew what would happen tomorrow. She'd still be in some form of shock – not a dazed shock as much as a denial. She'd go about her day as though nothing had happened, straining extra-hard for normalcy but falling just short of achieving it. Everything would be just a little different than yesterday. Nothing drastic, just the little things. Her food would taste a little different. The air would smell a little different. Colors would have an almost indiscernibly different hue.

At six in the morning, Myron got out of bed and showered. When he came back she was sitting up. 'Where are you going?' she asked.

'To see Pavel Menansi.'

'This early?'

'They'll think Aaron took care of the problem last night. I might catch them off guard.'

She pulled the covers over her. 'I've been thinking about what you said last night at dinner. About the connection to the Alexander Cross murder.'

'And?'

'Suppose you're right. Suppose something else happened that night six years ago.'

'Like?'

She sat upright, leaning against the headboard. 'Suppose Errol Swade didn't kill Alexander Cross,' she said.

'Uh-huh.'

'Well, suppose Valerie saw what really happened to Alexander Cross. And suppose that whatever she saw pushed her already battered psyche over the edge. She had already been weakened by what Pavel Menansi did to her. But now suppose whatever she saw was the ultimate cause of her breakdown.'

Myron nodded. 'Go on.'

'And now suppose years pass. Valerie gets stronger. She makes a remarkable recovery. She even wants to play tennis again. But most of all, she wants to face up to her darkest fear: the truth of what really happened that night.'

He saw where she was going with this. 'She'd have to be silenced,' he said.

'Yes.'

Myron slipped a pair of pants on. Over the past few months his clothes had begun a slow migration to Jess's loft. About a third of his wardrobe now resided here. 'If you're right,' he said, 'we now have two people who want to silence Valerie: Pavel Menansi and whoever killed Alexander Cross.'

'Or someone who wants to protect those two.'

He finished dressing. Jess hated his tie and told him to change it. He complied. When he was ready to leave, Myron said, 'You'll be safe this morning, but I want to move you someplace out of town for a little while.'

'For how long?' she asked.

'I don't know. Few days. Maybe longer. Just until I can get this situation under control.'

'I see,' she said.

'Are you going to fight me on this?'

She got out of bed and pattered across the room. She wore no clothes. Myron's mouth went a little dry. He stared. He could stare all day. She walked with the ease of a panther. Every movement was supple and marvelous and rawly sensual. She slipped into a silk robe. 'I know this is the part where I'm supposed to get all indignant and say that I'm not going to change my life,' she said. 'But I'm scared. I'm also a writer who could use a few days of solitude. So I'll go. No arguments.'

He hugged her. 'You're always a surprise,' he said.

'What?'

'Being reasonable. Who would have thought?'

'I'm trying to keep the mystery alive,' she said.

They kissed. Passionately. Her skin felt wonderfully warm.

'Why don't you stay a little longer?' she whispered.

He shook his head. 'I want to get to Pavel before Ache realizes what happened.'

'One more kiss then.'

He stepped away. 'Not unless you want to pack me in ice.' He blew her a kiss and left the bedroom area. Clumps of blood were stuck to the exposed brick wall by the door. Courtesy of Fishnet Lee's head.

Outside, Win was nowhere in sight, but Myron knew he was there. Jess would be safe until they moved her.

Pavel Menansi was staying at the Omni Park Central on Seventh Avenue, across the street from Carnegie Hall. Myron would have preferred to go in with backup, but it was better Win wasn't there. There had been a bond between Win and Valerie – more than just the family-friend variety. Myron didn't know what that bond was. Win cared about very few people, but for those select few he would go to any lengths. The rest of the world meant nothing to him. Somehow Valerie had entered that protective circle. Myron would have enough trouble keeping his own rage in check. If Win were here – if Win were to question Pavel about his 'affair' with Valerie – it wouldn't be a very pretty sight.

Pavel was staying in room 719. Myron checked his watch. Six-thirty. Not much activity in the lobby. The floor was being mopped. An exhausted family was checking out. Three kids, all whining. The parents looked like they could use a vacation. Myron walked purposefully onto an elevator, like he belonged. He pressed the button for the seventh floor.

The corridor was empty. When Myron reached the door to Pavel's room, he knocked. No answer. He knocked again. Still no answer. He tried once again. Nothing. He was about to go downstairs and try the house phone when a sound made him stop. He listened again. The sound was barely perceptible. He pressed his ear against the door.

'Hello?' he called out.

Crying. Faint. Growing stronger. The cries of a little girl.

Myron pounded the door this time. The crying picked up a little steam now, becoming more a sob. 'Are you okay?' Myron asked. More crying, but still no words. A minute or so more of this and Myron began to look for the familiar sight of the maid cart and her passkey. But it was six-thirty in the morning. The maid wasn't on her run yet.

Picking locks was not Myron's forte. Win was a lot better at it. Plus he didn't have the tools. Another cry from the room. 'Open the door,' he shouted. The only answer was more cries.

To hell with it, he thought.

Leading with his shoulder, Myron pile-drove his body into the door. It stung him pretty good, but the lock gave way. The cries were still muffled, but for a moment Myron forgot about them. Sprawled across the bed was Pavel Menansi. His eyes were wide open but unseeing. His mouth was frozen in a surprised oval. Dried, dark blood was caked on his chest where the bullet had entered.

He was naked.

Myron stared for a few moments before the renewed cries snapped him out of it. He turned to his right. The sound emanated from behind the bathroom door. Myron moved toward it. There was a plastic Feron's bag on the floor. The same kind they used at the US Open. The same kind they found at Val's murder.

The bag had a bullet hole in it.

In front of the bathroom door, jammed under the knob, was a chair. Myron kicked it out of the way and opened the door. A young girl was sitting on the tile, her knees pulled up to her chest. She was huddled in a corner against the toilet. Myron recognized her right away. It was Janet Koffman, Pavel's newest protégée. Fourteen years old.

She too was naked.

Janet looked up at him. Her eyes were large and red and puffy. Her lower lip quivered. 'We were just talking tennis,' she said in a dead voice. 'He's my coach. We were just talking about a match. That's all.'

Myron nodded. Janet started to cry again. He bent down and wrapped a towel around her. He reached out, but she shrank away.

'It's okay now,' he said, not knowing what else to say. 'You're going to be okay.'

37

Janet Koffman had stopped crying. She was sitting on the loveseat by the window. Her back was to the bed and hence Pavel's corpse. From what Myron could get out of her she had been in the bathroom when someone locked her in with the chair and killed Pavel. She hadn't seen a thing. She was still sticking to her other story too: she and her coach had been talking tennis. Myron chose not to probe into the small details – like why, for example, they would have this particular discussion in the nude.

He had called the police. They'd be here any minute now. The question was, what should he do with Janet? On the one hand, he wanted to protect her from all of this; on the other, he knew she had to deal with what she had been through, that she couldn't just pretend nothing had happened to her. So what should Myron do – tamper with a police investigation or expose her to the brutish ways of the cops and worse, the press? What message of shame would hiding the truth send her? Then again, what would happen to this young girl if the story hit the airwaves?

Myron didn't have a clue.

'He was a good coach,' Janet said softly.

'You did nothing wrong,' Myron said, again realizing how lame he sounded. 'Whatever else happens, remember that. You did absolutely nothing wrong.'

She nodded slowly, but Myron wasn't sure if she'd even heard him.

Ten minutes later the police arrived, led by Dimonte. Rolly looked like something the proverbial cat had dragged in. He was unshaven. His shirt was untucked and buttoned wrong. His hair was all over the place. He had sleep-buggers in both eyes. Still, the boots were nicely polished. He charged up to Myron. 'Returning to the scene of the crime, asshole?'

'Yeah,' Myron said, 'that's it.'

The press rounded the corner. Flashbulbs started strobing. 'Keep those assholes downstairs!' Dimonte hollered. Some uniformed cops pushed them back. 'Downstairs, I said! No one on this floor.'

Dimonte turned back to Myron. Krinsky came in and stood next to him. His pad was out.

'Hey, Krinsky,' Myron said.

Krinsky nodded.

'So what the hell happened?' Dimonte demanded.

'I came up to see him. I found him like this.'

'Stop fucking with me, asshole.'

Myron didn't bother with a retort. Cops were all over the place. The coroner was slitting a hole in Pavel's torso with a surgical scalpel. The liver area, Myron knew. Trying to get a liver temperature reading to find out time of death.

Dimonte spotted the Feron's bag on the floor. 'You touch this?'

Myron shook his head.

Dimonte bent down and looked at the bullet hole. 'Cute,' he said.

'You going to let Roger Quincy go now?'

'Why should I?'

'You didn't have squat on him before. Now you have less than squat.'

Dimonte shrugged. 'Could just be a copycat. Or' – he snapped his fingers – 'or it could be someone who wants to get Quincy off.' A smile. 'Someone like you, Bolitar.'

'Yeah,' Myron said, 'that's it.'

Dimonte stepped closer. He gave Myron the tough-guy glare again. Then, as though suddenly remembering it, he quickly whipped out his toothpick and put it in his mouth. He glared again and gnawed the toothpick.

'I was wrong before,' Myron said.

'What?'

'About the toothpick being cliché. It's actually very intimidating.'

'Keep it up, funny man.'

'It's too early for this, Rolly.'

'Listen, asshole, I want to know what you're doing here.'

'I told you. I came to see Pavel.'

'Why?'

'To talk about him coaching a player of mine.'

'At six-thirty in the morning?'

'I'm an early riser. It's why they call me Mr Sunbeam.'

'They should call you Mister Lying Sack of Shit.'

'Oooo,' Myron said. 'That hurt.'

Dimonte started gnawing on the toothpick with renewed vigor. You could almost hear something churn inside his head. 'So tell me, Bolitar,' he said with the beginnings of a smile, 'you came to the hotel to talk business. You took the elevator up to see our victim here. You knocked on the door. No one answered. Right so far?'

'Yep.'

'So then you kicked the door in, right?'

Myron said nothing.

Dimonte turned to Krinsky. 'That make sense to you, Krinsky? Kicking in the door like that?'

Krinsky looked up from his pad, shook his head, looked back down.

'You always do that when no one answers a door, asshole? Kick it down?'

'I didn't kick it. I used my shoulder.'

'Don't bullshit me, Bolitar. You didn't come here to talk business. And you didn't kick down the door just because no one answered.'

The coroner tapped Dimonte on the shoulder. 'Bullet to the heart. Clean shot. Death was instantaneous.'

'Time of death?' Rolly asked.

'He's been dead six, maybe seven hours.'

Dimonte looked at his watch. 'It's seven now. That would mean he was killed between midnight and one.'

Myron turned to Krinksy. 'And he didn't even see you use his fingers.'

Krinsky almost smiled.

Dimonte tossed out another glare. 'You got an alibi, Bolitar?'

'I was with a lady friend.'

'That Jessica Culver?'

'Correct.' Myron waited for Krinsky to look up. When he did, Myron said, 'Her number is 555-8420.'

Krinsky wrote it down.

'All right, Bolitar, now stop busting my balls. Why did you kick down the door?'

Myron hesitated. He looked at Dimonte. Dimonte looked back and said, 'Well?'

'Come with me,' Myron said in a quiet voice. He began to leave the room.

'Hey, where the fuck do you think you're going?'

'For once, Rolly, don't be an ass. Just shut up and follow me.'

To Myron's surprise Dimonte kept quiet. They went down the corridor in silence. Krinsky stayed at the crime scene. Myron stopped in front of a door, took out a key, and opened it. Janet Koffman was sitting on the bed. She was wearing a hotel bathrobe. If she realized they were there, she didn't show it. Janet rocked back and forth, humming to herself.

Dimonte looked a question at Myron.

'Her name is Janet Koffman.'

'The tennis player?'

Myron nodded. 'The killer locked her in the bathroom before he shot Menansi. I heard her crying when I knocked on the door. That's why I kicked it in.'

Dimonte looked at Myron. 'You mean she and Menansi were . . . ?'

Myron nodded.

'Christ, how old is she?'

'Fourteen, I think.'

Dimonte closed his eyes. 'We have someone down at the precinct,' he said softly. 'A doctor. She's good with this stuff. I'll talk to the Manhattan cop in charge about sneaking her out, see if he can keep the press away. I'll try to keep the victim's name out of the papers for a while.'

'Thank you.'

'I've seen this kinda thing before, Bolitar. The girl is going to need help.'

'I know.'

'Any chance she offed him herself? Frankly I wouldn't give a shit but . . .'

Myron shook his head. 'She was locked in from the outside with a chair. It couldn't have been her.'

Dimonte gave the toothpick a little chew. 'Thoughtful killer,' he said.

'What do you mean?'

'He didn't want the girl to see what happened. He made sure she had an alibi by locking her in with the chair. And most of all he saved her from going through any more of Menansi's hell.' He looked at Myron. 'I'd probably pin a medal on the guy if he hadn't also killed Valerie Simpson.'

Myron said, 'Me too.' It made him wonder.

38

The office was only about ten blocks away. Myron decided to walk it. Cars sat completely still on Sixth Avenue, though the lights were green and there was no visible construction. Everyone honked their horns. Like this ever does any good. A well-groomed man got out of a taxi. He wore a pin-striped suit, a gold Tag Heuer watch, and Gucci shoes. He also wore a green pinwheel hat and plastic Spock ears. New York – my kind of town.

Myron ignored the fumes and tried to think the whole thing through. The popular theory – the main theory, if you will – had gone something like this: Valerie Simpson had been abused by Pavel Menansi. Regaining her mental strength, she had decided to expose him. This exposure would have been detrimental to the financial well-being of TruPro and the Ache brothers. So they eliminated her before she could do any damage. It all added up. It all made sense.

Until this morning.

A major monkey wrench had been tossed into the main theory: Pavel Menansi had been murdered too, in a fashion similar to Valerie Simpson. Under the main theory, the murders of Valerie Simpson and Pavel Menansi were at cross-purposes. Why kill Valerie Simpson to protect Pavel Menansi, only to go ahead and kill Pavel Menansi? It didn't mesh. It wasn't profitable for TruPro or the Aches.

Of course, there was the possibility that Frank Ache had decided Menansi was too big a risk, that exposure was imminent and losses might as well be cut right now. But if Frank had wanted Pavel dead, he would have had Aaron do it. Pavel had been murdered between midnight and one. Aaron was dead by midnight. Myron mulled this over a bit and decided that Aaron's being dead made it extremely unlikely he was the killer. And moreover, if Frank had intended to kill Pavel, there would have been no reason to scare Myron off with the attack on Jessica.

On the street in front of him a pale woman with a bullhorn screamed that she had recently met Jesus face-to-face. She stuffed a pamphlet into Myron's hand.

'Jesus sent me back with this message,' she said.

Myron nodded, glanced down at the ink smears on the pamphlet. 'Too bad he didn't give you a decent printer.'

She gave him a funny look and went back to her bullhorn. Myron stuffed the pamphlet into his pocket and continued walking. His mind returned to the problem at hand.

Frank Ache wasn't behind Pavel's murder, he thought. To the contrary, Frank Ache wanted Pavel saved because Pavel meant mucho dinero to TruPro. Frank Ache had even brought Aaron in to protect Pavel. He had ordered Aaron to harm Jessica and to protect Pavel. Killing TruPro's main tennis drawing card would make no sense.

So what did that leave us?

Two possibilities. One, we were dealing with two separate killers with two separate agendas. Seeing an opportunity, Pavel's killer had left behind a Feron's bag to put the blame on Valerie's killer. Or two, there was some other linkage between Valerie and Pavel, one that was not readily apparent. Myron favored this possibility, and of course it led back to Myron's earlier obsession:

The murder of Alexander Cross.

Both Valerie Simpson and Pavel Menansi had been at the Old Oaks tennis club that night six years ago. Both had been attending the party for Alexander Cross. But so what? Let's suppose Jessica had been right this morning. Suppose Valerie Simpson had seen something that night, maybe even the identity of the real murderer. Suppose she'd been about to reveal the truth. Suppose that was why she'd been killed. How would that tie in to Pavel Menansi? Even if he had seen the same thing, he hadn't opened his mouth in years. Why would Pavel start now? It's not as though he'd come forward to help poor Valerie. So what is the connection? And what about Duane Richwood? How did he fit into this equation, if at all? And Deanna Yeller? And where was Errol Swade? Was he still alive?

He headed east three blocks and then turned down Park Avenue. The majestic (if not ostentatious) Helmsley Palace or Helmsley Castle or Helmsley whatever sat straight ahead, seemingly in the middle of the street; the MetLife building huddled over it like a protective parent. For eons the MetLife building had been something of a New York landmark known as the Pan Am building. Myron couldn't get used to the change. Every time he turned the corner he still expected to see the Pan Am logo.

Activity was brisk in the front of Myron's building. He headed past the modern sculpture that adorned the entrance. The sculpture was hideous. It looked very much like a giant intestinal tract. Myron had looked for a name on the sculpture once, but in a typical New York move, someone had pried off the name plaque. What someone did with an ugly sculpture's name plaque was beyond comprehension. Maybe they sold it. Maybe there was an underground market for name plaques from works of art – for those who couldn't afford actual stolen artworks and thus settled for the plaques.

Interesting theory.

He entered the lobby. Three Lock-Horne hostesses sat on stools behind a tall counter, smiling plastically. They wore enough makeup to double as cosmetic counter girls at Bloomie's. Of course, they didn't wear the official white lab coat of genuine Bloomie counter girls, so you could tell they weren't professional makeup people. Still, all three were attractive – model wanna-bes who found this more enjoyable (and put them in touch with more potential bigwigs) than waiting tables. Myron walked past them, smiled, nodded. None gave him the eye. Hmm. They must know how committed he was to Jessica. Yeah, that must be it.

When the elevator opened on his floor, he walked toward Esperanza. Her white blouse was a nice contrast against her dark, flawless skin. She'd have been great on one of those Bain de Soleil commercials. The Santa Fe tan without any sun.

'Hi,' he said.

Esperanza cupped the phone against her shoulder. 'It's Jake. You want to take it?'

He nodded. She handed him the phone.

'Hey, Jake.'

'Some girl did a partial autopsy on Curtis Yeller,' Jake said. 'She'll see you.'

Myron said, 'Some girl?'

'Mea culpa for not being politically sensitive,' Jake said. 'Sometimes I still refer to myself as black.'

'That's because you're too lazy to say African American,' Myron said.

'Is it African or Afro?'

'African now,' Myron said.

'When in doubt,' Jake said, 'ask a honky.'

'Honky,' Myron repeated. 'Now there's a word you don't hear much anymore.'

'Damn shame too. Anyway, the assistant ME is Amanda West. She seemed anxious to talk.' Jake gave him the address.

'What about the cop?' Myron asked. 'Jimmy Blaine?'

'No dice.'

'He still with the force?'

'Nope. He retired.'

'You have his address?'

'Yes,' Jake said.

Silence. Esperanza kept her eyes on her computer screen.

'Could you give it to me?' Myron asked.

'Nope.'

'I won't hassle him, Jake.'

'I said no.'

'You know I can find the address on my own.'

'Fine, but I'm not giving it to you. Jimmy is one of the good guys, Myron.'

'So am I,' Myron said.

'Maybe. But sometimes the innocent get hurt in your little crusades.'

'What's that supposed to mean?'

'Nothing. Just leave him alone.'

'And why so defensive?' Myron continued. 'I just want to ask him a couple of questions.'

Silence. Esperanza didn't look up.

Myron continued, 'Unless he did something he shouldn't have.'

'Don't matter,' Jake said.

'Even if he—'

'Even if. Good-bye, Myron.'

The phone went dead. Myron stared at it a second. 'That was bizarre.'

'Uh-huh.' Esperanza still stared at her computer screen. 'Messages on your desk. Lots of them.'

'Have you seen Win?'

Esperanza shook her head.

'Pavel Menansi is dead,' Myron said. 'Someone murdered him last night.'

'The guy who molested Valerie Simpson?'

'Yep.'

'Gee, I'm so brokenhearted. I hope I don't lose too much sleep.' Esperanza finally flicked a glance away from the screen. 'Did you know he was on that party list you gave me?'

'Yeah. You find any other interesting names?'

She almost smiled. 'One.'

'Who?'

'Think puppy dog,' Esperanza said.

Myron shook his head.

'Think Nike,' she continued. 'Think Duane's contact with Nike.'

Myron froze. 'Ned Tunwell?'

'Correct answer.' Everyone in Myron's life was a game show host. 'Listed as E. Tunwell on the list. His real name is Edward. So I did a little digging. Guess who first signed Valerie Simpson to a Nike deal.'

'Ned Tunwell.'

'And guess who had plenty of egg on his face when her career took a nosedive.'

'Ned Tunwell.'

'Wow,' she said dryly, 'it's like you're clairvoyant.' She lowered her eyes back to her computer screen and started typing.

Myron waited. Then: 'Anything else?'

'Just a very unsubstantiated rumor.'

'What?'

'The usual in a situation like this,' Esperanza said, her eyes still on the screen. 'That Ned Tunwell and Valerie Simpson were more than friends.'

'Get Ned on the phone,' Myron said. 'Tell him I need—'

'I already made the appointment,' she said. 'He'll be here at seven tonight.'

39

Dr Amanda West now worked as chief pathologist at St Joseph Medical Center in Doylestown, not too far from Philadelphia. Myron pulled into the hospital parking lot. On the radio was the classic Doobie Brothers song 'China Grove.' Myron sang along with the chorus, which basically consisted of saying 'Oh, Oh, China Grove' repeatedly. Myron sang it louder now, wondering – not for the first time – what a 'China Grove' actually was.

As he took a parking ticket from the attendant the car phone rang.

'Jessica is hidden,' Win said.

'Thanks.'

'See you at the match tomorrow.'

Click. Abrupt, even for Win.

Inside Myron asked the receptionist where the morgue was. The receptionist looked at him like he was nuts and said, 'The basement, of course.'

'Oh, right. Like on *Quincy*.'

He took the elevator down a level. No one was around. He found a door marked MORGUE, and again using his powers of deductive reasoning, quickly realized that this was probably the morgue. Myron the Medium. He braced himself and knocked.

A friendly female voice chimed, 'Come in.'

The room was tiny and smelled like Janitor-in-a-Drum. The decor theme was metal. Two desks facing each other, both metal, took up half the room. Metal bookshelves. Metal chairs. Lots of stainless steel trays and bins all over the place. No blood in them. No organs. All shiny and clean. Myron had indeed seen plenty of violence, but the sight of blood still made him queasy once the danger passed. He didn't like violence, no matter what he'd told Jessica before. He was good at it, no denying that, but he did not like it. Yes, violence was the closest modern man came to his true primitive self, the closest he came to the intended state of nature, to the Lockean ideal, if you will. And yes, violence was the ultimate test of man, a test of both physical strength and animalistic cunning. But it was still sickening. Man had – in theory anyway – evolved for a reason. In the final analysis, violence was indeed a rush. But so was skydiving without a parachute.

'Can I help you?' the friendly voiced woman asked.

'I'm looking for Dr West,' he said.

'You found her.' She stood and extended her hand. 'You must be Myron Bolitar.'

Amanda West smiled a bright, clear smile, which illuminated even this room. She was blond and perky with a cute little upturned nose – the complete opposite of what he'd expected. Not to be stereotyping, but she seemed a tad too sunny, too upbeat, for someone handling rotting corpses all day. He tried to picture her cheerful face splitting open a dead body with a Y-incision. The picture wouldn't hold.

'You wanted to know about Curtis Yeller?' she asked.

'Yes.'

'Been waiting six years for someone to ask,' she said. 'Come on in. There's more room in the back.'

She opened a door behind her. 'You squeamish?'

'Uh, no.' Mr Tough-guy.

Amanda West smiled again. 'There's nothing to see really. Just that some people get freaked out by all the drawers.'

He entered the room. The drawers. There was a wall of huge drawers. Floor to ceiling. Five drawers up. Eight across. That equals forty drawers. Mr Multiplication Tables. Forty dead bodies could fit in here. Forty dead rotting corpses that used to have lives and families, that used to love and be loved, that once cared and struggled and dreamed. Freaked out? By a bunch of drawers? Surely you jest.

'Jake said you remembered Curtis Yeller,' he said.

'Sure. It was my biggest case.'

'Pardon me if I sound out of line,' Myron said, 'but you look awfully young to have been an ME six years ago.'

'You're not out of line,' she said, still smiling sweetly. Myron smiled back with equal sweetness. 'I had just finished my residency and worked there two nights a week. The chief ME was with the corpse of Alexander Cross. Both bodies came in nearly the same time. So I did the prelim on Curtis Yeller. I didn't get the chance to do anything resembling a full autopsy – not that I needed one to know how he was killed.'

'How was he killed?'

'Bullet wound. He was shot twice. Once in the lower left rib cage' – she leaned to the side and pointed at her own – 'and once in the face.'

'Did you know which one was fatal?'

'The shot to the ribs didn't do much damage,' she said. Amanda West was, Myron decided, cute. She tilted her head a lot when she talked. Jess did that too. 'But the bullet in Yeller's head ripped off his face like it was Silly Putty. There was no nose. Both cheekbones were barely splinters. It was a mess. The shot was at very close range. I didn't get a chance to run all the tests, but I'd say the gun was either pressed against his face or no more than a foot away.'

442

Myron almost took a step back. 'Are you saying a cop shot him in the face at point-blank range?'

Water dripped into a stainless steel sink, echoing in the room. 'I'm just giving you the facts,' Amanda West said steadily. 'You draw your own conclusions.'

'Who else knows about this?' he asked.

'I'm not sure. It was a zoo in there that night. I usually worked alone, but there must have been half a dozen other guys with me on this one. None of them worked for the coroner's office.'

'Who were they?'

'Cops and government guys,' she replied.

'Government guys?'

She nodded. 'That's what I was told. They worked for Senator Cross. Secret service or something like that. They confiscated everything – tissue samples, the slugs I extracted, everything. They told me it was a matter of national security. The whole night was crazy. Yeller's mother even managed to get in the room once. She started screaming at me.'

'What was she screaming about?'

'She was very insistent that there should be no autopsy. She wanted her son back immediately. She got her wish too. For once the police acquiesced. They weren't interested in having anyone look too closely at this, so it worked out for all concerned.' She smiled again. ' Funny thing, don't you think?'

'The mother not wanting an autopsy?'

'Yes.'

Myron shrugged. 'I've heard of parents not wanting autopsies before.'

'Right, because they want the body preserved for a decent burial. But this kid wasn't buried. He was cremated.' She offered up another smile, this one more saccharine.

'I see,' Myron said. 'So any evidence of police wrongdoing would have been burned up with Curtis Yeller.'

'Right,' she said.

'So you think – what – someone got to her?'

Amanda West put her hands up in surrender. 'Hey, I said it was a funny thing. Not ha-ha funny, just strange funny. The rest is up to you. I'm just an ME.'

Myron nodded again. 'You find anything else?'

'Yes,' she said. 'And this too I found funny. Very funny.'

'Ha-ha funny or strange funny?'

'You decide,' she said. She smoothed her lab coat. 'I'm no ballistics expert, but I know a little something about bullet slugs. I pulled two slugs from Yeller. One from the rib cage, one from the head.'

'Yeah so?'

'The two slugs were of different calibers.' Amanda West put up her index finger. All traces of a smile were gone now. Her face was clear and determined. 'Understand what I'm telling you, Mr Bolitar. I'm not just saying two different guns here. I'm talking about different caliber. And here's the funny part: all the officers on the Philadelphia force use the same caliber weapon.'

Myron felt a chill. 'So one of the two bullets came from someone other than a cop.'

'And,' she continued, 'all those secret service men were carrying guns.'

Silence.

'So,' she said, 'ha-ha funny or strange funny?'

Myron looked at her. 'You don't hear me laughing.'

40

Myron decided to ignore Jake's advice. Especially after listening to Amanda West.

Finding Officer Jimmy Blaine's current address had not been easy. The man had retired two years ago. Still Esperanza found out he lived alone on some small lake in the Poconos. Myron drove through the wilderness for two hours until he pulled into what he hoped was the right driveway. He checked his watch. He still had plenty of time to see Jimmy Blaine and get back to the office in time for his meeting with Ned Tunwell.

The house was rustic and quaint, about what you'd expect to find nestled away in the Poconos. Gravel driveway. Dozens of small wooden animals guarded a front porch. The air was heavy and still. Everything – the weather vane, the American flag, the rocking chair, all the leaves and blades of grass – stood frighteningly motionless, as if inanimate objects had the ability to hold their breaths. As Myron climbed up the porch stairs, he noticed a modern-looking wheelchair ramp that also led to the front door. The ramp looked out of place here, like a doughnut in a health food store. There was no doorbell, so he knocked.

No one answered. Curious. Myron had called ten minutes ago, had heard a man answer, and hung up. Could be out back. Myron circled around the house. As he hit the backyard, the lake stared him in the face. It was a spectacular picture. The sun shone off the still – again, frighteningly motionless – water and made Myron squint. Placid. Tranquil. Myron felt the muscles in his shoulders start to unbunch.

Sitting in a wheelchair facing the lake was a man. A Saint Bernard lay by his feet. The dog too was frighteningly motionless. As Myron approached he saw that the man was whittling wood.

'Hi,' Myron called out.

The man barely raised his eyes. He wore a red T-shirt and a John Deere cap pulled down over a weathered face. His legs were covered with a blanket, even in this heat. There was a portable phone within reach. 'Hi.' He went back to whittling. If he was surprised or upset to have company he was certainly taking it all in stride.

'Beautiful day,' Myron said. Mr Engaging Neighbor.

'Yep.'

'Are you Jimmy Blaine?'

'Yep.'

Even without the wheelchair it was hard to picture this guy working the city bowels of Philadelphia for eighteen years. Then again, it was hard to picture the bowels of Philadelphia, period, when you were out here.

Silence. No birds or crickets or anything but the whittling.

After some time had passed, Myron asked, 'Had much rain this year?' Myron Bolitar, Salt of the Earth. Mr Farmer's Almanac.

'Some.'

'This your dog?'

'Yep. Name is Fred.'

'Hi, Fred.' Myron scratched the dog behind the ears. The dog wagged its tail without moving any other part of its body. Then it farted loudly.

'Great place you have here,' Myron tried. Yep, just two good ol' boys shooting the breeze. Eb and Mr Haney on *Green Acres*. Myron half expected denim overalls to materialize on his body.

'Uh-huh.' Whittle, whittle.

'Listen, Mr Blaine, my name is—'

'Myron Bolitar,' Blaine finished for him. 'I know who you are. Been expecting you.'

He shouldn't have been surprised. 'Jake called you?'

Blaine nodded without looking up from his whittling. 'He said you were stubborn. Said you wouldn't listen to him.'

'I just want to ask you a few questions.'

'Nothing I care to say to you though.'

'I'm not here to hound you, Mr Blaine.'

He nodded again. 'Jake told me that too. Said you were okay. Said you liked to right wrongs, is all.'

'What else did he say?'

'That you don't know how to mind your own business. That you're a wiseass. And that you're a major pain in the butt.'

'He left out snazzy dancer,' Myron said.

For the first time since he arrived Jimmy Blaine stopped whittling. 'You trying to right the wrong done to Curtis Yeller?'

'I'm trying to find out who killed him.'

'Simple,' Blaine said. 'Me.'

'No, I don't think so.'

That stopped him for a brief moment. He gave Myron the once-over and then began whittling again.

'Could you tell me what happened that night?' Myron asked.

'The boy pulled a gun. I shot him. That's it.'

'How far away were you when you shot him?'

He shrugged, whittled. 'Thirty feet. Maybe forty.'

446

'How many shots did you fire?'

'Two.'

'And he just dropped?'

'Nope. He swung around the corner with the other one – that Swade kid, I guess. They disappeared.'

'You shot a man in the face and ribs and he kept running?'

'I didn't say they kept running. The two of them were by a corner. They disappeared around it. Didn't know it at the time, but the Yellers lived right there. They must have climbed in a window.'

'With a bullet in his skull?'

Jimmy Blaine shrugged again. 'The Swade kid probably helped him,' he said.

'That's not how it happened,' Myron said. 'You didn't kill him.'

Blaine eyed him and then went back to his whittling. 'Second time you've said that,' he noted. 'You want to explain what you mean?'

'Two bullets hit Yeller.'

'I just told you I shot twice.'

'But two different caliber slugs were pulled out of him. One of the shots – the one in the head – was from close range. Less than a foot away.'

Jimmy Blaine said nothing. He concentrated hard on his whittling. It looked like he was sculpting an animal of some sort, like the ones on the front porch. 'Two different calibers, you say?' He aimed for nonchalance, but he wasn't making it.

'Yes.'

'That kid I shot didn't have a record,' Blaine continued. 'You know what the odds are of that? In that part of the city?'

Myron nodded.

'I checked up on him,' Blaine continued. 'On my own. His name was Curtis Yeller. He was sixteen years old. He did well in school. He was a good kid. He had a chance at a good life until that night.'

'You didn't kill him,' Myron said.

Blaine whittled with a bit more intensity now. He blinked a lot. 'How did you find out about those slugs?'

'The assistant ME told me,' Myron said. 'You never knew?'

He shook his head. 'I guess it makes sense though,' he said. 'Blame me for it. Why not? It's easier. It's a legit shooting. No one questioned it. IAD barely broke a sweat. It didn't hurt my record. Didn't hurt anyone. No harm done, they figured.'

Myron waited for him to say more, but he just kept whittling. Two long ears were now evident in the wood. Maybe he was making a rabbit. 'Do you know who really killed Curtis Yeller?' Myron asked.

There was a long moment of the same whittle-filled silence. Fred farted again and wagged his tail. Myron's eyes kept going back to the lake. He stared out at the silver water. The effect was hypnotizing.

447

'No harm done,' Jimmy Blaine said again. 'That's what they all probably thought. Good ol' Jimmy. We won't let him take the rap. It'll be washed clean from his record. No one will know. Hell, some of the guys will even treat him special – making a shooting like that. They'll say he saved his partner's life. Good ol' Jimmy will come out of this looking like a hero. Except for one thing.'

Myron was tempted to ask what, but he sensed the answer was coming.

'I saw that boy dead,' Blaine continued. 'I saw Curtis Yeller lying in his own blood. I saw his mother hold him in her arms and cry. Sixteen years old. If he was a street punk or a drug addict or . . .' He stopped. 'But he wasn't any of those things. Not this kid. He was one of the good ones. I found out later he never even touched the senator's kid. The other one – the Swade punk – he did the stabbing.'

Two ducks splashed madly for a second, then stopped. Blaine put down the whittling, then thinking better of it, picked it back up again. 'I replayed that night a lot of times in my head. It was dark, you know. There was barely any light. Maybe the Yeller kid wasn't going to fire the gun. Maybe what I saw wasn't even a gun. Or maybe none of that mattered. Maybe it was a legit shooting, but the pieces still never quite added up. I kept hearing the mother's screams. I kept seeing her press her dead boy's bloody face into her bosom. And I think about it, you know, and thinking ain't always a good thing for a cop to do. And four years later, the next time a kid is pointing a gun at me, I think about seeing another crying mother. I think long and hard. Too long.'

He pointed to his legs. 'And this is the result.' He changed tools and kept whittling. 'Nope, no harm done.'

Silence.

Myron now understood Jake's attitude on the phone. Jimmy Blaine had gone through enough. If he'd done wrong in the case of Curtis Yeller, he had already paid an enormous price. Problem was, Jimmy Blaine hadn't done wrong. He hadn't killed Curtis Yeller – legit shooting or not. In the end Jimmy Blaine was yet another victim of that night.

After some time had passed, Myron tried again. 'Do you know who killed Curtis Yeller?'

'No, not really.'

'But you have a thought.'

'A thought maybe.'

'You mind telling me?'

Blaine looked down at Fred, as if looking for an answer. The dog maintained his bear-rug pose. 'Henry and I – he was my partner – got the call at a little past midnight,' he began. 'The two suspects had stolen a car from a driveway three blocks from the Old Oak tennis club. A dark blue Cadillac Seville. We spotted a vehicle matching the description coming off the Roosevelt Expressway twenty minutes later. When we pulled up behind the stolen vehicle, the suspects sped off. We then engaged in a high-speed pursuit.'

His voice had changed. He was a cop again, reading from a notepad he had read too many times in the past. 'Henry and I followed the vehicle down an alley not far from Hunting Park Avenue, off Broad. The chase then proceeded on foot. At the time we had no identification on the two youths and thus no address. We only had the car. The chase proceeded for several blocks. As we turned a corner, the driver drew a firearm. My partner told him to freeze and drop his weapon. Yeller responded by aiming the firearm at Henry. I then fired two shots. The youth fell or stumbled out of sight beyond the next corner. By the time Henry and I turned the same corner, there was no sign of either youth. We figured that they were hiding in the nearby vicinity and awaited backup before proceeding. We secured the area as best we could. But the cops didn't get there first. The so-called secret service guys did.'

'Senator Cross's men?'

Blaine nodded. 'They called themselves "national security," but they were probably mob guys.'

'Senator Cross told me he had no mob connections,' Myron said.

Jimmy Blaine raised an eyebrow. 'You serious?'

'Yes.'

'The mob owns Bradley Cross,' Blaine said. 'More specifically, the Perretti family. Cross is a major gambler. I know he's also been arrested twice with prostitutes. One of his early opponents – this is back when he was just a congressman – ended up in the river during the primaries.'

'And you traced it back to Cross?'

'Nothing anyone could prove. But we knew.'

Myron considered this for a moment. Clearly, the beloved senator had lied to him. Big surprise. He had played Myron for a sucker. Another big surprise. Win was right. Myron always went astray when he believed the best about people. 'So what happened next?'

'The senator's hoods were at the scene almost immediately. Been monitoring our radio. We'd been told over the air to cooperate with them one hundred percent. A real community effort finding these two kids. I'm surprised we spotted them first. Mob goons are usually better at this stuff than we are, you know?'

Myron knew. The mob had all the advantages over the police. They were closer to the city's underbelly. They could pay top dollar. They didn't have to worry about rules or laws or constitutional rights. They could inspire genuine fear.

'So what happened?' Myron asked.

'We started combing the area with flashlights, checking garbage Dumpsters, the whole bit. Cops and goons hand in hand. We found nothing for a while. Then we heard some gunshots. Henry and I ran to some dumpy apartment adjacent to where I'd shot Yeller. But Senator Cross's men were already there.'

Blaine stopped. He leaned and gave Fred a good ear scratch. Fred still didn't move except for the thumping tail. Still scratching his dog, Blaine said, 'Well, you know what we found.' His voice was low and dead. 'Yeller was dead. His mother was cradling him in her arms. She went through all these stages. First she just kept calling out his name over and over. Sweetly sometimes. Like she was trying to wake him up for school. Then she stroked the back of his head and rocked him and told him to go back to sleep. We all stood around and watched. Even the goons didn't bother her.'

'What about the other gunshots?' Myron asked.

'What about them?'

'Didn't you wonder where they had come from?'

'I guess I did,' he replied. 'But I figured the security guys had shot after Swade. I didn't think they'd be dumb enough to admit it, but that's what I thought.'

'It never crossed your mind they might have shot Yeller?'

'No.'

'Why not?'

'I told you the mother went through stages.'

'Right.'

'Once she realized her boy wasn't waking up again, she started pointing fingers and screaming. She wanted to know who had shot her boy. She wanted to look the killer in the eyes, the murderer who had shot her son on the street in cold blood. She said that Swade had dragged her boy in like that. Already shot up and dead.'

'She said all that? That Swade dragged him in and that he was already shot?'

'Yes.'

Silence. No water rippling. No birds chirping. Not even whittling. Several minutes passed before Blaine looked up and squinted. Then he said, 'Cold.'

'What?' Myron asked.

'That mother. If she was lying about who killed her boy. I always wondered why there were no repercussions. The mother never made a fuss. She didn't go to the newspapers. She didn't press charges. She didn't demand an explanation.' He shook his head. 'But what could have made her do that to her own flesh and blood? How could they have gotten to her so fast? With money? With threats? What?'

'I don't know,' Myron said.

Jimmy Blaine finished whittling. It was a rabbit. Pretty good one too. A bird finally chirped, but it wasn't a pretty sound. More like a caw than a melody. Blaine spun his wheelchair around. 'You want something to eat?' he asked. 'I'm about to make lunch.'

Myron looked at his watch. It was getting late. He had to get back to the office for his meeting with Ned Tunwell. 'Thanks, but I really have to get going.'

'Some other time then. When you're all done with this.'

'Yes,' Myron said.

Blaine blew the wood dust off the rabbit. 'Still don't get it,' he said.

'What?'

He stared at his finished handiwork, turning the rabbit over in his hand, studying it from every angle. 'Could the mother have really been that frosty?' he asked. 'How much money did they offer her? How much fright did they put into her? Hell, is there enough money or frights in the world for a mother to do that to her son?' He shook his head, dropped the wooden rabbit into his lap. 'I just don't get it.'

Myron didn't get it either.

41

Myron got back into his Ford Taurus and headed east. He drove several miles without seeing a car. Mostly he saw trees. Lots of trees. Yes, the great outdoors. Myron was not an outdoors kind of guy. He didn't hunt or fish or do any of that. The appeal seemed clear, but it just wasn't for him. Something about being alone in the woods always reminded him of Ned Beatty in *Deliverance*. He needed people. He needed movement. He needed noise. City noise – as opposed to squeal-like-a-pig noise.

He now knew a lot more about the deaths of both Alexander Cross and Curtis Yeller than he'd known twenty-four hours ago, but he still didn't know if any of it was relevant to what happened to Valerie Simpson. And that was what he was after. Digging into a sensational six-year-old murder might be fun, but it was beside the point. He wanted Valerie Simpson's murderer. He wanted to find the person who had decided to snuff out that young, tortured life. Call it righting a wrong. Call it having a rescue or hero complex. Call it chivalry. Didn't matter. It was far simpler to Myron: Valerie deserved better.

The roads were still abandoned. The foliage on both sides of the road blurred into green walls. He started putting together what he knew. Errol Swade and Curtis Yeller had been spotted by Jimmy Blaine and his partner. A chase had ensued. Leaving aside the question of whether it was a legitimate shooting or not, Jimmy Blaine fired at Curtis Yeller. One of Blaine's bullets probably hit Curtis Yeller in the ribs, but the key fact is that somebody else shot Yeller in the head at close range. Somebody who was using a different caliber gun. Somebody who was not a cop.

So who shot Curtis Yeller?

The answer now seemed fairly obvious. Senator Cross's men – thugs or security forces or whatever they were – had been carrying firearms. Both Amanda West and Jimmy Blaine had confirmed that. They certainly had the opportunity. They certainly had the motive. It didn't matter if Cross had lied to Myron or not. Either way it would be in the senator's best interest for Curtis Yeller and Errol Swade to end up dead. Live suspects could talk. Live suspects could tell tales of drug use. Live suspects could counter the claim that Alexander Cross had died a hero. Dead men tell no tales. More important, dead men do not dispute spin doctors.

As for Errol Swade – the mysterious 'escapee' – he'd almost assuredly been killed, probably in that gunfire Jimmy Blaine heard. The senator's men could have hid the body and dumped it later. Not definite, but again most likely. Errol Swade had a lot working against him. He was no genius. He was six-four. Myron knew from personal experience it was difficult to hide when you were that big. The odds of Swade eluding the police dragnet for so long – not to mention the mob's underworld army – were, as they say, statistically insignificant.

The sun was beginning to lower. The beams were now positioned in that one spot high enough to be in Myron's eyes but still low enough to avoid the sun visor. Myron squinted and slowed. His mind shifted gears again, this time to the aftermath of the Yeller shooting. Somehow Curtis Yeller ended up in his mother's arms, and somehow somebody got to her. Through either money or fear of reprisal – probably a combination of both – Deanna Yeller had been convinced to let the death of her son slide.

There were problems with this scenario, of course. For example, the money. Deanna Yeller's son had been murdered six years ago – yet the first big deposit in her account had occurred five months ago. Why the time lapse? She could have been biding her time, hiding the money under a mattress or something. But that didn't feel right. On the other hand, if the money was indeed new, the questions became more focused: why, all of a sudden, was Deanna getting this money? Why, all of a sudden, had Valerie been murdered? And how did Pavel fit in?

Good questions. No answers yet, but good questions. Maybe Ned Tunwell would know something useful.

Something caught Myron's eye. He glanced up. A car grew suddenly large in the rearview mirror. A big car. Black with a tinted windshield so you couldn't see inside. The license plate was New York.

The black car moved to its right, disappearing from the rearview mirror and appearing in the passenger-side mirror. Myron watched its progress. The imprint in the mirror reminded him that objects may be closer than they appear. Thanks for the clue. The black car picked up a little speed. As it came alongside of him, Myron could see it was a stretch limousine. A Lincoln Continental stretch. Extra-long stretch. The side windows too were tinted so you couldn't look in. It was like staring into a pair of giant aviator sunglasses. Myron could see himself in the reflection. He smiled and waved. His reflection smiled and waved back. Handsome devil.

The limo was dead-even with Myron's car now. The back window on the driver's side began to slide open. Myron half expected an elderly man to stick his head out and ask for Grey Poupon. Imagine his surprise when, instead, a gun appeared.

Without warning the gun fired twice, hitting the front and back tires on the passenger side of Myron's car. Myron swerved. He fought to regain control. The car veered off the road. Myron twisted the wheel and skidded away from a tree. The Ford Taurus came to a stop with a thud.

Two men jumped out of the limousine and headed toward him. Both wore blue suits. One also wore a Yankees cap. Business suit, baseball cap – an interesting fashion combo. They also carried guns. Their faces were stern and ready. Myron felt his heart in his throat. He was unarmed. He didn't like carrying guns, not for some moral reason but because they were bulky and uncomfortable and he so rarely ever used one. Win had warned him, but who listens to Win on a subject like this? But Myron had been careless. He was pissing off some powerful people and he should have been better prepared. He should have at least kept one in the glove compartment.

A little late for self-admonishments. Then again he might never have the chance again.

The two men approached. Not knowing what else to do, Myron ducked out of sight. He started dialing the car phone.

'Get your ass out of the car,' one of the men barked.

Myron said, 'Take another step and I'll drop you where you stand.' Mr Bluff.

Silence.

Myron dialed furiously and hit the send button. At that exact moment, he heard a sound like a twig breaking and then static. The goon with the Yankees cap had snapped off his antenna. This wasn't good. Myron kept himself low. He opened the ·glove compartment and reached inside. Nothing but maps and registration. His eyes searched the floor anxiously for some sort of weapon. The only thing he saw was the car cigarette lighter. Somehow he doubted that it would be effective against two armed goons. Maps, registration card, cigarette lighter. Unless Myron suddenly became MacGyver, he was in serious trouble.

He could hear footsteps shuffling about now. Myron's mind raced for an answer. Nothing came to him. Then he heard the car door of the limo open again. A quiet curse followed. Sounded like 'Shit.' Then a deep sigh.

'Bolitar, I ain't here to play no fucking games.'

The voice sent a chill through Myron. Something hardened in his chest. New York accent. More specifically, a Bensonhurst accent. Frank Ache.

This was not good.

'Get the fuck out of the car now, ass-wipe. I ain't here to kill you.'

'Your men just shot out my tires,' Myron called back.

'Right, and if I wanted you dead, they would have shot out your fucking head.'

Myron mulled that one over. 'Good point,' he said.

'Yeah, how about this one? I got two AKs sitting in the back here. If I wanted you dead, I could have Billy and Tony spray-paint this piece of shit you call a car with them.'

'Another good point,' Myron said.

'Now get the fuck out here,' Frank barked. 'I don't got all goddamn day. Ass-wipe.'

Myron didn't really have a choice. He opened the car and stood. Frank Ache ducked back into the backseat. Billy and Tony scowled at him.

'Get in here,' Frank called out.

Myron walked to the car. Billy and Tony blocked his path. 'Give me your gun,' the one with the Yankees cap said.

'Are you Billy or Tony?'

'The gun. Now.'

Myron squinted at the baseball cap. 'Wait a second, I get it. Plugs, right?'

'What?'

'Wearing a baseball cap with a suit. You're covering up new hair plugs.'

The two men exchanged a glance. *Bingo*, Myron thought.

'Now, ass-wipe,' the cap man said. 'The gun.'

Ass-wipe. The goon word of the week. 'You didn't say please.'

Frank's voice came from inside the car. 'Jesus Christ, Billy, he don't have no piece. He was just yanking your hardware.'

Billy's scowl grew angrier. Myron smiled, turned his palms to the sky, shrugged.

Tony opened the door. Myron slid into the backseat. Tony and Billy moved into the front. Frank pressed a button and a partition slid up, separating the back compartment from the front seats. The limo had a wet bar and television with VCR. The inside was sort of a royal red, blood-red actually, which, knowing Frank's history, probably helped cut down on the cost of cleanings.

'Nice wheels, Frank,' Myron said.

Frank wore his customary garb – a velour sweat suit a couple of sizes too small. This one was green with yellow trim. The front zipper was down midway, like those guys in the seventies wore at discos. His gut was enormous enough to be mistaken for a multiple gestation. He was bald. He stared at Myron for several seconds before he spoke.

'You enjoy crawling up my ass crack, Bolitar?'

Myron blinked. 'Gee, Frank, there's an appetizing thought.'

'You're a crazy fuck, you know that? Why you always trying to piss me off? Huh?'

'Hey, I'm not the one who sent goons to rape his girlfriend,' Myron said.

Frank pointed his finger at Myron's chest. 'And what – you didn't have that coming? You didn't ask for that?'

Myron remained still. Stupid to raise Jessica with this man. Impossible as it seemed, you couldn't let it get personal. You had to separate, to stop thinking of Frank as the man who tried to do grievous harm to the love of your life. To think such thoughts would be at best counterproductive. At worst, suicide.

'I warned you,' Frank continued. 'I even sent Aaron so you'd know I was serious. You know what Aaron costs per day?'

'Not much anymore,' Myron said.

'Ho, ho, I'm dying of laughter,' Frank countered, but he wasn't laughing. 'I tried to be reasonable with you. I let you have that Crane kid. And how do you thank me? By fucking around with my business.'

'I'm trying to find a killer,' Myron said.

'And I'm supposed to give a rat's ass? You want to go play fucking Batman, fine, do it without costing me any money. Once you cost me money, you cross the line. Pavel meant money to me.'

'Pavel also slept with underage girls,' Myron said.

Frank held up his hands. 'Hey, what a guy does in the privacy of his own bedroom, that don't concern me.'

'You're so progressive, Frank. You voting Democratic now?'

'Look, ass-wipe, you want to hear I knew about Pavel? Fine, I knew. I knew Pavel fucked kiddies. So what? I work with guys who make Pavel Menansi looked like Mother Teresa. I can't go picking and choosing in my line of work. So I ask myself one simple question: Is the guy making me money? If the answer is yes, then that's it. That's my rule. Pavel was making me money. End of story.'

Myron said nothing. He was waiting for Ache to get to the point, which he sincerely hoped was not a bullet in the skull.

Frank took out a packet of chewing gum. Dentyne. He popped one in his mouth. 'But I ain't here to get in no philosophy talk with you. Fact is, Pavel is dead. He's not making me money anymore, so my rule don't apply no more. You see?'

'Yes.'

'I'm a simple businessman,' Frank went on. 'Pavel can't make me money no more. That means you and me don't have a beef no more. So you get to live. Wasting you would no longer be profitable to me. You understand?'

Myron nodded. 'Are we having a tender moment, Frank?'

Frank leaned forward. His eyes were small and black. 'No, ass-wipe, we're not. Next time I ain't gonna fuck around. Hiding your girlfriend won't help you. I'll find her. Or I'll waste someone else instead. Your mommy, your daddy, your friends – hell, even your fucking barber.'

'His name is Pierre. And he prefers the term "beauty technician."'

Frank looked him square in the eye. 'You fucking joking with me?'

'You just threatened my parents,' Myron said. 'What's the proper way to respond?'

Frank nodded slowly and sat back. 'It's over. For now.' He pressed a button and the partition slid down.

Billy said, 'Yes, Mr Ache?'

'Call a towing service for Bolitar's car.'

'Yes, Mr Ache.'

Frank turned back to Myron. 'Get the fuck out of my car.'

'No hug first?'

'Out.'

'Can I ask you one quick question?'

'What?'

'Did you have Valerie killed to protect Pavel?'

Frank grinned with bad, ferretlike teeth. 'Get out,' he said. 'Or I'll use your nuts for snack foods.'

'Right, thanks. Nice chatting with you, Frank, stay in touch.' He opened the door and got out.

Frank slid across the seat and leaned his head through the open door. 'You tell Win we talked, okay?'

'Why?'

'None of your business why. You just tell Win. Got it?'

'Got it,' Myron said.

Frank closed the door. The limo drove away.

42

Triple A got there pretty quickly. Myron reached his office at six-thirty. Ned wasn't there yet. Esperanza handed him his messages. He went into his office and returned calls.

Esperanza buzzed. 'The bitch. Line three.'

'Stop calling her that.' He picked up the phone. 'You're back at the loft?'

'Yes,' Jessica said. 'That didn't take long.'

'I work fast,' he said.

'And yet I never complain,' she said.

'Ouch.'

'So what happened?' she asked.

'Someone murdered Pavel Menansi. There's nothing for Ache to protect anymore.'

'It's that simple?'

'It's business. Business with these guys is very simple.'

'No profit, no kill.'

'The cardinal rule,' Myron said.

'Will you come over tonight?' she asked.

'Yes.'

'But one rule of our own,' she said.

'Oh?'

'No talking about Valerie Simpson or murder or any of this. We forget it all.'

'What will we do instead?' Myron asked.

'Screw each other's brains out.'

Myron said, 'I guess I can live with that.'

Esperanza leaned her head in and said, 'He's heeeee-ere.'

He nodded at Esperanza and said to Jessica, 'I'll call you later.'

Myron put the phone back in the cradle. He stood and waited. An evening alone with Jessica. Sounded perfect. It also sounded scary. Things were moving too fast. He had no control. Jess was back and things appeared to be better than ever. Myron wondered about that. Mostly he wondered if he could survive another crash like last time, if he could go through the pain again. He also wondered what he could do to protect himself, realized the answer was nothing, and wished he was better at putting up defenses.

Ned Tunwell practically leaped into his office, hand extended – like an enthusiastic late-show guest coming through a curtain. Myron half expected him to wave to the crowd. He pumped Myron's hand. 'Hey, Myron!'

'Hi, Ned. Have a seat.'

Ned's smile dropped at Myron's tone. 'Hey, there's nothing wrong with Duane, is there?'

'No.'

Still standing but his voice was panicky. 'He's not hurt?'

'No, Duane is fine.'

'Great.' The smile was back. Tough to keep a good man down. 'That match yesterday – he was fantastic. Fantastic, Myron. I tell you, the way he came back – it's all anyone's talking about. The exposure was awesome. Simply awesome. We couldn't have scripted it better. I practically wet myself.'

'Uh-huh. Sit down, Ned.'

'Sure.' Ned sat. Myron hoped he wouldn't leave a stain on the seat. 'Just a few hours away, Myron. The big day. The Saturday Semis. Big live crowd, huge TV audience. You think Duane's got a shot against Craig? Papers don't seem to think so.'

Thomas Craig, the second seed and the game's premier serve-and-volley player, was currently playing his career-best tennis. 'Yes,' Myron said. 'I think Duane's got a shot.'

Ned's eyes were bright. 'Wow. If he could somehow pull it off . . .' He stopped and just shook his head and grinned.

'Ned?'

He looked up. Wide-eyed. 'Yes?'

'How well did you know Valerie Simpson?'

Ned hesitated. The eyes dulled a bit. 'Me?'

Myron nodded.

'A little, I guess.'

'Just a little?'

'Yeah.' He flashed a nervous smile, struggled to hold it. 'Why, what's up?'

'I heard differently.'

'Oh?'

'I heard you were the one who got Nike to sign her. That you handled her account.'

He squirmed a bit. 'Yeah, well, I guess so.'

'So you must have known her pretty well then.'

'Maybe, I guess. Why are you asking me this, Myron? What's the big deal?'

'Do you trust me, Ned?'

'With my life, Myron. You know that. But this subject is painful for me. You understand?'

'You mean her dying and all?'

Ned made a lemon-sucking face. 'No,' he said. 'I mean her career plummet. She was the first person I signed for Nike. I thought she'd launch me to the top. Instead she set me back five years. It was painful.'

Another Mr Sensitive.

'When she flopped,' Ned continued, 'guess who took the fall? Go ahead, guess.'

Myron thought the question was rhetorical, but Ned waited with that expectant face of his. Myron finally said, 'Would that be you, Ned?'

'Damn straight, me. I was thrown to the bottom. Just dumped there. I had to start climbing up all over again. Because of Valerie and her collapse. Don't get me wrong, Myron. I'm doing okay now – knock wood.' He rapped his knuckles on the desk.

Myron knocked wood too. The sarcasm was lost on Ned. 'Did you know Alexander Cross?' Myron asked.

Both Ned's eyebrows jumped. 'Hey, what's the deal here?'

'Trust me, Ned.'

'I do, Myron, really, but come on . . .'

'It's a simple question: Did you know Alexander Cross?'

'I may have met him once, I don't remember. Through Valerie, of course. They were something of an item.'

'How about you and Valerie?'

'What about me and Valerie?'

'Were you two an item?'

He put his hand out in a gesture of *stop*. 'Hey, hold up. Look, Myron, I like you, I really do. You're an honest Joe. A straight shooter just like me—'

'No, Ned, you're not a straight shooter. You're jerking me around. You knew Alexander Cross. In fact you were at the Old Oaks tennis club the night he was murdered.'

Ned opened his mouth but no sounds came out. He managed to shake his head no.

'Here.' Myron stood and handed him the party guest list. 'In yellow highlighter. E. Tunwell. Ned né Edward.'

Ned looked down at the paper, looked up, looked down again. 'This was a long time ago,' he said. 'What does this have to do with anything?'

'Why are you lying about it?'

'I'm not lying.'

'You're hiding something, Ned.'

'No, I'm not.'

Myron stared down at him. Ned's eyes scattered, searching for safe haven and finding none. 'Look, Myron, it's not what you think.'

'I don't think anything.' Then: 'Did you sleep with her?'

'No!' Ned finally looked up and held a steady gaze. 'That damn rumor almost ended my career. It's a lie that slimeball Menansi made up about me. It's a lie, Myron, I swear.'

'Pavel Menansi told people that?'

Ned nodded. 'He is a sick son of a bitch.'

'Was.'

'What?'

'Pavel Menansi is dead. Someone killed him last night. Shot in the chest. Very similar to what happened to Valerie.' Myron waited two beats. Then he pointed his finger at Ned. 'Where were you last night?'

Ned's eyes were two golf balls. 'You can't think . . .'

Myron shrugged. 'If you've got nothing to hide . . .'

'I don't!'

'Then tell me what happened.'

'Nothing happened.'

'What aren't you telling me, Ned?'

'It was nothing, Myron. I swear—'

Myron sighed. 'You admit Valerie Simpson severely damaged your career. You admit you're still "pained" by what she did. You've also told me that Pavel Menansi spread rumors about you. In fact you referred to a recent murder victim as – and I quote – "a sick son of a bitch."'

'Hey, come on, Myron, that was just talk.' Ned tried to smile his way out of it, but Myron kept his face stern. 'It didn't mean anything.'

'Maybe, maybe not. But I wonder how your superiors at Nike are going to react to the publicity.'

The smile stayed in place, but there was nothing behind it. 'Hey, you can't be serious. You can't go around spreading rumors like that.'

'Why?' Myron asked. 'You going to kill me too?'

'I didn't kill anyone!' Ned shouted.

Myron feigned fear. 'I don't know . . .'

'Look, Valerie took me outside that night, okay, that's all. We kissed, but it went no further, I swear.'

'Whoa, back up a second,' Myron said. 'Start at the beginning. You were at the party.'

Ned slid to the tip of his chair, his words came fast now. 'Right, I was at the party, okay? So was Valerie. We arrived together. She was very excited because Alexander was going to announce their engagement. But when he backed out, she got really pissed off.'

'Why did he back out?'

'His father. He made Alexander call it off.'

'Senator Cross?'

'Uh-huh.'

'Why?' Myron asked.

'How the hell am I supposed to know? Valerie told me the man was a

461

major prick. She hated him. But when Alexander bowed to his whim like that, she blew her stack. She wanted revenge. A little payback.'

'And you were handy?'

Ned snapped his fingers. 'Right, exactly, I was handy. That's all. It wasn't my fault, Myron. I was at the wrong place at the wrong time. You understand, right?'

'So you two went outside,' Myron prompted.

'We went outside and found a spot behind a shed. We only kissed, I swear. Nothing more. Just kissed. Then we heard some noise, so we stopped.'

Myron sat back down. 'What noise?'

'First it was just someone hitting tennis balls. But then we heard raised voices. One of them was Alexander's. Then we heard this awful scream.'

'What did you do?' Myron asked.

'Me? Nothing at first. Valerie screamed too. Then she broke into a run. I followed her. I lost her for a second. Then I came around a bend and saw her up ahead just standing there. When I got to her I saw what she was staring at. Alexander was bleeding all over the grass. His friends were starting to run away. The big black guy was standing over the body. He had a tennis racket in one hand, a big knife in the other.'

Myron leaned forward. 'You saw the murderer?'

Ned nodded. 'Up close and personal.'

'And he was a big black guy?'

'Yep.'

'How many of them were there?'

'Two. Both black.'

So much for the setup theory. Unless Ned was lying, which Myron doubted. 'So what happened next?'

Ned paused for a second. 'You ever see Valerie in her prime? On the court, I mean.'

'Yes.'

'You ever see that look in her eyes?'

'What look?'

'Certain athletes get it. Larry Bird used to. Joe Montana. Michael Jordan. Maybe you used to too. Well, Val had it, and she had it now. The smaller black guy started screaming at the big one, saying stuff like, "Look what you did," "Are you crazy," stuff like that. Then they started to run. They ran right toward us. Me, I ran. I'm no fool. But not Val. She just stood there and waited. When they got close she let out this big scream and dove at the little guy. I couldn't believe it. She tackled him like a linebacker. They both ended up on the ground. The little guy whacked her with his tennis racket and managed to pull away.'

'Did you get a good look at them?'

'Pretty good, I guess.'

'Did you ever see pictures of Errol Swade?'

'Yeah, sure, his picture was on the news every day for a while.'

'Was it the same guy you saw?'

'Definitely,' he said without hesitation. 'No question about it.'

Myron mulled this over. They'd been there that night. At the Old Oaks Club. Myron had been wrong. Lucinda Elright had been wrong. Swade and Yeller were not just casual fall guys. 'So what did you two do then?' Myron asked.

'Hey, her career was in enough trouble. We didn't need this kind of press. So I brought her back to the party. Didn't say anything to anyone about it. Val was out of it anyway – in a real funk, but that wasn't any surprise. I mean, think about it. She takes me outside to cheat on her boyfriend at the exact moment he's getting murdered. Weird, huh?'

Myron nodded. 'Very.'

And, Myron thought, the kind of thing that would push a troubled soul over the final ledge.

43

Myron and Jessica kept their promise. They did not talk about the murders. They snuggled and watched *Strangers on a Train* on AMC while eating Thai takeout. They made love. They snuggled and watched *Rear Window* while downing some Häagen-Dazs. They made love again.

Myron felt light-headed. For one night he actually forgot all about the world of Valerie Simpson and Alexander Cross and Curtis Yeller and Errol Swade and Frank Ache. It felt good. Too good. He started thinking about the suburbs and the hoop in the driveway and then he made himself stop thinking such thoughts.

Several hours later the morning sunlight drop-kicked him back into the real world. The escape had been paradise and for a fleeting moment, as he lay in bed with Jessica, he considered wrapping his arms around her and not going anywhere. Why move? What was out there that could come close to this?

He had no answer. Jessica hugged him a little tighter, as though reading his thoughts, but it didn't last long. They both dressed in silence and drove to Flushing Meadows. Today was the big match. The last Tuesday of the US Open. The women's finals sandwiched by the men's semifinals. First match of the day featured the number-two seed, Thomas Craig, vs the tournament's biggest surprise, Duane Richwood.

After they passed through the gate Myron gave Jessica a ticket stub. 'I'll meet you inside. I want to talk to Duane.'

'Now?' she said. 'Before the biggest match of his career?'

'Just for a second.'

She shrugged, gave him a skeptical eye, took the ticket.

He hurried over to the players' lounge, showed his ID to the guard at the gate, and entered. The room was fairly unspectacular, considering that it was the players' lounge for a Grand Slam event. It reeked of baby powder. Duane sat alone in a corner. He had his Walkman on and his head tilted back. Myron couldn't tell if his eyes were opened or closed because, as always, Duane had on his sunglasses.

When he approached, Duane's finger switched off the music. He tilted his face up toward Myron. Myron could see himself in the reflection of the sunglasses. It reminded him of the windows in Frank's limo.

Duane's face was a rigid mask. He slowly slid the headphones off his ears and let them hang around his neck like a horseshoe. 'She's gone,' Duane said slowly. 'Wanda left me.'

'When?' Myron asked. The question was stupid and irrelevant, but he wasn't sure what else to say.

'This morning. What did you tell her?'

'Nothing.'

'I heard she came to you,' Duane said.

Myron said nothing.

'Did you tell her about seeing me at the hotel?'

'No.'

Duane changed tapes in the Walkman. 'Get out of here,' he said.

'She cares about you, Duane.'

'Funny way of showing it.'

'She just wants to know what's wrong.'

'Nothing's wrong.'

The sunglasses were disconcerting. He looked straight up at Myron; it appeared as though they were making eye contact, but who knew? 'This match is important,' Myron said, 'but not like Wanda.'

'You think I don't know that?' he snapped.

'Then tell her the truth.'

Duane's chiseled face smiled slowly. 'You don't understand,' he said.

'Make me understand.'

He fiddled with the Walkman, popping the tape out, pushing it back in. 'You think telling the truth will make it better, but you don't know what the truth is. You talking like "The truth will set you free" when you don't even know the truth. The truth don't always set you free, Myron. Sometimes the truth can kill.'

'Hiding the truth isn't working,' Myron said.

'It would if you'd let it lie.'

'Someone was murdered. That's not something you can just let lie.'

Duane put the Walkman's headphones back on his ears. 'Maybe it should be,' he said.

Silence.

The two men stared dares. Myron could hear the faint din coming from the Walkman. Then he said to Duane, 'You were there the night Alexander Cross was murdered. You were at the club with Yeller and Swade.'

The stares continued. Behind them, Thomas Craig lined up by the door. He carried several tennis rackets and what looked like an overnight bag. Security was there too with walkie-talkies and earplugs. They nodded toward Duane. 'Show time, Mr Richwood.'

Duane stood. 'Excuse me,' he said to Myron. 'I have a match to play.'

He walked behind Thomas Craig. Thomas Craig smiled politely. Duane did likewise. Very civil, tennis. Myron watched them leave. He sat there for a few minutes in the abandoned locker room. In the distance he heard the cheers as both men entered the court.

Show time.

Myron found his way to his seat. It was during the match – in the fourth set actually – when he finally figured out who murdered Valerie Simpson.

44

Stadium Court was packed by the time Myron sat down. Duane and Thomas Craig were still warming up, each taking turns lofting easy lobs for the other to slam away. The fans floated and mingled and socialized and made sure they were seen. The usual celebs were there: Johnny Carson, Alan King, David Dinkins, Renee Richards, Barbra Streisand, Ivana Trump.

Jake and his son Gerard came down to the box.

'I see you got the tickets okay,' Myron said.

Jake nodded. 'Great seats.'

'Nothing's too good for my friends.'

'No,' Jake said, 'I meant yours.'

Ever the wiseass.

Jake and Gerard chatted a moment with Jessica before moving up to their seats, which were by any stretch of the imagination excellently situated. Myron scanned the crowd. A lot of familiar faces. Senator Bradley Cross was there with his entourage, including his son's old chum Gregory Caufield. Frank Ache had shown up wearing the same sweat suit Myron had seen him in yesterday. Frank nodded toward Myron. Myron did not nod back. Kenneth and Helen Van Slyke were there too – surprise, surprise. They were sitting a few boxes over. Myron tried to catch Helen's eye, but she was trying very hard to pretend she didn't see him. Ned Tunwell and Friends (not to be confused with Barney and Friends, though the confusion would be understandable) were in their usual box. Ned too was doing his utmost not to see Myron. He seemed less animated today.

'I'll be right back,' Jessica said.

Myron sat. Henry Hobman was already in game mode. Myron said, 'Hi, Henry.'

'Stop messing with his head,' Henry said. 'Your job is to keep him happy.'

Myron didn't bother responding.

Win finally showed up. He wore a pink shirt from some golf club, bright green pants, white bucks, and a yellow sweater tied around his neck. 'Hello,' Win said.

Myron shook his head. 'Who dresses you?'

'It's the latest in sophisticated wear.'

'You clash with the world.'

'Pardon *moi*, Monsieur Saint Laurent.' Win sat down. 'Did you talk to Duane?'

'Just a little pep talk.'

Jessica returned. She greeted Win with a kiss on the cheek. 'Thank you,' she whispered to him.

Win said nothing.

They stood for the national anthem. When it was over, the English-accented voice on the loudspeaker asked everyone to lower their heads for a moment of silence to remember the great Pavel Menansi. Heads lowered. The crowd hushed. Someone sniffed. Win rolled his eyes. Two minutes later the match began.

The play was incredible. Both men were power hitters, but no one expected anything like this. The pace was like something from another planet. A far faster planet. The IBM serve speedometer drew constant 'Ooo's from the crowd. Rallies didn't last very long. Mistakes were made, but so were incredible shots. This was serve and volley in the old tradition taken to the tenth power. Duane was unconscious. He whacked at the ball with uncommon fury, as though the ball had personally offended him. Myron had never seen either man play better.

Win leaned over and whispered, 'Must have been some pep talk.'

'Wanda left him.'

'Ah,' Win said with a nod. 'That explains it. The shackles are off.'

'I don't think that's it, Win.'

'If you say so.'

Myron didn't bother. It was like talking colors with a blind man.

Duane won the first set 6–2. The second set went into a tie-breaker, which Thomas Craig won. As the third set opened, Win said, 'What have you learned?'

Myron filled him in, trying to keep his voice down. At one point, Ivana Trump shushed him. Win waved a hand in her direciton. 'She digs me. Big-time.'

'Get real,' Myron said.

During a change of sides in the third set, Win said, 'So first we believed that Valerie was eliminated because she knew something harmful about Pavel Menansi. Now we believe that she was eliminated because she saw something the night Alexander Cross was killed.'

'A possibility,' Myron said.

During the next change of sides, Myron felt a tap on his shoulder. He looked down – way down – and was surprised. 'Dr Abramson,' he said.

'Hello, Myron.'

'Nice to see you, Doc.'

'Nice to see you too,' she said. 'Your client is playing very well. You must be pleased.'

'I'm sorry,' Myron said. 'I can neither confirm nor deny that Duane Richwood is a client of mine.'

She didn't smile. 'Was that supposed to be funny?'

'Guess not,' Myron said. 'I didn't know you were a tennis fan.'

'I come every year.' She spotted Win. 'Hello, Mr Lockwood.'

Win nodded. 'Dr Abramson.'

'This is my friend Jessica Culver,' Myron said.

The two women shook hands and exchanged polite smiles. 'A pleasure,' Dr Abramson said. 'Well, I don't want to keep you. I just wanted to say a quick hello.'

'Can we talk a little later?' Myron asked.

'No, I don't think so. Good-bye.'

'Did you know that Kenneth and Helen Van Slyke are here?'

'Yes. And I also know they just stepped out for a moment.'

Myron looked toward their seats. Empty. He smiled. 'You crafty shrink. Coming over to say hello when they weren't looking.'

'And to say good-bye,' she said, returning the smile. She turned away and left. The match started up again. During the next change of sides, the Van Slykes returned. Myron leaned over to Win. 'How do you know Dr Abramson?'

'I visited Valerie,' he said.

'Often?'

Win didn't answer. He might have shrugged, might not. Either way it told Myron to mind his own business. Myron looked at Jessica. She shrugged too.

On the court Duane was growing more erratic, but he was still hitting enough winners to maintain the edge. He won the third set 7–5. He was up two sets to one – one set away from the US Open finals. The Nike box was animated. Hands were slapping Ned's back. Even Ned seemed to be perking up now. Hard to keep a good man down.

Senator Cross watched in silence. No one talked to him, and he talked to no one. Not even during breaks. He had met Myron's eyes only once. He stared for a long time, but did not move. Helen and Kenneth Van Slyke spoke to the people around them, but they both looked uncomfortable. Frank Ache adjusted his crotch and jabbered with Roy O'Connor, the president of TruPro. Frank looked comfortable. Roy looked like he wanted to puke. Ivana Trump glanced about her surroundings. Every time she looked near Win, he blew her kisses.

It was during a serve in the third set when Myron finally began to see it. It started small, a statement made by Jimmy Blaine that did not compute. Something about the foot chase in Philadelphia. The rest sort of tumbled into place. When the final piece clicked, he sat up.

Win and Jessica traded glances. Myron stared off.

'What is it?' Jessica asked.

Myron turned to Win. 'I need to talk to Gregory Caufield.'

'When?'

'Right away, next break. Can you get him alone?'

Win nodded. 'Done.'

45

In the tournament's first few rounds it was not uncommon for fifteen or more matches to be going on at the same time. The biggest names usually stayed on Stadium Court or the Grandstand, while other matches took place in smaller venues, some with no seating. Today those courts were so barren, Myron half expected a tumbleweed to blow through. He waited by court sixteen, a semimajor court. It had the most seating next to the Stadium and Grandstand, though less than most high school gyms.

He sat on an aluminum bench in the front row. The sun had gained strength and was now at its most potent. Every once in a while he heard cheers erupt from the Stadium's crowd a hundred yards or so away. Sometimes tennis fans sounded like they were having an orgasm during particularly brilliant points. It sort of built up slowly with a low oh-oh-oh, and then increased Oh-Oh, and finally the big OH-OH-OH, followed by a loud sigh and clapping.

Weird thought.

Distracting thought too.

He heard Gregory Caufield well before he saw him. That same creepy, money accent that Win possessed said, 'Windsor, where on earth are we going?'

'Just over here, Gregory.'

'Are you sure this couldn't wait, old boy?'

Old boy. Neither one of them was thirty-five yet and he was using the term *old boy*.

'No, Gregory, it can't.'

They rounded the corner. Gregory's eyes widened a bit when he saw Myron, but he recovered fast. He smiled and stuck out his hand. 'Hello, Myron.'

'Hi, Greg.'

His face flinched for a second. He was Gregory, not Greg.

'What's this all about, Windsor? I thought you had something private to tell me.'

Win shrugged. 'I lied,' he said. 'Myron needs to speak with you. He needs your cooperation.'

Gregory turned to Myron and waited.

'I want to talk to you about the night Alexander Cross was murdered.'

'I know nothing about it,' Gregory said.

'You know plenty about it, but I just have one question for you.'

'I'm sorry,' Gregory said. 'I must be getting back now.' He turned to leave. Win blocked his path. Gregory looked puzzled.

'Just one question,' Myron said.

Gregory ignored him. 'Please move out of my way, Windsor.'

Win said, 'No.'

Gregory could not believe what he was hearing. He half-smiled and put a hand through his unruly hair. 'Are you prepared to use force to keep me here?'

'Yes.'

'Please, Windsor, this is no longer amusing.'

'Myron needs your cooperation.'

'And I am not prepared to give it to him. Now I insist you move.'

Win did not move. 'Are you telling me you will not cooperate, Gregory?'

'That is precisely what I am telling you.'

Win's palm shot out and hit the solar plexus. The wind gushed from Gregory. He collapsed to one knee, his face pale and shocked. Myron shook his head at Win, but he understood what he was doing. To people like Gregory – actually, to most people – violence is abstract. They read about it. They see it in movies and in the newspapers. But it never really touches them. It simply doesn't exist in their world. Win had shown Gregory how quickly that can change. Gregory had now experienced physical pain from the hands of a fellow human being. He would be different now. Not just here, not just today.

Gregory held his chest. He was on the verge of tears.

'Do not make me strike you again,' Win said.

Myron stepped toward him but did not help him up. 'Gregory, we know all about that night,' he said. 'I have just one question. I don't care what you were doing out there. I don't care if you were snorting or shooting illegal substances. That doesn't interest me in the least. What you say will in no way incriminate you – unless you lie to me.'

Gregory looked up at him. His face was completely void of any color.

'They weren't robbing the club, were they?' Myron asked.

Gregory did not answer.

'Errol Swade and Curtis Yeller hadn't broken into the club to rob it,' Myron said. 'And they weren't there selling drugs either. Am I right? If I am, just nod.'

Gregory looked at Win, then back to Myron. He nodded.

'Tell me what they were doing,' Myron said.

Gregory didn't say anything.

'Just say it,' Myron continued. 'I already know the answer. I just need you to say it. What were they doing there that night?'

Gregory's breathing was returning to normal now. He stood up and looked Myron straight in the eye.

'What were they doing?' Myron asked. 'Tell me.'

And then Gregory Caufield said exactly what Myron had expected. 'They were playing tennis.'

46

Myron ran to his car.

Duane was ahead two sets to one, 4–2 in the fourth set. He was two games away from reaching the US Open finals, but that no longer seemed like such a big deal. Myron now knew what happened. He knew what happened to Alexander Cross and Curtis Yeller and Errol Swade and Valerie Simpson and maybe even Pavel Menansi.

He picked up the car phone and began placing calls. His second call was to Esperanza's house. She picked up.

'I'm with Lucy,' she said. Esperanza had been dating a woman named Lucy for a couple of months now. They seemed serious. Of course, Myron thought Esperanza was serious with a guy named Max just a few months earlier. Dating a Max, then a Lucy. Never a dull moment.

'Do you have the appointment book?' Myron asked.

'I got a copy on my computer here.'

'The last day Valerie Simpson was in our office, who had the appointment right before her?'

'Give me a second.' He heard her clack some keys. 'Duane.'

As he thought. 'Thanks.'

'You're not at the match?'

'No.'

'Where are you?'

'In my car.'

'Is Win with you?' she asked.

'No.'

'How about the witch?'

'I'm alone.'

'Swing by and pick me up then. Lucy's leaving anyway.'

'No.'

He hung up and switched on the radio. Duane was up 5–2. One game away. He dialed the home number of Amanda West, ME. Then he called Jimmy Blaine. It all checked out. Myron felt something very cold caress his spine.

His hand actually trembled when he called Lucinda Elright. The old teacher answered on the first ring.

'Can you see me today?' Myron asked.

'Yes, of course.'

'I should be there in a couple of hours.'

'I'll be here,' Lucinda said. She asked no questions, wanted no explanations. She simply said, 'Good-bye.'

Duane won the final set 6–2. He was in the finals of the US Open, but the postgame wrap-up was short for several reasons. First, the women's finals came up right on the heels of Duane's impressive win. Second, the colorful Duane Richwood had run out without doing any interviews. The radio broadcasters seemed surprised.

Myron was not.

He reached Lucinda Elright's apartment in less than two hours. He stayed less than five minutes, but the visit was the final confirmation Myron needed. There was no longer any doubt. He took the book and got back in his car. Half an hour later he parked in the driveway. Myron rang the doorbell. No smile this time when the door opened. No surprise this time either.

'I know what happened to Errol Swade,' Myron said. 'He's dead.'

Deanna Yeller blinked. 'I told you that the first time you came by.'

'But,' Myron said, 'you didn't tell me you killed him.'

47

Myron didn't wait for an invitation. He pushed past her. Again he was struck by the impersonal feel of this house. Not one picture. Not one remembrance. But now he understood why. The TV was tuned on the tennis match. No surprise there. The women were midway through the first set.

Deanna Yeller followed him.

'It must torture you,' he said.

'What?'

'Watching Duane on TV. Instead of in person.'

'It was just a fling,' she said in a monotone. 'It didn't mean anything.'

'Duane was just a one-nighter?'

'Something like that.'

'I don't think so,' Myron said. 'Duane Richwood is your son.'

'What are you talking about? I only had one son.'

'That's true.'

'And he's dead. They killed him, remember?'

'That's not true. Errol Swade was killed. Not Curtis.'

'I don't know what you're talking about,' she said. But there wasn't much conviction in her voice. She sounded tired, like she was going through the motions – or maybe she just realized that Myron was beyond buying the lies.

'I know now.' Myron showed her the book in his hand. 'Do you know what this is?'

She looked at the book, her face blank.

'It's the yearbook from Curtis's high school. I just got it from Lucinda Elright.'

Deanna Yeller looked so frail, a stiff breeze would send her crashing into the wall. Myron opened the yearbook. 'Duane has had a nose job since then. Maybe some other surgery too, I can't be sure. His hair is different. He's gotten a lot more muscular, but then again, he's not a skinny sixteen-year-old anymore. Plus he always wears sunglasses in public. Always. Who would recognize him? Who would even imagine Duane Richwood was a murder suspect killed six years ago?'

Deanna stumbled over to a table. She sat down. She pointed weakly to the chair across from her. Myron took it.

'Curtis was a great athlete,' Myron continued, fingering through the pages. 'He was only a sophomore, but he was already starting varsity football and basketball. The high school he went to didn't have a tennis team, but Lucinda told me that didn't stop him. He played as often as he could. He loved the game.'

Deanna Yeller remained still.

'You see, from the beginning I never bought the robbery angle,' Myron said. 'You were quick to call your son a thief, Deanna, but the facts didn't back it up. He was a good kid. He had no record. And he was smart. There was nothing to steal out there. Then I thought maybe it was a drug deal gone bad. That made the most sense. Alexander Cross was a user. Errol Swade was a seller. But that didn't explain why your son was there. I even thought for a while that Curtis and Errol had never gone to the club, that they were just scapegoats. But a fairly reliable witness swears he saw them both. He also said he heard tennis balls being hit at night. He also saw Curtis and Errol each carrying one tennis racket. Why? If you're robbing the place, you carry as many rackets as you can. If you're doing a drug deal, you don't carry any rackets. The answer was obvious in the end: they were there to play tennis. They jumped the fence not to rob the place, but because Curtis wanted to play tennis.'

Deanna lifted her head up. She was hollow-eyed. Her movements were sparse and slow. 'It was a grass court,' she said. 'He'd watched Wimbledon on TV that week. He just wanted to play on a grass court, that's all.'

'Unfortunately Alexander Cross and his buddies were outside getting high,' Myron went on. 'They heard Curtis and Errol. What happened next is not exactly clear, but I think we can probably take Senator Cross's word on this one. Alexander, high as a kite, created a conflict. Maybe he didn't like the idea of a couple of black kids playing on his court. Or maybe he really thought they were there to rob the club. It doesn't matter. What does matter is that Errol Swade took out a knife and killed him. It might have been self-defense, but I doubt it.'

'He just reacted,' Deanna said. 'Stupid kid saw a bunch of white boys, so he stabbed. Errol didn't know any different.'

Myron nodded. 'They ran away then, but Curtis got tackled in the bushes by Valerie Simpson. They struggled. Valerie got a good look at Curtis. A very good look. When you are fighting with someone you believed killed your fiancé, you don't forget the face. Curtis managed to break away. He and Errol jumped the fence and ran down the block. They found a car in a driveway. Errol had been arrested several times already for stealing cars. Breaking in and hot-wiring one was no problem for him. That's what first gave it to me. I talked to the officer who supposedly shot your son. His name is Jimmy Blaine. Jimmy said he shot the *driver* of the car, not the passenger. But Curtis wouldn't have been driving. That wouldn't make any sense. The driver was the experienced thief, not the good kid. So then it dawned on me: Jimmy Blaine didn't shoot Curtis Yeller. He shot Errol Swade.'

Deanna Yeller sat still as a stone.

'The bullet hit Errol in the ribs. With Curtis's help they managed to round the corner and crawl in through the fire escape. They made their way to your apartment. By now sirens were sounding all over the place. They were closing in on all of you. Errol and Curtis were probably in a state of panic. It was pandemonium. They told you what happened. You knew what this meant – a rich white boy stabbed at a fancy rich white club. Your son was doomed. Even if Curtis had only been standing there – even if Errol told the police that it was all his fault – Curtis was finished.'

'I knew more than that,' Deanna interjected. 'It'd been almost an hour since the murder. The radio already said who the victim was. Not just a rich white boy, but the son of a United States senator.'

'And,' Myron continued, 'you knew Errol had a long record. You knew it was his fault. You knew he was going away for good this time. Errol's life was over, and he had no one to blame but himself. But Curtis was innocent. Curtis was a good boy. He'd done everything right, and now because of the stupidity of his cousin, his life was about to be flushed away.'

Deanna looked up. 'But that was all true,' she insisted, sparking up just a bit. 'Can't deny any of that, can you? Can you?'

'No,' Myron said. 'I guess I can't. What you did next probably didn't take much thought. You'd heard the police fire two bullets. You saw only one in Errol. Most important, Curtis didn't have a record. His mug shot wasn't on file. His description wasn't on file.' He stopped. Her eyes were clear and on him. 'Whose gun was it, Deanna?'

'Errol's.'

'He had it with him?'

She nodded.

'So you took the gun. You pressed it against Errol's cheek. And you fired.'

She nodded again.

'You blew his face right off,' Myron continued. 'I wondered about that too. Why would someone shoot him up close in the face? Why not in the back of the head or the heart? The answer is, you didn't want anyone to see his face. You wanted him to be an unrecognizable lump. Then you put on your big act. You cradled him in your arms and cried while the police and the senator's hoods came crashing in. It was so simple really. I asked the medical examiner how they identified Curtis's body. She scoffed at such a ridiculous question. The usual way, she told me. The next of kin. You, Deanna. The mother. What else did they need? Why question that? The cops were thrilled you didn't want to make a big deal over it, so they didn't look too closely. And just to cement your plan, you were smart enough to have the body cremated immediately. Even if someone wanted to go back and check, the evidence was ashes.

'As for Curtis, his escape was easy. A nationwide manhunt began for Errol Swade, a six-foot four-inch man who looked nothing like your son. No one was looking for Curtis Yeller. He was dead.'

'It wasn't quite that easy,' Deanna said. 'Curtis and I were careful. Powerful men were in this. The police scared me, sure, but not as much as those men who worked for the senator. And then the papers all made that Cross boy out to be a hero. Curtis knew the truth. If the senator ever got a hold of my boy . . .' She shrugged away the obvious.

Myron nodded. He'd thought the same thing too. Dead men tell no tales. 'So Curtis spent the next five years underground?' he asked.

'I guess you could call it that,' Deanna said. 'He roamed around, scraped by on whatever he could. I sent him money when I had some, but I told him to never come back to Philadelphia. We'd arrange times to talk on public phones and stuff. He grew up on his own. He lived on the streets, but he was well-spoken enough to get some decent jobs. He worked for three years at a tennis club near Boston. He played all the time, even hustled a few games. I saved up enough for him to get a little plastic surgery done. Just some little touches, you know, in case he ran into someone he knew. Like you said, he got a lot bigger. He grew an inch and put on thirty pounds. He also wore those sunglasses, though I always thought that was going a little too far. No one's gonna recognize him, I thought. Not anymore. It'd been too long. Worst thing happen, someone might think he resembles a dead boy they used to know. I mean, five years passed. We thought he was safe.'

'That's why you started getting money recently,' Myron said. 'It wasn't a payoff. The money came from Duane's turning pro. He bought you this house.'

She nodded.

'And when I saw you two at the hotel that night, I immediately jumped to the conclusion that you were lovers. But it was actually a son visiting his mother. The embrace I saw when he left your room – it wasn't the embrace of lovers, but a mother hugging her son good-bye. In fact Duane hadn't slept around at all. That was an act on his part. Wanda was right all along. He loved her. He never cheated on her. Not with you. And not with Valerie Simpson.'

She nodded again. 'He loves that girl. He and Wanda are good together.'

'Everything was going just fine until Valerie spotted Duane in my office,' Myron continued. 'His sunglasses were off. She saw him up close, and like I said before, you don't forget the face of the man you think killed your fiancé. She recognized him. She stole his card from my Rolodex and called. What happened next, Deanna? Did she threaten to expose him?'

'There's some stuff we left out,' Deanna said. 'I just want to be clear, okay?'

Myron nodded.

'Curtis didn't know I was going to kill Errol that night,' she said. 'I just told him to hide in the basement. There was a closed-off tunnel down there. I knew he'd be safe for a while. I told Errol to stay with me, I'd fix his ribs. When Curtis was out of the room, I shot Errol.'

'Did Curtis ever learn the truth?'

'He figured it out later. But he didn't know then. He had nothing to do with it.'

'So what about Valerie? Was she going to talk?'

'Yes.'

Their eyes met.

'So you killed her,' Myron said.

For a few moments Deanna said nothing. She stared down at her hands, as though looking for something. 'She wouldn't listen to reason,' she said softly. 'Duane told me that Valerie called him. He tried to convince her she had the wrong man, but she wouldn't hear it. So I met up with her at the hotel. I tried to persuade her too. I told her he'd done nothing wrong, but she just kept talking this nonsense about not hiding things anymore – how she'd buried too many things and it had to all come out.' Deanna Yeller closed her eyes and shook her head. 'The girl left me no choice. I watched her hotel. I saw her rush out. I saw her rush to the matches, and I knew she was scared and I knew she was going to say something and I knew I couldn't wait anymore, that I had to stop her now or . . .' She sat still. Then she moved her hands off the table and folded them on her lap. 'I had no choice.'

Myron remained quiet.

'I did the only thing I could,' she said. 'It was her life or my son's life.'

'So for the second time you chose your son.'

'Yes. And if you turn me in, it'll all be for nothing. The truth will come out, and they'll kill my boy. You know they will.'

'I'll protect him,' Myron said.

'No, that's my job.'

Tires squealed in the driveway. Myron rose and looked out the window. It was Duane. He threw the car in park and leaped out.

'Keep him out,' Deanna said, suddenly out of her chair. 'Please.'

'What?'

She ran to the door and threw the dead bolt. 'I don't want him to see.'

'See what?'

But now Myron did see. She turned toward him. She had a gun in her hand. 'I've already killed twice to save him. What's a third?'

Myron looked for a safe place to dive, but for the second time in this case he'd been careless. He was out in the open. It would be impossible to miss. 'Killing me won't make it go away,' he said.

'I know,' she replied.

There was a pounding at the door. Duane shouted, 'Open up! Don't say anything to him!' More pounding.

Deanna's eyes welled with tears. 'Don't tell anyone, Myron. No need to say anything anymore. The guilty will have all been punished.'

She placed the barrel of the gun against her head.

'Don't,' Myron whispered.

From outside the door, Duane shouted, 'Mama! Open up, Mama!'

She turned toward the voice. Myron tried to reach her in time, but he had no chance. She pulled the trigger and made one final sacrifice for her son.

48

Time passed. Myron had to persuade Duane to leave his mother alone. It was what she would have wanted, Myron reminded him. When they were both far enough away, Myron placed an anonymous call to the Cherry Hill police. 'I think I heard a gunshot,' he said. He gave the address and hung up.

They met up at a stop along the New Jersey Turnpike. Duane was no longer crying.

'Are you going to tell?' Duane asked.

'No,' Myron said.

'Not even Valerie's mother?'

'I don't owe her anything.'

Silence. Then Duane started tearing again.

'Did the truth set you free, Myron?'

He ignored the question. 'Tell Wanda,' Myron said. 'If you really love her, tell her everything. It's the only chance you have.'

'You can't be my agent anymore,' Duane said.

'I know,' Myron said.

'There was no other way for her. She had to protect me.'

'There was another way.'

'What? If it was your kid, what would you have done?'

Myron didn't have the answer. He only knew that killing Valerie Simpson was not it. 'Are you going to play tomorrow?'

'Yes,' he said. He climbed back in his car. 'And I'm going to win.'

Myron did not doubt it.

It was late when he got back to New York. He parked the car at the Kinney lot and headed past the ugly intestinal sculpture and into the building. The security guard greeted him. It was Saturday night. Practically no one was there. But even on street level Myron had seen the light on.

He took the elevator to the fourteenth floor. The customary hubbub of activity at Lock-Horne Securities was absent. The floor was dark. Most of the computers had been turned off and covered with plastic, though a few were left on, the bizarre screen savers dancing streaks of lights across the desk. Myron walked toward the light in the corner office. Win was sitting at his desk, reading a book in Korean. He looked up when Myron entered.

'So tell me,' Win said.

Myron did. The whole story.

'Ironic,' Win said when he'd finished.

'What?'

'We kept wondering how a mother could care so little for her son when in reality the problem was just the opposite. She cared too much.'

Myron nodded.

Silence.

Then Win said, 'You know?'

'Yes.'

'How?'

'Dr Abramson,' Myron said. 'Your visiting Valerie enough for her to know your name. It got me thinking.'

Win nodded. 'I was going to tell you.'

'You didn't have to kill him,' Myron said.

'You're a child sometimes,' Win said. 'I did what had to be done.'

'You didn't have to kill him.'

'Frank Ache would have killed us,' Win said. 'The only reason he chose to back off was because Pavel Menansi was dead – ergo the profit was gone. By eliminating Pavel, I took away his motive. Our options were clear: we could have taken on the mob and eventually gotten killed, or we could exterminate a vermin. In the end, sacrificing scum saved our lives.'

'What else did you do to Ache?' Myron asked.

'What do you mean?'

'Frank didn't show up in the woods just to call off a hit. Something had scared him. He told me to mention our meeting to you.'

'Oh,' Win said, 'that.' He stood and grabbed his putter. He dropped a few golf balls on the floor. 'I sent him a little package.'

'What package?'

'One containing Aaron's right testicle. That, added together with Pavel's death, was enough to convince him that it would be in all of our interests to drop the matter.'

Myron shook his head. 'What separates you from Deanna Yeller?'

'Just one thing,' Win said. He lined up a putt and sank it. 'I don't fault her for what she did the night Alexander Cross was murdered. It was practical. It made sense. She didn't trust the justice system. She didn't trust a United States senator. In both cases, she was undoubtedly right. And what did she sacrifice? Her lowlife nephew who would have spent his life behind bars anyway. No, in that case we were the same.'

He lined up over the next putt and checked the lie. 'Where we differ, however, is that she killed an innocent person the second time around. I did not.'

'You're drawing a pretty thin line,' Myron said.

'The world is made up of thin lines, my friend. I was there. I visited Valerie every week in the institution. Did you know that?'

Myron shook his head. He was probably closer to Win than anyone, and he hadn't known that. He hadn't even known he knew Valerie Simpson.

Win took another putt. 'From the first moment I saw her in that godforsaken place I wanted to know what changed her. I wanted to know what monstrosity had deadened the spirit that had soared so. You were the one who figured it out. Pavel Menansi did that to her, just as he would have done it to Janet Koffman if I hadn't stopped him.' Win looked over at Myron. 'You already know this, but I'll say it just the same: the fact that killing Pavel helped us with Frank Ache was just a bonus. I would have killed him anyway. I really didn't need any justification.'

'There were other ways to make him pay,' Myron said.

'How?' Win scoffed. 'By arresting him? No one would press charges. And even if all was revealed as per your plan, what would happen to him? He'd probably write a book and go on *Oprah*. He'd tell the world how he'd been abused as a child or some such nonsense. He'd be an even bigger celebrity.' Win took another putt. Another make. 'We're not the same, you and I. We both know that. But it's okay.'

'It's not okay.'

'Yes, it is. If we were the same it wouldn't work. We'd both be dead by now. Or insane. We balance each other. It's why you're my best friend. It's why I love you.'

Silence.

'Don't do it again,' Myron said.

Win did not reply. He lined up another putt.

'Did you hear me?'

'It's time to move on,' Win said. 'This incident is in the past. You know better than to try to control the future.'

More silence. Win sank another putt.

'Jessica is waiting,' Win said. 'She told me to remind you about her new oils.'

Myron turned and left then. He felt unclean and unsure. But he knew Win was right: it was over. It would just take a bit of time for things to feel normal again. He would recover.

And, Myron thought as he headed into the elevator, what better way to start the healing process than with Jessica's oils?

Fade Away

For Larry and Craig,
the coolest brothers a guy could ever have.
If you don't believe me, just ask them.

Acknowledgement

The author wishes to thank the following for their help: Anne Armstrong-Coben, MD; James Bradbeer, Jr, of Lilly Pulitzer; David Gold, MD; Maggie Griffin; Jacob Hoye; Lidsay Koehler; David Pepe of Pro Agents, Inc.; Peter Roisman of Advantage International; and, of course, Dave Bolt. Any errors – factual or otherwise – are totally their fault. The author is not to blame.

1

'Just behave.'

'Me?' Myron said. 'I'm always a delight.'

Myron Bolitar was being led through the corridor of the darkened Meadowlands Arena by Calvin Johnson, the New Jersey Dragons new general manager. Their dress shoes clacked sharply against the tile and echoed through empty Harry M. Stevens food stands, Carvel Ice Cream carts, pretzel vendors, souvenir booths. The smell of sporting-event hot dogs – that sort of rubbery, chemically, yet nostalgically delicious aroma – wafted from the walls. The stillness of the place consumed them; there is nothing more hollow and lifeless than an empty sports arena.

Calvin Johnson stopped in front of a door leading to a luxury box. 'This may all seem a bit strange,' he said. 'Just go with the flow, okay?'

'Okay.'

Calvin reached for the knob and took a deep breath. 'Clip Arnstein, the owner of the Dragons, is in there waiting for us.'

'And yet I'm not trembling,' Myron said.

Calvin Johnson shook his head. 'Just don't be an ass.'

Myron pointed to his chest. 'I wore a tie and everything.'

Calvin Johnson opened the door. The luxury box faced midcourt. Several workers were putting down the basketball floor over the hockey ice. The Devils had played the night before. Tonight was the Dragons' turn. The box was cosy. Twenty-four cushioned seats. Two television monitors. To the right was a wood-paneled counter for the food – usually fried chicken, hot dogs, potato knishes, sausage and pepper sandwiches, that sort of stuff. To the left was a brass cart with a nicely stocked bar and minifridge. The box also had its own bathroom – this so the corporate high rollers would not have to urinate with the great unwashed.

Clip Arnstein faced them, standing. He wore a dark blue suit with a red tie. He was bald with patches of gray over both ears. He was burly, his chest still a barrel after seventy-some-odd years. His large hands had brown spots and fat blue veins like garden hoses. No one spoke. No one moved. Clip glared hard at Myron for several seconds, examining him from head to toe.

'Like the tie?' Myron asked.

Calvin Johnson shot him a warning glance.

The old man made no movement toward them. 'How old are you now, Myron?'

Interesting opening question. 'Thirty-two.'

'You playing any ball?'

'Some,' Myron said.

'You keep in good shape?'

'Want me to flex?'

'No, that won't be necessary.'

No one offered Myron a seat and no one took one. Of course the only chairs in here were the spectator seats, but it still felt weird to stand in a business setting where you're supposed to sit. Standing suddenly became difficult. Myron felt antsy. He didn't know what to do with his hands. He took out a pen and held it, but that didn't feel right. Too Bob Dole. He stuck his hands in his pockets and stood at a weird angle, like the casual guy in the Sears circular.

'Myron, we have an interesting proposition for you,' Clip Arnstein said.

'Proposition?' Always the probing interrogatory.

'Yes. I was the one who drafted you, you know.'

'I know.'

'Ten, eleven years ago. When I was with the Celtics.'

'I know.'

'First round.'

'I know all this, Mr Arnstein.'

'You were a hell of a prospect, Myron. You were smart. You had an unbelievable touch. You were loaded with talent.'

'I coulda been a contenda,' Myron said.

Arnstein scowled. It was a famous scowl, developed over some fifty-plus years in professional basketball. The scowl had made its first appearance when Clip played for the now-defunct Rochester Royals in the forties. It grew more famous when he coached the Boston Celtics to numerous championships. It became a legendary trademark when he made all the famous trades ('clipping' the competition, ergo the nickname) as team president. Three years ago Clip had become majority owner of the New Jersey Dragons and the scowl now resided in East Rutherford, right off Exit 16 of the New Jersey Turnpike. His voice was gruff. 'Was that supposed to be Brando?'

'Eerie, isn't it? Like Marlon's actually in the room.'

Clip Arnstein's face suddenly softened. He nodded slowly, giving Myron the doelike, father-figure eyes. 'You make jokes to cover the pain,' he said gravely. 'I understand that.'

Dr Joyce Brothers.

'Is there something I can do for you, Mr Arnstein?'

'You never played in a single professional game, did you, Myron?'

'You know very well I didn't.'

Clip nodded. 'Your first preseason game. Third quarter. You already had eighteen points that game. Not bad for a rookie in his first scrimmage. That was when fate took over.'

Fate took the form of big Burt Wesson of the Washington Bullets. There had been a collision, a searing pain, and then nothing.

'Awful thing,' Clip said.

'Uh huh.'

'I always felt bad about what happened to you. Such a waste.'

Myron glanced at Calvin Johnson. Calvin was looking off, arms crossed, his smooth black features a placid pool. 'Uh huh,' Myron said again.

'That's why I'd like to give you another chance.'

Myron was sure he'd heard wrong. 'Pardon?'

'We have a slot open on the team. I'd like to sign you.'

Myron waited. He looked at Clip. Then he looked at Calvin Johnson. Neither one was laughing. 'Where is it?' Myron asked.

'What?'

'The camera. This is one of those hidden camera shows, right? Is this the one with Ed McMahon? I'm a big fan of his work.'

'It's not a joke, Myron.'

'It must be, Mr Arnstein. I haven't played competitive ball in ten years. I shattered my knee, remember?'

'All too well. But as you said, it was ten years ago. I know you went through rehabilitation to rebuild it.'

'And you also know I tried a comeback. Seven years ago. The knee wouldn't hold up.'

'It was still too early,' Clip said. 'You just told me you're playing again.'

'Pick-up games on weekends. It's a tad different than the NBA.'

Clip dismissed the argument with a wave of his hand. 'You're in shape. You even volunteered to flex.'

Myron's eyes narrowed, swerving from Clip to Calvin Johnson, back to Clip. Their expressions were neutral. 'Why do I have the feeling,' Myron asked, 'that I'm missing something here?'

Clip finally smiled. He looked over to Calvin Johnson. Calvin Johnson forced up a return smile.

'Perhaps I should be less' – Clip paused, searched for the word – 'opaque.'

'That might be helpful.'

'I want you on the team. I don't much care if you play or not.'

Myron waited again. When no one continued, he said, 'It's still a bit opaque.'

Clip let loose a long breath. He walked over to the bar, opened a small hotel-style fridge, and removed a can of Yoo-hoo. Stocking Yoo-hoos. Hmm. Clip had been prepared. 'You still drink this sludge?'

'Yes,' Myron said.

He tossed Myron the can and poured something from a decanter into two glasses. He handed one to Calvin Johnson. He signaled to the seats by the glass window. Exactly midcourt. Very nice. Nice leg room too. Even Calvin, who was six-eight, was able to stretch a bit. The three men sat next to one another, all facing the same way, which again felt weird in a business setting. You were supposed to sit across from one another, preferably at a table or desk. Instead they sat shoulder to shoulder, watching the work crew pound the floor into place.

'Cheers,' Clip said.

He sipped his whiskey. Calvin Johnson just held his. Myron, obeying the instructions on the can, shook his Yoo-hoo.

'If I'm not mistaken,' Clip continued, 'you're a lawyer now.'

'I'm a member of the bar,' Myron said. 'I don't practice much law.'

'You're a sports agent.'

'Yes.'

'I don't trust agents,' Clip said.

'Neither do I.'

'For the most part, they're bloodsucking leeches.'

'We prefer the term "parasitic entities," ' Myron said. 'It's more PC.'

Clip Arnstein leaned forward, his eyes zeroing in on Myron's. 'How do I know I can trust you?'

Myron pointed at himself. 'My face,' he said. 'It screams trustworthiness.'

Clip did not smile. He leaned a little closer. 'What I'm about to tell you must remain confidential.'

'Okay.'

'Do you give me your word it won't go any farther than this room?'

'Yes.'

Clip hesitated, glanced at Calvin Johnson, shifted in his seat. 'You know, of course, Greg Downing.'

Of course. Myron had grown up with Greg Downing. From the time they had first competed as sixth graders in a town league less than twenty miles from where Myron now sat, they were instant rivals. When they reached high school, Greg's family moved to the neighboring town of Essex Fells because Greg's father did not want his son sharing the basketball spotlight with Myron. The personal rivalry then began to take serious flight. They played against each other eight times in high school, each winning four games. Myron and Greg became New Jersey's hottest recruits and both matriculated at big-time basketball colleges with a storied rivalry of their own – Myron to Duke, Greg to North Carolina.

The personal rivalry soared.

During their college careers, they had shared two *Sports Illustrated* covers. Both teams won the ACC twice, but Myron picked up a national championship. Both Myron and Greg were picked first-team All-American, both at the guard spots. By the time they both graduated, Duke and North Carolina had played each other twelve times. The Myron-led Duke had won eight of them. When the NBA draft came, both men went in the first round.

The personal rivalry crashed and burned.

Myron's career ended when he collided with big Burt Wesson. Greg Downing sidestepped fate and went on to become one of the NBA premier guards. During his ten-year career with the New Jersey Dragons Downing had been named to the All-Star team eight times. He led the league twice in three-point shooting. Four times he led the league in free-throw percentage and once in assists. He'd been on three *Sports Illustrated* covers and had won an NBA championship.

'I know him,' Myron said.

'Do you talk to him much?' Clip Arnstein asked.

'No.'

'When was the last time you spoke?'

'I don't remember.'

'Within the last few days?'

'I don't think we've spoken in ten years,' Myron said.

'Oh,' Clip said. He took another sip. Calvin had still not touched his drink. 'Well, I'm sure you heard about his injury.'

'Something with his ankle,' Myron said. 'It's day to day. He's in seclusion working on it.'

Clip nodded. 'That's the story we gave the media anyway. It's not exactly the truth.'

'Oh?'

'Greg isn't injured,' Clip said. 'He's missing.'

'Missing?' Again the probing interrogatory.

'Yes.' Clip took another sip. Myron sipped back, not an easy task with Yoo-hoo.

'Since when?' Myron asked.

'Five days now.'

Myron looked at Calvin. Calvin remained placid but he had that kind of face. During his playing days, his nickname had been Frosty because he never displayed emotion. He was living up to his name now.

Myron tried again. 'When you say Greg is missing—'

'Gone,' Clip snapped. 'Disappeared. Into thin air. Without a trace. Whatever you want to call it.'

'Have you called the police?'

'No.'

'Why not?'

Clip gave him the wave-off again. 'You know Greg. He's not a conventional guy.'

The understatement of the millennium.

'He never does the expected,' Clip said. 'He hates the fame. He likes to be on his own. He's even disappeared before, though never during a playoff drive.'

'So?'

'So there's a good chance he's just being his usually flaky self,' Clip continued. 'Greg can shoot like a dream, but let's face facts: the man is a couple of sandwiches short of a picnic. You know what Downing does after games?'

Myron shook his head.

'He drives a cab in the city. That's right, a goddamn yellow taxi cab in New York City. Says it keeps him close to the common man. Greg won't do appearances or endorsements. He doesn't do interviews. He doesn't even do the charity thing. He dresses like something out of a seventies sitcom. The man is a nut job.'

'All of which makes him immensely popular with the fans,' Myron said. 'Which sells tickets.'

'I agree,' Clip said, 'but that just underlines my point. If we call the cops it could damage both him and the team. Can you imagine the media circus if this got out?'

'It would be bad,' Myron admitted.

'Exactly. And suppose Greg is just hanging out in French Lick or whatever hickville town he goes to in the off-season, fishing or something? Christ, we'd never hear the end of it. On the other hand, suppose he's up to something.'

'Up to something?' Myron repeated.

'Hell, I don't know. I'm just talking here. But I don't need a goddamn scandal. Not now. Not with the playoffs coming up, you know what I'm saying?'

Not really, but Myron decided to let it go for now. 'Who else knows about this?'

'Just the three of us.'

The work crew rolled in the baskets. Two extras were kept in storage in case someone pulled a Darryl Dawkins and shattered a backboard. They then began putting down additional seats. Like most arenas, the Meadowlands holds more seats for basketball than hockey – in this case around a thousand more. Myron took another sip of Yoo-hoo and let it roll around his tongue. He waited until it slid down his throat before he asked the obvious question. 'So how do I fit in?'

Clip hesitated. His breathing was deep, almost labored. 'I know something of your years with the FBI,' he said finally. 'No details, of course. Not even vagaries really, but enough to know you have a background in this kinda stuff. We want you to find Greg. Quietly.'

Myron said nothing. His 'undercover' work for the feds, it seemed, was the worst kept secret in the continental United States. Clip sipped his drink. He looked at Calvin's full glass, then at Calvin. Calvin finally took a sip. Clip turned his attention back to Myron. 'Greg's divorced now,' Clip went on. 'He's basically a loner. All his friends – hell, all his acquaintances – are teammates. They're his support group, if you will. His family. If anyone knows where he is – if anyone's helping him stay hidden – it's got to be one of the Dragons. I'll be honest with you. These guys are a major pain in the ass. Spoiled, pampered prima donnas who think our purpose in life is to serve them. But they all have one thing in common: They see management as the enemy. Us against the world and all that crap. They won't tell us the truth. They won't tell reporters the truth. And if you approach them as some, uh, "parasitic entity," they won't talk to you either. You have to be a player. It's the only way to get on the inside.'

'So you want me to join the team so I can find Greg.'

Myron heard the echoes of hurt in his voice. It was unintentional, but he saw that both men heard it too. His face flushed in embarrassment.

Clip put a hand on his shoulder. 'I meant what I said, Myron. You could have been great. One of the greatest.'

Myron took a deep swig of his Yoo-hoo. No more sipping. 'I'm sorry, Mr Arnstein. I can't help you.'

The scowl was back. 'What?'

'I have a life. I'm a sports agent. I have clients to tend to. I can't just drop it all.'

'You'll get the player's minimum prorated. That's two hundred thousand dollars less whatever. And there's only a couple of weeks left until the playoffs. We'll keep you on till then no matter what.'

'No. My playing days are over. And I'm not a private investigator.'

'But we need to find him. He could be in danger.'

'I'm sorry. The answer is no.'

Clip smiled. 'Suppose I sweeten the pot.'

'No.'

'Fifty-thousand-dollar signing bonus.'

'I'm sorry.'

'Greg could show up tomorrow and you'd still get to keep that. Fifty grand. Plus a share of playoff money.'

'No.'

Clip sat back. He stared at his drink, dipped his finger into it, stirred. His voice was casual. 'You say you're an agent, right?'

'Yes.'

'I'm very friendly with the parents of three guys that will go in the first round. Did you know that?'

'No.'

'Suppose,' Clip said slowly, 'I guarantee you that one of them signs with you.'

Myron pricked up. A first round draft pick. He tried to keep his

497

expression cool – to do like Frosty – but his heart was thumping. 'How can you do that?'

'Don't worry about how.'

'It doesn't sound ethical.'

Clip made a scoffing noise. 'Myron, don't play choirboy with me. You do me this favor and MB SportsReps gets a first round draft pick. Guaranteed. No matter how this thing with Greg plays out.'

MB SportsReps. Myron's company. Myron Bolitar, ergo MB. Representing sports people, ergo SportsReps. Add it together: MB SportsReps. Myron came up with that name on his own but still no offers came in from major advertising companies to use his services.

'Make it a hundred-thousand-dollar signing bonus,' Myron said.

Clip smiled. 'You've learned well, Myron.'

Myron shrugged.

'Seventy-five thousand,' Clip said. 'And you'll take it so don't bullshit a bullshitter.'

The two men shook hands.

'I have a few more questions about the disappearance,' Myron said.

Using both armrests Clip rose and stood over Myron. 'Calvin will answer all your questions,' he said with a nod toward his general manager. 'I have to go now.'

'So when do you want me to start practicing?'

Clip looked surprised. 'Practicing?'

'Yeah. When do you want me to start?'

'We have a game tonight.'

'Tonight?'

'Of course,' Clip said.

'You want me to suit up tonight?'

'We're playing our old team, the Celtics. Calvin will make sure you have a uniform by game time. Press conference at six to announce your signing. Don't be late.' Clip headed toward the door. 'And wear that tie. I like it.'

'Tonight?' Myron repeated, but Clip was already gone.

2

After Clip left the box, Calvin Johnson allowed himself a small smile. 'I warned you it would be strange.'

'Serious strange,' Myron agreed.

'Finished with your nutritious chocolate beverage?'

Myron put down the can. 'Yeah.'

'Come on. Let's get you ready for the big debut.'

Calvin Johnson walked fluidly, back straight. He was black, six-foot-eight, thin but not gawky or disproportionate. He wore an olive Brooks Brothers suit. Perfectly tailored. Perfectly knotted tie. Perfectly shined shoes. His tightly kinked hair was receding, making his forehead overly prominent and shiny. When Myron matriculated at Duke, Calvin had been a senior at North Carolina. That made him around thirty-five years old, though he looked older. Calvin had enjoyed a solid pro career over eleven seasons. When he retired three years ago, everyone knew he'd end up in the front office. He started off as an assistant coach, moved to player personnel, and just recently was promoted to vice president and general manager of the New Jersey Dragons. These however were just titles. Clip ran the show. General managers, vice presidents, player personnel, trainers, even coaches all bent to his will.

'I hope you're all right with this,' Calvin said.

'Why wouldn't I be all right?'

Calvin shrugged. 'I played against you,' he said.

'So?'

'You were the most competitive son of a bitch I ever faced,' Calvin said. 'You'd stomp on someone's head to win. Now you're going to be a pissant bench-warmer. How's that going to sit with you?'

'I can handle it,' Myron said.

'Uh huh.'

'I've mellowed over the years.'

Calvin shook his head. 'I don't think so.'

'No?'

'You may think you've mellowed. You may even think you've got basketball out of your system.'

499

'I have.'

Calvin stopped, smiled, spread his arms. 'Sure you have. Just look at you. You could be the poster child for life after sports. A fine example to your fellow athletes. Your whole career crashed down around your ears, but you rose to the challenge. You went back to school – at Harvard Law no less. You started up your own business – a growing company in the field of sports representation. You still dating that writer?'

He meant Jessica. Their togetherness seemed to always be an iffy thing but Myron said, 'Yes.'

'So you got the education, the job, and the gorgeous girlfriend. Yep, on the outside you're happy and well adjusted.'

'On the inside too.'

Calvin shook his head. 'I don't think so.'

Everyone's Dr Joyce Brothers. 'Hey, I didn't ask to be put on the team.'

'No, but you didn't argue much either – except to up your price.'

'I'm an agent. That's what I do. I up the price.'

Calvin stopped and looked at Myron. 'Do you really think you have to be on the team to find Greg?'

'Clip seemed to think so.'

'Clip is a great man,' Calvin said, 'but he often has ulterior motives.'

'Like what?'

Calvin did not respond. He started walking again.

They reached the elevator. Calvin pressed the button and the doors immediately slid open. They stepped inside and began to descend. 'Look me in the eye,' Calvin said. 'Look me in the eye and tell me you never think about playing again.'

'Who doesn't *think* about it?' Myron countered.

'Yeah, but tell me you don't take it one step further. Tell me you never drift off and dream about making a comeback. Even now, when you're watching a game on TV, tell me you don't sit there and do a slow burn. Tell me you never watch Greg and think about all the adulation and fame. Tell me you never say, "I was better than him," because it's the truth. Greg is great. One of the top ten players in the league. But you were better, Myron. We both know that.'

'Long time ago,' Myron said.

Calvin smiled. 'Yeah,' he said. 'Right.'

'What's your point?'

'You're here to find Greg. Once he's found, you're gone. The novelty will be over. Clip will be able to say he gave you a chance, but you weren't up to the challenge. He'll still be the good guy with the good press.'

'Good press,' Myron repeated, remembering the upcoming press conference. 'One of his ulterior motives?'

Calvin shrugged. 'Doesn't matter. What does matter is that you understand you don't have a chance. You're only going to play during scrub time and we rarely win or lose by a lot so that doesn't happen and even if it does, even if you play spectacularly, we both know it's scrub time. And you won't play well because you are such a competitive son of a bitch, you need the points to mean something to the outcome of the game or you don't play your best.'

'I understand,' Myron said.

'I hope you do, my friend.' Calvin looked up at the numbered lights. The lights flickered in his brown eyes. 'Dreams never die. Sometimes you think they're dead, but they're just hibernating like some big old bear. And if the dream has been hibernating for a long time, that bear is going to wake up grumpy and hungry.'

'You should write country songs,' Myron said.

Calvin shook his head. 'Just giving a friend fair warning.'

'Much obliged. Now why don't you tell me what you know about Greg's disappearance?'

The elevator stopped and the doors opened. Calvin led the way. 'Not much to tell,' he said. 'We played against the Sixers in Philly. After the game Greg got on the bus with everybody else. When we got here, he got off the bus with everybody else. The last time anyone saw him he was getting into his car. The end.'

'How did Greg seem that night?'

'Fine. He played well against Philly. Scored twenty-seven points.'

'And his mood?'

Calvin thought about it. 'Nothing I noticed,' he said.

'Anything new going on in his life?'

'New?'

'Changes, that kind of thing.'

'Well, the divorce,' Calvin said. 'It's been nasty. I understand Emily can be quite difficult.' He stopped walking again and smiled at Myron. The Cheshire cat smile. Myron stopped but did not return the smile.

'Something on your mind, Frosty?'

The smile spread a bit farther. 'Weren't you and Emily an item at one time?'

'A lifetime ago.'

'College sweethearts, if I recall.'

'Like I said, a lifetime ago.'

'So,' Calvin said, starting to walk again, 'you were even better with the women than Greg.'

Myron ignored the comment. 'Does Clip know about my so-called past with Emily?'

'He's very thorough.'

'So that explains why you chose me,' Myron said.

'It was a consideration, but I don't think it's too important.'

'Oh?'

'Greg hates Emily. He'd never confide in her. But since this whole custody battle started there's definitely been a change in Greg.'

'How so?'

'For one thing, he signed a deal with Forte sneakers.'

Myron was surprised. 'Greg? An endorsement deal?'

'It's very hush-hush,' Calvin said. 'They're supposed to announce it end of the month, right before the playoffs.'

Myron whistled. 'They must have paid him a bundle.'

'A bundle and a half, I hear. Upwards of ten million a year.'

'Makes sense,' Myron said. 'A popular player who has refused to endorse any products for more than a decade – it's an irresistible draw. Forte does well with track and tennis shoes, but they're fairly unknown in the basketball world. Greg gives them instant credibility.'

'That he does,' Calvin agreed.

'Any idea why he changed his mind after all these years?'

Calvin shrugged. 'Maybe Greg realized he wasn't getting any younger and wanted to cash in. Maybe this whole divorce thing. Maybe he got whacked on the head and woke up with an iota of sanity.'

'Where's he been living since the divorce?'

'In the house in Ridgewood. It's in Bergen County.'

Myron knew it well. He asked for the address. Calvin gave it to him. 'What about Emily?' Myron asked. 'Where's she staying?'

'She and the kids are with her mother. I think they're in Franklin Lakes or thereabouts.'

'Have you done any checking yet – Greg's house, his credit cards, bank accounts?'

Calvin shook his head. 'Clip thought this thing was too big to trust to an agency. That's why we called you. I've driven past Greg's house a few times, knocked on the door once. No car in the driveway or garage. No lights on.'

'But no one's checked inside the house?'

'No.'

'So for all you know he slipped in the bathtub and hit his head.'

Calvin looked at him. 'I said, no lights on. You think he bathed in the dark?'

'That's a good point,' Myron said.

'Some hotshot investigator.'

'I'm a slow starter.'

They arrived at the team room. 'Wait here,' Calvin said.

Myron took out his cellular. 'Mind if I make a call?'

'Go ahead.'

Calvin disappeared behind the door. Myron turned on the power and dialed. Jessica answered on the second ring. 'Hello?'

'I'm going to have to cancel dinner tonight,' Myron said.

'You better have a good excuse,' Jessica said.

'A great one. I'll be playing professional basketball for the New Jersey Dragons.'

'That's nice. Have a good game, dear.'

'I'm serious. I'm playing for the Dragons. Actually, "playing" is probably not the right word. Might be more accurate to say I'll be getting fanny sores for the Dragons.'

'Are you for real?'

'It's a long story, but yes, I'm now officially a professional basketball player.'

Silence.

'I've never boffed a professional basketball player,' Jessica said. 'I'll be just like Madonna.'

'Like a virgin,' Myron said.

'Wow. Talk about a dated reference.'

'Yeah, well, what can I say. I'm an eighties kinda guy.'

'So, Mr Eighties, you going to tell me what's going on?'

'No time now. Tonight. After the game. I'll leave a ticket at the window.'

Calvin stuck his head back in. 'What's your waist? Thirty-four?'

'Thirty-six. Maybe thirty-seven.'

Calvin nodded and withdrew. Myron dialed the private line of Windsor Horne Lockwood III, president of the prestigious investment firm of Lock-Horne Securities in midtown Manhattan. Win answered on the third ring.

'Articulate,' Win said.

Myron shook his head. 'Articulate?'

'I said articulate, not repeat.'

'We have a case,' Myron said.

'Oh yippee,' he drawled in that preppy, Philly Main-Line accent of his. 'I'm enthralled. I'm elated. But before I completely wet myself, I must ask one question.'

'Shoot.'

'Is this case of your customary charity persuasion?'

'Wet away,' Myron said. 'The answer is no.'

'What? No moral crusade for brave Myron?'

'Not this time.'

'Heavens be, do tell.'

'Greg Downing is missing. It's our job to find him.'

'And for services rendered we receive?'

'At least seventy-five grand plus a first round draft pick as a client.' Now was not the time to fill Win in on his temporary career change.

'My, my,' Win said happily. 'Pray tell, what shall we do first?'

Myron gave him the address of Greg's house in Ridgewood. 'Meet me there in two hours.'

'I'll take the Batmobile,' Win said and hung up.

Calvin returned. He held out a purple-and-aqua Dragon uniform. 'Try this on.'

Myron did not reach for it right away. He stared at it, his stomach twisting and diving. When he spoke his voice was soft. 'Number thirty-four?'

'Yeah,' Calvin said. 'Your old number at Duke. I remembered.'

Silence.

Calvin finally broke it. 'Go try it on.'

Myron felt something well up in his eye. He shook his head. 'No need,' he said. 'I'm sure it's the right size.'

3

Ridgewood was a primo suburb, one of those old towns that still calls itself a village, where ninety-five percent of the students go on to college and no one lets their kids associate with the other five percent. There were a couple of strips of tract housing, a few examples of the mid-sixties suburban explosion, but for the most part Ridgewood's fine homes dated from an earlier, theoretically more innocent time.

Myron found the Downing house without any problem. Old Victorian. Very big but not unwieldy, three levels with perfectly faded cedar shingles. On the left side there was one of those rounded towers with a pointy top. Lots of outdoor porch space with all the Rockwellian touches: the kind of double swing where Atticus and Scout would share a lemonade on a hot Alabama night; a child's bicycle tipped on its side; a Flexible Flyer snow sled, though it hadn't snowed in six weeks. The required basketball hoop hung slightly rusted over the driveway. Fire Department 'Tot Finder' stickers glistened red and silver from two upstairs windows. Old oak trees lined the walk like weathered sentries.

Win hadn't arrived yet. Myron parked and rolled down a window. The perfect mid-March day. The sky was robin-egg blue. The birds chirped in cliché. He tried to picture Emily here, but the picture would not hold. It was far easier to see her in a New York high rise or one of those nouveau-riche mansions all done in white with Erté sculptures and silver pearls and too many gaudy mirrors. Then again he hadn't spoken to Emily in ten years. She may have changed. Or he may have misjudged her all those years ago. Wouldn't be the first time.

Funny being back in Ridgewood. Jessica had grown up here. She didn't like coming back anymore, but now the two loves of his life – Jessica and Emily – had something else in common: the village of Ridgewood. That could be added to the list of commonalities between the two women – stuff like meeting Myron, being courted by Myron, falling in love with Myron, crushing Myron's heart like a tomato under a stiletto heel. The usual fare.

Emily had been his first. Freshman year of college was late to lose one's virginity, if one were to listen to the boasts of friends. But if there had indeed been a sexual revolution among American teenagers in the late seventies/early eighties, Myron had either missed it or been on the wrong side. Women had always liked him – it wasn't that. But while his friends discoursed in great detail on their various orgylike experiences, Myron seemed to attract the wrong girls, the nice girls, the ones who still said no – or would have had Myron had the courage (or foresight) to try.

That changed in college when he met Emily.

Passion. It's a word bandied about quite a bit, but Myron thought it might apply here. At a minimum, unconfined lust. Emily was the type of woman a man labels 'hot,' as opposed to 'beautiful.' See a truly 'beautiful' woman and you want to paint or write a poem. See Emily and you want to engage in mutual fabric-ripping. She was raw sexuality, maybe ten pounds bigger than she should have been but those pounds were exquisitely distributed. The two of them made a potent mix. They were both under twenty, both away from home for the first time, both creative.

In a word: *kaboom.*

The car phone rang. Myron picked it up.

'I assume,' Win said, 'that you plan on having us break into the Downing residence.'

'Yes.'

'Then parking your car in front of said residence would not be a sound decision, would it?'

Myron glanced about. 'Where are you?'

'Drive down to the end of the block. Make a left, then your second right. I'm parked behind the office building.'

Myron hung up and restarted the car. He followed the directions and pulled into the lot. Win leaned against his Jaguar with his arms crossed. He looked, as he always did, as if he were posing for the cover of *WASP Quarterly.* His blond hair was perfectly in place. His complexion slightly ruddy, his features porcelain and high and a little too perfect. He wore khaki pants, a blue blazer, Top-Siders sans socks, and a loud Lilly Pulitzer tie. Win looked like what you'd picture a guy named Windsor Horne Lockwood III to look like – elitist, self-absorbed, wimpy.

Well, two out of three ain't bad.

The office building held an eclectic mix. Gynecologist. Electrolysis. Subpoena delivery service. Nutritionist. Women-only health club. Not surprisingly Win was standing near the entrance to the women-only health club. Myron approached.

'How did you know I was parked in front of the house?'

Keeping his eye on the entranceway Win motioned with his head. 'Up that hill. You can see everything with a pair of binoculars.'

A woman in her early twenties wearing a black Lycra aerobics suit walked out carrying a baby. It hadn't taken her long to get her figure back. Win smiled at her. The woman smiled back.

'I love young mothers,' Win said.

'You love women in Lycra,' Myron corrected.

Win nodded. 'There's that.' He snapped on a pair of sunglasses. 'Shall we begin?'

'You think breaking into that house will be a problem?'

Win made his I'll-pretend-you-didn't-ask-that face. Another woman exited the health club; sadly, this one did not warrant a Win smile. 'Fill me in,' Win said. 'And move away. I want to make sure they can see the Jag.'

Myron told him all he knew. Eight women came out in the five minutes it took to tell the story. Only two of them were awarded The Smile. One wore a tiger-striped leotard. She was treated to the Full-Wattage Smile, the one that almost touched Win's eyes.

Win's face did not seem to register anything Myron said. Even when he told him about taking Greg's temporary slot on the Dragons, Win went on staring hopefully at the health club door. Normal Win behavior. Myron finished up by asking, 'Any questions?'

Win bounced a finger against his lip. 'Do you think the one in the tiger-striped leotard was wearing any underwear?'

'I don't know,' Myron said, 'but she was definitely wearing a wedding band.'

Win shrugged. Didn't matter to him. Win didn't believe in love or relationships with the opposite sex. Some might take this for simple sexism. They'd be wrong. Women weren't objects to Win; objects sometimes got his respect.

'Follow me,' Win said.

They were less than half a mile from the Downing house. Win had already scouted it out and found the path with the least chance of being seen or arousing suspicion. They walked in the comfortable silence of two men who had known each other a long time and very well.

'There's one interesting aside in all this,' Myron said.

Win waited.

'Do you remember Emily Schaeffer?' Myron asked.

'The name rings a bell.'

'I dated her for two years at Duke.' Win and Myron had met at Duke. They had also been roommates for all four years. It had been Win who had introduced Myron to the martial arts, who had gotten him involved with Feds. Win was now a top producer at his Lock-Horne Securities on Park Avenue, a securities firm that had been run by Win's family since the market had first opened. Myron rented space from Win, and Win also handled all money-matters for MB SportsReps' clients.

Win thought a bit. 'Is she the one who used to make the little monkey noises?'

'No,' Myron said.

Win seemed surprised. 'Who was the one who made the little monkey noises?'

'I have no idea.'

'Maybe it was someone I was with.'

'Maybe.'

Win considered this, shrugged. 'What about her?'

'She used to be married to Greg Downing.'

'Divorced?'

'Yep.'

'I remember her now,' Win said. 'Emily Schaeffer. Built.'

Myron nodded.

'I never liked her,' Win said. 'Except for those little monkey noises. They were rather interesting.'

'She wasn't the one who made monkey noises.'

Win smiled gently. 'The walls were thin,' he said.

'And you used to listen in?'

'Only when you pulled down the shade so I couldn't watch.'

Myron shook his head. 'You're a pig,' he said.

'Better than a monkey.'

They reached the front lawn and proceeded to the door. The secret was to look like you belonged. If you scurried around back, hunched over, someone might take notice. Two men in ties approaching the door does not normally lead one to think thief.

There was a metal keypad with a little red light. The light was on.

'Alarm,' Myron said.

Win shook his head. 'Fake. It's just a light. Probably bought it at Sharper Image.' Win looked at the lock and made a tsk-tsk noise. 'A Kwiktight brand on a pro basketball player's salary,' he said, clearly disgusted. 'Might as well use Play-Doh.'

'What about the dead bolt?' Myron asked.

'It's not locked.'

Win already had out his strip of celluloid. Credit cards are too stiff. Celluloid worked much better – known as 'loiding the lock. In no more time than it would take with a key, the door was open and they were inside the front foyer. The door had a chute and the mail was all over the place. Myron quickly checked some postage dates. No one had been here in at least five days.

The decor was nice in a fake-rustic, Martha Stewart sort of way. The furniture was what they called 'simple country' where the look was indeed simple and the price outrageous. Lots of pines and wickers and antiques and dry flowers. The smell of potpourri was strong and cloying.

They split up. Win went upstairs to the home office. He turned on the computer and began to download everything onto floppy disks. Myron found the answering machine in a room that used to be called a 'den' but now went by such lofty titles as the 'California room' or 'great room.' The machine announced the time and date of each message. Awfully convenient. Myron pressed a button. The tape rewound and started playing. On the first message, which according to the digital voice was received at 9:18 P.M. the night Greg vanished, Myron hit bingo.

A shaky woman's voice said, 'It's Carla. I'll be in the back booth until midnight.' Click.

Myron rewound and listened again. There were lots of noises in the background – people chatting, music, glasses clinking. The call had probably been placed from a bar or restaurant, especially with that back-booth reference. So who was this Carla? A girlfriend? Probably. Who else would call that late to set up a meeting for even later that night? But of course this had not been just any night. Greg Downing had vanished sometime between the time this call was made and the next morning.

Strange coincidence.

So where did they meet – assuming Greg had indeed made their back-booth liaison? And why did Carla, whoever she might be, sound so shaky – or was this just Myron's imagination?

Myron listened to the rest of the tape. No other messages from Carla. If Greg hadn't shown up at said back booth, wouldn't Carla have called again? Probably. So for now, Myron could safely assume that Greg Downing had seen Carla sometime before his disappearance.

A clue.

There were also four calls from Martin Felder, Greg's agent. He seemed to grow more perturbed with each message. The last one said, 'Jesus, Greg, how can you not call me? Is the ankle serious or what? And don't go incom-municado on me now, not when we're wrapping up the Forte deal. Call me, okay?' There were also three calls from a man named Chris Darby who apparently worked for Forte Sports Incorporated. He too sounded panicked. 'Marty won't tell me where you are. I think he's playing a game with us, Greg, trying to up the price or something. But we had a deal, am I right? Let me give you my home number, okay, Greg? How bad's this injury anyhow?'

Myron smiled. Martin Felder's client was missing, but he was doing all he could to turn it into a positive lever. Agents. He pressed the mode button on the answering machine several times. Eventually the LCD screen scrolled to reveal the code number Greg had set to call in for messages: 317. A fairly new trick of the trade. Now Myron could call in anytime, press 317, and hear what messages had been left on the machine. He hit the redial button on the phone. Another fairly new trick. Find out who Greg called last. The phone rang twice and was picked up by a woman saying, 'Kimmel Brothers.' Whoever they were. Myron hung up.

Myron joined up with Win in the upstairs office. Win continued copying onto computer disks while Myron went through the drawers. Nothing particularly helpful.

They moved on to the master bedroom. The king-size bed was made. Both night tables were cluttered with pens and keys and papers.

Both.

Curious for a man who lived alone.

Myron's eyes swept the room and landed on a reading chair that doubled as a dressing dummy. Greg's clothes were strewn over one arm and the back. Normal enough, Myron guessed – neater than Myron, in fact, though that wasn't saying much. But looking again, he noticed something a tad strange on the other arm of the chair. Two articles of clothing. A white blouse and a gray skirt.

Myron looked at Win.

'They might belong to Miss Monkey Noises,' Win said.

Myron shook his head. 'Emily hasn't lived here in months. Why would her clothes still be on a chair?'

The bathroom, too, proved interesting. A large Jacuzzi on the right, a big steam shower with a sauna, and two vanities. They checked the vanities first. One contained a can of men's shaving cream, a roll-on deodorant, a bottle of Polo after-shave, a Gillette Atra razor. The other vanity had an open makeup case, Calvin Klein perfume, baby powder, and Secret Roll-On. A sprinkling of baby powder was on the floor near the vanity. There were also two disposable Lady Schick razors in the soap dish next to the Jacuzzi.

'He's got a girlfriend,' Myron said.

'A professional basketball player shacking up with some nubile lass,' Win remarked. 'Quite a revelation. Perhaps one of us should cry out, "Eureka."'

'Yes, but it raises an interesting question,' Myron said. 'If her boyfriend had suddenly vanished, wouldn't said lover have reported it?'

'Not,' Win said, 'if she were with him.'

Myron nodded. He told Win about the cryptic message from Carla.

Win shook his head. 'If they were planning on running away,' he said, 'why would she say where they were meeting?'

'She didn't say where. Only in a back booth at midnight.'

'Still,' Win said. 'It's not exactly the kind of thing you do before you disappear. Let's say that for some reason Carla and Greg decide to vanish for a little while. Wouldn't Greg know where and when to meet her before the fact?'

Myron shrugged. 'Maybe she was changing their meeting place.'

'From what? Front booths to back booths?'

'Damned if I know.'

They checked the rest of the upstairs. Not much doing. Greg's son's bedroom had racing-car wallpaper and a poster of Dad driving past Penny Hardaway for a layup. The daughter's room was done in Early American Barney – dinosaurs and purple. No clues. In fact there were no other clues until they reached the basement.

When they turned on the lights, Myron saw it right away.

It was a finished basement, a brightly colored playroom for the kids. There were lots of Little Tikes cars and big Legos and a plastic house with a sliding board. There were scenes from Disney movies like *Aladdin* and *The Lion King* on the wall. There was a television and a VCR. There was stuff too for when the kids got a little older – a pinball machine, a jukebox. There were small rocking chairs and mattresses and knock-around couches.

There was also blood. A fair amount of it in drips on the floor. Another fair amount smeared on a wall.

Bile nestled in Myron's throat. He had seen blood many times in his life, but it still left him queasy. Not so with Win. Win approached the crimson stains with something akin to amusement on his face. He bent to get a better look. Then he stood back up.

'Look at the bright side,' Win said. 'Your temporary slot on the Dragons may become more permanent.'

4

There was no body. Just the blood.

Using Glad sandwich bags he found in the kitchen, Win collected a few samples. Ten minutes later they were back outside, the lock on the front door reengaged. A blue Oldsmobile Delta 88 drove past them. Two men sat in the front seat. Myron glanced at Win. Win barely nodded.

'A second pass,' Myron said.

'Third,' Win said. 'I saw them when I first drove up.'

'They're not exactly experts at this,' Myron said.

'No,' Win agreed. 'But of course, they hadn't known the job would require expertise.'

'Can you run the plates?'

Win nodded. 'I'll also run Greg's ATM and credit card transactions,' he said. He reached the Jag and unlocked it. 'I'll contact you when I have something. It shouldn't take more than a few hours.'

'You heading back to the office?'

'I'm going to Master Kwon's first,' Win said.

Master Kwon was their tae kwon do instructor. Both of them were black belts – Myron a third degree, Win a sixth degree, one of the highest ranking Caucasians in the world. Win was the best martial artist Myron had ever seen. He studied several different arts including Brazilian jujitsu, animal kung fu, and Jeet Kun Do. Win the Contradiction. See Win and you think pampered, preppy panty-waist; in reality, he was a devastating fighter. See Win and you think normal, well-adjusted human being; in reality, he was anything but.

'What are you doing tonight?' Myron asked.

Win shrugged. 'I'm not sure.'

'I can get you a ticket to the game,' Myron said.

Win said nothing.

'Do you want to go?'

'No.'

Without another word, Win slipped behind the wheel of his Jag, started the engine, peeled out with nary a squeal. Myron stood and watched him speed away, puzzled by his friend's abruptness. But then again, to paraphrase one of the four questions of Passover: why should today be different than any other day?

He checked his watch. He still had a few hours before the big press conference. Enough time to get back to the office and tell Esperanza about his career shift. More than anyone else, his playing for the Dragons would affect her.

He took Route 4 to the George Washington Bridge. There was no waiting at the tolls. Proof there was a God. The Henry Hudson however was backed up. He swung off near Columbia Presbyterian Medical Center to get on Riverside Drive. The squeegee guys – the homeless men who 'cleaned' your windshield with a mixture of equal parts grease, Tabasco sauce, and urine – were no longer at the light. Mayor Giuliani's doing, Myron guessed. They had been replaced by Hispanic men selling flowers and something that looked like construction paper. He asked once what it was and had gotten an answer back in Spanish. As much as Myron could translate, the paper smelled nice and spruced up any home. Maybe that was what Greg used as potpourri.

Riverside Drive was relatively quiet. Myron arrived at his Kinney lot on 46th Street and tossed Mario the keys. Mario did not park the Ford Taurus up front with the Rolls, the Mercedes, Win's Jag; in fact, he usually managed to find a cozy spot underneath what must have been a nesting ground for loose-stooled pigeons. Car discrimination. It was an ugly thing, but where were the support groups?

The Lock-Horne Securities Building was on Park Avenue and 46th, perpendicular to the Helmsley building. High-rent district. The street bustled with the doings of big finance. Several stretch limos double-parked illegally in front of the building. The ugly modern sculpture that looked like someone's intestines stood pitifully in its usual place. Men and women in business attire sat on the steps, eating sandwiches too hurriedly, lost in their own thoughts, many talking to themselves, rehearsing for an important afternoon meeting or rehashing a morning mistake. People who worked in Manhattan learned how to be surrounded by others yet remain completely alone.

Myron entered the lobby and pressed the button for the elevator. He nodded to the three Lock-Horne Hostesses, known to everyone else as the Lock-Horne Geishas. They were all model/actress wanna-bes, hired to escort high rollers up to the offices of Lock-Horne Securities and look attractive while doing it. Win had brought the idea home after a trip to the Far East. Myron guessed this could be more blatantly sexist, but he wasn't sure how.

Esperanza Diaz, his valued associate, greeted him at the door. 'Where the hell have you been?'

'We need to talk,' he said.

'Later. You've got a million messages.'

Esperanza wore a white blouse – an absolute killer look against her dark hair, dark eyes, and that dark skin that shimmered like moonlight on the Mediterranean. Esperanza had been spotted by a modeling scout when she was seventeen, but her career took a few weird turns and she ended up making it big in the world of professional wrestling. Yes, professional wrestling. She'd been known as Little Pocahontas, the brave Indian Princess, the jewel of the Fabulous Ladies of Wrestling (FLOW) organization. Her costume was a suede bikini, and she was always cast as the good guy in the morality play that was professional wrestling. She was young, petite, tight-bodied, gorgeous, and though of Latin origin, she was dark enough to pass for Native American. Racial backgrounds were irrelevant to FLOW. The real name of Mrs Saddam Hussein, the evil harem girl in the black veil, was Shari Weinberg.

The phone rang. Esperanza picked it up. 'MB SportsReps. Hold on a moment, he's right here.' She flashed the eyes at him. 'Perry McKinley. It's his third call today.'

'What does he want?'

She shrugged. 'Some people don't like dealing with underlings.'

'You're not an underling.'

She looked at him blankly. 'You going to take it or not?'

Being a sports agent was – to use computer terminology – a multitasking environment with the capability of performing a variety of services with but a click of a button. It was more than simple negotiating. Agents were expected to be accountants, financial planners, real estate agents, hand-holders, personal shoppers, travel agents, family counselors, marriage counselors, chauffeurs, errand boys, parental liaisons, lackeys, butt-kissers, you name it. If you weren't willing to do all that for a client – to be what is known as a 'full service agency' – the next guy would be.

The only way to compete was to have a team, and Myron felt he had assembled a small yet extremely effective one. Win, for example, handled all the finances for Myron's clients. He set up a special portfolio for each player, met with them at least five times a year, made sure they understood what their money was doing and why. Having Win gave Myron a big leg up on the competition. Win was a near-legend in the financial world. His reputation was impeccable (at least in the financial world) and his track record unmatched. He gave Myron an instant 'in,' instant credibility in a business where credibility was a rare and heady concoction.

Myron was the JD. Win was the MBA. Esperanza was the all-purpose player, the unflappable chameleon who held it all together. It worked.

'We need to talk,' he said again.

'So we'll talk,' she said in a dismissing tone. 'First take this call.'

Myron entered his office. He overlooked Park Avenue in midtown. Great View. On one wall he had posters of Broadway musicals. On another there were movie stills from some of Myron's favorites: the Marx Brothers,

Woody Allen, Alfred Hitchcock, and a potpourri of other classics. On a third wall were photographs of Myron's clients. The client wall was a bit sparser than Myron would have liked. He imagined what it would look like with an NBA first rounder in the middle.

Good, he decided. Very good.

He strapped on his headset.

'Hey, Perry.'

'Jesus Christ, Myron, I've been trying to reach you all day.'

'Good, Perry. And you.'

'Hey, I don't mean to be impatient but this is important. You get anything on my boat?'

Perry McKinley was a golfer on the fringe, no pun intended. He was a pro. He made some money, but he wasn't a name anyone but big golf fans would recognize. Perry loved to sail and was in need of a new vessel.

'Yeah, I got something,' Myron said.

'What company?'

'Prince.'

Perry did not sound thrilled. 'Their boats are just okay,' he whined. 'Nothing great.'

'They'll let you trade in your old boat for a new one. You have to do five personal appearances.'

'Five?'

'Yep.'

'For a Prince eighteen-footer? That's too many.'

'They originally wanted ten. But it's up to you.'

Perry thought about it a moment. 'Ah, shit, okay the deal. But first I want to make sure I like the boat. A full eighteen-footer, right?'

'That's what they said.'

'Yeah, all right. Thanks, Myron. You're the best.'

They hung up. Bartering – an important component in the agent's multitasking environment. No one ever paid for anything in this business. Favors were exchanged. Trading products for some form of endorsement. Want a free shirt? Wear it in public. Want a free car? Shake hands at a few car shows. The big stars could demand serious payments in exchange for their endorsements. The lesser-known athletes happily seized the freebies.

Myron stared at the pile of messages and shook his head. Playing for the Dragons and keeping MB SportsReps afloat – how the hell was he going to pull it off?

He buzzed Esperanza. 'Come on in here please,' he said.

'I'm in the middle—'

'Now.'

Silence.

'Gosh,' she said, 'you're so macho.'

'Give me a break, huh?'

'No, really, I'm very frightened. I better drop everything and immediately do your bidding.'

Her phone fell. She sprinted in, feigning fear and breathlessness. 'Fast enough?'

'Yes.'

'So what is it?'

He told her. When he came to the part where he'd be playing for the Dragons, he was once again surprised to see no reaction. This was strange. First Win, now Esperanza. The two of them were his closest friends. They both lived for ridiculing him. Yet neither one of them had taken advantage of the obvious opening. Their silence on the subject of his 'comeback' was a tad unnerving.

'Your clients aren't going to like this,' she said.

'*Our* clients,' he corrected.

She made a face. 'Does it make you feel better to be patronizing?'

Myron ignored the comment. 'We have to turn this into a positive,' he said.

'How?'

'I'm not sure,' he said slowly. He leaned back in his chair. 'We can say that the publicity of all this will help them.'

'How?'

'I can make new contacts,' he said, the ideas coming to him even as he spoke. 'I can get closer to sponsors, learn more about them. More people will hear about me and indirectly my clients.'

Esperanza made a scoffing sound. 'And you think that's going to fly?'

'Why not?'

'Because it's bullshit. "Indirectly my clients." Sounds like trickle-down economics.'

She had a point. 'What's the big deal really?' he asked, palms to the ceiling. 'Basketball will only be a couple of hours a day. I'll be here the rest of the time. I'll have the cellular phone with me all the time. We just have to emphasize that I won't be there long.'

Esperanza looked at him skeptically.

'What?' he asked.

She shook her head.

'No, I want to know. What?'

'Nothing,' she said. She looked him straight in the eye, her hands resting on her lap. 'What does the bitch say about all this?' she asked sweetly.

Her pet name for Jessica. 'Will you please stop calling her that?'

She made a suit-yourself face, for once not arguing. There had been a time – long, long ago – when Jessica and Esperanza had at least tolerated each other. But then Jessica left, and Esperanza saw what it did to Myron. Some people held grudges. Esperanza internalized them. It didn't matter that Jessica had come back.

'So what does she think?' Esperanza asked again.

'About what?'

'About the prospects for peace in the Middle East,' she snapped. 'What do you think I mean? Your playing again.'

'I don't know. We haven't had a chance to talk about it much. Why?'

Esperanza shook her head again. 'We're going to need help in here,' she said, closing the subject. 'Someone to answer the phones, do some typing, that kind of thing.'

'You have someone in mind?'

She nodded. 'Cyndi.'

Myron blanched. 'Big Cyndi?'

'She could answer the phone, do some odd jobs. She's a good worker.'

'I didn't even know she could talk,' Myron said. Big Cyndi had been Esperanza's tag-team wrestling partner, fighting under the name of Big Chief Mama.

'She'll take orders. She'll do shit work. She's not ambitious.'

Myron tried not to wince at the thought. 'Isn't she still working at the strip joint as a bouncer?'

'It's not a strip joint. It's a leather bar.'

'My mistake,' Myron said.

'And she's a bartender now.'

'Cyndi's been promoted?' Myron said.

'Yes.'

'Well, I'd hate to sidetrack her burgeoning career by asking her to work here.'

'Don't be an ass,' Esperanza said. 'She works there nights.'

'What,' Myron said, 'Leather and Lust doesn't do a big lunch crowd?'

'I know Cyndi. She'll be perfect.'

'She scares people,' Myron said. 'She scares me.'

'She'll stay in the conference room. No one will see her.'

'I don't know.'

Esperanza rose smoothly. 'Fine, you find somebody. I mean, you're the boss. You know best. Me, I'm just a pissant secretary. I wouldn't dare question how you handle *our* clients.'

Myron shook his head. 'Low blow,' he said. He leaned forward, his elbows on his desk, his hands holding up his head. 'All right,' he said finally, releasing a deep breath. 'We'll give her a try.'

Myron waited. Esperanza stared back at him. After several seconds passed, she said, 'Is this the part where I jump up and down and say thank you, thank you?'

'No, this is the part where I leave.' He checked his watch. 'I got to talk to Clip about those bloodstains before the press conference.'

'Have fun.' She headed for the door.

'Hold up,' he called out. She turned and faced him. 'Do you have class tonight?' Esperanza took night classes at NYU Law school.

'No.'

'You want to go to the game?' He cleared his throat. 'You can, uh, bring Lucy, if you'd like.'

Lucy was Esperanza's latest love. Before Lucy she had dated a man named Max. Her sexual preference seemed to vacillate. 'We broke up,' she said.

'Oh, I'm sorry,' Myron said, not knowing what else to say. 'When?'

'Last week.'

'You didn't say anything.'

'Maybe because it's none of your business.'

He nodded. True enough. 'Well, you can bring a new, uh, friend, if you'd like. Or you can go yourself. We're playing the Celtics.'

'I'll pass,' she said.

'You sure?'

She nodded again, left the room. Myron grabbed his jacket and headed back to the lot. Mario tossed him his keys without looking up. He took the Lincoln Tunnel and hopped onto Route 3. He passed a huge and fairly famous appliance and electronics store called Tops. The billboard featured a giant nose jutted out over Route 3. The caption: Tops Is Right Under Your Nose. Very lifelike. The only thing missing were the giant nose hairs. He was only a mile or so from the Meadowlands when the car phone rang.

'I have some preliminaries,' Win said.

'Go ahead.'

'None of Greg Downing's accounts or credit cards have been accessed in the past five days.'

'Nothing?'

'Nothing.'

'Any cash withdrawals from his bank?'

'Not in the past five days.'

'How about earlier? Maybe he grabbed out a lot of money before he vanished.'

'It's being worked on. I don't know yet.'

Myron took the Meadowlands exit. He considered what this all meant. So far, not much, but it wasn't really good news. The blood in the basement. No sign of Greg. No financial activity. It wasn't really promising. 'Anything else?' Myron asked.

Win hesitated. 'I may soon have an idea where dearest Greg had that drink with fair Carla.'

'Where?'

'After the game,' Win said. 'I'll know more then.'

5

'Sports is folklore,' Clip Arnstein told the room full of reporters. 'What captures our imagination is not simply the winning and losing. It's the stories. The stories of perseverance. The stories of sheer will. The stories of hard work. The stories of heartbreak. The stories of miracles. The stories of triumph and tragedy. The stories of comebacks.'

Clip looked down at Myron from the podium, his eyes properly moist, his smile his most grandfatherly. Myron cringed. He fought back an intense desire to duck under the conference table and hide.

After a proper pause Clip turned back to the front. The reporters were silent. An occasional flashbulb burst forth. Clip swallowed several times as though summoning some inner resolve he'd need to continue. His throat slid up and down. He raised his moist eyes to the audience.

A little hammy, Myron thought, but all in all a fine performance.

The press conference was more crowded than Myron would've thought. Not a free seat and many reporters standing. Must have been a slow news day. Clip took his time, regaining his seemingly lost composure. 'A little over a decade ago, I drafted an exceptional young man, a player I believed was destined for greatness. He had a great jumper, a well-honed court sense, mental tenacity, and on top of all that was a fine human being. But the gods had other plans for that young man. We all know what happened to Myron Bolitar on that fateful night in Landover, Maryland. There is no reason to dredge up the past. But as I said when I opened this press conference, sports is folklore. Today the Dragons are giving that young man a chance to weave his own legend into the lush tapestry of sports. Today the Dragons are allowing that young man to try and recapture what was so cruelly snatched away from him all those years ago.'

Myron started squirming. His cheeks flushed. His eyes darted about, seeking a safe haven and finding none. He settled for looking at Clip's face, as per the media's expectations. He zeroed in on a cheek mole, staring so hard his vision began to mercifully blur.

'It won't be easy, Myron,' Clip said, turning now and addressing Myron directly. Myron kept his vision locked on the mole; he couldn't meet the gaze. 'No promises have been made to you. I don't know what happens from here. I don't know if this is the culmination of your story or the commencement of a brave new chapter. But those of us who love sports can't help but hope. It is in our nature. It is in the nature of all true combatants and fans.' Clip's voice started to crack.

'This is reality,' he went on. 'I have to remind you of that, Myron, much as I'd rather not. On behalf of the New Jersey Dragons I welcome you, a man of class and courage, to the team. We wish you nothing but the best. We know that no matter what happens to you on the court, you will bring honor to the entire Dragon organization.' He stopped, tightened his lips and managed a quick, 'Thank you.'

Clip held out a hand to Myron. Myron played his part. He stood to shake Clip's hand. Clip however had other ideas. He put his arms around Myron and pulled him toward him. The flashbulbs increased to the point of being a disco strobe. When Clip finally pulled back, he wiped his eyes with two fingers. Sheesh, the man put Pacino to shame. Clip held out an arm, ushering Myron to the podium.

'How does it feel to be back?' one reporter yelled out.

'Scary,' Myron replied.

'Do you really think you have what it takes to play at this level?'

'No, not really.'

The moment of honesty stopped them for a second. But only a second. Clip laughed and everyone else in the room followed suit. Figuring it was a joke. Myron didn't bother correcting them.

'Do you think you still have three-point shooting range?' another asked.

Myron nodded. 'I have the shooting range,' he said. 'I'm just not sure I have the making range.' A stolen joke but what the hey.

More laughs.

'Why the comeback so late, Myron? What convinced you to come back now?'

'The Psychic Friends Network.'

Clip stood and warded off further questions with a raised hand. 'Sorry, gang, that's it for now. Myron has to get suited up for tonight's game.'

Myron followed Clip out. They hurried down the corridor and into Clip's office. Calvin was already there. Clip shut the door. Before he sat down Clip asked, 'So what's the matter?'

Myron told him about the blood in the basement. Clip visibly blanched. Frosty's fingers tightened against the armrest.

'So what are you trying to say?' Clip snapped when he finished.

'Say?'

Clip gave an elaborate shrug. 'I don't get it.'

'There's nothing to get,' Myron said. 'Greg is missing. No one has seen him for five days. He hasn't used his ATM or credit card. And now there's blood in the basement.'

'In his kids' playroom, right? That's what you said before. The kids' playroom.'

Myron nodded.

Clip looked a question at Calvin then turned his palms to the sky. 'So what the hell does that mean?'

'I'm not sure.'

'It doesn't exactly add up to foul play, now does it?' Clip continued. 'Think it through, Myron. If Greg were murdered, for example, where is his body? Did the killer or killers take it with them? And what do you think happened here? The killers – what? – surprised Greg? Alone? In his kids' playroom where, I guess, Greg was playing with his little dolly? Then what happened? They killed him down there and dragged him out of the house without leaving traces of blood anywhere but in the basement?' Clip spread his hands. 'Does that make sense?'

The scenario had bothered Myron too. He sneaked a glance at Calvin. Calvin seemed deep in thought. Clip stood.

'For all we know,' Clip went on, 'one of Greg's kids cut himself playing down there.'

'Hell of a cut,' Myron said.

'Or a bloody nose. Christ, those things gush like mad. Could be nothing but a bloody nose.'

Myron nodded. 'Or maybe they were slaughtering chickens,' he said. 'Could be that too.'

'I don't need sarcasm, Myron.'

Myron waited a beat. He glanced at Calvin. Nothing. He glanced at Clip. Nada. 'It's getting opaque in here again.'

'Pardon?'

'You hired me to find Greg. I'm tracing down a major lead. Yet you don't want to hear it.'

'If you mean I don't want to hear that perhaps Greg has met with foul play—'

'No, that's not what I mean. You're afraid of something and it's not just that Greg may have met with foul play. I'd like to know what.'

Clip looked over at Calvin. Calvin nodded almost imperceptibly. Clip sat back down. His fingertips drummed the desktop. The grandfather clock in the corner ticked an imitating echo. 'Understand,' Clip said, 'that we have Greg's best interests at heart. We really do.'

'Uh huh.'

'You know anything about hostile takeovers?'

'I was alive in the eighties,' Myron said. 'In fact, someone recently remarked on what an eighties kinda guy I am.'

'Well, I'm undergoing one now.'

'I thought you were a majority owner.'

Clip shook his head. 'Forty percent. No one else owns more than fifteen percent. A couple of the minority shareholders have gotten together and are trying to oust me.' Clip made two fists and put them on his desk like paperweights. 'They say I'm too much a basketball mind and not enough a business mind. I should only be handling players and the on-court affair. They vote in two days.'

'So?'

'So right now the vote is very close. A scandal and I'm done.'

Myron looked at both men and waited a beat. Then he said, 'You want me to sit on this.'

'No, no, of course not,' Clip said quickly. 'I'm not saying that at all. I just don't want the press going berserk over what might be nothing. I can't afford to have anything unsavory uncovered now.'

'Unsavory?'

'Right.'

'Like what?'

'Hell if I know,' Clip said.

'But Greg might be dead.'

'And if that's the case, a day or two isn't going to help – cold as that might sound. And if something did happen to Greg, there might be a reason.'

'A reason?'

Clip threw up his hands. 'Hell, I don't know. You lift up a corpse or even a man in hiding and worms start to crawl out. You know what I mean?'

'No,' Myron said. But Clip went on.

'I don't need that, Myron. Not now. Not till after this vote.'

'Then you are telling me to sit on this,' Myron said.

'Not at all. We just don't want an unnecessary panic. If Greg is dead, we can't do him any good now anyway. If he's vanished, well, then you are his best hope to avoid media glare or to save him.'

They were still not telling him everything but Myron decided not to press it just now. 'Do you have any idea why someone would be watching Greg's house?'

Clip looked puzzled. 'Someone is watching his house?'

'I think so, yes.'

Clip looked over to Calvin. 'Calvin?'

'No idea,' Calvin said.

'I don't know either, Myron. Do you have any thoughts?'

'Not yet. One more question: did Greg have a girlfriend?'

Again Clip looked toward Calvin.

Calvin shrugged. 'He played around a lot. But I don't think there was anyone special.'

'Do you know any of the women he played around with?'

'Not by name. Some groupies, stuff like that.'

'Why?' Clip asked. 'You think he ran off with a broad?'

Myron shrugged and stood. 'Guess I better get to the locker room. It's almost game time.'

'Wait.'

Myron stopped.

'Please, Myron, I know it sounds like I'm being cold, but I really do care about Greg. Very much. I want him found alive and well.' Clip swallowed. The wrinkles in his skin looked more pronounced, like someone had just pinched them out a bit. His color was not good. 'If you can honestly tell me that revealing what we know to the public is best, I'll go along with it. No matter what the costs. Think about it. I want to do what's best for Greg. I care about him very much. I care about both of you. You're both fine young men. I mean that. I owe you both a great deal.'

Clip looked like he was about to cry. Myron wasn't sure what to make of all this. He decided to nod and say nothing. He opened the door and left.

As he approached the elevator Myron heard a familiar, husky voice say, 'If it isn't the Comeback Kid?'

Myron looked over at Audrey Wilson. She was wearing her customary sports-reporter garb: dark blue blazer, black turtleneck, what they called 'stone-washed' jeans. Her makeup was either light or nonexistent, her nails short and unpolished. The only splash of color could be found on her sneakers – bright aqua Chuck Taylor Cons. Her looks were completely unspectacular. There was nothing wrong with her features but nothing particularly right about them either. They were just there. Her straight black hair was cut short in a pageboy with bangs. 'Do I detect the scent of cynicism?' he asked.

Audrey shrugged. 'You don't really think I buy all this, do you?'

'Buy what?'

'Your sudden desire to' – she checked her notes – 'weave your own legend into the lush tapestry of sports.' She looked up, shook her head. 'That Clip can sure talk some shit, huh?'

'I have to get dressed, Audrey.'

'How about giving me the lowdown first?'

'The lowdown, Audrey? Gee, why not ask for a "scoop"? I love it when you reporters say that.'

She smiled at that. It was a nice smile. Full and open. 'Kinda defensive, aren't we, Myron?'

'Me? Never.'

'Then how about – to coin yet another cliché – a statement for the press?'

Myron nodded, put his hand to his chest in dramatic fashion. 'A winner never quits, and a quitter never wins.'

'Lombardi?'

'Felix Unger. It was on *The Odd Couple*, the one where Howard Cosell guest starred.'

He turned and walked toward the locker room. Audrey followed. She was probably the top female sports reporter in the country. She covered the Dragons for the East Coast's biggest newspaper. She had her own radio show on WFAN in a coveted time slot with huge ratings. She had a Sunday morning round-table talk show called *Talking Sports* on ESPN. And yet, like almost every other female in this male-dominated profession, there was something tenuous about her station, her career always a half-step from toppling over no matter how big she became.

'How's Jessica?' Audrey asked.

'Good.'

'I haven't spoken to her in a month,' she said with a singsong tone. 'Maybe I should give her a call. Sit down and have a heart-to-heart, you know.'

'Gee,' Myron said, 'that won't be transparent.'

'I'm trying to make this easier on you, Myron. There's something strange going on here. You know I'm going to find out what it is. Might as well just tell me.'

'I really don't know what you're talking about.'

'First Greg Downing leaves the team under mysterious circumstances—'

'What's mysterious about an ankle injury?'

'—then you, his old nemesis, take his place after being out of commission for the better part of eleven years. You don't find that strange?'

Great, Myron thought. On the job five minutes and already someone was voicing suspicion. Myron Bolitar, master of the undercover. They reached the door to the locker room.

'I gotta go, Audrey. We'll talk later.'

'Count on it,' she said. She smiled at him with a gentle mocking sweetness. 'Good luck, Myron. Knock them dead.'

He nodded, took a deep breath, and pushed open the locker-room door. Show time.

6

No one greeted Myron when he entered the locker room. No one broke stride. No one even looked at him. The room did not go quiet like something out of an old Western where the sheriff pushes open the creaking door and sashays into the saloon. Maybe that was the problem. Maybe the door needed to creak. Or maybe Myron had to work on his sashay.

His new teammates were sprawled about like socks in a college dorm. Three of them were draped over benches, semidressed and seminapping. Two were on the floor, a leg being held in the air by assistants, stretching quads and calves. A couple others were dribbling basketballs. Four were hobbling back to their lockers after getting taped. Almost all were chewing gum. Almost all were also listening to Walkmans, the tiny speakers jammed in their ears and blaring so loudly that they sounded like competing floor models at a stereo store.

Myron found his dressing area pretty easily. All the other lockers had bronze plaques with a player's name engraved on it. Myron's did not. It had a piece of white adhesive tape above it, the kind used to tape ankles, with the letters M. BOLITAR scrawled in black marker. It hardly inspired confidence or spoke commitment.

He glanced around for someone to talk to, but the Walkmans were the ideal room dividers. Everyone was in their own private space. Myron spotted Terry 'TC' Collins, the team's famed whining superstar, sitting alone in a corner. TC was the media's newest poster boy for the spoiled athlete, the guy 'ruining' the genteel world of sports 'as we know it,' whatever that meant. TC was a hell of a physical specimen. Six-ten, muscular, wiry. His cleanly shaven head glistened in the fluorescent light. Rumor had it TC was black though it was hard to see any trace of skin through the work of his tattoo artist. The obscure ink images blanketed almost all available somatic sites. Body piercing too appeared to be more of a lifestyle with TC than a hobby. The man looked like a nightmare version of Mr Clean.

Myron caught TC's eye, smiled, and nodded a hello. TC glared daggers and turned away. Making chums already.

His uniform was hung where it should be. His name had already been sewn on the back in block letters. BOLITAR. He stared at it for a moment or two. Then he quickly snatched it off the hanger and put it on. Everything caused bouts of déjà vu. The feel of the crumbly cotton. The shoelacelike tie-string on his shorts. The slight elastic tug at the waist when he put them on. The slight tightness of the top as it went over his shoulders. The practiced hands tucking in the tail. The lacing up of his high-tops. It all caused pangs. It was getting harder to breathe. His eyes blinked something back. He sat and waited until the feeling went away.

Myron noticed very few of the guys wore jock straps anymore, preferring those tight, Lycra shorts. Myron stuck with old dependable. Mr Old-Fashioned. Then he strapped a contraption onto his leg that was loosely labeled a 'knee brace.' Felt more like a metal compressor. The last thing he put on was his warm-ups. The bottoms had dozens of snaps up and down the legs, so a player could dramatically rip them off when called to go into a game.

'Hey, kid, how's it going?'

Myron stood and shook hands with Kip Corovan, one of the team's assistant coaches. Kip wore a plaid jacket that was about three sizes too small. The sleeves inched up to the forearms. The gut jutted out with great defiance. He looked like a farmer at the semiannual square dance. 'I'm doing fine, coach.'

'Great, great. And call me Kip. Or Kipper. Most people call me Kipper. Sit down, relax.'

'Okay.' Kipper?

'Great, happy to have you with us.' The Kipper pulled over a chair, turned it so the back faced Myron, and straddled it. His pants inseam didn't look happy with the move. 'I'll be honest with you, Myron, okay? Donny wasn't thrilled about this. Nothing personal, you understand. Just Donny likes to pick his own players. He don't like interference from upstairs, you know what I'm saying?'

Myron nodded. Donny Walsh was the head coach.

'Great, good. Donny's a straight guy though. He remembers you from the old days, liked you a lot. But we got a team heading for the playoffs. With a bit of luck we can lock up home-court advantage throughout the playoffs. It took a while to get the ducks all in a row. It's a balance, you know. Got to keep the ducks on an even keel. Losing Greg really knocked the wind from our sails, but we finally got those ducks back up. Now you come along, see. Clip doesn't tell us why, but he insists we add you to the roster. Fine, Clip is the big chief, no question. But we worry about getting our ducks back sailing straight, you see?'

The mixing of metaphors was making Myron dizzy. 'Sure. I don't want to cause any problems.'

'I know that.' He stood, put the chair back with a sweeping motion. 'You're a good guy, Myron. Always were a straight arrow. We need that now. A team-comes-first kinda guy, am I right?'

Myron nodded. 'A straight-sailing duck.'

'Great, fine. See you out there. And don't worry. You're not going to get in unless it's a blowout.' With that the Kipper hoisted his belt up over the gut and sauntered – almost sashayed – across the room.

Three minutes later, the Kipper shouted out, 'Gather round the board, boys.' No one paid any attention. He repeated this several times, tapping Walkman-entranced players on the shoulders, so that they would hear. It took a full ten minutes to get twelve professional athletes to move less than ten feet. Coach Donny Walsh strode in with great self-importance, took center stage, and began spilling out the tired clichés. This didn't mean he was a bad coach or anything. You play over a hundred games a season it's hard to come up with anything new.

The pep talk lasted a full two minutes. Some of the guys never bothered turning off their Walkmans. TC was busy taking off his jewelry, a task that took great concentration and a team of well-trained technicians. Another minute or two passed and then the locker-room door opened. Everyone removed their Walkmans and headed out. Myron realized they were heading for the court.

Game time.

Myron stood at the end of the line. He swallowed deeply. A cold rush swept through him. As he made his way up the ramp he heard a voice over the loudspeaker scream, 'And nowwwwww, your New Jersey Dragons!' Music blared. The jog quickened into a full trot.

The ovation was thunderous. The players automatically split into two makeshift lines for the lay-up drill. Myron had done this a zillion times before, but for the first time he really thought about what he was doing. When you were a star or a starter, you warmed up casually, loosely, unhurriedly. There was no reason to press it. You had the whole game to show the crowd what you could do. The scrubs – something Myron had never been – handled the warm-ups in one of two ways. Some went all out, slamming reverse dunks, doing windmill moves. In a phrase: showing off. Myron had always found this behavior sort of desperate. Others hung around the superstars, feeding them the ball, playing the mock defender like a boxer with a sparring partner. Cool by association.

Myron got to the front of the lay-up line. Someone passed him the ball. When you're warming up, you are subconsciously convinced that all eyes in the arena are on you, though in point of fact, most people were settling in or chatting or getting food or checking out the crowd and those that were watching couldn't care less what you did. Myron took two dribbles and laid the ball against the glass and in. Sheesh, he thought. The game hadn't started yet and already he didn't know what to do.

Five minutes later the lay-up lines disintegrated and players began to free shoot. Myron glanced into the stands for Jessica. She was not hard to spot. It was like a beacon hit her, like she came forward and the rest of the crowd stepped back, like she was the Da Vinci and the rest of the faces were but a frame. Jessica smiled at him and he felt a warmth spread through him.

With something close to surprise, he realized that this would be the first time Jessica had seen him play in anything but pick-up games. They'd met three weeks before Myron's injury. The thought made him pause. And remember. For a brief moment his mind dragged him back. Guilt and pain washed over him until a ball careened off the backboard and smacked him in the head. But the thought remained:

I owe Greg.

The buzzer sounded and the players moved to the bench. Coach Walsh blurted out a few more clichés and made sure each player knew whom they were covering. The players nodded, not listening. TC still glared. Game face, Myron hoped, but didn't really believe it. He also kept an eye on Leon White, Greg's roommate on the road and closest friend on the team. The huddle broke. The players from both sides approached the center circle, greeting one another with handshakes and hand slaps. Once out there, the players on both teams started pointing around, trying to figure out who was covering whom since no one had listened thirty seconds earlier. Coaches from both sides were up, yelling out the defensive assignments until the ball was mercifully tossed in the air.

Basketball is normally a game of momentum shifts, keeping things fairly close until the final minutes. Not tonight. The Dragons cruised. They led by twelve after one quarter, twenty points by halftime, twenty-six by the end of the third period. Myron started getting nervous. The lead was big enough for him to get in. He hadn't really counted on that. Part of him silently cheered on the Celtics, hoping they could stage enough of a comeback to keep his butt on the aluminum chair. But it was a no-go. With four minutes remaining the Dragons led by twenty-eight points. Coach Walsh shot a glance down the bench. Nine of the twelve players had already gotten in. Walsh whispered something to the Kipper. The Kipper nodded and walked down the bench, stopping in front of Myron. Myron could feel his heart beating in his chest.

'Coach is going to clear the bench,' he said. 'He wants to know if you want to go in.'

'Whatever he wants,' Myron replied, while sending out telepathic messages of no, no, no. But he couldn't tell them that. It wasn't in his nature. He had to play the good trooper, Mr Team-First, Mr Dive-On-The-Grenade-If-That's-What-The-Coach-Wants. He didn't know how else to do it.

A time-out was called. Walsh looked down the bench again. 'Gordon! Reilly! You're in for Collins and Johnson!'

Myron let loose a breath. Then he got mad at himself for feeling such relief. What kind of competitor are you? he asked himself. What kind of man wants to stay on the bench? Then the truth rose up and smacked him hard in the face:

He was *not* here to play basketball.

What the hell was he thinking? He was here to find Greg Downing. This was just undercover work, that's all. Like with the police. Just because a guy goes undercover and pretends he's a drug dealer doesn't make him a drug dealer. The same principle applied here. Just because Myron was pretending to be a basketball player didn't make him one.

The thought was hardly comforting.

Thirty seconds later, it started. And it filled Myron's chest with dread.

One voice triggered it. One beer-infested voice rising clearly above all others. One voice that was just deep enough, just different enough, to separate it from the usual cacophony of fandom. 'Hey, Walsh,' the voice cried out. 'Why don't you put in Bolitar?'

Myron felt his stomach plummet. He knew what was coming next. He had seen it happen before, though never to him. He wanted to sink into the floor.

'Yeah!' another voice crowed. 'Let's see the new guy!'

More shouts of agreement.

It was happening. The crowd was getting behind the underdog, but not in a good way. Not in a positive way. In the most blatantly patronizing and mocking way possible. Be-Nice-To-The-Scrub time. We've won the game. We want a few laughs now.

A few more calls for Myron and then . . . the chant. It started low but built. And built. 'We want Myron! We want Myron!' Myron tried not to slouch. He pretended not to hear it, feigning intense concentration on what was happening on the court, hoping his cheeks weren't reddening. The chant grew louder and faster, eventually disintegrating into one word, repeated over and over, mixed with laughter.

'Myron! Myron! Myron!'

He had to defuse it. There was only one way. He checked the clock. Still three minutes to go. He had to go in. He knew that wouldn't be the end of it, but it would at least quiet the crowd temporarily. He looked down the bench. The Kipper looked back. Myron nodded. The Kipper leaned over to Coach Walsh and whispered something. Walsh did not stand up. He simply shouted, 'Bolitar. In for Cameron.'

Myron swallowed and rose to his feet. The crowd erupted in sarcasm. He headed for the scorer's table, ripping off his sweats. His legs felt stiff and cramped. He pointed to the scorer, the scorer nodded and sounded the buzzer. Myron stepped on the court. He pointed at Cameron. Cameron jogged off. 'Kraven,' he said. The name of the man Myron would defend.

'Now reporting for Bob Cameron,' the loudspeaker began. 'Number 34. Myron Bolitar!'

The crowd went absolutely wild. Hoots, whistles, screams, laughs. Some might think they were wishing him well, but that was not really the case. They were wishing him well the same way you wish a circus clown well. They were looking for pratfalls and darn gone-it, Bolitar was their man!

Myron stepped on the court. This was, he suddenly realized, his NBA debut.

He touched the ball five times before the game ended. Each time it was met with cheer/jeers. He shot only once, from just inside the three point line. He almost didn't want to, knowing the crowd would react no matter what happened, but some things are just too automatic. There was no conscious thought. The ball went in with a happy swish. By now there were only thirty seconds left and thankfully most everyone had had enough and were heading to their cars. The sarcastic applause was minimal. But for those brief seconds when Myron caught the ball, when his fingertips found the groove, when he bent his elbow and cradled the ball half an inch above both palm and forehead, when the arm smoothed into a straight line, when the wrist flowed into a front curl, when the fingertips danced along the ball's surface and created the ideal backspin, Myron was alone. His eyes were focused on the rim, only the rim, never glancing at the ball as it arched its way toward the cylinder. For those few seconds there was only Myron and the rim and the basketball and it all felt very right.

The mood in the locker room was far more animated after the game. Myron managed to meet all of the players except TC and Greg's roommate Leon White, the one man he wanted to get close to most. Figures. He couldn't push it either, that would just backfire. Tomorrow maybe. He'd try again.

He stripped down. The knee began to tighten up, as though somebody had pulled all the tendons too taut. He slapped on an ice pack and fastened it with a stretch wrap. He limped to the showers, dried off, and was just finishing when he realized TC was standing over him.

Myron looked up. TC had his various pierce-jewelry in place. Ear, of course. Three in one, four in the other. One in his nose. He wore black leather pants and a black cut-off mesh tank top, giving one an excellent view of the ring on his left nipple and the one in the belly button. Myron couldn't make out what the tattoos were. They just looked like swirls. TC wore sunglasses now, the wraparound kind.

'Your jeweler must send you a hell of a Christmas card,' Myron said.

TC replied by sticking out his tongue and revealing another ring near the tip. Myron almost gagged. TC looked pleased by his reaction.

'You new, right?' TC said.

'Right.' Myron held out his hand. 'Myron Bolitar.'

TC ignored the hand. 'You gots to get thumped.'

'Excuse me?'

'Thumped. You the new guy. You gots to get thumped.'

Several other players started chuckling.

'Thumped?' Myron repeated.

'Yeah. You the new guy, right?'

'Right.'

'Then you gots to get thumped.'

More chuckling.

'Right,' Myron said. 'Thumped.'

'There you go.' TC nodded, snapping his fingers, pointed at Myron, left.

Myron finished dressing. Thumped?

Jessica was waiting for him outside the locker-room door. She smiled as he approached, and he smiled back, feeling goofy. She hugged him and gave him a brief kiss. He smelled her hair. Ambrosia.

'Ah,' a voice said. 'Now ain't this just too sweet?'

It was Audrey Wilson.

'Don't talk to her,' Myron said. 'She's the Antichrist.'

'Too late,' Audrey said. She put her hand through Jessica's arm. 'Jess and I are going out now to have a few drinks, talk over old times, that kind of thing.'

'God, you are shameless.' He turned to Jessica. 'Don't tell her anything.'

'I don't know anything.'

'Good point,' Myron said. 'So where are we going?'

'*We* are going nowhere,' Jessica said. She made a motion behind her with her thumb. Win was leaning against the wall, completely still and at ease. 'He said you'd be busy.'

'Oh.' Myron looked over at Win. Win nodded. Myron excused himself and made his way over.

Without preamble, Win said, 'The last cash transaction Greg made was at an ATM machine at eleven oh three P.M. the night he vanished.'

'Where?'

'Manhattan. A Chemical Bank near Eighteenth Street on the West Side.'

'It makes sense,' Myron said. 'Greg gets a call at nine eighteen P.M. from Carla. Carla tells him to meet her in the back booth. So he drives himself to the city and picks up cash before he sees her.'

Win looked at him with flat eyes. 'Thank you for that analysis of the obvious.'

'It's a gift really.'

'Yes, I know,' Win said. 'Moving right along, there are eight saloons within a four block radius of this particular ATM. I limited my search to those. Of the eight only two have what one might term a "back booth." The others had tables or dining facilities sans booths in the rear. Here are the names.'

Myron had long since gotten past asking how Win did it. 'You want me to drive?'

'I can't go,' Win said.

'Why not?'

'I'm going away for a few days.'

'When?'

'I leave from Newark airport in an hour,' Win said.

'This is sudden.'

Win didn't bother responding. The two men headed out the players' entrance. Five kids ran up to Myron and asked for his autograph. Myron obliged. One kid who looked to be around ten years old took back the paper, squinted at Myron's scrawl, and said, 'Who the hell is he?'

Another kid said, 'Some scrub.'

'Hey!' Win snapped. 'That's Mr Scrub to you.'

Myron looked at him. 'Thanks.'

Win made an it's-nothing gesture.

The first kid looked at Win. 'You anybody?'

'I'm Dwight D. Eisenhower,' Win replied.

'Who?'

Win spread his hands. 'Our blessed youth.' He walked away then without saying another word. Win was not big on good-byes. Myron reached his car. When he put the key in the door, he felt a slap on the back. It was TC. He pointed at Myron with a finger holding more jewelry than a Gabor-family reunion. 'Remember,' TC said.

Myron nodded. 'Thumped.'

'Exacto.'

Then he, too, was gone.

7

Myron arrived at MacDougal's Pub, the first bar on Win's list. The back booth was empty so he grabbed it. He sat there for a moment, hoping a psychic force would tell him if this was the place where Greg had met up with Carla. He felt nothing – positive or negative. Maybe he should hold a séance.

The waitress came over slowly, as if the effort of crossing the floor was synonymous with wading through deep snow and she should be rewarded for it. Myron warmed her up with one of his patented smiles. The Christian Slater model – friendly yet devilish. Not to be mistaken for the Jack Nicholson model which was friendly yet devilish.

'Hi,' he said.

She put down a Rolling Rock cardboard coaster. 'What can I get you?' she asked, trying to toss up a friendly tone and falling way short. You rarely find a friendly barmaid in Manhattan, except for those born-again waitresses at chains like TGI Friday's or Bennigan's where they tell you their name and that they'll be your 'server' like you might mistake them for something else, like your 'legal consultant' or 'medical advisor.'

'Got any Yoo-hoo?' Myron asked.

'Any what?'

'Never mind. How about a beer?'

She gave him flat eyes. 'What kind?'

Subtlety was not going to work here. 'Do you like basketball?' he asked her.

Shrug.

'Do you know who Greg Downing is?'

Nod.

'He told me about this place,' Myron said. 'Greg said he was here the other night.'

Blink.

'Did you work last Saturday night?'

Nod.

'Same station? I mean, this booth?'

Quicker nod. Getting impatient.

'Did you see him?'

'No. I got tables. Michelob okay?'

Myron looked at his watch, faked shock. 'Whoops, look at the time. I gotta go.' He gave her two dollars. 'Thanks for your time.'

The next bar on the list was called the Swiss Chalet. Not even close. A dive. The wallpaper was supposed to trick you into believing that the place was wood paneled; the effect may have worked better had the wallpaper not been peeling in so many spots. The fireplace had a flickering, Christmas-light log in it, hardly giving the place the desired ski-lodge warmth. For some reason there was one of those disco mirrored balls in the middle of the bar. No dance floor. No lights. Just the disco mirrored ball – another staple of authentic Swiss chalets, Myron surmised. The place had the stale smell of spilled beer mixed with just a hint of what might have been vomit, the kind of smell only certain bars or frat houses held, the kind where the odor had seeped into the walls like rodents that ended up dying and rotting.

The jukebox blared 'Little Red Corvette' by Prince. Or was it by the Artist Formerly Known As Prince? Wasn't that what he called himself now? But of course when 'Little Red Corvette' had been released he had been Prince. So which was it? Myron tried to reconcile this crucial dilemma, but it began to confuse him like one of those time paradoxes in the *Back to the Future* movies so he gave up.

The place was pretty empty. A guy with a Houston Astros baseball cap and bushy mustache was the sole patron seated at the bar. There was a man and woman semi-necking at a table in the center of the room – the most conspicuous table in the place, as a matter of fact. No one seemed to mind. Another male patron skulked around the back like he was in the adult movie area at his local video store.

Again Myron took the back booth. Again he struck up a conversation with a far more animated waitress. When he reached the part about Greg Downing telling him about the Swiss Chalet, she said, 'Yeah, no kidding? I only seen him in here once.'

Bingo.

'Would that have been Saturday night?'

She scrunched her face in thought.

'Hey, Joe,' the waitress shouted to the bartender. 'Downing was in here Saturday night, right?'

'Who the fuck wants to know?' Joe shouted back from his spot behind the bar. He looked like a weasel with mousy hair. Weasel and mouse. Nice combination.

'This guy and me, we was just talking.'

Joe Weasel squinted with beady, ferret eyes. The eyes widened. 'Hey, you're the new guy, right? On the Dragons? I saw you on the news. With the dorky name.'

'Myron Bolitar,' Myron said.

'Yeah, right, Myron. That's it. You guys gonna start hanging out here?'

'I don't know.'

'We get a pretty exclusive celebrity clientele,' Joe said, wiping the bar with what looked like a gas station rag. 'You know who was in here once? Cousin Brucie. The disc jockey. Real regular guy, you know.'

'Sorry I missed that,' Myron said.

'Yeah, well we've had other celebs, right, Bone?'

The guy with the Astros hat and bushy mustache pepped up and nodded. 'Like that guy who looked like Soupy Sales. Remember him?'

'Right. Celebrities.'

'Except that wasn't really Soupy Sales. Just someone who looked like him.'

'Same difference.'

Myron said, 'Do you know Carla?'

'Carla?'

'The girl Greg was with.'

'That her name? No, never got a chance to meet her. Didn't meet Greg either. He just kinda ducked in, cognito-like. We didn't bother them.' He sort of puffed out his chest like he was about to salute. 'At the Swiss Chalet, we protect our celebrities.' He pointed at Myron with the dishrag. 'You tell the other guys that, okay?'

'Will do,' Myron said.

'Fact, we weren't even sure it was Greg Downing at first.'

'Like with Soupy Sales,' Bone added.

'Right, like that. Except this was really him.'

'Guy looked like Soupy though. Great actor, that Soupy.'

'And what a nickname.'

'Talent all the way round,' Bone agreed.

Myron said, 'Had he ever been in here before?'

'The guy who looked like Soupy?'

'Moron,' Joe said, snapping the rag at Bone. 'Why the fuck would he want to know about that? He's talking about Greg Downing.'

'How the fuck was I supposed to know? I look like I work for one of those psychic networks or something?'

'Fellas,' Myron tried.

Joe held up a hand. 'Sorry, Myron. Believe me, this don't normally happen here at the Swiss Chalet. We all get along, right, Bone?'

Bone spread his arms. 'Who's not getting along?'

'My point exactly. And no, Myron, Greg isn't one of our regulars. That was his first time here.'

'Same with Cousin Brucie,' Bone added. 'He only came in that one time.'

'Right. But Cousin Brucie liked the place, I could tell.'

'He ordered a second drink. That shoulda told you something.'

'Right you are. Two drinks. Coulda just had one and left. Course, they were only Diet Cokes.'

Myron said, 'How about Carla?'

'Who?'

'The woman Greg was with.'

'What about her?'

'Had she been here before?'

'I never seen her here before. Bone?'

Bone shook his head. 'Nope. I woulda remembered.'

'What makes you say that?'

Without hesitation, Joe said, 'Serious hooters.'

Bone cupped his hands and stuck them in front of his chest. 'Major Charlies.'

'Not that she was good looking or anything.'

'Not at all,' Bone agreed. 'Kinda old for a young guy.'

'How old?' Myron asked.

'Older than Greg Downing, that's for sure. I'd say late forties. Bone?'

Bone nodded. 'But a first-rate set of ta-tas.'

'Humongous.'

'Mammoth.'

'Yeah, I think I got that,' Myron interrupted. 'Anything else?'

They looked puzzled.

'Eye color?' Myron tried.

Joe blinked, looked at Bone. 'Did she have eyes?'

'Damn if I know.'

'Hair color?' Myron said.

'Brown,' Joe said. 'Light brown.'

'Black,' Bone said.

'Maybe he's right,' Joe said.

'No, maybe it was on the lighter side.'

'But I'm telling you, Myron. That was some rack. Major guns.'

'Guns of Navarone,' Bone agreed.

'Did she and Greg leave together?'

Joe looked at Bone. Bone shrugged. 'I think so,' Joe said.

'Do you know what time?'

Joe shook his head.

'Bones, you know?' Myron tried.

The bill of the Astros hat jerked toward Myron like a string had been pulled. 'Not Bones, dammit!' he shrieked. 'Bone! No S at the end. Bone! B-O-N-E! No S! And what the fuck do I look like, Big Ben?'

Joe snapped the dishrag again. 'Don't insult a celebrity, moron.'

'Celebrity? Shit, Joe, he's just a scrub. Not like he's Soupy or something. He's a nobody, a zero.' Bone turned to Myron. The hostility was completely gone now. 'No offense, Myron.'

'Why would I take offense?'

'Say,' Joe said, 'you got a photograph? We can put your picture on the wall. You could autograph it to your pals at the Swiss Chalet. We should start like a celebrity wall, you know?'

'Sorry,' Myron said, 'I don't have one on me.'

'Can you send us one? Autographed, I mean. Or bring it next time you come.'

'Er, next time.'

Myron continued to question them but learned nothing more except Soupy Sales's birthday. He left and headed up the block. He passed a Chinese restaurant with dead ducks hung in the window. Duck carcasses, the ideal appetite whetter. Maybe Burger King should hang slaughtered cows in the window. Really draw the kids in.

He tried putting the pieces together a bit. Carla calls Greg on the phone and tells him to meet her at the Swiss Chalet. Why? Why there of all places? Did they not want to be seen? Why not? And who the hell is Carla anyway? How does all this fit into Greg's vanishing act? And what about the blood in the basement? Did they go back to Greg's house or did Greg go home alone? Was Carla the girl he lived with? And if so, why meet here?

Myron was so preoccupied he didn't spot the man until he almost bumped into him. Of course calling him a man might be a bit of an understatement. More like a brick wall doubling as a human being. He stood in Myron's way. He wore one of those pectoral-displaying ribbed T-shirts under an unbuttoned flower-patterned semi-blouse. A gold horn dangled between his near-cleavage. Muscle-head. Myron tried to pass him on the left. The brick wall blocked his path. Myron tried to pass him on the right. The brick wall blocked his path. Myron went back and forth one more time. Brick Wall followed suit.

'Say,' Myron said, 'you know the cha-cha?'

The brick wall showed about as much reaction as one might expect from a brick wall. Then again it wasn't one of Myron's better quips. The man was truly enormous, the size of your average lunar eclipse. Myron heard footsteps. Another man, this one on the large size but at least of the human variety, came up behind Myron. The second man wore fatigue camouflage pants, a popular new urban fashion trend.

'Where's Greg?' Camouflage Pants asked.

Myron feigned startled. 'What? Oh, I didn't see you.'

'Huh?'

'In those pants,' Myron said. 'You just blended into the background.'

Camouflage didn't like that. 'Where's Greg?'

'Greg?' Snappy retort.

'Yeah. Where is he?'

'Who?'

'Greg.'

'Greg who?'

'You trying to be funny?'

'What, you think this is funny?'

Camouflage looked over at Brick Wall. Brick Wall remained completely silent. Myron knew that there was a very real possibility of a physical altercation. He also knew he was good at such things. He also knew – or at least figured – that these two goons were probably good too. Despite Bruce Lee movies, one man defeating two or more quality opponents was nearly impossible. Experienced fighters were not stupid. They worked as a team. They never rushed one at a time.

'So,' Myron said. 'You guys want to catch a beer? Chat this through.'

Camouflage made a scoffing noise. 'We look like guys who like to chat?'

Myron motioned to Brick Wall. 'He does.'

There were three ways to get out of a situation like this unharmed. One was to run, which was always a good option. Problem was, his two adversaries were close enough yet spaced far enough to tackle and/or slow him down. Too risky. Second option: your opponents underestimate you. You act scared and cower and then whammo, you surprise them. Unlikely for Myron. Goons rarely underestimate a guy six-four, two-twenty. Third option: you strike first and hard. By doing this you increase the likelihood of putting one out of commission before the other one can react. This action however required a delicate balance. Until someone strikes, you really cannot say for sure that a physical altercation could not be avoided altogether. But if you wait for someone to strike, this option becomes null and void. Win liked option three. Then again Win liked option three even if there was only one opponent.

Myron never got the chance to make a selection. Brick Wall slammed a fist into the small of Myron's back. Myron sensed the blow coming. He shifted enough to avoid both the kidney and serious damage. At the same time he spun and delivered an elbow strike to Brick Wall's nose. There was a satisfying, crunching noise like a fist closing over a bird's nest.

The victory was short-lived. As Myron had feared, these guys knew what they were doing. Camouflage Pants struck at the same time, connecting where his comrade had failed. Pain erupted in Myron's kidney. His knees buckled but he fought it off. He doubled over toward Brick Wall and threw a back kick, his foot snapping out like a piston. His lack of balance threw off his aim. The blow landed on Camouflage's thigh. It didn't do much damage but it was powerful enough to push him away. Brick Wall was starting to recover. He groped blindly and found Myron's hair. He grabbed and pulled up. Myron pinned the hand with one of his own, digging his fingernails into the sensitive pressure points between the joints. Brick Wall screamed. Camouflage Pants was back. He punched Myron straight in the stomach. It hurt. A lot. Myron knew he was in trouble. He went down to one knee and bounced up, a palm strike at the ready. It connected with Brick Wall's groin. Brick Wall's eyes bulged. He dropped like somebody had pulled a stool out from under him. Camouflage Pants connected with a solid shot to the side of Myron's head. Numbness flowed into Myron's skull. Another blow landed. Myron's eyes began to lose focus. He tried to stand up but his legs wouldn't let him. He felt a kick land on a rib. The world began to spin.

'Hey! Hey, what you doing? Hey, you!'

'Stop it! What the fuck!'

In his haze Myron recognized the voices. Joe and Bone from the bar. Myron took the opportunity to scramble away on all fours. There was no need. Camouflage Pants had already helped Brick Wall to his feet. Both men ran.

Joe and Bone quickly came over and looked down at Myron.

'You okay?' Joe asked.

Myron nodded.

'You won't forget about sending us that autographed picture, will you? Cousin Brucie never sent one.'

'I'll send you two,' Myron said.

8

He convinced Joe and Bone not to call the cops. They didn't take much convincing. Most people do not like activities that involve law enforcement. They helped Myron into a taxi. The driver wore a turban and listened to country music. Multiculturalism. Myron spit out Jessica's SoHo address and collapsed into the ripped cushions. The driver wasn't interested in conversation. Good.

Myron mentally checked over his body. Nothing broken. The ribs would be bruised at worst. Nothing he couldn't play through. The head was another matter. Tylenol with codeine would help tonight, then he could move down to Advil or something in the morning. There was nothing much you could do for head trauma but give it time and control the pain.

Jessica met him at the door in her bathrobe. He felt, as he often did around her, a little short of breath. She skipped admonishments, drew a bath, helped him undress, crawled in behind him. The water felt good against his skin. He leaned back on her as she wrapped washcloths around his head. He let loose a deep, totally content breath.

'When did you go to medical school?' he asked.

From behind him Jessica kissed his cheek. 'Feeling better?'

'Yes, Doctor. Much better.'

'You want to tell me about it?'

He did. She listened in silence, her fingertips gently massaging his temples. Her touch was soothing. Myron imagined there were better things in life than being in this tub leaning back against the woman he loved, but for the life of him he couldn't think of any. The pain began to dull and slacken.

'So who do you think they were?' she asked.

'No idea,' Myron said. 'I imagine they're hired goons.'

'And they wanted to know where Greg was?'

'Seems so.'

'If two goons like that were looking for me,' she said, 'I might disappear too.'

The thought had crossed Myron's mind too. 'Yes.'

'So what's your next step?'

He smiled and closed his eyes. 'What? No lectures? No telling me it's too dangerous?'

'Too cliché,' she said. 'Besides, there's something else here.'

'What do you mean?'

'Something about all this you're not telling me.'

'I—'

She put a finger over his lips. 'Just tell me what you plan on doing next.'

He settled back down. Scary how easily she read him. 'I have to start talking to people.'

'Like?'

'His agent. His roommate, a guy named Leon White. Emily.'

'Emily. That would be your old college sweetheart?'

'Uh huh,' Myron said. Quick subject change before she started reading him again. 'How was your evening with Audrey?'

'Fine. We mostly talked about you.'

'What about me?'

Jessica began to stroke his chest. The touch slowly drifted away from being merely soothing. Her fingertips caressed his chest with a feather touch. Gently. Too gently. She was strumming him like Perlman on a violin.

'Uh, Jess.'

She shushed him. Her voice was soft. 'Your ass,' she said.

'My ass?'

'Yep, that's what we talked about.' To emphasize the point her hand cupped a cheek. 'Even Audrey had to admit it was edible, running up and down the court like that.'

'I have a mind too,' Myron said. 'A brain. Feelings.'

She lowered her mouth toward his ear. When her lips touched the lobe, he felt a jolt. 'Who cares?'

'Uh, Jess . . .'

'Shhh,' she said as her other hand slid down his chest. 'I'm the doctor here, remember?'

9

The ringing phone jabbed at the base of nerves in the back of his skull. Myron's eyes blinked open. Sunlight knifed through the slit in the curtain. He checked next to him in the bed – first with his hands, then with his eyes. Jessica wasn't there. The phone continued to blare. Myron reached for it.

'Hello.'

'So this is where you are.'

He closed his eyes. The ache in his head multiplied tenfold. 'Hi, Mom.'

'You don't sleep in your home anymore?'

His home was the basement of his parents' house, the same house in which he'd been raised. More and more he was spending his nights at Jessica's. It was probably a good thing. He was thirty-two; he was fairly normal; he had plenty of money. There was no reason to still be living with Mommy and Daddy.

'How's your trip?' he asked. His mother and father were on some tour of Europe. One of those bus tours that hit twelve cities in four days.

'You think I called at the Vienna Hilton's long distant rates to chitchat about our itinerary?'

'Guess not.'

'You know how much it cost to call from a hotel in Vienna? With all their surcharges and taxes and everything?'

'A lot, I'm sure.'

'I have the rates right here. I'll tell you exactly. Hold on. Al, what did I do with those rates?'

'Mom, it's not important.'

'I had it a second ago. Al?'

'Why don't you tell me when you get home?' Myron suggested. 'It'll give me something to look forward to.'

'Save the fresh remarks for you friends, okay? You know very well why I'm calling.'

'I don't, Mom.'

'Fine, then I'll tell you. One of the other people on this tour – the Smeltmans, very nice couple. He's in the jewelry business. Marvin, his name is. I think. They have a shop in Montclair. We used to drive by it all the time when you were a kid. It's on Bloomfield Avenue, near that movie theater. Remember?'

'Uh huh.' He had no idea what she was talking about but it was easier.

'So the Smeltmans talked to their son on the phone last night. He called them, Myron. He had their itinerary and everything. Just called his parents to make sure they were having a nice time, that kind of thing.'

'Uh huh.' Mom was in decompensation mode. There was no way to stop it. She could go in a heartbeat from the modern, intelligent woman he knew her to be to something out of summer stock *Fiddler on the Roof*. Right now she was Golda heading toward Yenta.

'Anyway the Smeltmans brag how they're on the same trip with Myron Bolitar's parents. Big deal, right? Who knows you anymore? You haven't played in years. But the Smeltmans are big basketball fans. Go figure. Their son used to watch you play or something, I don't know. So anyway the son – I think his name is Herb or Herbie or Ralph, something like that – he tells them you're playing professional basketball. That the Dragons signed you. He says you're making a comeback or something, what do I know? Your father is so embarrassed. I mean, complete strangers are talking about it and your own parents don't even know. We thought the Smeltmans were crazy.'

'It's not what you think,' Myron said.

'What's not what I think?' she countered. 'You shoot around in the driveway a little. Okay, no big deal. But I don't understand. You never even mentioned you were playing again.'

'I'm not.'

'Don't lie to me. You scored two points last night. Your father called Sports Phone. You know what it cost to call Sports Phone from here?'

'Mom, it's no big deal.'

'Listen to me, Myron, you know your father. The man pretends it doesn't mean anything. He loves you no matter what, you know that. But he hasn't stopped smiling since he heard. He wants to fly home right now.'

'Please don't.'

'Don't,' she repeated, exasperated. 'You tell him, Myron. The man is loo-loo, you know that. A crazy person. So tell me what's going on.'

'It's a long story, Mom.'

'But it's true? You're playing again?'

'Only temporarily.'

'What does that mean, "only temporarily"?'

Jessica's Call Waiting clicked in. 'Mom, I gotta go. I'm sorry I didn't tell you earlier.'

'What? That's it?'

'I'll tell you more later.'

Surprisingly she backed off. 'You be careful with your knee.'

'I will.'

He changed over to the other line. It was Esperanza. She didn't bother with hello.

'It's not Greg's blood,' she said.

'What?'

'The blood you found in the basement,' she said. 'It's AB positive. Greg's blood type is O negative.'

Myron had not expected to hear this. He tried to reconcile it in his head. 'Maybe Clip was right. Maybe it was one of Greg's kids.'

'Impossible,' she said.

'Why?'

'Didn't you take basic biology in high school?'

'Eighth grade. But I was too busy staring at Mary Ann Palmiero. What?'

'AB is rare. In order for a kid to have it, his parents have to be A and B or it's impossible. In other words, if Greg is O, then his kids can't be AB.'

'Maybe it's a friend's,' Myron tried. 'Maybe one of the kids had a friend over.'

'Sure,' Esperanza said. 'That's probably it. The kids have some friends over. One of them bleeds all over the place and nobody cleans it up. Oh and then by a strange coincidence Greg vanishes.'

Myron threaded the phone cord through his fingers like his hand was a loom. 'Not Greg's blood,' he repeated. 'Now what?'

Esperanza didn't bother responding.

'How the hell am I supposed to investigate something like this without getting anyone suspicious?' he went on. 'I have to ask people questions, right? They're going to want to know why.'

'I feel very sorry for you,' Esperanza said in a tone that made clear she was anything but. 'I got to get to the office. You coming in?'

'Maybe this afternoon. I'm going to see Emily this morning.'

'Is that the old girlfriend Win told me about?'

'Yes,' Myron said.

'Don't take any chances. Put on a condom now.' She hung up.

Not Greg's blood. Myron didn't get it. As he drifted off to sleep last night he had worked up a neat little theory that went something like this: the hoods were searching for Greg. Maybe they had roughed him up a bit, made him bleed a little. Just to show him they meant serious business. Greg had reacted by running away.

It all sort of fit. It explained the blood in the basement. It explained why Greg suddenly took off. Yep, all a very nice and neat equation: One beating plus one death threat equaled a man on the run.

Problem was, the blood in the basement was not Greg's. Kinda put a damper on the theory. If Greg had been beaten in the basement, then it would have been his blood. Greg would have bled his own blood, not someone else's. In fact, it was very difficult to bleed someone else's blood.

Myron shook his head. He needed a shower. A bit more deducing like this and the slaughtered-chicken theory would begin to pick up steam.

Myron soaped himself up, then turned his back to the shower and let the water cascade over his shoulders and down his chest. He toweled off and got dressed. Jessica was on the word processor in the other room. He had learned never to disturb her when the keyboard was clacking. He left a quick note and slipped out. He grabbed the 6 train up to midtown and walked to the Kinney lot on 46th Street. Mario tossed him the keys without glancing up from his paper. He picked up the FDR north at 62nd Street and took it to the Harlem River Drive. There was a slow down for right lane construction, but he made it to the George Washington Bridge in pretty good time. He took Route 4 through a place called Paramus, which was actually a giant mall pretending to also be a township. He veered to the right and passed the Nabisco building on Route 208. He was hoping for a factory Ritz-whiff, but today he got nothing.

As he pulled up to Emily's house, déjà vu swatted him in the back of the head like a father's warning blow. He had been here before, of course, during college breaks in their courting days. The house was brick and modern and fairly huge. It sat in a well-groomed cul-de-sac. The backyard was fenced. He remembered that there was a swimming pool in the back. He remembered that there was also a gazebo. He remembered making love with Emily in the gazebo, their clothes wrapped around ankles, the humidity coating their skin with a thin layer of sweat. The sweet bird of youth.

He parked the car, pulled the key out of the ignition, and just sat there. He had not seen Emily in more than ten years. Much had happened in the ensuing years, but he still feared her reaction to seeing him. The mental image of Emily opening the door, screaming 'Bastard,' then slamming it in his face was one of the reasons he hadn't worked up the nerve to call first.

He looked out the car window. There was no movement on the street. Then again there were only ten houses. He debated his approach and came up with nothing. He checked his watch, but the time didn't register in his head. He sighed. One thing was for sure: he couldn't sit here all day. This was a nice neighborhood, the kind where someone would spot him and call the police. Time to get a move on. He opened the door and stepped out. The development was at least fifteen years old but it still looked new. All the yards were just a little too sparse. Not enough trees and shrubbery yet. The grass looked like a guy with a bad hair transplant.

Myron walked up the brick path. He checked his palms. They were wet. He rang the doorbell. Part of him flashed back to earlier visits, his mind playing along with the long, still-familiar chime of the bell. The door opened. It was Emily.

'Well, well, well,' she said. Myron could not tell if the tone was one of surprise or sarcasm. Emily had changed. She looked a little thinner, a bit more toned. Her face was less fleshy too, accentuating the cheekbones. Her hair was cut shorter and styled. 'If it isn't the good one I let get away.'

'Hi, Emily.' Mr Big Opening.

'Here to propose?' she asked.

'Been there, done that.'

'But you didn't mean it, Myron. I wanted sincerity back then.'

'And now?'

'Now I realize sincerity is overrated.' She flashed him a smile.

'You look good, Emily,' he said. Get Myron on a roll and it's one good line after another.

'So do you,' she said. 'But I'm not going to help you.'

'Help me what?'

She made a face. 'Come on in.'

He followed her inside. The house was full of skylights and cathedral ceilings and white painted walls. Airy. The front foyer was done in some expensive tile. She led Myron to the living room. He sat on a white couch. The floors were beechwood. It was exactly the same as it was ten years ago. Either they had gotten the exact same couches again or their house guests had been exceptionally well behaved. There wasn't a spot on them. The only mess was a pile of newspapers in the corner. Mostly daily tabloids, from the looks of it. A *New York Post* front-page headline read SCANDAL! in huge 72 point print. Specific.

An old dog traipsed into the room on rigid legs. It looked like he was trying to wag his tail, but the result was a pitiful sway. He managed to lick Myron's hand with a dry tongue.

'Look at that,' Emily said. 'Benny remembers you.'

Myron stiffened. 'This is Benny?'

She nodded.

Emily's family had bought the overactive puppy for her younger brother Todd when Myron and Emily had first started dating. Myron was there when they brought the puppy home from the breeder. Little Benny had stumbled around with blinking eyes and then peed on this very floor. No one cared. Benny quickly got used to people. He greeted everyone by jumping on them, believing in a way only a dog could that no one would ever do him harm. Benny was not jumping now. He looked very old. He looked a brief step away from death. A sudden sadness swept through Myron.

'You looked good last night,' Emily said. 'It was nice seeing you back on the court.'

'Thanks.' The quips never stopped.

'Are you thirsty?' she asked. 'I could make you some lemonade. Like in a Tennessee Williams play. Lemonade for the gentleman caller, except I doubt Amanda Wingfield used a Crystal Light mix.' Before he could answer she disappeared around the corner. Benny looked up at Myron, struggling to see through milky cataracts. Myron scratched the dog's ear. The tail picked up a bit of velocity. Myron smiled sadly at Benny. Benny moved closer, as if he understood how Myron felt and appreciated the sentiment. Emily returned with two glasses of lemonade.

'Here,' she said. She handed him a glass and sat down.

'Thank you.' Myron took a sip.

'So what's next on your agenda, Myron?'

'Next?'

'Another comeback?'

'I don't understand.'

Emily gave him the smile again. 'First you replace Greg on the court,' she said. 'Maybe next you'll want to replace him in the bedroom.'

Myron almost gagged on his lemonade, but he managed to smother the sound. Going for the shock. Classic Emily. 'Not funny,' he said.

'I'm just having a little fun,' she said.

'Yes, I know.'

She put her elbow on the back of the couch and propped up her head with her hand. 'I see you're dating Jessica Culver,' she said.

'Yep.'

'I like her books.'

'I'll tell her.'

'But we both know the truth.'

'What's that?'

She leaned forward now and took a slow sip from her glass. 'Sex with her isn't as good as it was with me.'

More classic Emily. 'You're sure about that?' he said.

'Very sure,' she replied. 'I'm not being immodest. I'm sure your Ms Culver is quite skilled. But with me it was new. It was discovery. It was impossibly hot. Neither of us can ever recapture that rapture with anyone else. It'd be impossible. It would be like going back in time.'

'I don't compare,' Myron said.

With a smile and a tilt of the head, she said, 'Bullshit.'

'You don't want me to compare.'

The smile was unfazed. 'Come, come now, Myron. You're not going to give me that spiritual crap, are you? You're not going to tell me it's better because you share a deep and beautiful relationship and thus the sex is beyond something physical? That line would be so unbecoming on you.'

Myron did not respond. He didn't know what to say and he didn't feel very comfortable with the conversation. 'What did you mean before?' he asked, shifting gears. 'When you said you wouldn't help me.'

'Exactly what I meant.'

'What won't you help me with?'

Again the smile. 'Was I ever stupid, Myron?'

'Never,' he said.

'Do you really think I believed that comeback story? Or the one about Greg being' – she made quote marks in the air – ' "in seclusion" for an ankle injury? Your visit here just confirms my suspicion.'

'What suspicion?'

'Greg is missing. You're trying to find him.'

'What makes you think Greg is missing?'

'Please, Myron, don't play games with me. You owe me that much at least.'

He nodded slowly. 'Do you know where he is?'

'No. But I hope the bastard is dead and rotting in a hole.'

'Stop mincing words,' Myron said. 'Tell me how you really feel.'

The smile was sadder this time. Myron felt a pang. Greg and Emily had fallen in love. They'd been married. They had two children. What had torn that all apart? Was it something recent . . . or was it something in their pasts, something tainted from the beginning? Myron felt his throat go dry.

'When was the last time you saw Greg?' he asked.

'A month ago,' she said.

'Where?'

'A divorce court.'

'Are you two on speaking terms?'

'I meant what I said before. About him being dead and rotting.'

'I'll take that as a no.'

Emily nodded a suit-yourself.

'If he was hiding, do you have any idea where?'

'Nope.'

'No summer house? No place he liked to get away?'

'Nope.'

'Do you know if Greg had a girlfriend?'

'Nope. But I would pity the poor woman.'

'Have you ever heard the name Carla?'

She hesitated. Her index finger tapped her knee, an old gesture so familiar to him it almost hurt to watch. 'Wasn't there a Carla who lived on my floor at Duke?' she asked. 'Yes, Carla Anderson. Sophomore year, wasn't it? Pretty girl.'

'Anything more recent?'

'No.' She sat up, crossed her legs. 'How's Win?'

'The same.'

'One of life's constants,' she said. 'He loves you, you know. I wonder if he's a latent homosexual.'

'Two men can love each other and not be gay,' Myron said.

She arched an eyebrow. 'You really think so?'

He was letting her get to him. Bad mistake. 'Are you aware that Greg was going to sign an endorsement deal?' he asked her.

That got her attention. 'Are you serious?'

'Yes.'

'A big one?'

'Huge from my understanding,' Myron replied. 'With Forte.'

Emily's hands tightened. She would have made fists had her nails not been so long. 'Son of a bitch.'

'What?'

'He waited until the divorce had been finalized and I got squat. Then he signs the deal. That son of a bitch.'

'What do you mean, squat? Greg was still wealthy.'

She shook her head. 'His agent lost it all. Or so he claimed in court.'

'Martin Felder?'

'Yep. Didn't have a penny to his name. Son of a bitch.'

'But Greg still works with Felder. Why would he stay with a guy who lost his money?'

'I don't know, Myron.' Her voice was clipped and annoyed. 'Perhaps the son of a bitch was lying. It wouldn't be the first time.'

Myron waited. Emily looked back at him. Tears welled in her eyes but she bit them back down. She stood and walked to the other side of the room. Her back was now to him. She looked out the sliding glass doors into the fenced-in yard. The pool was covered with a tarp; random sticks and leaves clung to the aqua. Two children appeared. A boy of about ten chased a girl who looked to be eight. They were both laughing with faces wide and open and a little rosy from either cold or exertion. The boy stopped when he saw his mother. He gave her a big smile and wave. Emily raised her hand and gave a small wave back. The children ran on. Emily crossed her arms like she was hugging herself.

'He wants to take them away from me,' she said in a remarkably calm voice. 'He'll do anything to get them.'

'Like?'

'Like the sleaziest things you can imagine.'

'How sleazy?'

'None of your goddamn business.' She stopped. She still had her back to him. Myron could see her shoulders quake. 'Get out,' she said.

'Emily . . .'

'You want to help him, Myron.'

'I want to find him. There's a difference.'

She shook her head. 'You don't owe him,' she said. 'I know you think you do. It's your way. I saw the guilt in your face back then, and I could still see it the second I opened the front door. It's over, Myron. It had nothing to do with what happened to us. He never found out.'

'Is that supposed to make me feel better?' he asked.

She spun toward him. 'It's not supposed to make you feel better,' she snapped. 'It's not about you. I'm the one who married him. I'm the one who betrayed him. I can't believe you're still beating yourself up about it.'

Myron swallowed. 'He visited me in the hospital. After I got injured. He sat and talked with me for hours.'

'And that makes him a swell guy?'

'We shouldn't have done it.'

'Grow up,' she said. 'It was more than ten years ago. Gone and forgotten.'

Silence.

After some time had passed, Myron looked up at her. 'Could you really lose your kids?' he asked.

'Yes.'

'How far would you go to keep them?'

'As far as I had to.'

'Would you kill to keep them?' Myron asked.

'Yes.' No hesitation.

'Did you?'

'No.'

'Do you have any idea why some goons would be looking for Greg?'

'No.'

'You didn't hire them?'

'If I did,' she said, 'I wouldn't tell you. But if these "goons" want to hurt Greg, I'll do all I can to help them locate him.'

Myron put down the lemonade. 'I guess I better get going.'

She showed him to the door. Before she opened it, she put a hand on his arm. Her touch burned right through the material. 'It's okay,' she said gently. 'Let it go. Greg never found out.'

Myron nodded.

She took a deep breath and smiled again. Her voice returned to its normal tone. 'It was good to see you again, Myron.'

'Same here,' he said.

'Come back again, will you?' She was trying to hard to be casual. Myron knew it was just an act, one he had seen before. 'Perhaps we can have a quick fling for old times' sake. Couldn't hurt, right?'

One last grasp at the shock. Myron pulled away. 'That's what we said last time,' he said. 'And it still hurts.'

10

'It was the night before they got married,' Myron began. He was back at his office. Esperanza sat in front of him. Her eyes were on him, but he didn't know that. He stared at the ceiling, his fingers laced and resting on his chest. He had his chair tilted far back. 'Do you want the details?'

'Only if you want to tell me' Esperanza said.

He told her. He told her how Emily had called him. He told her how she came to his room. He told her that they'd both had too much to drink. He said that last one as a sort of trial balloon, but a quick glance at Esperanza blew that particular old balloon out of the sky. She interrupted with one question.

'How long after the draft did all this take place?'

Myron smiled at the ceiling. She was so damned perceptive. There was no reason to answer.

'I assume,' Esperanza continued, 'that this little tryst occurred sometime between the pro draft and your injury?'

'You assume correctly.'

'Ah,' she said with a small nod. 'So let me see if I got the true picture now. It's your senior year of college. Your team won the NCAA finals – a point for you. You end up losing Emily and she ends up engaged to Greg – a point for him. The draft comes. Greg is the seventh overall pick; you are eighth – point for Greg.'

Myron closed his eyes and nodded. 'You're wondering if I was trying to even the score.'

'Not wondering,' Esperanza corrected. 'The answer is obvious.'

'You're not helping.'

'You want help, go to a shrink,' she said. 'You want the truth, come to me.'

She was right. He took his hands off his chest. Keeping the fingers laced, he placed them behind his head. He put his feet on the desk.

'Did she cheat on you with him?' she asked.

'No.'

'You're sure?'

'Yes. They met after we broke up.'

'Too bad,' she said. 'It would have given you a nice out.'

'Yeah. Pity.'

'So this is why you feel obligated to Greg? Because you slept with his fiancée?'

'That's a big part of it, but there's more to it than that.'

'Like?'

'It's going to sound corny, but there's always been a bond between us.'

'A bond?'

Myron's line of vision traveled from the ceiling to his movie-still wall. Woody Allen and Diane Keaton were enjoying a Manhattan moment in *Annie Hall*. Bogie and Bergman leaned on Sam's piano back in the days when Paris had been theirs. 'Greg and I were once-in-a-lifetime competitors,' he said. 'And there is a special bond between competitors. Kinda like Magic Johnson and Larry Bird. You become defined by one another. It was like that with Greg and me. It was unspoken, but we both knew the bond was there.'

He stopped. Esperanza waited in silence. 'When I hurt my knee,' Myron continued, 'Greg visited me in the hospital. He showed up the very next day. I woke up from some pain medication and there he was. Sitting with Win. And I instantly understood. Win must have understood too, other-wise he would have thrown him out.'

Esperanza nodded.

'Greg stayed around too. He helped with rehab. That's what I mean by a bond. He was devastated by the news because when I got hurt, it was like a part of him was gone too. He tried to tell me why it meant so much to him, but he couldn't put it into words. It didn't matter. I knew. He just had to be there.'

'And you hurt your knee how long after you'd slept with his new bride?'

'About a month.'

'Did seeing him all the time help or hurt?'

'Yes.'

She said nothing.

'Do you understand now?' he asked. 'Do you see why I have to pursue this? You're probably right. Sleeping with Emily was probably nothing more than payback for not getting drafted before Greg. Just another stupid battle. But what kind of way was that for a marriage to start? I owe Greg Downing. It's that simple.'

'No,' she said. 'It's not that simple.'

'Why not?'

'Because too much of your past is resurfacing. First Jessica—'

'Don't start with that.'

'I'm not' she said calmly. Her voice was rarely calm when it came to Jessica. 'I'm just stating a fact. Jessica crushed you when she left. You never got over her.'

'But she's back now.'

'Yes.'

'So what's your point?'

'Basketball also crushed you when it left. You never got over it.'

'Sure I did.'

She shook her head. 'First you spent three years trying every possible remedy to fix your knee.'

'I just tried to get better,' he interjected. 'Nothing wrong with that, is there?'

'Nothing. But you were a pain in the ass. You pushed Jessica away. I'm not forgiving her for what she did to you. You didn't ask for that. But you played a part in her leaving.'

'Why are you bringing this all up?'

She shook her head. 'You're the one who's bringing it all up. Your entire past. Jessica and now basketball. You want us to watch you go through all this again, but we won't.'

'Go through what?'

But she didn't answer. Instead she asked, 'Do you want to know why I didn't go see you play last night?'

He nodded, still not facing her. His cheeks felt flush and hot.

'Because with Jessica, at least there's a *chance* you won't get hurt again. There's a chance the witch smartened up. But with basketball, there is no chance. You can't come back.'

'I can handle it,' he said, hearing those words yet again.

She said nothing.

Myron stared off. He barely heard the phone ring. Neither one of them moved to answer it. 'You think I should drop this?' he asked.

'Yes. I agree with Emily. She's the one who betrayed him. You were just a handy tool. If what happened somehow poisoned their relationship, it was her doing. It was her decision. You don't owe Greg Downing a thing.'

'Even if what you're saying is true,' he said, 'that bond is still there.'

'Bullshit,' Esperanza said. 'That's just a load of pedantic, macho bullshit. You're just proving my point. There's no bond anymore, if there ever was one. Basketball hasn't been a part of your life for a decade. The only reason you think the bond is still there is because you're playing again.'

There was a loud pounding on the door. The frame shook and almost gave way. Myron startled upright. 'Who's manning the phones?' he asked.

Esperanza smiled.

'Oh no.'

'Come in,' Esperanza said.

The door opened. Myron's feet fell to the floor. Though he had seen her many times before, his jaw still dropped open. Big Cyndi ducked in. She was mammoth. Six-five and over three hundred pounds. Cyndi wore a white T-shirt with the sleeves ripped off at the biceps. Her arms were the envy of

Hulk Hogan. Her makeup was more garish than it had been in the ring. Her hair was purple spikes; her mascara was also purple though a darker shade than her hair. Her lipstick was a red smear. Cyndi looked like something out of *Rocky Horror Picture Show*. She was the single most frightening sight Myron had ever seen.

'Hi, Cyndi,' Myron tried.

Cyndi growled. She held up her middle finger, turned, stepped back through the door, closed it.

'What the—'

'She's telling you to pick up line one,' Esperanza said.

'Cyndi's answering phones?'

'Yes.'

'She doesn't talk!'

'In person. On the phone she's very good.'

'Jesus Christ.'

'Pick up the phone and stop whining.'

Myron did so. It was Lisa, their contact at New York Bell. Most people think that only the police can get phone records. Not true. Almost every private eye in the country has a contact at their local phone company. It's just a matter of simply paying someone off. A month's phone record can cost you anywhere from one thousand to five thousand dollars. Myron and Win had met Lisa during their days with the feds. She didn't take money, but they always took care of her in some way or another. 'I got what Win wanted,' Lisa said.

'Go ahead.'

'The call at nine eighteen P.M. came from a public phone located in a diner near Dyckman Street and Broadway,' she said.

'Isn't that up near Two Hundredth Street?'

'I think so. You want the phone number?'

Carla had called Greg from a diner on 200th Street? Weirder and weirder. 'If you have it.'

She gave it to him. 'Hope that helps.'

'It does, Lisa. Thanks.' He held up the paper to Esperanza. 'Lookie what I got,' he said. 'A real live clue.'

11

To be fair, the Parkview Diner lived up to its name. You did indeed have a view of Lieutenant William Tighe Park across the street; it was smaller than the average backyard with shrubs so high you really couldn't see the landscaped garden within. A wire-mesh fence enclosed the grounds. Hung on the fence in several places were signs that read in big, bold letters: DO NOT FEED THE RATS. No joke. In smaller print the warning was repeated in Spanish: *No Des Comida a Las Ratas.* The signs had been placed there by a group calling itself the Quality of Life Zone. Myron shook his head. Only in New York would this be a problem – people who could not contain themselves from the seductive lure of feeding vermin. Myron glanced again at the sign, then the diner. Rats. Quite the appetite-enhancer.

He crossed the street. Two levels above the Parkview Diner, a dog squeezed his head through the grates of a fire escape and barked at passing pedestrians. The Parkview's green overhang was ripped in several spots. The letters were faded to the point of unintelligibility, and the support pole was bent so far that Myron had to duck to get to the door. There was a poster of a gyro sandwich in the window. Today's specials, according to a blackboard in the same window, included eggplant parmigiana and chicken à la king. The soup was beef consommé. There were permits from the City of New York Department of Buildings stuck on the door like car-inspection decals.

Myron entered and was immediately greeted by the familiar yet nonspecific smell of a Manhattan diner. Fat was in the air. Taking a deep breath felt as if it would clog an artery. A waitress with hair bleached to the point of straw offered him a table. Myron asked her for the manager. Using her pencil she pointed over her shoulder at a man behind the counter.

'That's Hector,' she said. 'He owns the place.'

Myron thanked her and grabbed a soda-fountain stool at the counter. He debated spinning himself in the seat and decided the act might be viewed as immature. Two stools to his right, an unshaven, perhaps homeless man with black Thom McAn sneakers and a tattered overcoat smiled and nodded. Myron nodded and smiled back. The man went back to his coffee. He raised his shoulders and huddled into the drink as though he suspected someone might try to swipe it in mid-sip.

Myron picked up a vinyl menu with cracked binding. He opened it but didn't really read it. There were a lot of worn index cards jammed into protective plastic cases announcing various specials. Worn was an apt description of the Parkview Diner, but it didn't fairly convey the overall impression. There was something welcoming and even clean about this place. The counter gleamed. So did the utensils and the silver milkshake maker and the soda fountain. Most patrons read a newspaper or gabbed with one another as if they were eating at home. They knew their waitress's name, and you could bet your last dollar she didn't introduce herself and tell them she was going to be their server when they first sat down.

Hector the owner was busy at the grill. Almost two P.M. It wasn't the height of the lunch hour, but business was still pretty brisk. He barked out some orders in Spanish, his eyes never leaving the food. Then he turned around with a polite smile, wiped his hands on a rag, and asked Myron if he could help him. Myron asked if he had a pay phone.

'No, sir, I'm sorry,' Hector answered. The Hispanic accent was there, but Hector had worked on it. 'There's one on the street corner. On the left.'

Myron looked at the number Lisa had given him. He read it out loud. Hector did several things at the same time. He flipped burgers, folded over an omelette, checked the french fries. His eyes were everywhere – the cash register, the clientele at both the tables and the counter, the kitchen to his left.

'Oh that,' Hector said. 'It's in the back. In the kitchen.'

'The kitchen?'

'Yes, sir.' Still polite.

'A pay phone in the kitchen?'

'Yes, sir,' Hector said. He was on the short side, thin under his white apron and polyester black pants. His nose had been broken several times. His forearms looked like steel cords. 'It's for my staff.'

'Don't you have a business phone?'

'Of course we do.' His voice spiked up a bit now, as if the question was an insult. 'We do a big takeout and delivery business here. Lots of people order lunch from us. We have a fax machine too. But I don't want my staff tying up the lines, you know? You get a busy signal, you give your business to someone else, yes? So I put a pay phone in the back.'

'I see.' An idea came to Myron. 'Are you telling me customers never use it?'

'Well, sir, if a customer truly insists, I would never refuse him.' The practiced politeness of a good businessman. 'The customer must come first at the Parkview. Always.'

'Has a customer ever insisted?'

'No, sir. I don't think any customers even know we have it.'

'Can you tell me who was using the pay phone at nine eighteen P.M. last Saturday?'

That question got his attention. 'Excuse me?' Myron started to repeat the question but Hector interrupted him. 'Why would you want to know that?'

'My name is Bernie Worley,' Myron said. 'I'm a product supervising agent with AT&T.' *A product what?* 'Somebody is trying to cheat us, sir, and we are not happy about it.'

'Cheat you?'

'A Y511.'

'A what?'

'A Y511,' Myron repeated. You start tossing the bull, your best bet is to just keep tossing. 'It's an electronic monitoring device built in Hong Kong. It's new on the market, but we're onto it. Sold on the streets. Somebody used one on your phone at nine eighteen P.M. on March eighteenth of this year. They dialed Kuala Lumpur and spoke for nearly twelve minutes. The total cost of the call is twenty-three dollars and eighty-two cents, but the fine for using a Y511 will be at least seven hundred dollars with the potential for up to one year in prison. Plus we'll have to remove the phone.'

Hector's face became a mask of pure panic. 'What?' Myron wasn't thrilled with what he was doing – scaring an honest, hard-working immigrant like this – but he knew that the fear of government or big business would work in a situation like this. Hector turned around and shouted something in Spanish to a teenager who looked like him. The teenager took over the grill. 'I don't understand this, Mr Worley.'

'It's a public phone, sir. You just admitted to a product supervising agent that you used the public phones for private use; that is, for your employees only and denying public access. This violates our own code, section one twenty-four B. I wouldn't report it normally, but when you add in the use of a Y511—'

'But I didn't use a Y511!'

'We don't know that, sir.' Myron was playing Mr Bureaucrat to the hilt; nothing made a person feel more impotent. There is no darker pit than the blank stare of a bureaucrat. 'The phone is on your premises,' Myron continued in a bored singsong voice. 'You just explained to me that the phone was only used by your employees—'

'Exactly!' Hector leaped. 'By my employees! Not me!'

'But you own this establishment. You are responsible.' Myron looked around with his best, bored expression – the one he learned while waiting on line at the Division of Motor Vehicles. 'We'll also have to check out the status of all your employees. Maybe we can find the culprit that way.'

Hector's eyes grew big. Myron knew this would hit home. There wasn't a restaurant in Manhattan that didn't employ at least one illegal alien. Hector's jowls slackened. 'All this,' he said, 'because someone used a pay phone?'

'What someone did, sir, was use an illegal electronic device known as a

Y511. What you did, sir, was refuse to cooperate with the product supervising agent investigating this serious matter.'

'Refuse to cooperate?' Hector was grasping at the possible life preserver Myron had offered up. 'No, sir, not me. I want to cooperate. I want to very much.'

Myron shook his head. 'I don't think you do.'

Hector bit down and set his polite meter on extra-strength now. 'No, sir,' he said. 'I want to help very much. I want to cooperate with the phone company. Tell me what I can do to help. Please.'

Myron sighed, gave it a few seconds. The diner bustled. The cash register dinged while the guy who looked homeless with the Thom McAn sneakers picked out greasy coins from a dirty hand. The griddle sizzled. The aroma from the various foods battled each other for dominance with none winning outright. Hector's face grew more and more anxious. Enough, Myron thought. 'For starters, you can tell me who was using the pay phone at nine eighteen P.M. last Saturday.'

Hector held up a finger imploring patience. He shouted something in Spanish to the woman (Mrs Hector maybe?) working the cash register. The woman shouted something back. She closed the drawer and walked toward them. As she drew closer, Myron noticed that Hector was suddenly giving him an odd look. Was he starting to see through Myron's rather husky load of bull-dooky? Perhaps. But Myron looked back at him steadily and Hector quickly backed down. He might be suspicious, but not suspicious enough to risk offending the all-powerful bureaucrat by questioning his authority.

Hector whispered something to the woman. She urgently whispered back. He made an understanding 'ah' noise. Then he faced Myron and shook his head.

'It figures,' he said.

'What?'

'It was Sally.'

'Who?'

'At least I think it was Sally. My wife saw her on the phone around then. But she said she was only on for a minute or two.'

'Does Sally have a last name?'

'Guerro.'

'Is she here now?'

Hector shook his head. 'She hasn't been here since Saturday night. That's what I mean by figures. She gets me in trouble and then she runs out.'

'Has she called in sick?'

'No, sir. She just up and left.'

'You got an address on her?' Myron asked.

'I think so, let me see.' He pulled out a big carton that read 'Snapple Peach Ice Tea' on the side. Behind him, the griddle hissed when fresh pancake batter touched down upon the hot metal. The files in the box were neat and color coded. Hector pulled one out and opened it. He shuffled through the sheets, found the one he was looking for, and frowned.

'What?' Myron prompted.

'Sally never gave us an address,' Hector said.

'How about a phone number?'

'No.' He looked up, remembering something. 'She said she didn't have a phone. That's why she was using the one in the back so much.'

'Could you tell me what Ms Guerro looked like?' Myron tried.

Hector suddenly looked uncomfortable. He glanced at his wife and cleared his throat. 'Uh, she had brown hair,' he began. 'Maybe five-four, five-five. Average height, I guess.'

'Anything else?'

'Brown eyes, I think.' He stopped. 'That's about it.'

'How old would you say she was?'

Hector checked the file again. 'According to this, she was forty-five. That sounds about right.'

'How long has she worked here?' he asked.

'Two months.'

Myron nodded, rubbed his chin vigorously. 'It sounds like an operative who goes by the name of Carla.'

'Carla?'

'A notorious phone fraud,' Myron continued. 'We've been after her for a while.' He glanced left, then right. Trying to look conspiratorial. 'Have you ever heard her use the name Carla or hear someone call her Carla?'

Hector looked at his wife. She shook her head. 'No, never.'

'Did she have any visitors? Any friends?'

Again Hector checked with his wife. Again the head shook. 'No, none that we ever saw. She kept to herself most of the time.'

Myron decided to push a little further and confirm what he already knew. If Hector balked at this stage, so what? Nothing ventured, nothing gained. He leaned forward; Hector and his wife did likewise. 'This may sound insensitive,' Myron whispered, 'but was this woman large chested?'

Both nods were immediate. 'Very large,' Hector said.

Suspicion confirmed.

He asked a few more questions, but any useful information had already been culled from these waters. Before leaving, he told them that they were in the clear and could continue to violate code section 124B without fear. Hector almost kissed his hand. Myron felt like a louse. *What did you do today, Batman? Well, Robin, I started off by terrorizing a hard-working immigrant's livelihood with a bunch of lies. Holy Cow, Batman, you're the coolest!* Myron shook his head. What to do for an encore – throw empty beer bottles at the dog on the fire escape?

Myron exited the Parkview Diner. He debated going to the park across the street, but suppose he became overcome by a lustful need to feed rats?

No, he couldn't risk it. He'd have to stay away. He began to head to the Dyckman Street subway station when a voice stopped him.

'You looking for Sally?'

Myron turned. It was the homeless-looking man with the Thom McAns from the diner. He sat on the pavement, his back leaning against the brick building. He had an empty plastic coffee cup in his hand. Panhandling.

'You know her?' Myron asked.

'She and I . . .' He winked and crossed his fingers. 'We met because of that damn phone, you know.'

'Really.'

Using the wall for support the man stood. His facial hair was whitish, not full enough to be a beard yet past the stage of a Miami Vice wanna-be. His long hair was black as coal. 'Sally was using my phone all the time. It pissed me off.'

'Your phone?'

'The pay phone in the back,' he said licking his lips. 'It's right by the back door. I hang out in the back alley a lot so I can hear it, you know? It's kind of like my business phone.' Myron couldn't guess his age. His face was boyish but leathered – from the passing years or hard living, Myron couldn't say. His grin was missing a couple of prominent teeth, reminding Myron of that beloved Christmas classic 'All I Want for Christmas Is My Two Front Teeth.' Such a nice song really. No toys, no Sega Genesis video game. The kid just wanted teeth. So selfless really.

'I used to have my own cellular,' the man continued. 'Two of them, as a matter of fact. But they got stolen. And the damn things are so unreliable, especially around the high buildings. And anyone can listen in with the right equipment. Me, I need to keep what I do secret, you see. Spies are everywhere. And they also give you brain tumors. The electrons or something. Brain tumors the size of beach balls.'

Myron kept his face blank. 'Uh huh.' Speaking of tossing the ball.

'So anyway Sally started using it, too. It pissed me off, you know? I mean, I'm a businessman. I got important calls coming in. I can't have the line tied up. Am I right?'

'As rain,' Myron said.

'See, I'm a Hollywood screenwriter.' He stuck out his hand. 'Norman Lowenstein.'

Myron tried to remember the fake name he used with Hector. 'Bernie Worley.'

'Nice to meet you, Bernie.'

'Do you know where Sally Guerro lives?'

'Sure. We used to be . . .' Norman Lowenstein crossed his fingers.

'So I heard. Could you tell me where she lives?'

Norman Lowenstein pursed his lips and used his pointer finger to scratch a spot near his throat. 'I'm not real good with addresses and stuff,' he said. 'But I could take you there.'

Myron wondered how big a waste of time this was going to be. 'Would you mind?'

'Sure, no problem. Let's go.'

'Which way?'

'The A train,' Norman said. 'Down to One Hundred Twenty-fifth Street.' They walked toward the subway.

'You go to the movies much, Bernie?' Norman asked.

'Much as the next guy, I guess.'

'Let me tell you something about movie-making,' he began, growing more animated. 'It's not all glamour and glitz. It's a dog-eat-dog business like no other, making dreams for people. All the back-stabbing, all that money, all that fame and attention . . . it makes people act funny, you know? I got this screenplay with Paramount right now. They're talking to Willis about it. Bruce Willis. He's really interested.'

'Good luck with it,' Myron said.

Norman beamed. 'Thanks, Bernie, that's real nice of you. I mean it. Real nice. I'd like to tell you what my flick is about, but well, my hands are tied. You know how it is. Hollywood and all the theft out there. The studio wants it kept hush-hush.'

'I understand,' Myron said.

'I trust you, Bernie, it's not that. But the studios insist. I can't blame them really. They got to protect their interests, right?'

'Right.'

'It's an action-adventure flick, that much I can tell you. But with heart too, you know? Not just a shoot-em-up. Harrison Ford wanted in, but he's too old. I guess Willis is okay. He's not my first choice, but what can you do?'

'Uh huh.'

One Twenty-fifth Street was not the nicest stop in the city. It was safe enough during the day, Myron surmised, but the fact that he was now carrying a gun made him feel a tad more secure. Myron did not like 'packing heat' and rarely did so. It was not that Myron was particularly squeamish; it had more to do with comfort. The shoulder holster dug into his armpit and made it itch like he was wearing a tweed condom. But after last night's soiree with Camouflage Pants and Brick Wall, it would be foolhardy to walk around unarmed.

'Which way?' Myron asked.

'Downtown.'

They headed south on Broadway. Norman regaled him with tales of Hollywood. The ins and outs. Myron nodded and kept walking. The farther south they headed, the better the area became. They passed the familiar iron gates of Columbia University, then turned left. 'It's right up here,' Norman said. 'Toward the middle of the block.'

561

The street was lined with low-rise apartments that were mostly used by Columbia's grad students and professors. Strange, Myron thought, that a diner waitress would live here. But then again nothing else about her involvement in all this made sense – why should where she lived? If she lived here at all, and not, say, with Bruce Willis in Hollywood.

Norman interrupted his thoughts. 'You're trying to help her, right?'

'What?'

Norman stopped walking. He was less animated now. 'All that stuff about being from the phone company. That was all crap, right?'

Myron said nothing.

'Look,' he said, putting his hand on Myron's forearm, 'Hector is a good man. He came to this country with nothing. He works his ass off in that diner. He and his wife and son – they slave there every day. No days off. And every day he's scared someone's going to take it all away from him. All that worry . . . it clouds the thinking, you know? Me, I got nothing to lose so I'm not afraid of anything. Makes it easier to see some stuff. Know what I mean?'

Myron gave a slight nod.

Norman's bright eyes dimmed as a bit of reality swept through him. Myron looked at him, really looked at him, for the first time. He made his eyes stop sweeping by him with barely a notice of age or height or even species. Myron realized that behind the lies and self-delusion lay the dreams of any man, the hopes and wants and needs that are the sole reserve of the human race.

'I'm worried about Sally,' Norman went on. 'Maybe that's clouding my thinking. But I know she wouldn't just up and leave without saying good-bye to me. Sally wouldn't do that.' He stopped, met Myron's eyes with his own. 'You're not from the phone company, are you?'

'No, I'm not.'

'You want to help her?'

'Yes,' Myron said. 'I want to help her.'

He nodded and pointed. 'In here. Apartment two E.'

Myron walked up the stoop while Norman stayed on the street level. He pressed the black button reading 2E. No one answered. No surprise there. He tried the entrance door, but it was locked. You had to be buzzed in.

'You better stay there,' he told Norman. Norman nodded, understanding. These buzzer-protected doors were mild deterrents to crime, but their true purpose was to prevent vagrants from coming in and setting up camp in the lobby. Myron would just wait. Eventually an occupant would leave or enter the building. While said occupant opened the door, Myron would enter as though he belonged. No one would question a man dressed in khakis and a button-down BD Baggies shirt. If Norman stood next to him, however, that same occupant might react differently.

Myron moved down two steps. When he saw two young women approach the door from the inside, he slapped his pockets as though looking for keys. Then he walked purposefully up to the door, smiled, and waited for them to push it open. He need not have bothered with the dramatics. The two young women – college students, Myron guessed – went through the portal without looking up or decelerating their oral activities. Both were talking nonstop, neither listening. They paid absolutely no attention to him. Amazing restraint really. Of course from this angle they couldn't see his ass, so their self-control was not only admirable but somewhat understandable.

He looked back at Norman, who thankfully waved him off. 'You go yourself,' he said. 'I don't want to cause a problem.'

Myron let the door close.

The corridor was pretty much what he expected. It was painted off-white. No stripes or designs. There were no wall-hangings other than a huge bulletin board that read like a schizophrenic political manifesto. Dozens of leaflets announced everything from a dance sponsored by the Native American Gay and Lesbian Society to poetry readings by a group calling itself the Rush Limbaugh Review. Ah, the college life.

He ascended a stairway lit by two bare bulbs. All this walking and stair climbing were starting to take a toll on his bad knee. The joint tightened up like a rusted hinge. Myron felt himself dragging the leg behind him. He used the railing for support and wondered what the knee would be like when he reached arthritis age.

The floor plan of the building was far from symmetrical. Doors seemed to be placed in the wall as though at random. Off in a corner, a good distance from the other apartments, Myron found the door marked 2E. The positioning made the apartment look like an afterthought, as if someone had spotted some extra space in the back and decided to add an extra room or two. Myron knocked. No answer. No surprise. He checked the corridor. No one in sight. He was thankful that Norman was not here because he wouldn't want someone to witness him breaking in.

Myron was not great at the lock-picking game. He had learned a bit over the years, but picking locks was a bit like playing a video game. You work at it enough, and eventually you move up levels. Myron hadn't worked at it. He didn't like it. He really didn't have much natural talent for it. In most cases, he relied on Win to handle the mechanical stuff, like Barney used to do on *Mission: Impossible*.

He examined the door and felt his heart sink. Even for New York the dead bolts were nothing short of impressive. Three of them stacked intimidatingly from six inches above the knob to six inches below the top frame. Top of the line stuff. Brand new, judging by the gleam and lack of scratches. This was a tad odd. Was Sally/Carla the extracautious type, or was there a more aberrant reason for such security? Good question. Myron looked at the locks again. Win would have enjoyed the challenge; Myron knew that any effort he made would be fruitless.

He debated kicking in the door when he noticed something. He moved closer and squinted into the door crack. Again something struck him as being odd. The dead bolts were not engaged. Why buy all these expensive locks and not use them? He tried the knob. It was locked, but that one would be easy to get through with the 'loid card.

He took out the card. He couldn't remember the last time he had used it. It looked pristine. Maybe never. He jammed it into the opening. Despite being an old lock it still took Myron almost five minutes to find the right spot to push the lock back. He gripped the knob. The door began to swing open.

It was open barely six inches when the odor attacked.

The bloodcurdling stench popped out into the hallway like pressurized gas. Myron felt his stomach dive and swoop. He gagged a little and felt a weight on his chest. He knew the smell, and dread filled him. He searched his pockets for a handkerchief and came up empty. He blocked his nose and mouth with the crook of his elbow, as if he were doing Bela Lugosi in *Dracula*. He didn't want to go in. He wasn't good at this type of thing. He knew that whatever image lay behind the door would stay with him, would haunt his nights and too often his days too. It would stay with him like a dear friend, tapping him on the shoulder every once in a while when he thought he was alone and at peace.

He pushed the door all the way open. The rancid smell permeated his meager protection. He tried to breathe through his mouth, but the thought of what he was sucking in made that option unbearable.

Fortunately, he didn't have to travel far to find the source of the odor.

12

'Whoa, Bolitar, new cologne?'

'Funny, Dimonte.'

NYPD homicide detective Roland Dimonte shook his head. 'Christ, what a stink.' He was out of uniform, but you wouldn't ever call him 'plainclothes.' He wore a green silk shirt and jeans that were too tight and too dark blue. The bottoms were tucked into purple snakeskin boots; the color faded in and out with any angle change, like some psychedelic Hendrix poster from the sixties. Dimonte gnawed on a toothpick, a habit he picked up, Myron surmised, when he spotted himself doing it in the mirror and decided it looked tough. 'You touch anything?' he asked.

'Just the doorknob,' Myron said. He had also checked the rest of the apartment to make sure there weren't any other gruesome surprises. There weren't.

'How did you get in?'

'The door was unlocked.'

'Really?' Dimonte raised an eyebrow and looked back at the door. 'The door is set to lock automatically when you close it.'

'Did I say unlocked? I meant, ajar.'

'Sure you did.' Dimonte did a bit more gnawing, shook his head. He ran his hand through greasy hair. Ringlets clung to his forehead, refusing to give ground. 'So who is she?'

'I don't know,' Myron said.

Dimonte scrunched up his face like a closed fist. Displaying very skeptical. Subtle body language was not Dimonte's forte. 'Little early in the day to be pulling my hardware, ain't it, Bolitar?'

'I don't know her name. It might be Sally Guerro. Then again it might be Carla.'

'Uh huh.' Toothpick chew. 'I thought I saw you on TV last night. That you were playing ball again.'

'I am.'

The coroner came over. He was tall and thin and his wire-rim glasses looked too big on the elongated face. 'She's been dead awhile,' he pronounced. 'At least four days.'

'Cause?'

'Hard to say for sure. Someone bludgeoned her with a blunt object. I'll know more when I get her on the table.' He looked at the corpse with professional disinterest, then back at Dimonte. 'They're not real, by the way.'

'What?'

He vaguely motioned toward the torso. 'Her breasts. They're implants.'

'Jesus Christ,' Dimonte said, 'you fiddling with dead bodies now?'

The elongated face sagged, his jaw dropping to somewhere around his navel. 'Don't even joke about that,' the coroner said in a stage whisper. 'You know what rumors like that could do to a guy in my business?'

'Get him promoted?' Dimonte said.

The coroner did not laugh. He gave Myron a wounded look, then Dimonte. 'You think that's funny, huh? Goddamn it, this is my career you're fucking around with!'

'Calm down, Peretti, I'm just playing with you.'

'Playing with me? You think my career is some kind of fucking joke? What the hell is wrong with you?'

Dimonte's eyes narrowed. 'Kind of sensitive about all this, Peretti.'

'You have to be in my position,' he said, back straightening.

'If you say so.'

'What the hell does that mean?'

' "The lady protests too much, methinks." '

'What?'

'It's Shakespeare,' Dimonte said. 'From *Macbeth*.' Dimonte looked over to Myron.

Myron smiled. '*Hamlet*.'

'I don't give a shit who said it,' Peretti protested. 'You shouldn't mess around with a man's reputation. I don't think any of this is funny.'

'Like I give a rat's ass what you think,' Dimonte said. 'You got anything else?'

'She's wearing a wig.'

'A wig? No kidding, Peretti. The case is as good as solved now. All we need to do is find a killer who hates wigs and fake tits. This is helpful, Peretti. What kind of panties was she wearing, huh? You sniff them yet?'

'I was just—'

'Do me a big favor, Peretti.' Dimonte made himself taller, hitched his pants. Signaling importance. Again the subtlety. 'Tell me when she died. Tell me how she died. Then we'll talk about her fashion accessories, okay?'

Peretti held up his hands in surrender and returned to the body. Dimonte turned to Myron. Myron said, 'The implants and wig might be important. He was right to tell you.'

'Yeah, I know. I just like busting his chops.'

'And the quote is, "Methinks the lady doth protest too much." '

'Uh huh.' Dimonte changed toothpicks. The one in his mouth was frayed like a horse's mane. 'You going to tell me what the fuck is going on, or am I going to drag you downtown?'

Myron made a face. 'Drag me downtown?'

'Don't bust my balls on this, Bolitar, okay?'

Myron forced himself to look at the bloodied corpse. His stomach did back flips. He was starting to get used to the smell, the thought of which was nearly as bad as the smell itself. Peretti was back at it, making a small slit to get to the liver. Myron diverted his gaze. The homicide crew from John Jay was setting up, taking photographs, that kind of thing. Dimonte's partner, a kid named Krinsky, quietly walked around and took notes. 'Why would she make them so big?' Myron wondered out loud.

'What?'

'Her breasts. I can understand the desire to enlarge them. All the pressures in this society. But why make them that big?'

Dimonte said, 'You're shitting me, right?'

Krinksy came over. 'All her stuff is in those suitcases.' He motioned with his hand to two bags on the floor. Myron had met Krinsky on maybe half a dozen occasions. Talking was not the kid's forte; he seemed to do it as often as Myron picked locks. 'I'd say she was moving out.'

'You got an ID yet?' Dimonte asked.

'Her wallet says her name is Sally Guerro,' Krinsky continued in a soft voice. 'So does one of her passports.'

They both waited for Krinsky to continue. When he didn't, Dimonte shouted, 'What do you mean, one of her passports? How many does she have?'

'Three.'

'Jesus Christ, Krinsky, talk.'

'One is in the name Sally Guerro. One is in the name Roberta Smith. One is in the name Carla Whitney.'

'Give me those.' Dimonte scanned through the various passports. Myron looked over his shoulder. The same woman was in all three pictures, albeit with different hair (ergo the wig) and different Social Security numbers. Judging by the amount of stamps, the woman had traveled extensively.

Dimonte whistled. 'Forged passports,' he said. 'And good ones too.' He turned more pages. 'Plus she has a couple of visits to South America here. Colombia. Bolivia.' The passports closed with a dramatic snap. 'Well, well, well. Looks like we got ourselves a nice, neat drug hit.'

Myron mulled over that bit of information. A drug hit – could that be part of the answer? If Sally/Carla/Roberta was dealing drugs, it might explain her connection with Greg Downing. She was his source. The meeting on Saturday night was nothing more than a buy. The waitress job was a cover. It also explained her using a pay phone and maintaining powerful door locks – tools of a drug dealer's trade. It made some sense. Of course, Greg Downing did not appear to be a drug user, but he would not be the first person to fool everyone.

Dimonte said 'Anything else, Krinsky?'

The kid nodded. 'I found a stack of cash in the bedside drawer.' He stopped again.

Dimonte gave him exasperation. 'Did you count it?'

Another nod.

'How much?'

'A little over ten thousand dollars.'

'Ten grand in cash, huh?' That pleased Dimonte. 'Let me see it.'

Krinksy handed it over. New bills, held by rubber bands. Myron watched while Dimonte shuffled through them. All hundreds. The serial numbers were sequential. Myron tried to memorize one of them. When Dimonte finished, he tossed the packet back to Krinsky. The smile was still there.

'Yep,' Dimonte said, 'it looks like things are coming together in a nice, neat, drug-hit package.' He paused. 'Only one problem.'

'What?'

He pointed at Myron. 'You, Bolitar. You're messing up my nice, neat drug-hit. What the hell are you doing—?' Dimonte stopped himself and snapped his fingers. 'Holy shit . . .' His voice sort of drifted off. He slapped the side of his own head. A small spark in his eyes expanded. 'My God!'

Again note the subtlety. 'You have a thought, Rolly?'

Dimonte ignored him. 'Peretti!'

The coroner looked up from the body. 'What?'

'Those plastic tits,' he said. 'Myron noticed they were huge.'

'Yeah, so?'

'How big?'

'What?'

'How big are they?'

'You mean like cup size?'

'Yeah.'

'I look like a lingerie manufacturer? How the fuck would I know?'

'But they're big, right?'

'Right.'

'Really big.'

'You got eyes, don't you?'

Myron watched the exchange in silence. He was trying to follow Dimonte's logic – a most treacherous trail.

'Would you say they were bigger than a water balloon?' Dimonte continued.

Peretti shrugged. 'Depends on the balloon.'

'Didn't you ever make water balloons when you were a kid?'

'Yeah, sure,' Peretti said. 'But I don't remember how big the balloons were. I was a kid then. Everything looks bigger when you're a kid. A couple years ago I went back to my old elementary school to visit my third grade teacher. She still works there, if you can believe it. Her name is Mrs Tansmore. I swear to God the building looked like a goddamn dollhouse to me. It was huge when I was a kid. It was like—'

'All right, moron, let me make this simple.' Dimonte took a deep breath. 'Could they be used for smuggling drugs?'

Silence. Everyone in the room stopped moving. Myron wasn't sure if he just heard the most idiotic thing in the world or the most brilliant. He turned toward Peretti. Peretti looked up, mouth open in fly-catching pose.

'Well, Peretti? Could it be?'

'Could it be what?'

'Could she stick dope in her boobs? Smuggle drugs through customs with them?'

Peretti looked at Myron. Myron shrugged. Peretti turned back to Dimonte. 'I don't know,' he said slowly.

'How can we find out?'

'I'd have to examine them.'

'Then what the fuck you staring at me for? Do it.'

Peretti did as asked. Dimonte smiled at Myron; his eyebrows did a little dance. Proud of his deduction. Myron remained quiet.

'Nope, no way,' Peretti said.

Dimonte wasn't happy with this report. 'Why the hell not?'

'There's hardly any scar tissue,' Peretti said. 'If she were smuggling drugs in there, they'd have to rip the skin open and sew it up. Then they'd have to do it again on this side. There's no sign of that.'

'You're sure?'

'Positive.'

Dimonte said, 'Shit.' Then he glared at Myron and pulled him into a corner. 'Everything, Bolitar. Now.'

Myron had debated how to handle it, but in truth he had no choice. He had to tell. He couldn't keep Greg Downing's disappearance a secret any longer. The best he could hope to do was keep it contained. He suddenly remembered that Norman Lowenstein was waiting outside. 'One second,' he said.

'What? Where the fuck you going?'

'I'll be right back. Just wait here.'

'Like hell.'

Dimonte followed him down the stairs and out onto the stoop. Norman wasn't there. Myron looked up and down the block. No sign of Norman. This was hardly a surprise. Norman probably ran when he saw the cops. Guilty or not, the homeless learn quickly to make themselves scarce when the authorities come calling.

'What is it?' Dimonte asked.

'Nothing.'

'Then start talking. The whole story.'

Myron told him most of it. The story almost knocked the toothpick out of Dimonte's mouth. Dimonte didn't bother asking questions, though he continuously stuck in exclamations of 'Jesus Christ!' and 'Frigging A,' whenever Myron paused. When Myron finished, Dimonte sort of stumbled back and sat on the steps of the stoop. His eyes looked unfocused for a few moments. He gathered himself together, but it took some time.

'In-fuckin'-credible,' he managed.

Myron nodded.

'Are you telling me no one knows where Downing is?'

'If they do, they aren't talking.'

'He just vanished?'

'That's how it appears.'

'And there's blood in his basement?'

'Yes.'

Dimonte shook his head again. He reached down and put his hand on his right boot. Myron had seen him do this before. He liked to sort of pet the boot. Myron had no idea why. Maybe he found the feel of snakeskin soothing. Reminiscent of the womb.

'Suppose Downing killed her and ran,' he said.

'That's a pretty big suppose.'

'Yeah, but it fits,' Dimonte said.

'How?'

'According to what you said, Downing was seen with the victim Saturday night. How much you want to bet that once Peretti gets her on the table we find the time of death around then?'

'Doesn't mean Downing killed her.'

Dimonte increased the speed of his boot-petting stroke. A man on Rollerblades skated by with his dog. The dog looked out of breath, trying to keep up. New product idea: Dog Rollerblades. 'Saturday night, Greg Downing and the victim get together at some gin joint downtown. They leave sometime around eleven o'clock. Next thing we know she's dead and he's vanished.' Dimonte looked up at Myron. 'That points to him killing her and running.'

'It points to a dozen things.'

'Like what?'

'Like maybe Greg witnessed the murder and got scared and ran. Maybe he witnessed the murder and was kidnapped. Maybe he was killed by the same people.'

'So where's his body?' Dimonte asked.

'It could be anywhere.'

'Why not just leave it here with hers?'

'Maybe they killed him someplace else. Or maybe they took his body because he's famous and they didn't want that kind of heat.'

He scoffed at that one. 'You're reaching, Bolitar.'

'So are you.'

'Maybe. Only one way to find out.' He stood. 'We got to get out an APB on Downing.'

'Whoa, hold up a second. I don't think that's a good idea.'

Dimonte looked at Myron as if he were something left unflushed in a toilet. 'I'm sorry,' he said feigning politeness. 'You must be mistaking me for someone who gives a rat's ass what you think.'

'You're suggesting putting out an APB on a major, beloved sports hero.'

'And you're suggesting I play favorites because he's a major, beloved sports hero.'

'Not at all,' Myron said, his mind racing. 'But imagine what happens when you call out this APB. The press gets it. You start getting that O.J. coverage. But there's a difference here. You got squat on Downing. No motive. No physical evidence. Nothing.'

'Not yet I don't,' Dimonte said. 'But it's early—'

'Exactly, it's early. Wait a little while, that's all I'm saying. And handle this one right because the whole world is going to look at everything you do. Tell those bozos upstairs to videotape every step. Leave nothing to chance. Don't let anyone come back later and say you tampered or contaminated something. Get a warrant before you go to Downing's house. Do everything by the book.'

'I can do all that and still put out an APB.'

'Rolly, suppose Greg Downing did kill her. You put out an APB, you know what happens? One, you look single-minded. You look like you got it in your head that Downing was the killer and that was it. Two, you got the press in your face – watching your every move, trying to beat you to the evidence, compromising and commenting on everything you do. Three, you drag Greg in here now and you know what bottom-feeders are stuck to him?'

Dimonte nodded and made a lemon-sucking face. 'Fucking lawyers.'

'A dream team's worth. Before you have anything, they're filing motions and suppressing whatever and, well, you know the routine.'

'Shit,' Dimonte said.

Myron nodded. 'You see what I mean?'

'Yeah, I do,' Dimonte said. 'But there's some stuff you forgot, Bolitar.' He gave Myron big-time toothpick gnawing. 'For example, if I issue an APB your little team investigation goes down the toilet. You lose out.'

'Could be,' Myron said.

Dimonte studied him with a small, uneven smile. 'That doesn't mean what you're saying is wrong. I just don't want you to think I don't see what you're up to.'

'You read me,' Myron said, 'like Vasco da Gama reads a map.'

Dimonte gave him hard eyes for a moment; Myron fought off the desire to roll his in return. 'So here's how we're going to play it. You're going stay on the team and you're going to continue your little investigation. I'm going to try to keep what you told me to myself as long' – he held up a finger for emphasis – 'as long as it benefits my case. If I find enough to haul Downing's ass in here, I put out the APB. And you are going to report everything to me. You are not going to hold back. Any questions?'

'Just one,' Myron said. 'Where do you buy your boots?'

13

On the ride to practice, Myron placed a call from the car phone.

'Higgins,' a voice answered.

'Fred? It's Myron Bolitar.'

'Hey, long time, no speak. How you doing, Myron?'

'Can't complain. You?'

'A thrill a minute here at the Treasury Department.'

'Yeah, I bet.'

'How's Win?' Higgins asked.

'The same,' Myron said.

'The guy scares the piss out of me, you know what I mean?'

'Yes,' Myron said, 'I do.'

'You two miss working for the feds?'

'I don't,' Myron said. 'I don't think Win does either. It got too restrictive for him.'

'I hear you. Hey, I read in the papers you're playing ball again.'

'Yep.'

'At your age and with that knee? How come?'

'Long story, Fred.'

'Say no more. Hey, you guys are coming down to play the Bullets next week. Can you get me tickets?'

'I'll do my best.'

'Great, thanks. So what do you need, Myron?'

'The wheres and why of about ten grand in hundred dollar bills. Sequentially wrapped. Serial number B028856011A.'

'How fast you need it?'

'Soon as you can get it.'

'I'll do my best. You take care, Myron.'

'You too, Fred.'

Myron held nothing back at practice. He let it all hang out. The feeling was awesome and overpowering. He entered his own zone. When he shot, it was like an invisible hand carried the ball to the cylinder. When he dribbled, the ball became part of his hand. His senses were heightened like a wolf's in the wilderness. He felt like he'd fallen into some black hole and emerged ten years earlier at the NCAA finals. Even his knee felt great.

Most of practice consisted of a scrimmage between the starting five players and the five who saw the most bench time. Myron played his best ball. His jumper was popping. He came off screens strong and ready to shoot. He even drove straight down the lane twice – into the teeth of the big men's domain – and came away the victor both times.

There were moments he completely forgot about Greg Downing and Carla/Sally/Roberta's mangled corpse and the blood in the basement and the goons who jumped him and yes, even Jessica. An exhilarating rush like no other flooded his veins – the rush of an athlete at his peak. People talked about a runner's high, a euphoria from a gland secretion when your body was pressed to its limit. Myron couldn't relate to that, but he understood the incredible highs and plunging depths of being an athlete. If you played well, your whole body tingled and tears of pure joy came to your eyes. The tingles lasted well into the night when you lay in bed with no chance of sleep and replayed your finest moments, often in slow motion, like an over-zealous sportscaster with his finger on the replay button. When you played poorly, you were surly and depressed and stayed that way for hours and even days. Both extremes were way out of proportion with the relevant importance of jamming a ball through a metallic circle or swatting a ball with a stick or throwing a sphere with great velocity. When you played poorly, you tried to remind yourself how stupid it was to get so caught up in something so meaningless. When you hit that rare high, you kept your internal big mouth shut.

As Myron dashed back and forth in the wave of basketball action, a thought sneaked in through the back door of his brain. The thought stayed on the fringes, hiding behind a couch, popping into view every once in a while before ducking back down again. *You can do this*, the thought taunted. *You can play with them.*

Myron's lucky streak continued when it came to his defensive assignment: Leon White, Greg's roomie-on-the-road and best friend. Myron and Leon bonded a bit while playing, the way teammates and even opponents often do. Whispering quick jokes in one another's ear while lined up chest-to-chest for an inbounds pass. Patting the other guy on the back when he made a nice play. Leon was a classy guy on the floor. No trash talk. Even when Myron burned his butt on a fade-away eighteen-footer, Leon offered only words of encouragement.

Coach Donny Walsh blew the whistle. 'That's it, fellas. Take twenty foul shots and go home.'

Leon and Myron exchanged a half-handshake, half-high-five the way only children and professional athletes can. Myron had always loved this part of the game, the almost soldierlike camaraderie; he hadn't had that in years. It felt good. The players partnered themselves up in groups of two –

one guy to shoot, one to rebound – and went off to different baskets. Myron lucked out again and hooked up with Leon White. They each snatched a towel and a water bottle and strolled past the bleachers. Several reporters were perched up there for the practice. Audrey was there, of course. She looked at him with an amused smile. He resisted the temptation to stick his tongue out at her. Or his ass. Calvin Johnson had been watching practice too. He wore a suit and leaned against the wall like he was posing for a candid picture. Myron tried to gauge his reaction during the scrimmage, but of course Calvin's expression remained unreadable.

Myron shot first. He stood at the foul line, feet spread shoulder length, his eyes on the front rim. The ball backspun through the hoop.

'I guess we're going to be roommates,' Myron said.

'That's what I heard,' Leon said.

'Probably won't be for very long.' Myron took another shot. Swish. 'When do you think Greg will be back?'

In one motion Leon grabbed the bouncing ball and swooped it back to Myron. 'I don't know.'

'How's Greg feeling? The ankle doing okay?'

'I don't know,' he said again.

Myron took another foul shot. Another swish. His shirt, heavy with sweat, felt right. He grabbed the towel and wiped his face again. 'Have you talked to him at all?'

'No.'

'That's funny.'

Leon passed the ball to Myron. 'What's funny?'

Myron shrugged, took four dribbles. 'I heard you two were tight,' he said.

Leon gave a half-smile. 'Where did you hear that?'

Myron released the ball. Another swish. 'Around, I guess. In the newspapers and stuff.'

'Don't believe everything you read,' Leon said.

'Why's that?'

He bounce-passed the ball to Myron. 'The press loves to build up a friendship between a white player and a black player. They're always looking for that Gale Sayers–Brian Piccolo slant.'

'You two aren't close?'

'Well, we've known each other a long time. I'll say that.'

'But you're not tight?'

Leon looked at him funny. 'Why you so interested?'

'I'm just making conversation. Greg is my only real connection to this team.'

'Connection?'

Myron started dribbling again. 'He and I used to be rivals.'

'Yeah, so?'

'So now we're going to be teammates. It'll be weird.'

Leon looked at Myron. Myron stopped dribbling. 'You think Greg still cares about some old college rivalry?' There was disbelief in his voice.

Myron realized how lame he was sounding. 'It was a pretty intense thing,' he said. 'At the time, I mean.' Extra lame. Myron didn't look at Leon. He just lined up the shot.

'I hope this don't hurt your feelings or nothing,' Leon said, 'but I've been rooming with Greg for eight years now. I've never heard him mention your name. Even when we talk about college and stuff.'

Myron stopped right before releasing the ball. He looked over at Leon, fighting to keep his face neutral. Funny thing was – much as Myron didn't want to admit it – that did hurt his feelings.

'Shoot already,' Leon said. 'I want to get out of here.'

TC lumbered toward them. He palmed a basketball in each hand with the ease most adults palm grapefruits. He dropped one of the balls and did a handshaking/slapping ritual with Leon. Then he looked over at Myron. His face broke into a big smile.

'I know, I know,' Myron said. 'Thumped, right?'

TC nodded.

'What exactly is thumped?'

'Tonight,' TC said. 'Party at my house. All will be revealed then.'

14

Dimonte was waiting for him in the Meadowlands parking lot. He leaned out of his red Corvette. 'Get in.'

'A red Corvette,' Myron said. 'Why aren't I surprised?'

'Just get in.'

Myron opened the door and slid into the black leather seat. Though they were parked with the engine off, Dimonte gripped the steering wheel with both hands and stared in front of him. His face was sheet-white. The toothpick hung low. He kept shaking his head over and over. Yet again, the subtlety. 'Something wrong, Rolly?'

'What's Greg Downing like?'

'What?'

'You fucking deaf?' Dimonte snapped. 'What's he like?'

'I don't know. I haven't spoken to him in years.'

'But you knew him, right? In school. What was he like back then? Did he hang out with perversive types?'

Myron looked at him. 'Perversive types?'

'Just answer the question.'

'What the hell is this? Perversive types?'

Dimonte turned the ignition key. The sound was loud. He hit the gas a bit, let the engine do the rev thing for a while. The car had been jacked up like a race car. The sound was, like, totally rad, man. No women were in the nearby vicinity to hear this human mating call or they would surely be disrobing by how. Dimonte finally shifted into gear.

'Where we going?' Myron asked.

Dimonte didn't answer. He followed the ramp that leads from the arena to Giants Stadium and the horse track.

'Is this one of those mystery dates?' Myron asked. 'I love those.'

'Stop fucking around and answer my question.'

'What question?'

'What's Downing like? I need to know everything about him.'

'You're asking the wrong guy, Rolly. I don't know him that well.'

'Tell me what you do know.' Dimonte's voice left little room for disagreement. His tone was less fake-macho than usual, and there was a funny quake in it. Myron didn't like it.

'Greg grew up in New Jersey,' Myron began. 'He's a great basketball player. He's divorced with two kids.'

'You dated his wife, right?'

'A long time ago.'

'Would you say she was left-wing?'

'Rolly, this is getting too weird.'

'Just answer the goddamn question.' The tone aimed for angry and impatient, but fear seemed to overlap them. 'Would you call her politics radical?'

'No.'

'She ever hang out with perversives?'

'Is that even a word? Perversives?'

Dimonte shook his head. 'Do I look like I'm in the mood for your shit, Bolitar?'

'Okay, okay.' Myron made a surrendering gesture with his hands. The Corvette swerved across the empty stadium lot. 'No, Emily did not hang out with perversives, whatever they are.'

They headed past the racetrack and took the other ramp back toward the arena. It became apparent to Myron that they were just going to circle the Meadowlands' vast expanse of paved lots. 'Let's get back to Downing then.'

'I just told you we haven't talked in years.'

'But you know about him, right? You've been investigating him; you've probably read stuff about him.' Gear shift up. Extra rev power. 'Would you say he was a revolutionary?'

Myron could not believe these questions. 'No, Mr Chairman.'

'Do you know who he hangs out with?'

'Not really. He's supposed to be closest to his teammates, but Leon White – that's his roommate on the road – seemed less than enamored. Oh, here's something that might interest you: after home games, Greg drives a taxi in the city.'

Dimonte looked puzzled. 'You mean he picks up fares and stuff?'

'Yes.'

'Why the fuck does he do that?'

'Greg is a little' – Myron searched for the word – 'off.'

'Uh huh.' Dimonte rubbed his face vigorously, as if he were polishing a fender with a rag. He did this for several seconds, not looking at the road; fortunately, he was in the middle of an empty parking lot. 'Does it make him feel like a regular guy or something? Could that be part of it? Getting closer to the masses?'

'I guess,' Myron said.

'Go on. What about his interests? His hobbies?'

'He's a nature boy. He likes to fish and hunt and hike and boat, that goyish stuff.'

'A back-to-nature type?'

'Sort of.'

'Like maybe an outdoor, communal guy?'

'No. Like maybe an outdoor, loner guy.'

'You have any idea where he might be?'

'None.'

Dimonte hit the gas and circled the arena. He came to a stop in front of Myron's Ford Taurus and put the car in park. 'Okay, thanks for the help. We'll talk later.'

'Whoa, hold up a second. I thought we were working together on this.'

'You thought wrong.'

'You're not going to tell me what's going on?'

His voice was suddenly soft. 'No.'

Silence. The rest of the players were gone now. The Taurus stood alone in the still, empty lot.

'It's that bad?' Myron said.

Dimonte kept frighteningly still.

'You know who she is, don't you?' Myron went on. 'You got an ID.'

Dimonte leaned back. Again he rubbed his entire face. 'Nothing confirmed,' he muttered.

'You got to tell me, Rolly.'

He shook his head. 'I can't.'

'I won't say anything. You know—'

'Get the fuck out of my car, Myron.' He leaned across Myron's lap and opened the car door. 'Now.'

15

TC lived in a turn-of-the-century, red brick mansion encircled by a six-foot, matching brick fence on one of the better streets of Englewood, New Jersey. Eddie Murphy lived down the block. So did three Forbes 500 CEOs and several major Japanese bankers. There was a security post by the driveway entrance. Myron gave the security guard his name. The guard checked his clipboard.

'Please park along the drive. The party is out back.' He raised the yellow-and-black striped gate and waved him through. Myron parked next to a black BMW. There were maybe a dozen other cars, all glistening from fresh washes and waxes or perhaps they were all new. Mostly Mercedes Benzes. A few BMWs. A Bentley. A Jag. A Rolls. Myron's Taurus stood out like a zit in a Revlon commercial.

The front lawn was immaculately manicured. Perfectly pruned shrubs guarded and clung to the brick facade. In stark contrast to this majestic setting was the rap music blaring from the speakers. Awful. The shrubs looked pained by the sound. Myron didn't necessarily hate all rap. He knew there was worse music out there – John Tesh and Yanni proved it every day. Some rap songs Myron found engaging and even profound. He also recognized that rap music had not been written for him; he didn't get it all, but he suspected that he wasn't supposed to.

The party was held in the well-lit pool area. The crowd of about thirty mingled about in a fairly subdued fashion. Myron was wearing a blue blazer, a button-down pinstripe shirt, a flower tie, J. Murphy casual loafers. Bolitar the Prep. Win would be so proud. But Myron felt frighteningly underdressed next to his teammates. At the risk of sounding racist, the black guys on the team – there were only two other white players on the Dragons right now – knew how to dress with style. Not Myron's style (or lack thereof), but definitely with style. The group looked like they were readying themselves for a Milan runway walk. Perfectly tailored suits. Silk shirts buttoned to the neck. No ties. Shoes polished like twin mirrors.

TC reclined in a lounge chair by the shallow end of the pool. He was surrounded by a bunch of white guys who looked like college students. They were laughing at his every word. Myron also spotted Audrey in her customary reporter's garb. She had added pearls for the occasion. Really dressing up. He barely had a chance to step toward them when a woman in her late thirties/maybe forty approached him. 'Hello,' the woman said.

'Hi.' The Wordsmith Strikes Again.

'You must be Myron Bolitar. My name is Maggie Mason.'

'Hi, Maggie.' They shook hands. Firm grip, nice smile.

She was dressed conservatively in a white blouse, charcoal-gray blazer, red skirt, and black pumps. Her hair was down and slightly mussed, as if she'd just released her bun. She was slim and attractive and would have been the perfect choice to play the opposing attorney on *LA Law*.

She smiled at him. 'You don't know who I am, do you?'

'Sorry, I don't.'

'They call me Thumper.'

Myron waited. When she didn't add anything, he said, 'Uh huh.'

'Didn't TC tell you about this?'

'He mentioned something about getting thump . . .' He stopped mid-word. She just smiled at him and spread her arms. After some time had passed, he said, 'I don't get it.'

'Nothing to get,' she said matter-of-factly. 'I have sex with all the guys on the team. You're new to the team. It's your turn.'

Myron opened his mouth, closed it, tried again. 'You don't look like a groupie.'

'Groupie.' She shook her head. 'God, I hate that word.'

Myron closed his eyes and pinched the bridge of his nose. 'Let me see if I'm getting this.'

'Go ahead.'

'You've slept with every guy on the Dragons?'

'Yes.'

'Even the married ones?'

'Yes,' she replied. 'Anyone who has been on the team since 1993. That's when I started with the Dragons. I started with the Giants in 1991.'

'Wait a second. You're a groupie for the Giants, too? The football Giants?'

'I told you. I don't like the term groupie.'

'What word would you be more comfortable with?'

She tilted her head a little and kept the smile. 'Look, Myron, I'm an investment banker on Wall Street. I work very hard. I like taking cooking classes and I'm a step-aerobics nut. All in all I am pretty normal by this world's standards. I don't hurt anybody. I don't want to get married or have a relationship. But I have this one little fetish.'

'You have sex with professional athletes.'

She held up her index finger. 'Only with the guys on the Giants and Dragons.'

'Nice to see team loyalty,' Myron said, 'in this era of free agency.'

Thumper laughed. 'That's pretty funny.'

'Are you telling me you've slept with every player on the Giants?'

'Just about. I have tickets on the fifty-yard line. After every game, I have sex with two players – one from the defense, and one from the offense.'

'Sort of like the game MVPs?'

'Exactly.'

Myron shrugged. 'Beats getting the game ball, I guess.'

'Yes,' she said slowly. 'It definitely beats getting a game ball.'

Myron rubbed his eyes. *Ground control to Major Tom.* He studied her for a moment. She seemed to be doing the same thing to him. 'So how did you get the nickname Thumper?' he asked.

'It's not what you think.'

'What's not what I think?'

'How I got the nickname. Everyone assumes it has something to do with screwing like a rabbit.'

'And it doesn't?'

'No, it doesn't.' She looked up in the air. 'How do I explain this delicately?'

'You're worried about delicacy?'

She gave him a mildly disapproving look. 'Don't be like that.'

'Like what?'

'Like some right-wing, narrow-minded, Pat Buchanan-type Neanderthal. I have feelings.'

'I didn't say you didn't.'

'No, but you're acting like it. I don't hurt anyone. I'm honest. I'm forward. I'm direct. I control what I do and to whom. And I'm happy.'

'Not to mention disease-ridden,' he heard himself say and immediately regretted it. The words had just slipped out; that happened to him sometimes.

'What?'

'I'm sorry,' he said. 'That was uncalled for.'

But he had hit a nerve. 'The men I have sex with always wear condoms,' she snapped. 'I get tested frequently. I'm clean.'

'I'm sorry. I shouldn't have said anything.'

She didn't stop. 'And I don't sleep with anyone I think might be infected with something. I'm careful that way.'

Myron bit his lip this time. No point. 'My mistake,' he said. 'I didn't mean it; I'm sorry. Please accept my apology.'

Her chest heaved, but she was calm now. 'Okay,' she said with an exhale. 'Apology accepted.'

Her eyes met his again. They smiled at each for far too long. Myron felt like a game-show contestant. A thought thankfully interrupted the semitrance. 'Did you sleep with Greg Downing?' he asked.

'In 1993,' she said. 'He was one of the first Dragons.'

How that must swell his bosom with pride. 'You still see him?'

'Sure. We're good friends. I'm friends with most of the guys afterwards. Not all, but most.'

'Do you two talk a lot?'

'Sometimes.'

'Recently?'

'Not the past month or two.'

'Do you know if he's seeing anyone?'

Thumper gave him a curious look. 'Why would you want to know about that?'

Myron shrugged. 'Just making conversation.' The Return of Mr Lame.

'It's an odd topic,' she said.

'I guess I've been thinking about him a lot. All this talk about my being on Greg's team and our history together. It just got me thinking.'

'It got you thinking about Greg's love life?' She wasn't buying it.

Myron sort of shrugged and mumbled something even he didn't understand. A laugh broke out from the other side of the pool. A group of his new teammates were enjoying a joke. Leon White was one of them. He met Myron's eye and nodded a hello. Myron nodded back. Myron realized that while no one seemed to be staring at them, all of his teammates had to know why Thumper had approached him. Again he felt like he was back in college, but this time the feeling didn't bring on the same happy nostalgia.

Thumper was busy studying him again, her eyes narrowed and focused. Myron tried to look neutral, but he felt like a doofus. Being so openly inspected did that to him. He tried to meet her gaze.

Thumper suddenly smiled widely and folded her arms. 'I get it now,' she said.

'What?'

'It's obvious.'

'What's obvious?'

'You want revenge,' she said.

'Revenge for what?'

The smile grew a bit, then relaxed. 'Greg stole Emily from you. Now you want to steal someone back.'

'He didn't steal her from me,' Myron said quickly. He heard the defensive tone in his voice and didn't like it. 'Emily and I broke up before they started dating.'

'If you say so.'

'I say so.' Mr Snappy Retort.

She let loose a throaty laugh and put a hand on his arm. 'Relax, Myron. I'm only teasing you.' She looked at him again. All of this eye contact was beginning to give Myron a headache. He stared at her nose instead. 'So are we going to do this?' she asked.

'No,' Myron said.

'If it's the fear of disease—'

'It's not. I'm involved with someone.'

'So?'

'So I don't cheat on her.'

'Who wants you to cheat? I just want to have sex with you.'

'And you think those two things are mutually exclusive?'

'Of course they are,' Thumper said. 'Our having sex should have absolutely no effect on your relationship. I don't want you to stop caring about your girlfriend. I don't want to be a part of your life. I don't even want to be intimate.'

'Gee, you make it sound so romantic,' Myron said.

'But that's just the point. It's not romantic. It's just a physical act. Sure, it feels great, but in the end it's just a physical act. Like shaking hands.'

'Shaking hands,' Myron repeated. 'You should write greeting cards.'

'I'm just telling you how it is. Past civilizations – ones far more intellectually advanced than us – understood that pleasure of the flesh was no sin. Associating sex with guilt is a modern, absurd hang-up. This whole concept of tying sex to possession is something we got from uptight Puritans who wanted to maintain control over their major possession: their wife.'

A history scholar, Myron thought. Nice to see.

'Where is it written,' she continued, 'that two people can't reach heights of physical ecstasy without being in love? I mean, think about how ridiculous that is. It's silly, isn't it?'

'Maybe,' Myron said. 'But I'll still pass, thank you.'

She shrugged a suit-yourself. 'TC will be very disappointed.'

'He'll get over it,' he said.

Silence.

'Well,' she said, clasping her hands together, 'I think I'll mingle. It was nice chatting with you, Myron.'

'A true experience,' Myron agreed.

Myron mingled a bit, too. He hooked up with Leon for a while. Leon introduced him to his wife, a blond sexpot named Fiona. Very Playmate-like. She had a breathy voice and was one of those women who made even the most casual conversation one long double entendre – so accustomed to using her physical charms that she did not know when to turn them off. Myron chatted with them both briefly and excused himself.

The bartender informed him that they were not stocking any Yoo-hoo. He took an Orangina instead. Not just orange soda, but Orangina. How European. He took a sip. Pretty good.

A hand slapped Myron's back. It was TC. He had foregone the *GQ*-suit look, opting for white leather pants and a white leather vest. No shirt. He wore dark sunglasses.

'Having a good time?' he asked.

'It's been interesting,' Myron said.

'Come on. I'll show you something.'

They walked in silence up a grassy hill away from the party. The incline grew steadily steeper, the music fainter. The rap had been replaced with an alternative group called the Cranberries. Myron liked their music. 'Zombie' was on right now. Dolores O'Riordan was repeatedly singing, 'In your head, in your head,' until she got tired and moved to repeating the word, 'Zombie, zombie' several hundred times. Okay, the Cranberries could work on their chorus lyrics, but the songs still worked. Good stuff.

There were no lights now, but a glow from the ones by the pool provided enough illumination. When they reached the plateau, TC motioned in front of them. 'There.'

Myron looked out, and the sight nearly took his breath away. They were up high enough to get an unimpeded, spectacular view of the Manhattan skyline. The sea of lights seemed to shimmer like beads of water. The George Washington Bridge looked close enough to touch. They both stood in silence for several moments.

'Nice, huh?' TC said.

'Very.'

He took off his sunglasses. 'I come up here a lot. By myself. It's a good place to think.'

'I would think so.'

They looked off again.

'Thumper talk to you yet?' Myron asked.

TC nodded.

'Were you disappointed?'

'No,' TC said. 'I knew you'd say no.'

'How?'

He shrugged. 'Just a feeling. But don't let her fool you. Thumper's good people. She's probably the closest thing I got to a friend.'

'What about all those guys you were hanging out with?'

TC sort of smiled. 'You mean the white boys?'

'Yeah.'

'Not friends,' he said. 'If tomorrow I stopped playing ball, they'd look at me like I'm pinching on a loaf on their sofa.'

'Poetically put, TC.'

'Just the truth, man. You in my position, you don't have no friends. Facts of life. White or black, it don't matter. People hang around me because I'm a rich superstar. They figure they can get something for free. That's all.'

'And that's okay with you?'

'Don't matter if it's okay,' TC said. 'It's the way it is. I ain't complaining.'

'Do you get lonely?' Myron asked.

'Too many people around to get lonely.'

'You know what I mean.'

'Yeah, I know what you mean.' TC sort of jerked his head from side to side, like he was trying to loosen up his neck before a game. 'Folks always talking about the price of fame, but you wanna know the real price? Forget that privacy shit. So I don't go out to the movies as much. Big fucking deal – where I come from you can't afford to go anyway. The real price is you ain't a person anymore. You're just a thing, a shiny thing like one of those Benzes out there. The poor brothers think I'm a golden ladder with goodies at every step up. The rich white boys think I'm a fancy pet. Like with O.J. Remember those guys who hung out in O.J.'s trophy room?'

Myron nodded.

'Look, I ain't complaining. Don't get me wrong. This is a whole lot better than pumping gas or working in a coal mine or something. But I always got to remember the truth: the only thing that separates me from any nigger on the street is a game. That's it. A knee going pop, like with what happened to you, and I'm back down there. I always remember that. Always.' He gave Myron hard eyes, letting his words hang in the crisp air. 'So when some hot babe acts like I'm something special, it ain't me she's after. You see what I'm saying? She's blinded by all that money and fame. Everyone is, male or female.'

'So you and I could never be friends?' Myron asked.

'Would you be asking me that if I was just some ignorant fool pumping gas?'

'Maybe.'

'Bullshit,' he said with a smile. 'People bitch about my attitude, you know. They say I act like everybody owes me. Like I'm a prima donna. But they just mad because I see through them. I know the truth. They all think I'm some ignorant nigger – the owners, the coaches, whatever – so why should I respect them? Only reason they even talk to me is because I can slam the ball through the hoop. I'm just a monkey making them money. Once I stop, that's it. I'm just another dumb slice of ghetto shit not fit to sit my black ass on their toilet.' He stopped then, as though out of breath. He looked back at the skyline. The sight seemed to rejuvenate him. 'You ever meet Isiah Thomas?' he asked.

'The Detroit Piston? Yeah, once.'

'I heard him doing this interview one time, must have been when the Pistons won those championships. Some guy asked him what he'd be doing if he wasn't a basketball player. You know what Isiah said?'

Myron shook his head.

'He said he'd be a United States senator.' TC laughed hard and high-pitched. The sound echoed in the still night. 'I mean, is the brother crazy or what? Isiah really believe that shit. A United States senator – who the fuck is he kidding?' He laughed again, but the sound seemed more forced now. 'Me, I know what I'd be. I'd be working in a steel mill, the midnight to ten

A.M. shift, or maybe I'd be in jail or dead, I don't know.' He shook his head. 'United States senator. Shit.'

'What about the game?' Myron asked.

'What about it?'

'Do you love playing basketball?'

He looked amused. 'You do, don't you? You buy all that "for the love of the game" bullshit.'

'You don't?'

TC shook his head. The moon reflected off his shaved pate, giving his head an almost mystical glow. 'It was never about that for me,' he said. 'Basketball was just a means to an end. It's about making money. It's about setting me up for life.'

'Did you ever love the game?'

'Sure, I guess I must have. It was a good place to go, you know? But I don't think it was the game – I mean, not the running and jumping and shit. Basketball was just what I was all about. Everywhere else I was just another dumb black boy, but on the basketball court, I was, well, the man. A hero. It's an incredible high, everyone treating you like that. You know what I mean?'

Myron nodded. He knew. 'Can I ask you something else?'

'Go ahead.'

'What's with all the tattoos and rings?'

He smiled. 'They bother you?'

'Not really. I'm just curious.'

'Suppose I just like wearing them,' TC said. 'That enough?'

'Yes,' Myron said.

'But you don't believe it, do you?'

Myron shrugged. 'I guess not.'

'Truth is, I do like them a little. The bigger truth is, it's business.'

'Business?'

'Basketball business. Making money. Lots of it. You know how much money I make in endorsements? A shit load. Why? Because outrageousness sells. Look at Deon. Look at Rodman. The more crazy shit I do, the more they pay me.'

'So it's just an act?'

'A lot of it, yeah. I like to shock, too, just my way. But mostly I do it for the press.'

'But the press is always ripping you apart,' Myron said.

'Don't matter. They write about me, they make me more money. Simple as that.' He smiled. 'Let me clue you in on something, Myron. The press is the dumbest animal on God's green earth. You know what I'm gonna do one day?'

Myron shook his head.

'One day I'll get rid of the rings and shit, and I'll start dressing nice. Then

I'll start talking polite, you know, giving them all yes-sirs and yes-ma'ams and start spitting out all that team-effort bullshit they like to hear. You know what'll happen? These same fucks that say I'm destroying the integrity of the game will be kissing my black ass like it's the Blarney Stone. They be talking about how I went through some sort of miraculous transformation. How now I'm a hero. But only thing that's really changed is my act.' TC gave him a big smile.

Myron said, 'You're a piece of work, TC.'

TC turned back to the water. Myron watched him in silence. He hadn't bought all of TC's rationalizations. There was more at work here. TC wasn't lying, but he wasn't exactly telling the truth either – or maybe he couldn't admit the truth even to himself. He hurt. He truly believed no one could love him, and no matter who you are, that hurts. It made you insecure. It made you want to hide and build fences. The sad thing was, TC was at least partially right. Who'd care about him if he wasn't playing professional basketball? If not for his ability to play a child's game, where would he be right now? TC was like the beautiful girl who wanted you to look down deep to find the soul within – but the only reason you'd bother trying was because she was beautiful. Get rid of that physical beauty – become the ugly girl – and nobody gives a damn about scratching the surface to find the beauty within. Get rid of TC's physical prowess and the same thing happens.

In the end, TC was not as off-the-wall as he appeared in public nor was he as put-together as he wanted Myron to think. Myron was no psychologist, but he was sure that there was more to the tattoos and body piercing than making money. They were too physically destructive for so pat an explanation. With TC, there were a lot of factors at work. Being a former basketball star himself, Myron understood some of them; being that Myron and TC came from completely different worlds, there were others he could not so readily grasp.

TC interrupted their joint solitude. 'Now I got a question for you,' he said.

'Shoot.'

'Why you really here?' TC asked.

'Here? As in your house—'

'On the team. Look, man, I saw you play when I was in junior high. In the NCAAs. You were great, okay? But that was a long time ago. You got to know you can't do it anymore. You had to see that at practice today.'

Myron tried not to look stunned. Had he and TC been at the same practice? But of course they had, and of course, TC was right. Didn't Myron remember the days when he was the team's superstar? Didn't he remember scrimmaging against the last five guys who would play their butt off while the starting five screwed around and played with no incentive? Didn't he remember how disillusioned those last became, fooling themselves into believing they were just as good as the first five when the first five were tired from real games and were just slacking off? And back then, Myron was in college. He played maybe twenty-five games a season – these guys played almost a hundred against vastly superior competition.

Good enough to play with these guys? Who had he been kidding?

'I'm just giving it a shot,' Myron said softly.

'Can't let go, huh?'

Myron said nothing. They fell back into a brief silence.

'Hey, I almost forgot,' TC said. 'I hear you're good friends with a big hotshot at Lock-Horne Securities. That true?'

'Yes.'

'Was he that slice of white bread you talking with after the game?'

Myron nodded. 'His name is Win.'

'You know Thumper works on Wall Street, right?'

'She told me,' Myron said.

'Thumper wants to change jobs. Think your friend could talk to her?'

Myron shrugged. 'I could ask him.' Win would certainly appreciate her outlook on the role of sex in ancient civilizations. 'Who does she work for now?'

'Small outfit. Called Kimmel Brothers. But she needs to move on, you know? They won't make her a partner, even though she busts her butt for them.'

TC said something else but Myron was no longer listening. Kimmel Brothers. Myron remembered the name immediately. When he'd hit the redial button on the phone at Greg's house, a woman had answered and said, 'Kimmel Brothers.' Yet Thumper had just told Myron she hadn't spoken to Greg in a month or two.

Coincidence? Myron thought not.

16

Thumper was gone.

'She came for you,' TC said. 'When it didn't happen she split. She got work tomorrow morning.'

Myron checked his watch. Eleven-thirty. Long day. Time for a little shut-eye. He made his good nights and headed for his car. Audrey was leaning against the hood, her arms folded across her chest, her ankles crossed. Pure casual.

'You going back to Jessica's?' she asked.

'Yes.'

'Mind giving me a lift?'

'Hop in.'

Audrey gave him the same smile he had seen back at practice. He had thought at the time she had been impressed with his play; now it was clearer that the amusement was more akin to ridicule than appreciation. He unlocked the doors in silence. She took off her blue blazer and laid it on the backseat; he did likewise. She wore a forest green turtleneck underneath it. She adjusted the neck part, folding it back an extra time. She took off the pearls and jammed them in the front pocket of her jeans. Myron started the car.

'I'm starting to put this thing together,' Audrey said.

Myron did not like the way she said it. Too much authority in her voice. Audrey hadn't needed a lift home, he was sure of that. She wanted to talk to him alone. That worried him. He gave her the good-natured smile and said, 'This doesn't have anything to do with my ass, does it?'

'What?'

'Jessica told me you two were discussing my ass.'

She laughed. 'Well, I hate to admit this,' she said, 'but it did look pretty scrumptious.'

Myron tried not to look too pleased. 'So you doing a story on it?'

'On your ass?'

'Yes.'

'Of course,' she said. 'I was thinking we could give it a big spread.'

Myron groaned.

590

'You're trying to change the subject,' she said.

'There was a subject?'

'I was telling you how I was putting this thing together.'

'That's a subject?'

He glanced at her. She was sitting with her left knee on the seat and her left ankle tucked under her so her entire body could face him. Audrey had a wide face and a few freckles, though he bet she had a lot more when she was a kid. Remember that tomboy who was kinda cute in your sixth grade class? Here she was all grown up. No beauty certainly. Not in the classic sense. But there was an earthy appeal to Audrey that made you want to reach out and hug her and roll in leaves on a crisp autumn day.

'It shouldn't have taken me so long to figure out,' she continued. 'It's pretty obvious in hindsight.'

'Am I supposed to know what you're talking about?'

'No,' she replied. 'You're supposed to continue to play dumb for a few more minutes.'

'My specialty.'

'Good, then just drive and listen.' Her hands were in constant gesturing motion, peaking and valleying along with her voice. 'See, I was waylaid by the whole poetic irony stuff. That's what I concentrated on. But your backgrounds as rivals is secondary in all this. It's not nearly as important as, say, your past relationship with Emily.'

'I have no idea what you're talking about.'

'You didn't play AAU. You didn't play in any summer league. You play in pick-up games at the Y maybe once week. Your major workout revolves around Master Kwon's place with Win – and they don't have a basketball court.'

'Is there a point?'

Her hands spread in disbelief. 'You haven't been honing your skills. You haven't played anyplace where Clip or Calvin or Donny would have seen you play. So why would the Dragons sign you? It doesn't make sense. Was the move strictly PR? Unlikely. The positive bump will be minimum, and if you fail – which, let's face it, is very likely – that good publicity will probably be nullified. Ticket sales are good. The team is doing well. They don't need a publicity stunt right now. So there has to be another reason.' She stopped and readjusted herself on the car seat. 'Enter the timing.'

'The timing?'

'Yes,' she said. 'Why now? Why sign you so late in the season? The answer is obvious really. There is only one thing about the timing that stands out.'

'And that is?'

'Downing's sudden disappearance.'

'He didn't disappear,' Myron corrected. 'He's injured. That's your precious timing. Greg got hurt. A spot opened up. I filled it.'

Audrey smiled and shook her head. 'Still want to play dumb, huh? Fine,

591

go ahead. You're right. Downing is supposed to be injured and in seclusion. Now I'm good, Myron, and for the life of me I can't find this secluded spot of his. I've called in all my best contacts and I can't get anything. Don't you find that a bit odd?'

Myron shrugged.

'Maybe,' she went on, 'if Downing really craved seclusion to fix his injured ankle – an injury which doesn't show up on any game tape, by the way – he could find a way. But if all he's doing is working on an injury, why work so hard at it?'

'So pain in the asses like you don't bother him,' Myron said.

Audrey almost laughed at that one. 'Said with such conviction, Myron. It's almost like you believe it.'

Myron said nothing.

'But let me just add a few more points and then you can stop playing dumb.' Audrey counted them off on ringless, slightly callused fingers. 'One, I know you used to work for the feds. That gives you some background in investigative work. Two, I know Downing has a habit of vanishing. He's done it before. Three, I know Clip's situation with the other owners. The big vote is coming up. Four, I know you visited Emily yesterday and I doubt you were there to restoke the flames.'

'How did you know about that?' Myron asked.

She just smiled and put her hand down. 'Add them up and there's only one conclusion: you are looking for Greg Downing. He's missing again. This time however the timing is much more critical; Clip's ownership vote and the playoffs are coming up. Your job is to find him.'

'You got a hell of an imagination, Audrey.'

'I do at that,' she agreed, 'but we both know I got this right so let's end playing dumb and cut to the heart of it: I want in.'

'Want in.' Myron shook his head. 'You reporters and your lingo.'

'I don't want to give you up,' she continued. Her knee was still up on the seat. Her face was as bright and expectant as a school kid's waiting for the final bell in May. 'I think we should team up. I can help. I got great sources. I can ask questions without worrying about blowing my cover. I know this team inside and out.'

'And what exactly do you want for this help?'

'The full story. I'm the first reporter to know where he is, why he vanished, whatever. You promise to tell only me; I get the full exclusive.'

They passed several sleazy motels and a potpourri of gas stations on Route 4. No-tell motels in New Jersey always gave themselves lofty names that belied their social station. Right now, for example, they were driving past the 'Courtesy Inn.' This fine establishment not only gave you courteous attention, but they gave it to you by the hour at a rate, according to the sign, of $19.82. Not twenty dollars, mind you, but $19.82 – so priced, Myron guessed, because it was also the year they last changed sheets. The CHEAP

BEER DEPOT, according to another sign, was the next building on Myron's right. Truth in advertising. Nice to see. The Courtesy Inn could learn a lesson from them.

'We both know I could report it now,' she said. 'It'd still be a pretty good scoop – reporting that Downing wasn't really injured and you're just here to find him. But I'd be willing to trade it in for a larger story.'

Myron thought it over as he paid the toll. He glanced at her expectant face. She looked wild-eyed and wild-haired, kind of like the refugee women coming off the boat in Palestine in the movie *Exodus*. Ready to do battle to claim her homeland.

'You have to make me a promise,' he said.

'What?'

'No matter what – no matter how incredible the story seems – you won't jump the gun. You won't report any of it until he's found.'

Audrey nearly leapt from her seat. 'What do you mean? How incredible?'

'Forget it, Audrey. Report whatever you want.'

'All right, all right, you have a deal,' she said quickly, hands raised in surrender. 'You had to know saying something like that would pique my interest.'

'You promise?'

'Yeah, yeah, I promise. So what's up?'

Myron shook his head. 'You first,' he said. 'Why would Greg vanish?'

'Who knows?' she replied. 'The man is a professional flake.'

'What can you tell me about his divorce?'

'Just that it's been acrimonious as all hell.'

'What have you heard?'

'They've been battling over the kids. They're both trying to prove the other is an unfit parent.'

'Any details on how they're going about that?'

'No. It's been kept pretty hush-hush.'

'Emily told me Greg had pulled some sleazy tricks,' Myron said. 'Do you know anything about that?'

Audrey chewed on her bottom lip for a few moments. 'I heard a rumor – a very unsubstantiated rumor – that Greg hired a private eye to follow her.'

'Why?'

'I don't know.'

'To film her maybe? Catch her with another man?'

She shrugged. 'It's just a rumor. I don't know.'

'You know the PI's name or who he works for?'

'Rumor, Myron. Rumor. A pro basketball player's divorce is hardly earth-shattering sports news. I didn't follow it that closely.'

Myron made a mental note to check Greg's files for any payment to an investigation firm. 'How was Greg's relationship with Marty Felder?'

'His agent? Good, I guess.'

'Emily told me Felder had lost Greg millions.'

She shrugged. 'I've never heard anything about that.'

The Washington Bridge was fairly clear. They stayed to the left and took the Henry Hudson Parkway south. On their right, the Hudson River sparkled like a blanket of black sequins; on their left was a billboard with Tom Brokaw displaying his friendly yet firm smile. The caption under his picture read: 'NBC News – Now More Than Ever.' Very dramatic. What the hell did it mean?

'How about Greg's personal life?' Myron continued. 'Girlfriends, that kind of thing?'

'You mean a steady?'

'Yes.'

She ran her fingers through the thick, curling locks, then rubbed the back of her own neck. 'There was this one girl. He kept it kind of secret, but I think they were living together for a while.'

'What's her name?'

'He never told me. I saw them together at a restaurant once. A place called the Saddle River Inn. He didn't look happy to see me.'

'What did she look like?'

'Nothing special from what I remember. She was a brunette. She was sitting so I couldn't tell you height or weight.'

'Age?'

'I don't know. Thirty-ish, I guess.'

'What makes you think they were living together?'

It seemed like an easy question, but she stopped and raised her eyes. 'Leon let something slip once,' she said.

'What did he say?'

'I don't remember anymore. Something about the girlfriend. Then he clammed up.'

'How long ago was this?'

'Three, four months ago. Maybe more.'

'Leon implied that he and Greg weren't really that close, that the media made a bigger deal out of it than it was.'

Audrey nodded. 'There is a tension there now, but I think it's just temporary.'

'Why would there be a tension?'

'I don't know.'

'How long have you noticed the tension?'

'Not long. Within the last two weeks maybe.'

'Anything happen recently between Greg and Leon that you're aware of?'

'Nope. They've been friends for a long time. Friends have disagreements. I didn't take it too seriously.'

Myron let loose a deep breath. Friends did indeed have disagreements, but the timing was curious. 'Do you know Maggie Mason?'

'Thumper? Of course.'

'Were she and Greg close?'

'If you mean did they screw—'

'No, I don't mean that.'

'Well, they screwed. That I'm sure of. Despite what Thumper claims, not every guy on the team has gotten thumped. Some have turned her down. Not many, I admit. But some. She hit on you yet?'

'Just a few short hours ago.'

She smiled. 'I assume you joined the few, the proud, the Unthumped?'

'You assume correctly. But what about her relationship with Greg? Are they close?'

'They're pretty close, I'd say. But Thumper is closest to TC. Those two are very tight. It's not purely sexual either. Don't get me wrong. I'm sure TC and Maggie have had sex and probably still do on occasions. But they're like brother and sister too. It's weird.'

'How do TC and Greg get along?' Myron asked.

'Not bad for team superstars. Not great either.'

'Care to elaborate?'

She paused, gathered her thoughts. 'For five years now, TC and Downing have shared the spotlight. I guess there is a mutual respect for each other on the court, but they don't talk off it. At least, not very much. I'm not saying they dislike each other, but playing basketball is a job like any other. You might be able to stand one another at work, but you don't want to see the person socially.' She looked up. 'Take the Seventy-ninth Street exit.'

'You still live on Eighty-first?'

'Yes.'

Myron took the exit and stopped at a traffic light on Riverside Drive.

'Now it's your turn, Myron. Why did they hire you?'

'It's like you said. They want me to find Greg.'

'What have you learned so far?'

'Not much.'

'So why were you so concerned I'd jump the gun and tell the story early?'

Myron hesitated.

'I promised not to say anything,' she reminded him. 'You have my word.'

Fair is fair. He told her about the blood in Greg's basement. Her mouth dropped open. When he told her about finding Sally/Carla's body, he feared her heart might give out.

'My God,' Audrey said when he finished. 'You think Downing killed her.'

'I didn't say that.'

She fell back against the seat. Her head lolled against the headrest as though her neck could no longer support her. 'Christ, what a story.'

'And one you can't tell.'

'Don't remind me.' She sat back up again. 'Do you think it'll leak soon?'

'It might.'

'Why can't I be the recipient of that leak?'

Myron shook his head. 'Not yet. We got a lid on this so far. You can't be the one to blow it off.'

Her nod was grudging. 'Do you think Downing killed her and ran?'

'There is no evidence of that.' He pulled up to her building. 'One last question,' he said. 'Was Greg involved in anything unsavory?'

'Like what?'

'Like is there any reason thugs would be after him?'

Again her excitement was palpable. The woman was like an electric current. 'What do you mean? What thugs?'

'A couple of thugs were watching Greg's house.'

Her face was positively glowing. 'Thugs? You mean like professional gangsters?'

'Probably. I don't know for sure yet. Can you think of anything that would connect Greg to thugs, or for that matter the murder of this woman? Drugs maybe?'

Audrey shook her head immediately. 'It can't be drugs.'

'What makes you so sure?'

'Downing is a health nut, a real Granola head.'

'So was River Phoenix.'

She shook her head again. 'Not drugs. I'm sure of it.'

'Look into it,' he said. 'See what you can come up with.'

'Sure,' she said. 'I'll look into everything we talked about.'

'Try to be discreet.'

'No problem,' she said. She got out of the car. 'Good night, Myron. Thanks for trusting me.'

'Like I had a choice.'

Audrey smiled and closed the car door. He watched her walk into the building. He put the car back in drive and headed back to Seventy-ninth Street. He got back on the parkway and continued south toward Jessica's. He was about to pick up his cellular phone and call her when the phone rang. The dashboard clock read 12:07 A.M. It had to be Jessica.

'Hello?'

It wasn't Jessica. 'Right lane, three cars behind you. You're being followed.'

It was Win.

17

'When did you get back?' Myron asked.

Win ignored the question. 'The automobile following you is the same one we spotted at Greg's house. It is registered to a storage facility in Atlantic City. No known mob connections, but that would seem to me to be a safe bet.'

'How long have you been following me?'

Again Win ignored him. 'The two men who jumped you the other night. What did they look like?'

'Big,' Myron said. 'One was absolutely huge.'

'Crew cut?'

'Yes.'

'He's in the car following you. Passenger seat.'

Myron didn't bother asking how Win knew about the thugs jumping him. He had a pretty good idea.

'They've been communicating on the telephone quite a bit,' Win continued. 'I believe they're coordinating with someone else. The phone activity picked up after your stop in Eighty-first Street. Hold on a second. I'll call you right back.' He hung up. Myron checked his rearview mirror. The car was still there, right where Win said it was. A minute later the phone rang again.

'What?' Myron said.

'I just spoke to Jessica again.'

'What do you mean, again?'

Win sighed impatiently. He hated explanations. 'If they are planning to jump you tonight, it is logical to assume it will be by her loft.'

'Right.'

'Ergo, I called her ten minutes ago. I told her to keep an eye out for anything unusual.'

'And?'

'An unmarked white van parked across the street,' Win answered. 'No one got out.'

'So it appears they are going to strike,' Myron said.

'Yes,' Win said. 'Should I preempt it?'

597

'How?'

'I could disable the car following you.'

'No,' Myron said. 'Let them make their move and see where it leads.'

'Pardon?'

'Just back me up. If they grab me, I may be able to get to the boss.'

Win made a noise.

'What?' Myron said.

'You complicate the simple,' Win said. 'Would it not be easier to simply take out the two in the car? We could then make them tell us about their boss.'

'It's that "make them" part I have trouble with.'

'But of course,' Win countered. 'A thousand pardons for my lack of ethics. Clearly it is far wiser to risk your own life than to make a worthless goon feel momentary discomfort.'

Win had a way of putting things that made very frightening sense. Myron had to remind himself that the logical was often more terrifying than the illogical – especially where Win was concerned. 'They're just hired help,' Myron said. 'They're not going to know anything.'

Pause. 'Fair point,' Win conceded. 'But suppose they simply shoot you.'

'That wouldn't make any sense. The reason they're interested in me is because they think I know where Greg is.'

'And dead men tell no tales,' Win added.

'Exactly. They want to make me talk. So just follow me. If they take me some place well guarded—'

'I'll get through,' Win said.

Myron did not doubt it. He gripped the steering wheel. His pulse began to race. Easy to dismiss the possibility of getting shot by reasonable analysis; it was another thing to have to park a car down the street from men you knew were out to hurt you. Win would have his eye on the van. So would Myron. If a gun came out before a person, the situation would be handled.

He got off the highway. The streets of Manhattan were supposed to be a nice, even grid. Streets ran north/south and east/west. They were numbered. They were straight. But when you got to Greenwich Village and SoHo, it was like a grid painted by Dali. Gone were the numerical roads for the most part, except when they twisted and turned between streets with real-live names. Gone was any pretext of straight or systematized.

Luckily Spring Street was a direct run. A bicyclist sped by Myron, but no one else was out. The white van was parked right where it was supposed to be. Unmarked, just as Jessica had said. The windows were tinted so you couldn't look in. Myron didn't see Win's car, but then again he wasn't supposed to. He moved slowly down the street. He passed the van. When he did, the van started its motor. Myron pulled into a spot toward the end of the block. The van pulled out.

Show time.

Myron parked the car, straightened out the steering wheel, turned the engine off. He pocketed the keys. The van inched forward. He took out his revolver and stuck it under the car seat. It wouldn't do him any good right now. If they grabbed him, they would search him. If they started shooting, shooting back would be a waste of time. Win would either remove the threat or not.

He reached for the door handle. Fear nestled into his throat, but he did not stop. He pulled the handle, opened the door, and stepped out. It was dark. The streetlights in SoHo were nearly worthless, like pen beams in a black hole. Lights drifting out from nearby windows provided more of an eerie kindle than real illumination. There were plastic garbage bags out on the street. Most had been torn open; the odor of spoiled food wafted through the air. The van slowly cruised toward him. A man stepped out from a doorway and approached without hesitation. The man wore a black turtleneck under a black overcoat. He pointed a gun at Myron. The van stopped, and the side door slid open.

'Get in, asshole,' the man with the gun said.

Myron pointed at himself. 'You talking to me?'

'Now, asshole. Haul ass.'

'Is that a turtleneck or a dickey?'

The man with the gun moved closer. 'I said, now.'

'It's nothing to get angry about,' Myron said, but he stepped toward the van. 'If it is a dickey, you can't tell. It's a very sporty look.' When Myron got nervous, his mouth went into overdrive. He knew it was self-destructive; Win had pointed that out to him on several occasions. But Myron couldn't stop himself. Diarrhea of the mouth or some such ailment.

'Move.'

Myron got in the van. The man with the gun did likewise. There were two more men in the back of the van and one man driving. Everyone was in black, except for one guy who looked to be in charge. He wore a blue pinstripe suit. His Windsor-knotted yellow tie was held in place by a gold tie bar at the collar. Euro-chic. He had long, bleached-blond hair and one of those tans that were a little too perfect to come from the sun. He looked more like an aging surfer boy than a professional mobster.

The van's interior had been custom designed, but not in a good way. All the seats had been ripped out except for the driver's. There was a leather couch in the back along one wall where Pinstripe sat alone. A lime-green shag carpet even Elvis would have found too garish ran along the van's floor and up the sides like a poor man's ivy.

The man in the pinstripe suit smiled; his hands were folded in his lap, very much at ease. The van started moving.

The gunman quickly searched Myron. 'Sit, asshole,' he said.

Myron sat on the carpeted floor. He ran his hand over the shag. 'Lime green,' he said to Pinstripe. 'Nice.'

'It's inexpensive,' Pinstripe said. 'That way we don't worry about bloodstains.'

'Thinking of overhead.' Myron nodded coolly, though his mouth felt very dry. 'That's smart business.'

Pinstripe did not bother with a response. He gave the man with the gun and dickey/turtleneck a look that made the man jolt upward. The man cleared his throat.

'This here is Mr Baron,' the gunman told Myron, indicating Pinstripe. 'Everyone calls him the B Man.' He cleared his throat again. He spoke like he'd been rehearsing this little speech, which, Myron surmised, was probably likely. 'He's called the B Man because he enjoys breaking bones.'

'Say, that must woo the women,' Myron said.

The B Man smiled with capped teeth as white as anything in those old Pepsodent commercials. 'Hold his leg out,' he said.

The man with the turtleneck/dickey pressed the gun against Myron's temple hard enough to leave a permanent imprint. He wrapped his other arm around Myron's neck, the inside of his elbow jammed into Myron's windpipe. He lowered his head and whispered, 'Don't even flinch, asshole.'

He forced Myron into a lying position. The other man straddled Myron's chest and pinned the leg to the floor. Myron had trouble breathing. Panic seized him, but he remained still. Any move at this stage would almost inevitably be the wrong one. He'd have to play it out and see where it went.

The B Man moved off the leather couch slowly. His eyes never left Myron's bad knee; his smile was a happy one. 'I'm going to place one hand on the distal femur and the other on your proximal tibia,' he explained in the same tone a surgeon might use with a student. 'My thumbs will then rest on the medial aspect of the patella. When my thumbs snap forward, I will basically rip off your kneecap laterally.' He met Myron's gaze. 'This will tear your medial retinaculum and several other ligaments. Tendons will snap. I fear it will be most painful.'

Myron didn't even try a wisecrack. 'Hey, wait a second,' he said quickly. 'There's no reason for violence.'

The B Man smiled, shrugged. 'Why does there have to be a reason?'

Myron's eyes widened. Fear hardened in his belly. 'Hold on,' he said quickly. 'I'll talk.'

'I know you will,' the B Man replied. 'But first you'll jerk us around a bit—'

'No, I won't.'

'Please don't interrupt me. It's very rude to interrupt.' The smile was gone. 'Where was I?'

'First he'll jerk us around,' the driver prompted.

'That's right, thank you.' He turned the white smile back to Myron. 'First, you'll stall. You'll do a song-and-dance. You'll hope we'll take you someplace where your partner can save you.'

'Partner?'

'You're still friends with Win, aren't you?'

The man knew Win. This was not a good thing. 'Win who?'

'Precisely,' B Man said. 'This is what I mean by being jerked around. Enough.'

He moved closer. Myron started to struggle, but the man jammed the gun in Myron's mouth. It struck teeth and made him gag. The taste was cold and metallic.

'I'll destroy the knee first. Then we'll talk.'

The other man pulled Myron's leg straight while the gunman took the revolver out of Myron's mouth and pressed it back against his temple. Their grips grew a bit tighter. The B Man lowered his hands to Myron's knee, his fingers spread like eagle's talons.

'Wait!' Myron shouted.

'No,' B Man replied calmly.

Myron started to squirm. He grabbed a loading handle on the floor of the van, the kind of thing used to tie down cargo. He held on and braced himself. He didn't have to wait very long.

The crash jarred them. Myron had been ready for it. No one else had. They all went flying, their grips slackening. Glass shattered. The scream of metal hitting metal filled the air. Brakes screeched. Myron held on until the van slowed. Then he curled into a ball and rolled out of harm's way. There were shouts and a door opened. Myron heard a shot being fired. Voices sounded in a cacophony of confusion. The driver ducked out through his door. The B Man followed, leaping like a grasshopper. The side door opened. Myron looked up as Win stepped in with his gun drawn. The man with the turtleneck/dickey had recovered. He picked up his gun.

'Drop it,' Win said.

The man with the turtleneck/dickey didn't. Win shot him in the face. He turned his aim toward the man who had straddled Myron's chest.

'Drop it,' Win said.

The man did. Win smiled at him. 'Fast learner.'

Win's eyes slid smoothly from side to side, never darting. Win barely moved, seeming to glide rather than walk. His movements were short and economical. He returned his eyes to his captive. The one still breathing.

'Talk,' Win said.

'I don't know nothing.'

'Bad answer,' Win said. He spoke with calm authority, his matter-of-fact tone more intimidating than any scream. 'If you know nothing, you are useless to me; if you are useless to me, you end up like him.' He vaguely motioned toward the still form at his feet.

The man held up his hands. His eyes were round and white. 'Hey, wait a sec, okay? It's no secret. Your buddy heard the guy's name. Baron. The guy's name is Baron. But everyone calls him the B Man.'

'The B Man works out of the Midwest,' Win said. 'Who brought him in?'

'I don't know; I swear.'

Win moved the gun closer. 'You're being useless to me again.'

'It's the truth, I'd tell you if I knew. All I know is the B Man flew in late last night.'

'Why?' Win asked.

'It's got something to do with Greg Downing. That's all I know, I swear.'

'How much does Downing owe?'

'I don't know.'

Win moved closer still. He pressed the barrel of the gun between the man's eyes. 'I rarely miss from this distance,' he said.

The man dropped to his knees. Win followed him down with the gun. 'Please.' His voice was a pained plea. 'I don't know nothing else.' His eyes filled with tears. 'I swear to God, I don't.'

'I believe you,' Win said.

'Win,' Myron said.

Win's eyes never left the man. 'Relax,' he said. 'I just wanted to make sure our friend here had confessed all. Confession is good for the soul, is it not?'

The man nodded hurriedly.

'Have you confessed all?'

More nods.

'You're sure?'

Nod, nod.

Win lowered the weapon. 'Go then,' he said. 'Now.'

The man didn't have to be told twice.

18

Win looked down at the dead body as though it were a bag of peat moss. 'We best depart.'

Myron nodded. He reached into his pants pocket and took out the cellular phone. A relatively new trick of the trade. Neither he nor Win had hung up after their call. The line was left open; Win had been able to hear everything that had gone on in the van. It worked as well as any bug or walkie-talkie.

They stepped into the cool night. They were on Washington Street. During the day the place was popping with delivery trucks, but at night it was completely silent. Someone would find a nasty surprise in the morning.

Win normally drove a Jaguar, but he had smashed a 1983 Chevy Nova into the van. Totaled. Not that it mattered. Win had several such vehicles he kept out in New Jersey to use for surveillance or activities just east of legal. The car was untraceable. The plates and paperwork were all phony. It would never lead back to anyone.

Myron looked at him. 'A man of your breeding in a Chevy Nova?' He tsk-tsked.

'I know,' Win said. 'Sitting in it almost gave me a rash.'

'If anyone at the club saw you . . .'

Win shuddered. 'Do not even think such a thought.'

Myron's legs still felt shaky and numb. Even as the B Man had reached down for his knee, Myron had known that Win would find a way to get to him. But the thought of how close he'd come to being crippled for life kept plucking at the muscles in his calves and thighs. He kept bending down and touching the bad knee, as if he couldn't believe it was still there. Tears brimmed in his eyes as he looked at Win. Win saw them and turned away.

Myron followed behind him. 'So how do you know this B Man?' he asked.

'He operates out of the Midwest,' Win said. 'He is also a superb martial artist. We met in Tokyo once.'

'What sort of operation does he run?'

'The usual assorted sundries – gambling, drugs, loan sharking, extortion. A bit of prostitution too.'

'So what's he doing here?'

'It appears that Greg Downing owes him money,' Win said, 'probably from gambling. The B Man specializes in gambling.'

'Nice to have a specialty.'

'Indeed. I would assume that your Mr Downing owes them a large sum of money.' Win glanced over at Myron. 'That's good news for you.'

'Why?'

'Because it implies that Downing is on the run rather than dead,' Win said. 'The B Man is not wasteful. He wouldn't kill someone who owes him a lot of money.'

'Dead men pay no debts.'

'Precisely,' Win said. 'On top of that he is clearly looking for Downing. If he killed him, he wouldn't need you to find him.'

Myron considered this for a moment. 'It sort of meshes with what Emily told me. She said Greg had no money. Gambling might explain that fact.'

Win nodded. 'Kindly fill me in on what else has occurred in my absence. Jessica mentioned something about finding a dead woman.'

Myron told him everything. As he spoke, new theories rushed forward. He tried to sort through them and organize them a bit. When he finished the recap, Myron went right into the first one.

'Let's assume,' he said, 'that Downing does owe lot of money to this B Man. That might explain why he finally agreed to sign an endorsement deal. He needs the money.'

Win nodded. 'Go on.'

'And let's also assume the B Man is not stupid. He wants to collect, right? So he would never really hurt Greg. Greg makes him money through his physical prowess. Broken bones would have an adverse effect on Greg's financial status and thus his ability to pay.'

'True,' Win said.

'So let's say Greg owes them a lot of money. Maybe the B Man wanted to scare him in another way.'

'How?'

'By hurting someone close to him. As a warning.'

Win nodded again. 'That might work.'

'And suppose they followed Greg. Suppose they saw him with Carla. Suppose they figured that Greg and Carla were close.' Myron looked up. 'Wouldn't killing her be a hell of a warning?'

Win frowned. 'You think the B Man killed her to warn Downing?'

'I'm saying it's possible.'

'Why wouldn't he just break one of her bones?' Win asked.

'Because the B Man wasn't personally on the scene yet, remember? He got in last night. The murder would have been the work of hired muscle.'

Win still didn't like it. 'Your theory is improbable, at best. If the murder was indeed a warning, where is Downing now?'

'He ran away,' Myron said.

'Why? Because he was afraid for his own life?'

'Yes.'

'And did he run away immediately after learning Carla was dead?' Win asked. 'On Saturday night?'

'That would be most logical.'

'He was frightened off then? By the murder?'

'Yes,' Myron said.

'Ah.' Win stopped and smiled at Myron.

'What?' Myron asked.

'Pray tell,' Win began with a lilt in his voice, 'if Carla's body was just discovered today, how did Downing know about the murder last Saturday night?'

Myron felt a chill.

'For your theory to hold up,' Win continued, 'Greg Downing would have to have done one of three things. One, he witnessed the murder; two he stumbled into the apartment after the murder; three, he committed the murder himself. Furthermore, there was a great deal of cash in her apartment. Why? What was it doing there? Was this money to help pay back the B Man? If so, why didn't his men take it? Or better yet, why didn't Downing take it back when he was there?'

Myron shook his head. 'So many holes,' he said. 'And we still haven't come up with what connection there is between Downing and this Carla or Sally or whatever her name is.'

Win nodded. They continued walking.

'One more thing,' Myron said. 'Do you really think the mob would kill a woman just because she happened to be with Greg at a bar?'

'Very doubtful,' Win agreed.

'So basically, that whole theory is blown to hell.'

'Not basically,' Win corrected. 'Entirely.'

They kept walking.

'Of course,' Win said, 'Carla could have been working for the B Man.'

An icy finger poked at Myron. He saw where Win was going but he still said, 'What?'

'Perhaps this Carla woman was the B Man's contact. She collected for him. She was meeting Downing because he owed a great deal of money. Downing promises to pay. But he doesn't have the money. He knows they are closing in on him. He has stalled long enough. So he goes back to her apartment, kills her, and runs.'

Silence. Myron tried to swallow, but his throat felt frozen. This was good, this talking it through. It helped. His legs were still rubbery from the incident, but what really bothered him now was how easily he had forgotten the dead man lying in the van. True, the man had jammed the barrel of a gun into his mouth and had not dropped his weapon when Win told him to. And true, the world was probably a better place without him. But in the past Myron would have still felt some remorse for this fellow human being; in all honesty, he didn't now. He tried to muster some sympathy, but the only thing he felt sad about was that he didn't feel sad.

Enough self-analysis. Myron shook it off and said, 'There are problems with that scenario too.'

'Such as?'

'Why would Greg kill her? Why not just run off before the back-booth meeting?'

Win considered this. 'Fair point. Unless something happened during their meeting to set him off.'

'Like what?'

Win shrugged.

'It all comes back to this Carla,' Myron said. 'Nothing about her adds up. I mean, even a drug dealer doesn't have a setup like hers – working as a diner waitress, hiding sequentially numbered hundred dollar bills, wearing wigs, having all those fake passports. And on top of that, you should have seen Dimonte this afternoon. He knew who she was and he was in a panic.'

'You contacted Higgins at the Treasury?' Win asked.

'Yes. He's tracing those serial numbers.'

'That could help.'

'We also need to get hold of the telephone records from the Parkview Diner. See who Carla called.'

They fell back into silence and kept walking. They didn't want to hail a taxi too close to the scene.

'Win?'

'Yes?'

'Why didn't you want to go to the game the other night?'

Win kept on walking. Myron kept pace. After some time, Win said, 'You've never watched a replay of it, have you?'

He knew he meant the knee injury. 'No.'

'Why not?'

Myron shrugged. 'No point.'

'No, there is a point.' Win kept walking.

'Mind telling me what that is?' Myron said.

'Watching what happened to you might have meant dealing with it. Watching it might have meant closure.'

'I don't understand,' Myron said.

Win nodded. 'I know.'

'I remember you watched it,' Myron said. 'I remember you watched it over and over.'

'I did that for a reason,' Win said.

'For vengeance.'

'To see if Burt Wesson injured you on purpose,' Win corrected.

'You wanted to pay him back.'

'You should have let me. Then you might have been able to put it behind you.'

Myron shook his head. 'Violence is always the answer for you, Win.'

Win frowned. 'Stop sounding melodramatic. A man committed a vile act upon you. Squaring things would have helped put it behind you. It's not about vengeance. It's about equilibrium. It's about man's basic need to keep the scales balanced.'

'That's your need,' Myron said, 'not mine. Hurting Burt Wesson wouldn't have fixed my knee.'

'But it might have given you closure.'

'What does that mean, closure? It was a freak injury. That's all.'

Win shook his head. 'You never watched the tape.'

'It wouldn't have mattered. The knee was still ruined. Watching a tape wouldn't have changed that.'

Win said nothing.

'I don't understand this,' Myron continued. 'I went on after the injury. I never complained, did I?'

'Never.'

'I didn't cry or curse the gods or do any of that stuff.'

'Never,' Win said again. 'You never let yourself be a burden on any of us.'

'So why do you think I needed to relive it?'

Win stopped and looked at him. 'You've answered your own question, but you choose not to hear it.'

'Spare me the Kung-Fu-grasshopper philosophical bullshit,' Myron shot back. 'Why didn't you go to the game?'

Win started walking again. 'Watch the tape,' he said.

19

Myron didn't watch the tape. But he had the dream.

In the dream he could see Burt Wesson bearing down on him. He could see the gleeful, almost giddy violence in Burt's face as he drew closer and closer. In the dream, Myron had plenty of time to step out of harm's way. Too much time really. But in this dream – as in many – Myron could not move. His legs would not respond, his feet mired in thick, dream-world quicksand while the inevitable approached.

But in reality, Myron had never seen Burt Wesson coming. There had been no warning. Myron had been pivoting on his right leg when the blinding collision befell him. He heard rather than felt a snap. At first there had been no pain, just wide-eyed astonishment. The astonishment had probably lasted less than a second, but it was a frozen second, a snapshot Myron only took out in dreams. Then came the pain.

In the dream Burt Wesson was almost on him now. Burt was a huge man, an enforcer-type player, the basketball equivalent of a hockey goon. He did not have much talent, but he had tremendous bulk and he knew how to use it. It had gotten him far, but this was the pros now. Burt would be cut before the start of the season – poetic irony that neither he nor Myron would play in a real professional basketball game. Until two nights ago anyway.

In the dream Myron watched Burt Wesson approach and waited. Somewhere in his subconscious, he knew that he would awaken before the collision. He always did. He lingered now in that cusp between nightmare and being awake – that tiny window where you are still asleep but you know it is a dream and even though it may be terrifying, you want to go on and see how it will end because it is only a dream and you are safe. But reality would not keep that window open for long. It never did. As Myron swam to the surface, he knew that whatever the answer was, he would not find it in any nocturnal voyage to the past.

'Phone for you,' Jessica said.

Myron blinked his eyes and rolled onto his back. Jessica was already dressed. 'What time is it?' he asked.

'Nine.'

'What? Why didn't you wake me?'

'You needed the sleep.' She handed him the phone. 'It's Esperanza.'

He took it. 'Hello.'

'Christ, don't you ever sleep in your own bed?' Esperanza said.

He was hardly in the mood. 'What is it?'

'Fred Higgins from Treasury is on the line,' she said. 'I thought you'd want it.'

'Pass it through.' A click. 'Fred?'

'Yeah, how you doing, Myron?'

'I'm okay. You got anything on those serial numbers?'

There was a brief hesitation. 'You stumbled into some heavy shit, Myron. Some very heavy shit.'

'I'm listening.'

'People don't want this out, you understand? I had to jump through all kinds of hoops to get this.'

'Mum's the word.'

'Okay then,' Higgins took a deep breath. 'The bills are from Tucson, Arizona,' he said. 'More specifically, First City National Bank of Tucson, Arizona. They were stolen in an armed bank heist.'

Myron shot up in the bed. 'When?'

'Two months ago.'

Myron remembered a headline, and his blood turned cold.

'Myron?'

'The Raven Brigade,' Myron managed. 'That was one of theirs, right?'

'Right. You ever work on their case with the feds?'

'No, never.' But he remembered. Myron and Win had worked on cases with a special and almost contradictory nature: high profile with the need for undercover. They had been perfect for such situations – who, after all, would suspect a former basketball star and a rich, Main Line prep of being undercover agents? They could travel in whatever circles they wanted to and not raise suspicion. Myron and Win didn't have to create a cover; their reality was the best one the agency had. But Myron was never full-time with them. Win was their fair-haired boy; Myron was more a utility fielder Win called in when he thought it necessary.

But of course he knew about the Raven Brigade. Most people with even a passing familiarity with sixties extremism knew about them. Started by a charismatic leader named Cole Whiteman, the Ravens had been yet another splinter group of the Weather Underground. They were very much like the Symbionese Liberation Army, the group that kidnapped Patty Hearst. The Ravens, too, attempted a high-profile kidnapping, but the victim ended up dead. The group had gone underground. Four of them. Despite the FBI's best efforts, the four escapees – including Cole Whiteman, who with his Win-like blond hair and WASPy background never looked the part of an extremist – had remained hidden for nearly a quarter-century.

Dimonte's bizarre questions about radical politics and 'perversives' no longer seemed so bizarre.

'Was the victim one of the Ravens?' Myron asked.

'I can't say.'

'You don't have to,' Myron said. 'I know it was Liz Gorman.'

There was another brief hesitation. Then: 'How the hell did you know that?'

'The implants,' Myron said.

'What?'

Liz Gorman, a fiery redhead, had been one of the founding members of the Raven Brigade. During their first 'mission' – a failed attempt to burn down a university chemistry lab – the police had picked up a code name on the scanner: CD. It was later revealed that the male members of the Brigade called her CD, short for Carpenter's Dream, because she was 'flat as a board and easy to screw.' Sixties radicals, for all their so-called progressive thoughts, were some of the world's biggest sexists. Now the implants made sense. Everyone Myron had interviewed remembered one thing about 'Carla' – her cup size. Liz Gorman had been famous for her flat chest – what better disguise than oversized breast implants?

'The feds and cops are cooperating on this one,' Higgins said. 'They're trying to keep this quiet for a while.'

'Why?'

'They got her place under surveillance. They're hoping to maybe draw out another member.'

Myron felt completely numb. He had wanted to learn more about the mystery woman and now he had: she was Liz Gorman, a famous radical who had not been seen since 1975. The disguises, the various passports, the implants – they all added up now. She wasn't a drug dealer, she was a woman on the run.

But if Myron had hoped learning the truth about Liz Gorman would help clarify his own investigation, he had been sadly mistaken. What possible connection could there be between Greg Downing and Liz Gorman? How had a professional basketball player gotten enmeshed with a wanted extremist who had gone underground when Greg was still a kid? It made absolutely no sense.

'How much did they get in the bank heist?' Myron asked.

'Hard to say,' Higgins answered. 'About fifteen thousand in cash, but they also blew open the safe-deposit boxes. Over a half million in goods have been declared for insurance purposes, but a lot of it is bullshit. A guy gets robbed, all of a sudden he was keeping ten Rolexes in the box instead of one – trying to rip off the insurance company, you know how it is.'

'On the other hand,' Myron said, 'anyone keeping illegal dollars in there wouldn't declare it. They'd just have to swallow the loss.' Back to drugs and drug money. The extremists in the underground needed resources. They'd been known to rob banks, blackmail former followers who had gone mainstream, deal drugs, whatever. 'So it could have been even more.'

'Right, hard to say.'

'You got anything else on this?'

'Nothing,' Higgins said. 'It's being kept sealed tight, and I'm not in the loop. I can't tell you how hard it was to get this, Myron. You owe me big.'

'I already promised you the tickets, Fred.'

'Courtside?'

'I'll do my best.'

Jessica came back into the room. When she saw Myron's face, she stopped and looked a question at him. Myron hung up and told her. She listened. Remembering Esperanza's crack, Myron realized that he had now spent four nights in a row here – a postbreakup world and Olympic record. He worried about that. It wasn't that he didn't like staying here. He did. It wasn't that he feared commitment or any of that other drivel; to the contrary, he craved it. But part of him was still afraid – old wounds that wouldn't heal and all that.

Myron had a habit of exposing too much of himself. He knew that. With Win or Esperanza it was okay. He trusted them absolutely. He loved Jessica with all his heart, but she had hurt him. He wanted to be tentative. He wanted to hold back, to not leave himself so open, but the heart don't know from stop. At least, Myron's didn't. Two primal internal forces were at odds here: his natural instinct to give all he had when it came to love vs the survival instinct of pain avoidance.

'This whole thing,' Jessica said when he had finished, 'is just too weird.'

'Yep,' he said. They had barely talked last night. He had assured her that he was all right and they had both gone to sleep. 'I guess I should thank you.'

'For what?'

'You were the one who called Win.'

She nodded. 'After those goons jumped you.'

'I thought you said you weren't going to interfere.'

'Wrong. I said I wasn't going to try to stop you. There's a difference.'

'True enough.'

Jessica started chewing on her bottom lip. She was wearing jeans and a Duke sweat shirt several sizes too large on her. Her hair was still wet from a recent shower. 'I think you should move in,' she said.

Her words hit him square in the jaw. 'What?'

'I didn't mean to just blurt it out like that,' she said. 'I'm not very good at beating around the bush.'

'That's my job anyway,' he said.

She shook her head. 'You pick the strangest times to be crude.'

'Yeah, I'm sorry.'

'Look, I'm not good at this stuff, Myron. You know that.'

He nodded. He knew.

She tilted her head to the side, shrugged, smiled nervously. 'It's just that I like having you here. It feels right.'

His heart soared and sung and quivered in fear. 'It's a big step.'

'Not really,' she said. 'You're here most of the time anyway. And I love you.'

'I love you, too.'

The pause lingered a bit longer than it should. Jessica jumped into it before it could do irreparable harm. 'Don't say anything now,' she said, rushing the words out in a gush. 'I want you to think about it. It was a dumb time to bring it up, with all this stuff going on. Or maybe that's why I chose now, I don't know. But don't say anything. Just think about it. Don't call me today. Or tonight. I'm going to your game, but then I'm taking Audrey out for a few drinks. It's her birthday. Sleep at your house tonight. Maybe we'll talk tomorrow, okay? Tomorrow?'

'Tomorrow,' Myron agreed.

20

Big Cyndi sat at the reception desk. 'Sat' was probably the wrong word. Talk about the proverbial camel trying to squeeze through the eye of the needle. The desk's four legs were off the floor, the top teetering on Big Cyndi's knees like a seesaw. Her coffee mug disappeared into the fleshy hands that resembled couch cushions. Her short spikes of hair had more of a pinkish hue today. Her makeup reminded him of a childhood incident involving melted Crayola crayons. She wore white lipstick, like something out of an Elvis documentary. Her size-3XL T-shirt read CLUB SODA NOT SEALS. It took Myron a few seconds to get it. Politically correct but cute.

Usually she growled when she saw Myron. Today she smiled sweetly and batted her eyes at him. The sight was far more frightening, like Bette Davis in *Whatever Happened to Baby Jane*, only on steroids. Big Cyndi pointed up her middle finger and bounced it up and down.

'Line one?' he tried.

She shook her head. The up and down gesture became more hurried. She looked up at the ceiling. Myron followed her gaze but he saw nothing. Cyndi rolled her eyes. The smile was frozen on her face, like a clown's.

'I don't get it,' he said.

'Win wants to see you,' she said.

It was the first time Myron had heard her voice, and it startled him. She sounded like one of those perky hostesses on a cable shopping network, the one where people call up and describe in far too much detail how much their lives were improved by purchasing a green vase shaped liked Mount Rushmore.

'Where's Esperanza?' he asked.

'Win's cute.'

'Is she here?'

'Win seemed to think it was important.'

'I'm just—'

'You're going to see Win,' Cyndi interrupted. 'You're certainly not checking up on your most valued associate.' The sweet smile.

'I'm not checking up. I just want to know—'

'Where Win's office is. It's two stories up.' She made a sound with her coffee that some might loosely label, 'slurping.' Moose in the tri-state area scattered in search of mates.

'Tell her I'll be back,' Myron said.

'But of course.' She batted her eyelashes. They looked like two tarantulas in death throes. 'Have a nice day.'

Win's corner office faced Fifty-second Street and Park Avenue. Major league view for Lock-Horne Securities' golden boy. Myron sank into one of the lush burgundy leather chairs. There were several paintings of fox hunts on the richly paneled walls. Dozens of manly men on horseback, dressed in black hats, red blazers, white pants, black boots, rode out armed with only rifles and dogs to chase down a small furry creature until they caught and killed it. Ah, gamesmanship. A tad overkill maybe. Like using a flame-thrower to light a cigarette.

Win typed on a laptop computer that looked lonely on the mono-expanse he called a desk. 'I found something of interest on the computer disks we made at Greg's house.'

'Oh?'

'It appears our friend Mr Downing had an e-mail address with America Online,' Win said. 'He downloaded this particular piece of mail on Saturday.' Win spun the laptop around so Myron could read the screen:

Subj:	Sex!
Date:	3–11 14:51:36 EST
From:	Sepbabe
To:	Downing22

Meet you tonight at ten. The place we discussed. Come. I promise you the greatest night of ecstasy imaginable.

—F

Myron looked up. 'Greatest night of ecstasy imaginable?'

'She has quite the writing flair, no?' Win said.

Myron made a face.

Win put a sincere hand to his heart. 'Even if she could not live up to such a promise,' he continued, 'one has to admire her ability to take risk, her dedication to her craft.'

'Uh huh,' Myron said. 'So who is F?'

'There is no profile for the screen name Sepbabe on line,' Win explained. 'That doesn't mean anything, of course. Many users don't have a profile. They don't want everyone knowing their real name. I would assume however that F is yet another alias for our dearly departed friend Carla.'

'We have Carla's real name now,' Myron said.

'Oh?'

'Liz Gorman.'

Win arched an eyebrow. 'Pardon?'

'Liz Gorman. As in the Raven Brigade.' He told Win about Fred Higgins's call. Win leaned back in his chair and steepled his fingers. As usual his face gave away nothing.

When Myron finished, Win said, 'Curiouser and curiouser.'

'It comes down to this,' Myron said. 'What connection could there possibly be between Greg Downing and Liz Gorman?'

'A strong one,' Win said, nodding toward the screen. 'The possibility of the greatest night of ecstasy imaginable, if one is to buy into the hyperbole.'

'But with Liz Gorman?'

'Why not?' Win almost sounded defensive. 'You shouldn't discriminate on the basis of age or implants. It wouldn't be right.'

Mr Equal Rights. 'It's not that,' Myron said. 'Let's pretend that Greg has the hots for Liz Gorman, even though nobody described her as much of a looker . . .'

'You're so shallow, Myron,' Win said with a disenchanted shake of the head. 'Did you ever consider the possibility that Greg saw beneath that? She did, after all, have large breasts.'

'As usual when discussing sex,' Myron replied, 'you've missed the point.'

'Which is?'

'How would they have hooked up in the first place?'

Win steepled his fingers again, bouncing the tips against his nose. 'Ah,' he said.

'Right, ah. Here's a woman who's been living underground for more than twenty years. She's traveled all over the world, probably never staying in one spot for very long. She was in Arizona robbing a bank two months ago. She's working as a waitress in a tiny diner on Dyckman Street. How does this woman hook up with Greg Downing?'

'Difficult,' Win allowed, 'but not impossible. There is plenty of evidence to support that.'

'Like?'

Win motioned to the computer screen. 'This e-mail is talking about last Saturday night, for one – the same night Greg and Liz Gorman met in a New York City bar.'

'In a dive bar,' Myron corrected. 'Why there? Why not go to a hotel or her place?'

'Perhaps because it is out of the way. Perhaps, as you implied, Liz Gorman would want to keep out of the public eye. Such a bar might be a good alternative.' He stopped steepling and lightly drummed his fingers on the desk. 'But you, my friend, are forgetting something else.'

'What?'

'The woman's clothes in Greg's house,' Win said. 'Your investigation has led us to conclude that Downing has a lover he was keeping secret. The question, of course is: why? Why would he work so hard to keep a love affair clandestine? One possible explanation is that the secret love was the infamous Liz Gorman.'

Myron wasn't sure what to think. Audrey had seen Greg at a restaurant with a woman that did not fit Liz Gorman's description. But what did that mean? It might have been another date. It might have been something innocent. It might have been a side affair, who knows? Still, Myron had trouble buying a romantic entanglement involving Greg Downing and Liz Gorman. Something about it just didn't wash. 'There must be a way of tracing down this screen name and finding the user's real identity,' he said. 'Let's make sure it checks back to Liz Gorman or one of her aliases.'

'I'll see what I can do. I don't have any contacts with America Online, but someone we know must.' Win reached behind him. He opened up the paneled door on his minifridge. He tossed Myron a can of Yoo-hoo and poured himself a Brooklyn Lager. Win never drank beer, only lager. 'Greg's money has been difficult to locate,' he said. 'I'm not sure there is very much.'

'That would fit into what Emily said.'

'However,' Win continued, 'I did find one major withdrawal.'

'How much?'

'Fifty thousand dollars in cash. It took some time because it came out of an account that Martin Felder holds for him.'

'When did he withdraw it?'

'Four days before he disappeared,' Win said.

'Paying off a gambling debt?'

'Perhaps.'

Win's phone rang. He picked it up and said, 'Articulate. Okay, put it through.' Two seconds later he handed the phone to Myron.

'For me?' Myron asked.

Win gave him flat eyes. 'No,' he said. 'I'm handing you the phone because it's too heavy for me.'

Everyone's a wiseass. Myron took the phone. 'Hello?'

'I got a squad car downstairs.' It was Dimonte in full bark. 'Get your ass in it now.'

'What's wrong?'

'I'm at fucking Downing's house, that's what's wrong. I had to practically suck off a judge to get the warrant.'

'Nice imagery, Rolly.'

'Don't fuck with me, Bolitar. You said there was blood in the house.'

'In the basement,' Myron corrected.

'Well, I'm in the basement right now,' he countered. 'And it's as clean as a baby's ass.'

21

The basement was indeed clean. No blood anywhere.

'There's got to be traces,' Myron said.

Dimonte's toothpick looked like it was about to snap between his clenched teeth. 'Traces?'

'Yeah. With a microscope or something.'

'With a . . .' Dimonte flapped his arms, his face crimson. 'What the hell good is traces going to do me? They don't prove a damn thing. You can't test traces.'

'It'll prove there was blood.'

'So what?' he shouted. 'You go through any house in America with a microscope and you're bound to find traces of blood. Who the fuck cares?'

'I don't know what to tell you, Rolly. The blood was there.'

There were maybe five lab cops – no uniforms, no marked cars – going through the house. Krinsky was there too. The videocamera in his hand was off right now. He also had what looked like manila files jammed into his armpit. Myron motioned to them. 'That the coroner's report?'

Roland Dimonte stepped in to block Myron's view. 'That ain't none of your business, Bolitar.'

'I know about Liz Gorman, Rolly.'

The toothpick hit the floor on that one. 'How the hell . . . ?'

'It's not important.'

'The fuck it ain't. What else do you know? If you're holding out on me, Bolitar—'

'I'm not holding out on you, but I think I can help.'

Dimonte narrowed his eyes. Señor Suspicious. 'Help how?'

'Just tell me Gorman's blood type. That's all I want to know. Her blood type.'

'Why the hell should I?'

'Because you're not a total numb nut, Rolly.'

'Don't give me that shit. Why do you want to know?'

'Remember I told you about finding blood in the basement?' Myron said.

'Yeah.'

'I left something out.'

Dimonte gave him the glare. 'What?'

'We tested some of the blood.'

'We? Who the fuck is . . .' His voice trailed off. 'Oh Christ, don't tell me that psycho-yuppie is in on all this?'

To know Win was to love him. 'I'd like to make a little trade.'

'What kind of trade?'

'You tell me the blood type in the report. I tell you the blood type we found in the basement.'

'Fuck you, Bolitar. I can arrest your ass for tampering with evidence in a police investigation.'

'What tampering? There was no investigation.'

'I could still nail your ass for breaking and entering.'

'If you could prove it. And if Greg were around to press charges. Look, Rolly—'

'AB positive,' Krinsky said. He ignored Dimonte's renewed glare and continued. 'It's fairly rare. Four percent of the populace.'

They both turned their attention to Myron. Myron nodded. 'AB positive. It's the same.'

Dimonte put up both hands and scrunched his face into perplexed. 'Whoa, hold up here. Just what the fuck are you trying to say? That she was killed down here and moved?'

'I'm not saying anything,' Myron said.

' 'Cause we didn't see any evidence of the body being moved,' Dimonte went on. 'None at all. Not that we were looking for it. But the bleeding pattern – I mean, if she was killed down here, there wouldn't have been so much blood at her apartment. You saw the mess there, right?'

Myron nodded.

Dimonte's eyes darted aimlessly. Myron could practically see the gears inside his head grinding to a halt. 'You know what that means, don't you, Bolitar?'

'No, Rolly, why don't you enlighten me?'

'It means the killer came back here after the murder. It's the only explanation. And you know who all this is starting to point to? Your pal Downing. First we found his fingerprints in the victim's apartment—'

'What's this?'

Dimonte nodded. 'That's right. Downing's fingerprints were by the door frame.'

'But not inside?'

'Yeah, inside. Inside the door frame.'

'But nowhere else?'

'What the hell's the difference? The fingerprints prove he was at the scene. What more do you need? Anyway, here's how it must have happened.' He stuck a new toothpick in his mouth. New toothpick for a new theory. 'Downing kills her. He comes back to his house to pack or

618

something. He's in a rush so he leaves a little mess in the basement. Then he runs away. A few days later he comes back and cleans it up.'

Myron shook his head. 'Why come down to the basement in the first place?'

'The laundry room,' Dimonte answered. 'He was coming down here to wash his clothes.'

'The laundry room is upstairs off the kitchen,' Myron said.

Dimonte shrugged. 'So maybe he was getting a suitcase.'

'They're in the bedroom closet. This is just a kids' playroom, Rolly. Why did he come down here?'

That stopped Dimonte for a moment. It stopped Myron too. None of this made much sense. Had Liz Gorman been killed here and dragged to her apartment in Manhattan? That didn't seem to make much sense based on the physical evidence. Could she have been injured down here?

Whoa, hold the phone.

Maybe the attack started here. Maybe there had been a scuffle in the basement. In the course of subduing or knocking her out, blood was spilled. But then what? Did the killer stick her in a car and drive to Manhattan? And then – what? – on a fairly active street, the killer parked a car, dragged her injured body up the stairs, entered her apartment, killed her?

Did that make any sense?

From the first level a voice cried down, 'Detective! We found something! Quick!'

Dimonte wet his lips. 'Turn on the video,' he told Krinsky. Videotaping all the relevant moments. Just like Myron had told him. 'Stay here, Bolitar. I don't want to have to explain your ugly mug being on the film.'

Myron followed but at a discreet distance. Krinsky and Dimonte headed up the stairs into the kitchen. They turned left. The laundry room. Vinyl yellow wallpaper with white chicks blanketed all four walls. Emily's taste? Probably not. Knowing Emily she'd probably never even seen the inside of a laundry room.

'Over here,' someone said. Myron stayed back. He could see that the dryer had been pushed away from the wall. Dimonte bent down and looked behind it. Krinsky arched over to make sure the whole thing was being filmed. Dimonte stood back up. He was trying like hell to look grim – a smile wouldn't look good on film – but he was having a rough time of it. He snapped on a pair of rubber gloves and lifted the item into view.

The baseball bat was covered with blood.

22

When Myron got back to the office, Esperanza was at the reception desk.

'Where's Big Cyndi?' Myron asked.

'Having lunch.'

The image of Fred Flintstone's car tipping over from the weight of his Bronto-ribs flashed in front of Myron's eyes.

'Win filled me in on what's been going on,' Esperanza said. She wore an aqua-blue blouse open at the throat. A gold heart on a slender chain dangled proudly against the dark skin of her sternum. Her always-mussed hair was slightly entangled in big hoop earrings. She pushed the hair back with one finger. 'So what happened at the house?'

He explained about the cleaned-up blood and the baseball bat. Esperanza usually liked to do other things while she listened. She wasn't right now. She stared square into his eyes. When she looked at you like that, there was such intensity it was sometimes hard to look back.

'I'm not sure I understand,' she said. 'You and Win found blood in the basement two days ago.'

'Right.'

'Since then, someone cleaned up that blood – but they left behind the murder weapon?'

'So it appears.'

Esperanza considered this for a moment. 'Could it have been a maid?'

'The police already checked on that. She hasn't been there in three weeks.'

'Do you have a thought?'

He nodded. 'Someone is trying to frame Greg. It's the only logical explanation.'

She arched a skeptical eyebrow. 'By planting and then cleaning up blood?'

'No, let's start from the beginning.' He grabbed the chair and sat in front of her. He had been going over it in his mind the whole ride back, and he wanted to talk it out. In the corner on his left, the fax machine sounded its digitally primordial screech. Myron waited for the sound to subside. 'Okay,' he said, 'first I'm going to assume that the killer knew Greg was with Liz

Gorman that night – maybe he followed them, maybe he was waiting for them near her apartment. Whatever, he knows they were together.'

Esperanza nodded, stood. She walked over to the fax machine to check the incoming transmission.

'After Greg leaves, the killer murders Liz Gorman. Knowing that Downing would make a good fall guy, he takes some blood from the murder scene and plants it at Greg's house. That will raise suspicion. To put the icing on the cake, the killer also takes the murder weapon and plants it behind the dryer.'

'But you just said the blood was cleaned up,' she interjected.

'Right. Here's where it gets a little tricky. Suppose, for example, I wanted to protect Greg Downing. I go into his house and find the blood. Now remember, I want to protect Greg from a murder rap. So what would I do?'

She squinted at the fax coming through. 'Clean up the blood.'

'Exactly.'

'Wow, thanks. Do I get a gold star? Get on with it already.'

'Just bear with me, okay? I would see the blood and clean it up. But – and here's the important part – the first time I was in that house I *never* saw the bat. That's not just in this example. That's real life. Win and I only saw the blood in the basement. No baseball bat.'

'Hold on,' she said. 'You're saying someone cleaned up the blood to protect Greg from a murder rap but didn't know about the bat?'

'Right.'

'Who?'

'I don't know.'

Esperanza shook her head. She moved back to her desk and hit some keys on her computer keyboard. 'It doesn't add up.'

'Why not?'

'Suppose I'm madly in love with Greg Downing,' she said, moving back to the fax machine. 'I'm in his house. For some reason I can't fathom, I'm in his kids' playroom. Doesn't matter where I am. Imagine I'm in my own apartment. Or I'm visiting your house. I could be anywhere.'

'Okay.'

'I see blood on the floor or on the walls or wherever.' She stopped, looked at him. 'What conclusion would you logically expect me to draw?'

Myron shook his head. 'I don't understand what you're saying.'

Esperanza thought a moment. 'Suppose you left here right now,' she began, 'and went back to the bitch's loft.'

'Don't call her that.'

'Whatever. Suppose when you walked in, you found blood on her walls. What would be your first reaction?'

Myron nodded slowly. Now he saw what she was getting at. 'I'd be worried about Jessica.'

'And your second reaction? After you found out she was okay?'

'Curiosity, I guess. Whose blood is it? How did it get there? That sort of thing.'

'Right,' she said with a quick nod. 'Would you think to yourself, "Gee, I better clean it up before the bitch gets accused of murdering somebody"?'

'Stop calling her that.'

Esperanza waved him off. 'Would you think that or not?'

'Not in that circumstance, no,' Myron said. 'So in order for my theory to hold water—'

'Your protector had to know about the murder,' she finished for him, back checking her computer for something. 'He or she would also have to know that Greg was somehow involved.'

Myron's head spun with possibilities. 'You think Greg killed her,' he said. 'You think he went back to his house after the murder and left behind some traces of the crime – like blood in the basement. Then he sent this protector back to the house to help cover his tracks.'

Esperanza made a face. 'Where the hell did you come up with that?'

'I just—'

'That's not what I think at all,' Esperanza said. She stapled the fax pages together. 'If Greg sent someone to get rid of the evidence, the weapon would be gone too.'

'Right. So that leaves us where?'

Esperanza shrugged, circled something on the fax page with a red marker. 'You're the great detective. You figure it out.'

Myron thought about it a moment. Another answer – one he prayed was wrong – came to him all at once. 'There's another possibility,' he said.

'What?'

'Clip Arnstein.'

'What about him?'

'I told Clip about the blood in the basement,' Myron said.

'When?'

'Two days ago.'

'How did he react?'

'He freaked, pretty much,' Myron said. 'He's also got motive – any scandal will destroy his chances of keeping control of the Dragons. Hell, that's why he hired me. To keep any trouble contained. Nobody else even knew about the blood in the basement.' Myron stopped. He leaned back and ran it through his mind again. 'Of course I haven't had a chance to tell Clip about Liz Gorman's murder. He didn't even know the blood wasn't Greg's. All he knew was that there was blood in the basement. Would he go that far just on that? Would he still risk covering it all up if he didn't know anything about Liz Gorman?'

Esperanza gave him a small smile. 'Maybe he knows more than you think,' she said.

'What makes you say that?'

She handed him the fax. 'It's the list of long distance calls made from the pay phone at the Parkview Diner,' she said. 'I already cross-checked it with my computer Rolodex. Look at the number I circled.'

Myron saw it. A call lasting twelve minutes had been made from the Parkview Diner four days before Greg's disappearance. The phone number was Clip's.

23

'Liz Gorman called Clip?' Myron looked up at Esperanza. 'What the hell is going on?'

Esperanza shrugged. 'Ask Clip.'

'I knew he was keeping something from me,' he went on, 'but I don't get it. How does Clip fit into this equation?'

'Uh huh.' She shuffled through some papers on her desk. 'Look, we got a ton of work to do. I mean, sports agent work. You have a game tonight, right?'

He nodded.

'So ask Clip then. In the meantime, we're just going around in circles here.'

Myron scanned the sheet. 'Any other numbers jump out at you?'

'Not yet,' she said. 'But I want to talk about something else for a minute.'

'What?'

'We have a problem with a client.'

'Who?'

'Jason Blair.'

'What's wrong?'

'He's pissed off,' she said. 'He's not happy with me handling his contract negotiations. He said he hired you, not some' – she made quote marks in the air with her fingers – ' "scantily clad wrestler with a nice ass." '

'He said that?'

'Yep. Nice ass. Didn't even notice my legs.' Esperanza shook her head.

Myron smiled. 'So what happened?'

Behind them the elevator dinged. Only one hit this part of the floor. The elevator opened directly into the reception area of MB SportsReps. Classy, or so he had been told. When the doors opened, two men came out. Myron recognized them right away. Camouflage Pants and Brick Wall. They were both armed. They aimed their guns at Myron and Esperanza. B Man stepped out behind them like he'd just been introduced on the Leno show. Big smile, acknowledging-the-crowd wave.

'How's the knee, Myron?' he asked.

'Better than your van.'

B Man laughed at that one. 'That Win,' he mused. 'The man is always a surprise. How did he know when to hit us?'

No reason not to tell. 'We kept the cellular phones on.'

B Man shook his head. 'Ingenious really. I'm very impressed.' He wore one of those suits that are just a tad too shiny and a pink tie. His shirt was french-cuffed and monogrammed with four letters: B MAN. Taking the nickname thing a little far. A thick, ropelike gold bracelet encircled his right wrist.

'How did you get up here?' Myron asked.

'Do you really think a few rent-a-cops are going to stop us?'

'I'd still like to hear,' Myron said.

B Man shrugged. 'I called Lock-Horne Securities and told them I was looking for a new financial advisor for my millions. An anxious young peon told me to come right up. I hit the twelfth floor on the elevator instead of the fifteenth.' He spread his hands. 'So here I am.' He smiled at Esperanza. What with the too-white teeth and the tan, it looked like he switched on a night-light.

'And who is this fetching creature?' he asked with a wink.

'My,' Esperanza said, 'what woman doesn't love to be called a creature?'

B Man laughed again. 'The little lady has gumption,' he said. 'I like that. I really do.'

'Like I care,' Esperanza said.

More laughter. 'May I indulge you a moment, Miss . . . ?'

'Moneypenny,' she finished for him. She said it with her best Sean Connery imitation. No Rich Little, but not bad either.

Another laugh from the B Man. The man was half-hyena. 'Would you please call Win down here? On the speakerphone if you don't mind. Tell him to come down unarmed.'

She looked at Myron. Myron nodded. She dialed. Over the speakerphone, Win offered up another, 'Articulate.'

Esperanza said, 'Some bottled blond with a bottled tan is down here to see you.'

'Ah, I've been expecting him,' Win said. 'Hello, B Man.'

'Hello, Win.'

'I assume you are in well-armed company.'

'That I am, Win,' B Man said. 'If you try anything, your friends won't make it out alive.'

' "Won't make it out alive"?' Win repeated. 'I expected better from you, B Man, really. I'll be down in a second.'

'Come unarmed, Win.'

'Not a chance. But there will be no violence. That I promise you.' The phone clicked off. For several moments everyone looked at one another as if wondering who was going to take the lead.

'I don't trust him,' B Man said. He pointed to Brick Wall. 'Take the girl in the other room. Duck down behind a desk or something. You hear any shooting, you blow her head off.'

The Brick Wall nodded.

B Man directed his attention to Camouflage Pants. 'Keep your gun on Bolitar.'

'Right.'

B Man took out his own weapon. When the elevator dinged, he squatted and aimed. The doors slid open, but it wasn't Win. Big Cyndi emerged from the elevator, not unlike a dinosaur emerging from its egg.

'Jesus Christ!' Camouflage Pants said. 'What the hell is that?'

Big Cyndi growled.

'Who is she, Bolitar?' B Man demanded.

'My new receptionist.'

'Tell her to wait in the other room.'

Myron nodded to her. 'It's okay. Esperanza's in there.'

Cyndi growled again, but she listened. She walked past the B Man on her way to Myron's office. His gun looked like a disposable lighter next to her. She opened the door, snarled one last time, and closed it.

Silence.

'Jesus Christ,' Camouflage Pants said again.

They waited approximately thirty seconds before the elevator dinged again. B Man got back into his squat and aimed. The doors slid open. Win stepped out. He looked mildly annoyed when he saw the weapon aimed his way. His voice was clipped. 'I told you there would be no violence.'

'You have information we need,' B Man said.

'I'm well aware of that,' Win replied. 'Now put that gun away and we'll talk civilly.'

The B Man kept his weapon on Win. 'You armed?'

'Of course.'

'Hand over your weapon.'

'No,' Win said. 'And it's not weapon. It's weapons. Plural.'

'I said—'

'And I heard you, Orville.'

'Don't call me that.'

Win sighed. 'Fine, *B Man.*' He shook his head as he said it. 'You are making this far more difficult than it has to be.'

'What's that supposed to mean?'

'It means that for an intelligent fellow, you too often forget that brute strength is not the only course. There are situations that call for restraint.'

Win lecturing on restraint, Myron thought. What next? Xaviera Hollander lecturing on monogamy?

'Think about what you've already done,' Win said. 'First, you have Myron roughed up by a pair of amateurs—'

'Amateurs!' Camouflage Pants didn't like that. 'Who you calling—'

'Shut up, Tony,' B Man said.

'You hear what he called me? An amateur?'

'I said, shut up, Tony.'

But Tony The Pants wasn't through yet. 'Hey, I got feelings too, B Man.'

The B Man gave him hard eyes. 'Your left femur, if you don't shut up.'

Tony closed his mouth.

The B Man looked back to Win. 'Sorry about the interruption.'

'Apology accepted.'

'Go on.'

'As I was saying,' Win continued, 'first you try to rough Myron up. Then you try to kidnap and cripple him. All for naught.'

'Not for naught,' B Man countered. 'We need to know where Downing is.'

'And what makes you think Myron knows?'

'You were both at his house. Then all of a sudden Bolitar is on Downing's team. As a matter of fact, he takes his place on the roster.'

'So?'

'So I'm not stupid. You two know something.'

'And what if we do?' Win said, hands spread. 'Why didn't you just ask? Did you ever even consider that possibility? Did you ever think that maybe the best course of action would be simply to ask?'

'I did ask!' Camouflage Pants jumped in. He was defensive now. 'On the street! I asked him where Greg was. He gave me lip.'

Win looked at him. 'Were you ever in the military?' he asked.

Pants seemed confused. 'No.'

'You are a worthless punk,' Win said in the same tone he might use when discussing a mixed stock report. 'A pitiful ectoplasm such as yourself wearing army fatigues is an affront to any man or woman who has ever experienced real combat. If I ever happen across you again donning any similar garb, I will hurt you severely. Do I make myself clear?'

'Hey—'

'You don't know this guy, Tony,' B Man interrupted. 'Just nod and shut up.'

Camouflage Pants looked hurt but he did as he was told.

Win turned his attention back to the B Man. 'We can help each other out in this situation,' he said.

'How?'

'It just so happens that we, too, are searching for the elusive Mr Downing. That is why I wish to make a proposal.'

'I'm listening.'

'First,' Win said, 'stop aiming the weapons at us.'

B Man gave him a funny look. 'How do I know I can trust you?'

'If I wanted you dead,' Win answered, 'I would have killed you last night.'

The B Man thought it over, nodded, lowered his weapon. He signaled

Camouflage Pants, who then did likewise. 'Why didn't you?' B Man asked. 'I probably would have killed you in the same situation.'

'That's what I mean about brute force,' Win said. 'About being wasteful. We need each other here. If I had killed you, I wouldn't be able to make this proposal today.'

'Fair enough. The floor is yours.'

'I assume that Mr Downing owes you a rather hefty sum.'

'Very hefty sum.'

'Fine,' Win said. 'You tell us what you know. We find him, no cost to you. When we do find him, you promise not to hurt him if he pays up.'

'And if he doesn't pay up?'

Win grinned and held his hands out, palms up. 'Who are we to interfere with the way you conduct your business?'

B Man thought about it, but not for very long. 'Okay, I can live with that,' he said. 'But I don't talk with the hired help around.' He turned to Camouflage. 'Go sit in the other room.'

'Why?'

'Because if someone decides to torture you, you'll know nothing.'

That answer seemed to make perfect sense to Camouflage. He went into Myron's office without another word.

'Why don't we?' Win suggested.

They did so. B Man crossed his legs and started right in. 'Downing is your basic gamble-a-holic,' he began. 'He had pretty good luck for a long time. That's a bad thing when a man has the itch. When his luck changed – as it must in the long run – he kept thinking he could win it back. They all do. When they have the sort of money that Downing has, I let them go. Let them dig their own grave. It's good for business. But at the same time, you have to keep an eye out. There is a fine line working here. You don't want them to end up digging to China either.' He turned and looked at Myron. 'You know what I'm saying?'

Myron nodded. 'China.'

'Right. Anyway, Downing started losing big. I'm talking very big here. He was never a prompt payer, but he was always good for it. I sometimes let the tab run as high as two-fifty or even three.'

'Hundred thousand?' Myron asked.

'Yeah.' B Man smiled. 'You don't know any gamblers, do you?'

Myron kept silent. He wasn't about to tell this slime bucket his life story.

'It's as bad as alcohol or heroin,' B Man went on. 'They can't stop themselves. In some ways, it's even worse. People drink and do drugs to escape despair. Gambling has that element, too, but it also offers you the friendly hand of hope. You always got hope when you gamble. You always believe that you're just one bet away from turning it all around. It's a catch-twenty-two. If you got hope, you keep on gambling. But with gambling, there's always hope.'

'Very deep,' Win said. 'Let's get back to Greg Downing.'

'Simply put, Greg stops paying his tab. It runs up to half a million. I start putting some pressure on him. He tells me he's flat broke, but I shouldn't worry because he's signing some big endorsement deal that will net him zillions.'

The Forte deal, Myron thought. Greg's sudden change of heart about endorsement money made more sense now.

'I asked him when this endorsement money will be coming in. He tells me in about six months. Six months? On a half-million-dollar debt and growing? I told him that's not good enough. He'd have to pay up now. He said he didn't have the money. So I ask for a show of good faith.'

Myron knew where this was going. 'He shaved points.'

'Wrong. He was *supposed* to shave points. The Dragons were favored by eight over Charlotte. Downing was going to see to it that the Dragons won by less than eight. No big deal.'

'He agreed?'

'Sure he did. The game was on Sunday. I dumped a ton on Charlotte. A ton.'

'And Greg never played,' Myron finished for him.

'You got it,' B Man said. 'The Dragons won by twelve. Okay, I figure Greg got hurt. Like the papers say. A freak injury, that's not his fault. Don't get me wrong. He's still responsible for what I lost. Why should I pay for his freak injury?' He paused to see if anyone was going to argue with his logic. No one bothered. 'So I waited for Downing to call me, but he never did. I'm owed close to two million by now. Win, you know I can't just sit back with that kind of thing, right?'

Win nodded.

'When was the last time Greg made a payment to you?' Myron asked.

'It's been a while. I don't know. Five, six months maybe.'

'Nothing more recent?'

'Nothing.'

They talked a bit more. Esperanza, Big Cyndi, Camouflage, and Brick Wall came back into the room. Win and B Man changed the topic to martial art buddies they had in common. A few minutes later B Man and his entourage left. When the elevator door closed, Big Cyndi turned and smiled widely at Esperanza. Then she began to skip in a circle. The floor shook.

Myron looked a question at Esperanza.

'That big guy,' Esperanza said, 'the one who was with us in the other room.'

'What about him?'

'He asked Cyndi for her phone number.'

Big Cyndi continued skipping with childlike abandon. The occupants of the floor beneath them were probably diving for cover like it was the last day of Pompeii. He turned to Win. 'Did you catch the fact that Greg hadn't paid anything in months?'

Win nodded. 'Clearly the fifty thousand dollars he withdrew before his disappearance was not to pay off gambling debts.'

'So what was it for?'

'To run, I imagine.'

'So he knew at least four days before the fact that he was going to take off,' Myron said.

'It would appear so.'

Myron thought about that for a moment. 'Then the timing of the murder can't just be a coincidence. If Greg planned to disappear, it can't be a coincidence that the day he takes off is the day Liz Gorman gets killed.'

'Doubtful,' Win agreed.

'You think Greg killed her?'

'The clues point in that direction,' Win said. 'I mentioned to you that the money had come from an account handled by Marty Felder. Perhaps Mr Felder has an answer.'

Myron wondered about that. Big Cyndi suddenly stopped skipping. She hugged Esperanza and made a la-la noise. Young love. 'If Felder knew Greg was going into hiding,' Myron said, 'why would he leave those messages on Greg's machine?'

'Perhaps to throw us off. Or perhaps he did not know Greg's intent.'

'I'll call him,' Myron said. 'See if I can make an appointment for tomorrow.'

'You have a game tonight, do you not?'

'Yes.'

'What time?'

'Seven-thirty.' Myron checked his watch. 'But I need to leave pretty soon if I want to talk to Clip first.'

'I'll drive,' Win said. 'I'd like to meet this Mr Arnstein.'

After they left, Esperanza went through the messages on the voice mail. Then she straightened out her desk. Her two photographs – one of her bearded collie Chloe getting Best in Breed at the Westchester Dog Show; the other of her as Little Pocahontas and Big Cyndi as Big Chief Mama, holding up their FLOW (Fabulous Ladies of Wrestling) tag-team title belts – had been knocked askew by Cyndi's knees.

As she stared at the photographs, something Myron said kept needling her. He was worried about timing. The timing of the murder. The timing of Downing's disappearance. But what about Liz Gorman's timing? What about the timing of her arrival in New York City? The bank in Tucson was robbed two months ago; Liz Gorman also started working for the Parkview Diner two months ago. A criminal on the run would want to get far away from the crime scene, yes, but to a place as populated as New York City? Why?

The more Esperanza thought about it, the more she grew bewildered. There had to be a cause and effect at work here. There had to be something about the bank heist that made Liz Gorman come out this way. Esperanza chewed on this for another minute or two. Then she picked up the phone and called one of Myron and Win's closest contacts at the bureau.

'They need everything you got on the Raven Brigade bank heist in Tucson,' Esperanza said. 'Can you send me a copy of the file?'

'You'll have it by tomorrow morning.'

24

Win and Myron shared a somewhat unusual passion for Broadway musicals. Right now, the stereo system in Win's Jag was pumping out the soundtrack from *1776*. A Continental Congressman cried out, 'Somebody better open up a window!' This led to fierce argument over the merits of opening said window (it was 'hot as hell in Philadelphia') vs keeping them closed ('too many flies'). Interspersed in this argument, people were telling John Adams to sit down. History.

'Who played the original Thomas Jefferson?' Win asked. He knew the answer. Life with Myron's friends was a nonstop quiz show.

'Movie version or stage?'

Win frowned. 'I don't do movie versions.'

'Ken Howard,' Myron answered.

'Correct. What is Mr Howard's most famous role?'

'The coach on the *White Shadow*.'

'Correct again. The original John Adams?'

'William Daniels.'

'Best known as?'

'The obnoxious surgeon on *St Elsewhere*.'

'The actress who portrayed Martha Jefferson?'

'Betty Buckley. Best known as Abby on *Eight Is Enough*.'

Win smiled. 'You are good.'

Myron stared out the window, the buildings and cars blurring into one pulsating mass, and thought about Jessica. Moving in with her. There was no reason not to. He loved her. She loved him. More than that, she had made the first move – the first time he could remember such a thing. In most relationships, one partner has more control than the other. It was just the natural order of things. Perfect balance was a hard thing to find. In their case, Jessica currently had the upper hand. Myron knew that – if he hadn't, Esperanza's constant references to his being 'whipped' would surely have made him aware. It didn't mean he loved her more or Jessica loved him less. Or maybe it did. Myron wasn't sure anymore. What he did know for sure was that moments where Jessica made the move – where she was the one exposing herself – were rare. Myron wanted to embrace it, encourage it. He had waited a long time for her to say such words to him. But something held him back. Like with TC, there were a lot of factors pushing and pulling at him.

His mind churned through the pros and cons, but no conclusions spewed forward. What he really wanted was to bounce his thoughts off someone. He deliberated best that way – by thinking out loud with a close friend. The problem was, who? Esperanza, his most dependable confidante, hated Jessica. Win . . . well, when it came to matters of the heart, Win was simply not your man; something in that nether region had shorted out a long time ago.

Still Myron heard himself say, 'Jessica asked me to move in.'

For a moment Win said nothing. Then: 'Do you get a full share of the playoff money?'

'What?'

'You joined the team late. Have you worked out what share of the playoff money you'll be getting?'

'Don't worry. It's taken care of.'

Win nodded. His eyes remained on the road. The speedometer hovered around eighty, a swiftness Route 3 was not built to bear. Win swerved lanes constantly. Myron had gotten somewhat used to Win's driving over the years, but he still kept his eyes averted from the front windshield.

'Are you staying for the game?' Myron asked.

'That depends.'

'On?'

'On if this Thumper will be there,' Win replied. 'You said she was seeking employment. Perhaps I can interrogate her at the same time.'

'What will you say?'

'That,' Win said, 'is a dilemma we both face. If you ask her about Downing's call, you blow your cover. If I ask her, she'll want to know the whys and wherefores. Either way, unless this Thumper is brain dead, she will be suspicious. Moreover, if she knows anything significant, she will most probably lie.'

'So what do you suggest?'

Win tilted his head as though in deep thought. 'Perhaps I'll bed her,' he concluded. 'Then I can make her talk while lost in the throes of passion.'

'She only sleeps with men on the Giants or the Dragons,' Myron said. Then he frowned and added, 'Bed her?'

Win shrugged. 'Just suggesting an alternative to whipping her with a rubber hose,' he said. 'Unless, of course, she's into that kind of thing.'

'Any other suggestions?'

'I'm working on it.' They took the exit to the Meadowlands in silence. On the CD player, Abigail Adams was telling John Adams that women in Massachusetts needed pins. Win hummed along with the music for a moment. Then he spoke. 'As far as Jessica goes' – he took one hand off the wheel and sort of waved it – 'I'm not the one to ask about such things.'

'I know.'

'You were miserable the first time she left,' he added. 'I don't know why you would risk going through that again.'

Myron looked at him. 'You really don't, do you?'

Win said nothing.

'That's sad, Win.'

'Yes,' he replied. 'So very tragic.'

'I'm serious,' Myron said.

Win put a dramatic forearm to his brow. 'Oh, what woe that I may never experience the depths of misery you plunged to when Jessica left. Pity this child.'

'You know there's more to it than that.'

Win put down the arm, shook his head. 'No, my friend, there is not. What was real was your pain. The rest of what you felt is the stuff of cruel delusion.'

'You really feel that way?'

'Yes.'

'About all relationships?'

Win shook his head. 'I never said that.'

'How about our friendship? Is that a cruel delusion too?'

'This isn't about us,' Win said.

'I'm just trying to understand—'

'There is nothing to understand,' Win interrupted. 'Do what you believe is best. As I said, I am not the one with which to have this discussion.'

Silence. The arena loomed in front of them. For years, it had been called the Brendan Byrne Arena, named for the unpopular governor who had been in office when the complex had been built. Recently, however, the sports authority needed to raise funds, so the name had been changed to the Continental Airlines Arena – not exactly musical, but then again the old name didn't exactly make you want to break out in song either. Brendan Byrne and his past lackeys cried foul over this affront. What a disgrace, they shouted with grave indignation. This was Governor Byrne's legacy. How could they sell him out like this? But Myron didn't have a problem with the name change. Which would you rather do – tax the people to collect twenty-seven million dollars or bruise a politician's ego? No contest when you thought about it.

Myron glanced over at Win. Win's eyes were on the road, his fingers tightly wrapped around the wheel. Myron's mind flashed back to the morning after Jessica left five years ago. He'd been moping around his house alone when Win knocked on the door. Myron opened it.

Without preamble, Win said, 'Come on. I'll hire you a girl. You need to get laid.'

634

Myron shook his head.

'Are you certain?'

'Yes,' Myron said.

'Do me a favor then.'

'What?'

'Don't go out and get drunk,' Win said. 'That would be such a cliché.'

'And what, getting laid isn't?'

Win pursed his lips together. 'But at least it's a good cliché.'

Then Win turned around and left. That had been it. They had never broached the subject of his relationship with Jessica again. It'd been a mistake to have brought it up now. Myron should have known better.

There were reasons Win was the way he was. Myron looked now at his friend and truly did pity him. From Win's vantage point, his life had been one long lesson in how to take care of himself. The results weren't always pretty, but they were usually effective. Win had not severed off his feelings or anything that dramatic, nor was he as robotic as he sometimes wanted people to think. But Win had learned not to trust or depend on others very much. There were not many people he cared about, but those he did were cherished with an intensity few ever experienced. The rest of the world meant very little to him.

'I'll get you a seat near Thumper's,' Myron said softly.

Win nodded, pulled into a parking spot. Myron gave his name to Clip's secretary and they were shown into his office. Calvin Johnson was already there, standing to Clip's right. Clip was behind his desk. He looked older today. His cheeks were grayer, and the skin around his jowls seemed looser. When he stood, it seemed to take more effort.

Clip eyed Win for a moment. 'This must be Mr Lockwood.'

He even knew about Win – again well prepared. 'Yes,' Myron said.

'He's helping us with our problem?'

'Yes.'

Introductions were made. Hands were shaken. Rear ends were seated. As was his custom in such situations, Win remained silent. His eyes slid from one side of the room to the other, taking in everything. He liked to study people for a while before speaking to them, especially in their home environment.

'So,' Clip began, forcing up a tired smile, 'what have we got?'

'When you first approached me,' Myron began, 'you were afraid I'd uncover something unsavory. I'd like to know what that something was.'

Clip tried to look amused. 'Nothing personal, Myron,' he began with a light chuckle, 'but if I knew that, I wouldn't have needed to hire you.'

Myron shook his head. 'Not good enough.'

'What?'

'Greg has disappeared before.'

'So?'

'So you never suspected anything unsavory then,' Myron said. 'Why now?'

'I told you. I have the owners' vote coming up.'

'That's your only concern?'

'Of course not,' Clip said. 'I'm worried about Greg too.'

'But you never hired anyone to find him before. What are you afraid of?'

Clip shrugged. 'Probably nothing. I'm just covering all my bases. Why? What have you found out?'

Myron shook his head. 'You never cover all your bases, Clip. You're a risk-taker. Always were. I've seen you trade popular, proven veterans for untested draft picks. I've seen you risk going for the steal rather than hoping your defense holds. You've never been afraid to lean over that edge, to risk it all.'

Clip smiled thinly. 'The problem with that strategy,' he said, 'is that you lose too. Sometimes you lose a lot.'

'What did you lose this time?' Myron asked.

'Nothing yet,' he said. 'But if Greg doesn't come back, it might cost my team a championship ring.'

'That's not what I meant. There's something more going on.'

'I'm sorry,' Clip said, spreading his hands. 'I really don't know what you're talking about. I hired you because it was the logical thing to do. Greg vanished. Now true, he's vanished before, but never this late in the season and never when we were so close to a championship. This simply isn't like him.'

Myron glanced over at Win. Win appeared to be bored.

'Do you know a woman named Liz Gorman?' Myron tried.

In the corner of his eye, Myron saw Calvin sit up a bit.

'No,' Clip said. 'Should I?'

'How about a woman named Carla or Sally?'

'What? You mean have I ever known a woman named—'

'Recently. Or any woman involved in some way with Greg Downing.'

Clip shook his head. 'Calvin?' Calvin also shook his head, but the shake was a little too lingering. 'Why do you ask?' Clip demanded.

'Because that's whom Greg was with the night he vanished,' Myron said.

Clip sat up, his words coming scatter-gun. 'Have you located her? Where is she now? Maybe they're together.'

Myron looked at Win again. This time, Win nodded ever so slightly. He'd caught it too. 'She's dead,' Myron said.

Any traces of color on Clip's face drained away. Calvin remained silent, but he crossed his legs. A big move for ol' Frosty. 'Dead?'

'Murdered, to be more specific.'

'Oh my God . . .' Clip's eyes leapt from one face to another, as though seeking some sort of answer or solace there. He found none.

'Are you sure you don't know the names Liz Gorman, Carla, or Sally?' Myron asked.

Clip opened his mouth, closed it. No sound came out. He tried again. 'Murdered?'

'Yes.'

'And she was with Greg?'

'He's the last known person to see her alive. His fingerprints are at the murder scene.'

'The murder scene?' His voice trembled, his eyes dazed. 'My God, the blood you found in the basement,' he said. 'The body was at Greg's house?'

'No. She was killed in her apartment in New York.'

Clip looked puzzled. 'But I thought you found blood in Greg's basement. In the playroom.'

'Yes. But that blood is gone now.'

'Gone?' Clip sounded both confused and annoyed. 'What do you mean, gone?'

'I mean somebody cleaned it up.' He looked straight at Clip. 'I mean somebody entered Greg's house in the past two days and tried to snuff out an unsavory scandal.'

Clip startled up at that one. Life came back into the eyes. 'You think it was me?'

'You were the only one I told about the blood. You wanted to keep the discovery secret.'

'I left that up to you,' Clip countered. 'I said I thought it was the wrong move, but I'd respect your decision. Of course, I would want to avoid a scandal. Who wouldn't? But I would never do something like that. You know me better than that, Myron.'

'Clip,' Myron said, 'I have the dead woman's phone records. She called you four days before the murder.'

'What do you mean she called me?'

'Your office number is in the phone records.'

He started to say something, stopped, started again. 'Well, maybe she called here, but that doesn't mean she spoke to me.' His tone was far from convincing. 'Maybe she spoke to my secretary.'

Win cleared his throat. Then he spoke for the first time since entering the office. 'Mr Arnstein?' he said.

'Yes.'

'With all due respect, sir,' Win continued, 'your lies are growing tiresome.'

Clip's mouth dropped. He was used to underlings kissing his rear, not to being called a liar. 'What?'

'Myron has a great deal of respect for you,' Win said. 'That's admirable. People do not earn Myron's respect easily. But you know the dead woman. You talked to her on the phone. We have proof.'

Clip's eyes narrowed. 'What kind of proof?'

'The phone records, for one—'

'—but I just told you—'

'And your own words, for another,' Win finished.

He slowed down, his expression wary. 'What the hell are you talking about?'

Win steepled his fingers. 'Earlier in this conversation, Myron asked you if you knew Liz Gorman or a woman named Carla or Sally. Do you recall that?'

'Yes. I told him no.'

'Correct. And then he told you – and I quote his exact words because they are relevant – "that's whom Greg was with the night he vanished." Awkward phrasing, I admit, but with a purpose. Do you recall your next two queries, Mr Arnstein?'

Clip looked lost. 'No.'

'They were – and again I quote exact words – "Have you located *her* yet? Where is *she* now?"' Win stopped.

'Yeah, so?'

'You said, *her*. Then you said, *she*. Yet Myron asked you if you knew Liz Gorman or Carla or Sally. From his wording, wouldn't it be natural to assume he was referring to three different women? A *they* rather than a she or her? But you, Mr Arnstein, immediately concluded that these three names belonged to one woman. Don't you find that odd?'

'What?' But Clip's anger was all bluster now. 'You call that evidence?'

Win leaned forward. 'Myron is being well compensated for his efforts here. For that reason, I would normally recommend that he continue working for you. I would advise him to mind his own business and take your money. If you wish to muck up your own investigation, who are we to interfere? Not that Myron would listen. He is a nosy man. Worse, he has this warped sense of doing right, even when it is not required.'

Win stopped, took a breath, leaned back again. Instead of steepling his fingers, he gently bounced the tips against one another. All eyes were on him. 'The problem is,' he continued, 'a woman has been murdered. On top of that, someone has tampered with a crime scene. Someone has also vanished and may very well be a murderer or another victim. In other words, it is now far too dangerous to remain in such a situation with blinders on. The potential costs outweigh the possible benefits. As a businessman, Mr Arnstein, you should understand that.'

Clip remained silent.

'So let us get to it, shall we?' Win spread his hands, then resteepled. 'We know the murder victim spoke to you. Either tell us what she said, or we shake hands and part company.'

'She spoke to me first.' It was Calvin. He shifted in his seat. He avoided Clip's eyes, but there was no need. Clip did not seem upset by the outburst.

He sank farther down in his chair, a balloon continuing to deflate. 'She used the name Carla,' Calvin continued.

With a small nod, Win settled back into his chair. He had done his part. The reins were back in Myron's hands.

'What did she say?' Myron asked.

'She said she had some kind of dirt on Greg. She said she could destroy the franchise.'

'What was the dirt?'

Clip came back into the fold. 'We never found out,' he chimed in. Clip hesitated a moment – to buy time or gather himself, Myron wasn't sure which. 'I didn't mean to lie to you, Myron. I'm sorry. I was just trying to protect Greg.'

'You spoke to her too?' Myron asked.

Clip nodded. 'Calvin came to me after she called. The next time she called we both spoke to her. She said she wanted money in exchange for silence.'

'How much?'

'Twenty thousand dollars. We were supposed to meet on Monday night.'

'Where?'

'I don't know,' Clip said. 'She was going to tell us the locale on Monday morning, but she never called.'

Probably because she was dead, Myron thought. Dead people rarely made phone calls. 'And she never told you her big secret?'

Clip and Calvin looked a question at each other. Calvin nodded. Then Clip turned back to Myron. 'She didn't have to,' Clip said with resignation. 'We already knew.'

'Knew what?'

'Greg gambled. He owed a lot of money to some very bad people.'

'You already knew about his gambling?'

'Yes,' Clip said.

'How?'

'Greg told me.'

'When?'

'About a month ago,' Clip said. 'He wanted help. I . . . I've always been something of a father figure to him. I care about him. I care about him very much.' He looked up at Myron, his eyes raw with pain. 'I care about you too, Myron. That's what makes this so hard.'

'Makes what so hard?'

But he shook it off. 'I wanted to help him, I convinced him to start seeing somebody. A professional.'

'Did he listen?'

'Greg started with the doctor just last week. A psychiatrist who specializes in gambling addictions. We also talked about him signing an endorsement deal,' he added. 'To pay off the gambling debt.'

'Did Marty Felder know about the gambling?' Myron asked.

'I can't say for certain,' Clip said. 'The doctor told me about the amazing lengths gamblers go to keep their addiction a secret. But Marty Felder handled most of Greg's money. If he didn't know, I'd be surprised.'

Behind Clip's head was a poster of this year's team. Myron looked at it a moment. The co-captains, TC and Greg, were kneeling in front. Greg smiled widely. TC sneered in typical fashion. 'So even when you first hired me,' Myron said, 'you suspected Greg's disappearance had something to do with his gambling.'

'No.' Then thinking further, Clip added, 'At least not in the way you think. I never thought Greg's bookie would harm him. I figured the Forte deal bought him time.'

'Then in what way?'

'I worried about his sanity.' Clip motioned to Greg's image on the poster behind him. 'Greg is not the most balanced person to begin with, but I wondered how much the pressure from the gambling debt weighed on his already questionable sanity. He loved his image, you know, strange as that might sound. He loved being a fan favorite more than the money. But if his fans learned the truth, who knows how they'd react? So I wondered if all of this pressure was too much for him. If maybe he had snapped.'

'And now that a woman is dead,' Myron asked, 'what do you think?'

Clip shook his head vehemently. 'I know Greg better than anyone. When he feels trapped, he runs away. He wouldn't kill anyone. I believe that with all my heart. He is not a violent man. Greg learned the dangers of violence a long time ago.'

No one spoke for several moments. Myron and Win both waited for Clip to elaborate. When he didn't, Win said, 'Mr Arnstein, do you have anything else to tell us?'

'No. That's all.'

Win rose without another word or gesture and walked out of the office. Myron sort of shrugged and started after him.

'Myron?'

He turned back to Clip. The old man was standing now. His eyes looked moist.

'Have a good game tonight,' he said softly. 'It's only a game, after all. Remember that.'

Myron nodded, discomfited yet again by Clip's demeanor. He jogged ahead and caught up with Win.

'Do you have my ticket?' Win asked.

Myron handed it to him.

'Describe this Thumper person please.'

Myron did. When they reached the elevator, Win said, 'Your Mr Arnstein is still not telling us the truth.'

'Anything concrete or just a hunch?'

'I don't do hunches,' Win said. 'Do you believe him?'

'I'm not sure.'

'You are fond of Mr Arnstein, are you not?'

'Yes.'

'Even though he has already admitted lying to you?'

'Yes.'

'Then let me present you with an interesting scenario,' Win said. 'Who, besides Greg, has the most to lose if his gambling addiction becomes public knowledge? Who, besides Greg, would have the greatest motive to keep Liz Gorman silent? And finally, if Greg Downing was about to become a terrible embarrassment to the franchise – to the point of devaluing if not destroying Clip Arnstein's chances of maintaining control – who would have the best motive to make sure Greg Downing disappeared?'

Myron did not bother answering.

25

The seat next to Thumper was open. Win took it and gave her the full-wattage smile.

'Good evening,' he said.

She smiled back. 'Hello.'

'You must be Ms Mason.'

She nodded. 'And you are Windsor Horne Lockwood III. I recognize you from the picture in *Forbes*.'

They shook hands, their eyes meeting. Their hands released one another; their eyes didn't. 'A pleasure to meet you, Ms Mason.'

'Please call me Maggie.'

'Yes, fine.' Win upped the smile for a moment. A buzzer sounded on the court. The first quarter was over. He saw Myron stand up to let his teammates sit. Seeing him dressed in a uniform on an NBA court hit Win in a very weird, unpleasant way. He didn't like to watch. He turned back toward Thumper. She looked at him expectantly.

'I understand that you are seeking employment with my firm,' Win said.

'Yes.'

'Do you mind if I ask you a few questions?'

'Please do.' She motioned a welcome with her hand.

'You are currently employed by Kimmel Brothers, are you not?'

'Yes.'

'How many traders do they currently engage?' Win asked.

'Less than ten,' she said. 'We're very small.'

'I see.' Win did the steepling, feigning consideration of her words. 'Do you work there on weekends?'

'Sometimes.'

'Weekend evenings?'

Her eyes narrowed just slightly, then relaxed back into place. 'Sometimes,' she repeated.

'How about last Saturday night?'

'Pardon me?'

'You know Greg Downing, do you not?'

'Of course but—'

'As you are no doubt aware,' Win continued, 'he has been missing since last Saturday night. Interestingly enough, the last call Mr Downing made from his home was to your office. Do you recall that phone call?'

'Mr Lockwood—'

'Please. Call me Win.'

'I don't know what you're trying to do here—'

'It's quite simple really,' Win interrupted. 'Last night, you told my associate Mr Bolitar that you had not spoken to Greg Downing in several months. Yet, as I have just told you, I have information that contradicts your statement. So there is a discrepancy here – a discrepancy that may cause some to view you, Ms Mason, as less than honest. I cannot have that at Lock-Horne Securities. My employees must be beyond reproach. For that reason, I'd like you to explain this contradiction.'

Win took out a bag of peanuts from his coat pocket. He shelled a few in the neatest manner imaginable, swept the shells with small movements into a second bag, then placed the peanuts into his mouth one at a time.

'How do you know Mr Downing called my office?' Thumper asked.

'Please,' Win said with a side glance. 'Let us not waste time with trivialities. His call is an established fact. You know it. I know it. Let us move beyond it.'

'I didn't work last Saturday night,' she said. 'He must have been calling somebody else.'

Win frowned. 'I grow weary of your tactics, Ms Mason. As you just admitted to me, yours is a small firm. I could call your employer, if you wish. I am sure he would be glad to tell Mr Windsor Horne Lockwood III if you were there or not.'

Thumper sat back in her chair, folding her arms across her chest, looking out at the game. The Dragons were up 24 to 22. Her eyes followed the course of the ball down the court. 'I have nothing more to say to you, Mr Lockwood.'

'Ah. No longer interested in a job?'

'That's right.'

'You misunderstand,' Win said. 'I don't mean just with Lock-Horne Securities. I mean with anybody, including your current employer.'

She turned to him. 'What?'

'There are two options here,' Win said. 'Let me spell them out for you clearly, so that you choose the one most suitable for you. One, you tell me why Greg Downing called you on Saturday night. You tell me why you lied to Myron about it. You tell me everything you know about his disappearance.'

'What disappearance?' she interrupted. 'I thought he was injured.'

'Option two,' Win went on. 'You continue to either stay silent or lie to me, in which case I will begin to circulate a rumor within our industry vis-à-vis your integrity. More specifically, I will let it be known that there are federal authorities looking into serious allegations of embezzlement.'

'But . . .' she started, stopped. 'You can't do that.'

'No?' He made an amused face. 'I am Windsor Horne Lockwood III. My word on such matters will not be questioned. You, on the other hand, will have difficulty finding employment as a hat check girl in a roadside Denny's when I'm through.' He smiled and tilted the bag her way. 'Peanut?'

'You're insane.'

'And you are normal,' Win countered. He looked down at the court. 'Say, that young towel boy is wiping a player's sweat off the floor. That must be worth' – he gave a big shrug – 'oh, I don't know. Fellatio at the very least, wouldn't you say?'

Win smiled at her sweetly.

'I'm leaving.' She started to stand.

'Would you sleep with me?' he asked.

She looked at him in horror. 'What?'

'Would you sleep with me? If you're very good, I may consider employing you at Lock-Horne.'

Her teeth were clenched. 'I'm not a prostitute,' she hissed.

'No, you are not a prostitute,' Win said, loud enough so that a few heads turned. 'But you are a hypocrite.'

'What are you talking about?'

Win motioned to her seat. 'Please sit down.'

'I'd rather not.'

'And I'd rather not have to shout.' He motioned again. 'Please.'

With wary eyes she did as he asked. 'What do you want?'

'You find me attractive, do you not?'

She made a face. 'I think you are the most repulsive man I have—'

'I am just speaking only about looks here,' Win said. 'The physical, remember? As you told Myron just last night, having sex is merely a physical thing. Like shaking hands – though with an analogy like that I question your partners' prowess. Now, at the risk of appearing immodest, I know that I am not physically unattractive. When you think back over the many Giants and Dragons you've bedded in your stellar career, surely there must be at least one that was less physically attractive than *moi*.'

Her eyes squinted. She looked intrigued and horror-stricken at the same time. 'Perhaps,' she allowed.

'Yet you will not sleep with me. That, my dear, is hypocritical.'

'How so?' Thumper countered. 'I'm an independent woman. I choose.'

'So you've told me,' Win said. 'But why do you choose only Giants and Dragons?' When she hesitated a bit too long, he smiled and wagged his finger. 'You should at least be honest as to why you made that particular choice.'

'You seem to know a lot about me,' Thumper said. 'Why don't you tell me?'

'Fine. You immediately announce this bizarre rule about Dragons and Giants and whatnot. You set limits. I do not. If I find a woman attractive, that is enough. But you need this random team affiliation. You use it as a fence to separate you.'

'Separate me from what?'

'Not from what. From so-called freewheeling sluts. As you just pointed out to me, you are not a prostitute. You choose, dammit. You are no slut.'

'That's right, I'm not.'

He smiled. 'But what is a slut? A woman who sleeps around? Well, no. That's what you do. You wouldn't criticize a fellow sister to the cause. So what exactly is a slut? Well, by your definition, there is no such thing. Except, of course, you needed to deny being a slut when I questioned you. Why?'

'Don't make it out to be more than it is,' Thumper said. 'Slut carries with it a negative connotation. That's the only reason I got defensive.'

Win spread his hands. 'But why should there be any negative connotation? If a slut is, by definition, a so-called loose woman, a woman who sleeps around, why not embrace the term with both legs? Why put up these fences? Why create these artificial limits? You use your team affiliations to announce your independence. But it announces the opposite. It announces that you are unsure and insecure.'

'And that's why I'm a hypocrite?'

'Of course. Go back to my request to sleep with you. Either sex is a purely physical act, in which case my brusque behavior with you now should have no bearing on it, or sex is something more than physical. Which is it?'

She smiled, gave a quick head shake. 'You're an interesting man, Mr Lockwood. Maybe I will sleep with you.'

'No good,' he said.

'What?'

'You'll be doing it simply to prove I'm wrong. That, my dear, is as pathetic and insecure as what you are currently doing. But we are getting sidetracked. That is my fault, I apologize. Are you going to tell me about your conversation with Greg Downing, or do I destroy your reputation?'

She looked dazed. It was what he wanted.

'Of course there is option three,' Win continued, 'which closely follows option two. That is, on top of having your reputation destroyed you face a murder charge.'

That made her eyes widen. 'What?'

'Greg Downing is a serious suspect in a murder investigation. If it is discovered that you in some way helped him, that would make you an accessory.' He stopped, frowned. 'But to be frank, I don't think the DA will get a conviction. No matter. I'll start with your reputation. We'll see how it goes from there.'

Thumper looked at him steadily. 'Mr Lockwood?'

'Yes.'

'Go fuck yourself,' she said.

Win rose. 'Undeniably a better option than present company.' He smiled and bowed. If he had a hat, he would have tipped it. 'Good day.'

He moved away, head high. There was, of course, a method to such madness. She would not talk. He knew that almost immediately. She was both smart and loyal. A dangerous albeit admirable combination. But what he had said would jar her. Even the best amongst us would panic or at the very least act. He would wait outside and follow her.

He checked the scoreboard. Midway through the second quarter. He had no interest in watching any more of this game. But as he reached the gate, a buzz came over the loudspeaker and then a voice said, 'Now coming in for Troy Erickson, Myron Bolitar.'

Win hesitated. Then he took another step for the exit. He did not wish to watch. But he stopped again and, still standing, he faced the court.

26

Myron sat at the far end of the bench. He knew that he wasn't going to play, but his chest was still wrapped in the steel bands of pregame jitters. In his younger days Myron had enjoyed the pressure of big-time competition, even when the jitters reached a level of near paralysis. They never lasted long after the opening tip. Once he had physical contact with an opponent or chased down a loose ball or shot a fade-away jumper, the butterflies flew off, the crowd's cheers and jeers dissolving into something akin to office background music.

Pregame jitters hadn't been a part of Myron's existence for over a decade, and he knew now what he'd always suspected: this nerve-jangled high was directly connected to basketball. Nothing else. He had never experienced anything similar in his business or personal life. Even violent confrontations – a perverted high if ever there was one – were not exactly like this. He had thought this uniquely sports-related sensation would ebb away with age and maturity when a young man no longer takes a small event like a basketball game and blows it into an entity of near biblical importance, when something so relatively insignificant in the long run is no longer magnified to epic dimensions through the prism of youth. An adult, of course, can see what is useless to explain to a child – that one particular school dance or missed foul shot would be no more than a pang in the future. Yet here Myron was, comfortably ensconced in his thirties and still feeling the same heightened and raw sensations he had known only in youth. They hadn't gone away with age. They'd just hibernated – as Calvin had warned him – hoping for a chance to stir, a chance that normally never came in one man's lifetime.

Were his friends right? Was this all too much for him? Had he not put this all behind him? He spotted Jessica in the stands. She was watching the action, that funny look of concentration on her face. She alone seemed unconcerned by his return, but then again, she had not been a part of his life in his basketball heyday. Did the woman he loved not understand, or did she—?

He stopped.

When you are on the bench, an arena can be a small place. He saw, for example, Win speaking with Thumper. He saw Jessica. He saw the other players' wives and girlfriends. And then, entering from a gate dead straight in front of him, he saw his parents. His eyes quickly fled back to the court. He clapped his hands and yelled out encouragement to his teammates, pretending to be interested in the outcome of the game. His mom and dad. They must have flown in early from their trip.

He risked a quick glance. They sat near Jessica now, in the family and friends section. His mom was staring back at him. Even from the distance he could see the lost look in her glassy eyes. Dad's eyes darted about, his jaw taut, as though he were summoning up a little extra before looking at the court straight on. Myron understood. This was all too familiar, like an old family film coming to life. He looked away again.

Leon White came out of the game. He grabbed an empty seat next to Myron. A towel boy draped his sweat top around his shoulders and gave him a squeeze bottle. Leon guzzled some Gatorade, his body glistened with sweat.

'Saw you talking with Thumper last night,' Leon said.

'Yeah.'

'You get some?'

Myron shook his head. 'I remain thump-less.'

Leon chuckled. 'Anyone tell you how she got that nickname?'

'No.'

'When she gets into it – I mean, when she gets really fired up – she's got this habit of thumping her leg up and down. Left leg. Always her left leg, you know. So she's like on her back and you're pumping her for all you're worth and then all of a sudden her left leg starts bopping up and down. You hear thump-thump, get it?'

Myron nodded. He got it.

'So if she don't do that – if a guy don't get Thumper thumping – it's like you haven't done your duty. You can't show your face. You hang your head.' Then he added, 'It's a pretty serious tradition.'

'Like lighting a menorah on Hanukkah,' Myron said.

Leon laughed. 'Well, not exactly.'

'You ever been thumped, Leon?'

'Sure, once.' Then he quickly added, 'But that was before I was married.'

'How long you been married?'

'Me and Fiona been married a little over a year.'

Myron's heart plummeted down an elevator shaft. Fiona. Leon's wife's name was Fiona. He looked up in the stands at the flashy, well-rounded blonde. Fiona began with the letter F.

'Bolitar!'

Myron looked up. It was Donny Walsh, the head coach. 'Yeah?'

'Go in for Erickson.' Walsh said it like the words were fingernail clippings he needed to spit out. 'Take the off guard spot. Put Kiley at the point.'

Myron looked at his coach as if he were speaking Swahili. It was the second quarter. The score was tied.

'What the fuck you waiting for, Bolitar? For Erickson. Now.'

Leon slapped his back. 'Go, man.'

Myron stood. His legs felt like strung-out Slinkys. Thoughts of murder and disappearances fled like bats in a spotlight. He tried to swallow but his mouth was bone dry. He jogged over to the scorer's table. The arena spun like the bed of a drunk. Without conscious thought he discarded his sweats on the floor like a snake changing skin. He nodded at the scorer. 'For Erickson,' he said. Ten seconds later, a buzzer sounded. 'Now coming in the game for Troy Erickson, Myron Bolitar.'

He jogged out, pointing to Erickson. His teammates looked surprised to see him. Erickson said, 'You got Wallace.' Reggie Wallace. One of the game's best shooting guards. Myron lined up next to him and prepared. Wallace studied him with an amused smile.

'SWB alert,' Reggie Wallace called out with a mocking laugh. 'Goddamn SWB alert.'

Myron looked at TC. 'SWB?'

'Slow White Boy,' TC told him.

'Oh.'

Everyone else was breathing deeply and coated with sweat. Myron felt stiff and unprepared. His eyes swung back to Wallace. The ball was about to be inbounded. Something caught Myron's eye and he looked up. Win stood near an exit. His arms crossed. Their eyes met for a brief second. Win gave a half nod. The whistle blew. The game began.

Reggie Wallace began the trash talk immediately. 'You got to be kidding me,' he said. 'Old-timer, I'm gonna make you my woman.'

'Dinner and a movie first,' Myron said.

Wallace looked at him. 'Lame retort, old man.'

Hard to argue.

Wallace lowered himself to a ready position. He shook his head. 'Shit. Might as well have my grandma cover me.'

'Speaking of making someone your woman,' Myron said.

Wallace looked at him hard, nodded. 'Better,' he said.

The Pacers inbounded the ball. Wallace tried to post Myron up under the basket. This was a good thing. Physical contact. Nothing unclasped those steel bands like battling for position. Their bodies bounced against one another with small grunts. At six-four, two-twenty, Myron held his ground. Wallace tried digging back with his butt, but Myron held firm, putting a knee into Wallace's backside.

'Man,' Wallace said, 'you are so strong.'

And with that, he made a move Myron barely saw. He spun off Myron's knee so quickly that Myron barely had time to turn his head. Seeming to use Myron for leverage, Wallace leaped high in the air. From Myron's vantage point, it looked like an Apollo spacecraft heading straight out of the arena. He watched helplessly as Wallace's outstretched hands grasped the lob pass at rim level. He seemed to pause in midair, then continue rising as though gravity itself had decided to freeze frame the moment. When Reggie Wallace finally began to descend, he pulled the ball behind his head before throwing it through the cylinder with frightening force.

Slam dunk.

Wallace landed with both arms spread for applause. His taunting chased Myron up court. 'Welcome to the NBA, has-been. Or never-was. Or whatever the fuck you are. Oh, man, was that pretty or what? How did I look going up? Be honest. Bottom of my sneakers look sweet, don't they? I'm so pretty. So very pretty. How did it feel when I slammed it in your face? Come on, old-timer, you can tell me.'

Myron tried to tune him out. The Dragons came down and missed a quick shot. The Pacers grabbed the rebound and headed back up court. Wallace faked going back inside and popped way out past the three point circle. He caught the pass and shot in one motion. The ball went in with a swish. Three pointer.

'Whoa, old man, did you hear that sound?' Reggie Wallace went on. 'That swish? There is no sweeter sound on earth. You hear me? No sweeter sound at all. Not even a woman crying out in orgasm.'

Myron looked at him. 'Women have orgasms?'

Wallace laughed. 'Touché, old-timer. Touché.'

Myron checked the clock. He'd been in for thirty-four seconds and his man had scored five points. Myron did some quick math. At that rate, Myron could hold Reggie Wallace to under six hundred points per game.

The boos started soon after. Unlike his youth, the crowd sounds did not fade into the background. They were not one indistinguishable blur of sound, a homecourt cheer to perhaps ride upon the way a surfer picks up a wave. Or a boo in a rival's arena – something you expect and even thrive on in a perverse way. But to hear your own fans boo your specific performance, to hear your home crowd turn against you – Myron had never experienced that before. He heard the crowd now as never before, as a collective entity of derision and as distinct voices making ugly catcalls. 'You suck, Bolitar!' 'Get that stiff outta there!' 'Blow out your other knee and sit down!' He tried to ignore them but each catcall punctured him like a dagger.

Pride took over. He would not let Wallace score. The mind was willing. The heart was willing. But as Myron soon saw, the knee was not. He was simply too slow. Reggie Wallace scored six more points off Myron that period for a total of eleven. Myron scored two off an open jumper. He took to playing what he used to call 'appendix' basketball; that is, certain players on the floor are like your appendix – they're either superfluous or they hurt you. He tried to stay out of the way and hit TC down low. He kept passing and moving away from the ball. When he saw a big opening and drove the lane near the end of the quarter, the Pacers' big center swatted the shot into the crowd. The boos were thunderous. Myron looked up. His mom and dad were still as two statues. One box over, a group of well-dressed men were cupping their hands around their mouths and starting a 'Bolitar Sucks' chant. Myron saw Win move quickly toward them. Win offered his hand to the cheer's leader. The leader took it. The leader went down.

But the odd thing was, even as Myron stunk up the joint, even as he continued to get beaten on defense and play ineffectively on offense, the old confidence remained. He wanted to stay in the game. He would still look for an opening, relatively unshaken, a man in denial, a man ignoring the mounting evidence that a crowd of 18,812 (according to the loudspeaker) could plainly see. He knew his luck would change. He was a little out of shape, that was all. Soon it would all turn around.

He realized how much that sounded like B Man's description of a compulsive gambler's rationale.

The half ended not long after that. As Myron headed off the court, he looked up again at his parents. They stood and smiled down at him. He smiled and nodded back. He looked toward the group of well-dressed booers. They were nowhere to be seen. Neither was Win.

Nobody spoke to him at halftime, and Myron didn't get in the rest of the game. He suspected that Clip had been behind his playing. Why? What had Clip been trying to prove? The game ended in a two-point victory for the Dragons. By the time they got into the locker room and began changing, Myron's performance was forgotten. The media surrounded TC, who had played a brilliant game scoring thirty-three points and grabbing eighteen rebounds. TC slapped Myron's back when he walked past him but said nothing.

Myron unlaced his sneakers. He wondered if his parents were going to wait for him. Probably not. They would figure he would want to be alone. His parents, for all their butting in, were actually pretty good at knowing when to make themselves scarce. They'd wait for him at home, staying up all night if they had to. To this day, his father stayed awake watching TV on the couch until Myron got home. Once Myron put the key in the lock, his father feigned sleep, his reading glasses still perched at the end of his nose, the newspaper lying across his chest. Thirty-two years old and his father still waited up for him. Christ, he was too old for that anymore, wasn't he?

Audrey peered tentatively around the corner and waited. Only when he signaled with a beckoning wave did she approach. She stuck her pad and pencil in her purse and shrugged. 'Look at the bright side,' she said.

'And that is?'

'You still have a great ass.'

'It's these pro shorts,' Myron said. 'They really mold and hold.'

'Mold and hold?'

He shrugged. 'Hey, happy birthday.'

'Thanks,' Audrey said.

' "Beware the Ides of March," ' Myron pronounced in dramatic fashion.

'The Ides are the fifteenth,' Audrey said. 'Today is the seventeenth.'

'Yeah, I know. But I never skip an opportunity to quote Shakespeare. Makes me look smart.'

'Brains and a good ass,' Audrey said. 'Who cares if you have no lateral movement?'

'Funny,' Myron said, 'Jess never complains about that.'

'At least not to your face.' Audrey smiled. 'Nice to see you so chipper.'

He returned the smile, shrugged.

Audrey looked around to make sure no one was in earshot. 'I got some info for you,' she said.

'On?'

'The private eye in the divorce case.'

'Greg hired one?'

'Either him or Felder,' she replied. 'I have a source who does electronics work for ProTec Investigations. They do all of Felder's work. Now my source doesn't know all the details, but he helped set up a videotaping at the Glenpointe Hotel two months ago. You know the Glenpointe?'

Myron nodded. 'The hotel on Route 80? Maybe five miles from here?'

'Right. My source doesn't know what it was for or what ended up on it. He just knows the work was for the Downing divorce. He also confirmed the obvious: this thing is usually done to catch a spouse in *flagrante delicto*.'

Myron frowned. 'This was two months ago?'

'Yep.'

'But Greg and Emily were already separated by then,' Myron said. 'The divorce was practically finalized. What would be the point?'

'The divorce, yes,' she agreed. 'But the child custody battle was just starting.'

'Yeah, but so what? She was a near-single woman having a sexual encounter. That kind of thing hardly proves parental unfitness in this day and age.'

Audrey shook her head. 'You are so naïve.'

'What do you mean?'

'A tape of a mother getting it on with some buck at a motel, doing lord-knows-what? We still live in a sexist society. It would be bound to influence a judge.'

Myron mulled it over, but it just wouldn't mesh. 'First of all, you're assuming the judge is both male and a Neanderthal. Second' – he sort of held up his hands and shrugged – 'it's the nineties for crying out loud. A woman separated from her husband having sex with another man? Hardly earth-shattering stuff.'

'I don't know what else to tell you, Myron.'

'You got anything else?'

'That's it,' she said. 'But I'm working on it.'

'Do you know Fiona White?'

'Leon's wife? Enough to say hello. Why?'

'She ever model?'

'Model?' She sort of chuckled. 'Yeah, I guess you'd call it that.'

'She was a centerfold?'

'Yep.'

'You know what month?'

'No. Why?'

He told her about the e-mail. He was fairly sure now that Ms F was Fiona White, that Sepbabe was short for September babe, the month, he bet, that she was a centerfold. Audrey listened raptly. 'I can check it out,' she said when he finished. 'See if she was a September playmate.'

'That would help.'

'It would explain a lot,' Audrey continued. 'About the tension between Downing and Leon.'

Myron nodded.

'Look, I gotta run. Jess is getting the car around back. Keep me posted.'

'Right, have fun.'

He finished up, toweled off, started dressing. He thought about Greg's secret girlfriend, the one who had been staying at his house. Could it possibly be Fiona White? If so, that would also explain the need for secrecy. Could Leon White have found out about it? That seemed logical based on his antagonism toward Greg. So where did that leave us? And how did this all tie in with Greg's gambling and Liz Gorman's blackmail scheme?

Whoa, hold the phone.

Forget gambling for a moment. Suppose Liz Gorman had something else on Greg Downing, a revelation equally if not potentially more explosive than laying down a few bets. Suppose she had somehow found out that Greg was having an affair with his best friend's wife. Suppose she had decided to blackmail Greg and Clip with this information. How much would Greg pay to keep his fans and teammates from learning about his betrayal? How much would Clip pay to keep that particular warhead from detonating in the midst of a championship run?

It was worth looking into.

27

Myron stopped at the traffic light that divided south Livingston Avenue and the JFK Parkway. This particular intersection had barely changed in the past thirty years. The familiar brick facade of Nero's Restaurant was on his right. It had originally been Jimmy Johnson's Steak House, but that had to be at least twenty-five years ago. The same Gulf station occupied another corner, small firehouse another, undeveloped land on the last.

He turned onto Hobart Gap Road. The Bolitar family had first moved to Livingston when Myron was six weeks old. Little had changed in comparison to the rest of the world. The familiarity of seeing the same sights over so many years was less comforting now than numbing. You didn't notice anything. You looked but you never saw.

As he turned up the same street where his dad had first taught him to ride that two-wheeler with a Batman reflector on the back, he tried to pay true heed to the homes that had surrounded him all of his life. There had been changes, of course, but in his mind it was still 1970. He and his parents still referred to the neighboring homes by their original owners, as though they were Southern plantations. The Rackins, for example, hadn't lived in the Rackin house for over a decade. Myron didn't know anymore who lived in the Kirschner place or the Roth house or the Parkers'. Like the Bolitars, the Rackins and the Kirschners and the rest had moved in when the construction was new, when you could still see some remnants of the Schnectman farm, when Livingston was considered the boonies, as far away from New York City at twenty-five miles as western Pennsylvania. The Rackins and the Kirschners and the Roths had lived a big chunk of their lives here. They'd moved in with infant children, raised them, taught them how to ride bicycles on the same streets Myron had learned on, sent them to Burnet Hill elementary school, then Heritage Junior High, finally Livingston High School. The kids had gone off to college, visiting only on college breaks. Not long after, wedding invitations went out. A few started displaying photos of grandchildren, shaking their heads in disbelief at how time flew. Eventually the Rackins and the Kirschners and the Roths felt out of place. This town designed to raise kids held nothing for them anymore. Their familiar homes suddenly felt too big and too empty, so they put them on the market and sold them to new young families with infant children who would too soon go off to Burnet Hill elementary school, then Heritage Junior High, and finally Livingston High School.

Life, Myron decided, was not that different from one of those depressing life insurance commercials.

Some neighborhood old-timers had managed to hang on. You could usually tell which houses belonged to them because – in spite of the fact that the children were grown – they had built additions and nice porches and kept their lawns well groomed. The Brauns and the Goldsteins were two who had done just that. And of course, Al and Ellen Bolitar.

Myron pulled his Ford Taurus into the driveway, his headlights sweeping across the front yard like searchlights during a prison break. He parked up on the blacktop not far from the basketball hoop. He turned off the ignition. For a moment he just stared at the basket. An image of his father lifting him so he could reach the basket appeared before him. If the image had come from memory or imagination, he could not say. Nor did it matter.

As he moved toward the house, outside lights came on via a motion detector. Though the detectors had been installed three years ago, they were still a source of unbridled awe for his parents, who considered this technological advance on a par with the discovery of fire. When the motion detectors were first put up, Mom and Dad spent blissful hours in disbelief testing the mechanism, seeing if they could duck under its eye or walk super slowly so that the detector would not sense them. Sometimes in life, it's the simple pleasures.

His parents were sitting in the kitchen. When he entered, they both quickly pretended they were doing something.

'Hi,' he said.

They looked at him with tilted heads and too-concerned eyes. 'Hi, sweetheart,' Mom said.

'Hi, Myron,' Dad said.

'You're back from Europe early,' Myron said.

Both heads nodded like they were guilty of a crime. Mom said, 'We wanted to see you play.' She said it gently, like she was walking on thin ice with a blowtorch.

'So how was your trip?' Myron asked.

'Wonderful,' Dad said.

'Marvelous,' Mom added. 'The food they served was just terrific.'

'Small portions though,' Dad said.

'What do you mean, small portions?' Mom snapped.

'I'm just commenting, Ellen. The food was good, but the portions were small.'

'What, did you measure it or something? What do you mean small?'

'I know a small portion when I see one. These were small.'

'Small. Like he needs larger portions. The man eats like a horse. It wouldn't kill you to lose ten pounds, Al.'

'Me? I'm not getting heavy.'

'Oh no? Your pants are getting so tight you'd think you were starring in a dance movie.'

Dad winked at her. 'You didn't seem to have any problem taking them off on the trip.'

'Al!' she shrieked, but there was a smile there too. 'In front of your own child! What's wrong with you?'

Dad looked at Myron, arms spread. 'We were in Venice,' he said in a way of explanation. 'Rome.'

'Say no more,' Myron said. 'Please.'

They laughed. When it died out his mother spoke in a hushed tone.

'You okay, sweetheart?'

'I'm fine,' he said.

'Really?'

'Really.'

'I thought you did some good things out there,' Dad said. 'You hit TC for a couple of nice passes on the post. Real nice passes. You showed smarts.'

Count on Dad to find the silver lining. 'I bit the big one,' Myron said.

Dad gave a staunch head shake and said, 'You think I'm saying this just to make you feel good?'

'I know you're saying this just to make me feel good.'

'It doesn't matter,' Dad said. 'It never mattered. You know that.'

Myron nodded. He did know. He had witnessed pushy fathers all his life, men who tried to live hollow dreams through their offspring, forcing their sons to carry a burden they themselves could never carry. But not his father. Never his father. Al Bolitar had never needed to fill his son with grandiose stories of his athletic prowess. He never pushed him, possessing the wondrous ability to appear almost indifferent while making it clear he cared intensely. Yes, this was a direct contradiction – sort of a detached attachment – but somehow Dad pulled it off. Sadly, it was unusual for Myron's generation to admit to such wonderment. His generation had remained undefined – shoehorned between the Beat Generation of Woodstock and the Generation X of MTV, too young when *thirty-something* had ruled the airwaves, too old now for *Beverley Hills, 90210*, or *Melrose Place*. Mostly, it seemed to Myron, he was part of the Blame Generation, where life was a series of reactions and counterreactions. In the same way those pushy fathers put everything on their sons, the sons came right back and blamed their future failures on the fathers. His generation had been taught to look back and pinpoint exact moments when their parents had ruined their lives. Myron never did. If he looked back – if he studied his parents' past feats – it was only to try to unravel their secret before he had children of his own.

'I know what it looked like tonight,' he said, 'but I really don't feel that bad.'

Mom sniffled. 'We know.' Her eyes were red. She sniffled again.

'You're not crying over—'

She shook her head. 'You've grown up. I know that. But when you ran out on the court again like that, for the first time in so long . . .'

Her voice died out. Dad looked away. The three of them were all the same. They were drawn to nostalgia like starlets to paparazzi.

Myron waited until he was sure his voice would be clear. 'Jessica wants me to move in with her,' he said.

He expected protests, at least from his mother. Mom had not forgiven Jessica for leaving the first time; Myron doubted that she ever would. Dad, as was his way, acted like a good news reporter – neutral, but you wondered what opinion he was making under those balanced questions.

Mom looked at Dad. Dad looked back and put a hand on her shoulder. Then Mom said, 'You can always come back,' she said.

Myron almost asked for a clarification, but he stopped himself and simply nodded. The three of them gathered around the kitchen table and began to talk. Myron made himself grilled cheese. Mom didn't do it for him. Dogs were domesticated, she believed, not people. She never cooked anymore, which Myron took as a positive thing. Her doting was all verbal, and that was all right with him.

They told him about their trip. He briefly and very vaguely sketched out why he was playing pro basketball again. An hour later he headed into his room in the basement. He had lived here since he was sixteen, the year his sister had gone off to college. The basement was subdivided into two rooms – a sitting area he almost never used except for company and hence kept clean, and a bedroom that looked very much like a teenager's. He crawled into bed and looked at the posters on the wall. Most had been up since his adolescence, the colors faded, the corners frayed near the thumbtacks.

Myron had always loved the Celtics – his father had grown up near Boston – and so his two favorite posters were of John Havlicek, the Celtics star of the sixties and seventies, and Larry Bird, the team's star of the eighties. He looked now from Havlicek to Bird. Myron was supposed to have been the next poster on the wall. It had been his boyhood dream. When the Celtics drafted him, it barely surprised him. A higher power was at work. It had been preordained that he would be the next Celtics legend.

But Burt Wesson slammed into him.

Myron put his hands behind his head. His eyes adjusted to the light. When his phone rang, he reached for it absently.

'We have what you're looking for,' an electronically altered voice said.

'Excuse me?'

'The same thing Downing wanted to buy. It'll cost you fifty thousand dollars. Get the money together. We'll call you with instructions tomorrow night.'

The caller hung up. Myron tried hitting star-six-nine to ring back, but the call was from out of the area. He lowered his head back to the pillow. Then he stared at the two posters and waited for sleep to claim him.

28

Martin Felder's office was on Madison Avenue in midtown, not far from Myron's own. The agency was called Felder Inc., the clever name making it very apparent that Marty wasn't on Madison Avenue as a hotshot advertising exec. A sprightly receptionist was all too happy to show Myron the way to Marty's office.

The door was already open. 'Marty, Myron is here to see you.'

Marty. Myron. It was one of those kind of offices. Everyone was a first name. Everyone was dressed in that new, neat-casual look. Marty, who Myron guessed was in his mid-fifties, wore one of those blue jean shirts with a bright orange tie. His thinning gray hair was plastered down, almost a comb over but not quite. His pants were Banana Republic green and crisply pressed. His orange socks matched the tie and his shoes looked like Hush Puppies.

'Myron!' he exclaimed, pumping Myron's hand. 'Great to see you.'

'Thanks for seeing me so soon, Marty.'

He waved a dismissing hand. 'Myron, please. For you, anytime.' They'd met a few times at different sporting and sports representative events. Myron knew that Marty had a solid reputation as a guy who was – to coin a cliché – tough but fair. Marty also had a knack for getting great media coverage for both himself and his athletes. He'd written a couple of how-to-succeed books which helped enhance his name recognition as well as his rep. On top of that, Marty looked like your favorite, self-effacing uncle. People liked him instantly.

'Can I get you a drink?' he asked. 'Caffè latte perhaps?'

'No thanks.'

He smiled, shook his head. 'I've been planning on calling you for the longest time, Myron. Please, have a seat.'

The walls were bare except for bizarre sculptures twisted out of neon light. His desk was glass, the built-in shelves fiberglass. There were no visible papers. Everything shone like the inside of a spaceship. Felder gestured to a chair in front of the desk for Myron; then he took the other chair in front of the desk. Two equals chatting it up. No desk to use as a divider or intimidator.

Felder started right in. 'I don't have to tell you, Myron, that you are quickly making a name for yourself in this field. Your clients trust you absolutely. Owners and managers respect and fear' – he emphasized the fear part – 'you. That's rare, Myron. Very rare.' He slapped his palms on his thighs and leaned forward. 'Do you enjoy being in sports representation?'

'Yes.'

'Good,' he said with a sharp nod. 'It's important to like what you're doing. Choosing a profession is the most important decision you'll ever make – more important even than choosing a spouse.' He looked up at the ceiling. 'Who was it that said, you may tire of your relationship with people but never of a job you love?'

'Wink Martindale?' Myron said.

Felder chuckled and offered up a shy, caught-himself smile. 'Guess you didn't come here to hear me drone on about my own personal philosophies,' he said. 'So let me put my cards on the table. Just flat out say it. How would you like to come work for Felder Inc.?'

'Work here?' Myron said. Job Interview Rule #1: Dazzle them with sparkling repartee.

'Here's what I'd like to do,' Felder said. 'I want to make you senior vice president. Your salary would be generous. You'd still be able to give all your clients the personal Bolitar attention they've come to expect, plus you'll have all the resources of Felder Inc. at your command. Think about it, Myron. We employ over one hundred people here. We have our own travel agency to handle all those arrangements for you. We have – well, let's call them what they are, shall we? – gofers who can deal with all those details that are so necessary in our business, freeing you up to tackle important tasks.' He raised a hand as if to stop Myron, though Myron hadn't moved. 'Now I know you have an associate, Miss Esperanza Diaz. She'd come aboard, too, of course. At a higher salary. Plus I understand she's finishing up law school this year. There'll be plenty of room for advancement here.' He gestured with his hands before adding, 'So what do you think?'

'I'm very flattered—'

'Don't be,' Felder interrupted. 'It's a sound business decision for me. I know good stock when I see it.' He leaned forward with a sincere smile. 'Let someone else be the client's errand boy, Myron. I want to free you up to do what you do best – recruit new clients and negotiate deals.'

Myron had no interest in giving up his company, but the man knew how to make it sound attractive. 'May I think about it?' he asked.

'Of course,' Felder said, raising his hands in surrendered agreement. 'I don't want to pressure you, Myron. Take your time. I certainly don't expect an answer today.'

'I appreciate that,' Myron said, 'but I actually wanted to talk to you about another matter.'

'Please.' He leaned back, folded his hands on his lap, smiled. 'Go right ahead.'

'It's about Greg Downing.'

The smile didn't budge, but the light behind it flickered a bit. 'Greg Downing?'

'Yes. I have a few questions.'

Still smiling. 'You realize, of course, that I cannot reveal anything that may fall under what I consider privileged.'

'Of course,' Myron agreed. 'I was wondering if you could tell me where he is.'

Marty Felder waited a beat. This was no longer a sales pitch meeting. It was now a negotiation. A good negotiator is frighteningly patient. Like a good interrogator, he must above all else be a listener. He must make his opponent do the talking. After several seconds, Felder asked, 'Why do you want to know that?'

'I need to speak with him,' Myron said.

'May I ask what this is about?'

'I'm afraid it's confidential.'

They looked at each other, both faces open and friendly, but now they were two card sharks who didn't want to show their hands. 'Myron,' Felder began, 'you have to understand my position here. I don't feel comfortable divulging this type of information without having at least some hint as to why you want to see him.'

Time to jar something loose. 'I didn't join the Dragons to make a comeback,' Myron said. 'Clip Arnstein hired me to find Greg.'

Felder's eyebrows dropped to half mast. 'Find him? But I thought he went into seclusion to heal an ankle injury.'

Myron shook his head. 'That was the story Clip told the press.'

'I see.' Felder put a hand to his chin and nodded slowly. 'And you're trying to locate him?'

'Yes.'

'Clip hired you? He chose you himself? It was his idea?'

Myron answered in the affirmative. There was a faint smile on Felder's face now, like he was enjoying an inside joke. 'I'm sure Clip already told you that Greg had done this kind of thing before.'

'Yes,' Myron said.

'So I don't see why you should be all that concerned,' Felder said. 'Your help is appreciated, Myron, but it is really not necessary.'

'You know where he is?'

Felder hesitated. 'Again, Myron, I ask you to put yourself in my position. If one of your clients wanted to stay hidden, would you go against his wishes or respect his rights?'

Myron smelled a bluff. 'That would depend,' he said. 'If the client was in big trouble, I'd probably do whatever I could to help him.'

661

'What sort of big trouble?' Felder asked.

'Gambling, for one. Greg owes a lot of money to some awfully unpleasant fellows.' Still no reaction from Felder. In this case, Myron read it as a good thing. If most people had just heard that a client owed money to mobsters, they would show some sort of surprise. 'You know about his gambling, don't you, Marty?'

Felder's words were slow, as if he were weighing each one separately with a hand scale. 'You are still new in this business, Myron. With that comes a certain enthusiasm that is not always well placed. I am Greg Downing's sports representative. That gives me certain responsibilities. It is not a carte blanche to run his life. What he or any other client does on his own time is not, should not, and cannot be my concern. For all our sakes. We care about every client, but we are not parental substitutes or life managers. It's important to learn this early on.'

The Cliff Notes summary: he knew about the gambling.

Myron asked, 'Why did Greg withdraw fifty thousand dollars ten days ago?'

Again Felder showed no reaction. He was either beyond being surprised by what Myron knew or he had the ability to shut off any connection between his brain and facial muscles. 'You know I can't discuss that with you – or even confirm that such a withdrawal took place.' He slapped his palms against his thighs again and mounted a smile. 'Do us both a favor, Myron. Think about my offer and drop this other matter. Greg will pop up soon. He always does.'

'I wouldn't be so sure,' Myron said. 'He's in real trouble this time.'

'If you are talking about his alleged gambling debts—'

Myron shook his head. 'I'm not.'

'Then what?'

So far, the man had given Myron nothing. Letting on that he knew about the gambling problem was a lay-up. He had realized Myron knew about it. To deny it would make him look either incompetent for not knowing or dishonest for making a strong denial. Marty Felder was shrewd. He would not misstep. Myron tried shifting direction. 'Why did you videotape Greg's wife?'

He blinked. 'Pardon?'

'ProTec. That's the name of the agency you hired. They set up videotape surveillance at the Glenpointe Hotel. I'd like to know why.'

Felder looked almost amused. 'Help me understand this, Myron. First you say that my client is in deep trouble. You claim you want to help him. Then you start making allegations about a videotape. I'm having trouble following you.'

'I'm just trying to help your client.'

'The best thing you can do for Greg is to tell me all you know. I am his advocate, Myron. I am truly interested in doing what's best for him – not what might be best for the Dragons or Clip or anybody else. You said he was in trouble. Tell me how.'

Myron shook his head. 'First you tell me about the videotape.'

'No.'

There you have it. Top-notch negotiating getting down to basics. Soon they'd been sticking tongues out at each other, but for now both faces remained pleasant. They were playing the waiting game. Who would be the first to crack? Myron ran down the situation in his mind. The cardinal rule of negotiating: Don't lose sight of what you want and what your opponent wants. Okay. So what did Felder have that Myron wanted? Information on the fifty thousand dollars, the videotape, and maybe some other stuff. What did Myron have that Felder wanted? Not much. Myron had made him curious when he mentioned big trouble. Felder might already know what trouble Greg was in, but he would still want to know what Myron knew. End analysis: Myron needed the information more. He would have to move. Time to up the ante. And no more delicacy.

'I don't have to be the one asking you these questions,' Myron said.

'What do you mean?'

'I could have a homicide detective ask them.'

Felder barely moved, but his pupils expanded in a funny way. 'What?'

'A certain homicide detective is this close' – Myron held up his thumb and index finger close together – 'to putting out an APB on Greg.'

'A homicide detective?'

'Yes.'

'But who was killed?'

Myron shook his head. 'First the videotape.'

Felder was not a man to jump. He refolded his hands on his lap, looked up, tapped his foot. He took his time, considering the pros and cons, the costs and benefits, all that. Myron half-expected him to start charting graphs.

'You never practiced as an attorney, did you, Myron?'

Myron shook his head. 'I passed the bar. That's about it.'

'You're lucky,' he said. He sighed and made a tired gesture with his hands. 'You know why people make all the jokes about lawyers being scum? It's because they are. It's not their fault. Not really. It's the system. The system encourages cheating and lying and basic scummy behavior. Suppose you were at a Little League game. Suppose you told the kids that there were no umpires today – that they would have to umpire themselves. Wouldn't that lead to some pretty unethical behavior? Probably. But then tell the little tykes that they must win, no matter what. Tell them that their only obligation is to winning and that they should forget about things like fair play and sportsmanship. That's what our judicial system is like, Myron. We allow for deceit in the name of an abstract greater good.'

'Bad analogy,' Myron said.

'Why's that?'

'The part about no umpires. Lawyers have to face judges.'

'Not many of them. Most cases are settled before a judge sees it. You know that. But no matter, my point is made. The system encourages attorneys to lie and distort under the guise of the client's best interest. That best-interest crap has become an all-purpose excuse for anything goes. It's ruining our judicial system.'

'Fascinating, really,' Myron said. 'And all this relates to the video-tape . . . ?'

'Very directly,' Felder said. 'Emily Downing's lawyer lied and distorted the truth. She did it to an unethical and unnecessary extreme.'

'Are you talking about the child custody case?' Myron asked.

'Yes.'

'What did she do?'

He smiled. 'I'll give you a hint. This particular claim is made now in one out of every three child custody cases in the United States. It has become almost standard practice, tossed about like rice was at the actual wedding, though it destroys lives.'

'Child abuse?'

Felder did not bother with an answer. 'We felt that we needed to quell these malicious and dangerous untruths. To balance the scales, so to speak. I'm not proud of that. None of us are. But I'm not ashamed either. You can't fight fair if your opponent insists on using brass knuckles. You must do what you can to survive.'

'What did you do?'

'We videotaped Emily Downing in a rather delicate situation.'

'When you say delicate, what exactly do you mean?'

Felder stood up and took a key from his pocket. He unlocked a cabinet and pulled out a videotape. Then he opened another cabinet. A TV and VCR faced them. He placed the tape in the machine and picked up the remote. 'Your turn now,' he said. 'You said Greg was in big trouble.'

It was time for Myron to give a little. Another cardinal rule of negotiation: don't be a pig and just take. It'll backfire in the long run. 'We believe a woman may have been blackmailing Greg,' he said. 'She has several aliases. Usually Carla but she may have used the names Sally or Liz. She was murdered last Saturday night.'

That one stunned him. Or at least he acted stunned. 'Surely the police don't suspect Greg—'

'Yes,' Myron said.

'But why?'

Myron kept it vague. 'Greg was the last person seen with her the night of the murder. His fingerprints were at the murder scene. And the police found the murder weapon at his house.'

'They searched his house?'

'Yes.'

'But they can't do that.'

Already playing the ready-to-distort lawyer. 'They got a warrant,' Myron said. 'Do you know this woman? This Carla or Sally?'

'No.'

'Do you have any idea where Greg is?'

'None.'

Myron watched him, but he couldn't tell if he was lying or not. Except in very rare instances, you can never tell if a person is lying by watching their eyes or their body language or any of that stuff. Nervous, fidgety people tell the truth too, and a good liar could look as sincere as Alan Alda at a telethon. So-called 'students of body language' were usually just fooled with more certainty. 'Why did Greg take out fifty thousand dollars in cash?' Myron asked.

'I didn't ask,' Felder said. 'As I just explained to you, such matters were not my concern.'

'You thought it was for gambling.'

Again Felder didn't bother responding. He lifted his eyes from the floor. 'You said this woman was blackmailing him.'

'Yes,' Myron said.

He looked at Myron steadily. 'Do you know what she had on him?'

'Not for sure. The gambling, I think.'

Felder nodded. With his eyes looking straight ahead, he pointed the remote control at the television behind him and pressed some buttons. The screen brightened into gray static. Then a black and white image appeared. A hotel room. The camera seemed to be shooting from the ground up. No one was in the room. A digital counter showed the time. The setup reminded Myron of those tapes of Marion Barry smoking a crack pipe.

Uh oh.

Could that be it? Having sex would hardly be grounds to show unfitness as a parent, but what about drugs? What better way to balance the scales, as Felder had put it, than to show the mother smoking or snorting or shooting up in a hotel room? How would that work on a judge?

But as Myron was about to see, he was wrong.

The hotel room door opened. Emily entered alone. She looked around tentatively. She sat on the bed, but then got back up. She paced. She sat down again. She paced again. She checked the bathroom, came right back out, paced. Her fingers picked up whatever object they could find – hotel brochures, room service menus, a television guide.

'Is there any sound?' Myron asked.

Marty Felder shook his head no. He was still not looking at the screen.

Myron watched transfixed as Emily continued to go through her nervous ritual. Suddenly she froze in place and turned to the door. Must have heard a knock. She approached tentatively. Looking for Mr Goodbar? Probably,

Myron surmised. But when Emily turned the knob and let the door swing open, Myron realized he was wrong again. It was not Mr Goodbar who entered the hotel room.

It was Ms Goodbar.

The two women talked for a bit. They had a drink from the room's minibar. Then they began to undress. Myron's stomach coiled. By the time they moved to the bed, he had seen more than enough.

'Turn it off.'

Felder did so, still not looking at the screen. 'I meant what I said before. I'm not proud of that.'

'What a guy,' Myron said.

So now he understood Emily's ferocious hostility. She had indeed been taped in *flagrante delicto* – not with another man, but with a woman. Certainly no law against it. But most judges would be influenced. It was the way of the world. And speaking of the way of the world, Myron knew Ms Goodbar by another nickname:

Thumper.

29

Myron walked back to his office, wondering what it all meant. For one thing, it meant that Thumper was more than a harmless diversion in all this. But what exactly was she? Had she set up Emily or had she, too, been taped unaware? Were they steady lovers or participants in a one-night stand? Felder claimed he didn't know. On the tape, the two women hadn't appeared to be all that familiar with each other – at least, not in the small portion he had watched – but he was hardly an expert on the subject.

Myron cut east on 50th Street. An albino wearing a Mets cap and yellow boxer shorts on the outside of ripped jeans played an Indian sitar. He was singing the seventies classic 'The Night Chicago Died' in a voice that reminded Myron of elderly Chinese women in the back of a laundromat. The albino also had a tin cup and a stack of cassettes. A sign read 'The Original Benny and His Magical Sitar, only $10.' The original. Oh. Wouldn't want that imitation albino, sitar, AM seventies music, no sir.

Benny smiled at him. When he reached the part of the song where the son learns hundred cops are dead – maybe even the boy's father – Benny began to weep. Moving. Myron stuffed a dollar into the cup. He crossed the street, his thoughts reverting back to the videotape of Emily and Thumper. He wondered now about the relevance. He'd felt like a dirty voyeur for watching the tape in the first place, and now he felt that way for rehashing it in his mind. It was, after all, probably no more than a bizarre aside. What possible connection could there be in all this to the murder of Liz Gorman? None that he could see; then again he still had trouble seeing how Liz Gorman fit in with Greg's gambling or how she fit in at all.

Still, the video undoubtedly raised a few fairly major issues. For one thing, there was the abuse allegations made against Greg. Was there anything to them, or as Marty Felder had indicated, was Emily's attorney just playing hardball? And hadn't Emily told Myron she would do anything to keep her kids? Even kill. How did Emily react when she learned about the videotape? Spurred on by this awful violation, how far would Emily go?

Myron entered his office building on Park Avenue. He exchanged a brief elevator smile with a young woman in a business suit. The elevator reeked of drugstore cologne, the kind where some guy decides that taking a shower is too time-consuming so he opts for sprinkling himself with enough cologne to glaze a wedding cake. The young woman sniffed and looked at Myron.

'I don't wear cologne,' he said.

She didn't seem convinced. Or perhaps she was condemning the gender in general for this affront. Understandable under these circumstances.

'Try holding your breath,' he said.

She looked at him, her face a seaweed green.

When he entered his office, Esperanza smiled and said, 'Good morning.'

'Oh no,' Myron said.

'What?'

'You've never said good morning to me before. Ever.'

'I have, too.'

Myron shook his head. '*Et tu*, Esperanza?'

'What are you talking about?'

'You heard about what happened last night. You're trying to be – dare I say it? – nice to me.'

The fire in her eyes flamed up. 'You think I give a shit about that game? That you got your butt burned at every turn?'

Myron shook his head. 'Too late,' he said. 'You care.'

'I do not. You sucked. Get over it.'

'Nice try.'

'What, nice try? You sucked. S-U-C-K-E-D. A pitiful display. I was embarrassed to know you. I hid my head in shame when I came in.'

He bent down and kissed her cheek.

Esperanza wiped it off with the back of her hand. 'Now I got to get a cootie shot.'

'I'm fine' he said. 'Really.'

'Like I care. Really.'

The phone rang. She picked it up. 'MB SportsReps. Why yes, Jason, he is here. Hold on a moment.' She put a hand over the receiver. 'It's Jason Blair.'

'The vermin who said you had a nice ass?'

She nodded. 'Remind him about my legs.'

'I'll take it in my office.' A photograph on the top of a stack of papers on her desk caught his eye. 'What's this?'

'The Raven Brigade file,' she said.

He picked up a grainy photo of the group taken in 1973, the only shot of the seven of them together. He quickly found Liz Gorman. He hadn't gotten a good look at her, but from what he saw, there was no way anyone would ever imagine that Carla and Liz Gorman were one and the same. 'Mind if I keep this for a few minutes?' he asked.

'Suit yourself.'

He moved into his office and picked up the phone. 'What's up, Jason?'

'Where the fuck have you been?'

'Not much. How about you?'

'Don't play smart guy with me. You put that little lady on my contract and she fucked it all up. I got half a mind to leave MB.'

'Calm down, Jason. How did she fuck it up?'

His voice cracked with incredulity. 'You don't know?'

'No.'

'Here we are, hot in the middle of negotiating with the Red Sox, right?'

'Right.'

'I want to stay in Boston. We both know that. But we have to make a lot of noise like I'm leaving. That's what you said to do. Make them think you want to switch teams. To up the money. I'm a free agent. This is what we got to do, right?'

'Right.'

'We don't want them to know I want to be on the team again, right?'

'Right. To a degree.'

'Fuck to a degree,' he snapped. 'The other day my neighbor gets a mailing from the Sox, asking him to renew his season tickets. Guess whose picture is on the brochure saying I'm gonna be back? Go ahead. Guess.'

'Would that be yours, Jason?'

'Damn straight mine! So I call up little Miss Nice Ass—'

'She's got great legs too.'

'What?'

'Her legs. She's not that tall, so they're not very long. But they're nicely toned.'

'Will you quit fucking around here, Myron? Listen to me. She tells me the Sox called up and asked if they could use my picture in the ad, even though I wasn't signed. She tells them to go ahead! Go right fucking ahead! Now what are those Red Sox assholes supposed to think, huh? I'll tell you what. They think I'm gonna sign with them no matter what. We lost all our leverage because of her.'

Esperanza opened the door without knocking. 'This came in this morning.' She tossed a contract on Myron's desk. It was Jason's. Myron began to skim through it. Esperanza said, 'Put the pea brain on the speakerphone.'

Myron did.

'Jason.'

'Oh Christ, Esperanza, get the fuck off the line. I'm talking to Myron here.'

She ignored him. 'Even though you don't deserve to know, I finalized your contract. You got everything you wanted and more.'

That slowed him down. 'Four hundred thou more per year?'

'Six hundred thousand. Plus an extra quarter-million on the signing bonus.'

'How the . . . what . . . ?'

'The Sox screwed up,' she said. 'Once they printed your picture in that mailer, the deal was as good as done.'

'I don't get it.'

'Simple,' she said. 'The mailer went out with your picture on it. People bought tickets based on that. Meanwhile I called the front office and said that you'd decided to sign with the Rangers down in Texas. I told them the deal was almost final.' She shifted in the chair. 'Now, Jason, pretend you are the Red Sox for a moment. What are you going to do? How are you going to explain to all those ticket holders that Jason Blair, whose picture was on your latest mailer, won't be around because the Texas Rangers outbid them?'

Silence. Then: 'To hell with your ass and legs,' Jason said. 'You got the most gorgeous set of brains I ever laid eyes on.'

Myron said, 'Anything else, Jason?'

'Go practice, Myron. After the way you played last night, you need it. I want to talk over the details with Esperanza.'

'I'll take it at my desk,' Esperanza said.

Myron put him back on hold. 'Nice move,' he said to her.

She shrugged. 'Some kid in the Sox marketing department screwed up. It happens.'

'You read it very well.'

Her tone was exaggerated monotone. 'My heaving bosom is swelling with pride.'

'Forget I said anything. Go take the call.'

'No, really, my goal in life is to be just like you.'

Myron shook his head. 'You'll never have my ass.'

'There's that,' she agreed before leaving.

Left alone, Myron picked up the Raven Brigade photo. He located the three members still at large – Gloria Katz, Susan Milano, and the Raven's enigmatic leader and most famous member, Cole Whiteman. No one had drawn the press's attention and ire more than Cole Whiteman. Myron had been in elementary school when the Ravens went into hiding, yet he still remembered the stories. For one thing, Cole could have passed for Win's brother – blond, patrician-featured, well-to-do family. While everyone else in the picture was scraggly and long haired, Cole was fresh shaven with a conservative haircut, his one sixties concession being sideburns that went down a tad too far. Hardly your Hollywood-cast, radical leftist. But as Myron had learned from Win, looks could often be deceiving.

He put down the photograph and dialed Dimonte's line at One Police Plaza. After Dimonte snarled a hello, Myron asked him if he had anything new.

'You think we're partners now, Bolitar?'

'Just like Starsky and Hutch,' Myron said.

'God, I miss those two,' Dimonte said. 'That hot car. Hanging out with Fuzzy Bear.'

'Huggy Bear,' Myron said.

'What?'

'His name was Huggy Bear, not Fuzzy Bear.'

'Really?'

'Time's short, Rolly. Let me help if I can.'

'You first. What have you got?'

Another negotiation. Myron told him about Greg's gambling. Figuring that Rolly had the phone records too, he also told him about the suspected blackmail scheme. He didn't tell him about the videotape. It wouldn't be fair, not until he spoke to Emily first. Dimonte asked a few questions. When he was satisfied, he said, 'Okay, what do you want to know?'

'Did you find anything else at Greg's house?'

'Nothing,' Dimonte said. 'And I mean, nothing. Remember how you told me you found some feminine doo-dads in the bedroom? Some woman's clothes or lotions or something?'

'Yes.'

'Well, someone got rid of them too. No sign of any female apparel.'

So, Myron thought, the lover theory rears its ugly head once again. The lover comes back to the house and cleans up the blood to protect Greg. Then she covers her own tracks too, making sure that their relationship remains a secret. 'How about witnesses?' Myron asked. 'Anybody in Liz Gorman's building see anything?'

'Nope. We canvassed the whole neighborhood. No one saw nada. Everybody was studying or something. Oh, another thing: the press picked up the murder. The story hit the morning editions.'

'You gave them her real name?'

'You crazy? Of course not. They think it's just another breaking and entering homicide. But get this. We got an anonymous tip called in this morning. Someone suggested we check out Greg Downing's house.'

'You're kidding.'

'Nope. Female voice.'

'He's being set up, Rolly.'

'No shit, Sherlock. By a chick no less. And the murder didn't exactly make a big news splash. It was stuck in the back pages like every other unspectacular homicide in this cesspool. Got a little extra juice because it was so close to a college campus.'

'Have you looked into that connection?' Myron asked.

'What connection?'

'Columbia University being so close by. Half of the sixties movements started there. They must still have some sympathizers in the ranks. Maybe someone there helped Liz Gorman.'

Dimonte gave a dramatic sigh. 'Bolitar, do you think all cops are morons?'

'No.'

'You think you're the only who thought of that?'

'Well,' Myron said, 'I have been called gifted.'

'Not in today's sports section.'

Touché. 'So what did you find out?'

'She rented the place from some whacko, fanatic, leftist, commie, pinko so-called Columbia professor named Sidney Bowman.'

'You're so tolerant, Rolly.'

'Yeah, well, I lose touch when I keep missing those ACLU meetings. Anyway, this pinko won't talk. He says she just rented from him and paid in cash. We all know he's lying. The feds grilled him, but he got a team of faggot, liberal lawyers down here to spring him. Called us a bunch of Nazi pigs and stuff.'

'That's not a compliment, Rolly. In case you don't know.'

'Thanks for clueing me in. I got Krinsky trailing him right now, but he's got nothing. I mean, this Bowman's not a retard. He's got to know we're watching.'

'What else have you got on him?'

'Divorced. No kids. He teaches a class in existential, worthless-in-the-real-world bullshit. According to Krinsky he spends most of his time helping the homeless. That's supposed to be his daily ritual – hanging out with hobos in parks and shelters. Like I said, a whacko.'

Win entered the office without knocking. He headed straight for the corner and opened the closet door, revealing a full-length mirror. He checked his hair. Patted it though every strand was perfect. Then he spread his legs a bit and put his arms straight down. Pretending to be gripping a golf club. Win slowly began to turn into a backswing, watching his motion in the mirror, making sure the front arm remained straight, the grip relaxed. He did this all the time, sometimes stopping in front of store windows while walking down the street. This was the golf equivalent, Myron surmised, to the weight lifters who flex whenever they happen past their reflection. It was also annoying as all hell.

'Got anything else, Rolly?'

'No. You?'

'Nothing. I'll talk to you later.'

'Can hardly wait, Hutch,' Dimonte said. 'You know something? Krinsky's so young he doesn't even remember the show. Sad, ain't it?'

'Today's youth,' Myron said. 'They got no culture.'

Myron hung up. Win continued to study his shot in the mirror. 'Fill me in please,' he said. Myron did. When he finished Win said, 'This Fiona, the ex-playmate. She sounds like a perfect candidate for a Windsor Horne Lockwood III interrogation.'

'Uh huh,' Myron said. 'But why don't you first tell me about the Windsor Horne Lockwood III interrogation of Thumper?'

Win frowned at the mirror, adjusted his grip. 'She is rather closed mouthed,' he said. 'So I took a distinctive tack.'

'What tack is that?'

Win told him about their conversation. Myron just shook his head. 'So you followed her?'

'Yes.'

'And?'

'And there is not much to report. She went to TC's house after the game. She slept over. No calls of any consequence were made from his residence. Either she was not rattled by our conversation, or she doesn't know anything.'

'Or,' Myron added, 'she knew she was being followed.'

Win frowned again. He either didn't like Myron's suggestion or he'd spotted a problem with his swing. Probably the latter. He turned away from the mirror and glanced at Myron's desk. 'Is that the Raven Brigade?'

'Yes. One of them looks like you.' Myron pointed to Cole Whiteman.

Win studied it for a moment. 'While the man is indeed handsome, he lacks both my sense of style and my striking, debonair good looks.'

'Not to mention your humility.'

Win put out his hand. 'Then you understand.'

Myron looked at the picture again. He thought again about what Dimonte said about Professor Sidney Bowman's daily routine. Then it came to him all at once. Ice flooded his veins in a gush. In his mind he changed around Cole's features a bit, imagined distortions from plastic surgery and twenty years of aging. It didn't fit exactly, but it was close enough.

Liz Gorman had disguised herself by perverting her most distinguishing characteristic. Wouldn't it make sense to assume that Cole Whiteman had done the same?

'Myron?'

He looked up. 'I think I know where to find Cole Whiteman.'

30

Hector was not thrilled to see Myron back at the Parkview Diner.

'We think we found Sally's accomplice,' Myron said.

Hector cleaned the counter with a rag.

'His name is Norman Lowenstein. Do you know him?'

Hector shook his head.

'He's a homeless man. He hangs out in the back and uses your pay phone.'

Hector stopped cleaning. 'You think I'd let a homeless man in my kitchen?' he said. 'And we don't even have a back. Take a look.'

The answer did not surprise Myron. 'He was sitting at the counter when I was here the other day,' he tried. 'Unshaven. Long black hair. Tattered beige overcoat.'

Still working the rag over the Formica, Hector nodded. 'I think I know who you mean. Black sneakers?'

'Right.'

'He comes in a lot. But I don't know his name.'

'Did you ever see him talk to Sally?'

Hector shrugged. 'Maybe. When she was his waitress. I really don't know.'

'When was he here last?'

'I haven't seen him since the day you came in,' Hector said.

'And you never met him?'

'No.'

'Or know anything about him?'

'No.'

Myron wrote down his phone number on a scrap of paper. 'If you see him, please call. There's a thousand dollar reward.'

Hector studied the phone number. 'This your work number? At AT&T?'

'No. It's my personal phone.'

'Uh huh,' Hector said. 'I called AT&T after you left last time. There's no such thing as Y511 and there's no employee named Bernie Worley.' He did not look particularly upset, but he wasn't dancing the hula either. He just waited, watching Myron with steady eyes.

'I lied to you,' Myron said. 'I'm sorry.'

'What's your real name?' he asked.

'Myron Bolitar.' He gave the man one of his cards. Hector studied it for a moment.

'You're a sports agent?'

'Yes.'

'What does a sports agent have to do with Sally?'

'It's a long story.'

'You shouldn't have lied like that. It wasn't right.'

'I know,' Myron said. 'I wouldn't have done it if it wasn't important.'

Hector put the card in his shirt pocket. 'I have customers.' He turned away. Myron debated explaining further, but there was no point.

Win was waiting for him on the sidewalk. 'Well?'

'Cole Whiteman is a homeless man who calls himself Norman Lowenstein.'

Win waved down a taxi. A driver in a turban slowed down. They got in. Myron told him where to go. The driver nodded; as he did, his turban buffed the taxi's ceiling. Sitar music blew forth from the front speakers, plucking at the air with razor-sharp nails. Awful. It made Benny and His Magical Sitar sound like Itzhak Perlman. Still it was preferable to Yanni.

'He looks nothing like that old picture,' Myron said. 'He's had plastic surgery. He grew his hair and dyed it jet black.'

They waited at a traffic light. A blue TransAm pulled up next to them, one of those souped-up models that hip-hopped up and down while playing music loud enough to crack the earth's core. The taxi actually started shaking from the decibel level. The light turned green. The TransAm sped ahead.

'I started thinking about how Liz Gorman had disguised herself,' Myron continued. 'She'd taken her defining attribute and stood it on its head. Cole was the well-bred, clean-cut, rich boy. What better way to stand that on its head than to become an unkempt vagrant?'

'A *Jewish* unkempt vagrant,' Win corrected.

'Right. So when Dimonte told me that Professor Bowman liked to hang out with the homeless, something clicked.'

The turban barked, 'Route.'

'What?'

'Route. Henry Hudson or Broadway.'

'Henry Hudson,' Win replied. He glanced over at Myron. 'Continue.'

'This is what I think happened,' Myron said. 'Cole Whiteman suspected Liz Gorman was in some kind of trouble. Maybe she hadn't called him or met up with him. Something. The problem was, he couldn't check it out himself. Whiteman hasn't survived underground all these years by being stupid. He knew that if the police found her, they'd set a trap for him – the way they're doing right now.'

'So,' Win said, 'he gets you to go in for him.'

Myron nodded. 'He hangs around the diner, hoping to hear something about "Sally." When he overhears me talking to Hector he figures I'm his best bet. He gives me this weird story about how he knows her from using the phone at the diner. Claimed they were lovers. The story didn't really mesh, but I didn't bother questioning it. Anyway, he takes me to her place. Once I'm inside, he hides and waits to see what happens. He sees the cops come. He probably even sees the body being taken out – all from a safe distance. It confirms what he probably suspected all along. Liz Gorman is dead.'

Win thought about it a moment. 'And now you think Professor Bowman may be contacting him when he visits with the homeless?'

'Yes.'

'So our next goal is to find Cole Whiteman.'

'Yes.'

'Amongst the wretched unbathed in some godforsaken shelter?'

'Yes.'

Win looked pained. 'Oh goodie.'

'We could try to set a trap for him,' Myron said. 'But I think it'll take too long.'

'Set a trap how?'

'I think he's the one who called me on the phone last night,' Myron said. 'Whatever blackmail scheme Liz Gorman was running, it's natural to think that Whiteman was in on it too.'

'But why you?' Win asked. 'If he has dirt on Greg Downing why would you be the target of his extortion?'

It was a question that had been gnawing at Myron too. 'I'm not sure,' he said slowly. 'The best guess I can come up with is that Whiteman recognized me at the diner. He probably figures that I'm closely connected to Greg Downing. When he couldn't reach Greg, he decided to try me.'

Myron's cellular phone rang. He flicked it on and said hello.

'Hey, Starsky.' It was Dimonte.

'I'm Hutch,' Myron said. 'You're Starsky.'

'Either way,' Dimonte said, 'I think you'll want to get your butt over to the precinct pronto.'

'You got something?'

'Only if you call a picture of the killer leaving Gorman's apartment something,' Dimonte said.

Myron almost dropped the phone. 'For real?'

'Yep. And you'll never guess what.'

'What?'

'It's a she.'

31

'Here's the deal,' Dimonte said. They were threading their way through a veritable United Nations of cops, witnesses, and whatnots. Win was waiting outside. He didn't like cops, and they didn't exactly feel like taking him out for ice cream. Best for all if he kept his distance. 'We got a partial image of the perp on a videotape. Problem is, it's not enough to make an ID. I thought maybe you'd recognize her.'

'What kind of videotape?'

'There's a shipping garage on Broadway between One Hundred Tenth and One Hundred Eleventh streets, east side of the block,' Dimonte said. He remained a pace ahead of Myron, moving briskly. He kept turning behind him to make sure Myron was keeping up. 'They handle home electronics. You know how that is – every worker steals like it's a Constitutional right. So the company set up surveillance cameras all over the place. Videotape everything.' Still moving he shook his head, awarded Myron a toothpick-less smile and added, 'Good old big brother. Every once in a while somebody tapes a crime instead of a bunch of cops beating up a perp, you know what I'm saying?'

They entered a small interrogation room. Myron looked into a mirror. He knew it was one-way glass – so did anybody with even a passing knowledge of cop shows or movies. Myron doubted anybody was on the other side, but he stuck his tongue out just in case. Mr Mature. Krinsky was standing by a television and a VCR. For the second time today, Myron was going to watch a video. He trusted this one would be more tame.

'Hey, Krinsky,' Myron said.

Krinsky barely nodded. Mr Loquacious.

Myron looked over at Dimonte. 'I still don't see how a shipping garage camera could have gotten the killer on tape.'

'One of the cameras is by the truck entrance,' Dimonte explained. 'Just to make sure nothing falls off the truck as it's leaving, if you know what I mean. The camera catches part of the sidewalk. You can see people walking by.' He leaned up against the wall and motioned Myron to sit in a chair. 'You'll see what I mean.'

Myron sat. Krinsky hit the play button. Black and white again. No sound again. But this time the shot was from above. Myron saw the front end of a truck and behind it, a glimpse of the sidewalk. Not many people walked by; the ones that did were barely more than distant silhouettes.

'How did you come up with this?' Myron asked.

'With what?'

'This tape.'

'I always check for this stuff,' Dimonte said, hitching up his pants by belt loops. 'Parking garages, storage houses, any of those places. They all have surveillance cameras nowadays.'

Myron nodded. 'Good work, Rolly. I'm impressed.'

'Wow,' Dimonte said, 'now I can die happy.'

Everyone's a wiseass. Myron turned his attention back to the screen. 'So how long is each tape?'

'Twelve hours,' Dimonte replied. 'They change them at nine A.M. and P.M. Eight camera setup. They keep each tape for three weeks. Then they tape over them.' He pointed his fingers. 'Here she comes now. Krinsky.'

Krinsky pressed a button and the tape froze.

'The woman who just entered the picture. On the right. Heading south, which would be away from the scene.'

Myron saw a blurry image. He couldn't see a face or even gather much about her height. She wore high heels and a long overcoat with a frilly neck. Hard to tell much about her weight either. The hair however was familiar. He kept his tone neutral. 'Yeah, I see her.'

'Look at her right hand,' he said.

Myron did. There was something dark and long in it. 'I can't make it out.'

'We got it blown up. Krinsky.'

Krinsky handed Myron two large black and white photographs. The woman's head was enlarged in the first one, but you still couldn't see any facial features. In the second picture, the long, dark object in her hand was clearer.

'We think it's a plastic garbage bag wrapped around something,' Dimonte said. 'Kind of an odd shape, wouldn't you say?'

Myron looked at the photo and nodded. 'You figure it's covering up a baseball bat.'

'Don't you?'

'Yeah,' Myron said.

'We found plastic garbage bags just like that one in Gorman's kitchen.'

'And probably half the kitchens in New York City,' Myron added.

'True enough. Now look at the date and time on the screen.'

On the top left-hand side of the screen, a digital clock read 02:12:32 A.M. The date was early Sunday morning. Just hours after Liz Gorman had been at the Swiss Chalet bar with Greg Downing.

'Did the camera get her coming the other way?' Myron asked.

'Yeah, but it's not too clear. Krinsky.'

Krinsky hit the rewind button. Several seconds later, he stopped and the picture came back on. The time now read 01:41:12. A little more than thirty minutes earlier.

'Coming now,' Dimonte said.

The image almost flew past. Myron only recognized the woman by the long overcoat with the frilly neck. This time, she was carrying nothing in her hand. Myron said, 'Let me see the other part again. All the way through.'

Dimonte nodded at Krinsky. Krinsky found it and hit play. While Myron still couldn't see the woman's face, her walk was another matter. And a person's walk could be fairly distinctive. Myron felt his heart crawl up into his throat.

Dimonte was studying him through squinting eyes. 'You recognize her, Bolitar?'

Myron shook his head. 'No,' he lied.

32

Esperanza liked to make lists.

With the Raven Brigade file in front of her, she jotted down the three most important factors in chronological order:

1. The Raven Brigade robs a bank in Tucson.
2. Within days, at least one of the Ravens (Liz Gorman) was in Manhattan.
3. Soon after, Liz Gorman made contact with a high-profile professional basketball player.

It didn't flow.

She opened the file and briefly scanned the 'brigade's' history. In 1975 the Ravens had kidnapped Hunt Flootworth, the twenty-two-year-old son of publishing giant Cooper Flootworth. Hunt had been a classmate at San Francisco State of several of the Ravens, including both Cole Whiteman and Liz Gorman. The famous Cooper Flootworth, never one to sit around idly and let others handle his affairs, hired mercenaries to rescue his son. During their raid, young Hunt was shot at point-blank range in the head by one of the Ravens. No one knew which one. Of all the brigade members at the scene four managed to escape.

Big Cyndi skipped into the office. The vibrations rolled Esperanza's pens off the desk.

'Sorry,' Cyndi said.

'It's okay.'

'Timmy called me,' Cyndi said. 'We're going out Friday night.'

Esperanza made a face. 'His name is Timmy?'

'Yeah,' Cyndi said. 'Isn't that sweet?'

'Adorable.'

'I'll be in the conference room,' Cyndi said.

Esperanza turned back to the file. She flipped ahead to the Tucson bank heist – the group's first in more than five years. The robbery took place as the bank was closing. The feds believed one of the security guards was in on it, but so far they had nothing more than the guard's left-leaning background. About $15,000 in cash was taken, but the robbers took the time to blow the safe-deposit boxes. Risky. The feds theorized that the Ravens had somehow found out that drug money was stored there. The bank cameras showed two people dressed head to toe in black with black ski masks. No fingerprints or hairs or fibers. Nada.

Esperanza read through the file again, but nothing new exploded from the pages. She tried to imagine what the past twenty years had been like for the surviving Ravens, constantly on the run, never sleeping in the same place very long, leaving and reentering the country, relying on old sympathizers you were never sure you could completely trust. She grabbed her piece of paper and made some more notes:

Liz Gorman—>Bank Robbery—>Blackmail

Okay, she thought, follow the arrows. Liz Gorman and the Ravens needed funds, so they robbed the bank. That worked out. It explained the first arrow. That was a gimme anyway. The real problem was that second connection:

Bank Robbery—>Blackmail.

Simply put, what about the bank robbery had led her to the East Coast and her scheme to blackmail Greg Downing? She tried to write down possibilities.

1. Downing was involved in the bank robbery.

She looked up. It was possible, she surmised. He needed the money for gambling debts. He might do something illegal. But this hypothesis still did not answer the biggest question in all this: how did they meet? How did Liz Gorman and Greg Downing hook up in the first place?

That, she felt, was the key.

She wrote a number two. And waited.

What other link could there be?

Nothing came to mind so she decided to try it from the opposite end. Start with the blackmail and go back. In order to blackmail Downing, Liz Gorman had to have stumbled across something incriminating. When? Esperanza drew another arrow:

Bank Robbery<—>Blackmail

Esperanza felt something like a tiny pinprick. The bank robbery. Something they found at the bank robbery led to the blackmail scheme.

She quickly shuffled through the file, but she already knew that it wasn't there. She picked up the phone and dialed. When the man answered, she said, 'Do you have a list of the people who were renting safe-deposit boxes?'

'Somewhere, I guess,' he replied. 'Why, you need it?'

'Yes.'

Deep sigh. 'All right, I'll start looking. But tell Myron he owes me for this. Owes me big.'

When Emily opened the door, Myron said, 'Are you alone?'

'Why, yes,' she replied with a coy smile. 'What do you have in mind?'

He shoved past her. Emily stumbled back, her mouth an open circle of surprise. He headed straight for the foyer closet and opened it.

'What the hell are you doing?'

Myron did not bother answering. His hands pushed hangers left and right in a frenzy. It didn't take long. He pulled the long overcoat with the frilly neck into view. 'Next time you commit a murder,' he said, 'dispose of the clothes you wore.'

She took two steps back, her hand fluttering toward her mouth. 'Get out,' she hissed.

'I'm giving you one chance to tell the truth.'

'I don't care what you're giving. Get the fuck out of my house.'

He held up the coat. 'You think I'm the only one who knows? The police have a videotape of you at the murder scene. You were wearing this coat.'

Her body slackened. Her face looked like she'd been on the receiving end of a palm strike to the solar plexus.

Myron lowered the coat to his side. 'You planted the murder weapon at your old house,' he said. 'You smeared blood in the basement.' He turned and half-pounced into the living room. The pile of tabloids was still there. He pointed at it. 'You kept searching the papers for the story. When you read about the body being found, you made an anonymous call to the police.'

He glanced back at Emily. Her eyes were unfocused and glazed.

'I kept wondering about the playroom,' Myron said. 'Why, I kept asking myself, would Greg go down there of all places after the murder? But of course that was the point. He wouldn't. The blood could remain undetected for weeks if need be.'

Emily made two fists at her sides. She shook her head, finally finding her voice. 'You don't understand.'

'Then tell me.'

'He wanted my kids.'

'So you framed him for murder.'

'No.'

'This isn't the time to lie, Emily.'

'I'm not lying, Myron. I didn't frame him.'

'You planted the weapon—'

'Yes,' she interrupted, 'you're right about all that. But I didn't frame him.' Her eyes closed and reopened, almost like she was doing a minimeditation. 'You can't frame somebody for something they did.'

Myron stiffened. Emily stared at him stone faced. Her hands were still tightened into small balls. 'Are you saying Greg killed her?'

'Of course.' She moved toward him, taking her time, using the seconds the way a boxer uses an eight count after a surprise left hook. She took the coat from his hands. 'Should I really destroy it, or can I trust you?'

'I think you better explain first.'

'How about some coffee?'

'No,' Myron said.

'I need some. Come on. We'll talk in the kitchen.'

She kept her head high and walked the same walk Myron had watched on the tape. He followed her into a bright white kitchen. The kitchen gleamed in tiled splendor. Most people probably thought the decor was to die for; Myron thought it resembled a urinal at a fancy restaurant.

Emily took out one of those new coffee presses people were using. 'You sure you won't have some? It's Starbucks. Kona Hawaiian blend.'

Myron shook his head. Emily had regained her senses now. She was back in control; he'd let her stay there. A person in control talks more and thinks less.

'I'm trying to figure out where to begin,' she said, adding hot water to the press. The rich aroma immediately filled the air. If this was a coffee commercial, one of them would be saying 'Ahhhh' right about now. 'And don't tell me to begin at the beginning or I'll scream.'

Myron held up his hands to show he would do no such thing.

Emily pushed a little on the plunger, met resistance, pushed again. 'She came up to me one day in the supermarket of all places,' she said. 'Out of the blue. I'm reaching for some frozen bagels, and this woman tells me she has uncovered something that could destroy my husband. She tells me that if I don't pay up, she's going to call the papers.'

'What did you say?'

'I asked her if she'd need a quarter for the phone.' Emily chuckled, stopped pressing, stood upright. 'I figured it was a joke. I told her to go ahead and destroy the bastard. She just nodded and said she'd be in touch.'

'That was it?'

'Yep.'

'When was this?'

'I don't know. Two, three weeks ago.'

'So when did you hear from her next?'

Emily opened a cabinet and took out a coffee mug. The mug had a picture of some cartoon character. The words WORLD'S GREATEST MOM were emblazoned on the side. 'I'm making enough for two,' she said.

'No thank you.'

'You sure?'

'Yes,' Myron said. 'What happened next?'

She bent down and peered into the coffee press like it was a crystal ball. 'A few days after this, Greg did something to me . . .' She stopped. Her tone was different now, the words coming slower and with more care. 'It's like I told you last time you were here. He did something awful. The details aren't important.'

Myron nodded but said nothing. No reason to raise the videotape now and knock her off her stride. Facilitate her – that was the key.

'So when she came back and told me Greg was willing to pay big for her silence, I told her I'd pay more to make her talk. She told me it would cost a lot. I told her I didn't care how much. I tried to appeal to her as a woman. I went so far as to tell her about my situation, how Greg was trying to take my kids away from me. She seemed to sympathize, but she also made it clear that she couldn't afford to be philanthropic. If I wanted the information, I'd have to pay up.'

'Did she tell you how much?'

'One hundred thousand dollars.'

Myron held back a whistle. Serious double dipping. Liz Gorman's strategy was probably to keep collecting from both of them, bleeding them both for as long as she thought it was safe. Or maybe she was hitting hard and fast because she knew she would have to go underground again. Either way, it made sense from Liz Gorman's perspective to collect from all interested parties – Greg, Clip, and Emily. Take money for silence. Take money to sing. Blackmailers have the loyalty of election-year politicians.

'Do you know what she had on Greg?' he asked.

Emily shook her head. 'She wouldn't tell me.'

'But you were prepared to pay her a hundred grand?'

'Yes.'

'Even though you didn't know what it was for?'

'Yes.'

Myron gestured with both hands. 'How did you know she wasn't just a crackpot?'

'The truth? I didn't know. But I was going to lose my kids, for chrissake. I was desperate.'

And, Myron thought, Emily had shown that desperation to Liz Gorman who, in turn, took full advantage of it. 'So you still have no idea what she had on him?'

Emily shook her head. 'None.'

'Could it have been Greg's gambling?'

Hre eyes narrowed in confusion. 'What about it?'

'Did you know Greg gambled?'

'Sure. But so what?'

'Do you know how much he gambled?' Myron asked.

'Just a little,' she said. 'A trip to Atlantic City once in a while. Maybe fifty dollars on a football game.'

'Is that what you thought?'

Her eyes moved over his face, trying to read it. 'What are you saying?'

Myron looked out the back window. The pool was still covered, but some of the robins had returned from the yearly aliya to the south. A dozen or so crowded a bird feeder, heads down, wings flapping happily like dog tails. 'Greg is a compulsive gambler,' Myron said. 'He's lost away millions over the years. Felder didn't embezzle money – Greg lost it gambling.'

684

Emily gave him a little head shake. 'That can't be,' she said. 'I lived with him for almost ten years. I would have seen something.'

'Gamblers learn how to hide it,' Myron said. 'They lie and cheat and steal – anything to keep on betting. It's an addiction.'

Something in her eyes seemed to spark up. 'And that's what this woman had on Greg? The fact that he gambled?'

'I think so,' Myron said. 'But I can't say for sure.'

'But Greg definitely gambled, right? To the point where he lost all his money?'

'Yes.'

The answer kindled Emily's face with hope. 'Then no judge in the world would award him custody,' she said. 'I'll win.'

'A judge is more likely to give the kids to a gambler than a murderer,' Myron said. 'Or someone who plants false evidence.'

'I told you already. It's not false.'

'So you say,' Myron said. 'But let's get back to what happened with the blackmailer. You were saying she wanted a hundred grand.'

Emily moved back to her coffee press. 'That's right.'

'How were you to pay her?'

'She told me to wait by a pay phone outside a Grand Union supermarket on Saturday night. I was supposed to get there at midnight and have the money ready. She called at midnight on the dot and gave me an address on One Hundred Eleventh Street. I was supposed to get there at two in the morning.'

'So you drove to One Hundred Eleventh Street at two in the morning with one hundred thousand dollars?' He tried not to sound too incredulous.

'I could only raise sixty thousand,' she corrected.

'Did she know that?'

'No. Look, I know this all sounds crazy, but you don't understand how desperate I was. I would have done anything at this point.'

Myron understood. He had seen up-close how far mothers would go. Love twists; maternal love twists absolutely. 'Go on,' he said.

'When I turned the corner, I saw Greg come out of the building,' Emily said. 'I was stunned. He had his collar up, but I could still see his face.' She looked up at Myron. 'I was married to him a long time, but I've never seen his face like this.'

'Like what?'

'So filled with terror,' she replied. 'He practically sprinted toward Amsterdam Avenue. I waited until he turned the corner. Then I approached the door and pressed her apartment button. Nobody answered. I started pressing other buttons. Somebody finally buzzed me in. I went upstairs and knocked on her door for a while. Then I tried the knob. It was unlocked. So I opened the door.'

Emily stopped. A trembling hand brought the cup up to her lips. She took a sip.

'This is going to sound awful,' she went on, 'but I didn't see a dead human being lying there. I only saw my last hope of keeping my kids.'

'So you decided to plant evidence.'

Emily put down the cup and looked at him. Her eyes were clear. 'Yes. And you were right about everything else, too. I chose the playroom because I knew he'd never go down there. I figured that when Greg got back home – I didn't know he'd run – the blood would be safe. Look, I know I went too far, but it's not like I was lying. He killed her.'

'You don't know that.'

'What?'

'He might have stumbled across the body the same way you did.'

'Are you serious?' Her tone was sharp now. 'Of course Greg killed her. The blood on the floor was still fresh. He was the one who had everything to lose. He had motive, opportunity.'

'Just as you do,' Myron said.

'What motive?'

'You wanted to set him up for murder. You wanted to keep your children.'

'That's ridiculous.'

'Do you have any proof your story is true?' Myron asked.

'Do I have what?'

'Proof. I don't think the police are going to buy it.'

'Do you buy it?' she asked him.

'I'd like to see proof.'

'What do you mean, proof?' she snapped. 'Like what? It's not like I took pictures.'

'Any facts that back up your story?'

'Why would I kill her, Myron? What possible motive could I have? I needed her alive. She was my best chance of keeping my kids.'

'But let's assume for a moment that this woman did indeed have something on Greg,' Myron said. 'Something concrete. Like a letter he wrote or a videotape' – he watched for a reaction – 'or something like that.'

'All right,' she said with a nod. 'Go ahead.'

'And suppose she double-crossed you. Suppose she sold the incriminating evidence to Greg. You admit Greg was there before you. Maybe he paid her enough so that she'd back out of your agreement. Then you go into her apartment. You find out what she's done. You realize your one chance at keeping your kids is gone. So you kill her and pin it on the man who had seemed to have the most to gain from her death: Greg.'

Emily shook her head. 'That's nuts.'

'You hated Greg enough,' Myron continued. 'He played dirty with you; you'd play dirty back.'

'I didn't kill her.'

Myron took another look at the robins, but they were gone. The yard looked barren now, stripped of any life. He waited a few seconds before he turned back toward her. 'I know about the videotape of you and Thumper.'

A quick bolt of anger hit Emily's eyes. Her fingers clutched the coffee mug. Myron half-expected her to throw it at him. 'How the hell . . . ?' Then her grip suddenly slackened. She backed away. She sort of shrugged into a slouch. 'It doesn't matter.'

'It must have made you furious,' he said.

She shook her head. A small sound like a chuckle escaped from her lips. 'You just don't get it, do you, Myron?'

'Don't get what?'

'I wasn't looking for revenge. The only thing that mattered was that the tape could take away my kids.'

'No, I do get it,' Myron countered. 'You'd do anything to keep your kids.'

'I didn't kill her.'

Myron shifted gears. 'Tell me about you and Thumper,' he said.

Emily snorted a derisive laugh. 'I didn't think you were that type, Myron.'

'I'm not.'

She picked up her coffee mug and took a deep sip. 'Did you watch the whole tape from beginning to end?' she asked in a tone somewhere between flirtatious and furious. 'Did you hit the slow motion button a few times, Myron? Rewind and replay certain parts over and over? Drop your pants to your knees?'

'No to all of the above.'

'How much did you see?'

'Just enough to know what was going on.'

'Then you stopped?'

'Then I stopped.'

She regarded him from behind the mug. 'You know something? I actually believe you. You're that kind of goody two-shoes.'

'Emily, I'm trying to help.'

'Help me or Greg?'

'Help get to the truth. I assume you want that too.'

She shrugged noncommittally.

'So when did you and Thumper . . . ?' He made vague coming-together motions with his hand.

She laughed at his discomfort. 'It was the first time,' she replied. 'In all respects.'

'I'm not judging—'

'I don't care if you are or not. You want to know what happened, right? It was my first time. That little whore set me up.'

'How?'

'What do you mean, how?' she countered. 'You want me to go into details – how many drinks I had, how I was feeling lonely, how her hand started up my leg?'

'I guess not.'

'Then let me give you the quick capsule: she seduced me. We'd flirted innocently a few times in the past. She invited me to the Glenpointe for drinks. It was like a dare on myself – I was drawn and repelled, but I knew I wouldn't go through with it. One thing led to another. We went upstairs. End of capsule.'

'So you're saying Thumper knew you were being filmed?'

'Yes.'

'How do you know? Did she say anything?'

'She didn't say anything. But I know.'

'How?'

'Myron, please stop asking so many goddamn questions. I just know, okay? How else would anyone know to set up a camera in that room? She set me up.'

That made sense, Myron thought. 'But why would she do it?'

Her face registered exasperation. 'Christ, Myron, she's the team whore. Didn't she fuck you yet? Or no, let me guess. You refused, right?'

Emily stormed away into the living room and collapsed on a couch. 'Get me the aspirin,' she said. 'They're in the bathroom. In the medicine chest.'

Myron shook out two tablets and filled a cup with water. When he came back, he said, 'I have to ask you about one more thing.'

She sighed. 'What?'

'I understand you made allegations against Greg,' he said.

'My attorney made allegations.'

'Were they true?'

She put the pills on her tongue, took some water, swallowed. 'Some of them.'

'How about the ones about him abusing the children?'

'I'm tired, Myron. Can we talk more later?'

'Were they true?'

Emily looked into Myron's eyes, and a cold gust of air blew across his heart. 'Greg wanted to take my kids away from me,' she said slowly. 'He had money, power, prestige on his side. We needed something.'

Myron broke the eye contact. He walked toward the door. 'Don't destroy that coat.'

'You have no right to judge me.'

'Right now,' he said, 'I don't want to be near you.'

33

Audrey was leaning against his car. 'Esperanza told me you'd be here.'

Myron nodded.

'Jesus, you look like hell,' she said. 'What happened?'

'Long story.'

'And one that you will soon tell me in riveting detail,' Audrey added. 'But I'll go first. Fiona White was indeed a Miss September in 1992 – or as that particular rag calls it, the September Babe-A-Rama.'

'You're kidding.'

'Nope. Fiona's turn-ons include moonlit walks on the beach and cozy nights by a fireplace.'

He smiled in spite of himself. 'My, what originality.'

'Her turn-offs include shallow men who only care about looks. And men with back hair.'

'Did they list her favorite movies?'

'*Schindler's List*,' Audrey said, 'And *Cannonball Run II*.'

He laughed. 'You're making this up.'

'All except the part about being the September Babe-A-Rama in 1992.'

Myron shook his head. 'Greg Downing and his best friend's wife,' he sighed. In a way, the news sort of buoyed him. Myron's ten-year-old indiscretion with Emily no longer seemed quite so bad. He knew that he shouldn't find comfort in such logic, but man takes solace where he can find it.

Audrey motioned toward the house. 'So what's up with the ex?'

'Long story.'

'You said that already. I got time.'

'I don't.'

She held up her palm like a cop directing traffic. 'Not fair, Myron. I've been a good girl. I've been running your errands and keeping my big mouth shut. Not to mention the fact that I got zippo from you for my birthday. Please don't make me start with the exposure threats again.'

She was right. Myron gave her an abbreviated update, leaving out two parts: the Thumper videotape (no reason anyone had to know about that) and the fact that Carla was the infamous Liz Gorman (it was simply too big a story; no reporter could be trusted to keep it off the record).

Audrey listened intently. Her page-boy cut had grown a little too long in the front. Hairs dangled close to her eyes. She kept sticking out her lower lip and blowing strands off her forehead. Myron had never before seen this particular gesture done by anybody over the age of eleven. It was kind of sweet.

'Do you believe her?' Audrey asked, motioning again to Emily's house.

'I'm not sure,' he replied. 'Her story sort of makes sense. She had no motive to kill the woman, except to frame Greg and that's reaching.'

Audrey tilted her head as if to say, maybe yes – maybe no.

'What?' he asked.

'Well,' she began, 'isn't there a chance that we're looking at this from the wrong perspective?'

'What do you mean?'

'We assume that this blackmailer had dirt on Downing,' Audrey said. 'But maybe she had dirt on Emily.'

Myron stopped, looked back at the house as though it held some answers, looked back at Audrey.

'According to Emily,' Audrey went on, 'the blackmailer approached her. But why? She and Greg aren't together anymore.'

'Carla didn't know that,' Myron replied. 'She figured Emily was his wife and would want to protect him.'

'That's one possibility,' Audrey agreed. 'But I'm not sure it's the best one.'

'Are you saying that they were blackmailing her, not Greg?'

Audrey turned her palms skyward. 'All I'm saying is that it could work the other way too. The blackmailer might have had something on Emily – something Greg would want to use against her in the child custody case.'

Myron folded his arms and leaned against the car. 'But what about Clip?' he asked. 'If they had something on Emily, why would he be interested?'

'I don't know.' Audrey shrugged. 'Maybe she had dirt on both of them.'

'Both of them?'

'Sure. Something that could destroy them both. Or maybe Clip thought whatever it was – even if it was about Emily – would distract Greg.'

'Any guesses?'

'Not a one,' Audrey said.

Myron mulled it over for a few seconds, but nothing came to him. 'There's a chance,' he said, 'we'll find out tonight.'

'How?'

'The blackmailer called. He wants to sell me the information.'

'Tonight?'

'Yep.'

'Where?'

'I don't know yet. He's going to call. I got my home line forwarded to the cellular.'

As if on cue, the cellular rang. Myron took it out of his pocket.

It was Win. 'The dear professor's schedule was posted on his office door,' he said. 'He is in class for another hour. After that, he has open office hours so the kiddies can whine about grades.'

'Where are you?'

'On Columbia's campus,' Win replied. 'By the way, Columbia women are fairly attractive. I mean, for the Ivy Leagues and all.'

'Glad you haven't lost your powers of observation.'

'Indeed,' Win said. 'Have you finished speaking to our girl?'

Our girl was Emily. Win did not trust cellular phones with names. 'Yes,' he said.

'Goodie. What time should I expect you then?'

'I'm on my way.'

34

Win was sitting on a bench near the Columbia gate on 116th Street. He was wearing Eddie Bauer khakis, Top-Siders without socks, a blue button-down Oxford, and a power tie.

'I'm blending in,' Win explained.

'Like a Hasid at Christmas mass,' Myron agreed. 'Is Bowman still in class?'

Win nodded. 'He should be exiting that door in ten minutes.'

'Do you know what he looks like?'

Win handed him a faculty handbook. 'Page two ten,' he said. 'So tell me about Emily.'

Myron did. A tall brunette dressed in a black, skintight cat suit strolled by with her books pressed up against her chest. Julie Newmar on Batman. Win and Myron watched her closely. Meow.

When Myron finished, Win didn't bother with any questions. 'I have a meeting at the office,' he said as he stood. 'Do you mind?'

Myron shook his head and sat down. Win left. Myron kept his eye on the door. Ten minutes later students began to file out the door. Two minutes after that, Professor Sidney Bowman followed suit. He had the same unkempt, academic beard as in the photo. He was bald but kept his fringe hair ridiculously long. He wore jeans, Timberland boots, and a red flannel shirt. He was either trying to look like a working stiff or Jerry Brown on the campaign trail.

Bowman pushed up his spectacles and kept walking. Myron waited until he was out of sight before following. No rush. The good professor was indeed heading for his office. He crossed the grassy commons and disappeared into yet another brick building. Myron found a bench and sat down.

An hour passed. Myron watched the students and felt very old. He should have brought a newspaper. Sitting for an hour without reading material meant he had to think. His mind kept conjuring up new possibilities and then dismissing them. He knew he was missing something, could see it bobbing in the distance, but every time he reached out it ducked back down below the surface.

He suddenly remembered that he had not checked Greg's answering machine today. He took out his cellular phone and dialed the number. When Greg's voice came on, he pressed 317, the code numbers Greg had programmed into the machine. There was only one message on the tape, but it was a doozy.

'Don't fuck with us,' the electronically altered voice said. 'I've spoken to Bolitar. He's willing to pay. Is that what you want?'

End of message.

Myron sat very still. He stared at a brick, ivyless wall. He listened to a tone for a few seconds and did nothing. What the hell . . . ?

'. . . *He's willing to pay. Is that what you want?*'

Myron pressed the star button to have the message replayed. Then he did it again. He probably would have listened for a fourth time, had Professor Bowman not suddenly appeared at the door.

Bowman stopped to chat with a couple of students. The conversation grew animated, all three displaying fervent, academic earnest. College. Continuing their undoubtedly weighty discourse, they walked off campus and down Amsterdam Avenue. Myron pocketed the phone and kept his distance. At 112th Street, the group separated. The two students continued south. Bowman crossed the street and headed toward the Cathedral of St John the Divine.

St John the Divine's was a massive structure and interestingly enough, the largest cathedral in the world in terms of cubic square feet (St Peter's in Rome is considered a basilica by this statistic, not a cathedral). The edifice was like the city that housed it: awe-inspiring yet worn. Towering columns and gorgeous stained-glass windows were surrounded by signs like HARD HAT AREA (though it dated back to 1892, St John the Divine's has never been completed) and THE CATHEDRAL IS PATROLLED AND ELECTRO-NICALLY MONITORED FOR YOUR PROTECTION. Wooden planks plugged holes in the granite facade. On the left side of this architectural wonder were two prefab aluminum storage barracks that brought back memories of the opening credits of *Gomer Pyle*. On the right was the Children's Sculpture Garden featuring the Peace Fountain, an enormous sculpture that inspired several moods, none of them peaceful. Images of severed heads and limbs, lobster claws, hands reaching out from the dirt as though trying to escape hell, a man twisting the neck of a deer all whirled together to create an atmosphere that was more Dante meets Goya than languid tranquillity.

Bowman headed down the driveway on the cathedral's right. Myron knew that there was a homeless shelter down that way. He crossed the street and tried to keep his distance. Bowman passed a group of apparently homeless men – all dressed in threadbare synthetics and pants with plunging butt-lines. Some waved and called out to Bowman. Bowman waved back. Then he disappeared through a door. Myron debated what to do. There was no choice really. Even if it meant blowing his cover, he had to go in.

He passed the men, nodded, smiled. They nodded and smiled back. The shelter entrance was a double black door with chintzy lace curtains. Not far from it were two signs – one reading SLOW CHILDREN AT PLAY and the other CATHEDRAL SCHOOL. A homeless shelter and a children's school side by side – an interesting yet working combo. Only in New York.

Myron entered. The room was packed with frayed mattresses and men. A smell like a used bong after an all-nighter singed his nostril hairs. Myron tried not to make a face. He spotted Bowman talking to several men in one corner. None of them was Cole Whiteman aka Norman Lowenstein. Myron glanced about the unshaven faces and hollow eyes, his gaze swinging left to right.

They spotted each other at exactly the same time.

From across the room, their eyes locked for perhaps a second, but that was long enough. Cole Whiteman turned and ran. Myron followed, threading his way through the throngs. Professor Bowman spotted the disturbance. Eyes afire, he jumped in Myron's path. Myron lowered his shoulder and flattened him without breaking stride. Just like Jim Brown. Except Jim Brown had to do it against guys like Dick Butkus and Ray Nitzchke opposed to a fifty-year-old college professor who probably didn't weigh 180 even with the soft gut. Still.

Cole Whiteman disappeared out a back door, slamming it behind him. Myron went through it not long after. They were outside now, but only briefly. Whiteman disappeared up a metal stairway and back into the main chapel. Myron followed. The inside was very much like the outside – spectacular examples of art and architecture mixed in with the tattered and tacky. The pews, for example, were cheap folding chairs. Lush tapestries hung upon granite walls with seemingly no organization. Ladders were melded into thick columns.

Myron spotted Cole heading back out a nearby door. He sprinted after him, his heels echoing up through the giant arched ceiling. They were back outside. Cole headed down below the cathedral and through heavy fire doors. A sign read ACT PROGRAM. It looked like a basement school or day-care center. Both men raced down a hallway lined with beat-up, metallic lockers. Cole turned right and disappeared behind a wooden door.

When Myron pushed the door open, a darkened stairway greeted him. He heard footsteps below him. He trotted down, the light from above dwindling with each step. He was descending deep into the cathedral's subdwelling now. The walls were cement and clammy to the touch. He wondered if he was entering a crypt or tomb or something equally creepy, if indeed there was equally creepy. Did American cathedrals have crypts, or was that only in Europe?

By the time he reached the bottom step, Myron was bathed in darkness, the light from above little more than distant glint. Great. He stepped into a black hole of a room. He cocked his head, listening for a sound like a dog on a hunt. Nothing. He felt for a light switch. Again nothing. The room had a bone-chilling, windless cold. A damp smell permeated his surroundings. He didn't like it down here. He didn't like it at all.

He inched forward blindly, his arms outstretched like Frankenstein's monster. 'Cole,' he called out. 'I just want to talk to you.'

His words echoed hard before fading out like a song on the radio.

He kept going. The room was still as . . . well, as a tomb. He had moved about five feet when his outstretched fingers hit something. Myron kept his hand on the smooth, cold surface. Like marble, he thought. He traced down. It was a statue of some sort. He felt the arm, the shoulder, to the back, down a marble wing. He wondered if it was some kind of tombstone decoration and quickly withdrew his hand.

He stayed perfectly still and tried to listen again. The only sound was a rushing in his ears, like seashells were pressed against them. He debated going back upstairs, but there was no way he could do that. Cole knew now that his identity was in danger. He would go into hiding again and not resurface. This was Myron's only chance.

He took another step, leading now with his foot. His toe hit something hard and unyielding. Marble again, he figured. He circled around it. Then a sound – a scurrying sound – made him freeze in his tracks. It had come from the ground. Not a mouse. Too big for a mouse. He cocked his head again and waited. His pulse raced. His eyes were just beginning to adjust to the darkness, and he could make out a few shadowy, tall figures. Statues. Lowered heads. He imagined the serene expressions of religious art on their faces, looking down at him with the knowledge they were embarking on a journey to a better place than the one in which they dwelled.

He took another step, and cold fingers of flesh grabbed his ankle.

Myron screamed.

The hand pulled and Myron fell hard against the cement. He kicked his leg loose and scrambled backward. His back slammed into more marble. A man giggled madly. Myron felt the hairs on the nape of his neck stand up. Another man giggled. Then another. Like a group of hyenas were encircling him.

Myron tried to get to his feet, but midway up, the men suddenly pounced. He didn't know how many. Hands dragged him back to the floor. He threw a blind fist and connected square into a face. Myron heard a crunching sound and a man fell. But others reached their target. He found himself sprawled on the wet cement, fighting blindly and frantically. He heard grunts. The stench of body odor and alcohol was suffocating, inescapable. The hands were everywhere now. One ripped off his watch. One grabbed his wallet. Myron threw another punch. It hit ribs. Another grunt and another man fell.

Somebody turned on a flashlight and shone it into his eyes. It looked like a train heading toward him.

'Okay,' a voice said, 'back off him.'

The hands slid off like wet snakes. Myron tried to sit up.

'Before you get any cute ideas,' the voice behind the flashlight said, 'take a look at this.'

The voice put a gun in front of the flashlight.

Another voice said, 'Sixty bucks? That's fuckin' all? Shit.'

Myron felt the wallet hit him in the chest.

'Put your hands behind your back.'

He did as the voice asked. Someone grabbed the forearms, pulling them closer together, tearing at the shoulder tendons. A pair of handcuffs were snapped on his wrists.

'Leave us,' the voice said. Myron heard the rustling movements. The air cleared. Myron heard a door open, but the flashlight in his eyes prevented him from seeing anything. Silence followed. After some time passed, the voice said, 'Sorry to do this to you, Myron. They'll let you go in a few hours.'

'How long you going to keep running, Cole?'

Cole Whiteman chuckled. 'Been running a long time,' he said. 'I'm used to it.'

'I'm not here to stop you.'

'Imagine my relief,' he said. 'So how did you figure out who I was?'

'It's not important,' Myron said.

'It is to me.'

'I don't have any interest in bringing you down,' Myron said. 'I just want some information.'

There was a pause. Myron blinked into the light. 'How did you get involved in all this?' Cole asked.

'Greg Downing vanished. I was hired to find him.'

'You?'

'Yes.'

Cole Whiteman laughed deep and hearty. The sound bounced around like balls of Silly Putty, the volume reaching a frightening crescendo before mercifully fading away.

'What's so funny?' Myron asked.

'Inside joke.' Cole stood, the flashlight rising with him. 'Look, I have to go. I'm sorry.'

More silence. Cole flicked off the flashlight, plunging Myron back into total blackness. He heard footsteps receding.

'Don't you want to know who killed Liz Gorman?' Myron called out.

The footsteps continued unimpeded. Myron heard a switch and a dim lightbulb came on. Maybe forty watts. It didn't come close to fully illuminating the place, but it was a hell of an improvement. Myron blinked away black spots left over from the flashlight assault and examined his surroundings. The room was jammed with marble statues, lined and piled up without reason or logic, some tilted over. It wasn't a tomb, after all. It was some bizarre, church-art storage room.

Cole Whiteman came back over to him. He sat cross-legged directly in front of Myron. The white stubble was still there – thick in some spots, completely missing in others. His hair jutted up and out in every direction. He lowered the gun to his side.

'I want to know how Liz died,' he said softly.

'She was bludgeoned with a baseball bat,' Myron said.

Cole's eyes closed. 'Who did it?'

'That's what I'm trying to find out. Right now, Greg Downing is the main suspect.'

Cole Whiteman shook his head. 'He wasn't there long enough.'

Myron felt a knot in his stomach. He tried to lick his lips but his mouth was too dry. 'You were there?'

'Across the street behind a garbage can. Like Oscar the fucking Grouch.' His lips smiled, but there was nothing behind it. 'You want no one to notice you? Pretend you're homeless.' He stood up in one fluid motion, like some kind of yoga master. 'A baseball bat,' he said. He pinched the bridge of his noise, turned away, and lowered his chin to his chest. Myron could hear small sobs.

'Help me find her killer, Cole.'

'Why the fuck should I trust you?'

'Me or the police,' Myron said. 'It's up to you.'

That slowed him. 'The cops won't do shit. They think she's a murderer.'

'Then help me,' Myron said.

He sat back down on the floor and inched a bit closer to Myron. 'We're not murderers, you know. The government labeled us that and now everyone believes it. But it's not true. You understand?'

Myron nodded. 'I understand.'

Cole gave him a hard look. 'You patronizing me?'

'No.'

'Don't patronize me,' Cole said. 'You want me to stay and talk, don't you dare patronize me. You stay honest – I'll stay honest.'

'Fine,' Myron said. 'But then don't hand me the "we're not killers, we're freedom fighters" line. I'm not in the mood for a verse of "Blowin' in the Wind."'

'You think that's what I'm talking about?'

'You're not being prosecuted by a corrupt government,' Myron said. 'You kidnapped and killed a man, Cole. You can dress it up in all the fancy language you want, but that's what you did.'

Cole almost smiled. 'You really believe that.'

'Wait, don't tell me; let me guess,' Myron said. He feigned looking up in thought. 'The government brainwashed me, right? This whole thing has been a CIA plot to crush a dozen college students who threatened to undermine our government.'

'No,' he said. 'But we didn't kill Hunt.'

'Who did?'

Cole hesitated. He looked up and blinked back what looked like tears. 'Hunt shot himself.'

His reddening eyes looked to Myron for a reaction. Myron remained still.

'The kidnapping was a hoax,' Cole went on. 'The whole thing was Hunt's idea. He wanted to hurt his old man so he figured what better way than to take his money and then embarrass the shit out of him? But then those assholes surprised us and Hunt chose another revenge.' Cole's breathing grew deep and erratic. 'He ran outside with the gun. He screamed, "Fuck you, Dad." Then he blew his own head off.'

Myron said nothing.

'Look at our history,' Cole Whiteman said, his voice a semiplea. 'We were a harmless group of stragglers. We protested at antiwar rallies. We got stoned a lot. We never committed one act of violence. None of us even had a gun, except for Hunt. He was my roommate and best friend. I could never hurt him.'

Myron didn't know what to believe; more to the point, he didn't have time now to worry about a twenty-year-old homicide. He waited for Cole to continue, to let him talk out the past, but Cole remained still. Finally, Myron tried to update the subject. 'You saw Greg Downing go into Liz Gorman's building?'

Cole nodded slowly.

'She was blackmailing him?'

'Not just her,' he corrected. 'It was my idea.'

'What did you have on Greg?'

Cole shook his head. 'Not important.'

'She was probably killed over it.'

'Probably,' Cole agreed. 'But you don't need to know the specifics. Trust me.'

Myron was in no position to push it. 'Tell me about the night of the murder.'

Cole scratched at his stubble hard, like a cat on a post. 'Like I said,' he began, 'I was across the street. When you live underground, you have certain rules you live by – rules that have kept us alive and free for the last twenty years. One of them is that after we commit a crime, we never stay together. The feds look for us in groups, not individuals. Since we've been in the city, Liz and I have made sure we were never together. We only communicated by phone.'

'What about Gloria Katz and Susan Milano?' Myron asked. 'Where are they?'

Cole smiled without mirth or humor. Myron saw the missing teeth and wondered if they were part of the disguise or something more sinister. 'I'll tell you about them another time,' he said.

Myron nodded. 'Go on,' he said.

The lines in Cole's face seemed to deepen and darken in the bare light. He took his time before continuing. 'Liz was all packed and ready to go,' he said finally. 'We were going to score the cash and get out of the city, just like I planned. I was just waiting across the street for her signal.'

'What signal?'

'After all the money was collected, she'd flicker the lights three times. That meant she'd be down in ten minutes. We were going to meet at One Hundred Sixteenth Street and take the One train out of here. But the signal never came. In fact, her light never went off at all. I was afraid to go check on her for obvious reasons. We got rules about that, too.'

'Who was Liz supposed to collect from that night?'

'Three people,' Cole said, holding up the pointer, middle man, and ring man. 'Greg Downing' – he dropped ring man – 'his wife what's-her-name—'

'Emily.'

'Right, Emily.' The middle finger went down. 'And the old guy who owns the Dragons.' His hand made a fist now.

Myron's heart contracted. 'Wait a second,' he said. 'Clip Arnstein was supposed to show up?'

'Not supposed to,' Cole corrected. 'He did.'

A back coldness seeped into Myron's bones. 'Clip was there?'

'Yes.'

'And the other two?'

'All three showed up. But that wasn't the plan. Liz was supposed to meet Downing at a bar downtown. They were going to make the transaction there.'

'A place called the Swiss Chalet?'

'Right.'

'But Greg showed up at the apartment too?'

'Later on, yeah. But Clip Arnstein arrived first.'

Win's warning about Clip came back to him. You like him too much. You're not being objective. 'How much was Clip supposed to pay?'

'Thirty thousand dollars.'

'The police only found ten thousand in her apartment,' Myron said. 'And those bills were from the bank robbery.'

Cole shrugged. 'Either the old man didn't pay her or else the killer took the money.' Then, thinking it through a little more he added, 'Or maybe Clip Arnstein killed her. But he seems kind of old, don't you think?'

Myron didn't answer. 'How long was he inside?'

'Ten, fifteen minutes.'

'Who came by next?'

'Greg Downing. I remember he had a satchel. I figured it had the money in it. He was in and out fast – couldn't have been more than a minute. And he still had the satchel on him when he came out. That's when I started to worry.'

'Greg could have killed her,' Myron said. 'It doesn't take long to hit someone with a baseball bat.'

'But he wasn't carrying a bat,' Cole said. 'The satchel wasn't big enough for one. And Liz had a bat in her apartment. She hated guns, so she kept it for protection.'

Myron knew that no bat had been found at Gorman's apartment. That meant the killer must have used Liz's. Could Greg have gone upstairs, entered her apartment, found the bat, killed her with it, run out – all in such a short time?

It seemed doubtful.

'What about Emily?' Myron asked.

'She came in last,' Cole said.

'How long was she there?'

'Five minutes. Something like that.'

Time enough to gather the evidence to plant. 'Did you see anybody else go in and out of the building?'

'Sure,' Cole said. 'Lots of students live there.'

'But we can assume that Liz was already dead by the time Greg Downing arrived, right?'

'Right.'

'So the question is, who do you remember going in between the time she got back from the Swiss Chalet and the time Greg arrived? Besides Clip Arnstein.'

Cole thought about it and shrugged. 'Mostly students, I guess. There was a real tall guy—'

'How tall?'

'I don't know. Very.'

'I'm six-four. Taller than me?'

'Yeah, I think so.'

'Was he black?'

'I don't know. I was across the street and the light wasn't too good. I wasn't watching that closely. He might have been black. But I don't think he's our man.'

'Why do you say that?'

'I watched the building until the next morning. He never came back out. He must have lived there or at least stayed with someone overnight. I doubt the killer would've hung around like that.'

Tough to argue, Myron thought. He tried to process what he was hearing in a cold, computerlike way, but the circuits were starting to overload. 'Who else did you remember seeing? Anybody stand out?'

Cole thought again, his eyes wandering aimlessly. 'There was one woman who went in not long before Greg got there. Now that I think of it, she left before he got there too.'

'What did she look like?'

'I don't remember.'

'Blonde, brunette?'

Cole shook his head. 'I only remember her because she wore a long coat. The students all wear windbreakers or sweat shirts or something like that. I remember thinking she looked like an adult.'

'Was she carrying anything? Did she—'

'Look, Myron, I'm sorry. I gotta get moving.' He stood and looked down at Myron with a hollow, lost expression. 'Good luck finding the son of a bitch,' he said. 'Liz was a good person. She never hurt anyone. None of us did.'

Before he could turn away, Myron asked, 'Why did you call me last night? What were you going to sell me?'

Cole smiled sadly and began to walk away. He stopped before he reached the door and turned back around. 'I'm alone now,' he said. 'Gloria Katz was shot in the initial attack. She died three months later. Susan Milano died in a car crash in 1982. Liz and I kept their deaths a secret. We wanted the feds searching for four of us, not two. We thought it would help us stay hidden. So you see, there is only one of us left now.'

He had the bone-weary look of a survivor who wasn't so sure the dead weren't the lucky ones. He rambled back over toward Myron and unlocked the handcuffs. 'Go,' he said.

Myron rose, rubbing his wrists. 'Thank you,' he said.

Cole merely nodded.

'I won't tell anyone where you are.'

'Yeah,' Cole said. 'I know.'

35

Myron sprinted to his car and dialed Clip's number. Clip's secretary answered and told him that Mr Arnstein was not in at the moment. He asked her to transfer the call to Calvin Johnson. She put him on hold. Ten seconds later, the call was put through.

'Hey, Myron,' Calvin said, 'what's up?'

'Where's Clip?'

'He should be here in a couple of hours. By game time anyway.'

'Where is he now?'

'I don't know.'

'Find him,' Myron said. 'When you do, call me back.'

'What's going on?' Calvin asked.

'Just find him.'

Myron disconnected the call. He opened the car window and took deep breaths. It was a few minutes after six. Most of the guys would already be at the arena warming up. He headed up Riverside Drive and crossed the George Washington Bridge. He dialed Leon White's number. A woman answered.

'Hello?'

Myron disguised his voice. 'Is this Mrs Fiona White?' he asked.

'Yes, it is.'

'Would you like to subscribe to *Popular Mechanics*? We have a special going on for a limited time.'

'No, thank you.' She hung up.

Conclusion: Fiona White, the Sepbabe and promisor of night ecstasy, was home. Time to pay her a little visit.

He took Route 4 and got off at Kindermack Road. Five minutes later, he was there. The house was a semi-nouveau ranch with orange-tinged brick and diamond-shaped windows. This particular architectural look was all the rage for maybe a two-month span in 1977, and it had aged about as well as the leisure suit. Myron parked in the driveway. On either side of the cement walkway were low-rise iron fences with plastic ivy snaked through them. Classy.

He rang the bell. Fiona White opened the door. Her green, flower-print blouse hung open over a white leotard. Her bleached-blonde hair was tied in a bun that was falling apart, spare strands dangling down over her eyes and ears. She looked at Myron and frowned. 'Yes?'

'Hi, Fiona. I'm Myron Bolitar. We met the other night at TC's house.'

The frown was still there. 'Leon isn't here.'

'I wanted to talk to you.'

Fiona sighed and crossed her arms under the ample bosom. 'What about?'

'Can I come inside?'

'No. I'm busy right now.'

'I think it would be better in private.'

'This is private,' she said, her face unyielding. 'What do you want?'

Myron shrugged, conjured up his most charming smile, saw it would take him nowhere. 'I want to know about you and Greg Downing.'

Fiona White's arms dropped to her side. She suddenly looked horror-stricken. 'What?'

'I know about your e-mail to him. Sepbabe. You were supposed to meet last Saturday for the' – Myron made quote marks with his fingers – ' "greatest night of ecstasy imaginable." Do you recall that?'

Fiona White went to close the door. Myron stuck his foot in the way.

'I've got nothing to say to you,' she said.

'I'm not trying to expose you.'

She pushed the door against his foot. 'Get out.'

'I'm just trying to find Greg Downing.'

'I don't know where he is.'

'Were you having an affair with him?'

'No. Now leave.'

'I saw the e-mail, Fiona.'

'Think what you want. I'm not talking to you.'

'Fine,' Myron said, moving back and throwing up his hands. 'I'll talk to Leon instead.'

Her cheeks flushed. 'Do whatever you want,' she said. 'I did not have an affair with him. I did not see him last Saturday night. I don't know where he is.'

She slammed the door.

Gee, that went well.

Myron headed back to his car. As he reached the door, a black BMW with tinted windows rocketed up the street and screeched to a halt in the driveway. The driver's door opened and Leon flew out like an escaped bird.

'What the fuck you doing here?' he snapped.

'Take it easy, Leon.'

'Fuck take it easy,' he shouted. Leon ran up and stuck his face within an inch of Myron's. 'What the fuck you doing around here, huh?'

'I came by to see you.'

'Bullshit.' The spittle hit Myron's cheeks. 'We're supposed to be in the arena in twenty minutes.' He pushed Myron in the chest. Myron stumbled back. 'Why you here, huh?' Leon pushed again. 'What are you sniffing after?'

'Nothing.'

'You think you'd find my wife alone?'

'It's nothing like that.'

Leon lined himself up for another push. Myron was ready. When Leon's hand reached him, Myron's right forearm shot across his body, pinning Leon's hands helplessly against Myron's chest. Myron bent at the waist, bending Leon's wrists back the wrong way. The pressure forced Leon to drop to one knee. Myron's right hand slid until it met Leon's left. He grabbed it and quickly executed an elbow lock. Leon winced.

'You calm?' Myron asked.

'Motherfucker.'

'That doesn't sound like calm, Leon,' Myron applied a little pressure to the elbow. Joint locks were about controlled pain. They worked by bending joints in ways they were never intended to bend. The more the bend, the more the pain. But go too far and the joint dislocated or the bone broke. Myron was careful.

'Greg is missing again,' Myron said. 'That's why I'm on the team. I'm supposed to find him.'

Leon was still on his knees, his arm locked and upright. 'So what does that have to do with me?'

'You two have had a falling out,' Myron said. 'I want to know why.'

Leon looked up at him. 'Let go of me, Myron.'

'If you attack me again—'

'I won't. Just let go already.'

Myron waited another second or two, then did as Leon asked. Leon rubbed his arm and stood. Myron eyed him.

Leon said, 'You're here because you think Greg and Fiona were getting it on.'

'Were they?'

He shook his head. 'Not from a lack of trying though.'

'What do you mean?'

'He's supposed to be my best friend. But he's not. He's just another fucking superstar who takes what he wants.'

'Including Fiona.'

'He tried. Tried like hell. But she's not like that.'

Myron said nothing. Not his place.

'Guys are always hitting on Fiona,' he went on. 'Because of the way she looks. And the whole racial thing. So when I saw you here when you figured I wouldn't be around . . .' He shrugged into silence.

'Did you ever confront Greg?' Myron asked.

'Yeah,' he said. 'A couple of weeks ago.'

'What did you say to him?'

Leon's eyes narrowed, suddenly wary. 'What does this have to do with finding him?' he asked, suspicious now. 'You trying to pin this on me?'

'Pin what on you?'

'You said he's disappeared. You trying to pin that on me?'

'I'm just trying to find out where he is.'

'I got nothing to do with it.'

'I didn't say you did. I just want to know what happened when you confronted him.'

'What do you think happened?' Leon countered. 'The motherfucker denied it. He made this big point of swearing he'd never sleep with any married woman – especially his best friend's wife.'

Myron sort of gulped at that one. 'But you didn't believe him.'

'He's a superstar, Myron.'

'That doesn't make him a liar.'

'No, but it makes him something different. Guys like Greg and Michael Jordan and Shaq and TC . . . they ain't like the rest of us. They got their own thing going. Everyone else is a fucking underling to them. The whole planet is set up to cater to their whims, you know what I'm saying?'

Myron nodded. In college he had been one of those who got to breathe the rarified air of superstardom. He thought again about the bonds superstars shared. He and Greg had not exchanged more than five words before Greg visited him in the hospital, but there had been a bond. They both knew. Superstars share that rarefied air with very few. As TC had told him, it does indeed isolate in a very bizarre, often unhealthy way.

And with that thought came something of a revelation. Myron took a step back.

He'd always thought that if Greg was in trouble, he'd go to his closest friend for help. But that wasn't the case. If Greg had indeed stumbled across the dead body and panicked, if he had seen all his problems – the gambling debts, the threat of exposure, the divorce, the child custody case, the blackmail, the probability of being a suspect in a murder – closing in on him, who would he go to for help?

He'd go to the guy who understood him best.

He'd go to the guy who could best relate to the unique troubles of superstardom.

He'd go to the guy who shared that rarefied air with him.

36

Myron wasn't sure what to do next.

In truth, he had nothing more than a suspicion. There was no proof. No real evidence. But it could potentially answer a lot of questions. Why, for example, had Thumper helped set up Emily on videotape? By all accounts, she was not particularly close to Greg.

But she was to TC.

Again the superstar bond. Greg had feared losing his kids in a custody battle. That's about as big a worry as a person can have. So whom did he turn to for help?

TC.

When Win had leaned on Thumper last night, letting her know that he was searching for Greg, whom had she warned?

TC.

No proof, of course. But it felt very right.

Myron could now put a lot of it together. Greg was under incredible strain – not the best situation for a man of his questionable mental fortitude to be ensnared. What had gone through his mind when he saw Liz Gorman dead on the floor? He'd have to have known that he would be the prime suspect in her murder. As Emily had pointed out, Greg had motive, opportunity, and was at the murder scene. Emily saw that. It was why she set him up. Greg must have seen it too.

So what did he do?

He ran.

Seeing Liz Gorman dead had been the final straw. But Greg had also known that he could not do it alone. People would be looking for him this time. He needed help. He needed time and space.

So whom did Greg reach out to?

The guy who understood him best. Who could relate to the unique troubles of superstardom. Who shared that rarefied air with him.

Myron stopped at a red light. He was close, so goddamn close. TC was helping Greg hide; he was sure of it. But of course, TC was only part of the solution. None of this answered the central question in all this:

Who killed Liz Gorman?

706

He put his mind on rewind and reviewed the night of the murder. He thought about Clip being the first of the three to arrive. In many ways, Clip was now his best suspect. But Myron still saw big problems with that scenario. What was Clip's motive, for example? Yes, Liz Gorman's information may have been detrimental to the team. The information may have even been potent enough for him to lose the vote. But would Clip pick up a baseball bat and murder a woman over that? People kill for money and power all the time. Would Clip?

But there was still a larger problem at work here, one that Myron could not get around no matter how hard he tried. Emily was the one who planted the blood and murder weapon at Greg's house. That was established and that made sense. Okay, fine. We know who planted the evidence . . .

. . . but who cleaned it up?

There were only three logical choices: 1. Greg Downing, 2. someone trying to protect Greg, or 3. the killer.

But it couldn't have been Greg. Even if you accept the semi-impossible premise that Greg went back into his house after going into hiding, how did he find the blood? Did he just happen to go down into his playroom? No. It was too ridiculous. The only way Greg would have gone down there was if he'd known the blood had been planted.

Myron froze.

That was it. Whoever had cleaned up the blood had known what Emily had done. They didn't just stumble across it by accident. So how did they find out? From Emily? Uh uh, no way. Emily would be the last person to say anything. Could she have been spotted in the act? Again, the answer was a resounding no. If that had been the case, the bat would have been removed too. More to the point, the blood would have been cleaned up right away – *before* Myron and Win found it. The timing of the clean-up was crucial – it'd happened after Myron and Win had revealed their discovery. That meant Myron and Win were the leak.

So whom had they told?

The finger pointed back to Clip.

He turned on Route 3 and entered the Meadowlands complex. The arena loomed before him like a large UFO on a white landing pad. Did Clip Arnstein murder Liz Gorman and clean up the blood? Myron wrestled with the possibility, but he didn't like it. How had Clip gotten inside Greg's house? There were no signs of forced entry. Had he picked the lock? Doubtful. Did he have a key? Doubtful. Did he hire a professional? Still doubtful. Clip hadn't even let a private investigator do a simple credit card check on Greg for fear word would get out. Whom would he trust to clean up the blood of a person he murdered?

And something else still jabbed at Myron with a sharpened, steel point: the woman's clothes in the bedroom. They had been packed away too. Why would Clip remove all traces of a secret girlfriend? Why would anybody?

The different scenarios swirled in Myron's head like rubber ducks in a whirlpool. He concentrated again on the mystery girlfriend. Could it have been Fiona White? She wasn't talking, but Myron firmly believed that she was not the one. How could Fiona have lived with Greg and kept it hidden from a husband as obsessively jealous as Leon? Perhaps there had been some entanglement between Greg and Fiona – a casual fling in a motel room or something – but Myron no longer believed even that. The more he thought about it, the 'greatest night of sexual ecstasy' epistle was more of a come-on than the talk of two familiar lovers. It seemed more logical that Greg was telling Leon the truth when he said he would never sleep with another man's wife. The thought gave Myron's old shame new life.

A commercial came on the radio. A very hip man and a very hip woman were enjoying a Molson's Golden far too much. They spoke in low voices and laughed at each other's lame jokes. Myron switched it off.

He still had more questions than answers. But when he picked up his cellular phone to check Greg's answering machine, his fingers began to tremble. Something tightened his chest, making it hard to breathe. This feeling, however, was not like pregame jitters. In fact, it was the furthest thing from them.

37

Myron rushed by Clip's secretary.

'He's not in there,' she cried.

Ignoring her, he opened the office door. The lights were off and the room was empty. He spun back toward the secretary. 'Where is he?'

The secretary, a classic battle-ax who had probably been with Clip since the Coolidge Administration, put her hands on her hips. 'I don't have the slightest idea,' she huffed.

Calvin Johnson came out of the adjoining office. Myron approached him. He waited until they were inside Calvin's office and the door was closed. 'Where is he?'

Calvin held up his hands. 'I don't know. I tried his house, but there was no answer.'

'Does he have a car phone?'

'No.'

Myron shook his head and began pacing. 'He lied to me,' Myron said. 'The son of a bitch lied.'

'What?'

'He met with the blackmailer.'

Calvin raised an eyebrow. He moved to the chair behind his desk and sat down. 'What are you talking about?'

'The night she was murdered,' Myron said, 'Clip went to her apartment.'

'But she wasn't supposed to meet with us until Monday,' Calvin said.

'Did you hear her say that?'

Calvin plucked at his chin with his thumb and pointer. The track lights from above his desk reflected off the receding forehead. His face remained the ever placid pool. 'No,' he said slowly. 'Clip told me.'

'He lied to you.'

'But why?'

'Because he's hiding something.'

'Do you know what?'

'No,' Myron said. 'But I intend to find out tonight.'

'How?'

'The blackmailer still wants to sell,' Myron said. 'I'm his new buyer.'

Calvin tilted his head. 'I thought you said the blackmailer was dead.'

'She had a partner.'

'I see,' Calvin said with a slow nod. 'And you're meeting tonight?'

'Yep. But I don't know when or where. He's supposed to call.'

'I see,' Calvin said again. He made a neat fist and coughed into it. 'If it's something damaging. I mean, something that could affect the outcome of the vote tomorrow . . .'

'I'll do whatever is right, Calvin.'

'Of course. I didn't mean to imply otherwise.'

Myron rose. 'Let me know when he gets here.'

'Sure.'

Myron entered the locker room. TC was in his pregame pose – sprawled on a chair in the corner with a Walkman plugged into his ears, his eyes blazing straight ahead and unmoving. He did not acknowledge Myron. Leon was also there. He, too, studiously avoided Myron's gaze. Not surprising.

Audrey approached. 'How did it go with—?'

Myron shook his head to silence her. She nodded, understanding. 'You okay?' she asked.

'Fine.'

'You think they can hear us?'

'I'm not taking any chances.'

Audrey looked left, then right. 'You find something new?'

'Plenty,' Myron said. 'You should have your story tonight. And then some.'

The gleam in her eye expanded. 'You know where he is?'

Myron nodded. The locker room door opened. Calvin popped his head in. He leaned over and spoke to the Kipper for a moment. When he left, Myron noticed that he turned right, which led to the exit, as opposed to left which would have taken him back to his office.

The cellular phone in Myron's pocket rang. He looked up at Audrey. Audrey looked back. He moved closer to the corner and picked it up.

'Hello?'

An electronically altered voice said, 'You got the money?'

'You got lousy timing,' Myron said.

'Answer my question.'

Leon pulled up his gym shorts. TC stood and bobbed his head in rhythm to the music.

'I have it,' Myron said. 'I also have a game tonight.'

'Forget the game. Do you know Overpeck Park?'

'The one in Leonia? Yeah, I know it.'

'Turn in the right side off Route Ninety-five. Then go down a quarter-mile and make another right. You'll see a cul-de-sac. Park there and look for a flashlight. Approach with both your hands raised.'

'Do I get to say a password?' Myron asked. 'I loves passwords.'

'Fifteen minutes. Don't be late. And for the record, I know your superhero partner is in his Park Avenue office. I have a man watching it. If he leaves between now and then, the deal is off.'

Myron turned off the phone. It was coming to a head now. In fifteen minutes it would all be over – one way or another. 'Could you hear?' he asked.

Audrey nodded. 'Most of it.'

'There's going to be some weird stuff going down,' Myron said. 'I need an unbiased journalist to record it. You want to come along?'

She smiled. 'That was a rhetorical question, right?'

'You'll have to keep on the floor in the backseat,' he went on. 'I can't risk having you spotted.'

'No problem,' she said. 'It'll remind me of my high school dates.'

Myron turned toward the door. His nerves were as frayed as an old horse whip. He tried to look nonchalant as they exited. Leon was lacing up his sneakers. TC remained still, but this time his eyes followed them out.

38

Rain beat down, blackening the pavement. Cars were just starting to enter the arena lot in force. Myron took the back exit over the New Jersey Turnpike and onto the northbound lanes just past the final toll booth. He veered to the right, staying on Route 95.

'So what's going on?' Audrey asked.

'The man I am about to meet,' he said, 'killed Liz Gorman.'

'Who's Liz Gorman?'

'The blackmailer who was murdered.'

'I thought her name was Carla.'

'That was an alias.'

'Wait a minute. Isn't Liz Gorman the name of some sixties radical?'

Myron nodded. 'It's a long story; I don't have time to go into details. Suffice to say the guy we're about to meet was part of the blackmail scheme. Something went awry. She ended up dead.'

'Do you have evidence?' Audrey asked.

'Not really. That's what I need you for. You have your microcassette player?'

'Sure.'

'Let me have it.'

Audrey reached into her purse and handed it up front.

'I'm going to try to get him to talk,' Myron said.

'How?'

'By pushing the right buttons.'

She frowned. 'You think he'll fall for that?'

'Yeah, I do. If I push the right ones.' He picked up the car phone. 'I have two separate phones here: the car phone and the cellular in my pocket. I'm going to dial the car phone with the cellular and keep the line open. This way, you can listen in. I want you to take down every word. If something happens to me, go to Win. He'll know what to do.'

She leaned forward and nodded. The windshield wipers whipped shadows across her face. The rain picked up its tempo, glistening the road in front of them. Myron took the next exit. A sign reading Overpeck Park greeted them a quarter-mile later.

'Get down,' he said.

She disappeared from view. He made the right turn. Another sign told him the park was closed. He ignored it and proceeded ahead. It was too dark to see anything, but he knew there were woods on his left and a horse stables straight ahead. He made the first right. The car's headlights danced across a picnic area, illuminating tables, benches, garbage cans, a swing set, a sliding board. He reached the cul-de-sac and stopped the car. He killed the lights, turned off the engine, and dialed the car's number on his cellular. He answered with the car's speakerphone so Audrey could listen in. Then he waited.

For several minutes nothing happened. The rain pelted down on the roof like tiny pebbles. Audrey remained still in the back. Myron put his hands back on the wheel and felt his grip tighten. He could hear his heart thumping in his chest.

Without warning, a beacon of light sliced through the night like a reaper's scythe. Myron shaded his eyes with his hand and squinted. He slowly opened the car door. The wind had picked up now, spraying the rain into his face. He hefted himself out of the car.

A male voice, distorted by the elements, shouted, 'Put your hands up.'

Myron raised them above his head.

'Open your coat. I know you're carrying a gun in a shoulder holster. Take it out with two fingers and toss it onto the seat of the car.'

Keeping one hand in the air, Myron unbuttoned his coat. He was already drenched from the rain, his hair matted against his forehead. He took out the gun and put it on his car seat.

'Close the door.'

Again Myron obeyed the voice.

'Do you have the money?'

'First I want to see what you brought,' Myron said.

'No.'

'Hey, be reasonable here. I don't even know what I'm buying.'

A brief hesitation. 'Come closer.'

Myron stepped toward the light, ignoring the symbolism. 'Whatever you're selling,' he said, 'how do I know you haven't made copies?'

'You don't,' the voice said. 'You'll have to trust me.'

'Who else knows about this?'

'I'm the only one,' the voice said, 'who is still alive.'

Myron picked up the pace. His hands were still in the air. The wind whipped into his face. His clothes were sopping. 'How do I know you won't talk?'

'Again, you don't. Your money buys my silence.'

'Until someone ups the bid.'

'No. I'm leaving after this. You won't hear from me again.' The flashlight flickered. 'Please stop.'

Ten feet in front of him stood a man wearing a ski mask. He had a flashlight in one hand and a box in the other. He nodded at Myron and lifted the box. 'Here.'

'What is it?'

'First, the money.'

'For all I know, the box is empty.'

'Fine. Go back to your car and leave then.' The man in the ski mask turned around.

'No, wait,' Myron said. 'I'll get the money.'

The ski mask faced Myron again. 'No games.'

Myron headed back to the car. He had moved about twenty paces when he heard the gunshots. Three of them. The noises did not startle him. He slowly turned around. The man with the ski mask was down. Audrey was running toward the still body. She was carrying Myron's gun.

'He was going to kill you,' Audrey cried. 'I had to shoot.'

Audrey kept running. When she reached the still body, she ignored it and scooped up the box. Myron slowly walked toward her.

'Open it,' he said.

'Let's get out of this rain first. The police—'

'Open it.'

She hesitated. No thunder bellowed. No lightning struck.

'You were right before,' Myron said.

Audrey looked puzzled. 'About what?'

'I was looking at this the wrong way.'

'What are you talking about?'

Myron took another step toward her. 'When I asked myself who knew about the blood in the basement,' he began, 'I only remembered Clip and Calvin. I forgot I told you. When I wondered why Greg's lover would have to keep her identity a secret, I thought about Fiona White and Liz Gorman. Again I forgot about you. It's hard enough for a woman to get respect as a female sports reporter. Your career would be ruined if anybody found out you were dating one of the players you covered. You had to keep it quiet.'

She looked at him, her face a wet, white blank.

'You're the only one who fits, Audrey. You knew about the blood in the basement. You had to keep a relationship with Greg a secret. You had a key to his house so access would be no problem. And you were the one who had a motive to clean up the blood in order to protect him. After all, you killed to protect him. What's cleaning up some blood?'

She brushed her hair away from her eyes and blinked into the rain. 'You can't seriously believe that I—'

'That night after TC's party,' Myron interrupted, 'when you told me how you had put it all together. I should have wondered then. Sure, my joining the team was unusual. But only somebody with a personal connection – somebody who truly knew that Greg had vanished and why – would have been able to come up with it so fast. You were the mystery lover, Audrey. And you don't know where Greg is either. You cooperated with me not because you wanted the story, but because you wanted to find Greg. You're in love with him.'

'That's ridiculous,' she said.

'The police will comb the house, Audrey. They'll find hairs.'

'That doesn't mean anything,' she said. 'I interviewed him a couple of times—'

'In his bedroom? In his bathroom? In his shower?' Myron shook his head. 'They'll also comb the murder scene now that they know about you. There'll be evidence there too. A hair or something.' He took another step toward her. Audrey raised the gun with a quivering hand.

'Beware the Ides of March,' Myron said.

'What?'

'You were the one who pointed it out to me. The Ides are the fifteenth of March. Your birthday was the seventeenth. March seventeenth. Three-one-seven. The code Greg set on his answering machine.'

She pointed the gun at his chest. 'Turn off the tape recorder,' she said. 'And the phone.'

Myron reached into his pocket and did as she asked.

Tears and rain mixed together and cascaded down her cheeks. 'Why couldn't you just keep your mouth shut?' she wailed. She pointed to the still body on the wet grass. 'You heard what he said: no one else knows. All the blackmailers are dead. I could have destroyed this thing' – she held up the box – 'once and for all. I wouldn't have had to hurt you. It would have finally been over.'

'And what about Liz Gorman?'

Audrey made a scoffing noise. 'That woman was nothing more than a conniving blackmailer,' she said. 'She couldn't be trusted. I told Greg that. What was to stop her from making copies and bleeding him dry? I even went to her house that night and pretended I was an ex-girlfriend with an ax to grind. I told her I wanted to buy a copy. She said sure. Don't you see? Paying her off would do no good. There was only one way to keep her quiet.'

He nodded. 'You had to kill her.'

'She was just a low-life criminal, Myron. She'd robbed a bank, for chrissake. Greg and I . . . we were perfect together. You were right about my career. I had to keep our relationship a secret. But not much longer. I was going to get transferred to another beat. Baseball. The Mets or Yankees. Then we could be open about it. It was going so well, Myron, and then this low-life bitch comes along . . .' Her voice drifted off with a hard shake of the head. 'I had to think about our future,' she said. 'Not just Greg's. Not just mine. But our baby's too.'

Myron's eyes closed in pain. 'You're pregnant,' he said softly.

'Now do you see?' Her wide-eyed enthusiasm was back, though it took on a more twisted dimension now. 'She wanted to destroy him. Destroy us. What choice did I have? I'm not a killer but it was either us or her. And I know how it looks – Greg running off and not telling me. But it's just the way he is. We've been together for more than six months. I know he loves me. He just needed time.'

Myron swallowed. 'It's over now, Audrey.'

She shook her head and held the gun with both hands. 'I'm sorry, Myron. I don't want to do it. I'd almost rather die first.'

'It doesn't matter.' Myron took another step. She moved back. The gun trembled in her hand. 'They're blanks,' he said.

Her eyes squinted in confusion. The man in the ski mask sat up like Bela Lugosi in an old Dracula film. He pulled off the mask and showed his badge. 'Police,' Dimonte shouted. Win and Krinsky came over the crest. Audrey's mouth formed a perfect circle. Win had made the fake blackmailer call; Myron had set his cellular phone's volume on high to be sure Audrey overheard it. The rest was easy.

Dimonte and Krinsky made the arrest. Myron watched, no longer feeling the rain. After Audrey was put into the back of a cruiser, he and Win walked toward the car.

'Superhero partner?' Myron said.

Win shrugged.

39

Esperanza was still in the office when the fax machine rang. She crossed the room and watched the machine begin to spew out paper. The facsimile was addressed to her attention, from the FBI:

Re: FIRST CITY NATIONAL BANK – TUCSON, ARIZONA
Subject: Renters of Safe-Deposit Boxes.

She'd been waiting for this transmission all day.

Esperanza's theory on the blackmail plot had gone something like this: The Raven Brigade robbed the bank. They hit the safe-deposit boxes. People keep all kinds of things in those. Money, jewelry, important documents. That was what hooked the timing together. Simply put, the Raven Brigade had found something in one of those boxes that was damaging to Greg Downing. Then they hatched their little blackmail scheme.

The names came out in alphabetical order. Esperanza read down the list while the paper was still being transmitted. The first page ended in the Ls. No name was familiar. The second page ended in the Ts. No name was familiar. On the third page, when she reached the Ws, her heart leapt into her throat. Her hand fluttered to her mouth, and for a moment she feared that she might scream.

It took several hours to sort through the mess. Statements had to be taken. Explanations made. Myron told Dimonte practically the whole story. He left out the videotape of Thumper and Emily. Again, it was nobody's business. He also left out the part about meeting up with Cole Whiteman. Myron somehow felt he owed him. For her part, Audrey would not talk at all, except to ask for a lawyer.

'Do you know where Downing is?' Dimonte asked Myron.

'I think so.'

'But you don't want to tell me.'

Myron shook his head. 'He's not your business.'

'Ain't that the truth,' Dimonte agreed. 'Go on. Get out of here.'

They were downtown at One Police Plaza. Myron and Win walked out in the city night. Large municipal structures consumed the neighboring area.

Modern bureaucracy in its most extreme and intimidating form. Even this late at night, you could visualize lines of people heading out the door.

'It was a good plan,' Win said.

'Audrey is pregnant.'

'I heard.'

'Her baby will be born in jail.'

'Not your doing.'

'She thought it was her only way out,' Myron said.

Win nodded. 'She saw a blackmailer who stood in the way of all her dreams. I'm not so sure I would have behaved any differently.'

'You don't commit murder to stave off life's inconveniences,' Myron said.

Win didn't argue, but he didn't agree either. They kept walking. When they reached the car, Win said, 'So where does that leave us?'

'With Clip Arnstein,' Myron said. 'He has some explaining to do.'

'You want me to come along?'

'No. I want to talk to him alone.'

40

By the time Myron arrived at the arena, the game was over. Cars tapped the exits, making it hard to go the opposite way. Myron managed to weave through. He showed his ID to the guard and drove into the players' lot.

He ran to Clip's office. Someone called his name. He ignored it. When he reached the outer office door, he tried the knob. It was locked. He was tempted to break it down.

'Yo, Myron.'

It was one of the towel boys. Myron forgot the kid's name. 'What's up?' he said.

'This came for you.'

The kid handed Myron a manila envelope.

'Who dropped this off?' Myron asked.

'Your uncle.'

'My uncle?'

'That's what the guy said.'

Myron looked at the envelope. His name was scrawled across the front in giant block letters. He tore it open and turned it upside down. First, a letter slid out. He shook again and a black cassette tape fell into the palm of his hand. He put the cassette down and unfolded the letter.

Myron,

I should have given this to you at the cathedral. I'm sorry I didn't, but I got too caught up in Liz's murder. I wanted you to concentrate on catching the killer, not on this tape. I was afraid it would distract you. I still think it will, but that doesn't give me the right to keep it from you. I just hope you stay focused enough to find the bastard who killed Liz. She deserves justice.

I also wanted to tell you that I'm thinking about turning myself in. Now that Liz is gone, there's no reason to keep hiding. I spoke to some old lawyer buddies about it. They've already started reaching out to all the mercenaries Hunt's father hired. They're sure one of them will corroborate my story. We'll see.

Don't listen to this tape alone, Myron. Listen to it with a friend.
Cole

Myron folded the letter. He had no idea what to think. He glanced down the corridor. No sign of Clip. He jogged toward the exit. Most of the players had already left the arena. TC, of course. Last in, first out. Myron got in his car and turned the key. Then he stuck the tape into the car's player and waited.

Esperanza tried dialing Myron's car phone. No answer. Then his cellular. Same deal. He always carried his cellular. If he wasn't picking up, it was because he didn't want to. She quickly dialed Win's cellular. He picked up on the second ring.

'Do you know where Myron is?' she asked.

'He went to the arena.'

'Go find him, Win.'

'Why? What's wrong?'

'The Raven Brigade robbed the safe-deposit boxes. That's where they got the information they used to blackmail Downing.'

'What did they find?'

'I don't know,' she said, 'but I have a list of the people who rented the boxes.'

'So?'

'One was rented to a Mr and Mrs B. Wesson.'

Silence.

Win said, 'Are you sure it's the same B. Wesson who injured Myron?'

'I already checked,' she said. 'The B stands for Burt, listed on his application as a thirty-three-year-old high school basketball coach. It's him, Win. It's the same Burt Wesson.'

41

Nothing.

Myron fiddled with the volume knob. Static feedback screeched through the car speakers. He turned it down a second, then back up. He heard muffled sounds, but he had no idea what they were. Then the sounds faded away.

Silence.

Two minutes of blank tape passed before Myron finally heard voices. His ears perked up, but he couldn't make out much. Then the voices grew a little louder, a little clearer. He leaned closer to the speaker and suddenly he heard a gruff voice with frightening clarity:

'*You have the money?*'

A hand reached into Myron's chest, grabbed his heart, and squeezed. He hadn't heard the voice in ten years, but recognition was instantaneous. It was Burt Wesson. What the hell—?

Then the second voice jarred him like a body blow:

'*I got half now. A thousand dollars now. You get the other half when he goes down . . .*'

Myron's entire body shuddered. A flash of rage unlike anything he had ever known warmed and then engulfed him. His hands tightened into fists. Tears forced their way forward. He remembered wondering why the blackmailers had contacted him to buy the dirt on Greg; he remembered Cole Whiteman's laugh and Marty Felder's ironic smile when they'd learned that he'd been hired to find Greg Downing; he remembered the voice on Greg's answering machine saying, 'He's willing to pay. Is that what you want?'; and most of all, he remembered Greg's pained face at the hospital all those years ago. It hadn't been a bond that brought Greg to Myron's bedside.

It'd been guilt.

'*Don't hurt him too bad, Burt. I just want Bolitar banged up for a few games . . .*'

Something in the deep recesses of Myron's mind snapped like a dry twig. Without conscious thought, Myron shifted into reverse.

'*Look, I really need the money. Can't you give me another five hundred?*

They're going to cut me soon. It's my last scrimmage and then I'm unemployed . . .'

He straightened out his car and shifted into drive. His foot pressed down upon the pedal. The speedometer climbed. Myron's face twisted into a mask of incognizant fury. Tears sheeted down his cheeks but no sound came with them. He drove without really seeing.

When he reached the Jones Road exit, Myron wiped his face with his sleeve. He turned into TC's driveway. The security gate blocked his path.

The guard stepped out of his little hut. Myron waved him closer to the car. When the guard was fully out of the box, Myron showed the gun.

'Move and I'll blow your head off.'

The guard's hands went up. Myron got out of the car and opened the gate. He ordered the guard inside the car. The car roared up the driveway. Myron slammed on the brake just feet before the front door. He jumped out on the run and without hesitating, he kicked in TC's front door. He ran into the den.

The television was on. TC looked up, startled. 'What the fuck—?'

Myron bounded across the room, grabbed TC's arm, twisted it behind his back.

'Hey—'

'Where is he?' Myron demanded.

'I don't know what—'

Myron pulled up on the arm. 'Don't make me break it, TC. Where is he?'

'What the fuck are you—?'

Myron silenced him by pushing the arm farther up his back. TC cried out, his huge frame bent at the waist to lessen the pressure. 'Last time I ask,' Myron said. 'Where's Greg?'

'I'm here.'

Myron let go and spun toward the voice. Greg Downing stood in the doorway. Myron did not hesitate. Letting out a guttural scream, he pounced.

Greg put up his hands, but it was like quieting a volcano with a squirt gun. Myron's fist landed square in Greg's face. Greg toppled back from the assault. Myron fell on him, his knee landing in his ribs. Something cracked. He straddled Greg's chest and threw another punch.

'Stop!' TC shouted. 'You're gonna kill him.'

Myron barely heard him.

He cocked his other fist, but TC was on him before he could throw it. Myron rolled with the tackle, digging his elbow into TC's solar plexus. When they hit the wall, the air whooshed out of TC, his eyes bulging as he gasped for air. Myron rose. Greg was scrambling away. Myron vaulted over the couch. He grabbed Greg by the leg and pulled him toward him.

'You fucked my wife!' Greg shouted. 'You think I didn't know? You fucked my wife!'

The words slowed Myron, but they didn't stop him. Through his tears, he threw another punch. Greg's mouth filled with blood. Myron cocked his fist again. A hand of iron reached out and grabbed his arm, holding it in place.

'Enough,' Win said.

Myron looked up, his face distorted by confusion and rage. 'What?'

'He's had enough.'

'But it's like you said,' Myron pleaded. 'Wesson did do it on purpose. Greg hired him.'

'I know,' Win said. 'But he's had enough.'

'What the hell are you talking about? If it was you—'

'I'd probably kill him,' Win finished for him. He looked down and something flickered in his eyes. 'But you wouldn't.'

Myron swallowed. Win nodded again and let go of Myron's wrist. Myron let his arm fall to his side. He got off Greg Downing.

Greg sat up, coughing blood into his hand. 'I followed Emily that night,' Greg managed through the hacks. 'I saw you two . . . I just wanted payback, that's all. You weren't supposed to get hurt that bad.'

Myron swallowed and breathed deeply. The adrenaline rush would soon ebb, but for now it was still there. 'You been hiding here since the beginning?'

Greg touched part of his face, winced, then nodded. 'I was afraid they'd think I killed that woman,' he said. 'And I had the mob chasing me and the custody battle and my girlfriend is pregnant.' He looked up. 'I just needed some time.'

'Do you love Audrey?'

Greg said, 'You know?'

'Yes.'

'Yeah,' Greg said, 'I love her a lot.'

'Then give her a call,' Myron said. 'She's in jail.'

'What?'

Myron didn't elaborate. He'd hoped throwing that in Greg's face would give him some sort of perverse pleasure, but it didn't. All it did was remind him that he was far from blameless in this.

He turned and walked away.

Myron found Clip alone in that same corporate skybox they'd met in when this all began. He was looking down at the empty court, his back to Myron. He didn't move when Myron cleared his throat.

'You knew all along,' Myron said.

Clip said nothing.

'You went to Liz Gorman's apartment that night,' Myron continued. 'She played the tape for you, didn't she?'

Clip clasped his hands behind his back. Then he nodded.

'That's why you hired me. This wasn't all a coincidence. You wanted me to find out the truth.'

'I didn't know how else to tell you.' Clip finally turned and faced Myron. His eyes were dazed and hazy. All color was gone from his face. 'It wasn't an act, you know. The emotion at the press conference . . .' He lowered his head, gathered himself, raised it again. 'You and I lost touch after your injury. I wanted to call you a thousand times, but I understood. You wanted to stay away. The injury never leaves the great ones, Myron. I knew it would never leave you.'

Myron opened his mouth but nothing came out. His entire being felt exposed and raw. Clip came closer. 'I thought this would be a way for you to learn the truth,' Clip said. 'I also hoped this would be something of a catharsis. Not a complete one. Like I said, it never leaves the great ones.'

For several moments, they both just stood and stared.

'You told Walsh to play me the other night,' Myron said.

'Yes.'

'You knew I wouldn't be able to match up.'

Clip nodded slowly.

Myron felt the tears come back to his eyes. He blinked them down.

Clip set his jaw. There were tiny tremors in his face, but he stood rigid. 'I wanted to help you,' he said, 'but my reasons for hiring you were not all altruistic. I knew, for example, that you'd always been a team player. You loved that aspect of basketball, Myron – being part of a team.'

'So?'

'My plan included making you feel like a member of the team. A real member. So much so that you would never hurt us.'

Myron understood. 'You figured that if I bonded with my teammates, I wouldn't blow the whistle when I learned the truth.'

'It's not in your nature,' Clip said.

'But it will come out,' Myron said. 'There's no way to avoid it now.'

'I know that.'

'You could lose the team.'

Clip smiled, shrugged. 'There are worse things,' he said. 'Just as you now know there are worse things than never being able to play again.'

'I always knew,' Myron said. 'I just maybe needed a reminder.'

42

He and Jessica sat on the couch in her loft. He told her everything. Jess hugged her knees and rocked back and forth. Her eyes looked pained.

'She was my friend,' Jessica said.

'I know.'

'I wonder.'

'What?'

'What would I have done in the same situation? To protect you.'

'You wouldn't have killed.'

'No,' she said. 'I guess not.'

Myron watched her. She looked on the verge of tears. He said, 'I think I learned something about us in all this.'

She waited for him to elaborate.

'Win and Esperanza didn't want me to play again. But you never tried to stop me. I was afraid that maybe you didn't understand me as well as they do. But that wasn't the case at all. You saw what they couldn't.'

Jessica studied his face with a penetrating gaze. She let go of her knees and slid her feet to the floor. 'We've never really talked about this before,' she said.

He nodded.

'The truth is, you never mourned the end of your career,' Jessica went on. 'You never showed weakness. You stuffed it all in some internal suitcase and moved on. You tackled everything else in your life with a smothering desperation. You didn't wait. You seized whatever was left and pressed it against you, afraid your whole world was as fragile as that knee. You rushed off to law school. You ran off and helped Win. You frantically clung to whatever you could.' She stopped.

'Including you,' he finished.

'Yes. Including me. Not just because you loved me. Because you were afraid of losing more than you already had.'

'I did love you,' he said. 'I still do.'

'I know. I'm not trying to put this all on you. I was an idiot. It was mostly my fault. I admit that. But your love back then bordered on the desperate. You channeled your grief into a grasping need. I was afraid of suffocating. I don't want to sound like an amateur shrink, but you needed to mourn. You needed to put it behind you, not suppress it. But you wouldn't face it.'

'You thought my playing again would make me face it,' he said.

'Yes.'

'It's not like this was a cure-all.'

'I know,' she said. 'But I think it helped you let go a little.'

'And that's why you think now is a good time for me to move in.'

Jessica swallowed hard. 'If you want,' she said. 'If you feel ready.'

He looked up in the air and said, 'I'll need more closet space.'

'Done,' she whispered. 'Whatever you want.'

She snuggled into him. He put his arms around her, pulled her close, and felt very much at home.

It was a sweltering morning in Tucson, Arizona. A big man opened his front door.

'Are you Burt Wesson?'

The big man nodded. 'Can I help you with something?'

Win smiled. 'Yes,' he said. 'I think you can.'